THE COMPLETE ENCYCLOPEDIA OF ELVES, GOBLINS, AND OTHER LITTLE CREATURES

THE COMPLETE
ENCYCLOPEDIA
OF
ELVES,
GOBLINS,
AND
OTHER LITTLE
CREATURES

SECRETS REVEALED
BY
Pierre Dubois

ILLUSTRATED BY
Claudine & Roland Sabatier

ABBEVILLE PRESS PUBLISHERS
New York   London

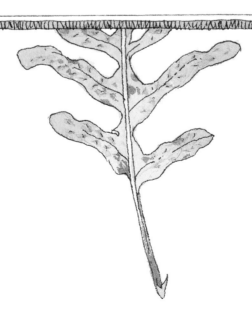

For His Royal Highness Prince Charles, sovereign and protector of the green hills . . .

. . . and for Nils, on wild Elves' wings

FOR THE ENGLISH EDITION
Editor: Molly Dorozenski
Copy editors: Eric Abbott, Ashley Benning
Production editors: Marie Dessaix, David Fabricant
Production manager: Louise Kurtz
Translators: American Pie, London; Translate-A-Book, Oxford, UK
Typesetter: Julia Sedykh
Jacket designer: Misha Beletsky

First published in the United States of America in 2005 by Abbeville Press

First published in France in two volumes, *La grande encyclopédies des Elfes* (2003) and *La grande encyclopédies des Lutins* (1992), by Éditions Hoëbeke, Paris

First edition
10 9 8 7 6 5 4 3 2 1

Library of Congress Cataloging-in-Publication Data

Dubois, Pierre, 1945-
[Grand encyclopédies des elfes. English]
The complete encyclopedia of elves, goblins, and other little creatures / secrets revealed by Pierre Dubois.— 1st ed.
    p. cm.
Translation and merged edition of: La grande encylopédies des elfes and La grande encyclopédies des lutins.
Includes bibliographical references.
ISBN 0-7892-0878-4
1. Elves—Encyclopedias. 2. Goblins—Encyclopedias. I. Dubois, Pierre, 1945– Grande encyclopédies des lutins. English. 2005. II. Title.

GR549.D82 2005
398'.45—dc22
                                        2005018443

For bulk and premium sales and for text adoption procedures, write to Customer Service Manager, Abbeville Press, 137 Varick Street, New York, NY 10013 or call 1-800-ARTBOOK.

Table of Contents

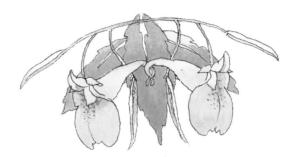

PART I

ELVES

The Lure of Elves

My garland will stay with you: the flowers are the "thoughts": the forget-me-nots, the buttercups, the little roses are my childhood and they symbolize it: daisies for the purest moments.
—Mélanie Saskia Dubois

"Let's go for a walk in the woods while the Elves are there"; let's open up the clear valleys; let's sit beneath the cherry trees. The hedge is in blossom: the blackthorn, its branches covered in frost-dust; the white hawthorn with its May time scent; the elderflower and the dog rose. Petals falling on the pages of the book dust it with bridal veils, virginal wings, the scent of orchards. This moment must be seized at once: delay a few chapters and the leaves will turn yellow, the meadows will be mown, and the two notes of the cuckoo will be lost to silence.

A breath of autumn touches the pages, bringing with it a hint of smoke—a frieze of fast-vanishing thoughts—which winter grasps and freezes onto the window glass. In her dream, the child transforms frost into butterflies.

"Let's go for a walk in the woods while the Elves are there." In the curtain of foliage, the wind ruffles the words that have taken refuge among images that no longer make us dream and which will soon be relegated to the attic.

Many years will be needed, many rainy days, of lost loves and forsaken quests, an accumulation of dust and spiders' webs, before, at last, a wish will be granted, a rediscovered wreath that blooms again. Open the book to the first page as on the first day, only to find its dawn light a little misted over. The gaze of a child is necessary for the magic to return: Is there anything of that refuge of childhood wonder, lost among force of habit, left in us? Even if it is only a breath on the dying embers among the ashes—as at the edge of a dream you set a candle to guide and welcome anyone who takes it up in their turn?

We crack the tome to the same page to which it opened all by itself when we first stopped there to gaze at that vision of miraculous renewal. We leaf through it now in the hope that we may catch a memory of the soul, or the light of bygone days, once upon a time slipping from legendary skies onto the gleaming roofs of fairy tales. We wish to hear again the sounds of the river flowing past the mill, the Water Sprites playing near the washerwomen, and in the town square, the cheerful din of market days when the Elves with pointed noses furtively came to pinch things from the stalls. We wish for the hills to part again, allowing us to glimpse the Siths riding by moonlight on silvery nights. The transparent-winged Ouphs in their courtly costumes would return to gather pollen from the lilacs—lilacs so blue and close enough to pick . . .

If we listen carefully, we can still hear the little refrain, the three notes so precious that all liturgies return to them.

At the bottom of pages, we sometimes find little finger stamps on the soft sandy shores, which are like hesitant footprints

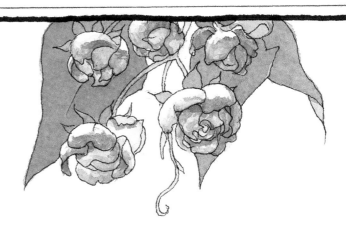

on the threshold of Elfiria. Of course, these are the footsteps we must follow one by one. Plant your heavy soles on that delicate path, but crush nothing. Forget everything about the weight of years and false certainties and hear the songbird calling beyond the path . . .

"Let's go for a walk in the woods while the Elves are there."

Such an invitation becomes a kiss that withers on the lips if not taken at the moment it is privately offered.

I'd so love to restore them to their primal beauty—this thought from a poem by Kathleen Raine flutters among the leaves and then opens like a buttercup in the meadow, offering itself for contemplation, for picking, for pressing between the pages. Its message remains there, gently fading and diffusing its happy essence upon the fiber of the paper. Sweet tears will later make it bloom again, propagating its gleam of a golden age to gardens and white-winged books.

When the bird flies away, it discovers the hidden door that has always been enclosed by ivy and honeysuckle in the hope of a possible return.

But where during all this time have the Elves been hiding along the brambly ways?

Throughout the years, I rediscovered them by being attuned to the flutter of a wing, to a crystal tinkling, to pale fleeting shapes in silent places, to scents, to stray grains of saffron upon the moorland fires, and to moss on ancient trees and the cairns' gray stones. From hill to hill, from rath to rath, in circles, on hilltops where the grass grows tall, they gather. All the sites where ancient beliefs claim their kingdoms spread: the grassy road of Hututu; the Brig 'o Doon near Shanter; the Old Clapper Bridge at Dartmeet, which you must cross when the day is over; the top of Hallowmount that looms over Fairford at the Welsh border; Cwn Pwcca at the bottom of the valley of Clydach, which Shakespeare considered to be the elfin valley of his *Midsummer Night's Dream;* the "Elfin Hideout" near Chagford in Devonshire; the blue combes of the Chiltern and Malvern Hills; the Eildon Hills on the Borders; the bright heather on Kielder; under the great oak with its holly pentacle at Comper in Brocéliande; at Ruynes in Margeride, where the shadow of the castle keep shelters the Dragon; Ben Bulben in Sligo, where no one goes without a reason; here and there if you follow remote and winding roads.

Strangely, I have never met one of those warlike Elves questing for the ring, but these were not the ones for which I searched. The only hero of this line of iron and fire—King Eochaidh, killed in the battle of Moytura where Tuatha Dé Danaan clashed with Fir Bolg—lay under a mound of stone in a field not far from Cong. Nearby a weary, ancient tree tells the distressing story to those who lean against its gloriously gashed trunk.

On a cold and rainy winter's day in the ancient, spongy Aberfoyle cemetery, by the tomb of Reverend Kirk, the sky is gaping slightly, so that a pale pathway of light can be glimpsed leading from the mossy slab to the neighboring hills. It stretches as far as the great pine tree, stopping at its foot as if to show the place where the "Shepherd of the Siths" was imprisoned within its bark for having revealed their Elfin secrets. All around it

leaves rustle and moan, though there is not a breath of wind.

At the edge of Dartmoor lies Lewtranchard Manor, filled by Sabine Baring Gould with mysterious presences gathered in the course of her walks among the bogs, the tors, and the ruins haunted by Pixies, Elves, and Ghosts. A Black Huntsman roams the moor as soon as night falls, and even if you see him only rarely, you can distinctly hear his horse's galloping feet striking the pathways. I sometimes hear him still.

Under the sacred vault of oaks in Wintsman Wood, time is abolished and becomes eternal. On some nights, Elves dressed in moss and lichen emerge from among the rocks piled there long ago by the guardians of the tors and engage in strange rituals. I have found traces of bonfires, dance circles, and curious garlands of feathers and cord tied to the branches.

Wait by the grove where tradition says they appear, and they will come out somewhere else where you did not expect them. So it is with Elves: they do not answer calls, and offerings cannot lure them.

Living in the company of these stubborn little creatures is like a caper of the spirit—an acrobatic feat that makes or breaks you, for better or worse. Consorting with Fairies is a subtle adventure, a matter of charms and spells, a seduction and giving of your heart, and the approach to Elves is a flight towards fleeting beings in a fleeting world. This surrender is very dangerous because it also opens the way to delusory visions of flight, to wild shores, and the refuge of shadows. Elfland is the rediscovered world of childhood before childhood. It is a valley of no return. Those who reach it—because they feel the lure of the Elves—will become kings or queens of shadows and never again feel the attraction of the fallen world of mortals.

If one day you are led by chance or some obscure reason to cross the mirror water here below, it will be through "Elf Thought," the voice of the Love-Talker, and doubtless, before disappearing again into the far-off mists, like the piper, you will take many children's hearts with you.

There, each one of us finds what we
*   dreamed about*
All those we had lost
There each of us finds all those we dreamed
*   about*
Everything we had lost

Or you remain in exile. Wandering between two worlds, you will follow the trail of dreams to the farthest reaches of mysterious lands, along causeways, along rivers and gray canals; you will walk the margins of books and notebooks, plunder cloudy skies, distil perfumes, and study pictures for a clue. You will become an enchanter or a wraith.

Winged, diaphanous swarm, goldenhelmeted warriors, magicians with hoarfrost beards, scaly monsters, mischievous imps of the Brocéliande moss, hideous, crazed, pale, midnight phantoms. These creatures haunt the summer skies, the black snow, the bright rivers, and the shadow of the undergrowth, each able to walk out of mirrors and follow us step by step, each ready to fire the Elf-shot at a twist in the path. They breathe their magic breath and disappear into the mists of the road.

Here the book is rediscovered with its

labyrinthine words, encrusted images, pages to turn which themselves turn over our captive memories.

In a picture book, first of all there must be pictures. Pictures fascinate children, even before words create windows for their imagination. They are garden squares open to all horizons: to islands, the bush, constantly renewed geographies. Neither walls nor fences, nor rows of leeks and cabbages can enclose their cavalcades. The child forgets the spadework that digs the road to escape. All the colors and the Dream Elves just appear.

A beautiful picture is a picture that dreams, that is born of itself. Like a threshold, it invites us to step over, to visit the pages of the garden, and to run along its paths where its words bloom. To discover at the bottom of the garden, behind the gooseberry bushes, the land of the March hare and the hidden staircase leading to all the books. It gives access to the library of Elfland where books write themselves and tell their own story as you turn the pages. But on the other hand, pictures do not blossom of their own accord. You have to draw them, you have to color them, and you have to dream them before they can dream themselves.

Roland and Claude Sabatier know this well, and with a pen and a brush they have made the blank page bloom with all the fauna and flora of Elfiria.

They are attentive, serious, amused, or gently disturbed; for years they have planted their easels at the top of a mound that looms over Grimoirie, and day after day they have drawn the portrait of those who pass by, charming the mistrustful Goblins, Fairies, and Elves—Claudine with her gentle eyes, Roland with little drops of drink, tidbits, and bombardon concerts . . .

Let the song continue!

—Pierre Dubois
Elfologist
(June 2003)

Origins and Geneses of Elfery

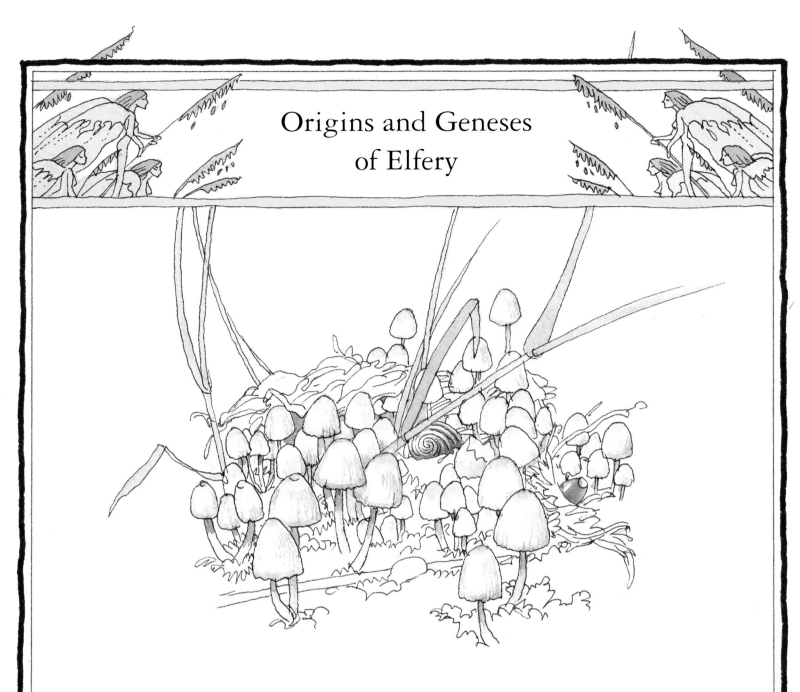

You Learn on the Fly That Which Can't Be Learned

The fairies, ye ken.
—Mr. Gibb, librarian,
from Sir Walter Scott's *Letters on Demonology and Witchcraft*

I t's easier to follow back an endless chain than to embark on the path of the Elves. It's best to answer those seeking the origin of Alfs, Elves, or Others with pointed ears, with the terse reply: "We don't know much at all; in fact, we scarcely know a thing," and to add, like the cuckoo, "Go and see for yourself . . . it's that way!" Leave them at the corner of the pearly wood with a few blades of grass in their pocket. They'll lose their way back.

Those who study and search too hard for the Elves and the gates of Elfland, Elfhame, or Elferia risk passing them by. "Mortals do not see fairies—the generalization is as nearly a rule as anything in this turning world can be. It is certain that they cannot be seen by those who are looking for them." Those who seek elves have minds so full of preconceived ideas about what they are looking for that they no longer see anything. This according to the disturbing and delightful Sylvia Townsend Warner—Lolly Willow Warner—who shared their existence, reporting even the subtlest details of the habits and customs of the Afrites of Brocéliande, where there have never actually been any Elves.

No one who has ever seen them, met them, or followed them home under the golden vaulted hills was ever looking for them. Their heads were filled with other matters: they were gathering herbs, pebbles, or wood, or were chasing an escaped cow away from the hedge. The exception is children, Tabhaisvers, those born with a caul, Lorialés, paladins in stories, and blackbird musicians.

Elves can be found in books—the magic books of Grimoirie—but on the "path of life" it is always the Elves themselves who decide on meetings. Those unwise people or dream doctors—like the unfortunate Reverend Kirk of Aber-

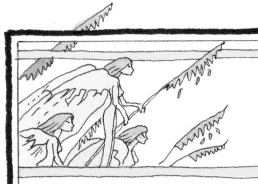

Origins and Geneses
of Elfery

foyle—who took unreasonable risks to force their way through the "barricades mystérieuses" to study Elves too closely did not come to a happy ending, as we shall see later on.

Sometimes people manage to see them just out of the corner of their eye, but a moment later a goat, a tree stump, a mocking hare, a dragonfly is there instead . . . or nothing at all. Moreover, there is no reason to be pleased to see them, as their appearance often brings misfortune.

Usually, it's when you are not thinking about them at all—or are hoping to be forgotten by them, as night falls along the country road—that one of the flying cohort of Gyre Carlin, Fir Darrig, or Sluaghs alights in a single bound on your shoulder and carries you away for miles in the wrong direction, to set you down hanging from a church steeple. Or some screeching moorland Fuaths amuse themselves by making you drink a cup of stagnant pond water. Or Rhi'Mellen bites your heel. Or you are suddenly whisked away by a beautiful broomstick-rider and forced to satisfy all your darkest desires during a night lasting a hundred years. Or you are devoured by a Palis in the depths of the desert. Or forced by the Siths to take part in their endless circle dance . . .

To cross paths with one who has come from the "Pale Country" is a source of great discomfort, but at the same time fabulous miracles . . .

When you have just arrived a few steps from the Passage, what do you decide to do: Do you disdain the cautious warnings, the old fears descended from stories and ancient beliefs? Do you leave the decision to the little Elfin cousin still at play somewhere inside you—calling to adventure, to rediscovery of the Golden Age—and leap over the frontier despite all the risks and perils? Or do you finally turn your back on the enchanted shores of the mirror—which small girls in organdie dresses and small boys fallen out of their cradles have never been afraid to leap over in one bound—and go home, congratulating yourself on your wise choice?

Be careful! On the other side you can be devoured, imprisoned in a tower till the end of your days, or condemned to dance, twist, and leap, with your heart in ashes and your feet on fire for ever. In Never Neverland blood-thirsty Indians, a hungry crocodile, and the terrible Captain Hook roam every corner of the island, and in Elfland there are Devaldas and Trolls everywhere, but aren't the disguised monsters here below, who have become official, patented, self-endorsed, even more terrifying?

You can always pretend you entered accidentally, inadvertently, without intending mischief, and search in your pockets for a present to offer in compensation—it must be precious, not in cash value, but sacred—with a "fetishistic" value. A ball still laden with a thousand laughs from ancient games, a pretty peb-

ble, a mummified spinning top, a lucky charm, or a little toy pig-with-a-heart—anything you are attached to like a treasure—may do, especially if your hand trembles slightly as you hold out the offering. Respectful fear is also a sort of "password." If you carry a broom flower in your coat lining, nothing too bad can happen to you.

Elves do not appreciate intruders, especially not braggarts who breach their gates as conquerors. Take off your hat and greet them very politely. Elves deserve respect; they are a hundred times older than our world and know more about it than all of our scholars. Stay vigilant; do not accept anything to drink from them, or anything to eat. Do not take part in their dancing—ever—even if the most delightful Elfin lady invites you. Remember the song—and above all, avoid vexing them.

Elves are not Goblins or Dwarves, with whom you can discuss working down in the mine, harvesting, or gardening. With these creatures who have come out of the earth, the ground, it is possible to strike up friendships; you can offer them a beer, grasp them by the shoulder, and then let them have a corner in an attic or stable in return for some small services. Not with Elves.

Neither are Elves fairy godmothers, loving mother-goddesses who welcome us on our first day and watch over our cradle, while their skilful hands weave the mysterious threads of our destiny. Fairy godmothers, despite the poisonous Carabosses, always safeguard the precious dreams of our buried childhood. Elves are something else.

In his *Letters on Demonology and Witchcraft,* Sir Walter Scott writes that Elves are part of the most pleasant legacy with which imagination has endowed us. True, a wonderful dazzling imagery floats about them, but it is so dazzling that it mystifies us. The people of the "Pale Kingdom" are above all great enchanters, masters of illusion and phantasmagoria. These moon-favorites' kingdom lies in the liquid depths of mirrors, the changing and tempestu-

Origins and Geneses
of Elfery

ous skies of dreams, the endlessly rustling gold and silver of the leaves, and the timeless moment of the mirage slipping between fluid shapes. These aerial sprites reside on the borders of night and dawn, offering occasional glimpses of pale dark walls and vanishing towers.

Among all the peoples of the "Gentry of the Others," the Elf—born of the contrary and the impalpable, ice and fire, dark and light—is certainly the most complex and shyest creature, the most extravagant, the least accessible of all, but that is good because the mysterious must remain so in order to keep its magic power.

Take it as said
What will be revealed to you today
Tomorrow once day has dawned
The frontier crossed
will be taken back from you.

The Invisible Kingdom

Kingdom of elsewhere
Whose time is: bygone
Whose place is: far away.

—Kathleen Raine

Between night and day, shadow and light, the Dream dreams a Creature, and frees it from its confused imaginings. This creature is an Elf. Between snow and flame, sky and water, the Dream dreams a shore and sets the Elf upon it.

Between the innocence of fallen angels, the malice of nightmare, and the kindness of birds, the Dream abandons the child to the refuge of Elfiria, then departs and disappears . . .

Very pretty romantic things have been written about Elves—fine stories—as well as frightening things, and lots of silly things. All have added their notes, their refrains, their couplets to the song, so that the music has become so discordant that the Elves have taken it over to play it for themselves. This tune is called *Alpeich*, "the Elf King's Song." When mortals hear it, they cannot prevent themselves from dancing, jigging, jumping, and whirling until they fall down exhausted, with their heart in ashes and their feet on fire.

To escape from this enchantment a very skillful fiddler must break the curse by playing the same tune backwards, without mistaking a single note, which has never been done.

It is said, repeated, murmured about Them . . .

. . . that they are fallen angels, who at the time of Lucifer's great rebellion were unable to choose between Good and Evil, and found themselves wandering forever between Eden and Hell, sky and earth, the visible and invisible, in search of their lost souls.

. . . that they are Cain's children driven out by God after the murder of Abel *(Beowulf)*.

. . . that the Elves are the souls of generations that disappeared long ago but who continue to have relations—sometimes friendly and sometimes hostile—with the living, and that the living join the Elf people after death (H.F. Feiberg, *Der Kobold*).

. . . that at the beginning of the world, when the sky split to pour down all the heavenly flora and fauna onto the earth, at the same time the creator of all things sent

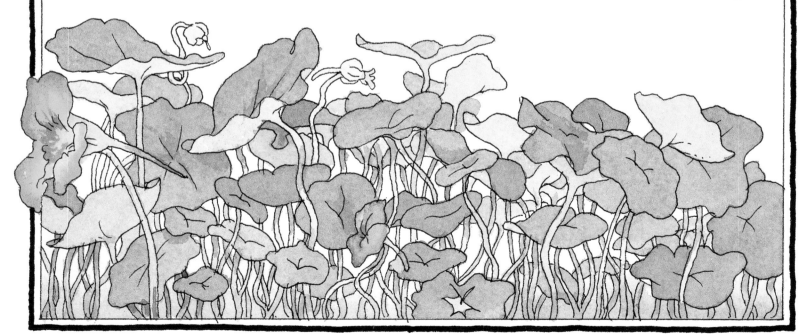

Origins and Geneses
of Elfery

his most skilful workers to till the earth and get it ready for humans, whose attentive and invisible neighbors these workers, the Elves, remain (J. Uréthère, *Les Anges, les Elfes, les Nains et les Démons*).

It is said that the reason Elves steal children from mortals is because they are required to pay an annual tribute of a life to the infernal regions. They prefer to pay their tribute to the prince of Tartary in the form of human children rather than from among their own (Thomas Campbell).

Elves love pleasure. We know that they have spent the night hunting when in the morning the horses in the stable are found worn out and sweating. Elves dress in gray or black and also wear a little red cap with a few flowers tucked into it. Their flocks graze invisibly among the flocks of earth people. Elves dance in the moonbeams on silent nights and frolic in broad daylight in deserted places. If a passerby approaches, they change themselves into trees, stones, and bushes (J. Collin de Plancy).

It is said that they are the elementary spirits of the air and the materialization of natural forces, split into two families: the white Elves and the black Elves. The white Elves are luminous, more beautiful than the sun, with brilliant skin, golden hair, and eyes bright as stars. They wear foxglove hoods or a cap with a bell on it and glass shoes. They gambol all day through the fields distributing kindnesses here and there. If a human being finds one of their bells or one of their glass slippers in the meadow, the Elf who lost it will grant their every wish. They are skilful artisans and build magnificent structures. The other family of Elves is extremely dangerous, misshapen, and black as tar. With their poisoned breath they breathe out nightmare, madness, and curses powerful enough to make sheep dizzy, bring fever, colic, hives, acne, sleeping sickness, and death. They suck blood and kill people and cattle by shooting them with invisible lightning arrows—*Elfe-skud,* or Elf-shot. If a single ray of sunshine touches a night Elf, that Elf is immediately turned to stone.

Light or dark, their capricious character makes them formidable. Although they are no taller than a young girl's thumb, Elves can lift granite blocks or shake and rock the foundations of a house . . .

They are said to be tiny, winged, fluttery, and light, like butterflies gleaning nectar from honey-laden lilac blossoms. . . or pale and evanescent, merging with the moonlit mists of pools and ponds. They have been seen as iron-clad, sword-wielding giants, throwing themselves into battle, and as skinny, lively imps with pointed ears and slit goat lips. Also as cherubs and little monkeys . . . Half-woman, half-wolf, they have been seen haunting the desert sands.

Lovecraft imagined them sticky, roughly sketched, hideously dragging up silt from the depths of gorges . . . The theosophists Geoffrey Hudson and C.W. Leadbeater saw their transparent shining shapes surrounding lonely sick people with a benevolent bluish aura.

One day, for William Blake, they brought one of their people to earth, wrapping its body in a rose petal under the primroses in his garden.

They are said to be descended from the Pairikas or Peris of Persia, which some say is the birth place of the Elves. Heine wrongly thought they were familiars of the moorlands of Languedoc.

"No higher than a chanterelle mushroom, taller than the tallest pine"; snowy, opaline, luminescent, more liquid than rain, or monstrously black, tentacular, hairy—the Elves play each of these parts in turn, changing shape at the slightest breath, and they keep their secrets buried in dreams . . .

From the depths of the ancient swarming ages of the skies
Snatched by the winds from the dreams and nightmares of the gods.

Origins and Geneses of Elfery

The Other Side of the Hedge

Night sighs slip through the grass.
— Rupert Chawner Brooke

Now that we have gathered a fistful of knowledge about Elves, let us forget it all; let us trust our inspiration to the cuckoo. Mid-May is the best time to leap over the hedge in a single bound. But you must have first ruffled up your hair with a fistful of buttercups and trodden blades of grass. You must have looped a tendril of ivy around your arm and splashed your brow with the dew of oblivion. Crossing over requires you to put seven drops of your blood onto seven leaves in the undergrowth. It is best to choose high noon, because daybreak and twilight are dubious times, favorable to the Elves' contrary, goatish humor. You would have to be a complete lunatic to risk it at night.

In the leap, the crossing over, you feel fresh and vegetal, as if there were mirror-lights glistening on your skin. It's as if a brisk October breeze suddenly encircled your soul, carrying with it the whirling golden leaves. You don't understand how you have managed to pass through the bramble thicket and undergrowth without getting scratched or how you shed the veil that masked an array of new perceptions from you: the suddenly limpid message of the birdsong, the sharp light on the shape of things, and the presence of the spirit among light and scented pathways. Each step brings a renewed awareness, the happy recollection of adventures long forgotten because you had huddled up inside yourself through force of habit. Flowers, grass, and streams have regained the brightness of their original colors. The squirrel does not run away, the foxgloves tinkle sweetly, and the messenger jay clearly sings out his greeting: "Turlututat pointed hat."

Sitting on a water lily, the frog wears a crown, and when you glance back at the bank, you see your first Elf.

He is not very big, only the size of a small monkey, but lively, hopping about, with his pointed ears and narrow eyes, a red holly berry for each pupil. His skin is a flecked, golden brown and tightly molded to a spindly, sinewy body bristling with hairs and leaves. He whips the air with his long tail.

You offer him your grandfather's old fob watch, which has no hands but whose casing gleams with memories.

Then, perhaps, the Elf will take you farther into his realm, to the wisest of the ageless Elves, who will come out of his oak tree, and assemble the pale Elf people to hear him tell you their story.

First, he will speak about flowers, which all Elves love, and elfin voices from all the other places—mountains, marshes, jungles, and plains—will be heard in his. The hoarse low voices of the desert Elves, the liquid murmuring voices of the fenland Elves, the chattering of those of the bush, and the icy echo of mountaintop moans; each light or dark voice will join in, mingling in the flow of time eternal:

> *Elf, Alp, Elbe, Ylfe, Alfar, Alf.*
> *Elv: river, albus: white.*
> *Albh: is brilliant white.*
> *Elbe: clear springs, the swan . . .*
> *Elfe, Alp, Alf, Ylfe.*
> *Alfar: the dazed song of luminous flight through the air.*
> *Alf, Elfe, Elv, Aelfwine: friend of Elves.*
> *Aelfsiden: Elf magic . . .*
> *Alfablot: Elf sacrifice . . .*

His voice runs on and streams down his misty beard, through his hair plaited into the branches. He tells how memories spring from his head crowned with antlers thick with the bark of centuries. He recalls the age when time still knew nothing about tomorrows. It was an age without beginning or end: one cold endless night and one endless sunny day, facing each other in the garden of space where the gods themselves dreamed. Others dreamed of soaring up towards the dreaming gods until they finally did and found themselves in a deluge of fire and ice, hurtling through an immensity of stars, pieces of night and day, fragments of sun and moon, stardust, and the dreams of the worlds.

The wizened elder Elf tells of the arrival of the gods, dark and light, and their first descent on the gray rugged road to an unknown land with its own sky . . .

He tells how the gods sent their "Dream People" to arrange the world and how they were instructed to plant forests, construct mountains, dig valleys, spread seas, lay the beds of rivers, and build on this world the majestic palaces the gods had imagined.

The ancient ageless Elf hesitates and sighs before countenancing the suspicion that once the spectacle of the new world was complete, the "Dream People" were

Origins and Geneses of Elfery

abandoned there. Once the final course of the rainbow dissipated, they were there like the founding angels of a magic island, in exile . . .

The people of the dreams of light—the Liosálfar—then claimed the snowy mountaintops, the sunny places, mirages, and the reflections on lake waters. The people of the dark dreams—the Svartálfar—dug deep underground, secreting themselves away in mines and the darkness of night . . .

The others, the undecided—the Dokkálfar—remained on the borders of dawn and twilight, between Alfheim, the kingdom of the Elves, home of the white Elves, and Svartálfaheim, the kingdom of the Alfs, home of the black Elves.

The humans who came later made all that into legends.

The Elf draws himself up to his full height to talk about the Golden Age of the Elves, their battles, their quests, their glories, and their loves. With the butt of his serpent rod, he traces luminous signs in the air under the dark arch of leaves, to evoke the ancient magic powers, and perhaps they still make the ground shake a little . . .

Once, they were handsome and tall and brave . . . no other dream equaled theirs in splendor, when riding snowy unicorns they set out to battle the Fomoirés, the black Ogres, or the dragons, bearing on their armbands the favors of matchlessly beautiful ladies. In reverie, he goes on to describe the cavalcades, the castles chiseled in gold and crystal, libraries where the books lit up as you turned the pages, and the feasts of the May Queen with their harp music . . . Elves flew through the air at the speed of light and passed through walls at will until men of little faith claimed that they had wings . . . and, in doing so, shrank them. For, year after year, human dreams invaded the ancient dreams of the gods and, in doing so, weakened them. Enchantment no longer sprang from the soul's belief . . .

Hook-nosed Elf
I forbid you to breathe in my face!
I forbid you, Elf, to smoke,

To crawl, to climb!
Elf children, demons
Take your claws off me!

Thus humans threw curses against the Elves of light—confusing the beneficent healing Elves with demons.

This moved the good Elves to join their dark brethren of the night and the ones who are between dogs and wolves. They became invisible in order to survive. Thereafter, they caught each passing dream and insinuated themselves into it, so that they could reign over each shadowy place and each particle of light. All that's needed is a firefly, a child's dream, a lost and fearful traveler, a moment of bewil-

derment, a blackout, or a screen that goes suddenly dark.

They appear in mirrors and inhabit the quick-growing grass that cracks the concrete humans have spread over the dreamwork of the gods; ever a step or two away, they are just behind the hedge where the cuckoo is calling.

While the Elfin Elder has been telling his story, other creatures have come to join him, leaping down from the high trees in a single bound, or gently coming to rest, folding their wings in silence. They have come out from under mushrooms, bracken ferns, river eddies, and the spangled naked thighs of duckweed. Some have arrived on horseback, on horses with plaited silver manes. Dressed in green, they carry their bows slung across their shoulders. At his feet a circle of Elves dressed in red flower corollas sit embroidering bonnets. Evening has fallen, and his voice has become fainter and fainter, calm, detached . . . Now it describes the flowers that the ancient sage loves best: euphorbia, hellebores, aconites, lisianthus, columbines, abelias, and epidum, which are the Elves' own flowers. The voice of the old Elf under the oak tree—clarion of Alfheim, Elferia, Elfland—and the moon shining down are eternal for the blossoms that he names.

Somewhere in the shadowy thicket, an invisible hand tunes a fiddle. It must be time for the dance:

Dance, dance
Turn, twist, and leap
On the dry grass, the branch stripped bare
Your heart in ashes, your feet on fire.

Perhaps you will want to stay on with them.

IN THE DAWN TWILIGHT

I'd love to know where to find a dawn
for this dark night we have in us.
—Victor Hugo

The Dawn Elves are like the first light of daybreak when night is passing. A few grains of saffron diluted with a dewdrop at the sky's birth, but which the moon bird can still carry off with a black sweep of its wings. . . and snuff the candle.

They are like hard-packed snow imprisoned in ruts and dense hedgerows, which *The Distaff Almanac* calls "wolf snow":

As long as it's there
Cold and wolf keep in step.

The blackbird, disturbed by the snow's presence, does not dare give breath to its tuneful trills, which chaffinches and warblers will pick up later and carry from bush to bush. They haunt this silence. They disturb themselves by their own presence, one foot already in the morning, the other kept back in the dark. The heart split in two on a hilltop offers one half to a daffodil marriage and the other to the poisonous flora of midnight. The queen of darkness takes her time flattering them, holding them by her side with a thousand sweet nothings. "Take care, children," she warns, hiding her delicate profile from the coming day, "for out there you will fade too fast." But the children want to run through the meadows and the woods, leap over fences and rivers, and push back the approach of evening with their endless games. "Don't you love me any more?" simpers the Beauty of the Night, knowing how to promise intoxicating dreams and open all doors to the night's magic.

The Dawn Elves remain undecided about the choice between light and dark. This state of mind, we may well say, gives rise to pretences; it leads to lying, trickery, and mischief. Can you fault the innocent dawn hawthorn that it pricks itself with thorns?

HEIGHT:
A rather short human, a child, or a midget.

APPEARANCE:
They are skinny and look like mortals but with exaggerated features. Very pale, they give an impression of lightness, as if they had shed the "organic weight" of mortals. They have a lively expression. Their hair is long and whitish. Most of the women are rather pretty.

CLOTHING:
Whether richly or modestly dressed, they all wear green, with flower bells or little silver bells attached to their ankles and wrists.

HABITAT:
The skies of Scotland, the Shetland Isles, the Hebrides, or the Irish islands.

FOOD:
They take advantage of their invisibility to snatch food and drink from human tables.

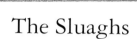

The Sluaghs

Lady Fergusson! Alas the Sluaghs will never carry us off!

—Lord Brett,
The Darling Loulou's Story

Sometimes in the evening, above isolated villages in the Borders, the Lowlands, or the far-off Highlands, you can hear a muffled sound of coming and going on the rooftops. Those who hear this buzzing stand in their doorways, sniff the sky above, and gaze into the shadows in vain. There is no storm cloud in the air, no wind in the trees, no bird flight, no wing beat, not one. Nothing. Just this rippling murmur—that is all. Yet just because nothing can be seen does not mean there is nothing there. On the contrary. People duck indoors feeling disturbed; they make the sign of the cross, barricade their doors and shutters, and pray for those who still hang about out of doors, because a fool ought to know that it's the worse time of the year to go out after nightfall . . .

*After the harvests, just before Halloween
When Good Neighbors get ready to leave
The troop appears in the twilight.
Some ride on buns, others on beans.
They are all dressed in green,
richly attired, large or small,
The Fairy King with the Elfin Queen
and all their court of Sluaghs carried on the wind.*

. . . according to the poem that everyone knows by heart.

At Dunblane near Aolla, in Menstrie Glen, although night has fallen, a peasant and his cart are hurrying to finish plowing a furrow, when suddenly the tumult of a race through the air breaks out above him. Too bad for him if he would rather not attend. One can't refuse an invitation to a Sluagh race. No one can resist! Here he is riding a broom made of twigs.

*Slender fairies! Slender fairies!
Wind travelers! Wind travelers!
On the way to Cruinau!*

They arrive at Cruinau and whirl round the castle, where a banquet is laid out. Like a flock of starlings, they descend on the tables, drinking, eating, partying—and yet they remain invisible under the guests' noses. Then the lord of the Elves calls again:

*Sky Elves! Sky Elves!
Wind travelers! Wind travelers!
To Stirling for the dance. Let's go!*

And in a single flight they are off through the castle locks as quick as lightning and back up in the clouds. Then the peasant adds his own couplet to the song:

*Hounds! Hounds! Run ahead! Run ahead!
To Dunblane, to Menstrie Glen return!*

And all at once the whole airborne company disappears. The peasant finds himself alone with his cart in the field to finish his furrow.

BEHAVIOR:

These airy twilight Alfs are neither good nor bad. They are very attached to the world of the dead; they are sort of ferrymen or guides, who happily accompany the people they meet out walking on certain evenings to the shadow kingdom of the Fairies. They roam in a pack, especially between evening and midnight.

ACTIVITIES:

During their rides above fields and villages, the Sluaghs may kill cats, dogs, and cattle by shooting them with poisonous arrows. These arrows are not lethal to humans but can enchant or daze them.

Occasionally, Sluagh armies clash in the air. It is unwise to put your nose out of doors when you hear sounds of their battles or of their love affairs.

Dvorovoï

There is no sweeter song than that of the ogre who has repented.
—*Mythology Tamed*, P. Noctiflore

In Slavic mythology, Svarog is the father of the gods. He produced Dajbog, the sun, and Svarogitch, fire. Svarog then expanded his brood to include Messiatz, the moon; the Jorios, sisters of the dawn; Vetcherniaia Zvezda, the evening star; Striborg, the wind god; Warplis, the storm; and Erisvork, the tempest. Each produced multitudes of young Spirits as enthusiastically as their father. These grandchildren of Svarog were so full of pride that they rebelled against him, the creator of the Skies and the Earth. So Svarog chased them out of his kingdom and flung them to the four corners of the horizon. Those who fell into the steppes, forests, mountains, and wild waters remained wicked and capricious, while those who fell into house chimneys and farmyards became kind and useful in their contact with the simple, peaceful folk of those days. The familiar genie Donvoi and his wife Domovikla belong to that generation. Dvorovoï landed on top of a hill: confident in his powerful ancestry, he took possession of all his eyes could see, driving out Rod and Tchor, the protectors of the tribes, and had himself consecrated tsar and god. The people were ordered to bow down to him.

Dvorovoï lived like a tyrant for many years. Fierce, cruel, and envious, he made each person give him what he or she held dearest. He took away a certain lord's youngest daughter and forced her to live with him for thirty-five years, without ever undoing her hair, which he had plaited into a braid so long, that it swept the floor behind her. And whenever she remained absent for too long he drew her to himself. One day, a young peasant, who had loved her since her childhood, broke her chain and ran away with her to marry her. One night, in search of firewood, the peasant wandered momentarily away from the camp where he and his love were hiding, and he heard a great shout followed by a frightful laugh. Returning, he found the unhappy girl dead, swinging from her braid, which had been tied to the branch of a tree by Dvorovoï.

Tsar Dvorovoï reigned for many years over the country in this gruesome fashion.

APPEARANCE:

After his marriage he changed a lot. Dvorovoï with his lordly and arrogant mien developed a hefty paunch in the belly, and he also shrunk. His cheeks are bluish because his blood is blue. His dreamy green eyes disappear under thick snow-white eyebrows. His huge beard is also snowy. He allows it to grow to hide his rotund shape. Despite his excess fat due to good food, he has remained strong and vigorous. It is better not to cross him when he loses his temper once a year.

CLOTHING:

He dresses like a peasant. He wears a red belt. He wears his shoes on the wrong feet and buttons up his caftan wrongly. He hides his baldness with an astrakhan hat embroidered with a heart.

HABITAT:

A comfortable home under an isba. His children go to sleep in the places they take care of: stable, cowshed, forge, garden shed, or under the roots of the trees they protect. In certain homes, the Dvorovoï progeny share the same attributes as the Nursery Bogies and sleep in the children's room.

It was his happy meeting with Kikimora that encouraged him to water down his vodka and become the genius of the home. However, it cannot be said that the lady was ever one of the most alluring.

Thin enough to frighten the priests, Kikimora's body resembled old skin draped over chicken bones; she had emaciated, claw-like arms, a hollow, hairy chest, shoulders like salt-cellars, and a sort of mole's head with a curling swan's beak and fishy eyes under a mop of hair, topped with horns and two batlike ears. Kikimora was also a real slattern, always badly dressed with a grimy shawl on her head (except when busy cooking—then she wears an impeccably clean apron). We can't pretend that love is not blind!

Nevertheless, this Alfygenetic throwback drove the king wild. In the evenings, he could be heard sobbing with love and seen trying to make himself appear handsome, gentle, and kind; by day, he worked at transforming the bramble into flower and fruit, yellowing the fields with golden wheat spattered with passion-red poppies, and softening the rough forest floor with moss, bluebells, and the quivering bells of lily of the valley. For her sake, he took up spade and rake and planted a vegetable garden, becoming so benevolent that his grateful people venerated him as the Father of Isba.

Ever since, the husband and wife have watched over the crops in both the literal and the figurative sense. Dvorovoï makes the crops and cattle prosper; he protects and enriches the house. Kikimora looks after the birds and helps the farmer's wife with her housework. But if the housewife has an arm as hollow as an elder-branch and is lazy, Kikimora brings muddle and

discord, breaks the china, and tickles the children at night, until the exasperated husband throws his incompetent wife out of the house. The only way to be reconciled with Kikimora is to go into the forest to gather ferns and prepare a mixture with which to paint all the walls. Dvorovoï and Kikimora watch over farms, helped by their equally kind children: Perseias watches over the flocks, Moloch takes care of the little domestic animals, Krukis shoes the horses, and Ratainitza brushes and grooms them. Giwoitis calms all din and racket. Matergabria oversees the kitchen. Dugnai looks after the bakery, Kricco and Krinis tend the orchard, and Zozim charms the bees in the hive. Krimba, the eldest, has made his home in Bohemia. In the evening all of them sing as they keep watch.

Despite his resolution to be good and all his qualities, Dvorovoï may sometimes lose control and slip back into his former ways. To appease him it is necessary to lay a fistful of sheep's wool, something shiny, and a large slice of cake outside his door, and say with emphasis: "Tsar Dvorovoï, master and kind little neighbor, I offer you this gift as a sign of gratitude: look after the cattle and feed them well."

If that is not enough to calm him down, you can punish him by pricking the wood of a fence with a fork. He feels the pricks.

FOOD:
Too much, but it's so difficult to resist.

BEHAVIOR/ACTIVITIES:
Mati-Syra-Iembia (Damp Mother Earth) predicts the future for those who can understand her and Dvorovoï taught humans how to listen: a peasant can dig into the earth with his stick, apply his ear to it, and listen to what the earth says. If he hears a sound like the noise of a heavily laden cart with bells and laughter, the harvest will be good. If the hole merely cracks like an empty nutshell, the harvest will be bad. To know if someone is telling the truth, put a clump of earth on his head, and the Dvorovoï will make his soul speak.

In Poland, Datan, Tawah, and Lawkapatin preside over successful farming. Gentle Mazanna looks after the orchard crop. Cattle are under the care of Walgiris, and lambs provided for by Kurwaitchin. Kremara, the beer-drinker, and his cousin, Pripartchis, fatten pigs.

HEIGHT:
Tiny.

APPEARANCE:
Take an Elizabethan court at the moment of its greatest splendor, with its king, its queen, its princes and princesses, counts and countesses, its favorites, followers, knights, poets, troubadours, its astrologers, fools, adventurers, its generals, ministers and captains . . . and all the pages, servants, cooks, kitchen lads . . . and reduce them to the size of ants. This is what they are like. The Elfins, unlike the Ouphs, have wings whose texture, scale-quality, and color increase according to their degree of nobility.

Elfins and Ouphs

Can you hear, can you hear
faint trotting on the holly?
—William Pearce, *La jolie ronde*

Of course, you have to stretch your neck out, look carefully, and listen well, but above all, you must stand about, muse, and forget that time is madly racing by.

It is September—autumn's May-time—and the hedge is a wonder: the blackberry is a rich black mouthful, the sloe is dark blue, and the hawthorn is vermilion.

Brush aside a leaf.

You don't see them at first. You have to get used to looking and learn that this luminous and airy buzz, this crystalline twittering, is not caused by swarms of pollinating insects. It is caused by the conversations and frolics of a sumptuous royal court. There is nothing nobler or more precious than the court of King Pwyll and Queen Phylline.

Under the golden dome, laced with branches of wild hop, the king and queen sit, side by side, on their thrones upon the virginal cushion of a water lily dragged from a nearby pond—what a gigantic effort! Despite their fragile and dainty appearance, nothing and nobody can alter the will of the Ouphs and the Elfins.

You will not find any ladybugs or trotting beetles near their majesties Pwyll and Phylline, but princes in ceremonial costume, crowned duchesses, pretty ladies, jugglers, strolling actors, and a star-studded magician gifted with "second sight."

In embossed, strawberry-colored, high-waisted velvet dress, daffodil and partridge-gray doublets, plumed caps, and pointed hennins—veiled with light, or topped with adamantine antennas, the company of the king and queen walk about, flirt, philosophize, pluck lute strings, and dance in a circle . . .

Courtship
You think it's a pair of butterflies resting on a flower, until they detach themselves from a kiss, and you see that they are two lovers, gently parting, holding hands as they go off to the decorative shade of the clematis. A nasturtium leaf serves as a parasol for their gentle vows. She rests her blond head upon a morning glory and listens to him reciting lines by Thomas Campion, which he has learned by heart in order to please her.

Work and Play
In a flowered labyrinth, the prince of Little Windsor, accompanied by his vassals, shouts "Tally Ho!" as he plays at hunting the Countess of Petticoat Tails. They rush to the left through a green corridor, turn twice to the right, once to the left, and come to a dead end. They all bump into each other and leave again laughing. On the other side of the topiary hedges, young people engage in races riding on crickets or in contests of jumping over parasol, chanterelle, and sheep's-foot mushrooms.

On a bed of autumn crocuses interspersed with honesty, two elegant ladies, all in blue, exchange gossip from the bedchambers and antechambers, while playing croquet.

Farther off in the woods, others

gather feathers shed in the autumn molting, left lying on the ground.

Higher up in the undergrowth, a joyful crowd hastens to shake down the beechnuts and the vermilion, starchy whitebeam berries. A wine barrel tap is fixed to the apples, and the nectar flows out, spreading its sweet scent.

Battle

The tocsin sounds from the top of the old medlar tree. The trumpets blare out the summons to assemble; from all sides, the guards come running, armed to the teeth, to take up their positions on the ramparts. The black menace comes down from the sky in a flurry of wings: it's a hungry shrike that has come to fill his larder with tender little Elfins and plump little Ouphs. At the command of their captains, the archers take up their positions on the battlements. Wearing coats of armor made of barley grains, the soldiers push cannons and catapults along the parapets. The cannons are set to fire; the culverins are loaded.

"Fire!" shouts King Pwyll, brandishing his sword. The broadside of thistle prickers and cannonballs of hardened nuts shoots out and hits the bird in the flank, but it is not enough to make him retreat. Another salvo roars out, hitting his wing at point blank range. This is still not enough to defeat him. The shrike flies up and up, gathers height, and charges again, driving straight at them—beak pointing forwards!

Quickly, King Pwyll sends in the winged cavalry of light Elfins and the heavier Ouphs, mounted on wasps, horseflies, and hornets to attack the foe.

At first, the caparisoned army swarms forward, buzzing, to attack the enemy in serried ranks. Within a few inches of his beak, the squadron disperses and, quick as lightning, encircles the enemy, attacking from all sides at once. The bird of prey does not know where to hit back with wing, claw, and beak. He becomes agitated and his plumage blazes, as King Pwyll, astride a big horned stag beetle, dashes straight for him with his lance at the ready. The bird's heart is pierced. The shrike screams in agony and falls in a whirl to the earth.

From her balcony, Queen Phylline, proud of her king's exploit, sends kisses to the heavens.

Funerals

Yesterday evening Dame Grindelline died. From her deathbed she asked to be brought a mirror in which to see herself one last time. She gave a final satisfied sigh as she admired her reflection, unchanged for centuries, and then her body fell back gently onto the white sheet.

They carried her, wrapped in a rose leaf, and placed her standing upright under the hedge, allowing her fingertips to stick out. Children will see her fingers as petals lying on the grass and will say, "Look, here are some autumn crocuses." And if they come back in March, they will say, "Look, here are some spring crocuses."

CLOTHING:
The wardrobe of an Elizabethan court, adapted to each rank and profession.

HABITAT:
A floral palace hidden in the hedges of eternal England.

FOOD:
Small dishes in the big ones and even smaller in the small.

BEHAVIOR:
It is said that the Ouphs and the Elfins are nothing but literary creations. It is said that they were born from the bucolic dreams of Elizabethan poets. It is said that they are not descended from the great founding Elves, and that they have no past. This is why certain writers and learned mythologists have criticized their butterfly wings, their crystalline antennae, and their dainty ways, saying they are only good for use in decorating plates and preaching morality in silly children's books. Fortunately, marvelous poets and playwrights have loved them dearly. Shakespeare and Spenser not only spent a lot of time with them but have also gone to join them deep within the immortal theatre of the hedge.

ACTIVITIES:
They guard the beauty and purity of the language in its Golden Age, as well as the song of the blackbird and the chaffinch.

HEIGHT:
> *That of a boy aged seven.*

APPEARANCE:
> *Everything in his exuberant physiognomy expresses impish mischief and quicksilver liveliness! His bright, naughty eyes, his slit, laughing mouth, his cheeky, grinning face, his snub nose, his sticking-out, pointed ears, his thrusting chin . . . and the stubborn little horns. There is something goatish about him, something of Pan, Robin Goodfellow, and the nocturnal Bacchantes of the hills.*

CLOTHING:
> *Green doublet, the Elves' color, whose spirit he is. Pointed shoes and green cap. But he has also been seen dressed as a goat, in leaves. He has even been seen quite naked!*

HABITAT:
> *Oberon's fairy court in India. But each day, each night, at every moment, he haunts and crisscrosses each hill, wood, grove, moor, river, road, and country district of England, where he is always hopefully expected.*

Puck

. . . Puck, alias Robin Goodfellow, alias Nick O'Lincoln, alias Lob-lie-by-the-Fire . . .
— Rudyard Kipling,
Rewards and Fairies

P UCK'S WEEK:
Monday:
Get up with the dawn, ask it if it has slept well, and wake up the country with a flamboyant cock-a-doodle-do. Have a Breakfast of fresh lettuce, then circle the earth—by way of gymnastics—in just forty minutes.

Water the new flowers: the wood anemones, the starry celandines, the violets, and the primroses, and with two notes recall the cuckoo to our home woods. Chase away the last of the snow. Visit old Mother Goose in her shoe—and don't forget to take her my shoes to mend!

Scatter rosehip itching powder on the chasubles in the sacristy. Join Dan and Una on the hill and, by the magic of the oak, the ash, and the hawthorn, carry them back to the time when no one dreamed of building walls of cement and stone in the enchanted domains. Then onto a well-earned nap under the big willow before going to unhook the fishes from the bait on fishing lines, splash the washerwomen, tangle the washing, and spatter it with elderberry ink. Twist up Master Dick's hop vines, send his cow to graze on Saturn . . .

and, before flirting with Morpheus, say goodnight to the cuckoo.

Tuesday:
Lulla, Lulla, Lullaby! Lulla, Lulla Lullaby!
This is Tuesday
Market day in Tewkesbury!
Lulla, Lulla, Lullaby! Lulla, Lulla Lullaby!
Turn myself into a mad bull!
Lulla, Lulla, Lullaby! Lulla, Lulla Lullaby!
And spread panic, turbulence, turn the town upside down!

Wednesday:
Take advantage of the passage of Mercury to fetch from the astral waters the seaweed crystals that have been promised to Peaseblossom, Cobweb, Moth, and Mustardseed, so that they can finish making Titania's train before May Day . . . Then roam, never stop roaming! Leading the goblin band, from evening until morning, roam all the roads. Wander the streets of Windsor! Stop up the chimneys to fill the inns with smoke, open the rabbit hutches, shake weathercocks and inn signs, and topple matrons head over heels. Keep roaming!

Then, drowsy with laughter, tricks, and jokes, fall asleep on a crescent moon.

Thursday:
On this jester night my task is to amuse Oberon and his noble shadow court: to cheer up the ancient faces of the oaks, I become a Will-o'-the-Wisp. Will-o'-the-Wisp, Jack-a-Lantern, Kit-Candle-Stick, and Hinky Punk, I will be: to make the nocturnal woodruff gatherers smile, and amuse those who tread on moss, or sleep under the chanterelle mush-

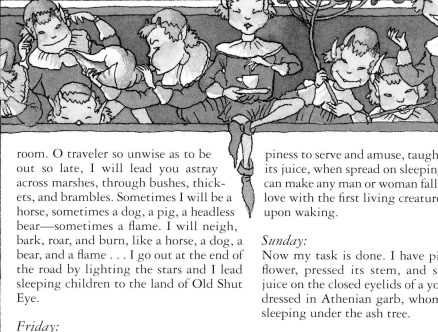

room. O traveler so unwise as to be out so late, I will lead you astray across marshes, through bushes, thickets, and brambles. Sometimes I will be a horse, sometimes a dog, a pig, a headless bear—sometimes a flame. I will neigh, bark, roar, and burn, like a horse, a dog, a bear, and a flame . . . I go out at the end of the road by lighting the stars and I lead sleeping children to the land of Old Shut Eye.

Friday:
Recall that the knot in my handkerchief is an invitation to have my portrait taken by Arthur Rackham for his illustrations to *A Midsummer Night's Dream.* I will not ask him for a penny on the condition that in return he reduces the size of my ears and the point of my chin. I hope I will meet some pretty models—Bottom led me to understand that the master's studio was not without beautiful creatures in a state of undress. Then tea at five o'clock in the Fairies' Club on the Snow Hill oak branch, followed by a conference on the subject of Katharine Briggs' brilliant work: *The Anatomy of Puck* . . . then a mischievous return by way of the Ring O'Bells and the pubs of York, and, to finish, a dance on the Hestercombe Garden lawns.

Saturday:
Go and find a flower for my beloved master—the great King Oberon—and be careful not to get the wrong kind. Wander over moors, hills, woods, and markets to find Shakespeare's "little western flower, before milk-white, now purple with love's wound," the one pierced by Cupid's arrow which is sharp enough to shatter a hundred thousand hearts. "Maidens call it love-in-idleness." My noble master, whom I have had the honor and hap-

piness to serve and amuse, taught me that its juice, when spread on sleeping eyelids, can make any man or woman fall madly in love with the first living creature they see upon waking.

Sunday:
Now my task is done. I have picked the flower, pressed its stem, and spread its juice on the closed eyelids of a young man dressed in Athenian garb, whom I found sleeping under the ash tree.

> *Flower of this purple dye,*
> *Hit with Cupid's archery,*
> *Sink in apple of his eye.*
> *When his love he doth espy,*
> *Let her shine as gloriously*
> *As the Venus in the sky.*
> —Shakespeare,
> *A Midsummer Night's Dream*

This is the formula word for word. This is the enchantment in the dream. . . .

FOOD:
What he can pinch and also the youth-apples of Avalon, the month-of-May elixirs from Elfiria, nettle soup, elder juice, cuckoo flower, and primrose and dandelion wine.

BEHAVIOR:
Spirit of the hills, prince and wanderer of the night, the Fairies' jester, by his countless tricks and disguises, Puck, the best known but most elusive of Elves, has decked himself in a stunning Harlequin costume, borrowing brightly colored diamonds from the costumes of his neighbors: the Pixies, Brownies, Boggart, Pooka, the turbulent marsh, moorland, wood and hill spirits, Peghs, Will-o'-the-Wisps, and even from the devil himself. But there is only one Puck!

ACTIVITIES:
More mischievous than wicked, he fraternizes with poets and children and only attacks those who deserve it. But he is also a scatterbrained and muddling magician. Many tales and stories tell of the comic consequences of his blunders.

The Loireag

Anything that could be spun, the Loireag span it, day and night she span.

—Kathleen Weedling

Mother Crook was so miserly that she wouldn't even have given away her egg-boiling water. Distaff in hand, she was watching her three cows graze early in the morning on the grassy slopes of Snowhill, when her sharp eye caught sight of a big ball of mist-colored wool. She picked it up to examine it. It was no ordinary thread. The silk was as fine as a thread spun by a spider on meadow dew, and as strong as a steel blade. It must have been the work of a Loireag, who had come to spin the night before. The Loireag must have dropped the ball from her apron. Bad luck for her if she had lost it!

Of course, it would have been more honest if Mother Crook had left it in plain sight on a stone, so that the Spinner could find it again. But she was so greedy! Already she could see the fine stockings, handkerchiefs, bonnets, and lace she could make from the ball and sell in the market. Already she could hear the pennies rattling in her pocket . . .

But as she was busy handling it, she dropped the ball, which rolled away before her. In order to grab it Mother Crook had to quickly discard her distaff on the side of the road. Eagerly, she stretched out both of her hands to catch it, but it rolled away and kept on rolling!

Like a Will-o'-the-Wisp, it rolled sometimes behind her and sometimes in front, but it always slipped from her grasp.

Breathlessly, she ran through the hamlet's fields. Without even noticing, she climbed the steep mountain slopes of Lochboisdale in pursuit of the ball. At last she managed to grab, not the ball she coveted, but the length of thread unwinding behind it.

Despite the rocks she had to climb, the ruts in which she twisted her feet, and the brambles that tore at her clothes, Mother Crook couldn't contain her joy. Straining with effort, she held fast and kept winding the thread round her hands, wrists, and arms.

Soon Mother Crook was as tightly enmeshed as a fly in a spider's web; she wound the thread round herself a few more times, hobbling her legs. It infuriated her, but she resigned herself to break-ing the thread by biting through it. Suddenly the ball she had pursued for so long disappeared in a single giddy bound. At the same time, the whole skein of thread she had such trouble gathering unwound out of her hands and fingers. Nothing remained—not a single bit of thread!

And old Mother Crook again ran after the ball, which taunted her by bouncing off her face!

That evening her husband found the three cows grazing on the hillside grass alone and the distaff abandoned at the roadside but no sign of Mother Crook.

Year after year she has continued to chase the ball of "mist-colored" thread through the mists and moors of an unknown country.

When you find a ball of thread in the morning grass, pick it up, if you like—but make sure you give it back to the Loireag who has lost it.

HEIGHT:
As small as an infant in a cradle.

APPEARANCE:
Tiny, pale, flaxen-haired, rather rustic looking, with long clever fingers and a very intense gaze. Loireags leave behind them a scent of fresh laundry.

CLOTHING:
Like the inhabitants of the Western Isles of Scotland, but so finely woven that you can see the mist through them. Misty white and green, so pale that you think you are seeing a mirage. Their lace apron is always full of balls of thread, wool, needles, and shuttles in all sizes.

HABITAT:
The isles of Uist, Benbecula, and Barra. Especially splendid dwellings at the summit of Ben More.

FOOD:
They adore milk and cream. Sometimes you can surprise them when they are attached to a cow's teats sucking the milk out.

BEHAVIOR:
These ladies of dawn and twilight are highly respected by the elf and fairy world for their skill in spinning and weaving. They are also very rich and courted by the Brownies and Siths from all over Scotland. The Loireags fear nobody and are not afraid to confront those who approach their home too closely.

ACTIVITIES:
They spin, weave, and supervise all the making of cloth and clothes in Elfiria, and also in the mortal world of the Western Isles of Scotland.

Blue Men of the Minch

And your sister?
She pisses blue—why, have you got something to dye?

The Shiant Islands are two pale cliffs rising out of the gray-blue water between the misty isles of Harris and Lewis in the Outer Hebrides. Travelers to enchanted isles and old fishermen with memories full of marvels will tell you that they are really the two visible fragments of the hidden kingdom—hidden on a "floating rock" anchored in the Minch Strait—of the Blue Men of the Minch, and their Elfin people with salty blue skin.

Local people know about them, but strangers do not; this is a great pity, as a little knowledge would prevent a lot of shipwrecks, storms, and drowning.

Once, some salmon fishermen, who had come from far away to cast their nets in the Minch, were surprised to find a naked man—they thought he was blue with cold—caught in their nets. As they dragged him brutally onto the bridge, the man began to threaten them and spit with such rage that the fishermen were terrified he might attack them. They tied him up even tighter, so that it was impossible for him to struggle, as he could move neither his arms nor his legs. No sooner had the ship set sail again than they saw two other men, just as naked and blue, advancing in their wake, so fast that soon they were able to grab hold of the boat.

Then the prisoner rose with a single bound, broke his bonds as if they were spider's webs, and jumped overboard to rejoin those who had come to save him. All three dived with such force that they made a hole in the water, a chasm so deep that the ship was swallowed up in it.

Another time, an old man from Scalpay was coming back from the inn along a stony path, grumbling as he drew upon his pipe that had gone out, and cursing the night winds. He looked for a niche in a rock for shelter from the wet. Then he noticed a blue light, like a window cut into a cave. Scarcely had he taken three steps towards it when the ground gave away beneath his feet and he found himself tumbling down a pit into the depths. Thus Ouald Mac Fubis came into contact with the underground kingdom of the Blue Men of the Minch.

It could not be said that the salty blue Elves received him badly. He was presented to the king and all the king's court of naked blue people began to dance.

Never had the old man tasted such fine gin, eaten better fish, or embraced prettier women. The next day he took one of them home with him, the most beautiful of all, whom the king had offered him as a bride. She was a real beauty, with eyes the color of waves in summer, sky-colored hair, and soft skin.

She was the best, most attentive, and loving of wives, except that if she was crossed in any way, she became furious.

And it was in the course of one these domestic scenes that Ouald Mac's cottage was struck by lightning and set on fire, then crushed and inundated with rain. After that he became a vagabond without a home, wandering ever since from inn to inn to tell his story.

HEIGHT:
The same as humans.

APPEARANCE:
Like humans except that their skin and hair is blue and salty.

CLOTHING:
Naked. The king wears a shining cobalt crown; warriors wear shell helmets. They do not need weapons. Instead of arrows, sword, and lance, they unleash thunder by snapping their fingers.

FOOD:
Delicacies of fish, seafood, and seaweed spiced with saffron.

HABITAT:
A gigantic sapphire, turquoise, and blue diamond palace with a crystal-dome for a ceiling. It has squares, avenues, gardens, buildings, libraries, and sea museums.

BEHAVIOR:
Powerful Elves of the sea, their blue skin and blood show their high nobility. In Elfiria, they occupy the same place in the sea as the Daoine Sidhe do on the hills. They are intelligent, merry, and helpful. Clever fishermen, they are also brave and redoubtable fighters. They have never suffered defeat, except at the hands of time. They are a people becoming extinct. The degradation of the ocean is a curse against which they cannot or will not fight . . .

ACTIVITIES:
Fishing, singing, the arts, philosophy, exploration, and the study of infinite liquids. They can unleash storms, tempests, and tidal waves, or they can make the waves calm and kind. They charm whales and disturb mermaids.

HEIGHT:
A little man.

APPEARANCE:
His impish mischief can be read on his face. His complexion is ruddy and dry. His eyes are twinkling and bright. But he can frighten the population by taking the shape of a fierce giant on all fours.

CLOTHING:
The Fir Darrig—the "red man"—is dressed in vermilion, crimson, scarlet, and carmine, from the peak of his tricorn hat to the soles of his shoes. He wears a flamboyant waistcoat and a long cloak, and often bears a sword.

HABITAT:
The whole of Ireland, but especially Kerry, Donegal, and the region of Munster. They live in former forts, Dun Siths, hollow hills, and ruined inns, but also frequent Tir-Nan-Og and the enchanted isles.

The Fir Darrig
or Fir Dhearga

He sat down by the fire, closed his eyes, and smoky stories came out of his pipe.
—Peggy Lee, *Donegal's Songs*

Diarmid Bawn loved smoking his pipe and playing the bagpipes. He rented a little farm in the hills above the Killarney Lakes. Every evening after supper he'd go and sit on a little stone wall that surrounded his property, attach the bellows to his arm, and begin playing for the wind and the heather and all those who live in them. Afterwards he would take out his clay pipe and his tobacco and reward himself by blowing a few delightful smoke rings.

One night he was very disappointed when he took his pouch out of his pocket and did not find a shred of tobacco in it. Swearing in anger, he was magically transported to a Dun Sith, an Elfin fort, at Lady View crossroads. He had barely gathered his wits, when, suddenly, he saw—the Lord preserve us—a whole host of little people dressed in red, decked out and armed for war, as they rallied round a person who appeared to be their general.

"Is everyone ready?" he shouted, drawing his sword.

"No, your Majesty," replied the captain. "You need a horse to lead us, because otherwise we will be defeated."

Diarmid Bawn knew he had come upon the army of the kingdom of Fir Darrig assembled in full force. He tried to tiptoe away, but he heard a voice summoning him. "Where are you off to, Sir Diarmid Bawn, the piper, whose melodies delight us every evening? You are big, strong, and solid. Come here, so that I can make you my horse."

And before Diarmid Bawn could get away, the king touched him with his saber, turned him into a warhorse, and mounted him. "Tally Ho! Fir Darrig! Charge!"

They charged into the air and soared above the vast ocean, until they landed on a dark island where cohorts of hairy dwarves awaited them. The two armies

threw themselves on one another in a fury. Arrows flew, bodies fell, and blood flowed in a ceaseless stream. The Dwarf troops increased continually, until the Fir Darrig found themselves overrun and driven back to the shore.

Diarmid Bawn was keeping a low profile, when suddenly one of the Fomoirés, stabbed him under his right eye with a sword thrust. Engaged, he flew into a fury and charged forward with his head down, entering into the fray, and spreading devastation. Soon all that remained was a big pile of hairy Dwarves and a few fugitives escaping as fast as they could. The battle had been won.

Then to reward Diarmid Bawn, "the best horse of all," the general with a long white beard commanded: "Every man is to give him a fistful of tobacco," and they flew back over the vast ocean. Returning to the ancient Dun Sith, they disappeared into the mountain mist.

When Diarmid Bawn looked about him, the sun was rising, and he thought it had all been a dream, until he saw a big heap of tobacco at the entrance to the old fort and heard a voice close beside him whisper in his ear: "All that tobacco is for you, because of your brave conduct in the battle. Henceforth, whenever I need a horse, a Fir Darrig will come and fetch you, because I never rode a better charger than Diarmid Bawn."

Truly, that is what the voice said.

FOOD:
Traditional Irish cooking. They are greedy eaters and great drinkers, sometimes drinking too much poteen.

BEHAVIOR/ACTIVITIES:
Sometimes benevolent, always mischievous, usually sly, they are always playing tricks on mortals: changing their brides into sows, hiding their cattle, turning the horses they are riding into all kinds of creatures.

They are brave and warlike, but also good musicians and excellent singers. They play for all the balls and parties in Elfiria.

HEIGHT:

The tallest are nine inches (22 cm), but the majority measure between four and six inches (9 to 15 cm). Some are no bigger than one inch (2 cm).

APPEARANCE:

Hudson, from whom most descriptions of manikins derive, distinguishes several species. He says that meadow manikins are like young children of about three years old: chubby-cheeked, with a happy, smiling expression. Their eyes are small and bright, and their ears poke out from under their hats. Oak manikins are ruddy, as if they had been exposed to rough weather. Their eyes are slanted and do not have a human expression. He calls those with a brick-colored complexion the "Reds": their head is a special shape. It is very flat at the sides and there is a sort of ledge from the center of their brow, down their nose to their chin. The "Greens" are like small children in miniature, with big heads, plump bodies, thin legs, and pointed feet. The "Mole Manikins" are short, thick, and gruff in appearance. They look older, less lively, and wear long beards. They are surrounded by a grayish light as if they were smoking a pipe. Some species of Manikin have little oval wings on their backs, made of some shining semi-transparent stuff, which quiver and tremble.

CLOTHING:

This varies according to the species. Hudson says that garden manikins wear a loose, dark red-brown costume reaching to their hips, with short trousers and gray stockings, large scalloped collars, and aprons with many pockets. Woolen caps. Tree manikins wear a pointed hat and a little costume with a long collar, so long that it is like a cape falling from their shoulders. Red manikins wear clothes that strongly resemble Elizabethan dress; they look padded and quilted. They wear a very strange pointed hat, which is crimson and decorated with an acorn or little bell. The smallest ones are molded into a sort of skin-tight green body suit, rather like a lizard or frog's skin. It covers their head except for their faces, which are sometimes painted or gilded.

Manikins, Manneken, and Little Mannequins

Mr. Untel claims to have seen something extraordinary, which I myself have not been able to observe. So I cannot form an absolute opinion on the subject. But on the other hand, I have no reason to doubt what he says a priori: it's quite possible that what he says is true.

—Dr. J.P. Crouzet

Mr. Geoffrey Hudson was a happy man. We do not know what kind star gave him his particular gift: the Manikin Little People revealed themselves to each of his senses quite naturally, without him expressing the least desire that they should do so. As soon as he went out shopping or to get some air in the garden, he saw, felt, and heard the imperceptible.

He sniffed the soft evening air. Immediately, the air he breathed became sweeter and soon he spotted the Little Manikin busily scenting the flowers with his honeysuckle and the essence of mock orange.

His eye wandered over the beds of pansies, where processions of Manikins emerged, engaged in folding up the petals to shelter them from the chilly night air. Hudson raised his eyes and saw another Manikin smoking his pipe astride a branch.

Theosophists, Hawthorn doctors, and students of elf lore state that this rare "clairvoyance" and "clairaudience" is gained gradually at the price of strenuous ascesis—fasting and purification. But in the case of Geoffrey Hudson, none of that was required. A few days after he had given in the cap and big patent leather bag that went with his job at the section depot, as he stood in his shirtsleeves about to dig some cabbage, he raised his eyes and saw them. He shut his eyes immediately, opened them again, and they were still there.

As a confirmed materialist, he went to consult the local doctor, complaining about fatigue causing him visual troubles.

The doctor found he had a young man's

vision and a clear head; that he was, in fact, as healthy as a horse.

The doctor prescribed three or four chamomile flower compresses per week and beef broth every day. Mr. Geoffrey Hudson went home reassured. He was even more reassured because the Little Manikins did not seem at all interested in his presence. They were there, as the birds were, pecking about on the path and searching for stuff with which to build their nests. "Each one was busy with its own affairs," he wrote that night in his big oilskin-covered diary, which had been given to him as a retirement present by his work colleagues.

He enjoyed seeing them as you enjoy seeing a bold robin displaying his bright breast in the pale winter landscape. Between hoeing two rows, he stopped to roll a cigarette and sit down on the wheelbarrow. He watched them coming and going incessantly, busily engaged in absurd little tasks whose purpose he could not fathom but which, he gathered from the Manikins' zealous expressions, they regarded as vitally important. When he was out walking in the woods, he would encounter them round a tree stump, or on a mushroom bank. Resting on his stick, he would stay there for hours, writing things down in his notebook.

They never came closer together than one yard apart; they never tried to win each other over. They inhabited two separate alien worlds, living their lives in the same space without friendship or hostility.

As a child, Mr. Hudson had heard stories of Elves and other little creatures, notably the Dartmoor Pixies, for whom the locals left out bowls of clotted cream, so that they would grant them good harvests and tools that would work of their own accord. But Mr. Hudson did not ask them for anything. He enjoyed himself too much gardening, looking after his own tools, and savoring the fruits of his labor to want anyone to do it for him and deprive him of this peaceful pleasure. Moreover, he knew that kind of dealing generally ended very badly; the day would come when it was payback time, and the price was sometimes high.

Hudson never got anything out of the affair and did not say a word to anyone. Indeed, whom could he have confided in? He did not go to the inn and was such a silent and discreet soul that people did not even see him pass by.

Did he also prefer to keep quiet out of modesty? Was he afraid of being thought mad? Or did he simply fear he might lose the presence of these familiar little creatures that no one else could see? "The Little Manikins work in the grass, run about aimlessly here and there, simply flitting somewhere like butterflies in the sun," he wrote. And what were you doing, dear Mr. Hudson; were you so different from your little Elfin gardeners?

HABITAT:
They live inside the places from which they emerge. They disappear to mingle with a bank, undergrowth, mushrooms, and all the natural elements surrounding them.

FOOD:
Perhaps they absorb a vital essence from the air, which they then infuse into trees, plants, and flowers.

BEHAVIOR/ACTIVITIES:
Well before Geoffrey Hudson's notebook, we can read in Pétrus Barbygère's Elfin Chronicles *that little manikins, mannekens, and mannequins represent the most common type of elementary Elves. He says the manikin or country Elf is the one that comes to mind when in the evening stories are told of Little People. They are the ones the pencil draws when you mechanically try to represent them. The manikin makes innocents laugh and accompanies truant children. Everywhere he hops, dances, and twitters, becoming as essential as the air we breathe.*

They are sensitive to pollution and decimated by chemical emissions, genetically modified crops, and herbicides. Today, they have become immune. They plant and will continue to plant the eternal meadows in the asphalt and concrete.

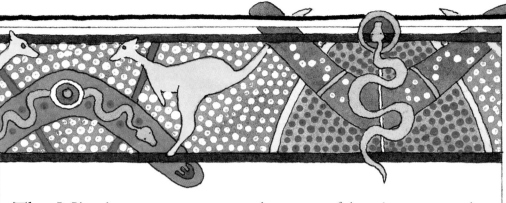

HEIGHT:
About twenty-four inches (60 cm).

APPEARANCE:
We know certain elements of their physiognomy from the portraits of themselves they have painted on the walls of caves and rocks, and from descriptions of them passed down in Toolalla oral tradition. They are very graceful, very delicate, and slender as koala leaves. They are so light that they cannot go out on windy days, because gusts of wind would carry them off or break them in two. Their gaze is lit by sky and fire. Exceptional hearing enables them to discern the slightest sound of footsteps, crawling, or rustling miles away so that they are able to disappear into the narrowest of crevices.

CLOTHING:
Loincloths made of leaves and necklaces and bracelets made of shiny metal, plaited leather, and shells.

HABITAT:
Australia. Spacious, comfortable caves, superbly decorated, under the Arnhem plateau.

FOOD:
They hunt and fish.

The Mimi

Lord, now lettest thou thy servant depart in peace, according to thy word . . .
—Luke 2:29

Gooroondoodilbaydilbay, the southern wind, had driven poor Toolalla far into the bush. Now he was wandering about, parched with thirst, over the sand and past the shriveled trees. He was also hungry and afraid. He was afraid of meeting Walgaru, the stone and wooden man, Yurunggur, the snake, or Mamu, the cannibal. In his fist he clasped the heavy boomerang, but he felt lost. A thorn had wedged itself deep in his foot, forcing him to limp and causing him to burn with fever.

Then young Toolalla raised this prayer: "I promise anyone who comes to help me to serve them for half my life."

As soon as he had uttered these words, he heard a rustling sound in front of him, he saw pebbles moving, and then a wonderful little creature emerged from under the ground. Soon he was followed by dozens more of these tiny creatures, who were just as splendid as the one who seemed to be their leader.

"We have heard your prayer, and it shall be granted," said the little leader in a strange language, like the language of birds, but which Toolalla was somehow able to understand. The creature signaled and the rocks obeyed. They rolled open magic doors into the mountain and Toolalla entered the heart of the Mimi Kingdom.

As soon as he crossed the threshold his pain ceased, the thorn was no longer in his foot, he was no longer hungry or thirsty, and his tiredness was gone. Toolalla felt happier than he had ever been before. His happiness lasted all through the time of his service. The work he had to do was not hard. He carried the game killed by the Mimi on his back and propped up their caves with big beams, which he cut from tree trunks in the forest, and which by some unknown magic seemed to him as light as little sticks. He helped to grind the colors the Mimi used to paint their large frescoes. In the evening he brought in the flocks of wallabies, dingoes, pythons, and kangaroos. Toolalla was treated as a

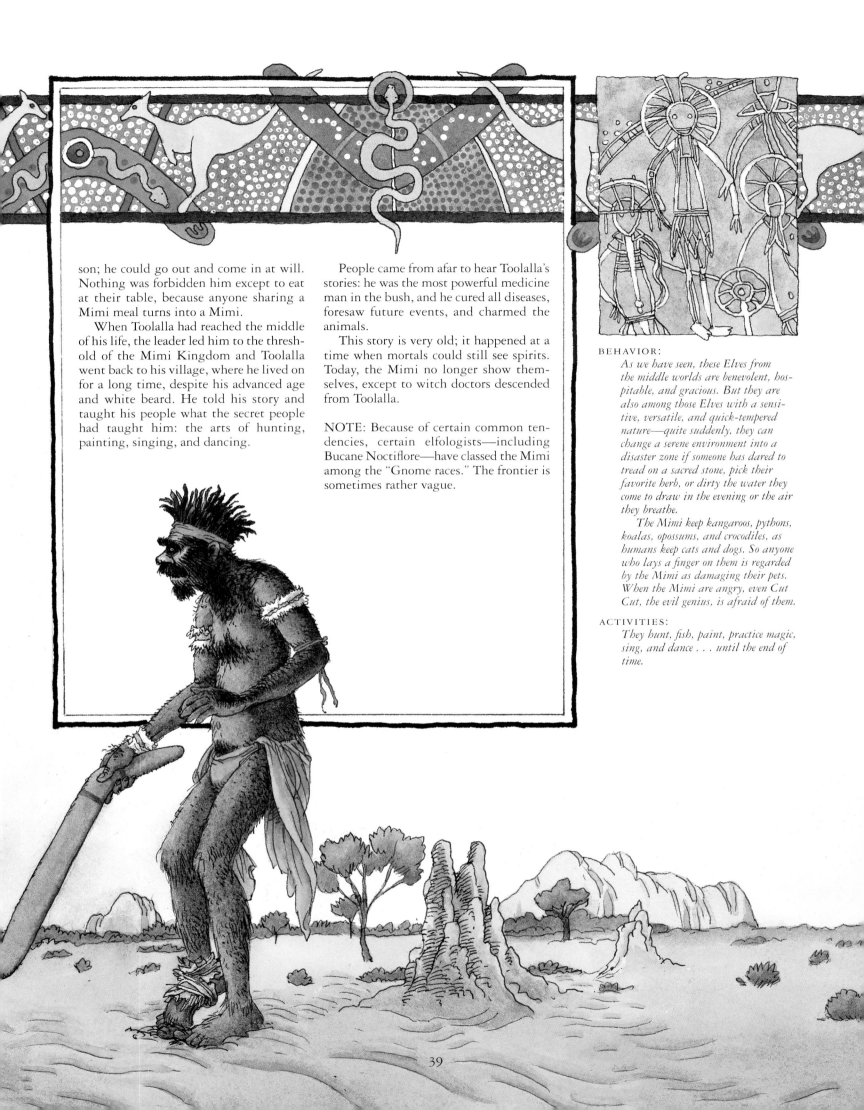

son; he could go out and come in at will. Nothing was forbidden him except to eat at their table, because anyone sharing a Mimi meal turns into a Mimi.

When Toolalla had reached the middle of his life, the leader led him to the threshold of the Mimi Kingdom and Toolalla went back to his village, where he lived on for a long time, despite his advanced age and white beard. He told his story and taught his people what the secret people had taught him: the arts of hunting, painting, singing, and dancing.

People came from afar to hear Toolalla's stories: he was the most powerful medicine man in the bush, and he cured all diseases, foresaw future events, and charmed the animals.

This story is very old; it happened at a time when mortals could still see spirits. Today, the Mimi no longer show themselves, except to witch doctors descended from Toolalla.

NOTE: Because of certain common tendencies, certain elfologists—including Bucane Noctiflore—have classed the Mimi among the "Gnome races." The frontier is sometimes rather vague.

BEHAVIOR:
As we have seen, these Elves from the middle worlds are benevolent, hospitable, and gracious. But they are also among those Elves with a sensitive, versatile, and quick-tempered nature—quite suddenly, they can change a serene environment into a disaster zone if someone has dared to tread on a sacred stone, pick their favorite herb, or dirty the water they come to draw in the evening or the air they breathe.

The Mimi keep kangaroos, pythons, koalas, opossums, and crocodiles, as humans keep cats and dogs. So anyone who lays a finger on them is regarded by the Mimi as damaging their pets. When the Mimi are angry, even Cut Cut, the evil genius, is afraid of them.

ACTIVITIES:
They hunt, fish, paint, practice magic, sing, and dance . . . until the end of time.

The Co-Walker

HEIGHT:
Same as the person they are reflecting.

APPEARANCE:
Same as the person whose physiognomy they borrow and mimic. When the co-walker is still only a shadow, he is visible only to cats and dogs, which cause confusion by gazing at an empty space.

CLOTHING:
The same goes for their clothes. However, despite all his efforts, the Co-Walker is not a perfect reproduction of the original. The clear, expert eye of Tabhaisver is never deceived because there is always a detail that is wrong.

HABITAT:
It seems that they can live at the same time in an "underground" limbo and the "overground" environment of their "victim."

FOOD:
Same as their mortal double. The Tabhaisver often see them sitting down to table during funeral banquets.

BEHAVIOR/ACTIVITIES:
The Reverend R. Lewtranchard considers them to be Elves who have wandered onto the frontier between day and night, and have never been able to choose between light and darkness, or good and evil. That is why a mortal with an indecisive spirit suits them well.

The Co-Walkers' role is very mysterious and complex. Sometimes they behave like simple ghosts. At times they behave like guardian angels, and at other times they behave like malignant demons determined to destroy their victim in order to take his place.

Sometimes they take pity on a solitary person and become the secret familiar companions of abandoned children or the attentive friends of forgotten old people.

As he did so he got a horrible shock, for though just then a cloud sailed across the moon he saw, in spite of the sudden darkness around him, his own image.
—Bram Stoker, *The Sands of Crooken*

A man finishes work and goes home. Every evening at the same time, he takes the same road, along the same pavement, meets the same people, goes up the same steps, lingers for a moment at the same baker's shop window, and then carries on the same way until he reaches his own front door. He puts the key into the lock and goes inside.

His dog welcomes him with unexcited but cheerful barking. His wife then mechanically embraces him. He hangs his jacket in the closet and sits down in his armchair until supper is ready . . . and this has been going on for so many years that it would be boring to count them.

One day, on the same road he always takes, he gets the impression that he is being followed. But when he looks back, he sees the same scene he always sees. Nevertheless, from this point on, he always feels the same sense of unease as he goes home by his accustomed route. He sniffs a scent, a scent that he recognizes without being able to place it. He catches the sound of a footstep that echoes his own, and a shadow that quickly disappears whenever he looks back. Now the presence follows him so closely that he is afraid. So he hurries along the streets and rushes up the steps, his footfalls echoing behind him.

Then one day, something happened. Unlike all the preceding nights, he left his work and did not feel the threatening shadow waiting for him. He went on his way home almost jauntily. At last he went indoors, satisfied that all he could hear was the echo of his own feet on the stairs.

He called out happily, "It's me." But no one came to meet him, neither his wife, nor his dog. They were too busy in the sitting room entertaining a guest sitting in the armchair with only his back visible from the door.

When the man approached his wife and dog, it was as if they looked without seeing him, and when the Other turned round, he found he was facing himself.

From then on he had no real existence, no one could see or hear him, eternally treading the same immemorial path. Perhaps tomorrow he will attach himself to some passerby as their shadow.

Candle Tip and Candle Nick

Each year they conjure up a certain number of tormenting spirits...
—John Flanders, *Ingoldsby Legends*

Allistair Pruffle had the unusual job of being a smoking hat representative. He offered all kinds of hats for smokers: all sizes, all shapes, all prices, and in all materials. He could provide a black crepe skullcap for an inconsolable widower, a Highlander's tartan bonnet, astrakhan hats with silver tassels, or a hat of linsey-woolsey, or velvet, with macramé trimmings or…

He was a jovial, Pickwickian little man, apparently open-handed. But you would have been wrong to think so, because this impulsive bonhomie was in fact the cover for a secret vice: Allistair Pruffle was a miser! He even economized on candle ends—once he had finished his daily sales, he'd sneak into churches to snuff out all the burning candles and purloin them.

One day Allistair Pruffle chose the flourishing little town of Tappington to present his new autumn collection, for he knew it was a very pious parish.

Slightly to the edge of the town, the church's square tower stood in the middle of the cemetery, surrounded by venerable old oaks haloed in October gold.

A sign pinned under the portrait of its patron saint indicated the locations of treasures to be discovered. There were some remarkable pieces, of which Allistair Pruffle took no notice. He was busy looking out for dancing lights in the shadows. But he found nothing at all! Not a single candle, not even a little one, flickered under the arches. Desperately disappointed, he was about to slide away, when suddenly a tall bright flame attracted his gaze to the middle of an aisle, along which he had already walked several times. It was a noble-looking candle. It was as long as your arm, a fine ivory white. It sent up to heaven a light as splendid as an angel star. In the twinkling of an eye, he had snaffled it and put it in his bag.

Home in his attic, Allistair Pruffle wanted to light his short pipe by the faint light of the oil lamp, but it went out and the poor little man found himself in the dark.

He groped for the stolen candle. It lit of its own accord. Allistair Pruffle had no time to be surprised, because all at once the candle changed shape, twisted itself out of his hand, and transformed itself into a luminous little dwarf, who was looking at him threateningly.

"Good evening," he said. "My name is Candle Tip."

No sooner had he reached out his hand than Allistair Pruffle began to scream.

All that was found of him were his smoking hats, lying in nasty pool of warm candle wax.

HEIGHT:
Of a candle.

APPEARANCE:
Candle Tip has a twin brother, Candle Nick, who is as devilish and mischievous as himself. They look like imps. However, their skin is neither dry nor dark, but pale as wax. Likewise their faces do not look evil but, on the contrary, have the chubby cheeks, snub nose, bright eyes, and smile and dimples of a cheerful, naughty child.

Their bushy hair is red and curly; their ears are pointed. When they are angry, they can be very frightening as their faces change to look like hideous gargoyles.

CLOTHING:
Tight-fitting. Golden-brown waistcoat, red trousers, shiny stockings, and scarlet Beelzebub cloak.

HABITAT:
England. They particularly like Tappington, where both of them are called Trill. They only appear where candles are burning.

FOOD:
No information.

BEHAVIOR:
They are candle imps. According to John Flanders, author of Ingoldsby Legends, *they are little jokers from the spirit world. Richard Harris Barham describes them, in his unusual work* Lanterns of the Dead and Mystic Lighting, *as Elves fallen from twilight and the half-darkness, among the Imps or Impets.*

ACTIVITIES:
They spend their time playing tricks on those who deserve it: rascals, misers, and all evildoers.

HEIGHT:
Hyter Sprites are not very big.

APPEARANCE:
Slight, graceful, and pleasant to look upon. Their very pale, delicate skin looks as if it were powdered with gold dust. Their features are fine, with big almond-shaped eyes, and a small mouth. They are so light that they can cross moving sands and fens without sinking into them. Birds by day, Elves by night, sometimes they can be seen in a group together, mixing in both their shapes.

CLOTHING:
Even when they take their original shape as Elves, they have exchanged forever the dresses, doublets, and elegant clothes they once wore for a coat of feathers.

HABITAT:
Misty towers and the Lincolnshire Fens.

FOOD:
Seeds, saffron grains, and leftovers from feasts.

BEHAVIOR:
These little-winged, twittering Elves—light as twilight and soft as dawn's misty shadow—enchant the silent coastlands with their presence . . . They remind us of the fragility and futility of material riches, the brevity of reigns, and—on the other hand—the eternity of legends.

ACTIVITIES:
They fly about over sands and waters.

The Hyter Sprites

The Fens begin somewhere but nowhere do they finish. Only the winged spirits know their full extent.

—Edwin D. Pluckley

Once upon a time there was just one expanse of endless fens between the three towers of Lincoln, standing on their cliff, and the enchanted isles. On market days you could see and hear the pretty little crowd of Elves and Hyter Sprites crossing the Fens with their baskets, and hopping between the reeds so as not to get their feet wet. It was delightful to watch them climbing Steep Hill, freshly beribboned, before spreading out among the stalls to make their purchases. At noon they went to the inns, applauded the jugglers, and never failed to respond to the piper's invitation to dance.

They bought eggs, vegetables, and ham, which they paid for with packets of gold dust. The men went to the tailors to order fashionable clothes. The ladies went to the dressmakers, corset-makers, and haberdashers. At the evening bell, as heavily laden as peddlers, they departed single file, a little drunk on beer and mead, and hopped off to their enchanted isles. When they arrived at Holbeach Saint Matthew, a gentle puff of wind carried them over the Wash, and little by little, they were lost to sight in the misty horizon.

They were seen coming and going in this way until the arrival of the pirates from the North. Ancient local stories tell why and how they disappeared.

Between Woodhall Spa and Horncastle, the Viking Way still winds. That is where the pirates settled. One day they fell upon a flock of graceful, female Hyter Sprites coming home from the market, and, being savages, they raped them all. All the Hyter Sprites were so hurt, so shocked, that not a single one of them wanted to keep her original shape, which had been spoiled. They asked the magician of their enchanted isle to change them into sand swallows, and, in order to join them in their new shape, the men changed into swifts.

Since then the magician has sunk with his island into the depths of oblivion . . . but the Hyter Sprites fly, chirp, swirl, and hop around among the reeds and the new flowers of the Fens. You can see them perching in the trees and on church towers on market days. They only reappear in their Elfin beauty during the buttercup season. However, if someone found the magician's book and recited the bird formula from it, it is said that the Hyter Sprite kingdom would be born again, as it used to be . . .

The Fériers

Throughout the year, they make the finest days.
—Emma Phrodyte, Night and Day

The Lincolnshire Hyter Sprites and the Suffolk Fériers join in a single flight above the fens and peck at the golden-shadowed sands . . .

Once the Fériers' domain, with its tall forests of towers and belfries, outdid the powerful capital of the kings of East Anglia. At that time Dunwich, with its twelve churches, stood proudly by the sea. The two cities, the Elf city and the human one, both looked out to sea, and from the sea came fine white sailing ships from Holland, laden with Flanders cloth, Bruges lace, big round, blond cheeses, and bulbs which bloomed into chalice-shaped flowers of every color the moment the fine weather came. The people of Dunwich built their houses with brick gables and fretted stonework, on the beach, as near as possible to the sea. As they wanted to encroach into the sea, they built dikes, despite the Elves warning them not to, warning them to leave the waves to sailors, mermaids, and tritons, for "the earth is fruitful enough not to want to till the waves as well." But the humans would not listen.

"They can't give advice," they retorted. "The Fériers can say what they like, because they live off air; they do not have to work. They only have to dig into their treasures to be rich!"

So they built dams extending into the sea, drove stilts into the shifting sands, and built on surf and wind.

You cannot defy the ocean gods for long. One of them breathed on the water and the rumbling waves poured inland. At that time the Fériers and humans used to intermarry and do business together, so the Elves tried to intervene with their watery sisters, but the Nereids and the Selkies were inflexible. The only concession the Fériers could gain was that the tidal wave would be spread out over many long years, and that the waves would not nibble away more than a handful of sand per day.

Slowly, year by year, handful by handful, one grain of sand then another, the houses and streets of Dunwich were lost to the sea. The churches with their cemeteries and their dead sank beneath the waves.

So that they would not also be drowned, the Fériers changed their splendid city into dunes and heath land, and changed themselves into avocets, gulls, bitterns, and marsh harriers. Every sunset the Férier towers rise again and are illuminated. The Elfin court reinhabits them for the night, and every morning they all fly away and evaporate with the dew.

HEIGHT:
The Fériers are not very big.

APPEARANCE:
There is so little physical difference between the Fériers and their cousins the Hyter Sprites that only an elfologist raised on the four rivers of milk from the graceful Audumbla might be able to tell some vague difference. Master Expansyve says that they quite often confuse themselves.

CLOTHING:
Sea-bird feathers, unless they are feeling nostalgic at the crescent moon—then they wear the elegant clothes of their Elfin wardrobe.

HABITAT:
Sands and dwarf heathers of Suffolk.

FOOD:
Dream grain from harvests of yesteryear. Birdlike appetites.

BEHAVIOR:
Scarcely better or worse than the Hyter Sprites.

ACTIVITIES:
They fly about over the sands and waters.

HEIGHT:
Like a bird or a one-legged Indian.

APPEARANCE:
Colored like the bird Coculus Cornutus, he looks like a skinny dwarf, sunburned and long-haired. He constantly hops about on his one leg, attached to a large foot.

CLOTHING:
A few feathers and always a red hat.

FOOD:
The products of his hunting and fishing or what he steals from kitchens, cellars, shops, and market stalls.

BEHAVIOR:
Together with Boïtatá, Ouroutaou, Iara, Boïuna, Saci Pererê is an Elfin subject of the moon goddess Jaci. He has the dancing brightness of a moonbeam. He is a midnight Elf, a singer-dancer-tightrope walker on a silken silver rope. He is neither good nor bad. This former son of Moroubixabas, a sorcerer from fierce ages past, has become an "odd bird," a joker.

ACTIVITIES:
In the primitive legends, he obeyed the moon goddess Jaci and helped her to enrich the local fauna with new species. He was bad-tempered and frightened humans by summoning the elements and savage beasts against them. His character has improved since then, and his bad deeds are limited to mischievous tricks.

Saci Pererê and the Moon Elves

Lady Pyle said that the Moon Elves were like the Goblins that danced in Cornwall gardens.
—Ida Rentoul Outhwaite

Saci Pererê (or Saci Cererê, or Mati Taperê) is the best-known and most mischievous Elf in Brazil today. He is now a sort of Goblin-figure, with a red cap—a laugher, a joker and a trickster—but in the olden days he was worse.

The story of his birth itself is not very edifying: once upon a time a Pirahiba—from the Tupi *pira* (fish) and *ahiba* (bad)—with a wrinkled brow and striped belly, devoured all who came to fish in the waters where she lived . . . So the Indians decided to get rid of her. They plaited a long liana rope and fastened a fat child onto it as bait. Then they threw it out into the middle of the lake. No sooner had the fishing line dropped below the surface of the water than the Pirahiba greedily snapped through the rope with her teeth, took the bait, and swam off.

Then a sage advised the chiefs of the mourning tribes: "My children," he said, "this Pirahiba is the dark spirit of a moon sorcerer. If you really want to catch it, use a rope plaited from your own wives' hair."

The wives all gave up their hair and braided a rope, to which another fat child was fastened as bait . . . and this time they finally caught the Pirahiba.

The sage said, "Kill it! Open its belly and you will find a bird, which is the soul of the moon sorcerer's son. Be sure you do not let it fly away, because if it manages to sing 'Tinkouan,' we are all lost."

They opened the Pirahiba's belly, but the bird managed to escape and sing "Tinkouan!"

All at once the sky grew dark, the earth shook, fear was born among the Indians, who had not known it up until then, and they were all overwhelmed by the furious waters.

They called the bird Saci Pererê, which means "mother of the souls that appear on the road."

Boïtatá

From the Tupi *mboï* (snake) and *tata* (fire), this Brazilian Will-o'-the-Wisp is Saci Pererê's companion. It lures into the abyss those who are guilty of setting fire to their fields on purpose or for profit. It has a lot to do with the arsonists of the Amazon forests. Boïtatá also shows passersby the hidden graves of those who have been murdered.

Ouroutaou

As this bird only sings by moonlight, Brazilian mestizos today call it Maen de lua, which means "mother of the moon." However, it is actually the child of the moon goddess Jaci. It's a close relative of Saci Pererê, whom it resembles.

From the Tupi *ourou* (bird) and *taou* (ghost). Ouroutaou likes to perch on a branch and sing sad, staccato tunes. The melody gives rise to love dreams and soothes the pain of unhappy lovers.

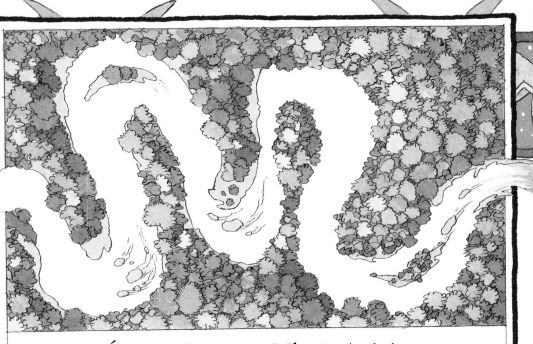

Boiúna, Íara, and the Moons of Love

*Next to nothing: a little sand, a little moon
in a thimbleful of water.
The rest, my beautiful one, in the lap of the
gods.*

—Sophie Saint-Acheul

Jaci cast her jade, emerald, and pearl necklace into the pale sand beneath the waters, and it came to life, unwinding in the undulating current until it stretched from bank to bank, the full length of the river, growing larger still as the waters rose. Jaci, the Tupi moon deity, then traced with her fingernails other rivers and the serpentine tail of her creation extended into each of them, growing even longer. She named her creature Boiúna and tasked it to protect all the rivers and streams.

The moon serpent Boiúna is the guardian and mistress of freshwater rivers, streams, lakes, canals, and ponds. Her sibilant hiss sends shudders up and down men's spines and drains them of their life force.

Boiúna had no mate or lover but longed to be a mother. Each night, she would look up at Jaci in silent reproach, urging the moon deity to give her a daughter as beautiful as the dream child she saw reflected on the surface of the water. So Jaci took her most precious moonstone bracelet and cast it into the pale sand beneath the waters.

And Íara, the daughter of Boiúna, saw the light of day in the middle of the night.

Mboïa-Arárá

Mboïa-Arárá is from the Tupi words *mboï* (snake) and *arárá* (macaw) and describes the multicolored plumage of this moon water Elf who watches over young virgins. Ancient Tupi custom held that if a young girl of the tribe was suspected of being unchaste, she was led to a small island in the middle of a lake and offerings were placed around her. The snake would circle the island, hissing loudly. If the young girl was still a virgin, he would consume only the sacrificial offerings. But, if she had lost her virginity, Mboïa-Arárá's immense jaws would open, and she would be devoured.

Cariré and Catiti

These two followers and servants of Roudá, the Tupi Goddess of Love, assume the shapes of the full moon and the crescent moon. Cariré, the full moon, causes fruit to ripen and nurtures in a lover's heart the fond memory of his beloved. Catiti, the crescent moon, prevents a lover from harboring memories of anyone other than his distant mistress.

HEIGHT:
It is believed that when Boiúna uncoils, she grows large enough to fill all rivers and streams. Her beloved daughter Íara can survive in the tiniest pool of water.

APPEARANCE:
One is a serpent, the other a beautiful young girl—and yet they look alike. They have the same aqueous form, and Íara's magnificently full head of hair is oddly reminiscent of the reeds that Boiúna sends rippling in her wake.

CLOTHING:
It is believed that precious stones found in the silt by local Indians are vestiges of Boiúna's sloughed skin. Íara reveals her seductive charms by appearing completely nude.

HABITAT:
In Brazilian freshwater rivers and streams, and in the recesses of a palace built of sapphires, emeralds, and other precious minerals which is the envy of the water nymphs.

FOOD:
Boiúna devours animals and the occasional fisherman and sucks the blood out of old men's bodies. Íara is far less demanding, content to drink fresh water and feed off the love of those she holds in thrall.

BEHAVIOR:
Boiúna is the guardian of fresh water and is also known by the Tupi as Maen d'Agua (Mother of the Waters). Her daughter Íara is both a moon and a water Elf, with all the features typically associated with water nymphs, nixies, and river sirens.

ACTIVITIES:
Regardless of her busy life, Íara likes nothing better than resting on a bed of still water. Boiúna, by contrast, has a fondness for capsizing canoes and for driving children insane, although she also provides fish and fertilizes the land. Her hissing and chanting also call down much-needed rain to help the cassava crop grow.

The Siths or Sleagh Maith

You proclaim our power, then be now our prey.
—Falconer

HEIGHT:
Never very tall and frequently very short, even miniscule. Invisible most of the time.

APPEARANCE:
As described by the Reverend Kirk.

CLOTHING:
Outlandish and variegated, with a weave akin to a spider's web.

HABITAT:
Scotland; in hill caverns, Dun Siths, and Sithbruaich.

FOOD:
The "astral and spiritual essence" of plants and fruit, animals, and even humans (who fall asleep close to a Dun Sith).

BEHAVIOR:
The Sleagh Maith, Siths, "Good People," "Good Neighbors," or "People of Peace" all have features in common with the Daoine Sidhe in Ireland, although they appear to be somewhat more complex and distinctly more timid.

ACTIVITIES:
It would be less than prudent to go into any great detail. The Scots of old used to protect their animals from the Siths and their Elf-shot by the simple measure of ploughing arabesque furrows to confuse their aim.

The Reverend Robert Kirk of Aberfoyle was a *tabhaisver*, a clairvoyant who professed to see beyond appearances, a man who had the gift of second sight, who perceived things otherwise hidden, who straddled this world and the vast and mysterious landscapes of Elfland, rubbing shoulders with its inhabitants.

In the village of Aberfoyle, Kirk was known as the *Fairies Minister*. He was held in great esteem as a man of learning, and his mentors remembered him as an excellent and diligent student. No doubt the Little People of the Siths had long since had him in their sights, but it was only after he was called to the parishes of Balquhider and Aberfoyle in his native Trossachs that the Sleagh Maith chose to reveal themselves and invite him into the mirage-like clearings that comprise their kingdom.

The Trossachs countryside is indeed an enchanted land, with purple moors, wooded ravines, and steep escarpments overlooking dark silver lochs. The mist is whiter there, the light more subtle than elsewhere. Elfiria is all around; its presence can be felt on every breath of air or tuft of heather. Here, the Reverend Kirk was in his element, at one with the spirit world.

When he was not on the pulpit or otherwise engaged on his round of duties as a Presbyterian cleric, the Reverend *wrote*. He hunched over the pages of the Holy Scripture, which he was endeavoring to translate into Irish Gaelic. But he also daydreamed by the open window as the sky darkened towards evening, his pen poised over the inkwell. Was he daydreaming, or was he lost in contemplation of what he and he alone could see?

Kirk would set aside his erudite scholarship for a moment in order to describe the luminous procession of Siths that paraded before his eyes. Light and translucent, they slipped in and out of moonbeams and surfed across the mist. They were silver-haired, with crowns of pearls atop their flowing manes. Their banners were deployed, and their diamond-encrusted helmets and suits of armor glittered. Their wings beat furiously as they shifted drifts of hoar frost to their storerooms. They came and they went, fading in and out, bursting like bubbles, flying off suddenly only to return and regroup.

Kirk took copious notes. They were "intermediate beings" between man and angel, he concluded, with light, fluid, astral-like bodies, like wisps of cloud, at their most visible in the evening twilight. Then, one by one, the Siths faded and disappeared. No sound was heard other than that of a croaking frog or the interminable scratch of a quill pen on parchment.

Every day, week in, week out, the Reverend Kirk climbed the hill to the top of the Dun-Sith and wandered across the ridge, peering into every nook and cranny and turning over one rock after another, checking behind bushes, or sifting through the heather. He watched for hours on end.

As evening set in, he came down the hill, aching all over from his exertions, with his clothing full of burrs, withered leaves, or moss, and his three-cornered hat covered in twigs. His pockets bulged with all manner of curious objects and with scribbled notes that he would later transcribe with the utmost care.

The Reverend Kirk had the rare good fortune to witness the Siths first hand. Kirk would describe them as delicate, immaterial, spongelike creatures whose only form of sustenance appeared to be an alcoholic beverage they gulped like air. But he later learned that others fed off plant extracts and rare essences and that some ate corn fresh from the ground. Some nibbled furtively while others pecked and scratched "like mice or carrion crows."

One day, on the banks of Loch Katrine in the lee of Ben Venue, Kirk chanced upon the Siths at work. The womenfolk appeared to be skilled at weaving, knitting, and embroidery. Their spider's web garments and their evanescent rainbow-colored dress were already familiar to him, but he noted that some were wearing plaid or outlandish costumes. It seems that Kirk took advantage of the situation on this and other occasions to venture into a Sithbruaich and inspect their houses while they were at work. How else would he have been able to describe their dwellings with such detail?

Sith houses, it seemed, were beautiful and imposing although, except in very unusual circumstances, they were sadly invisible to the naked eye (much like Rackland and other enchanted islands). Their lamps, so Kirk recorded, were fashioned from pinecones and burned indefinitely; fires blazed in the hearth, but there was no trace of fuel.

The Reverend Kirk would crouch behind a low drystone dyke and look on as the Siths launched their Elf-shot from catapults and cordless bows. They took aim and let fly at domestic animals, using the farm furrows to gauge distance and trajectory. Their projectiles were fashioned from yellow flint with a barbed arrowhead. The Siths hurled them as they would a dart or javelin, fatally wounding the innards but never breaking the skin.

The Reverend Kirk was being foolhardy. He was venturing too close. He even kept a collection of Elf-shot on his sideboard! He was asking for trouble but, undaunted, he persisted in collating information about the Siths. He failed to take precautions, often making little or no effort to keep hidden from sight. Over

time, he began to understand their signs and spoken language. One day, he promised himself, he would be able to share their thoughts.

As far as Kirk could tell, the Siths were not religious, inasmuch as they professed no love for or devotion towards God, the author of all things. They appeared to live longer than humans but they *did* die or, at least, disappear. They shared one belief: that, like the sun and the changing seasons, life goes round in smaller or larger circles, reinventing itself with each revolution.

The Reverend Kirk had learned too much. He had revealed too much. He had trespassed on their inner beliefs, on the secrets of their souls.

The year is 1692. A considerable time has elapsed since the *Fairies Minister* first scaled Sithbruaich in quest of the Siths. It has been four years since his impressive Gaelic hymnal was published. But, more importantly, he has just finished his manuscript recording everyday life among the Siths. His treatise tells of a "Secret Empire" and relates the principal curiosities that can still be observed to this day by people in the Scottish Lowlands—curiosities, moreover, that are *particular to* Scotland. It describes the "nature and doings" of subterranean and largely invisible creatures commonly known as Elves, Fauns, Fairies, and the like, as described by "one with the gift of Second Sight."

The Reverend Robert Kirk is forty-two years old. He has only a few more days left to live.

Early one morning his corpse is discovered wrapped in his robe and spread-eagled against the slopes of a Sithbruaich still shrouded in mist. What conceivable reason could there have been for him to venture out so early to visit the forbidden kingdom of the Siths?

Sir Walter Scott would later take the view that the Elves, "a jealous and irritable race" that inveighs against any and all who even dare to call them such, were mortally offended by the temerity of the late reverend, who had seen fit to delve into their affairs and disclose them to the public at large.

Meanwhile, to this day, every local knows that the body of the *Fairies Minister* does not lie buried in its tomb in the east wing of the ruins of Aberfoyle church. Instead, it was spirited away by vengeful Siths and condemned to wander the hillsides above the town, doomed to find no final rest until the Day of the Last Judgment . . .

HEIGHT:

Not as tall as he appears at first sight and, even when fully grown, never taller than a child. Can shrink, but never to a size smaller than a mouse.

APPEARANCE:

Pleasant and attractive on the whole, but difficult to describe since he always seems to appear through a dream-like veil and is never completely visible. His almond-shaped eyes are large and bright, his cheeks are prominent, and his mouth is full and fleshy, with teeth like those of a rabbit. His chin is pointed, as are his ears, and his hair is long and brown. On the whole, his appearance gives a hybrid effect, a cross between an animal of sorts and a young prince.

CLOTHING:

Wears a large, pointed hat decorated with a raven's feather and smokes a reed-pipe. His clothes are a play of light and shade, their outlines blurred in much the same way as his features. There is undergrowth and hedgerow here, and the pallid rays of an April sun falling on a clutch of cowslips. He carries a scepter-like dart with a sharp and magic point. At night, he dons a black cape dusted with moonbeams. The leather pouch hanging from his broad belt is where he keeps the wishes sent to him by young children.

HABITAT:

Hedgerows and overgrown gardens. His home is a citadel of greenery set amid meadows and woods, and close by running water. There is a well-known Hututu pathway near Avesnes in northern France (between Haut-Lieu and Boulogne-on-Elfe), but the Hututu can live anywhere one finds parks and gardens, such as in Kent or the Cotswolds in England, where they can be seen most evenings.

The Hututu and His Little People

First Mademoiselle and then yourself
In this joyous round of love
  —Saint-Yves Liaudaine,
    A Liturgy of Field and Wood

Young Claire rose as the first rays of the morning sun framed the curtain at her window. She had plans that day. If only life were always this simple, she thought to herself. She had spent most of the night tending to her father, who professed to be so ill that he made her promise yet again she would always be on hand to care for him and help heal his scars.

Claire was barely ten, but her angel eyes were shadowed with fatigue.

Ever since her mother had left when Claire was only two, her father had taken to his bed. Claire was a lonely child, entrusted to the care of a holier-than-thou grandmother who treated her as badly as the Ugly Stepsisters treated Cinderella. She took great delight in punishing Claire, locking her into a dark broom closet. She was a sanctimonious witch who went on more pilgrimages to Lourdes than most people have hot dinners. Claire was never happier than when she managed to sneak out of the farmhouse and walk in the meadows and along the hedgerows. She clambered out of the window, crossed the barnyard, where her kittens purred a greeting, eased open the gate, and set off, happy as any lark, down the path to Hututu Land.

Her step was light and her spirits high. Butterflies fluttered by and birdsong filled the air. She was no longer lonely. Crickets chirped a cheery hello and assured her today would be a lovely day. Her pretty little pointed face was as radiant as any bride of Elfiria.

The grass felt soft and pleasant under her feet, and the hedgerows and bramble bushes grew thicker. As she walked along, she recited out loud the now-familiar names she had given to the places she passed. She trod the "Path of the Mouse" and entered the "Glade of Lament," then skirted "Graignette's Hideaway" (where the little shepherd girl had taken refuge when pursued by the "Black Hunter" and his pack of hounds). She started out down the "Prince's Path" which led (as such paths almost invariably do) to the "Bower of the Sleeping Beauty," deep in Hututu Land.

Claire came to a tiny clearing and lay on her back, gazing up at the clouds.

She waited for the Hututu and his Little People . . .

They came, walking side by side out of the shade of the elderberry trees and the hawthorns. They were so alike that it was hard to tell one from the other. As they approached, the murmur of their voices was magnified by the vaulting of honeysuckle and hazel branches. It swelled to a crescendo as the host of the gaudily dressed yet graceful creatures fluttered into the clearing.

One figure balanced on the tip of Claire's nose for a second or two, then settled on the Hututu's pointed cap and

started to dance. Claire had never seen anything like it. She watched as the exquisite creature balanced on the tips of her toes, pirouetting, curtseying, throwing the occasional kiss, and waving her little hand in greeting. She was wearing a doll's dress so neatly cut and stitched that it must have been sewn by nimble fingers from another world.

The miniscule figures were everywhere now, surging out of the greenery and skipping from one petal to the next, bouncing gently on a supple twig, then twirling for a moment in the air before landing headfirst on a wild rose or settling astride a ripe berry. Claire was treated to a bewildering and exuberant display of athleticism and grace.

Then the Hututu raised his pointed scepter and all was still.

Claire nodded in timid acknowledgment, gently stroking the dusty wings of a Hazelnut and smiling at the Blackcurrants, the Hawthorns, the Wild Cherries, and all the other little creatures. She was transported to a vast chamber with an ogival window and a vaulted ceiling, lit by stars and Chinese lanterns. She and the Hututu looked into each other's eyes and saw the sparkle there. The prince spoke in the measured tones of his familiar, the blackbird. The interwoven cupola of blackthorn branches covered the whole of Earth, he explained. It was the work of the Blackcurrant Moles. And the Fays with the languid eyes were like that because they were here to replenish their stock of belladonna extract.

Then his expression changed and grew more serious. He draped a long skein of tangled ivy around Claire's shoulders and spoke soothingly to her: "Later, when you are a grown woman and your heart opens to love, always, always place your trust in ivy . . ."

Standing there, surrounded by the Hedgerow People, Claire took everything in and understood completely.

FOOD:

> *Fruits of the Four Seasons; also enjoys wheat waffles with cheese, pancakes, pies, and the tasty treats brought to him by children. Sips blackberry and other fruit cordials.*

BEHAVIOR:

> *The Hututu is the prince of hedgerows and glades, a chiaroscuro Elf who fascinates children and leads them off on the path to Elfiria; his name is sometimes associated (not without some justification) with the Pied Piper of Hamelin.*

ACTIVITIES:

> *The Hututu is the guardian of the* boscage, *farmland crisscrossed with hedgerows and trees. Whenever a farmer pulls down a hedge or uproots a tree, the Hututu immediately plants the seeds of another in its place. He is always accompanied by a blackbird familiar, whose black plumage stands for the color of night and whose bright yellow beak represents the bright light of day, symbolizing the Hututu's sovereignty. The Hututu hates cats and promptly changes them into snails, worms, or insects before feeding them to pet birds, field mice, or shrews. Children adopted by the Hututu become Hututu themselves; one of the most celebrated "inheritors" in this respect is the young Dickson in Frances Hodgson Burnett's* The Secret Garden.

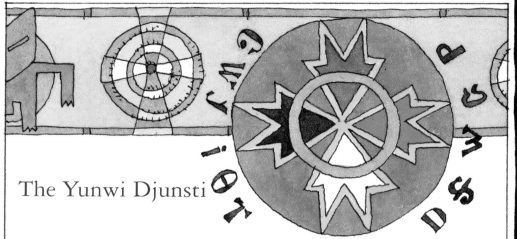

The Yunwi Djunsti

Give me savage creatures as friends and neighbors, not beings that are submissive . . .
—Henry David Thoreau

The fertile and verdant Black Belt lies in the southeastern United States; it is a vast expanse of undulating terrain that lies south of the Appalachian Mountains and stretches west as far as the Mississippi River. Dense forests cover the land, and lush vegetation harbors plentiful game and an abundance of fruit. Before the Palefaces ever set foot on this land, the area was inhabited by Native American tribes—the Creek, the Choctaw, the Chickasaw, and the Cherokee among them—who lived like Adam and Eve in the Garden of Eden.

The tribes held that the universe was made up of three worlds, each distinct but each linked to the other two. Above, as one might expect, was the Upper World; below was the Lower World. The Middle World was the world of humans, animals, and plants, a round island suspended from the heavens at the four cardinal points. A bird's-eye view would reveal a cross within a circle, since the island was divided into four equal parts by lines that led at right angles from north to south and from east to west.

The Upper World was that of the gods, a stable and ordered world that exemplified harmony, equilibrium, and purity. By contrast, the Lower World spawned madness and pollution. This was where the chthonian spirits dwelled: they were harbingers of fertility and invention, certainly, but also the wellsprings of chaos.

In the Beginning, there were only these two juxtaposed worlds, the Upper and the Lower, and they were in conflict with each other. But, over time, the Middle World emerged. The denizens of the Upper and Lower Worlds pounced on it, digging valleys, smoothing plains, and creating mountains with powerful blows. Soon, however, they tired of their labors. This Middle World was no fit place for gods, they reasoned, and promptly abandoned it, leaving it to humankind, although here and there amid the flora and the fauna they would record their presence in the guise of demigods, heroes, divine messengers, and intermediaries.

Among the bestiary bequeathed to the Middle World was a fabled monster: the Uktena, half-moose, half-winged serpent, whose fetid breath could kill. The Uktena was as tall and broad as a tree and, between its horns, there was a magnificent diamond—the Ulunsuti—which sustained its brilliance by consuming blood. From the depth of its celestial flanks sprang small creatures with godlike properties, among them the Yunwi Djunsti . . .

The Cherokees handled the situation well. After all, they were intelligent and far-sighted enough to comprehend that Mother Earth did not belong exclusively to them and that it was only fitting that they share her bounty with others. The Cherokees were prudent farmers, whose plots of land did not encroach on the domains of the spirits and the fairies. They hunted and fished in sufficient measure to feed themselves and did not kill indiscriminately. In exchange, the Yunwi Djunsti protected the Cherokee crops, brought rain in times of dire drought, conjured up the sun when bad weather threatened to destroy the fields of maize, and led the hunters towards herds of buffalo and other prey.

In sum, the Yunwi Djunsti and the Cherokees proved to be good neighbors, although the Elementals (as the Yunwi Djunsti were often known) would participate in all manner of mischief and foolish

HEIGHT:
About twenty-eight inches (70 cm).

APPEARANCE:
Once, other than in terms of their diminutive stature, they resembled Cherokees; today, however, they have become virtually invisible (and it is actually considered bad luck to see them). They are said to have long black hair which hangs down to the ground.

CLOTHING:
Their clothing was very stylish, with embroidered hide tunics and capes decorated with beads and fringe. They wore leather belts and high-cut, brightly-colored leggings. They once wore bandanas around their heads, and necklaces, medallions, and silver breastplates around their necks, but all these have been abandoned in favor of white garments that are as diaphanous as they are themselves.

HABITAT:
They have resisted any attempt to move them from their ancient tribal lands. There are four distinct tribes: the Yunwi Djunsti of the Mountains, who live in comfortable caves high up on the summit of almost inaccessible peaks; the Yunwi Djunsti of the Rhododendrons, who live under bushes in the far recesses of hollowed-out galleries and caves; and the Yunwi Djunsti of the Heath, who are every bit as vindictive and dangerous as the fourth strain, the Yunwi Djunsti of the Prairie.

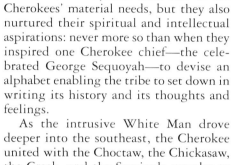

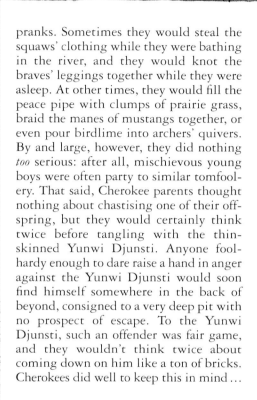

pranks. Sometimes they would steal the squaws' clothing while they were bathing in the river, and they would knot the braves' leggings together while they were asleep. At other times, they would fill the peace pipe with clumps of prairie grass, braid the manes of mustangs together, or even pour birdlime into archers' quivers. By and large, however, they did nothing *too* serious: after all, mischievous young boys were often party to similar tomfoolery. That said, Cherokee parents thought nothing about chastising one of their offspring, but they would certainly think twice before tangling with the thin-skinned Yunwi Djunsti. Anyone foolhardy enough to dare raise a hand in anger against the Yunwi Djunsti would soon find himself somewhere in the back of beyond, consigned to a very deep pit with no prospect of escape. To the Yunwi Djunsti, such an offender was fair game, and they wouldn't think twice about coming down on him like a ton of bricks. Cherokees did well to keep this in mind…

The Yunwi Djunsti took care of the Cherokees' material needs, but they also nurtured their spiritual and intellectual aspirations: never more so than when they inspired one Cherokee chief—the celebrated George Sequoyah—to devise an alphabet enabling the tribe to set down in writing its history and its thoughts and feelings.

As the intrusive White Man drove deeper into the southeast, the Cherokee united with the Choctaw, the Chickasaw, the Creek, and the Seminole peoples to form the Five Civilized Tribes. This was a clever move, not only to prevent themselves from being swamped by a colonizing culture, but to assert their own cultural identity. If the newcomers had agreed to share the immense tracts of land, an independent American Indian state might well have joined the Union a few generations later. But the Palefaces were adamant: they wanted *all* the land in order to farm, graze livestock, and develop plantations.

The worst was yet to come, when the first gold nugget was discovered.

Corruption, treachery, exploitation, and, worst of all, violence were to follow. The Five Civilized Tribes were driven from their ancient hunting grounds in the course of a few short years, from 1832 to 1839. They were displaced and "resettled" on "Indian Territory" reservations in the far-off and hostile dust bowl of Oklahoma. Thousands of Indian men, women, and children perished of starvation and disease, or were cut down by sword and bullet in what was to prove a veritable "Trail of Tears."

It was then and only then that the Yunwi Djunsti turned evil. Not evil by choice, as the white settlers often were, but evil out of necessity.

FOOD:
Wild berries, game, and fish. They refuse to ingest genetically modified, hydrogenated, or otherwise industrially adulterated White Man's food.

BEHAVIOR:
The Yunwi Djunsti have evolved like any other species that has been exploited and endangered. They appear only very rarely. but then to inflict harm or death on those who disturb them. It is said that twins have the faculty to see them as they were at The Beginning.

ACTIVITIES:
The archetype of the benign white Elf has been rendered malevolent by the advent and intervention of "civilization." The Yunwi Djunsti are now intermediate Elves, intermittently cheerful in their natural habitat, yet prone to turn evil at the approach of an enemy or outsider. The Yunwi Djuntsi cause travelers to lose their way in the desert or fall to their death in the mountains. They unleash floods, avalanches, landslides, and earthquakes to avenge the Cherokee Earth Mother with whom they once bonded.

HEIGHT:
Frequently very tall.

APPEARANCE:
*Impressive. The face combines the beauty
of a primitive deity with the features
of a Wise One. He sports a crown of
leaves and branches on his head, and
has a long ivy beard, a thickset trunk,
and powerful limbs. Very frightening
if angered: can uproot himself and
advance threateningly, his voice boom-
ing and his tread thundering against
the forest floor. His skin coruscates
with the glitter of multicolored emeralds and his eyes are a gray-green.*

CLOTHING:
Leaves, bark, and moss.

The Green Man

*I heard, or thought I heard, a whispering
sound like the wind through grasses, saw, had
no doubt that I saw, the growth of ivy on a
near-by oak ripple and turn its leaves to and
fro, as if the wind, but there was no wind.*
—Kingsley Amis, *The Green Man*

When the wind changes and the menace of an impend-ing storm hangs over the peaceful Low Country land-scape, the cock perched on the weather vane atop the mill shrieks a warning and the miller hurriedly places by the door a poplar branch moistened with seven drops of blood to appease the Green Man. If he doesn't, he knows that Peere Baboe and his leafy demons—Niakhaert, Flab-baert, Knippers, Giptenessen, Djipten, and the hirsute elves of Bloedkoets—will soon appear to demand the return of wood cut from their forest in order to build his mill. They will come to reclaim their own, tearing out every post and plank, every beam and stake, every floorboard and every step, every door and every window frame. When you take wood from the Green Man's forest, you must always, *always* offer him seven drops of blood in exchange for the sap he has lost.

The Green Man lives deep in the heart of the forest and watches over his veg-etable kingdom. Touch a leaf, handle a twig, or uproot a plant and the Green Man will sense it. And woe betide those who infringe upon his laws.

The trappers and woodsmen of the Wild West also feared the Green Man. They described him as a hybrid, a protean amalgam of maple, sequoia, and fir, a powerfully-muscled Bigfoot, a green man-eater. When the low-lying branches of a tree scraped across the roof of their log cabin, they would exchange anxious glances, wondering who among them had been foolish enough to transgress. And, once they discovered the culprit, they would throw him out-of-doors without a second thought, abandoning him to the grim vengeance of the Green Man.

In the magic forest of Brocéliande in deepest Brittany, the Green King was a giant of a man covered in ivy so dark green it was almost black. He had only one foot and only one eye. He sat on his throne and bonded with his subjects, the mighty oaks that ringed the castle of Comper. And he would bellow like the great god Pan, sum-moning to his leafy court the leguminous alfalfa, the moss gatherers, the butterflies and moths, the worms, the chanterelle Elves, the lascivious grass-eaters, and the assorted fauna of the forest.

In Denmark, he was the fierce Löviska, friend only to the Trolls (whom he fre-quently chastised for sharpening their nails on his trunk). He lived on the north-facing slopes, sheltering under a canopy of blue firs. At night, he would take up his oversize flute hewn from a fir trunk and play a plaintive melody to attract the spir-its of mist and rain, who settled on branches and roots and spun their delicate filament of pearl drops.

In Prussia, he was Puskait the Irasci-ble, who detested the sound of gunshots and chased off any interloper who ventured

FOOD:

Folk legend sometimes holds that the Green Man is a man-eater. In fact, he lives off his own natural tree-sap and off the forest around him, with its plentiful supply of extracts and essences. He drinks large quantities of rainwater.

HABITAT:

Lives everywhere from primeval jungle to the most modest copse or grove. He is often to be found in orchards.

BEHAVIOR:

Folklore, legend, and the popular imagination have saddled the Green Man with a bad reputation. The Ageless Ones call him "The Greening" and see him as a symbol of eternity, Elfish wisdom, and the continuity of the Green Kingdom.

The Green Man is hardly ever a completely freestanding tree. In most instances, he is "affiliated" to the Matrix Tree, the Hiranyagarbha, or "Golden Embryo"; he lives apart from the trunk but draws energy, sustenance, and wisdom from it. He typically lives in the topmost branches, and only Green Men who are suffering from a wasting disease or who have fallen from grace are to be found living in the roots.

ACTIVITIES:

The Green Man is mobile and, as a result, can roam at will everywhere in the forest. He finds lost children and takes them home, he comes to the aid of travelers who have taken the wrong road, and he has words of comfort for souls in pain. He most enjoys replying to metaphysical questions but is happy to answer any and every question put to him. Unfortunately, he talks in parables that only the initiated can follow and interpret. Those who are solely preoccupied with their own material welfare, however, and who approach him as one might a fortune-teller, will be sadly disappointed, for all they will hear is a series of creaks and groans coming from the leaves and branches. Once they return home, they will no doubt tell all and sundry what they have learned from the Green Man, but it will prove to be sterile nonsense couched in the undecipherable language of the woods.

into his forest domain to threaten his livestock and his favorite boars. In Poland, he was Botura, who guaranteed an excellent harvest (in exchange, naturally, for a copious supply of vodka). In Finland, he was Tuometar, who delighted in felling trees across the snow-covered roads to block the sleds of those out hunting for "his" wolves.

But it is in England that the Green Man is most in evidence. His bold priapic silhouette is carved into the chalk of hillsides and his beautiful godlike features are sculpted in stone in churches up and down the country. He stands as a symbol of fecundity and renascent nature, presiding over seasonal festivals and carnivals. He is wood personified and is omnipresent—in the knotted bark, the panoply of leafy branches, the gnarled and twisted roots, the densely-coiled ivy. When he sits in quiet meditation, winter is upon us. When he gently exhales, spring begins.

The Green Man is the zealous guardian of the sacred oaks of Wistman's Wood, the Mayor Oak in Sherwood Forest, the woods of Grantchester Meadows, the Royal Oak at Boscobel, the beeches of Needwood Forest, and the thick foliage of Edwinstow, under which Robin wed his Maid Marion. His voice is heard at Knutsford, calling villagers to the maypole dance.

The Green Man has many names: Robin, the Green; Jack in the Green; Bodach na Criobhe Moire; Owlad; Mech Dick; and the Oak Man . . .

HEIGHT:

The Daoine Sidhe can assume any shape or form at will. When first seen, they are small, but once they have worked their magic, they grow to their true height.

APPEARANCE:

Their angelic beauty is marred only by their sad eyes and their pointed ears. Their hair is as blond as light or as dark as night, their complexion pale and at times streaked with saffron. Their movements are delicate, but as fast as fleeting beams of light or shadows.

The Daoine Sidhe

My thoughts were with Tir-Nan-Og.
—Lord Dunsany

One day in May, the Tuatha Dé Danaan started to shrink; they gradually vanished into their fortified strongholds in the hills. They took the name Daoine Sidhe and from that day on, the good people of the valleys started to recount tales about the Hidden Ones.

The Tuatha Dé Danaan had once been the stuff of legend, spoken of in the same breath as saints, but no more tangible than a golden glow across the evening hills. Only the fools, poets, and fairy doctors knew there was more to them than that.

It was not until the Daoine Sidhe themselves elected to sally forth from their kingdom on their tiny white horses with braided and silver-speckled manes, that strange things started happening: large black sheep began to appear among the flocks, golden coins were found in the hearths, and the wheat yield improved inexplicably. It was only then, when the Daoine Sidhe again began to show themselves—sometimes no taller than the width of a man's hand, at other times fully-grown—that stories began to circulate. When folks gathered of an evening in the inn, some hair-raising tales were told. Yet there were other stories too, of episodes many would have been more than happy to have witnessed firsthand.

As one story followed another and chance encounters became more frequent, a picture gradually emerged of these fabled creatures concealed beneath the hills. Over time, people gradually came to be familiar with their likes and dislikes, to understand what they would tolerate, to learn what it took to be good neighbors.

All this happened piecemeal and on a hit-or-miss basis. For a time, everything was at sixes and sevens—as is only right and proper when dealing with Elves!

Michael Kerney of Moytura left home one morning to gather firewood on the hillside. He climbed up as far as the rath of The Others, where he came across a circular patch of green surrounded by a shallow ditch and the remains of a low wall, sometimes used as a sheep pen. Michael thought no more of it. The place had once been a major fortification, however, and the Shee who lived beneath it did not take kindly to someone trampling all over their domain; they liked it even less when people started rooting around there in the hope of finding a crock of gold.

That day, had Michael Kerney seen fit, he could have cut as much brushwood as he wanted. But Kerney had other plans. He knew the risk he was about to take, but he persisted in hacking away at the hawthorn bush that grew in the middle of the small enclosure. As he repeatedly swung his sickle in a wide arc, he heard his name being called out: not once, but twice, and then a third time. Michael Kerney paid no heed and kept on doing what he was doing.

When Kerney awoke the following morning, he discovered that his head had been shaved and that he was completely bald. His hair was never to grow back again. And, from that day on, every time he planted something, a mysterious hand would come in the night and uproot his crops before they had a chance to grow and ripen.

Michael Kerney died in abject poverty and misery.

Then there was the tale of the farmer couple who settled on land near Cong and built a pretty little house there, with a

thick thatch roof, whitewashed walls, and green doors and shutters. The village elders had warned them that they were building across the Path of the Shees, the route they always took when they rode on a clear May night from one knoll to another. The couple refused to heed the elders' advice and sent them packing, telling them to mind their own business.

There are none so blind as will not see and none so deaf as will not hear, thought the elders. They shrugged their shoulders and told the couple to do as they saw fit.

One night, a tiny figure dressed in green stopped by the farm cottage and politely asked the couple to build a second door in the back wall. The front door was in a perfect position, the figure explained, but there was a problem: "they" could find no proper exit at the back. The couple listened, and then slammed the door in his face.

On the night of May 1, there was a huge fracas. Tiny feet pattered to and fro and bells rang out. The following morning, the cottage had been demolished, and the couple had fled.

Paddy Flynn of Ballygawley married a highborn Shee, the daughter of King Darby, who gave in dowry a selection of his best animals and everything they might wish for, to set up house together. Paddy and his bride were madly in love, but it is a well-known fact that marriages between Elves and mortals are risky affairs at best.

When a Shee marries, she always imposes a number of conditions on her husband-to-be. In Paddy's case, there was one condition only. Should Paddy ever strike her three times, then . . .

Paddy laughed off the suggestion that he would ever raise a hand to his bride. He would smother her in kisses, not blows, he promised with a smile. And Paddy was true to his word. The two of them lived happily together for eighteen years and had many children. Despite the passage of time, the Shee was still as pretty and young as on the day they had wed. Then, one day when she appeared particularly attractive, Paddy slapped her gently on the backside. She immediately began to sob: a first blow had been struck.

A year later, when Paddy was teaching his eldest boy how to wield the traditionally Irish blackthorn cudgel known as a *shillelagh*, his wife inadvertently got in the way. The second blow had been struck.

"Damn this *shillelagh*!" shouted Paddy in anger, hurling the offending cudgel against the wall. The *shillelagh* bounced back off the wall and hit the Shee: the third and final blow.

The Shee's eyes filled with tears. She embraced her husband and children, and then set off into the fields where the cattle were grazing. They at once stopped feeding and followed her. The beasts in the barn also heard her voice, stopped feeding, and followed her. She said a few words to the calf they had slaughtered that morning and the animal came down from the meat hook on which it had been suspended. It followed her. A lamb killed and dressed the previous evening stirred itself and followed her, as did the salted pork joints that had been laid out to cure in the country air. Next, she called out to the furniture. Chairs and tables and sideboard and wardrobes followed her, as did pots and pans and buckets and bowls. They all sprouted feet and marched along behind her. Soon, the house was stripped bare.

The Shee led this curious procession into the hills, where doors magically opened, and she and everything with her disappeared back into the belly of the mountain, into the kingdom of the Daoine Sidhe.

CLOTHING:
According to Darby O'Gill, who saw them one moonlit night in May as they moved from one rath to another near Ballylee: "They were dressed like the noblest of kings and queens, as if they were on their way to church or to a grand wedding." Their favorite color is green, but they have also been known to wear red or gray headgear.

HABITAT:
Raths, forts, and Dun Siths, magnificent palaces hidden under the mounds and hills of the Irish countryside.

FOOD:
Sweetmeats dusted with saffron.

BEHAVIOR:
They maintain the ways of their ancestors, the Tuatha Dé Danaan, but mingle with mortals.

ACTIVITIES:
Like their fathers before them.

THE LUMINOUS SNOWS

It is essential to understand that there are two suns, one spiritual, for those who live in the spirit world, and the other natural, for those who live in the natural world. Failing to appreciate this means understanding nothing about creation.

—Emanuel Swedenborg,
Conversations with Angels

Come, my king. Assume your crown of white flame and blue sulfur with its coruscating cascade of diamonds and sapphires!

—George Sand

The reader and traveler standing on the threshold of this frontier of fire must beware, must be mindful of legends such as those of Icarus and Prometheus, and be alert to the seductiveness of fragile, ephemeral wings, which are dangerous when carelessly exposed to heat and the Beings of Light.

This landscape is a pure wave of pleasure upon which one can soar effortlessly towards infinite summits, abandoning the senses to the heady mix of incense, the flaming nectar of the chalice, and the mysterious alchemy of Athanor, the primal Beings of Shadow.

The snows here are translucent and soft as a loved one's skin. A single thought suffices to invoke undiluted beauty. Every secret is revealed. Regrets and sorrows melt away like nocturnal ghosts disappearing at daybreak.

Soon, the mysteries of our tomorrows will be revealed . . .

HEIGHT:
  *Extremely tall in ancient times,
  almost giants.*

APPEARANCE:
  *Depicted in the Lebanese Legend of
  Loegaire as white warriors with tousled hair that gleams like gold. They
  are powerful yet graceful sons of royalty whose strength remains forever
  undiminished. Their cold blue eyes
  attest to their strength and determination and their teeth gleam white as
  driven snow.*

The Tuatha Dé Danaan

*May it not even be that Death shall unite us
to all romance, and that some day we shall
fight dragons among blue hills . . .*
  —William Butler Yeats

When Jadgh the Soothsayer Magician entered the gates of King Rory's castle on the blue hill known to this day as Shuheen, the birds that came in his train turned to their jackdaw cousins and others on the walls, announcing that Jadgh of the Endless Roads was about to sing. There was a fluttering of frenzied wings as one after another they came down off their high perch and clustered around the windows in order to hear his song.

"Would you hear songs of the King-dom of Darès de Dana?" asked the bard, unslinging his harp from his back and plucking a few chords. And Rory, the Dreamer King, at once called him to his chambers. All who wished to listen were made welcome. They sat on the black-and-red tiled floor of the Great Hall, or found whatever vantage point they could, some standing on the ramparts, others crowding the streets that sloped up to the castle. Doors and windows were thrown open that all might hear the chant of Jadgh the Soothsayer Magician on the blue hill known as Shuheen.

The king sat on his throne of veined marble, his head bowed, with one arm around the slender shoulders of his queen.

He pointed a heavily-bejeweled finger and the portals of the past were opened: "Sing to us of the colors of the spring dawn, when the oars churn the sea and the prow plunges through the blue of the waters."

Not long before, the Tuatha Dé Danaan, the children of Dé Dana, had lived on celestial islands. Their most fer-vent wish had been to set sail in their ancient craft in search of new lands to conquer, to throw off their wings, and to explore beaches, rocks, and grass. They had come ashore here in Ireland, a land ever ready to welcome strangers, dream-ers, and angels.

Legend has it that Jadgh's harp was made from the whitened bones of sea-horses. The limpid and indescribably har-monious melodies that resonated in every heart came from strings of gold plucked from the hair of the Queen of Merrows. And such was the beauty of the instru-ment that the gods chanted songs of the Ancient Times in accompaniment, evok-ing the Great Father, Dagda, whose mas-sive four-wheeled chariot crunched over and swept aside the bones of his enemies like hailstones under a horse's hooves. One end of Dagda's chariot brought Death, it was said, while the other brought Life.

Then there was Go Vannon, who forged Dagda's armor and weapons and who brewed a pernicious potion that conferred eternal life; the valiant Ludd of the Silver Hand; Gywdion, the Master of All the Arts; the warrior Morrigain; Midir, the Bowman of the Shades; Angus, whose kisses were transformed into birds chirp-ing love songs that enchanted and bore away all who heard them; and, not least,

Brigit, whose words written to the music of Angus brought poetry to the Irish valleys. They carried with them the Invincible Sword of Nuada, the Lance of Lug, the bottomless cauldron of Dagda, and Fal, the Stone of Destiny, which cried out when the legitimate king of the Emerald Isle placed his foot upon it.

Before them lay the Plain of Pillars of Muytora, the Mag Tuireadh where the Formoré, the monstrous Army of the Sea, lay in wait.

Jadgh clutched his harp even closer to his breast and plucked the strings with his long fingers and nails, sending ripples of anticipation among the enemy ranks; only the shouted orders of the generals were to be heard over an expectant silence as the armies prepared to hurl themselves one upon the other. The crowd shuddered when the charge was sounded and when steel clashed on steel and when the earth trembled beneath their feet. Double-edged swords and axes pounded helmets and split body armor, while gnarled hurley-sticks splintered against breastplates, and shields and lances probed through chain mail deep into the flesh beneath. The Tuatha Dé Danaan were again poised to carry the day, just as they had done before, when they routed the Fir Bolg, the "bag-men," at the Battle of Moytura.

Like surf pounding on a beach, a roar went up as Jadgh proclaimed the victory. The final chords from his harp, and the spell of the narrative, died away. The crowd was about to call for another song of battle when the queen, resting her head on the shoulder of the Dreamer King,

intervened to call for a gentler lay, where the song of warriors would give way to the more dulcet tones of love.

Jadgh listened to the beating of his own heart and set music to the rhythm of it, recounting the saga of Etain, that most beautiful and most coveted lady of the Golden Age, who was reincarnated more than once. When Dagda's son, Midir the Proud, first saw her, he was immediately smitten and took her to wife. But Midir was already husband to Fuamnach, who in a fit of jealousy—and with the connivance of a Druid priest—changed Etain into first a pool, then a sea, and finally a fly. (When all was said and done, this was an age when magic reigned supreme and every miracle was possible.) Then, one day, Etar, the spouse of an Ulster warrior, swallowed the fly and some months later gave birth to Etain, who emerged as fresh and beautiful as ever but, sadly, with no memory of Midir. Recalling nothing of her former love for him and feeling ready to love again, she welcomed the advances of the powerful Eochaid, the King of All Ireland, and went with him to his palace in Tara, where they were married and lived a long and happy life.

Jadgh the minstrel suddenly hit a sustained note that made the audience catch its breath. "It is said that the amorous destiny of the beautiful Etain did not end there," said Jadgh. And the bevy of courtly ladies, sitting there in the palace of King Rory on the still blue slopes of Shuheen, heaved a collective sigh of relief.

Jadgh recounted how Midir the Proud discovered the truth about his beloved

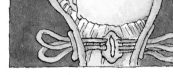

CLOTHING:

Elegantly cut and tailored. Colors were striking, never more so than in the case of Midir, whose body armor and coat of mail were forged from an alloy that no steel could ever pierce, then beautifully decorated and heightened with gold. Claudius Expansyve writes in his People of Danu, *published in Dublin in 1892, that the jewelry of the Tuatha Dé Danaan glittered from afar like "camp fires in the night."*

HABITAT:

Originally in fortresses and sumptuous palaces on hilltops all over Ireland, but later confined to hillside caves and grottoes, under raths and forts, beneath Ben Bulben and other mountains, and on the enchanted islands of Tir-Nan-Og or Hy-Bresail.

FOOD:

Prodigious eaters but with refined tastes. Their dishes were without fail flavored with saffron. That said, the Great Dragda's favorite food was a porridge made from milk, flour, and pork and goat fat. He required it in sufficient quantities to satisfy the appetites of fifty normal men; the dish was meted out from a wooden ladle reputed to be so enormous that a man and a woman could comfortably sleep inside it.

BEHAVIOR:

The Tuatha Dé Danaan—the tribe of the goddess Dana—were legendary deities and founding fathers of Ireland. The Book of the Dun Cow, the oldest existing Irish manuscript–written by Maelmuiri, grandson of Conn-Na-M-Bacht, who died in 1106–maintains that the origins of the Tuatha Dé Danaan are unknown. It is nonetheless believed they could have been descendants of celestial creatures banished from Paradise, which is to say, fallen angels. This, in turn, could also be an allusion to the Titans of Greek legend, who were hurled by even more powerful deities into the depths of Tartarus, the deepest region of Hades. According to ancient legend, the Titans initially lived in Greece and aided the Athenians in their war against the Syrians before going off to practice magic in the towns of Fabias, Gorias, and Finias. They arrived in an Ireland occupied by the Fir Bolgs and the odious sea creatures, the Formorians.

The Titans brought with them their legendary four talismanic skills: Magic, Art, Fertility, and the Science of Agriculture. Their reign was destined to be of short duration, however. Newcomers sailed into Ireland's Kenmare Estuary at the beginning of May one year: Ith and Bilé, two deities from the Empire of the Dead, together with their son Mile and his eight sons and their retinue. The Milesians, as this new tribe became known, waged a bloody campaign against the Tuatha Dé Danaan. The latter were defeated and sought refuge in hillside caves and hillocks. They took to calling themselves by a new name—Aes Sidhe (the Hillock Race), most commonly abbreviated to "Sidhe" or "Shee."

In his Elfin Chronicles, however, J. Sfar the Younger inclines to the view that their flamboyant reign did not last long because, irrespective of their own considerable power and strength, they were quite willing to relinquish their lands without putting up too much of a fight, content to leave Ireland "lock, stock, and barrel" to the Milesians, while they—the Tuatha Dé Danaan—went in search of the celestial islands of their birth, unhappy with their lot as banished gods condemned to live out their lives here on Earth.

spouse, how she had been born again as graceful as ever and was now living in the palace of Tara as wife to Eochaid. Midir wasted no time. He donned a disguise and visited Eochaid, challenging him to a game of chess, a game at which both excelled, although Midir had magic on his side. An unsuspecting Eochaid played and lost. Check and mate: Midir took Eochaid's knights, his rooks, and—above all—his queen, the beautiful Etain. So the story goes and who is to say otherwise?

As soon as the deed was done, Midir carried Etain off on his white charger. Vowing that the treacherous rogue would pay for his misdeeds, Eochaid summoned his princes, knights, and vassals and set about training them to hunt Midir down. This was easier said than done, because Midir was, among other things, the King of the Elves. He was believed to be living in one of Ireland's enchanted places, but Ireland was brimful of enchanted places, so Eochaid set to digging them up one by one, demolishing caves and dismantling old stone circles.

It was a year and a day before Eochaid finally came upon Midir's palace. Once he crossed the threshold, however, he saw not one but ten, twenty, thirty, fifty Etains standing before him. Each resembled the next, as alike as two peas in a pod. Eochaid could only wring his hands in despair.

Powerful as he was among mortals, he was impotent in the face of such magic and wizardry. Perhaps the magic of love would yet save the day? It did: the true Etain stepped out of the magic circle where the King of the Elves had imprisoned her. The spell was broken and she at once recognized her beloved husband Eochaid. The two embraced. Nothing would ever part them ever again.

Jadgh's harp was still. He looked around the throng and spoke: "From that day of defeat onwards, the power of Midir and the Tuatha Dé Danaan declined. They retreated farther and farther into their mounds and finally disappeared when the children of Mil robbed them of their memories."

But no one was listening now in the castle of Rory the Dreamer King on the blue hill of Shuheen. The king, the queen, and the assembled courtiers had gradually faded away, leaving nothing behind except dim shadows. And folk passing the hillside where Jadgh sat on a mound of ruins would point and say, "There he is, the mad Jadgh, who still harps on about the Elves and the gods."

The Tuatha Dé Danaan initially had little truck with humans and dealt only with the gods. They lived in palaces with gardens that were perpetually in bloom and

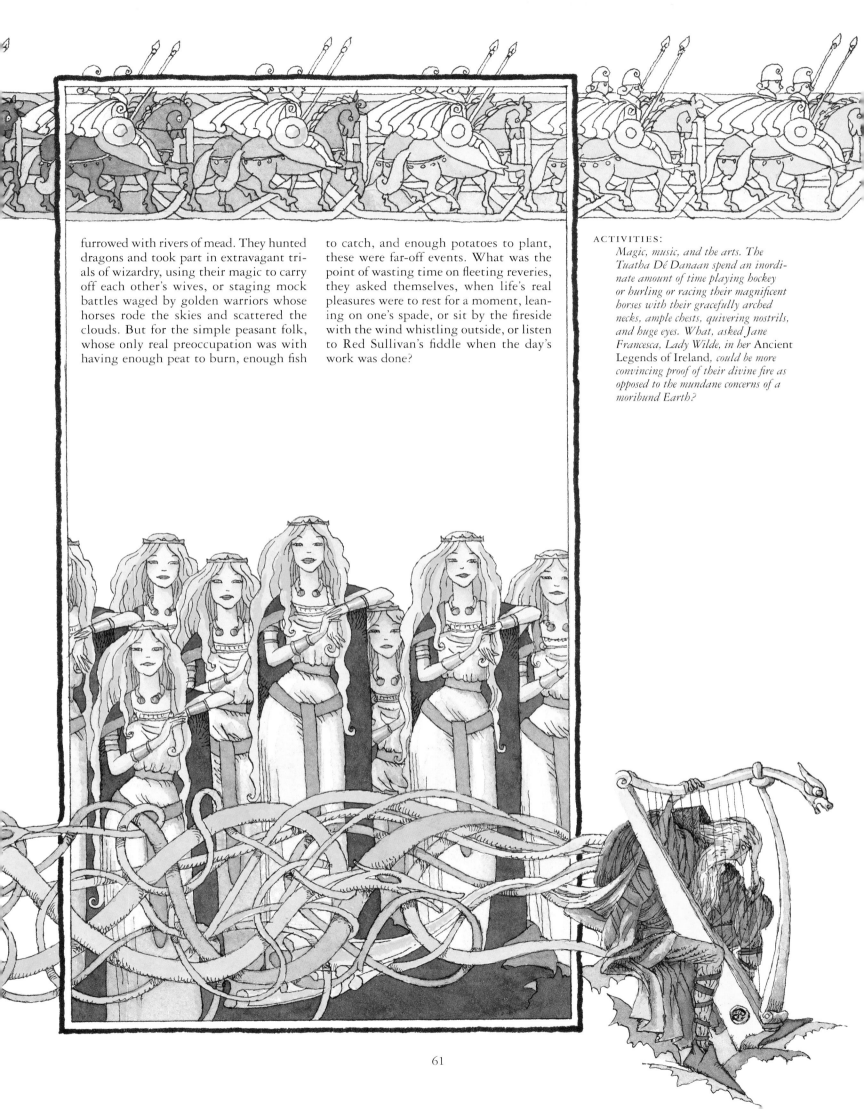

furrowed with rivers of mead. They hunted dragons and took part in extravagant trials of wizardry, using their magic to carry off each other's wives, or staging mock battles waged by golden warriors whose horses rode the skies and scattered the clouds. But for the simple peasant folk, whose only real preoccupation was with having enough peat to burn, enough fish to catch, and enough potatoes to plant, these were far-off events. What was the point of wasting time on fleeting reveries, they asked themselves, when life's real pleasures were to rest for a moment, leaning on one's spade, or sit by the fireside with the wind whistling outside, or listen to Red Sullivan's fiddle when the day's work was done?

ACTIVITIES:

Magic, music, and the arts. The Tuatha Dé Danaan spend an inordinate amount of time playing hockey or hurling or racing their magnificent horses with their gracefully arched necks, ample chests, quivering nostrils, and huge eyes. What, asked Jane Francesca, Lady Wilde, in her Ancient Legends of Ireland, *could be more convincing proof of their divine fire as opposed to the mundane concerns of a moribund Earth?*

The Vendoise and the Vendoiselles

A gentle cyclone, a queen tricked out in a prodigious opera set of boscage greenery.
—Julien Gracq, *Shallow Waters*

At first, it seems little more than a distant yet sustained dyslalia, the whisper of a zephyr caught perhaps in the branches of a tree, the sibilant lisp of dried leaves, or the muted sound of rippling water. The sounds emanate from underneath a bush or from deep within the gnarled branches of a weeping willow by the riverbank. The Vendoiselles are there but still unseen, lying dormant and fossil-like in the leafy folds until suddenly the fancy takes them and they explode in a starburst of movement.

This is "La Vendoise": a whirlwind cluster of featherlight, will-o'-the-wisp, wind-borne sprites emerging from their hiding places to swirl and eddy on the wind.

Only a few Vendoiselles venture out initially. Some hop and skip and slide down banks of moss before settling on a bead of pollen and taking to the air. Others cling to dandelion umbrellas and drift slowly upwards on the breeze. Others still recline languidly on rafts of leaves that float gently down the stream. Their hair hangs loose as silk and their cheeks glow with pleasure as they submit to the vagaries of the changing wind, gliding high above the meadows, twisting this way and that. They settle for a second, then launch themselves again on the wind, soaring straight up like a lark until they reach their apogee, where they pause for a second before plummeting back earthwards on a madcap toboggan ride, veering sharply away to crest a ridge, and settling softly once again in the forest glade below.

By this time, other Vendoiselles have joined them, their graceful and slender bodies spiraling into the far distance. The air is alive with them now, as they flit across the golden corn and ruffle the surface of the stream, coating its banks with snowlike petals. They settle on the blades of a watermill, and then veer away again to skim across the hawthorn bushes and hedgerows, alight on haystacks, and pirouette around the weathervane atop the village church. They hover for a moment over a cemetery and touch down gently, inviting the souls of dead children to emerge and play hopscotch among the clouds.

La Vendoise is a display that knows no seasons: it can occur day-in, day-out, year after year, for there is always a wind of some kind or other and—as is well known—the wind is a friend to Elves and Sprites. Some Vendoiselles like it best in the fall, when the breezes are mild and soft and imbued with a curious melancholy, whereas the more mischievous prefer the winter winds, the dreamers love those of spring, and the flirtatious revel in the hot winds of summer. On occasion, the Vendoiselles will meet up with spirits of the air and winds, fall in love, and marry (it is said that is where draughts come from). At other times, the Vendoiselles are joined by the Dames Sauvages, the wild female spirits of the thickets and the sandy seashores, and by the Fountain Nymphs, who scale their bodies down in order to play their part, swirling colorful arabesques against the sky. And, it is believed, the Vendoiselles accompany migrating birds on their journey south towards sunnier climes.

One day, so the story goes, a Vendoiselle came across a familiar sight, a house set in a stony clearing, with a small garden flanked by thriving hedgerows. The Vendoiselle paused for a second, confused, but as she floated downwards and came closer, she recognized something. The outline of a face (of a father or mother, perhaps, or of another loved one), the trunk of a seed tree, the hollow of a natural spring, or

HEIGHT:
Perennially miniscule; a nothingness, a grain of sand, the tiniest puff of wind.

APPEARANCE:
The Vendoiselles are quicksilver sprites, so tiny and so multifaceted as to defy description. Their appearance changes with the changing seasons: May sprites have the vivacity of spring flowers—pinks, primroses, hyacinths, umbellifers—whereas October sprites glitter like wisps of silver cloud.

CLOTHING:
In essence, nude, but appear to be wearing diaphanous garments as they flit from flower to flower on breaths of wind.

HABITAT
Traditionally in mossy crevices or abandoned bird's nests, in the fold of dried leaves, in fissures in the rocks, in the hollows of a tree, in the tangle of a thicket, on a barleycorn, a drop of water, or a cherrystone, but often simply cradled on the breeze or reclining on a sugar-candy cloud . . .

perhaps even her own shadow she had once cast aside on a river bank.

She flitted from one to the next, bidding farewell to these familiar sights, and then touched down as gently as a filament of spiderweb brushes over a meadow in autumn. She saw to her astonishment that she had landed on leaves floating in a pond familiar to her from her childhood. She paused for a moment to get her bearings and drink in the atmosphere, savoring the perfumes and essences she had once known and long since left behind. Days later, her childhood sweetheart came across her image reflected in the pool as she sheltered there under a water-lily pad. It is said that a Vendoiselle must remain where she lands until another Vendoiselle comes by. Then, and only then, can she be reborn and set off again on her enchanted flight . . .

BEHAVIOR:
Too diaphanous and too illusive to be described with any degree of accuracy. What is certain, however, is that they are never wicked or harmful.

ACTIVITIES:
When they tire of playing, drifting endlessly to and fro, or racing about the skies, the Vendoiselles help pollinate other plants and trees. They act as guides and guardians to birds and try (in vain) to prevent air pollution. They lead dead souls to enchanted islands, singing en route to soothe children in pain and promising them dreams of wonderful voyages. They also light up the skyways to help Father Christmas steer his sleigh in safety.

HEIGHT:
Approximately the size of a butterfly or a butterfly dream.

APPEARANCE:
As graceful, light, free, and luminous as anything one might imagine, with wings like spring flower petals and voices like the song of the chaffinch or the magic trill of the cuckoo.

CLOTHING:
The stuff dreams are made of and beyond one's wildest imaginings. A multicolored bonnet, perhaps, or a ribbon of tiny bells, with slippers made of dew, the whole enveloped in an acacia leaf and a lily petal; or simply without any clothes at all.

HABITAT:
By the endless pediment of the Mountain of the Gods, or simply everywhere in Italy.

FOOD:
Anything you can imagine, provided it tastes of kisses . . .

BEHAVIOR/ACTIVITIES:
Born of an impossible dream of a God of Darkness, their task is to make other impossible dreams come true for those who dream of the Farfarelli.

The Farfarelli

And did he dream of Cybele, of the fiery Vesta, or of Juno?

—Pilumnus

What schoolboy has never daydreamed in class, letting his mind drift beyond the schoolroom windows, and forgetting momentarily where he is and what he is doing? In seconds, the desks and books and blackboard vanish, and the droning voice of the teacher is consigned to a bottomless pit. The world outside beckons and nothing seems more natural than to reach out and touch the phantoms and Chimerae that fill the air outside. And, when the bell rings at the end of day and a winged Gryphon has set them gently down again, they file out two by two. A waiting parent inquires of them what they have learned in school that day, but they just smile and keep their secrets to themselves, clutching in the palm of their hand the memories of dreams dreamed that day.

So it was with the obscure Little God of Darkness. A minor deity, he too dreamed the dreams of schoolchildren closeted in the penumbra of the classroom.

Do et des—I give to you that you may give to me. But Jupiter had bequeathed the Little God of Darkness nothing save a tiny patch of shade. And he would sit there in the dark, looking out towards the light, and waiting in vain for someone to visit his domain. But mortals are afraid of the dark and shun it. Once or twice a month at best, some surly gray-haired Shade would come by to register a death or two, but then the curtain would fall, and all would be plunged into darkness.

There are many people like the Little God of Darkness in this world—clerks who work at desks secreted in some dim and forgotten back office or toil their anonymous lives away behind a cash desk. When the weekend comes, however, they shed their chrysalis of drab work clothes and don the brightly colored vestments of the jungle to seek out birds of paradise that most museum curators would give their right arm to see. They look for adventure, for new experiences that help them to forget their mundane nine-to-five weekday existence. And, in that respect, they have the edge on the minor deities: gods, as we all know, work twenty-four hours a day, seven days a week, for eternity. What would happen to the world if some god or other were not on hand to work his magic?

The Little God of Darkness was not free to leave his post. He sat there day after day, keeping his files in order, and attending to his duties as keeper of penumbra and chiaroscuro, guardian of the shadows and the dark. But *his* mind wandered too, as he dreamed increasingly of light.

It should not be forgotten that in days of yore the gods believed that there was no limit to what they could achieve and that their destiny was without end. But Jupiter and his powerful cohorts had miscalculated (they had always had a tendency to count their chickens before they hatched): for them, it had all started out like a vacation destined never to end—until, suddenly one morning, the first leaf dropped from the trees, the grass began to wither, and the first snowflake quietly fell. In the heavens, the indestructible Pantheon creaked and groaned as the first cracks in the edifice started to appear. One by one, even the most powerful deities fell victim to that most fatal of viruses, the Wind of Change.

Down below, meanwhile, the Little God of Darkness toiled away the hours, oblivious to what was happening, until one day, when a lone microbe, gasping for breath, fell down a staircase and landed at

his feet. He sneezed, and died right there on the spot.

Untold years later, when a cleaning firm was hired to sweep out what was left of the Ancient Palace of Elysium, an employee entrusted with tidying the basement brushed aside the labyrinthine cobwebs and uncovered a door into a cave of sorts. The employee was afraid of the dark, but he braved the cave just long enough to discover a small jute sack next to a pile of ashes. He picked the sack up and threw it out of a window as he ran from the building.

The sack hit the ground outside and split open. Inside were the dreams of the Little God of Darkness. They burst in the air like a fireworks display, but quickly faded on contact with the ambient air. The Little God of Darkness had dreamed of flowers he would never touch and smell, of birds he would never see, of rainbow-winged water nymphs he would never meet or love, of all manner of dreams that would forever be unfulfilled.

And his dreams, the Farfarelli, danced and floated in the ether above the earth, waiting only to make real the dreams of any mortals fortunate enough to catch them in the palms of their hands.

The Févert

You shall always find me in the woods . . .
—Sylvia Townsend Warner,
Laura Willowes

HEIGHT:
> *Pleasantly tall.*

APPEARANCE:
> *Appears in whatever form or guise women and young girls dream of in the first flush of April. Dark and brooding, burning with a mysterious passion and a sense of wild abandon. Everything about him is geared to attraction, seduction, charm, and sensuality. He is irresistible and has an aura of danger that attracts rather than repels, that fascinates rather than alarms. He is described in many ways, and each description varies, although there is general agreement that he is decidedly male and a compound of every woman's most secret dreams and most intimate longings. His body is that of a beast, sprouting foliage, thorns, and moss. In many ways, he recalls similar creatures such as the Green Man, the Green Hunter, and Ganconer, who is the son of Pan.*

CLOTHING:
> *Covered in ivy when inside the forest, but commonly attired as a forester or gamekeeper when outside it.*

The Févert—the Green Man of the Woods—puts in a first appearance in early spring, after the cuckoo's call has been heard for a third time. He contrives to meet and greet women and young girls walking at the edge of the woods, emerging suddenly and as if by chance, to ask them if they would care for a stroll in the forest. His smile is as dazzling as a shaft of sunlight. They follow him into the forest—not willingly, as they invariably claim afterwards, but compelled, very much against their better judgment, and all the while calling on their guardian angel to come to their aid while desperately clutching hold of branches and twigs and tufts of grass and roots.

All their efforts to resist come to nothing. They do their best to escape, to turn back at the entrance to the forest, but every step takes them a yard closer. The Févert, meanwhile, talks incessantly, whispering endearments in their ear, laughing gaily, and cooing like an amorous blackbird. His eyes—those incredible eyes, as they all admit later—are those of the Devil himself.

He flatters and cajoles—"You are more beautiful than the heavens themselves," he says—as his arms circle their waists, like the celebrated Magic Belt that nothing or no one can unbuckle. And, as he carries them ever deeper into the forest, they know it is pointless to resist and dangerous to fight against the inevitable.

They sink into his arms and are led through the woods to a coppice. Hedgerows part before them, branches mysteriously move aside, and nettles and thistles shrink underfoot. There is no natural clearing in the woods, but there is no need: the trees draw back to reveal a moss-covered bed with sheets of hyacinth and soft pillows of gauze-like flora.

They lie together. And whatever their names—Gladys, Marion, Alice, Julia, Charlotte, or Sophia—they all tell a similar tale of how this handsome stranger dressed in green undresses and caresses them, whispering protestations of love and intimacy in such mellifluous tones that the words themselves are simultaneously full of meaning and meaningless.

He explains why leaves are sometimes star-shaped and why the cattail dances on the banks of the stream. He conjures up images of wild abandon, of birds joyously mating, of the intoxicating transports of desire. His kisses are gentle as butterfly wings and his touch as heady as the scent of spring flowers.

It may be no more than a fleeting impression, but his eyes seem to dilate as the lids retract to reveal pupils like those of some wild animal. His pointed ears are like stag-horn fern fronds and, as he bends to kiss yielding lips, his backlit features are like some moss-covered mask with a crown of branches.

His victims feel as if their hands are bound together. Tendrils of ivy bruise their thighs. A tangle of creepers encircles them, and twigs and small branches press like probing tongues against their flesh as he pulls their breasts to him. The rich smell of fallow earth wafts in their nostrils as they are submerged in this vertiginous sylvan embrace. As the rather prudish Victorian, Lady C., discreetly recorded in her secret diary: "It was as if I was welcomed and fêted only to be absorbed before being released again into the real world." To her, it seemed that the Févert metamorphosed into all manner of different creatures—a dragonfly, a vixen, a bullfinch, a salamander, a water beetle, a screech owl, a sea anemone, and a water nymph—and was at various times redolent of fresh-mown hay, heather, and a softly-scented mist. She recalled the "exquisite fragrance of wild cherries" and the "intoxication" of singing like a nightingale. And she asked a somewhat rhetorical question: "Who could resist the temptation of having been, if only for once, the essence and soul of a rose, plucked and held close to another's lips, then changed into sparkling glass?"

By her own account, Lady C. gave herself willingly time and again, while all around her the air was permeated by the fragrance of pollen and sap and fresh flowers, whose only mission in life was to be beautiful. "I was an apple blossom waiting for the visit of the honeybee."

When the elderberries ripen and the first fog draws a veil slowly over the meadow, the Févert leaves abruptly without saying his farewells. Ladies still walk near the entrance to the woods as if nothing had ever happened there. From time to time, one of them finds herself with child, but she carries the burden lightly and, at birth, the infant evaporates into thin air, like a wayward wind on an April day.

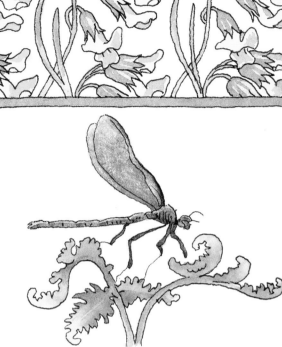

HABITAT:
> *Found in woods and forests from around the end of March until the early days of September. His only known domicile is amid the foliage. It would seem that he returns to Elfiria before the winds of autumn blow the leaves off the trees and strip the forest bare.*

FOOD:
> *Quintessential forest fare.*

BEHAVIOR:
> *Despite his given name, the Févert or Fayvert—literally, "the Green Fairy"—is not a fairy at all, but an Elf associated with the return of spring and the advent of longer days. The Church has done its level best to demonize him, in much the same way as it has Robin Goodfellow, Pan, and Puck, making out that this minor sylvan spirit of fecundity and the life force is some sort of succubus that must be exorcised and driven from his natural habitat. Like his kindred spirits, however, the Févert has stayed the course: even when the sacred oaks of his "sylvan court of love" have been cut down, uprooted, and replaced by chapels and calvaries, the Févert happily goes about his business of seducing susceptible women and young girls and transforming them into wood nymphs and Elves.*

ACTIVITIES:
> *Those who have spent some time in his company tend to remain tight-lipped about the experience, although some snippets of information emerge from time to time, notably if one reads between the lines of letters and diaries prudently tucked away in drawers containing items of intimate apparel . . .*

HEIGHT:
   Varies.

APPEARANCE:
   Also varies. There are thousands of them, each possessing a more or less humanoid form. Some Nats are a magnificent yellow color, whereas others have animal traits (frogs, eagles, elephants, wild ducks, crocodiles, fish, and the like). Wicked Nats are monstrous red-eyed creatures who assume the appearance of ogres, witches, and warlocks.

CLOTHING:
   The Nats wear traditional Burmese garments, typically saffron robes and fine silks, with gold jewelry.

HABITAT:
   They inhabit the Land of the Nats on the summit of Mount Meru in the six regions that lie between the world of mortals and the dwelling-place of the Brahmans. The lush vegetation that covers the extinct volcano known as Mount Poppa is the Burmese equivalent of Mount Olympus. Nats also live in little houses found at street corners and crossroads.

FOOD:
   Nats thrive on offerings such as cereals, fruit, meat, vegetables, and flowers. The Wicked Nats are gluttons and man-eaters.

BEHAVIOR:
   The term "Nats" is applied to spirits of three distinct categories: those from the animist or spirit world, those from the pantheon of Hindu deities, and those of Buddhist inspiration. The Burmese refer to Nats (or Naq) as "Elfin Spirits."

ACTIVITIES:
   Nats can perform both good and bad deeds. Buddha provides for Man's spiritual welfare, whereas Nats provide for Man's material needs.

The Nats

Of an evening, I seemed to see a swarm of Nats alighting on floating gardens . . .
   —Aline Locatelli, *A Burmese Journal*

"To the lords of the rivers, we offer up in sacrifice this chicken, this goat, and this pigeon that we may be granted abundant crops of rice, cotton, and sesame; that the seven rivers shall protect us from wild boar, tigers, big birds, small birds, and the tiger cats; that farmers everywhere shall live in continued good health and that they shall prosper and be happy."

Such is the prayer intoned by the Burmese farmhand as he places his offering before the dwelling-place of the Nats.

In Burma, there are as many Nats as there are wishes in the human heart. The Nats have been there since the dawn of time. Of a person's thousand daily gestures and thousand upon thousand thoughts, one must be reserved for the Nats.

Thirty-seven is a lucky number: thirty-seven repetitions of the same phrase are needed to invoke Buddha, and thirty-seven incantations are required to summon the Nats. The Nats originally numbered thirty-seven also, but the demands made on them by mortals were so numerous that their numbers grew to meet the need. Every single day another Nat appeared.

It should perhaps be explained that even the lowliest members of the human race can become Nats. In ancient times, this was emphatically not the case. To accede to the elevated status of a Nat, one had to have been a hero or to have achieved great things. Today, all it takes is a few good deeds . . .

For instance, when one Nat was a mortal, he was very poor. One day, he sat down to eat his simple noonday meal in the field where he had been mowing. Out of the goodness of his heart, he offered a grain or two of rice to a raven. He was immediately changed into a Nat Prince with an escort of five hundred princesses. Similar gestures elsewhere were similarly rewarded. A poor man worked all hours of the day and night to pay for the funeral of a family member. A poor woman alone in a land of men took time to wash the feet of a monk, then offered him water and a place to sleep. Both were rewarded by being changed into Nats. It takes only a little gesture, but one must prove oneself *capable* of such a gesture . . .

As a minor deity, the Nat has to respond to every prayer and request, however modest. A Nat has to be everywhere at once, secreted in a grain of rice *and* hiding in the holy ash of an incense stick. It is hard to imagine what a Nat must go through to reward the just and punish the guilty. A Nat may be created in error, in which case he is known as a *Naq Hsô* ("a Wicked Nat") or a *Meisha Naq* (a "wrong Nat"). The example that springs most readily to mind is that of King Bodiçaq, who accidentally partook of human flesh—and, sadly, acquired a taste for it. He was banished from his kingdom because he was depopulating it. Bodiçaq took refuge in a pool covered in lotus blossom and was changed into a malevolent glutton who devoured everyone who came near his lair.

A young girl offers her most precious flower to a River Nat
And, on the far bank, a handsome prince appears and comes towards her . . .

The Fire-God Agni

I burn unquenched as a flame and consume myself.

—Friedrich Nietzsche

Once there was a young maiden by the name of Poulama, who was courted by two lovers at same time.

These were no ordinary lovers. One was called Bhrgu, a name which means "born of flame." He was extremely wise and the father of all the Bhrgu, the messenger deities of the winds who conveyed to earth tales of the gods' benevolence. The other was a demon as wicked and ugly as all of his kind, with fanglike teeth and twisted horns; he was a vulgar type who blasphemed every time he opened his mouth. Strange to relate, however, the beautiful Poulama favored the demon. Bhrgu wept inconsolably and refused to eat. He tore great tufts from his beard and trumpeted to all that he would never allow his beloved to fall into the hands of this degenerate incubus.

According to the popular poet Dalim Kumar, Bhrgu decided to kidnap Poulama and marry her according to Vedic tradition and ritual. He crept quietly into her house by the light of a moonbeam, lifted the sleeping Poulama from her bed, and carried her off into the night.

When the demon heard what had happened, he unleashed a thunderous roar of anger and caused a star to fall, turning the prosperous province of Chandrapur into a wilderness. Then, seething with anger, he set off in search of the Fire God Agni.

Some say that Agni is wise, good, and all-knowing, but others hold him to be wicked and capricious. There is a simple explanation: Agni has two heads, one of a good spirit, the other that of a wicked spirit. He is as fire itself, which both provides warmth and burns and destroys. Agni, like so many other gods, carries the seeds of both good and evil and has always been admired for his equitable provision of fire to every hearth, rich and poor alike.

Agni listened to the demon's case. Bhrgu had entered Poulama's house by treachery and stealth, complained the demon. He had made off with the demon's bride-to-be. He implored Agni to help him, to reveal their hiding place.

Agni is all-knowing and all-feeling because he is a friend to Vaiu, the incorruptible God of the Wind and Air, who keeps him continually informed of every sound and odor. "I see them beyond the fragrant magnolias, lying side by side in a cave nestled in a mango grove," he replied.

History does not record if Poulama was happy or not to be reunited with her demon. What *is* known, however, is that yet another star fell from the heavens that day when Bhrgu's howl of anguish punctured the air. Snorting with resentment and venomous rage, he made haste to Agni's temple and cursed the Fire God for having aided his rival. But Agni was unrepentant: "I have done nothing save respond to what was asked of me. I, too, can rant and rave and cast evil spells, but I respect the Wise Ones and I hold my anger in check. It is not I who crept into another's garden to steal his bride-to-be."

Bhrgu listened to Agni's words and knew they were just. Contrite, he gave this reply: "As the heat and light of the Sun nurture and purify all Nature, so do the flames of the Fire-God Agni purge all that is base."

From that time onwards, throughout the region we now know as the Indies, the people offered sacrifices and portions of clarified butter to feed the three fires of Agni in exchange for their own continued security and happiness . . .

HEIGHT:
An imposing figure usually portrayed seated or riding sidesaddle on a blue ram with red horns.

APPEARANCE:
Has been described as a "red colossus" with three legs and seven arms. His eyes, eyebrows, hair, and beard are black as ink. Seven beams of light emanate from his body. His three legs correspond to the three sources of fire: the Sun, lightning, and terrestrial fire.

CLOTHING:
Agni wears a red, ochre, and saffron loincloth with a corded Brahman sash and a necklace of fruit. His symbols are an axe, wood, a whistle, a flaming torch, and a sacrificial spoon.

HABITAT:
In the Temple of Agni and in every hearth from the most humble to the most prosperous. He also lives in the waters and in the heavens, near the Sun's core.

FOOD:
Agni devours all that is set before him, including (it is written) his own parents, whom he ate at birth. He also feeds on the various oblations of clarified butter that the faithful pour into his fiery mouth.

BEHAVIOR:
Agni was born as a result of two dry Arani branches being rubbed together, but is also credited as being the off-spring of the union between earth and sky. His soul is twofold and dispenses both light and darkness.

ACTIVITIES:
Agni is the divine spirit of the Cosmic Hearth. He hurled into the darkest night a handful of burning embers that now form the Milky Way. He uses shafts of lightning to pierce the clouds and bring fertile rain. He is a go-between to gods and mankind—and the former are in awe of him as he knows the ways of mortals. He watches over every hearth and wards off evil spirits.

The Undines

They dwell in water and breathe it as we do air; astonished as we are that they can live in water, they are equally astonished that we can live in air.

—Paracelsus

HEIGHT:

About five feet (1.6 m) tall when standing on tiptoe.

APPEARANCE:

The Undines, or Water Nymphs, are slim and exceedingly pretty, with figures as supple and flowing as the water that is their natural element. Their long hair is sometimes blond and sometimes green and is often crowned with water plants and flowers. Their lips are coral pink, their eyes a sparkling green. Despite this, one D. Schlapp-Schwanz records in his Lexicon of Water Spirits *that the menfolk were often described in ancient legend as monsters with palm leaves on their heads, possessing big eyes with thick lashes, a hideous mouth, faces punctured by twigs and branches, and bodies covered in scales. They had hedgehog-like backs with a sharp dorsal fin. The womenfolk were scarcely less ugly, except that their breasts were "as smooth as a siren's belly."*

CLOTHING:

Their garments are typical of those worn in the Court of Nicchus as the Palace of the Nixies was sometimes known. The male Undines wear helmets encrusted with precious stones (which enable the occasional outside visitor to the Water World to breathe underwater) and body armor studded with emeralds. The female Undines wear bright-colored gowns ornately decorated with gemstones. They are readily identified when they appear on dry land, because the hems of their gowns are always soaking wet . . .

HABITAT:

The Undines live in a fabulous crystal, gold, and coral palace under the oceans and freshwater lakes of the North.

For those who have not heard it before, here is the tale of Colas Cha Cha.

Colas Cha Cha was a ferryman who traveled all day long from one bank of the Semois River to the other. Those who wished to cross had only to walk down the gentle slope until they reached his flat-bottomed boat moored among the reeds. Colas Cha Cha was sure to be waiting there, probably fishing. The traveler would slip him a penny, and Colas Cha Cha would take to the oars. There was no conversation. People used to say he was as garrulous as a fish, even that he looked like one, what with his big round eyes. Some even said he was every bit as stupid as a fish, but that's a cruel thing to say . . .

The fact is, people made fun of Colas Cha Cha, but he was the one they sought out if someone drowned and had to be recovered from the river, or if there was a risk of flooding. Colas rarely spent time in the village, preferring the company of aquatic animals. His home was a simple hut built on piles and thatched with reeds and old fishnets. He spent most of his time there, breathing in the dank odors and counting off the seasons one by one.

Early one morning, when white wisps of mist still drifted across the riverbank, he emerged from his hut to find a young girl waiting by his boat. Her dress was soaking wet and clung to her slender frame. Her long fair hair rippled like two brooks around her face and drops of water speckled her cheeks. She seemed to have been in the water, thought Colas Cha Cha. "Do you wish to cross to the other bank?" asked Colas. "I've just come from there," she answered. Without warning, she thrust ice-cold lips against his. Her scent was that of the river in spring, her kiss like diving into the depths of a whirlpool.

Over the years, poets, novelists, academics, and mythologists of considerable renown have written some interesting and quite beautiful descriptions of the Undines or Water Spirits. But who knows if their descriptions of those dreamlike creatures and their habitat are accurate? Colas Cha Cha, for one, knew nothing of the writings of Albrecht von Scharfenberg or Heinrich von Neustadt or Heinrich von dem Türmlein, and he was oblivious to the courtly adventures of knights such as Kamphyant, Huldbrand, or Siegfried of Ardemont. As a consequence, Colas Cha Cha was blissfully unaware of the risks run by a mortal who dared to fall in love with a

was prepared to risk the wrath of the Elves. And every time he was near water—walking by a river, passing a fountain, or drawing from a well—there was the danger that the water would overflow, drowning him and dragging him down to the kingdom of Undine.

Entwined in each other's arms and deeply in love, however, Colas Cha Cha and his Undine paid no heed to these dire warnings.

The village of Bohan lies in the Ardennes and the villagers of old busied themselves forging iron nails and growing tobacco. Like other villages in the region—Vresses, Hautes-Rivières, and elsewhere along the valleys of the Semois and the Meuse—the inhabitants of Bohan were accustomed to hearing the chatter of river spirits. They would often say of them as they might of other animals, such as deer or wild boar that approached their houses in the depths of winter, that "they'll do no harm as long as they keep their distance." That being the case, they took little notice of Colas Cha Cha, other than to remark that "he'd done well for himself." The Undine didn't worry them unduly: she was not really an outsider, bearing in mind that Water Tritons had been a common sight around the region since time immemorial.

So Colas Cha Cha and his Water Nymph lived their fairy tale and now, when he met people in the village, there was always a smile on his lips. He fished and she sold his catch in the village marketplace. And, for his part, he was careful not to get his feet wet. But then, one cold winter's day when the river had iced over, Colas Cha Cha made a fatal mistake. He was determined to take her skating, forgetting in his enthusiasm that "ice" was simply frozen water . . .

They had barely taken three steps when the Undine was snatched from below and dragged down through the ice. She held tightly to the hand of Colas Cha Cha and he was dragged down with her.

His body was never found, but that is probably because the two of them are still alive. At least that is what everyone in a little village in the Ardennes desperately wishes to believe.

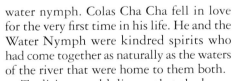

water nymph. Colas Cha Cha fell in love for the very first time in his life. He and the Water Nymph were kindred spirits who had come together as naturally as the waters of the river that were home to them both.

Tradition would dictate that the beautiful Water Nymph should have pointed out what might happen if he broke certain rules. It was a well-known fact that anyone marrying an Undine should avoid taking her on the water and should *never ever* anger her when she was in physical contact with her element. If that happened, the Water Nymph would immediately return to where she had originally come from. Worse, the marriage would not be void, and the abandoned husband could only marry another woman if he

FOOD:
Raw, smoked, boiled, or grilled fish flavored with saffron.

BEHAVIOR:
These Elfin spirits of the waters and the rainbow have inspired more tales than those enshrined in Arthurian legend. Ancient bards and minstrels have recounted their long, rich history, which is carried on the murmur of the waves and written on beaches, rocks, and reefs. One can hear them still on evenings when the wind blows.

ACTIVITIES:
The Undines no longer whip up storms or carry off princesses, and the mariner need no longer fear they will attack his vessel. In fact, they rarely show themselves at all these days, although the females of the species occasionally surface to dally with a mortal who is reckless enough—or so much in love—that he is prepared to follow them back underwater. A word of caution, however: young men who enter the Water Kingdom of Nicchus typically emerge again several days later as men old before their time.

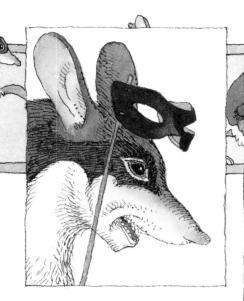

The Pilous

Let us return now to the village and leave this dream-like meadow until the morrow.
—Joseph Cressot, *Le pain au lièvre*

HEIGHT:

Not much bigger than a field mouse or a dormouse.

APPEARANCE:

Something of a cross between a field Elf and an animal. They have all the supple agility of a squirrel coupled with the wiry strength of a fox. The upper portion of the face is similar to that of a dormouse. There are distinctive dark spectacle-like markings around the eyes. The eyes themselves glitter like elderberries. The ears are disproportionately large and set far apart. The muzzle is pointed. A mischievous smile plays around the mouth. Hands and arms are Elfin, but paws and tail are decidedly dormouse-like. The body is slight yet muscular. A soft, furry fleece covers the back, shoulders, chest, and belly. The hair covering their paws is long. The females are strikingly beautiful and coquettish.

CLOTHING:

Their soft, fleecy coat suffices. It changes from green in the summer months to russet in the fall, and goes gray and then white in winter.

In Northwestern France, these creatures are known affectionately as the *Pilous* on account of their downy coats resembling soft flannel nightdresses. The Pilous have no material possessions and they have no need of them since they have everything they could possibly desire in their natural habitat. Their treasures are not padlocked away in some strongbox, but displayed all around them. Their diamonds, it is said, are the stars sprinkled carelessly across the night sky.

Like the cuckoo and the cricket, the Pilous are content to have a twig on which to perch. When a white rim of frost tinges the hedgerows of a morning, however, the parasitical cuckoo searches out an abandoned nest and the cricket goes cap-in-hand to his friend, the ant, and begs for food. Not so the Pilous: they move indoors, install themselves in eaves and attics, or forage for grain in winter larders. This is what they do now and have done ever since the days of Adam and Eve. In exchange, nothing was ever asked of them other than that they grace meadows, woods, hedgerows, and riverbanks with their cheerful presence, especially at harvest time. As time passed and the Old World went into decline, these lovable creatures continued to roam freely over the land like nomads or gypsies.

At the first flush of spring, the Pilous take to their beloved fields and meadows and nibble the first sweet shoots of dandelion, cress, and cardamom. They rejoice in larksong and the gurgling waters of the nearby stream, and watch as the birds cavort in the skies above. They build their little love-nests on the hillsides and look on as their newborns chirp and squawk in delight at the prospect of a bountiful summer. Their days are spent scavenging for food to nourish the youngsters: ripening cherries and radishes and the first strawberries that thrust through the rich dark earth. Come August, the Pilous feast on tender ears of corn and sip the last drops from bottles that the harvesters have discarded in the fields. And when lightning flashes and thunder rolls, they revel in the downpour that churns and swells the waters of the nearby river. Then September is upon them: spiders weave their gossamer webs along the hedgerows, wild mushrooms are in abundance in the woods, schoolboy pockets bulge with rosy apples, and the moon is framed by a soft veil of rime.

It is time to return to the eaves and attics. The rafters rattle gently as if a bag of nuts has been emptied and rolled across them. And people lie in bed and listen and shrug and grumble that "the field mice are back." But the older generation will nod and smile: "the *Pilous* are back," *they* will say.

Not only are they back, they have returned in greater numbers. And they make their presence felt on quiet evenings when housewives sit at their sewing or peel chestnuts or darn socks while husbands rack their brains over the family accounts. Their claws can be heard scratching on the attic floor, and the noise will only get louder if one has the audacity to call out to them to stop. It's best to ignore them, let them have their way.

According to Dr. Taupin, who practices in the village of Pipriac, there was the time when four young girls came back late from a country dance in the village of Messac. They'd had more than a drop to

drink and they decided to spend the night at the farmhouse owned by the parents of one of the girls. They were laughing and giggling from the effect of the pints of cider and were in no mood to call it a day. Instead, they decided to pile into one bed—all four of them—for a final round of gossip. Suddenly, there was a scraping noise as footsteps sounded on the ceiling above. One, two, one, two. It was as if someone was marching to and fro up there. The four girls knew that it had to be the Pilous, but they were in the mood for a laugh, so they all called out together: "Pity, there aren't more of you. Then you could make even *more* noise!"

The footsteps paused for a split second, then started up again. Only now, there *were* more of them. Many, many more. The attic floorboards started to vibrate and the mas-

sive wooden support beams on the ceiling started to quiver and shake until the ceiling finally gave way, crashing down on the bed below. The Pilous were furious. They stripped the girls naked and forced them to dance until the floor gave way, then the floor below, then the floor after that until the quartet found themselves shivering and naked in the cellar. Fortunately for them, there was a tiny window in the basement and they were able to crawl out into the cold night. Otherwise, as Dr. Taupin has pointed out, who knows if they would have even lived to tell their tale?

Pilous take to attics in September, come down chimneys Christmas Eve,
But when cuckoos sing in April, they know it's time to leave . . .

Salamanders

HEIGHT:
As long as a typical marshland lizard, but can also be as tiny as a single spark. May take the form of a half-burnt log, a jet of pure flame, or even that of a slender and elongated human figure.

APPEARANCE:
Depends on the type of "Fire Spirit" involved. The Salamander can appear as a Triton (or water-salamander), as a dancing ember, or as an alchemist's Mandragora (mandrake). Descriptions vary accordingly. Salamanders are spoken of in terms of "glowing shadows, tapering like a skyrocket and as large as a child, with a sickly, pale yellow face," according to Heinrich Heine. Alternatively, they may be as described by Paracelsus: "Slender, graceful, and coruscating in their purity."

Their skin is smooth, delicate, and elegantly textured, their hair absolutely impervious to fire.

CLOTHING:
According to Heinrich Heine, Salamanders wear tightly fitting scarlet- and gold-embroidered jerkins and breeches, and invariably have on their heads a small gold crown studded with rubies. At other times, however, they can be decked out in fiery silk and incandescent gemstones, wearing a long cape that is ablaze but never seems to be consumed by fire.

Form of all forms! Soul, Spirit, Harmony, and Aggregate of all things!
—The Salamander Prayer

Light is the perennial source and symbol of spiritual illumination, and the alchemy of dreams is a composite of water, air, earth, and fire. When better then to dream of Salamanders than by the light of early dawn?

Young Lalia was untroubled by such lofty thoughts as she crouched low beside the pool and watched for Salamanders, her button nose inches from the surface of the water. She often watched and waited for hours on end until the pale yellow mud at the bottom of the pool shivered imperceptibly and yielded up its secrets.

Secrets. The secrets that had puzzled and intrigued philosophers since the beginning of Time. The same secrets that, over the centuries, had spawned indecipherable hermetic formulae, cryptic alphabets, and an arcane plethora of anecdote and legend. What it all amounted to was this: that Salamanders are the Spirits of Fire, Elves of the igneous element that thrive in flames as Undines thrive in water; that these creatures exhibit the most subtle and ephemeral qualities of fire; and that they emerge when fire has reached its apogee. The initiated also know them as Vulcanians or Aetnians, though they are commonly called by other, less flattering names: "Newts," "Rogues," "Tritons," "Pimpernels," "Sallies," and so on.

Salamanders have a bright, shiny skin and are agile, quicksilver spirits able to foretell the future as accurately as they can recite the past. They serve mankind by revealing that which is hidden. Above all, the Salamander is the quintessential cicada, the alchemist's Jiminy Cricket. When it is set on hot coals and begins to dance, it alerts its owner that the time is opportune to transform base metal into gold.

Salamanders reveal themselves to philosophers, clairvoyants, and children. This is perhaps why young Lalia can see them clearly as they flit among the reeds and show their faces among the pond algae. But what do these sharp-eyed and gold-flecked amphibian creatures have in common with the Spirits of Fire? To some, they are simply batrachians, like any common frog or toad; to others, however, they are of the spirit world. Might the answer be that they are like a flower, whose glorious petals and simple leaves all stem from a common root?

Lalia sings softly to herself as a Salamander runs casually across her outstretched hand, as if it might tell her fortune from the lines on her palm: "Salamander, Salamander, who are you, I wonder?" She collects them in a bowl of water warmed by the sun and adds a grain or two of sand along with, as an afterthought, a sprig of figwort. She examines them through her magnifying glass, watching closely as they twist and turn, seeming to change shape and color by the second. Soon, she will take them home with her to admire these incandescent arabesques. And she will ask them to reveal their secrets. How does one find the way in and out of Elfiria? How does one learn the language of kittens and finches? They will explain. And they will comfort her when she is sad or when an infuriatingly dense teacher deems Lalia's schoolwork unsatisfactory. Ancient wisdom holds that the Salamander extinguishes fires, soothes burns, and *also* grants sincerely held wishes. If you would like a woman's hair to fall out, for example, all you have to do is to recite this incantation to your pet Salamander: *hoc Salamandra caput aut saeva novacula nudet.* It's as simple as that . . .

The school bell sounds in the distance. It is time to hurry back. The schoolmistress is already standing by the entrance, impatiently ushering latecomers inside. She is even more short-tempered than usual this morning, perhaps because of the irritating itch caused by the cheap wig that covers her bald pate.

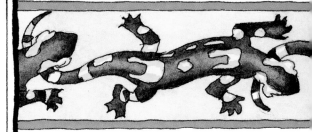

HABITAT:
Everywhere where there is fire, including the Alesh-Majim, dragonfly pools, and the site of the Philosopher's Stone. Bergerac locates them in the bituminous lava that flows beneath Etna, Vesuvius, and the Red Cape, whereas Gervais de Tilbury places them in the much-maligned mountains of Sicily.

FOOD:
Salamanders feed off of their own fire.

BEHAVIOR:
The Aetnians are tight-lipped and stay well clear of mankind, except for alchemists, magi, philosophers, and witches. It is dangerous to be in their vicinity, say their detractors, because they harbor the Devil. But wise men venerate them. Salamanders live longer than other Elementals.

ACTIVITIES:
Salamanders instructed Prometheus in the art of capturing and preserving fire and also taught alchemists how to transform metals. The Spirits of Fire are also responsible for fashioning the treasures that are subsequently entrusted to the Spirits of the Air, the Gnomes of the Earth, and the Undines of the Waters. They shed light, both literally and metaphorically, although they have since delegated this task to the Scintillae.

Yuki-Onna

And there she is, nude and white and tall.
—Victor Ségalen

HEIGHT:

The Yuki-Onna, the Snow Woman of the Mountains, is actually on the small side, although those that have met her invariably claim she is very large indeed.

APPEARANCE:

The Yuki-Onna is exceptionally beautiful. Fashioned from the purest crystal, she is a splendid white. When darkness falls, she buries herself deep in the virginal snow.

CLOTHING:

She wears a white gown, a mantle of snow, and a veil of frost, her whole attire the antithesis of the black she is at pains to dissimulate. Her accoutrements are tinged with the lightest of pale blues; her aura is the palest shade of pink, and her crown midnight-black.

HABITAT:

She walks the high roads and byroads of Japan when the snows form a bridge between her world and the world of men. It is said that the flowers of spring can sometimes tempt her to venture into the fields as late as the month of May.

Mosaku and Minokichi, father and son, were returning home after a day in the forest when they were caught in a violent snowstorm. Minokichi was no more than eighteen years old. Buffeted by the driving wind and freezing with cold, they struggled onward until they reached a ferryman's cabin, hoping against hope that he would take them across the river and enable them to get home as soon as possible. But the ferryman's hut was empty and his boat was moored on the far side of the river. They decided to take refuge for the night in the ferryman's hut, where they could light a fire and wait out the storm. But there was neither a fireplace nor logs in the hut, the sole items of furniture being two straw sleeping mats spread out on the hard cabin floor. That would have to do, they told themselves, as they huddled there back-to-back in a vain effort to share their body heat. The father, exhausted, started to snore.

The howling wind outside pounded against the roof and door and, alarmed by the noise and chilled to the bone, Minokichi was unable to sleep. He was afraid that the storm might take a turn for the worse, tearing off the roof and demolishing the thin walls. His teeth chattered and he shivered under his flimsy straw blanket.

After what seemed an age, the sound of the wind lulled Minokichi to sleep, despite the freezing cold. When he was awakened, it was not by noise, but by a sudden silence. He felt snowflakes on his cheek and he was gripped by fear. The eerie Light of the Snows (*yuki-aleari*) silhouetted a figure in the wide-open doorway. He held his breath as the tall and slender figure stooped over his companion. He saw now that it was the figure of a beautiful yet deathly pale young woman. She breathed her icy breath on Mosaku. Minokichi tried to speak. No sound came from his lips, but he had moved just enough to draw attention to himself. The woman slowly turned and looked at him, her frozen glance chilling him to the bone. He took in her frost-encrusted lips and her chiseled, supernatural features and knew then he would never forget the sight of this figure carved, as it were, from the ivory of the moon.

She gently bent over him and started to breathe on his face. He shuddered and the cruel face above him betrayed the faintest of smiles. "I had intended to take life from you as I have already taken it from your father," she said, "but you are so young that I will take pity on you. But I give you fair warning: should you ever breathe a word of what you have witnessed here this night to anyone, even to your own mother, I shall know. And I shall seek you out and kill you. Mark my words well!"

With that, she turned and vanished into the night.

Almost one year to the day later, Minokichi was on his way home from a day's work when he met a young woman on the road. He glanced at her out of the corner of his eye and saw that she was extremely

beautiful, lithe, and comely. He greeted her, and she replied in a voice as delightful as the song of any bird. He slowed down and walked alongside her, engaging her in conversation. It transpired that she had a lovely name—O-Yuki (the Japanese word for "snow")—and that she had recently been orphaned. She was on her way to Yedo to find work as a domestic servant.

The closer they came to the parting of the ways, the more determined Minokichi became not to let her out of his sight. His heart thumped against his ribs like a bird trapped in a cage.

They passed close by his house and he begged her to enter. His mother warmly welcomed the young woman and, captivated by O-Yuki's ways, invited her to share their evening meal. Then, mindful of the dangers that lurk in the woods after dark, she offered O-Yuki a bed for the night.

O-Yuki never got as far as Yedo. She stayed on in Minokichi's home as his wife and as his mother's "honored daughter-in-law." By the time the old lady finally passed away, cradled in the arms of her daughter-in-law, she could boast of ten grandchildren, each more handsome than the next, each with a complexion as white as driven snow. The villagers sensed that O-Yuki had been blessed by the Spirits; how else, they reasoned, could she have kept her youthful looks and shown no signs of aging? And, in all truth, O-Yuki still had the same cherry-blossom freshness that Minokichi had so admired that very first day they met.

One winter evening, as the snow whistled around the thatched cottage, O-Yuki put the children to bed and settled down to her sewing near the glowing stove. Her skin was as delicate and translucent as the finest porcelain. As he sat there, listening to the wind blowing ever more fiercely, Minokichi's mind was drawn inexorably to a night such as this so many years ago. He studied his wife's profile intently.

"When I look at you like this, with the soft lamplight behind you, I am reminded of something terrible that happened years ago, when I was only eighteen. It was a woman as beautiful as you

yourself are. In fact, you are uncommonly like her," he said.

O-Yuki did not look up from her sewing. She wound a thread around a finger and snapped it off. She gave a sigh and asked: "Where did you see this woman? Tell me about her."

Minokichi told her, voicing a secret he had vowed to keep forever. He spoke slowly, like a drowning man struggling back to the surface. The violent snowstorm. The ferryman's cabin in the mountains. Old Mosaku's silent death. The pale form bent over his own chest. "It was the only time in my life that I have ever seen a creature as beautiful as you. I am certain she was a spirit, a supernatural being. She was so white. So cold. To tell the truth, I've never been certain whether it was a nightmare or whether I genuinely saw the Snow Woman of the Mountains."

At these words, O-Yuki threw her sewing into the fire and stood up in such a fury that Minokichi recoiled in alarm.

"It is I! I am whom you saw that night! O-Yuki! And didn't I give you fair warning that I would seek you out and kill you if ever you disclosed what happened in the storm that night? If it weren't for the children sleeping next door, believe me, I would keep my word this very instant! You have ruined everything and we are lost to each other forever. I shall leave the children with you. Try to take good care of them because you'll rue the day if you ever give them cause to complain!"

While she spoke, the door creaked slowly open and her voice was gradually lost on the howling wind. The snow grew denser and denser until it and O-Yuki were as one, until she disappeared in a flurry of frost and ice.

NOTE: *There is no reason whatsoever to regard Yuki-Onna as related in some way to the White Ladies or the Ladies of the Mountains. Instead, Yuki-Onna is closer to the legendary and malevolent "Frozen-Nippled Woman" whose permanent abode is in the Alps. The latter lures her victims to the roadside by exhibiting her opulent breasts, and then clasps them in her icy embrace until they freeze to death.*

FOOD:
The Yuki-Onna feeds off the breath of mortals, but is otherwise content to seek nourishment in the luminous brilliance of the snows or the icy winds of winter.

BEHAVIOR:
Neither good nor bad. Yuki-Onna is, quite simply, the Woman of the Mountain Snows, the Lady Spirit of Winter, the Diana of the Frosts; she is a celebration of branches encrusted with ice, of drifting snow, of the delights a child takes in winter. She is unrelentingly beautiful, this creature from the Vale of Ivory, but she can also be cruel, and as hard and unyielding as a block of ice.

ACTIVITIES:
Many legends tell of the Snow Woman and her encounters with mortal men. Such unions, however, almost invariably end tragically, more often than not when a husband makes a fatal mistake or simply dares to infringe upon the rules of the game. And then it is all over: she disappears in a whirlwind of snow and ice, leaving behind at most a single silver tear, a solitary snowdrop in the early spring thaw.

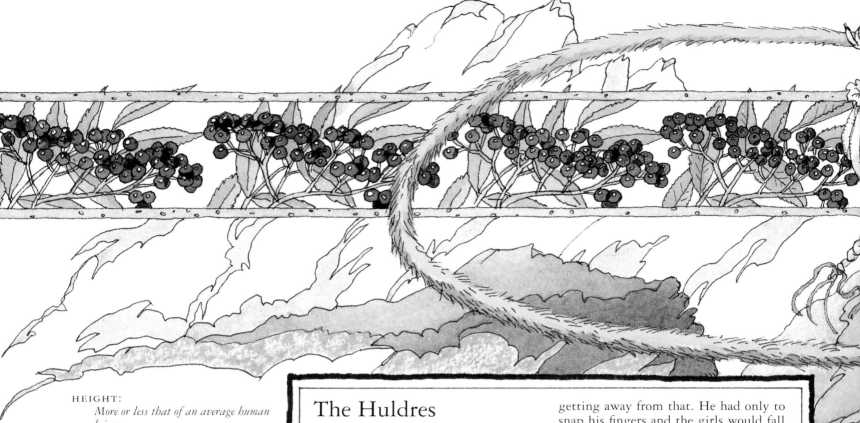

HEIGHT:

More or less that of an average human being.

APPEARANCE:

The Huldres remain, as a rule, invisible until they assume human form, at which point they are virtually indistinguishable from ordinary mortals—except for one significant difference, of course, namely the long cow's tail which they are careful to conceal under their clothing. They also have a deep hollow in the middle of their back. The female is decidedly more graceful than the male; the latter is presentable enough, but a little on the coarse side.

CLOTHING:

The male Huldre wears traditional peasant dress, with a red cape that conceals his many secrets. He wears a bonnet that renders him invisible. The female dresses in a long blue, green, and white skirt and bodice, which is cinched at the waist by a red belt, with red thigh-length stockings. Her thick hair flows down her back. The shawl knotted around her neck keeps her invisible.

HABITAT:

The Huldrefolk are sometimes called The Hidden Ones, because their kingdom is situated under the mist-shrouded hills and mountains of deepest Norway. Those who marry a Huldre are allowed to visit there, and invariably return with glowing reports of vast underground cities fashioned from precious metals and gemstones. Elsewhere throughout the Norwegian countryside, the Huldres build distinctly more modest dwellings, especially on protected "greenfield" sites. Anyone imprudent enough to build next to a Huldre's dwelling will have his house burned down or smashed to smithereens by an irascible Troll. The Huldrefolk are kin of the Huldufólk who inhabit Iceland.

The Huldres

The prettiest of girls by the water's edge
Sings songs of love and of Spring,
But have you ne'er heard her glacial dirge
When the snows of Winter set in?
—Einar Tambarskjelve,
Norske Folkeviser (Folk Songs of Norway)

On ancient runic calendars, *Vetrnaat* marks the impending arrival of the Long Chill and, not long after, a cross placed next to *Fyribod* indicates the official start of Winter (*Finbul*).

The Huldres emerge during *Vetrnaat*, when the weather changes, and roam the open countryside, prospecting for a husband or wife from the world of mortals. Many a young man and many a young girl have been taken in by their charms. At some risk to themselves, one might add.

This should *not* be taken to mean that marrying a Huldre is *necessarily* a bad thing. Huldres can be lovable and loving. Spending an entire winter with one's own kind is already something of a strain, so you can imagine that being cooped up all winter in the company of an Alf may not be a particularly inviting prospect! That said, some people have managed to get through it. One can only assume they were very much in love . . .

The female Huldre is much harder to please than her male counterpart. Gudbrand Endrelo was among those who discovered as much, to his peril. Gudbrand prided himself on being the best catch in the village. He was handsome, there's no

getting away from that. He had only to snap his fingers and the girls would fall over themselves to please him. Gudbrand knew he was onto a good thing, claiming, "All I have to do is pick them up!" When the conversation turned to marriage, Gudbrand was equally forthright: "Why choose one when I can have them all? Besides, all the others would be so distraught that they'd probably throw themselves in the river or string themselves up! No, no, marriage is not for me."

One fine morning in September, Gudbrand was sitting all by his lonesome, his cap set rakishly in his head. He was whittling a piece of reed, fashioning a simple flute, and he didn't see the young girl approaching him. Nor did he see her coiling her cow's tail and tucking it into her petticoat or undoing a couple of the top buttons of her bodice. Gudbrand was startled by her sudden laughter.

"That's a pretty flute," she said. "Let me have it for a moment. I'll show you how to play it."

Gudbrand handed the flute over. She put it to her lips and played a series of notes. Gudbrand felt his heart pounding against his ribs like never before. He had never seen anything like her: beautiful skin, golden hair, slim and nimble fingers. To hell with all the others, he thought, this is the one for me. She was simply gorgeous and he was determined to marry her. It never crossed his mind that the lady in question might have something to say on that score. But, as soon as he had made his intentions known, she did precisely that.

"I'll marry you, but only on three conditions: The first is that you are not to discover who I am until our wedding day.

The second is that you tell no one that we are engaged to be married. And the third and last condition is that we shall not see each other again until after Fyribod."

Gudbrand was taken aback, but he was in love. He accepted her three conditions.

"Then, if you keep your promise, I shall be yours." With that, she handed him back his flute and disappeared into the reeds as quickly as she had arrived.

Gudbrand immediately went around the village and the neighboring farms telling everyone of his good fortune. He shouted it from the rooftops: he was going to marry a young lady who was as beautiful as she was rich. He strutted up and down the streets of the village, preening like a peacock. He bought round after round of drinks and invited all and sundry to the Big Day. The wedding, he assured everyone, would be a grandiose affair, all pomp and circumstance. There would be a carriage drawn by twelve plumed horses, with a train of footmen wearing gold-braided, three-cornered hats. There would be musicians and cooks hired especially for the occasion—not locally, but

from the big city. It would be a wedding feast to end all wedding feasts.

Gudbrand had broken one condition with a vengeance, so it was only to be expected that he would break another. He scoured the countryside, looking for a manor house where his fiancée might have hidden herself away. He hunted high and low, but there was no trace of her. It didn't really matter, he told himself. Today was Fyribod and she would be here soon.

Gudbrand waited by the cluster of reeds where they had first met and fallen so madly in love. There was no sign of her. She's probably still standing in front of a mirror, he decided, getting herself all gussied up. To kill time, he took his flute out of his jacket pocket, put it to his lips, and began to play. But the reed flute had dried out and the only sound he could conjure from it was a succession of squeaks and groans.

"Bravo!" came a voice from close by. "Bravo, Gudbrand! Gudbrand, the breaker of promises! Gudbrand, the liar!"

He could feel the hair rising on the back of his neck as his beloved stormed out of the reeds, her face contorted in anger.

"You pathetic creature!" she raged. "Your heart is as dried-up as your miserable little flute! You don't deserve me!"

Gudbrand, angered now, responded in kind: "You're the one who'll regret this! I can have hundreds of girls like you any time I choose!"

"But they're not Huldres like I am!"

She reached beneath her skirts and uncoiled her immensely long cow's tail. Wielding it like a whip, she struck Gudbrand with all her might. The blow was so violent that it knocked him to the ground.

He remained there.

Motionless . . .

FOOD:

Huldres are not big eaters. They eat a little bit of everything, but always in moderation.

BEHAVIOR:

Opinions differ as to their origins. Claudius Expansyve assigns them to the Trolls, but Pétrus Barbygère, in his Elfin Chronicles, *makes the case that they began when Huldra of the Liósálfar, the Elves of the Light, lost her incandescence by venturing into the penumbra of mists and burrows. Unlike a Troll, a huldre fears neither the sun nor Holy Scripture (even if her tail falls off when she enters a church or consecrated building).*

ACTIVITIES:

The Huldres often fend off inquisitive mortals with the words: "You show us yours and we'll show you ours!" It's no great secret, on the other hand, that Huldres love music and delight in playing by night. The Huldre slaat *is a dirge-like chant, but its monotonous and repetitive tones are soothing and not unattractive.*

HEIGHT:

Tiny embers which flicker and grow in size when a breath of wind blows down the chimney. Never taller than a large cat or a three-year-old child, however.

APPEARANCE:

These Small Elves of the Flame are predictably fiery and lively. They have pointed ears and their feet are colored red. They are as slender as twigs despite the amount they consume. Their frizzy hair crackles. Two flames shoot out from their middle and from their lower back in the case of the Kochlöeffelmannele and the Firmannele. The former can change into a fire-rat, the latter into a cat with orange fur. The Grauwiwele, meanwhile, can turn into a little red mouse.

CLOTHING:

They flicker and dance to and fro totally naked.

HABITAT:

Bellies, pipes, and conduits of stoves in Alsace.

FOOD:

Traditional Alsatian fare (in massive quantities).

BEHAVIOR:

Born of stellar friction in the far corners of Elfiria. In Die Sagen des Elsusses *("Alsatian Myth and Legend"), authored by Bertold Braunkopf and published in Colmar in 1898, it is noted that "a falling star" (which is to say, a meteorite) came down a long, long time ago in a pretty valley not far from Riquewiller, Kaysersberg, Turckheim, or perhaps Drachenbrom, and that miniscule "creatures of fire" emerged from it and have since lived inside stoves all over the region.*

ACTIVITIES:

Granted, they are thieves and always hungry, not to say a mite vicious and more than a tad dangerous, but they fire the ovens of Alsace and are indispensable to the region's culinary and gastronomic heritage.

The Kochlöeffelmannele, Firmannele, and Grauwiwele

The cook at the White Horse Inn couldn't help noticing that someone or something was repeatedly stealing her tastiest morsels . . .
—Olympe Gevin-Cassal

Surrounded by pink pots and pans, Kathel Huck of the venerable White Horse Inn has, since the crack of dawn, been hard at work preparing the midday banquet to be hosted by Grand Master Kasper Storck of the Guild of Noble Vintners. Kathel, no spring chicken herself, has concocted the menu for a four-course meal designed to satisfy the healthiest of appetites. First up will be her legendary *lewerknepfle,* followed by pan-fried Sundgau carp and *fleischschnacka,* a regional specialty meat dish with stuffing. Then, to do justice to the Pinot Noir, there will be a succulent *hasepfeffer,* a stew of jugged hare, followed by a cockerel braised in white Riesling and garnished with *spaetzele,* and, last but by no means least, a regal *baekenofe,* a slow-baked stew of various meats. Needless to say, the meal will be rounded off by portions of Muenster cheese with caraway seeds, and a selection of tarts and sweetmeats.

Kathel makes ready her salting-tub and fetches her cooking utensils from the sideboard, then opens her storeroom only to find that the cupboard is . . . bare! The

bacon has vanished into thin air, along with the pork liver, the breadcrumbs, the eggs, the carefully seasoned and marinated beef, the horseradish, the jugged hare, the potatoes, the pastry, the cheeses, the fresh double cream, and the brandy-soaked plums!

There is nothing left in her larder. The Kochlöeffelmannele, the Firmannele, and the Grauwiwele must have crept out and stolen her provisions.

The Kochlöeffelmannele, the Firmannele, and the Grauwiwele are the thieving fire Alfs that live in the belly of the *kunst,* the massive stove and oven installation that is the pride and joy of cooks and housewives all over Alsace. This is more than a simple oven; it is the centerpiece of every Alsatian home. It is decorated with patterned ceramic tiles and copper fitments burnished to a mirrorlike sheen, with doors and recesses and ovens of every conceivable shape and size. It throbs and pulsates as it coddles and simmers and bakes and poaches and roasts and grills. It positively *sings.*

Inside the *kunst* is another world entirely, a mysterious and complex universe hidden from human eyes. It is said that it looks like a petrified landscape seething with heat, complete with houses, streets, taverns made of molten gold, and towering forests of flame. This is home to the Alfs of the Flame. How they ever manage to survive in there is a perpetual mystery. They are potentially dangerous, but never malicious—provided, that is, that they are left to their own devices.

Besides, who would risk the Devil's wrath by reaching into the flames?

The Erdwible and Erdmännle

Special places are the likeliest places for these meetings.
—Alain Kauss, *Le Monde des Esprits* (The World of Spirits)

In his collection of tales and legends from Alsace, Olympe Gevin-Cassal tells us that the Erdwible is the female Elf of that region. It seems he is still bedazzled by a childhood memory of his meeting with the "little women of the earth." He reports that they are most often encountered when the lily of the valley and strawberries are in season and that, in days gone by, many children saw them while out gathering fruit.

"Not here, little ones," they would say in their reedy, pure voices, "there are adders' nests here, but look over there . . ."

They are visible only for an instant, and they have fled from those who have forgotten that the moors, the meadows, and the woods are living things.

You would think you were seeing whirling eddies of dried leaves, acacia thorns, insects gathering pollen, or a cluster of mushrooms on the path, but when you look again, they are magicked away. The deceptive disguise vanishes each time and reveals an Erdwible.

There are soon more of them bobbing up and down than there are daisies on the bank, along with their little husbands, the Erdmännle, and the greedy berry pickers, the Beeremanneler, who point out the path which you must follow if you wish to share their "exquisite light," to melt away into "timeless time."

In the winter, beneath the dark fir trees, in the windy hollows of the slopes, where the snow is more dense and bluish and protected from thawing, the Erdwible indulge in a thousand cold-weather games, snugly wrapped up in mouse-skin coats and the downy feathers of birds. They summon children to attend endless balls at their ice palace, sculpted by their skillful little silver chisels, and to witness dreams of frost princes and princesses. And at midnight, just as the stones change color, they grant the most beautiful wishes that are made upon stars . . . and sometimes even bring a deceased person back to life, at the request of a Fairy soul.

HEIGHT:
Less than one ell (45 in./114 cm).

APPEARANCE:
Erdwible and Erdmännle are as perfectly alike as twins, except that they are of the opposite sex. They look as though they are made from the moon and the sun, and their hair is made from the rays. However, it is said that they have webbed feet like geese.

CLOTHING:
Erdwible are very particular about their appearance, and are fond of jewels, rich fabrics, and beautiful finery. They sport crowns—or bonnets of foxglove blossoms—on their heads and belts of gemstones around their waists. The Erdmännle also wears a bonnet of red foxglove. He is dressed in brown, and his tiny crystal lantern is set like a jewel on the front of his gold belt.

HABITAT:
Alsace. The wooded mountains of Sundgau are their favorite retreat.

FOOD:
Morning dew, fruit syrups, and wines. Fresh or cooked raspberries and blueberries served on gold and silver dishes.

BEHAVIOR:
Some regard these miraculous Aelfbeorht Little People as fallen angels, but it is nonetheless true that they lived valorously and wisely at the zenith of the Golden Age.

ACTIVITIES:
We are told that the Erdwible is a beneficent spirit: helpful, lighthearted, sensitive, and radiant. The Erdmännle is said to be less amiable than his wife, very rarely revealing himself. He does not deign to set the lost traveler back on the right path until the wayward soul has humbly asked him to do so.

The Tengu

The high, sacred mountains are therefore not
here to provide a panoramic view over the earth;
on the contrary, they represent the mysterious
and intangible essence of its spirit.
—Simon Schama,
Le paysage et la mémoire
(Landscape and Memory)

HEIGHT:

*The Tengu are tall, but variable
according to the time of day. They
grow taller, longer, and then shrink
with the shadows and lights that
play upon the rocks.*

APPEARANCE:

*The Greater Tengu are imbued with
nobility: their fine features chiseled
from marble, their cheeks colored
carmine with rouge. Their long, soft
hair is snow-white. Vast sun-wings
surround their lofty silhouettes with
a halo of light. The body, which has
a fluid appearance, seems hewn from
the high mountain air. They become
hideous when they are angry. The
Lesser Tengu, who are rather dark
and squat, have a more savage physiognomy, at once animal and vegetable. Their wings are shorter and
less transparent. Their eyes sparkle
both day and night. Their hands and
feet end in claws. Their very mobile
faces, inclined to grimaces and laughter, are reminiscent of monkey faces.
All Tengu sport a very, very long and
grotesque nose.*

CLOTHING:

*A robe as white as frost, with trim
as red as the blood of the setting sun,
a golden crown, and a fan of multicolored feathers for those who belong to
the Greater Tengu. The others wrap
themselves in a tight sheath of leaves
rather similar to that worn by Green
Men, and they wear black bonnets on
their heads.*

HABITAT:

*The mountains of Japan, amid the
tall pines and cedars. All trees are the
property of the Tengu, who are conse-
quently present in all the woodwork of
houses. There are numerous "Tengu
rocks."*

A Zen parable tells us that a hunter
once went off into the mountains. The mountain is a temple, and he who goes there
climbs towards enlightenment. But
although he had been searching these
sacred places since *tatsu-no-hoko*—the
hour of the dragon—he had not yet
reached his goal. What mattered to *him*
was the trail of his quarry on the short
grass, a tuft of hair on the bramble, or a
hoofprint amid the stones. He advanced
very softly as the animals do, controlling
his breathing in the high altitude, and
moving more slowly with the effort. The
animal must have halted here, for it had
recently bitten into a mound of leaves.
Anxious, alerted by a sound or by the
silence, it had remained tense, its muzzle
quivering before it merged with the vegetation in one invisible movement.

The man listened, watched, and sniffed
at the air. He could not yet see, but the
murmur of the stream was beginning to
pulse through his veins. The stones would
begin to speak like the forest that surrounded him.

Walking in the mountains is like beginning to learn the language of the birds.

Leaning against a rock, as motionless as
a tree stump, the hunter could now make
out the sound of wings beating; it was a
struggling crow, caught in the mouth of a
snake. It swallowed it down. The crow's
shape could still be seen writhing at the
bottom of the snake's interminable gullet.

The hunter did not move. Taking advantage of the snake's fleeting vulnerability, a
fox had leaped onto it and was already
tearing it apart and devouring it.

The hunter still did not move, for it
was now the bear's turn to seize the fox, to
snap its spine, and to chew on its entrails.

The hunter lifted his weapon; it was
his turn to kill now. He took aim at the
animal. He was about to fire and was
holding his breath . . . but what was that
voice among the leaves telling him?
What was that voice in the far-off river
saying? If he killed the bear, what would
then kill him? If he killed the bear, then
he would be part of the chain of killers
that were themselves killed and eaten;
soon it would be his turn to meet a predator that would kill him. And the hunter
shivered, for he sensed that it was already
on its way.

He fled.

When he got home, he heard a voice
calling to him from the trees, a voice that
was composed of the wind, the rain, the
whistling of birds, the babbling of rivers,
and the growling of animals.

The hunter shivered; he recognized the
silhouette clad in leaves, seated on the big
cedar branch, with its black hat above its
shining eyes. He immediately recognized
the Tengu's long red nose and respectfully
bowed.

"Hear me!" the Tengu cried. "You did
well to spare the bear, hunter; you are very
lucky that you acted wisely, because I was
making ready to come and eat you . . ."

The parable adds that the hunter went
home and never again killed any animal.

The mortal in the story encountered a
Lesser Tengu—identifiable by the black
cap, the claws, and the suit of leaves.
Doubtless, it was acting on the instructions of a Greater Tengu, to whom the
mountains belong. It is he who reigns
over the fauna, the flora, and all those
whose footsteps lead them to his lands.
This Master-Spirit of the area had to
watch the man's choice attentively from
the top of his snowy summit. Since he was
satisfied, he did not move. If he had done
so, he would have moved with breathtaking speed: just the length of the time it
takes to swoop down with wind, thunder,
and stone, to cast his victim into hell . . .

The hunter had the good fortune to
understand the language of the peaks,
which is the language of the Tengu.

The Kokuö of Tokoyö, the governor of
Horai, and the king of the empire of the
Fairies, held them in great esteem and
never failed to ask the opinion of the
"Elves of the snowy skies": "At once gods
and demons, these Spirits of the mountains have souls similar to their kingdom,
where the sun and the moon come to be
born and reborn, and where the sacred
flower blooms. Beauty and wisdom flow
in these vast expanses . . . but he who
comes and shatters the peace disturbs
Harmony and awakens the volcano."

FOOD:

Very fond of rice cakes—botamochi—which lumberjacks place as offerings to them before cutting down any tree. They are also ogres; tales from the Shinto tradition often refer to them as having the appetite of a tiger.

BEHAVIOR:

They originated in China and are affiliated with the T'ien Kou. Described as shooting stars, or mountain demons who came from the sky amid fire and thunder, or creatures disguised as winged dogs who were thieves and who ate children. They can also be seen as Spirits of the vengeful and arrogant dead.

ACTIVITIES:

The Greater Tengu have very few. They are contemplative, and through their silence they maintain the balance of the High Places. They sense any intrusion by strangers onto the surface of their mountains, and can divine their intentions and their thoughts; they can influence them, make them lose their way, crush them under rocks; or, on the contrary, use them to spread forth the lotus seed they possess within them unwittingly. The Lesser Tengu frequently serve as "help-meets" to the Greater; they do errands, look after the mountain and the forests, and oversee the lumberjacks' work. But, most often, they indulge joyfully in their favorite pastime: practical jokes!

HEIGHT:

The Tylwyth Teg appear to be young people by day, slightly taller than mortals, but at night, on the moors, when they sing and dance, they measure only six inches in height.

APPEARANCE:

Their appearance is comparable to singing angels, according to one observer. Very often they are invisible: only one in four people can see them. They are pretty, graceful, and radiant. The moon's gleam produces a mirror effect on their skin and reflects back light around the locations where they take form, appearing to light false, bluish fires on the crests of the hills.

CLOTHING:

Rich but simple: tunics, and light, satin-smooth gowns, green in color, cut for dancing and comfort. On their heads they wear bonnets the same shape and hue as a broom-flower. They are naked during the May celebrations. The Bendith y Mamau are poorly dressed.

FOOD:

They eat neither flesh nor fish, but dairy products, from which they make dishes flavored with saffron.

HABITAT:

Wales, Isle of Man. The region of their birth is Caer Gwydion, an Elfin island located approximately between Saturn and Offaly; but at present they occupy the intermediate world. They were once numerous on Mount Llwydiarth and around Lake Llwydiarth.

BEHAVIOR:

A variety of origins are attributed to these benevolent Elves: they are said to be the children of the Ellyllon and the Gwagged Annwn; or Fir Bolg, driven out by the invasion of the Tuatha Dé Danaan.

ACTIVITIES:

Dance, sing, and play music. Their favorite instrument resembles a sort of large and very melodious hunting horn, with strange arabesques, and with strings like a harp.

Tylwyth Teg, Sleiglh Beggey, and Bendith y Mamau

A hundred maidens, white as lilies and all ranged in a circle, were dancing with delight.
—Spenser, *The Fairie Queen*

Perhaps the Tylwyth Teg will come this evening. When the good folk of Wales and the Isle of Man went up to bed, they were always careful to put down a piece of cake, to stoke up the fire, and to draw the most comfortable bench nearer to the flame—leaving a pinch of tobacco on the stone hearth was also greatly appreciated. One last glance at the kitchen to make sure that it was clean and then the place was left to the Tylwyth Teg . . . With their ears glued to the door, the master and mistress of the house listened as little footsteps entered, and blushed with pride at the admiring whistles and compliments uttered by the Fairy Folk as they discovered that the room had been carefully prepared for them. "What a beautiful, clean dwelling," they said. "How tasty this cake is. Old Meg is without a doubt the finest cake-maker for miles around!" These words of appreciation were a sure sign that they would leave a few gold pieces behind them as a gift, when the cock's crow called them back beneath the moorland mounds.

If they did not receive a warm welcome, however, the house would be sacked and turned upside down. But who would be mad enough to tempt the devil and show such disrespect to these extremely generous little beings, whom they had been taught to venerate since their own infancy, and indeed since the dawn of time!

The Tylwyth Teg king, Gwydion-ab-don, dwells with Queen Gwenhidw, at Caer Gwydion in the clouds. Old Welsh women call the little cumulus clouds gathered together in a blue sky "Queen Gwenhidw's sheep."

In the county of Carmarthenshire, the Tylwyth Teg take the name of Bendith y Mamau, "Divine Mothers" or "Holy Mothers." Scrawnier and drabber than their cousins, they take children from their cradles and leave in their place a hideous Crimbil, which must be mistreated and thrown in the river if the parents want to get their baby back.

It is said that in the times when the Lord walked the earth, he stopped at the door of a cottage where a mother lived with her twenty children. As the task of bringing up so many noisy offspring was becoming more burdensome to her by the day, she entrusted half of them to the protection of the Divine One. But after they had left, the good woman regretted what she had done and rushed after them, intending to take them back. Alas, she never found them again: the children had become Bendith y Mamau . . . forever sorrowful and yearning for affection.

Ellyl and the Ellyllons

There, I discovered beings that I did not know.
—Julien Darmian,
Les chemins paladins
(The Paladin Ways)

There were three of them, singing as they came back together from the fair at Cwnaman: Master Robin Gwyndal, a merchant; Cuthbert Pugh, the curate; and Lwyfog Hafodydd, who had always been known for sitting outside his front door, doing nothing. The three of them were strolling along arm in arm, singing—or rather they were massacring a pretty love song that sounds pleasant when lightly hummed, but which they were bellowing as though it were a drinking song.

Then, abruptly halting the triumphal march, Master Robin Gwyndal staggered a few strides to a tree and emptied more beer than water onto some mushrooms.

Immediately the sound of small, protesting voices was heard, and some tiny creatures were seen emerging from the shadows, wet through, shaking themselves and distinctly displeased. There is no excuse for this kind of boorish behavior, especially when there is a lady among those one has just humiliated. Moreover, there were several such ladies, as graceful and white as milkweed in the moonlight.

It was Lwyfog Hafodydd, the layabout, who first found his voice, stammered out apologies, and spoke of a terribly unhappy love affair, which had caused the drunkard to seek comfort in the bottom of a barrel.

It was skillfully done, but the Ellyllons remained circumspect.

Then one of them, no doubt their leader, for he was holding a sort of scepter, came forward and asked:

"Where are you going like that?"

"We are going back home, to Aberpennar," answered the companions in unison.

"How do you want to go there? In the wind, on the wind, or under the wind?" he asked again, addressing his question to the curate, Cuthbert Pugh.

Cuthbert Pugh, whose aspirations as a man of the Church predisposed him to the heavenly itinerary, answered that he preferred the idea of traveling above the wind, and immediately found himself plucked off the ground and thrown up into the air, where he spun round, and—so it appears—where he will keep on spinning round until the Day of Judgment.

Questioned next, Robin Gwyndal, who had been made cautious by the curate's unfortunate choice, suggested in a trembling voice that a journey beneath the wind might be more judicious. He felt most ill at ease, and found himself immediately dragged at lightning speed across the ground, through hedges, thorns, brambles, and bushes until he arrived at his front door, half-dead, torn, broken, and bleeding. Afterwards, he was nicknamed Y Trwyn, "big broken nose."

As for Lwyfog Hafodydd—not such a bad fellow—who had humbly left the choice up to the Ellyl, he went back home, a little more swiftly than usual.

HEIGHT:
Very small, scarcely taller than two to three mushrooms.

APPEARANCE:
Very graceful. Light, pale, and diaphanous. Slightly bluish and luminescent, less ethereal and more like a Goblin with a twisted mouth.

CLOTHING:
A charming mixture of the traditional Elfin and Welsh costumes. The Ellyllon ladies and young girls wear gowns the colors of the moon and stars, to which they like to add the Welsh tall hat, a cashmere shawl, petticoats, and shoes with silver buckles. Or they may be naked, barely veiled by lunar silk and flower petals.

HABITAT:
They are found in all the green valleys of Wales, under old trees, lindens, cairns, rocks, and mountains.

FOOD:
They dine exclusively on poisonous toadstools and "Fairy butter": a sort of semisolid, slightly sweetened mousse that oozes from the roots of old trees, and from moon-flowers on nights of the Asraïs.

BEHAVIOR:
The word "ellyl" can be translated as "wandering spirit" or "Elf": this small, ethereal creature of the Welsh mountains gave its name to the poisonous toadstool "Bwyd Ellyllon," as well as to the bells of the purple foxglove, which are called "Menyg Ellyllon," or "Ellyllon's Gloves." It is no doubt that through contact with the harsh realities of this earthly world, little by little those slender moon Elves were transformed into these malicious, playful, and mischievous little beings. They enjoy only the company of their own kind and, although benevolent, can prove dangerous.

HEIGHT:

About two feet (60 cm), but can shrink to pass through a keyhole, or to make himself invisible.

APPEARANCE:

He was formerly a flame. Subsequently, across the centuries, he took on diverse appearances: that of a small, hairy demon with horns and a limp, and eventually a sort of little man blackened with soot, with a hole in his hand, affiliating him with the devil. He has also been seen walking on all fours, his eyes phosphorescent, his face pointed like a cat's. At the end of the eighteenth century, the term "duende" was used to designate the "brothers," which perhaps prompted the visionary painter Francisco Goya to depict them as grimacing and hideous, dressed in hooded monastic habits.

CLOTHING:

Naked, or dressed in a red cassock, an orange bonnet, a dark hood, and a short gray cape: all fiery and ashen hues of the hearth.

HABITAT:

Called Tardo in Galicia, Trasgu in Asturias, Pisadiel around Navia, Duendos in Valencia, and Pasadelo in Portugal, the Duende haunts the fireplaces, hearths, and furnaces of the entire Iberian Peninsula. In the Belgian Ardennes, a poltergeist closely resembling El Duende exists, called "Spratchen de Wandjons," that is to say, "cockroach crusher."

El Duende

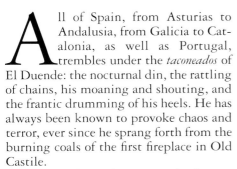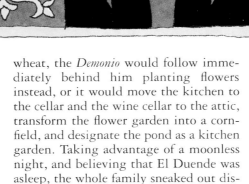

. . . coxiba,
y los cuernos y el rau se tapaba
con un gorrete por la mor del xelu . . .
— F. Gonzales Pietro,
El Folklore artístico asturiano

All of Spain, from Asturias to Andalusia, from Galicia to Catalonia, as well as Portugal, trembles under the *taconeados* of El Duende: the nocturnal din, the rattling of chains, his moaning and shouting, and the frantic drumming of his heels. He has always been known to provoke chaos and terror, ever since he sprang forth from the burning coals of the first fireplace in Old Castile.

In the eighteenth century, the famous Benedictine Brother Benito Jerónimo Feijóo, an enlightened thinker and author of the *Teatro crítico universal*, pointed to the misdeeds of one El Duende in his *Cartas eruditas* (1786). El Duende had taken refuge in a house in Barcelona, and Brother Tomas de Puigjamer of Montserrat was going to try and drive him out with his rifle. This was a dangerous mission, for El Duende clings to his prey like an octopus. There is also the story of the poor soldier haunted by one of them, which had got into his kit bag and followed him everywhere, without even bothering to hide. It danced a veritable sarabande on his belly as soon as he went to bed, then jumped from bed to bed, through all the rooms, until the authorities were obliged to put the entire barracks under lock and key.

Still today, we can lament the abandonment of many fine dwellings, farms, monasteries, and castles set in the beautiful Iberian countryside, because of the undesirable Duende or Trasgo, the familiar demons of those *cuentos y legendas* that are without question the true chronicles of "popular history."

F. Martinez y Martinez, in *Cosas de la Mena Terra*, tells us that a country family from Valencia, driven to despair by a Duende's "services," decided to move house. It wasn't that he was evil, but his way of regimenting the household's affairs was so unpredictable and invasive that the farmer could no longer decide anything without El Duende's interference. If, for example, the fancy took him to sow some wheat, the *Demonio* would follow immediately behind him planting flowers instead, or it would move the kitchen to the cellar and the wine cellar to the attic, transform the flower garden into a cornfield, and designate the pond as a kitchen garden. Taking advantage of a moonless night, and believing that El Duende was asleep, the whole family sneaked out discreetly on tiptoe. They loaded everything they could onto a donkey and abandoned the farm as if they were escaping from prison. But the wife said suddenly:

"We've forgotten the flour-dressing mill!"

"Go back and see if you can find it," her husband ordered her. Then a little voice was heard, announcing from within the parcels on the donkey's back: "Don't worry, I brought it!" It was El Duende.

Defeated, the family went home.

The only way to get rid of him is to ask him to collect and count seeds or lentils that you have thrown on the ground: as there is a *furacu* (hole) in his hand, the seeds fall through. He is incapable of carrying out his task, and he becomes angry and leaves the premises, never to return.

But why should one *want* to get rid of this ancient, protecting god, this fire spirit, this *friend* believed by the Romans to be a direct descendant of the souls of the dead: the Duende is diabolical and destructive towards those who reject him, but loyal and generous towards those who open their arms to him. A place by the hearth or near to the furnace is enough to make him happy, and to ensure abundance within the household.

Unfortunately, each tale, fable, or legend of El Duende describes how, across the centuries, owing to the persecutions of a Church bled dry of divine dreams and to the rigid planning of a dehumanized society, the gods of fire and the hearth and the spirits of deceased relatives have become domestic spirits, demons, and finally simple poltergeists. Hope resides in the dreamer who is still capable of leaving the window open to let in the bright rays of the Wishing Star!

FOOD:
He is not greedy, being content with little: a spoonful of grain, a bowl of milk, or a piece of bread.

BEHAVIOR:
This poltergeist is a complex mixture of the dark Elf of nightmares and the fire spirit. He has been compared to the English Puck, the French Will-o'-the-Wisp, and, a little lightheartedly, the Swiss Trolls!

ACTIVITIES:
He performs all the duties of a good and faithful domestic spirit when he is regarded as such. If not, his actions are those of the worst poltergeist. He is nocturnal, sleeping all day and emerging only at dusk. He proves himself to be very dangerous if you spit into the fire he protects or throw eggshells into it. It is said that when the flames sing, El Duende is happy.

HEIGHT:
> The size of a twelve-year-old child.

APPEARANCE:
> The Asraï are extremely beautiful but slightly built, so fragile and fluid that one would think it possible to see right through them. They have the precious bodies of aquatic dancers, slender, oval faces with blue lips, eyes of water, and long hair that is very pale green and phosphorescent. Webbed feet. The Asraï shine in the darkness: it is the Asraï who cause the sort of lightning flash effect that is seen from time to time, passing fleetingly across dark water.

CLOTHING:
> Naked.

HABITAT:
> The depths of the cold, dark waters of the most isolated lakes and ponds of Cheshire, Shropshire, and the Welsh Borders.

FOOD:
> Condensation, the moon's mist above smooth waters, and the incense from water lilies.

BEHAVIOR:
> These darkness-loving but radiant Elves flourish in the shadows and are extremely timid. The Ageless Ones consider them great prophets and protectors of fresh water.

ACTIVITIES:
> Mysterious. They garden the deep-water flora, from which they collect herbal infusions and philters for lake-dwelling Fairies. They teach the frogs to sing, play the harp, and greet those who have drowned, whom they initiate into the slower life of the sleeping waters.

NOTE:
> Anyone mad enough to have the bad idea of wanting to capture one should know that once an Asraï is taken from the water, it must be wrapped immediately in waterweed, for its touch is so icy that it can cause deep, terrible burns.

The Asraï

A charming specter which is carried off by
 a breath of air
And which, having been, is no more!
—Théophile Gautier

The Asraï flourish in the nights of mid-May. It takes three nights for the Asraï to be reborn. At this time, two great wonders come to pass. Deep within the hedged farmland, at the dawn of the cuckoo, Sleeping Beauty lies listless beneath the brambles; upon receiving the prince's kiss, she awakens and brings back the spring. At the farthest edge of the woods, on the night of the nightingale, the moon's kiss on the water awakens the Asraï. It takes her three nights to rise up from the depths of the waters and bring the lake back to life.

On the first night, the Ageless Ones emerge from the Land-Beneath-the-Mounds, leave the enchanted isles, slip out of the kingdom of dreams, and descend from the skies, the trees, and the hills. Then—guided by the clear song of the nightingale—they head for the endless shadow of the woods.

Intoxicated by the scent of the ivy and the wet earth, the Fairy People make their way towards the cradle of water and moon.

They assemble around the lake, sit down, and gaze upon the smooth, black, silent waters.

On the second night, they wait.

On the third night, the nightingale wakes them at the curved edge of the bank. The bird cannot be seen, only heard.

The Ageless People gaze into the depths of the star-field.

The water's mirror seems to be disturbed by a strange effervescence; a pale glimmer can be glimpsed as it blossoms from the very depths of the abyss. It is like an echo of the moon's rays.

Beginning with this kiss at the water's surface, as the air and the water are illuminated, the Asraï blossoms forth.

She will live for a century in the most secret depths of the ponds and lakes. She will live for a century, unless she touches earth, unless daylight or the hand of a man should brush her too-pale skin.

A fisherman from Shropshire had heard that an "unimaginably delectable" Asraï sometimes rose to the surface of a lake deep in the forest, to pay homage to the moon.

He knew how to trap her, and he went to the middle of the lake at midnight, in a boat, and waited until the moon shone at its zenith and the nightingale sang.

When the Asraï emerged from the water, he cast his net and pulled her towards him. She weighed no more than a breath of air. He wrapped her in water-weed, laid her at the bottom of the boat, and started rowing towards the bank, as quickly as he could. The fisherman heard the Asraï moaning and pleading with him in a most melodious language, whose words he could not understand.

Her voice was no more than a whisper by the time they reached the bank. The fisherman bent down to pick up his prey, but there was nothing left . . . only a little water at the bottom of the boat.

Pechs, Peghts, Pechts, Pehts

They danced by the light of the moon,
The moon,
The moon,
They danced by the light of the moon . . .
—Edward Lear

It is raining too hard for the child to be allowed out. Although he is being kept indoors as a punishment, the child who has been shut in has as many open doors as he could wish for, hidden in the depths of his hole-pocked pockets. Very softly, he asks the window Spirit, "Let me through." The reflective glass is a mirror page; the transparent glass is an imaginary sky. The two mingle and pass through each other. This is well understood by those children who, as soon as the walls close in on them, steal away and escape to rediscover endless, joyful dances beneath the nasturtiums' lanterns and green umbrellas.

On the garden path, one such boy performs a kind of hopping, skipping dance while reciting ritual rhymes. In answer, a little hunchbacked creature greets him from behind a hunchbacked beet root; out of the thin, bald leeks comes a thin, bald Pech; the big fat cabbage unfurls, revealing a big fat Pech; and a scrappy patch of salsify spits out a dirty Pech.

The puny child dancing amidst them in his little garden at Kirriemuir is James Matthew Barrie. He is a sad child. He desperately loves his mother, who prefers the ghost of his dead brother; she sees him as he was before the accident, laughing as he skated on the ice. The little deceased boy is more alive than James in the maternal heart he so covets. James stays with his nose pressed against her door all day in the vain hope that she will open it again. He longs for her sweet, pretty words and the kisses that blossom on her rosy lips. Day by day, he will grow older; day after day, obliged to move farther away from the scented cradle of those arms in which the little dead child rests and smiles forever. There is nowhere else he wants to be. He is a lost boy.

He is a lost boy, and even if he forces himself not to grow in order to resemble his brother in every respect, he has fallen from the cradle too soon. He is a shadow, barely attached to the edge of his window on the world, and he risks being let loose by one of his mother's painful sighs. One sigh, one sigh wet with tears, and there he goes . . . into the heavens of the gardens and the enchanted isle of the red-currant bushes where he will no longer be alone, for the Pechs are there. They are careful to gather up lost children.

This will not be the first or the last "Once upon a time." Ever since the very first cry for help by a child who had wandered from its home, a Pech has answered. A Pech can always be counted on to spring out of the briar patch, out of the golden seed of a midnight fern, to be a child's companion in games and affectionate reveries . . .

HEIGHT:
Some two and one-half feet (80 cm) tall.

APPEARANCE:
Originally uncouth and rough-hewn, they have been softened by their friendship with lost children. Their skin has grown lighter, and their eyes have become brighter. Richard Doyle, the great dreamer of Elves, Goblins, and Fairies, drew and painted wondrous and very precise portraits of the little Pech people. For the most part they are red-haired and have a look in their eyes that is both mischievous and affectionate.

CLOTHING:
The Pechs have rather eclectic clothes: silky, warlike, pretty, and neat, but more often than not, downright messy! However, it is known that they always wear strange braided shoes, which they take off when it rains and use as umbrellas.

HABITAT:
They live underground, in the Scottish earth, where they originate, but there are also Pechs in Northumberland, Yorkshire, Somerset, and the Shetland Isles.

FOOD:
Imaginary game animals, since it disgusts them to "kill for real." Lots of nice, pretend things to eat.

BEHAVIOR:
According to Lewis Spence, the word pech or pecht in Scotland denotes a very ancient type of Elfin creature, akin to a Brownie. This impish Elf, the most common and popular in Scotland, is, according to Pétrus Barbygère, the radiant counterpart to the dark Akkas, both of them having emerged from the belly of the giant Ymir.

ACTIVITIES:
They are credited with building numerous edifices and the majority of the cairns and dolmens in Scotland. Gentle, amiable, attentive, joyful, and playful, they nurture and accompany the reveries of childhood, and gather up lost children, to whom they offer the keys to an enchanted kingdom, the infinite escape into the heavens of the imagination.

The Sylphs

In a cowslip's bell I lie;
There I couch when owls do cry.
On the bat's back do I fly,
After sunset, merrily,
Merrily, merrily, shall I live now,
Under the blossom that hangs on the bough . . .
—William Shakespeare

HEIGHT:

*From six feet to a few inches
(1.8 m to 8 cm).*

APPEARANCE:

*A Sylph is lighter and swifter than
lightning bolts. Its body is as perfect
as the spirit of creativity. It has the
beauty and brilliance of a flower in
the sun, the fluidity of water gushing
forth from the glacier, the whiteness of
Christmas snow, and wings as fine as
June mist. Its eyes contain glints of
dawn and sunset. Its scent is sweeter
than the scent of mock orange or honeysuckle after the rain. It flies with the
silvery, shimmering movement of a
field of rye, bending as the wind passes.
It can make itself invisible, or take on
the form of the most hideous Harpy if
it senses that it is in danger.*

FOOD:

*It feeds on the purest essences, which it
seeks out where they are abundant.*

CLOTHING:

*Gowns of dawn, tunics of sky and
frost, and rainbow capes. The Sylphides
are swathed in the sun's muslin.*

So sings Ariel, the Sylph, in Shakespeare's *The Tempest*; he also sings,
accompanied by Aeolian harps, in
the work of Goethe and other
poets. Indeed, he sings wondrously—as
we shall see—and flies and breathes in the
scents of the flowers, but the Sylph is not
just some graceful, simplistic "extra" for a
Christmas pantomime!

At the start of the Carolingian era, the
Sylphs revealed themselves to humans,
appearing out of the blue upon admirably
constructed airborne vessels, which traveled according to the whims of the wind.
The people thought at first that they were
Stormbringers, who had taken to the air
to whip up storms and bring down hail
upon the harvests. As this sight reoccurred
several times, scholars, theologians, and
legal advisers soon agreed with the people. The wise Charlemagne and, after him,
Louis le Débonnaire imposed serious pun-
ishments on all these would-be tyrants of
the air.

So the clergy and experts in the study
of demonology promptly propelled the
Sylph to the head of the demonic
menagerie; they accused it of being
demon of the air just as the Undine is the
demon of the earth, and the Salamander is
the demon of fire!"

If Elves *in general* are spirits of the air,
then the Sylph is *the* Spirit of the Air: it
represents the earliest appearance of spiritual life in the ether, while down below,
in the water, the thinnest hint of material
seed struggled for existence. A Sylph is a
feeling of life, an intelligence, which
materialized harmoniously on contact with
the positive currents of space. It fed upon

"psychic particles" emanating from mete-
orites and from other cosmic phenomena.
It is also said that it is a source of dreams
about the philosopher's stone, condensed
from the alchemical achievements of the
Elementals. And that the winds, rain,
snow, hail, and rainbows are the external
expressions of its feelings.

After the creative explosion—the Big
Bang—sounds were passed on through
the celestial vibrations, sounds that the
Sylphs heard first, in their purest and
most absolute form. It is this original det-
onation that gave the notes of music to
the Sylphs, as well as unleashing their first
impulse to live.

The anatomy of the Sylph's mouth is
constructed in such a way as to express the
harmony of the fundamental song of the
emotions. Those who are able to perceive
their speech hear "a voice that seems to
come from the throat, both low and nasal,
almost discordant to a novice's ears, and
which generates high-pitched frequencies
that have come down from the heavens to
proclaim the Lost Word." This supra-har-
monic song is a veritable elemental Symphony, which brings knowledge and
supreme happiness to its listener. Those
who have been touched by its raw, perfect,
uncontrolled sounds as children often
become prisoners of this sound, incapable
of adapting to the demands of earthly
existence. It is claimed that the masked
stranger who appeared in order to commission a *Requiem* from Mozart in his last
days was a Sylph who had come to open
up the way for him to master their ineffa-
ble harmonies.

Throughout history, mages and sorcerers from all philosophies and religions have
tried to capture the energy of the songs of
the Sylphs, by condensing the songs into
words, sounds, and vowels spoken according to repetitive, regular, incantatory
rhythms: magic words and invocations
capable of commanding the elemental
forces through the power of the Word.

Prayers, poems, children's nursery
rhymes, and the sounds of certain musical
instruments are said to be distant echoes
of the Sylphs' heritage.

HABITAT:
The vast, galactic expanses. Numerous chronicles report that travelers, mountain climbers, and explorers have experienced visions of wondrous cities suspended above clouds, forests, or mountains. These are the cities of the Sylphs, reflected by atmospheric phenomena. Accounts locate a few Sylphs on Prospero's island, near Naples.

BEHAVIOR:
The Sylph is faithful to a Sylphide for all his life; their dazzling but intangible union gives birth to a radiant soul, which will assume bodily form. In the days of yore, the attic of a French house was called the "sylphirie" (Littré): It is in these secret and mysterious high places, where the dreamy house's memories were kept, that the last Sylphs stored the vestiges of their Golden Age.

ACTIVITIES:
Guardians of the celestial universes. They transcend the beauties of nature through the mere fact of their presence, and distribute gifts to the chosen children of men who are capable of maintaining and safeguarding the treasure of the Golden Age.

Anhangá and the Servants of Guaraci

And then Anhangá emerged from the wood in the form of a stag.
—Gustavo Barroso, *Indian Legends*

Among the ancient Tupi people, whose tribal name means "sons of the god Tupan," there was a renegade tribe, which took pleasure in war, rape, and pillage: these were the Tupinamba.

It was in the days when animals knew that they had been created to feed human beings, and they knew also that some of the strongest among them could eat humans, that such were the natural laws of the jungle, that one fed on another, that the fauna fed on the flora, which one day in its turn would suck out the marrow of the corpses that had been returned to the ground . . . and no one thought of rebelling, for they all knew that Tupan had acted wisely. So, when the doe met the hunter, she knew that her death would not be pointless. She knew that the hunter would address her with respect and gratitude before firing his arrow into her heart. He would ask her forgiveness for stealing away her life, and would add that he himself would offer her his flesh later, when in turn he had become a doe and she a hunter. For each carries the seed of the other in himself, and everything is one.

However, it was quite different with the Tupinamba, who killed without need-

ing to eat, just for the pleasure of killing and causing suffering.

Once, a Tupinamba was pursuing a doe, which was still suckling her fawn. With one blow of his *tacápe*—his club—he first injured the little one, in order to make it cry out and attract the mother, who was swifter. Hearing its moans, and mad with the pain of the mother, the doe came back and approached the bushes where her torturer lay in wait. His arrow plunged deep into her throat, but before all of her blood had spilled out, she called upon Tupan, father of all things, entrusting him with the life of her fawn, and demanding vengeance for herself and those dear to her. Tupan heard her and turned to Guaraci, the sun, who gathered up the doe's breath; he mingled it with his own breath and kneaded them together for a moment in his own hands, before mixing in a little bit of everything in the world. He then sent Anhangá down to earth. Anhangá was loved by all the good Indians, but detested and feared by the others . . .

When the Tupinamba hunter stood up to gaze in triumph upon his victim, a voice made it clear to him that he had been the plaything of a mirage created by Anhangá, and that his cruelty had just plunged him into a nightmare.

At his feet, in the place of the doe, lay the corpse of his mother, whom he had killed with his own hands.

HEIGHT:
That of a giant stag.

APPEARANCE:
When Anhangá dwells in the divine realms, he is described as a fine athlete of Indian appearance, with sun-colored hair, which he inherits from his father; and the large, gentle eyes of a doe, which he has inherited from his mother. To the Indians of Brazil, he always appears in the form of a white stag with fiery eyes, with a crown of impressive antlers on his head.

CLOTHING:
Even when he returns to the blessed lands of Tupan, Anhangá retains his immaculate stag's skin, which he wears like a plaid.

HABITAT:
The jungles of Brazil.

FOOD:
Often, he threatens to devour men and women who do not respect his laws and who hunt game animals, but it is not known if this is true.

BEHAVIOR/ACTIVITIES:
A radiant, forest-dwelling Alf linked with the sun, he is one of the four spirits who protect the natural realm governed by Guaraci. He guards the game animals from the atrocities of bad hunters, whom his anger may pursue beyond death. He is the master of nightmares and fills the sleep of both the living and the dead with terrifying visions.

Cáapóra

The second servant of the sun spirit Guaraci, he is the companion of Anhangá. Guardian of the Brazilian fauna, he prevents the extermination of all the animals of the forest. From morning till evening, he roams the forests at the head of an immense herd of wild boars—*caetetous*—riding on the largest of them himself.

Present-day natives believe that it is wise to carry tobacco when they go out hunting, because Cáapóra likes it a great deal, and it is the only way to mollify him.

Ouirapourou

This other servant of Guaraci reigns solely over the world of the birds. It seems that Father Tupan created him from a few drops of happiness, one note of song, and one ball of light. From that day on, he has lived in the form of a small Amazonian bird, whose song is so sweet, so melodious that all the other birds fall silent to hear it.

Those who succeed in obtaining the stuffed body or a few feathers of this "singing Elf" will have happiness all their lives. It is said to be the most precious of talismans.

Ouaouiára

Ouaouiára is the last spirit of Guaraci's solar quartet. He governs the flowers and rivers, and protects the fish and all aquatic fauna. According to Couto de Magalhäens, when he sees a young girl and finds her to his taste, the Ouaouiára leaves his *bôto* (dolphin) skin and, when night comes, approaches her house, singing. His song is melodious and attracts Indian girls to the riverbanks. He then seduces them; the first children born to young girls of the Tupi tribes are almost always attributed to Ouaouiára. He sometimes catches them unawares, when they are bathing, and carries them down into the depths of the river. On nights of the full moon, it is common to see *bôtos* coming to dance and sing in the river to attract the young girls from the neighboring villages.

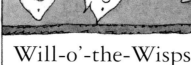

HEIGHT:
From a candle stub to a raging fire.

APPEARANCE:
As changeable as the flames of a brazier. They can appear as cockerels, fire goats, candles, fire ships, crowns, sheaves, chariots, firebrands, children, birds, butterflies, or solitary lanterns moving mysteriously between heaven and earth.

CLOTHING:
Gowns of blue flames, top hats half consumed by fire, and clogs made from embers. All kinds of bonnets, cravats, jackets, hoods, and tiaras of fire.

FOOD:
Feeds in the same way that fire feeds.

HABITAT:
They are known across Europe and beyond the geographical borders established by man. It would take too long to list all their habitats. Their preferred locations are moors, rivers, marshes, shores, oceans, melancholy pools, old cemeteries, bridges, and hidden paths.

The place that has the largest number of Will-o'-the-Wisps is in Normandy, above the Briouze marsh: there blaze the sinful souls of all the inhabitants of a town that was swallowed up long ago.

Will-o'-the-Wisps

A smoldering wick he shall not quench.
—Matthew 12:20

We know the ancestors' rituals for attracting the good graces of the "Little Red Beings." The Ancients invoked the Hindu fire spirit Agni and his ten flaming servants, the *Dackchalis* (fingers). Other instances of this phenomenon can be found: in the Finistère Will-o'-the-Wisp, Yan-Gan-Y-Tan, with his ten fiery fingers; in Lithuania, with the fiery court of the underground sun god, Pécollos; and in the Lumerelles, whose fiery hair lit up the dances of the ancient fairy folk upon the mounds in the Blessed Time.

In Auvergne, the souls of children who have died unbaptized are called Brandons (firebrands) or Illayés, and emerge from limbo at night, to search among the travelers for a godfather who will open up the gates of paradise to them.

The old people of the Geer valley in the Ardennes give the name of Escaufeûr or Flambia to a mysterious ball of fire as big as the mouth of an oven, of which solitary walkers are justifiably terrified.

The Fouleto of Burgundy is a light that lingers by rustic bridges. It helps those who offer it payment to cross; others will meet with misfortune.

In the Vosges, the Culards haunt the marshy lands where the sphagnum mosses grow. They bring about the downfall of those who are unwise enough to follow them, by giving the water the appearance of firm ground, and firm ground the appearance of water.

The Flambelle is a little crown of fire, which is seen on Midsummer night above Fief Lake (Loire-Atlantique).

The Vuurman, Vierman, Schoovert, Sjoverik, or Schoeffer walks each night on the banks of the Meuse; it burns with a long, bright flame.

At Kieldrecht, a man perished in a state of mortal sin. By night, he is still aflame, in the form of a burning sheaf, which is where his name comes from: De Brandende Schoof.

The lanes of the Belgian Ardennes are set aflame by a coterie of flaming spirits: *rodje gate* (red goat); *roudje bonnète* (red bonnet); and *rodje cotchét* (red cockerel).

It is said that the Fléolles that follow the flat boats on the great Brière River are the souls of those whom the druids sacrificed on the nearby rocks.

The Foulta of the Jura of Bern is a small imp, whose legs end in flames.

The Swiss Feu Belluet resembles a sort of bluish phosphorescent butterfly.

The Dourallichten, Stalkeersen, Doodkeersen, and Stallichter are all little human skeletons with small candles in the place of the hearts. *Paotrick he shod tan*, "the little boy who carries the fire," holds a flaming brand and flutters like a moth above the meadows and the marshes.

Major Rogers' famous Rangers spoke of "fox fires" running the length of the Mohawk River, and scaling the tall trees around Fort Ticonderoga, which frightened the Indians.

In the heather around Champigny, on the night of the *Brandende Schaper*, the "fire shepherd" can be seen. This shepherd found a purse filled with silver one day and dared to say, under oath, that he had not pocketed anything: "If I am lying, may I burst into flames here and now," he added. Scarcely had he finished before he began to burn like a piece of kindling in the hearth . . . and his torture continues to this very day.

Sometimes the Will-o'-the-Wisps, dancing on the streams, allow themselves to be carried to the sea. The Grand Légendaire has given numerous explanations for the blazing waves. These burning waves are called *marcremo* (sea fire), *brâsi* (burning coal), the cordon of fire, marine flames, the water's teeth, and the sea's thirst.

When these fires leave the waters to festoon the rocks on the shores, or to become dancing flower petals of fire on the masts and rigging of ships, they become known as flammeroles, furoles, goulaouennred, wandering candles, or devil's fire. This is also the origin of what is most often called Saint Elmo's fire.

Fishermen in the English Channel believe that the Northern Lights are made up of countless clouds of minuscule Firefly-Fairies, which they call marionettes.

Will-o'-the-Wisps are "Elfin luminescences," and there is nothing human about them. These are the invisible Flambettes, and all we can see of them are the torches they hold in their hands. The Hannequets are little men walking in the woods at night, wearing red flames like a bonnet. The Herlequins, Herliquins, Hennequins, Lumerelles, and Keleren are all nocturnal dancers.

One should neither mock a Will-o'-the-Wisp nor whistle or point at it. To get rid of one, you must throw it a piece of copper with a hole in the center, or plunge a knife into the earth, on which it might injure itself. Given a needle, it will amuse itself by passing backwards and forwards through the eye, and forget all about you.

BEHAVIOR:

The Jos, fire spirits, multiply like the flames of a fire, and Will-o'-the-Wisps are equally prolific. Specialists argue about their origins: Some contend that they are the souls of unbaptized children, the tormented souls of the drowned, the souls of individuals who died in a state of mortal sin, or the souls of witches, crooks, money-lenders, bailiffs, or murder victims. Others see them as the ghosts of old Elementals. Demonologists incline towards "fugitives from Hell"; spiritualists, towards "prisoners of limbo," ill at ease in this intermediate world, who question humans as well as Fairy Beings about what is to become of them. As for Barbygère, he claims that "Will-o'-the-Wisp Elves" are the sparks and brands of the original soul and of the fire of creation, while "Will-o'-the-wisp Alfs" fell from the final explosive disintegration of the Golden Age.

ACTIVITIES:

If the happy, Elfin Will-o'-the-Wisps express their lunar joy by dancing and fluttering, others wander to expiate their sins, tormenting passersby. They guard treasures and victimize humans with their hatred by drowning them or pushing them off the tops of cliffs.

TOWARDS THE CLOSE OF DAY

*Rowan gathered at eventide, and slipped
    beneath my glove,
The first one I meet must be my true love.*
                                                —Marie Gevers

When the watchman of the moors sets spark to his lantern at eventide, he extinguishes all the lights of day: the fading umbel of the elder tree, the cattail's candles, and the dancing lamps of the water lilies on the lake. Each light will cease after a lantern is lit against the menaces unleashed by the night. When people are at last freed from work and the cares of the day, and should let their souls glide towards peace and calm, an anxious murmur disturbs rational thought. Between dog and wolf, the werewolf creeps in. This is the moment when familiar, well-known shapes slowly become distorted, lengthen, and unmask themselves, then emerge from the shadows and set off to roam the countryside on all fours.

However, not all of these shad-
ows are evil; on the contrary, it is the fear they engender, the fact that they make people run away, that makes some of them grind their teeth.

They say that perhaps they too would like to be able to sit down by the fire in the evenings, share supper, bounce children on their knees, and tell them stories of the world of Elves, filled with beauty, humor, and lessons in wisdom. But doors and windows are closed to their pointed ears. And beautiful Marion, encountered by chance in a corner of the wood, will never be sufficiently kindhearted to embrace them, unless she is the kind of woman who would offer herself up to worse . . .

As one evening follows another, the dark Elves have grown darker . . . Little by little, the crawling shadows have come to join them, wiping good intentions from their memory. Now, they roam in savage bands, baying about the great woodland Alliance; and the women of the moon, who are more seductive and las-civious, do not push them away on summer nights . . .

HEIGHT:

The size of a triton, but may become gigantic. The Cantal Drac is so small that it is often confused with a Goblin.

APPEARANCE:

Drachs, Draci, Drakins, Drakes, Dracken, Draks, Krats, and Fire-Drakes are handsome aquatic men with powerful bodies. They have noble features: blue eyes, green hair and beards, and scaly skin that is cold, but soft to the touch. They very often change their appearance, from a grain of wheat to a stormy bolt of lightning, from a dragon to the worst monster of the murkiest depths. Dracs have been seen posing as peaceable washerwomen, as snakes that coil themselves round their prey and strangle them, as bright-eyed peddlers with charming smiles, and even as black donkeys or horses.

There's a handkerchief lying on the edge of the path. You pick it up and blow your nose . . . and the Drac is twisting it. Over there is a knife that someone has lost; the finder slips it into his pocket. It begins to open up, gets bigger, cuts through his pants, and escapes, leaving the unfortunate man cut and bleeding on the road, and yelling, "I had you! I had you! I had you!" The echo answers back, "I stab you, I stab you."

CLOTHING:

Armor and a crown of the same color, made of the same indefinable material.

The Drac

What mystery pervades a well!
The water lives so far–
A neighbor from another world
—Emily Dickinson

One day, beautiful Jeanneton went down to the river to bathe. The Drac, Lord Draci, finding her to his liking, abducted her and married her in his beautiful underwater castle. After six months, seeing that she was growing bored, the king of the waves attached a gold chain to her left foot. It was as fine as a single hair, but as strong as a bar of steel, and seven hundred leagues in length. Thus she could come and go, and run about in the liquid meadows. Each evening, when the water's sky was growing dark, she'd sing:

The Drac has stolen me away
And has bound me by the foot
With a gold chain
Drac, pull on the chain
Bear me away into the depths . . .

The Drac then hauled on the chain and Jeanneton returned. But it is always the same with Fairy Creatures and love; one day a handsome prince arrives to steal their beautiful bride from them! A king's son, who had just come to the water to drink, met Jeanneton, broke the chain, and took her away.

Inconsolable, the Drac became extremely wicked. He raised storms and caused floods, sickness, and drowning. He searched everywhere for the infidel; his eye was in every well. Every time a girl passed by his river lair, he dragged her in, thinking that in her fickle gaze he had rediscovered Jeanneton's eyes. Often, he ate the girl so as to retain her soul.

Dracs can take on any form, including the human body, in order to show themselves in public, but most often they indicate their presence by making gold cups and rings float to the surface of the water, tempting women. The women enter the water to claim the treasure and suddenly disappear beneath the surface. This happens above all to women who are breastfeeding; Dracs abduct them in order to feed the children that girls like Jeanneton have left behind.

One woman who was washing her laundry on the banks of the Rhone noticed a floating box filled with jewels; she swam out to seize it, but the box drifted away from her like a boat, and when the washerwoman reached a deep place, the Drac abducted her and instructed her to feed his son. After seven years she returned home, and her husband and friends scarcely recognized her. She told them wondrous things: that Dracs fed on the flesh of men they had seized and that they sometimes took on human form. One day, while she was still at Lord Draci's palace, he gave her a cake to eat, containing "the flesh of the secretary bird." By chance, she touched one of her eyes with a little fat from the cake, and from that moment had the power to see clearly underwater. This is how she was able to make her way through the aquatic forests and find her way home. Once she had reached the riverbank and was making her way to her village, she happened to meet another Drac, who had assumed the form of a peddler. Unthinkingly, she greeted him as aquatic beings greet each other underwater. "With which eye did you recognize me?" he asked. Naively, she showed him; the Drac placed his finger upon the woman's eye and she lost her power.

This true story proves that, deep down, Dracs are good. A Morgan le Fay or a Morgana would have torn her eye from her head or blinded her by spitting venom in her face. However, the Drac is no longer the romantic and magnanimous sovereign he used to be; the beautiful girl's treason turned him into a water-ogre, who is feared everywhere. Rivers, lakes, wells, stables, cellars, caves, houses, forests, and oceans, but also the air and the wind, are now his hunting fields, where nobody is safe from his metamorphoses.

FOOD:

Allegedly, human flesh! His favorite delicacies are swallows and swifts. As soon as spring comes, he goes off hunting in the form of a winged, invisible dragon. It is for this reason that the birds, who are alone in their ability to see him, fly in a zigzag pattern, and suddenly change direction to escape him.

HABITAT:

Ancient underwater castles built in rivers, lakes, and springs in Auvergne, Lozère, the Hautes-Alpes, Languedoc, and Dauphiné.

BEHAVIOR:

In Remarkable Memories of a Drac Brought to the Knowledge of the Learned Man, *the autobiography of a certain Sire Dracy, long regarded as a forgery before being rediscovered and authenticated, the author describes the Drac as being the Prince of the Elves, with a brave heart and a fine mind, and skilled from birth in the subtle arts of metamorphosis. In more than a thousand pages of exploits worthy of the Baron du Crac, which read like an adventure serial, we discover beneath the boastfulness an individual as disenchanted and touching as King Arthur on the last night of Camelot.*

ACTIVITIES:

Hunting, fishing, and playing bad practical jokes. It is not rare for certain "Goblin-like" Dracs to run inns in a few verdant corners of Auvergne. The Chronicles of the Black Pudding insinuate that one Drac may be maintaining close and strange relations with Monsieur and Madame Poum.

HEIGHT:
Rather tall.

APPEARANCE:
A sort of archaic, uncouth satyr, as tousled, hairy, and rough as the landscape from which it comes, and which he knows in minute detail. The eyes are said to have the same depth and color as Highland lochs, sometimes bright and clear, sometimes as dark as the abysses of Loch Ness. It walks heavily, and its manners are awkward and often indecent. Certain legends have it that its reddish pelt helps it blend in with the heather, which explains the belief in its invisibility.

CLOTHING:
Its own fur. It becomes angry if it is offered clothes.

HABITAT:
According to Perthshire Scenes *by the Reverend Graham, successor at Aberfoyle to the famous Reverend Kirk, the Coire-nan-Uriskin, a romantic valley near Ben Venue, is the place where the Uruisgs meet. They live in isolated caves, in the most inaccessible parts of the Scottish mountains. However, one can read in Armstrong's* Gaelic Dictionary *that "each manor has its own Uruisg and, in each kitchen beside the fire, an empty chair is left for it."*

FOOD:
It hunts, fishes, and collects berries. It likes milk and mortals' cooking, on which it feasted in the days when it helped on farms.

The Urisk

Different places on the face of the earth have different vital effluence, different vibration, different chemical exhalation, different polarity with different stars: call it what you like. But the spirit of place is a great reality.
—D. H. Lawrence,
Studies in Classical American Literature

One day, the fine weather brought an Urisk out of his cave. The slopes were covered with heather in full bloom, flooding the valley right to the bottom with waves of deep purple. The spectacle was so dazzling that, touched by so much beauty, the gruff Alf felt that the heather was calling to him. He felt a desire to wade in it. He let himself be carried along. He laughed as he gamboled among the heather, grunting with pleasure, letting himself fall down and roll and then getting up again farther down, drunk on sap, surrounded by bees, and with his fleece covered in purple twigs.

Usually, Urisks are melancholy by nature; so, seized by these new feelings of lightheartedness, he forgot caution and the time . . . and the night soon closed in around him.

Urisks do not like venturing forth once darkness has fallen on the glen. He searched for shelter. Close to the Eas à Phollchair waterfall, not far from Poolewe, he found a little cottage with a thatched roof. A light was shining in the window, and he knocked.

Knock. Knock. He entered without waiting to be invited in . . . By the fireplace, a housewife was in the process of cooking something that smelled deliciously of butter and hot milk.

Of course, she recognized a savage from the mountains straight away. Even though they had recently become peaceable and even somewhat fearful of mankind, it had not always been the case: the memory of the terror they inspired was still very fresh. It was said that in the old days the Urisks came down in bands from the summits and attacked the isolated farms, that they pillaged and burned, violated the women, and massacred the inhabitants no matter what their age or sex . . . before disappearing into the darkness as suddenly as they had come.

The woman, who remembered the stories that her grandmother had told her, knew also that he must not be vexed; she must be amiable and speak to the beast softly with a smile. As he asked her name, she answered him: "Nobody." *You never know*, she thought. You don't give out your baptismal name just like that to a pagan who doesn't even have one!

He considered this a very pretty first name, just right for her little house and the countryside that surrounded it, and also perfectly suited to the desire he now had to spend the night there, with her, perhaps in her bed, and to stay there while the hills were covered with flowers.

Sensing this, the woman started to tremble. She had been told all too often that you could refuse them nothing! And her husband was so far away . . .

So she offered him a good plateful of porridge. No matter how uncouth and smelly they may be, they know a good thing when they see it!

"I won't say no!" the beast proclaimed.

But she emptied the whole of the burning-hot cooking pot onto his knees. The cry of pain he let out made the house shake; horribly scalded, he made a single bound to the river to soothe his burns with cool water.

He then climbed back up to the wild peaks where the Urisks live, with his pelt singed and his skin peeling, and when—ready to avenge him—his fellow Urisks asked who had burned him, he grunted: "Nobody, it was Nobody."

This story of the Urisk, (sometimes

called the Urwisg or Ourisk) is the best known and most widespread of Urisk stories.

Famous bards have each in turn created many versions of this story, but the "fireside storytellers" know plenty of others. One, for example, tells how the chief of the MacFarlanes of Arrochar had abducted an Uruisg (the female of the species) to make her the wet nurse for his son. The male Urisk, drunk with pain at the loss of his companion, began to prowl around the chief's castle, waiting for an opportunity to take vengeance. For a long time, he watched the chief's wife when she took walks at the foot of the walls, and one day he ambushed and jumped on her, tearing off her breasts with his teeth. He was pursued, tracked down, caught, and hanged from a large tree at Rudha Ban, or "White Point." By way of vengeance, the Uruisg then poisoned the child she was caring for, by applying a poultice of poisonous herbs to its heart. It is said that the "half-savage" depicted on the arms of the MacFarlanes represents the Uruisg of the story.

Another tale tells how an Uruisg haunted the "Corrie of the Howlings." She showed herself in the form of an appealing shepherdess to the young men who passed by, and invited them in among the trees to enjoy the games of love. The son of one clan chieftain was wary, having discovered two little horn-buds under the beauty's abundant hair, and unwisely tried to refuse her. She immediately resumed her original form. "Both goat and witch, her skin was like a grayish leather and thick as a blacksmith's apron," he said. The same tale has it that "she could crush a hazelnut between her nose and her chin and cause a horrible, cruel snake to crawl out of her chest and bite a reluctant lover on the throat."

From time to time, in spite of everything, these wild Alfs can prove generous. This often depends on the way one behaves towards them; in the tale *The King of Lochlann's Three Daughters*, the hero meets an Uruisg, her fur whitened with age, who asks him for something to eat. He gives her a piece of meat and, in gratitude, she builds—right before his eyes—a ship that sails as well on land as on the sea, and in which he will be able to continue his adventurous journey. . .

BEHAVIOR:

George Henderson remarks that popular etymology has it that its name derives from ur-uirg, a creature which lives in lakes and waterfalls, while the Gaelic arrusg expresses clumsiness and awkwardness, both characteristic of the Urisk. In any event, he prefers a Nordic origin, deriving from the Scandinavian expression ofreskja, or gift of twofold sight: a person who can see hidden and invisible creatures. The origin of this "ancient Lord of the mountains" remains rather mysterious. For some, it is the result of crossbreeding between dark Alfs and ancient Picts. The Brownie, a domesticated Urisk, is supposedly the fruit of its lovemaking with the brown Dwarves and Dunter.

ACTIVITIES:

They were once known as warriors, then as workers on farms and as millers' lads; a sort of melancholy seems to have taken hold of them after this diminishment. They are dreamy and contemplative, set apart from the world, but this is perhaps merely one stage in the course of their destiny.

NOTE:

They have sometimes been confused with the Cughtagh or Ciuthach, their neighbors; with the Scandinavian Meming; and with the brown Dwarf of the moors, with whom they share numerous similarities, and which Walter Scott brings into The Lady of the Lake.

The Liderc

If you are indeed my husband, tell me where all my beauty spots are, and my secret nooks; tell me everything you know about me . . .
—János Erdélyi, *Népdalok és Mondâk*

How pretty János's betrothed is, with her heart-shaped face, and her plaited black hair with silk ribbons. She looks like a bouquet of flowers made from folded paper, cut out and unfolded into a lacy garland. Her rounded arms in her puffed sleeves, her bosom pert in her tightly fitting, embroidered bodice, and her legs sleek in red boots amid starched, full, pleated petticoats: she is a doll. There is a look in her eyes that says *love me*.

But *love me* with the immense and faithful love of a child.

This is what the May Queen songs say . . . that she coos so wondrously that in the village she is called Furulya, from the name of a flute with a voice as clear as that of the blackbird.

But Furulya is sad. János has gone off to war, and now the roses have gone from her cheeks too. But the weeping mouth, the sorrowful eyes, and the sighing breast of a woman in mourning often give men a taste for desire. Many are hoping that the fine fellow she is waiting for never returns from the front. They prowl around the house; they look out for the postman, and hope for a letter announcing his death. At the sound of a piercing cry of despair from behind the shutters, they would run up to console the young widow. But the beautiful girl does not weaken, does not crack; on the contrary, one would say that her lips are blossoming again and that, curiously enough, the colors are returning to her face! See the sparks of light in her eyes, and behold her sashay and swivel her lovely, curving waist!

It *is* strange, and yet a sufficiently close watch is being kept on her for people to know that there is no lover, concealed beneath a rock. They would know. Anyone would think she was smiling at the angels, like a woman in the throes of a blissful love affair, and when evening comes, through the glass they spy her making herself beautiful, getting ready for the night . . . and not for far-off János.

No secrets can be kept in a small village, and the mystery quickly does the rounds of all the houses. It is said by gossips in the know that each night at midnight, a blue star comes to shine on the ridgepole of her roof, before slipping over the threshold and entering her room.

"The little one is in danger," announces an old woman who has knowledge of the arts of sorcery. "Little Furulya has fallen prey to the Liderc. For the moment, he seduces and spoils her; tomorrow, he will devour her from the inside."

"Just think," she continues, "he will exhaust her with love. Gnaw away at her body from the inside. He will leave nothing but one bone. It is high time to act before it is too late."

In the morning, at cockcrow, the old woman goes to find Furulya, to warn her that the handsome János she thinks she has found again is in fact a trickster demon, who only wants her soul. In answer to the girl's protestations of innocence, the old woman asks only if Furulya's enthusiastic visitor has ever taken off his boots. She tells the stunned young girl that if she requires proof, she has only to steal the imposter's left boot and throw it into the fire. She will see then that he has the foot of a rooster.

That is what Furulya did, that very night. Reluctantly, but she did it and she saw what she had to see: the black Alf appeared as he truly was—half billy goat and half chicken—before disappearing up the chimney in a puff of smoke.

Time passed. János did not return. Furulya never married. The Alf had eaten her beauty and nobody wanted her any more.

HEIGHT:
Of a chicken, a monkey, or a slender man.

APPEARANCE:
Generally he shows himself in one of three ways: as a bluish, flickering light, as a plucked chicken, or in the form of the loved one who is absent, with one chicken's claw instead of a human left leg.

CLOTHING:
Traditional Hungarian costume.

HABITAT:
Hungary. A regular visitor to the czardas, inns on the major routes.

FOOD:
Greedily breathes in the carnal appetites of the women who are besotted with him.

BEHAVIOR:
The behavior of an incubus, a particularly depraved vampire Alf.

ACTIVITIES:
His only goal is to exhaust his conquest to the point of death. Hungarian legends (see Magyarsáy Neprajza *by Zoltán Szabolcsi) also speak of the existence of certain domestic Lidercs, similar to hairy Gnomes; they offer their help to farmers, but it is dangerous to accept it, for once they have accomplished the task on the spot, they immediately demand another one, which they carry out even more swiftly. They must then be found impossible tasks, like bringing water or sand in a sieve or a colander, otherwise, once they have no more work to do, there is a risk that they will take apart the house, the outbuildings, and the entire settlement, stone by stone.*

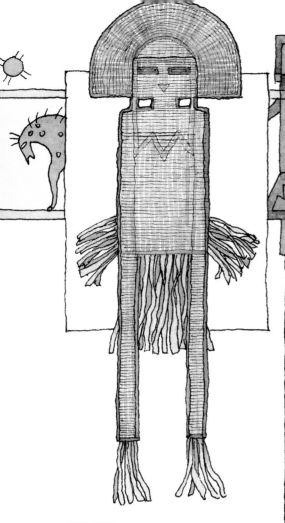

HEIGHT:
Medium.

APPEARANCE:
A Red Indian Venus, the Ho'ok is delectable. The features of a wild adolescent, at once sensual and innocent. A curvaceous, shapely body that fans the flames of love. Long red hair. Very large, almond-shaped eyes, which burn like fire. The teeth of a carnivore, and the hands and feet of a wild animal.

CLOTHING:
Animal-skin tunic, fringed in the Indian fashion.

HABITAT:
The caves of Baboquivari Mountain and the surrounding deserts, as far as Tucson.

FOOD:
The flesh of children.

BEHAVIOR/ACTIVITIES:
These solar ogresses are as embittered, solitary, and frustrated as old maids leading the cruel, idle life of the Harpies.

The Ho'ok

The old man said: it is a very long and very complicated story.
—Sophie Guillin, *Ma grosse Biesse*

The story of the Ho'ok is not easy to follow for anyone who is not an American Indian, and is not familiar with the mythology of the Tohono O'odham—the people of the Sonoran Desert.

Nevertheless, let us try to understand by traveling back into the light of that Age when legends were born. Let us sit downstream, and drift back upstream with the tales; on one of the banks, beside the water, a young girl is sitting, beautiful as the day. She smooths her long, shining hair and smiles at her reflection. It is a beautiful day to marry, she thinks. At that very thought, a red ball comes along and splashes her.

The ball belongs to two valiant young warriors who are racing to catch it. The one who does will marry the beautiful girl. But the girl picks up the ball before they do and hides it under her dress.

"No, I haven't seen it," she answers the boys when they question her.

She takes the trophy back home and shows it to her parents.

"We shall prepare the nuptial bedroom while we wait for your suitor," they say, not knowing that their daughter has deceived her two betrothed.

Time passes, but nobody arrives; no suitor comes to claim her. And yet the beautiful girl's belly takes on the roundness of a woman great with child. This is because the red ball, made from the sun's dust, is growing in her belly.

After nine months, the beauty gives birth to a little girl with red hair as beautiful as the day, but whose hands and feet are those of an animal.

The more she grows, the more wicked she becomes. She bites and scratches the other children with such ferocity that her mother, threatened with being driven out of the tribe, is obliged to part with her. She takes her far into the desert and sends her to find her father. She points to an enormous red ball laid upon a bed of heat clouds and says: "Go. That is your father. Keep walking south, and do not stop; go to him, he will welcome you . . ."

The beauty knows that her daughter is a Ho'ok, that she is not of this world and will not find any mortal to love her here.

"Go," she says, and the little Ho'ok sets off without turning around. She walks south without stopping, as she was told, but the sky grows turbulent, darkens, and soon hides her father under a cloak of darkness. Then she lies down and goes to sleep, thinking that the greatest part of the journey is done and that tomorrow she will sleep in the arms of her father. But the sky is full of mysteries and, in the morning, when she wakes up, her father has arisen on the other side.

The Ho'ok knows that she is not of this world, that nobody here in this world wants her, and that only her father can love her; so, without waiting, she sets off again in the other direction. She walks towards him without stopping and her father moves away again. Sometimes he rules the north, sometimes the west, and sometimes the east. Each time she thinks she can reach him, the night hides him from her eyes.

It is exhausting and sad, and as she wanders her despair is transformed into anger.

One day, she finds a red, deep cave. Perhaps this is where he comes to sleep. She will settle there and wait for him . . . and wait for years. At night, when hunger overcomes her, she goes out and sneaks

into the villages, stealing babies and young children, which she then devours. Each night, she is very hungry.

The Itoi is a medicine man, who is very old and very wrinkled, with long, white hair. He is so pale and so thin that you would think him weak, but he is immensely powerful. It is he whom the Tohono O'odham consult in his hermitage to the west of Baboquivari Mountain, to beg him to rid them of the Ho'ok.

He tells the tribal elders that a great ceremony of dances must be organized and the Ho'ok invited to it. She will be flattered and accept the invitation.

The Ho'ok dances for three days and three nights with the Tohono O'odham. In readiness, the Itoi prepares a very strong tobacco with drugs and herbs that cause sleep and dreams, and the Ho'ok smokes it constantly. It takes three days and three nights, and hundreds of pipes to cloud her mind. Finally, she falls into a stupor. Her eyes roll in their sockets, but she can no longer see. Her limbs can no longer move. She is carried to her cave and the door is sealed, then warriors set fire to it, feeding the flames until her whole lair goes up in smoke.

The Tohono O'odham rejoice, believing that they have been freed forever from the Ho'ok, but from her smoke, her ashes, and her scattered bones her terrible daughters are born. They still haunt the Sonora desert and its people.

You can meet them upstream or downstream of the tales, seated on the banks of a dried-up river.

The Fuaths

HEIGHT:
From the size of a salmon to the size of a walrus.

APPEARANCE:
Very disparate. It is very difficult to describe them, as they are all so different from each other. Apart from a few exceptions, the Fuaths are repulsive, hairy, savage, and menacing.

CLOTHING:
Naked, or covered in dirty, faded finery that is always wet.

HABITAT:
Scotland; the Borders and the Lowlands as well as the Highlands. Grottoes created in the depths of the lochs, or in the rocky banks of rivers. There are Fuaths in the Shetland Islands and in rare corners of England.

FOOD:
Fish, livestock, human flesh.

BEHAVIOR:
"Fuathan" is a general term to designate the Fuaths or Voughs. Petrus Barbygère calls the Fuaths "industrious and peaceable Elves, who built lake towns on the largest and most frequented lochs in the Highlands, and lived there by crafts and trade until invaded, massacred, and dispersed by hordes from the south. Forced to take refuge underwater, their prolonged stay in the darkness embittered them, little by little, and degraded their blood, so that they became the sly, venomous creatures we deplore."

ACTIVITIES:
They hunt, fish, and laze around when they are not indulging in cruel games at the expense of those who disturb them.

The man who is absorbed believes that nothing can be perceived beyond the cricket's song . . .
—Henry David Thoreau

You're sitting on a rock set like the head of a watchman in the middle of the heather; the valleys stretch endlessly towards the mountains, whose peaks extend into the distance, along with the skies. There is nothing around except an eagle wheeling overhead, which seems to be chasing the sound of its own voice, with great flaps of its wings. Apart from this, the glen is deserted, hollow with silence. Your eyes have nothing to rest upon but the treeless expanse. There is nothing but the slopes, smoothed by the winds. You try to focus on a blade of grass or the petals of a flower, but the eye is drawn by the emptiness and moves farther into the distance.

There is nothing to be heard, not even the prayer of an insect or the bleating of a solitary goat.

Down below is the dark loch, deep, so deep, and obscured by a layer of leaves, with no sound of a spring. You think you are alone. You are mistaken.

Your shadow stretches as far as the spongy bank and the stagnant water, which is so flat and motionless that you throw a pebble into it, to bring it to life. This is a mistake.

What were they saying in the inn yesterday evening: that above all, you mustn't throw pebbles into the waters of the lochs and mountain rivers. And why is that? Because it disturbs those who live in them. The fish? "Not really."

What else were they talking about in the inn last night between two pints of beer, washed down with whiskies? They were saying that the Fuaths didn't like it at all that strangers, who think they know everything and know nothing at all, come and drop stones on their heads when they are peacefully enjoying the underwater coolness, seated there on their doorsteps.

And one of the drinkers in the bar, the most talkative, started to reel off a load of gibberish about two lovers who were having fun and making a lot of noise, skimming stones over by Ettrick Water. The Green Glaistig rose from her bed in fury, dripping wet and clad in her robe of waterweed. After copiously garlanding them, she invited them to spend the evening at her home, and they followed her to her house beneath the waves. During the night, it seems, the Green Glaistig sneaked up on the lad, and in the morning, when the girl awoke, she did not find him there.

"He went off fishing and said not to wait for him," said the Green Glaistig to the girl, presenting her with a meal.

After a while, the Glaistig asked her if she had enjoyed the meat dish she had just eaten, and as the girl said yes, the Green Glaistig told her, "That was your betrothed."

This is the sort of story the old Scots love to tell, deep in isolated valleys, to frighten strangers.

And what's more, the Green Glaistig isn't the worst of all the Fuaths!

See all that horrible seething mass, rising towards the surface: those round and bloody eyes, those horns, those scales, and those snapping jaws . . .

There surely won't be enough time to list them all.

There is the Wulver with its incredible speed; he is armless, but with skilful, powerful legs. His whole body is covered with short, brown hair. Despite his horrible wolf's head, he is quite benevolent and spends his time sitting on his little rock, fishing. Sometimes he even leaves a few fish on the windowsills of elderly people who he knows are in need. As long as he isn't disturbed, he doesn't attack anyone; but if he is, he crushes the bones of these irritating individuals.

There is the Fideal, half human, half dragon—but not a very large dragon, only the size of a small calf. Even so, he will swallow a fellow in one mouthful, even if he isn't hungry.

Peallaidh: the Shaggy One. Physically, it resembles the Urisk, but it is much more evil in nature.

The evocative name of Beithir, the shadowy and solitary Fuath of the Highlands, which also haunts ruins and caves, means "snake" *and* "lightning"!

Shellycoat: pretty and sly, she takes her name from the noisy cloak of shells that covers her supple, green naiad's body. When Shellycoat is bored, she leaves her lake dwelling and goes to haunt the old tower of Gorrenberry in the Borders. There, she lets out the heartrending cries of a drowning woman, and lures those who hurry to help her into quicksand or whirlpools.

The Ceab—the Killing One—is always thirsty for blood. He kills everything that passes within reach: man, woman, child, or beast.

The mysterious and angry Cuachag's territory is mainly around Glen Cuaich in Invernesshire, but he enjoys hunting and visiting the other lochs by means of underground rivers. Because of his grayish, tapering body and his long neck, which sticks up above the water, he has been confused more than once with the famous Nessie of Loch Ness.

The Brollachan is a Fuath from Sutherland, described as "rough and hairy." In Gaelic, the name denotes "someone in rags," or naked. There are both males and females. They have yellow hair, green clothing, large round eyes, and a tail—but no nose. They are killed by light. J. F. Campbell tells of a family by the name of Munro who, in the past, married with the Voughs, and their offspring had tails and breasts covered with fish skin, for at least four generations.

Beware of the Glaistig. She is a sort of Jekyll and Hyde, who likes to change her personality. Sometimes dressed in a Banshee's shroud, she slips across the misty moorlands, crying mournfully "to weep for the death of her favorites." Or again, half woman and half goat, she climbs towards the summits to go gallivanting with the hairy Urisks.

It is said that in her benevolent form, she goes into farms to help with household work, guard the cows, and take care of the children and old people, whom she treats with affection. But like her sister the Green Glaistig, she is above all an implacable killer.

And then there is the black, spongy creature, all claws and gaping maw: the one whose name we don't have time to mention . . .

The Devalpa

You are the first he has not strangled; he has never abandoned those over whom he has gained mastery, not until after he has suffocated them.
—Story of Sinbad the Sailor

HEIGHT:
Five feet (1.5 m).

APPEARANCE:
Pallid, frail, and lined and bent by age and rheumatism. Sparse, white hair and a gray beard. He always has a timid, affectionate, imploring air, even when his tentacles are tightening around you and he is proving merciless. As regards their texture, the arms and legs resemble the limbs of a cow, as does its tail.

CLOTHING:
A long, worn-out, gray djellabah.

HABITAT:
The deserts of Arabia and a few unknown islands.

FOOD:
Fruit and the energy of his victims.

BEHAVIOR/ACTIVITIES:
We know nothing about this sort of wandering, solitary Alf, for apart from Sinbad the Sailor, nobody has ever emerged alive from his clutches. Arabian mythologists, Boudjema Djedid among others, who nickname him "the old man of the sea," state that he used to reign over a vast sea kingdom before the water receded, and that it is the vestiges of this that he seeks tirelessly. That is why he smells so strongly of salt.

In the desert one should be wary of everything, of everything unknown, even if it is a gouty old man with a bent back, an honest smile, and eyes that are brimful of goodness. He seems so exhausted, this old man who is staggering with fatigue on tired, frail legs, and he pleads with such innocence: "Could you please carry me for a moment?" Nobody suspects him, not for a moment. For fear that he will fall, you bend down and hoist him carefully onto your shoulder, so as not to break his bones.

He is so light that you might think you are picking up a feather, but then you suddenly feel yourself sink beneath a crushing burden.

The Devalpa has trapped his prey. It is too late to react. His mass weighs you down and paralyzes you; the weight, pressed against the nape of the neck, slowly numbs the brain. The Devalpa has doubled in volume; his chest is now as broad as a barrel, and from it other arms and other legs emerge, and tentacles that tighten around the waist and the limbs, while a tail like a whip forces you to keep walking, running as he dictates . . .

It is over: the Devalpa has tightened his grip. You walk, you keep going forward, you hurry all day long . . . and at night, when you fall exhausted on the sand, he remains hooked onto your shoulders. You sleep under this sort of hump, which stifles your dreams of escape.

It is futile to hope that his attention will wander, to believe that you can take him by surprise and throw him over your head: he is a sucker and a tourniquet. As soon as you make to free a muscle, his grip immediately tightens again, compresses your heart, and leaves you breathless, asphyxiated on the ground by way of a warning.

You cannot expect any help from anybody: the gods and the saints are not listening to you. The Devalpa has wiped away your destiny amid the desert sands. The wind has passed, and nothing more remains. Only your two legs, to carry him to the end . . .

One day, sooner or later, maybe tomorrow, he will leave the carcass of his worn-out steed in the hollow of a dune and, seated on a stone, he will wait for another unwary traveler to pass by.

It was during his fifth voyage that Sinbad the Sailor encountered the Devalpa. And, though he may lay claim to being a clever and valiant hero, strengthened by his countless experiences in confronting every sort of monster, like the biggest simpleton, he fell headfirst into its trap . . .

Two rocs, carrying rocks in their giant claws, had just got the better of his ship, and as the waves had cast him up on an unknown shore, he explored its solitary wastes.

"When I had walked a little way across the island," he recounted later, "I spotted an old man who seemed completely worn out. He was sitting on the edge of a stream;

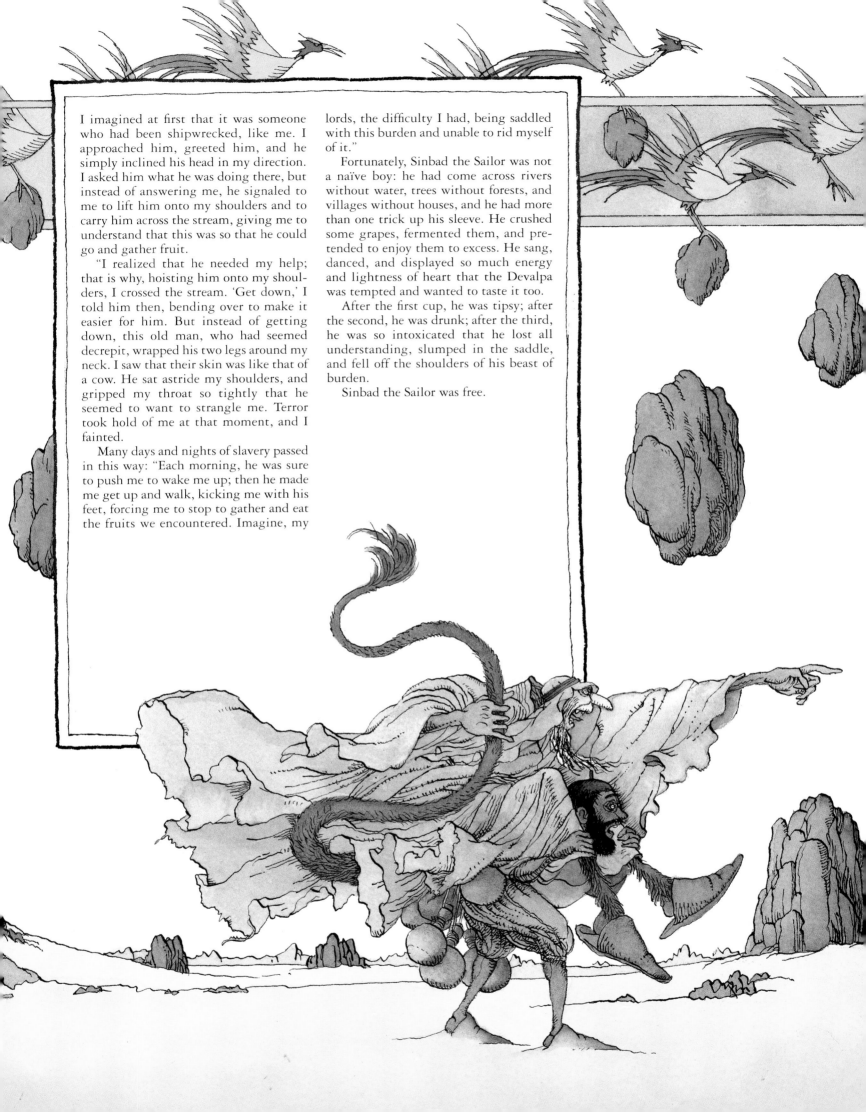

I imagined at first that it was someone who had been shipwrecked, like me. I approached him, greeted him, and he simply inclined his head in my direction. I asked him what he was doing there, but instead of answering me, he signaled to me to lift him onto my shoulders and to carry him across the stream, giving me to understand that this was so that he could go and gather fruit.

"I realized that he needed my help; that is why, hoisting him onto my shoulders, I crossed the stream. 'Get down,' I told him then, bending over to make it easier for him. But instead of getting down, this old man, who had seemed decrepit, wrapped his two legs around my neck. I saw that their skin was like that of a cow. He sat astride my shoulders, and gripped my throat so tightly that he seemed to want to strangle me. Terror took hold of me at that moment, and I fainted.

Many days and nights of slavery passed in this way: "Each morning, he was sure to push me to wake me up; then he made me get up and walk, kicking me with his feet, forcing me to stop to gather and eat the fruits we encountered. Imagine, my lords, the difficulty I had, being saddled with this burden and unable to rid myself of it."

Fortunately, Sinbad the Sailor was not a naïve boy: he had come across rivers without water, trees without forests, and villages without houses, and he had more than one trick up his sleeve. He crushed some grapes, fermented them, and pretended to enjoy them to excess. He sang, danced, and displayed so much energy and lightness of heart that the Devalpa was tempted and wanted to taste it too.

After the first cup, he was tipsy; after the second, he was drunk; after the third, he was so intoxicated that he lost all understanding, slumped in the saddle, and fell off the shoulders of his beast of burden.

Sinbad the Sailor was free.

HEIGHT:
  The size of whatever creature's appearance it borrows, or . . . nothing.

APPEARANCE:
  That of whoever's appearance it borrows, or a shadow of bad aspect. The cabalist Abraham Athanarius, the famous and fiendish A. A. of Noli-me-Tangere, who forced it to appear before him in order to complete his Diabolical Teratology, described it as being pale and scrofulous, leaf-shaped, and borne upon two tadpole feet. He added that it left behind it a trail of downy hair and foul breath.

CLOTHING:
  According to A. A., it always appears in a sort of long flannel coat.

HABITAT:
  Eastern Europe, in the cellars of oblivion.

FOOD:
  Kosher.

BEHAVIOR:
  The Dybbuk is not, as has often been claimed, the tormented spirit of a dead person in search of a body, but a sort of demon Alf, which uses "migrant souls" in the manner of a vehicle, in order to seize their fluidity and enter the body of a living person to possess it.

ACTIVITIES:
  Prowling and hunting without respite, the Dybbuk is attracted by cries, tears, and lamentations. Talismans, pious objects, sincere prayers, alembroth, or salt of wisdom may drive it away.

The Dybbuk

"Are you a man . . . or a spirit?" he asked, not without effort.
"I do not know that myself, Lampoon. Perhaps both at once."
  —John Flanders,
  The Mysterious Man of the Rain

One day, a man of little virtue who was traveling by sea fell overboard in a storm and drowned. He had a heavy soul, and his body, instead of floating back up, was lost in the deep sands. After several weeks and the work of the crabs and fish, when there was nothing left of the man but fleshless bones, his freed soul was beached on a shore and began his lamentable wanderings on the earth. In Judaic mythology, these souls in distress are called *gilgul*. When they are corrupted by sin, as this one was, they find that they are the prey of the Dybbuk. Now, one such demon happened to be prowling nearby, and it melted into the lost soul of the drowned man and directed his ectoplasmic envelope to the nearest village. Seeing a handsome, sturdy lad taking the air outside his front door, the Gilgul-Dybbuk rushed at him and invaded him.

The young man, renowned for his good humor and peaceable nature, suddenly developed a furious madness, rushed howling into the house he had just built, and started to destroy it with blows from an ax. He insulted the neighbors who came in vain to calm him. He foamed at the mouth, spat, and uttered horrible blasphemies.

In the end, they sent for the rabbi.

The rabbi asked him: "Who are you?"

When the holy man addressed it, the Dybbuk began to tell of the life of the gilgul whose soul he had possessed just before seizing the body of the poor madman. He told of his dissolute existence. He confessed his miserable deeds and made the listeners shiver as he described his horrible death-throes in the wild sea. There were so many signs of sincere con-

trition that each listener was in turn won over by grace, and felt the need to lighten his own conscience. And each time, the rabbi gave his blessing, with the result that the Dybbuk *himself* asked to be exorcised in the end.

Ritually, the Dybbuk emerges from the borrowed body by the tongue or the little finger. Once pacified by the sanctity of so much confession, this one flew out of the open window as lightly as a butterfly . . .

Once freed, the young man awoke immediately, completely astonished to see everyone gathered in his home, which he noticed someone had severely damaged—for once you have been delivered, you do not remember being possessed.

This story of the Dybbuk, taken from the *Book of the Mayseh,* is one of the rare few that end well. Most often the demon refuses to leave the body, fights tooth and nail, and does not abandon it until he has led it into the ways of vice, crime, and all maledictions, right to the doors of hell.

The Dybbuk does not necessarily attack those who are the guiltiest; he also interferes in the lives of the innocent. All it takes is a moment's inattention—simple absentmindedness—and the demon pops up where he is least expected. In the same way, one must take care when entering the ritual bath, the *mikvah*, for one may emerged inhabited by a Dybbuk who was hiding at the bottom of the water.

A few other phantom Elves:

Yezer Ha-Ra

This is the worst of all, the blackest Alf, who haunts rabbinic writings. He is hidden in every soul, where he cooks up the most abject temptations and lovingly prepares the ground for odious crimes, rapes, and debauchery of all kinds. No soul escapes this torment and none are more haunted than the souls of the rabbis, whom Yezer Ha-Ra eagerly harasses.

Yezer Ha-Ra is especially dangerous at the end of synagogue on Thursday night.

The Meurli

This dark, mad Alf enjoys frequenting places where tragic deeds have occurred, for there he is sure to meet ghosts of all sorts, whose emaciated bodies he immediately borrows, as well as their shrouds, which he likes to shake in all directions while laughing sinisterly.

The Forso

This is a dead Alf who is so bored that he often leaves the tree in which his corpse is laid, to go and stir up discord in the houses of those who have neglected him. He must then be distracted by bringing out the bones of his ancestors, painting their skulls, and exhibiting them close to the dwellings.

They are feared in the islands of Northern Australia, and in New Guinea.

The K'uei

In China, these are the embittered spirits of those who died accidentally or were murdered. Rendered furious by this unjust fate, they prowl every night in the form of skeletons, their skulls covered with a devil mask, and slaughter the fishermen who fall into their clutches.

In India, they are known as Pretas.

Páng Che, Páng Chiao, Páng Chu

These are the good ladies of the dead who, in China, occupy the corpse between the time of death and the burial. These beautiful and divine Elves help the souls to make their perilous journey between the two worlds. They may, however, abandon the deceased to his sad fate if the rituals are not properly respected, or if the family falls asleep instead of keeping vigil.

The Kayeri

In the rainy season
The Kayeri weep.

—Sir William McPherson,
The Rivers of South America

The rainy season is a season that the Cuiva people fear, for it is the time when the fearsome Kayeri come back up from their underground caves. They come up through the holes of anthills, at first no bigger than moles; they choose a large tree that stands sturdily on its root ball and sneak beneath it. Then, transformed into mushrooms, ficuses, durians, or tambourissa, they wait for the great rains to come and make them grow bigger.

Once they have reached the appreciable size of a giant ogre in a fairy tale, the Kayeri separate and go their separate ways across the forest. It is then that troubles really start to rain down for the Cuiva.

Everywhere, the Kayeri are stealing the herds, devouring the cows, and abducting girls. Nobody is safe.

Only yesterday, a man went out hunting with his two daughters. They had insisted on keeping him company, and of course, despite his reprimands, they chattered, squabbled, and made too much noise. "Stop that, you'll make the game run away and attract the Kayeri," he said.

It was no use! They stuffed their mouths with fruit and, while chasing each other, spat the stones in each others faces. Of course, they soon tired of these games, and although their father had warned them about the Kayeri, they decided to go back home—quite alone.

Off they went. Hardly had they turned the corner when the hunter heard them shouting at the end of the path.

A Kayeri was abducting them. It was no use struggling; they were going to end their lives without ever seeing daylight again. They would die under one of the anthills, after years of sweeping, cooking cow soup, and washing the Kayeri dishes.

Fortunately for them, in the rainy season, hunters are always careful to carry a bone arrow in their quivers. This is the only weapon that the Kayeri fear.

The hunter shouted to his daughters to cover the eyes of the "cow-eater." They covered its hideous head with their blouses, and the Kayeri, blinded, stopped running and staggered about with arms outstretched, repeating "mu, mu, mu," the only words it knew.

The hunter was now a few paces from it. He drew his bow and, holding his breath so that his hands would not shake, aimed carefully at the middle of the back, the vulnerable point he had to hit with his first shot. If he missed the target, he and his daughters were done for. Just one arrow . . .

He drew, aimed, and fired.

The sharp dart quivered as it plunged into the flesh.

"Mu, mu, mu," the Kayeri cried again, in a fading voice, before jumping into the river and turning into a stone.

Then all three, without further ado, ran off to their hut in the middle of the village and barricaded themselves inside, while all the forest echoed to the sounds of sticks hitting tree trunks and the painful cries of "Mu, mu, mu."

That is what the rest of the Kayeri do when one of them dies.

HEIGHT:
Of a mushroom's cap, then a mole, and finally a giant.

APPEARANCE:
It is first a mushroom, a fruit, a sort of acorn. The rain turns it into a very ugly giant, with cabbage-leaf ears, an anteater's snout, and globular, red eyes under eyebrows of moss. Its mouth is very large and filled with teeth capable of crushing cows' bones. Its heavy, powerful body has the consistency of a mushroom. The vegetation that covers it is dripping with moisture. It smells very strongly of decomposing wood. When it walks, its big, flaccid feet make sounds like footsteps wading through mud.

CLOTHING:
Its impermeable fleece is sufficient, but on its head it wears a greenish-blue or sometimes yellow hat.

HABITAT:
The Kayeri lives underground in South America, in deep caves hollowed into labyrinths.

FOOD:
Exclusively cows.

BEHAVIOR/ACTIVITIES:
A seasonal type of forest-dwelling Alf, which only appears in the rainy seasons. Dangerous, quick-tempered, and a thief. Wild, uncouth, but not very crafty. It is absolutely impossible for a human to hope to enter into friendly contact with one. Even other Alfs avoid them.

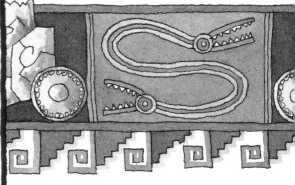

The Munuane

This song of the water, which is like the crackling of the fire and like memory.
—Léa Silhol, *Contes de la tisseuse*
(Tales of the Weaving Woman)

There is no shame in fearing the Munuane. If the Sikuani Indians fear him, it is because he is fearsome. Nobody but the son of the sorcerer and the moon dared venture into his territory, and still fewer go there to do harm to the fish, his subjects! Whoever kills a fish wounds the spirit of Munuane and enrages him.

Despite the danger, the son of the sorcerer once went back upriver to the place where it branched and mingled with the marsh, and entered the perilous kingdom. He climbed a tree, whose twisted trunk created an arch above the water, settled himself there, and started firing arrows at all the fish that passed. Then he climbed down to collect his booty, but when he pulled out his arrows, there was nothing left at all, not even the tips of the bones that had been broken. This was a bad sign. The boy wisely climbed back into the tree. He knew he was in very great danger, for the Munuane is everywhere.

The boy began whistling, in the way the Munuane despises. The lord of the marshes responded to this high-pitched, mocking whistle by sliding onto his raft of mossy reeds. Slowly, he advanced; if his movements and thoughts are slow, it is because his mind is that of the marsh—stagnant, murky, and disturbing. His gaze is lethal; one look draws his prey towards him and carries it off. As an archer, he is infallible.

The sorcerer's son knew all this, as the secrets of the marsh had been revealed to him in his moon-cradle. He was careful not to move a muscle. Very gently, he fixed an arrow to the string of his bow, but the Munuane had already sensed him. As the Munuane fired his infallible shaft, the boy held before his chest the stone talisman he had brought, and the talisman deflected the lethal shot. But the force of impact knocked him off balance, and he fell into the Munuane's boat.

Before the craft reached the dock made up of human femurs, the boy dove into the treacherous waters and began to swim with all his might.

If he had not been the sorcerer's son, the Munuane would have reached him,

captured him, and thrown him into the cooking pot. His shamanic powers protected him; he reached a tree and hung on to it, asking it to grow, to bend over and to span the lagoon, in order to set him down on the bank close to his village. However, he knew that the Munuane, despite his slowness, would not abandon his prey. He waited until nightfall, and then all through another day . . . and at last the Munuane appeared. Finally, it came close enough for the boy to take advantage of the secret he alone knew, the precise point at which to strike.

The eyes of the king of the marshes are set deep in his knees, and that is where the boy knew to strike in order to kill him.

The spirit of his father guided the boy's hand as he fired his arrow straight into its target.

Since then, the Sikuani never again lacked for fish. Or at least, not until civilization came and poisoned their fishing grounds.

HEIGHT:
Six and one-half feet (2 m) or more.

APPEARANCE:
Long, thin, and very slow, he seems to be suffering from intense depression. Greenish-gray skin. His yellowish head resembles a deflated ball, or a veiny pig's bladder, and features a wide, toothless mouth. His skull is covered with long, straight, gray hair, which mingles with sprigs of waterweed and small aquatic plants. Those who have seen him naked state that his emaciated body is covered in scales and that he has a dorsal fin. His hands and feet are webbed and have claws. The lidless eyes, sunk deep into the knees, shine an intense green.

CLOTHING:
A sort of wide, long robe, bluish-green in color, which is always damp and seemingly mildewed. He wears a bow like a bandolier. His quiver contains only one arrow, for he never misses his target.

HABITAT:
A horrible hut on stilts, whose structure is composed of the bones of his victims. He lives in the marshes of South America.

FOOD:
He eats the flesh of those who come and profane his kingdom by threatening the fish, snakes, and other reptiles, which he regards as his beloved children.

BEHAVIOR/ACTIVITIES:
This type of aquatic Elf ogre was formerly a powerful god who protected the waters, the springs, and the rivers of Elfland. He now has only the fish and the small fry of poor fishing villages. It is thought that he is responsible for marsh fevers, that he charms mosquitoes, and that he teaches the frogs music.

The Dodo

Do-do-dogson.

—Lewis Carroll

The Dodo Dryophilus, whose strong legs and imposing beak resemble those of the extinct Dodo of the Mascarene Islands, could be funny. But it isn't. Anyone who suddenly sees him swooping down towards him from his hiding place has little desire to laugh. One blow of the beak to the top of the skull is like a spoon cracking an egg to get at the yolk. Thereafter, two talons come down and stab the shoulders, and the skull offers up its delectable contents.

Between breakfast and midday, two Ghanaian women were drawing water from a blue river. One, as beautiful as a big, golden coconut, was laughing and splashing about, for she was happy on account of the baby she was carrying in her womb. The other, thin and sharp as a knife blade, was seeking to do harm, and waiting for the right moment.

It came. As soon as her laughing companion turned her shapely, carefree back to enter the water, she filled her pitcher with heavy pebbles and dirt. Then she slipped away among the low banana trees. Later, the happy young woman decided to return home and tried to lift the pitcher to balance it on her head, but she could not even manage to get it off the ground. "What to do?" she panted between attempts. Her breath smelled of vanilla, cocoa, and caramel.

Now, the Dodo of the woods is first and foremost a nose. All the accoutrements of feathers, scales, lumpy feet, and wings are really nothing more than the incongruous appendices to feverish nostrils. The Dodo smells so efficiently that, from the top of his eyrie, he quickly detected the delicate breath, its owner, and the scent of an unborn baby.

He likes child-women, and still more the children of child-women, and it was like a reassuring Jean Valjean that he seized the handle of this exotic Cosette's burden, lifted it up, and invited her to follow him along the path to the village.

"Do you like cucumber sandwiches?" he asked, for it is one of the characteristic features of the tree-dwelling Dodo that it carries on random conversations with young child-women.

True, the beautiful girl ought to have been wary, and should have declined to accept anything from it, but child-women have no suspicion. When they reached a spot behind a bush laden with English muffins and watercress, he drew aside his capacious overcoat to reveal his true identity.

It was too late now for regrets. She had accepted his help. She must pay the Dodo his due.

"If the child you are carrying is a girl, she shall be my wife."

"Don't forget!" he squawked, before disappearing.

Months later, she wondered what she could do to hide the little girl who had now been born.

Hide in a corner and hope that he would not find out? Or pray that he would forget? But she did not realize the villainies her jealous neighbor was capable of: she had gone deep into the forest to proclaim to the Dodo that the baby had been born. She went again, years later, to tell him that the little girl was growing in grace and in beauty. The last time she went to him it was to announce that the girl was going to be married, and that the whole village was preparing for the wedding, which was to take place the following day!

Just as the ceremony started, the Dodo arrived in its multicolored ceremonial plumage, with its beak waxed and its claws manicured.

"I thank you for keeping her for me, for bringing her up so well, and for taking so much trouble to offer me this lavish wedding!"

Then the mother turned to her husband to tell the secret that she had never dared reveal to him.

"Give me your daughter," demanded the Dodo.

The father offered everything he possessed, and as that was not enough for the Dodo's demands, he gave him the guests as well.

But that was not enough either, and the Dodo ate the groom, the father, and the mother. He ate everyone before kissing the terrified bride, who begged the spirits of the sky to help her. In response, a knife fell from the clouds and the Dodo, as greedy as ever, swallowed that as well. In a single movement it cut him in half—freeing the guests, the father, the mother, and the groom—so that the wedding could continue.

HEIGHT:
Variable.

APPEARANCE:
The Dodo is as baroque and extravagant as one of those puzzle-animals that emerge, completely lopsided, from a Lewis Carroll opera hat belonging to Charles Lutwidge Dodgson. He possesses the snakelike intestinal piping of the Jabberwock, the incandescent abdomen of the dragonfly, and the lamentable wings that the Borogroves drag around. Take a pelican, a dragon, a Snark, an ostrich, a large tortoise, a calf, a toucan, a rhinoceros, a pterodactyl, and a Victorian professor in all his regalia; light a stick of dynamite and place it underneath; and then reassemble the bits in the order in which they fall back to earth. That's him.

CLOTHING:
A long African-style robe and loincloth, with gussets of the finest tweed, and pants with gold and silver braid. In the evening, he wears a robe made from feathers and down. Often wears an opera hat.

HABITAT:
They proliferate in Ghana, deep in forests where things have no name. It inhabits a small house amid a nest of branches, built in a very tall tree, which the native people call a "lightning conductor tree."

FOOD:
Fresh flesh, tea, and cucumber or watercress sandwiches . . . and little girls in a pie. It swallows in the same way as a pelican, though its digestion is more reminiscent of the python.

BEHAVIOR:
This great, frustrated, stuttering, melancholy Dodo Dryophilus has been classified by the honorable president of the Darling Honeys, Lord C. Brette, between the dark Alfs and the bird-Elves of the Garuda type.

HEIGHT:
The tapering figure of a fox, or of a seductive creature with voluptuous curves.

APPEARANCE:
That of a superb vixen with a bushy tail and green eyes, or that of a young woman who is so alluring that none can resist her. A sensual mouth, full-lipped over sharp teeth, a narrow face with prominent cheekbones, and a pointed nose. And, in countries where the women have hair as black as jet, her wild, abundant locks shine like a burning bush. Her shapely body is fashioned as an appeal to lust and carnal desire. When the Kitsune turns herself into a vixen, she retains something of her womanly appearance, and when she is a woman, the vixen that quivers beneath cannot be forgotten. However, whether she displays herself as a woman or a fox, the Kitsune can never completely mask her diabolical nature.

CLOTHING:
Apart from her pelt, and the fan of her tail, she prefers to go naked, but may dress extremely elegantly when she happens to be hunting in bars, discotheques, and other meeting places in big cities. She then hides her all-too-identifiable mane beneath a wig.

The Kitsune

"But who is she, or anyway, what is she?" asked the Ashigaru. "A fox-woman?"
—Lafcadio Hearn

In Japan, it is after two o'clock in the morning that the Beings of the night—ghosts, vampires, dark Alfs—wander at large. They awaken at the hour of the Rat, crawl out of their tombs, emerge from the paddy fields, the abandoned temples, and the marsh fogs, to sneak between the frail sotobas in the cemeteries, and go out hunting along the roads.

The Rokuro-Kubi does not leave her thicket of bamboo, but sends her head to seek out food on its own. It is like a grimacing ball, which rolls and jumps along the alleyways; it leaps at the throat of a passerby or a drunk lying on the pavement in a sake-induced stupor. It bites, plunges its canine teeth deep into the veins, and slakes its thirst. Only then, full to the brim with blood, does it return to reattach itself to its mistress's shoulders. There are others, too, whose hunger lures them outside: the insatiable Gaki, who flutter around the sleeper's pillow, enchanting his dreams before stealing the breath of life; the terrifying Shiryo of the trees; and the discreet Ikiryo, who hides from all except its victims at the moment of surrender. The most dangerous by far, because she is the most seductive, has not yet emerged.

She waits for the butchery to end, for the meat-seeking mob to go home before choosing her prey. During this time, in the moonlight, she adorns herself, makes herself up, and combs her red hair. She is a coquette with a delicate palate, who cannot countenance the hunt without the spice of love.

By day, in her nimble animal form, she has scoured the countryside, slid under thickets, and staked out the dwellings in search of a choice morsel. She flows into the shadows and advances until she is very close to the chosen one. She studies his habits and—unbeknownst to the unfortunate fellow—is already influencing him, catching him in the coils of her plot.

What could awaken this young, handsome lad in the middle of the night, and draw him from his bed?

Under the arch of a bridge, a young girl is waiting for him, more beautiful than any other. It seems to this young man that his eyes are opening for the very first time. All it takes is one kiss from her, and a garden of new perceptions opens up to him. There are exquisite tastes on her lips, infinite scents; there is a whirlpool of emotions when their limbs entwine.

He needs this silken nakedness and does not want to leave, although she urges him to flee when her face grows more slender, sharper.

"Go," she tells him, "and come back to me tomorrow. At the same time . . . here." When the first glimmers of dawn turn her hair to flame, he retreats . . .

He did not dream it; his skin bears the passionate marks that she left, and a lingering, musky aroma. His entire body is sluggish from his amorous frolics. From now on, he will never love anyone but her. He wants to marry her. His fiancée's laughter now seems so coarse, her waist so thick, and her smell sickening. She and those like her seem so heavy and clumsy, with their slow movements. How time weighs upon him now, and how pointless his work seems. Doing the same thing a hundred times over, when all it does is separate him from the time when everything brightens and awakens. With this woman, he wants to be so light: he doesn't walk, he runs, he dances, he flies. He keeps his eye on the window constantly, waiting for the sun to set, waiting for the moment when the birds gather together and praise the sky on the threshold of the night.

The first star is the lantern that guides his steps towards her.

At the sight of the first star, he cannot stand still. He paces like a caged tiger, and his parents and his friends are worried by the look in his eyes, as if he is constantly seeking an escape.

He is either pacing about or lying prostrate; he gets irritated over nothing. You would think he was about to bite. He's no longer entirely in his right mind, and you can see clearly that from day to day he is growing weaker, despite all the raw meat he devours. The more time passes, the more his eyes burn with an evil fire, the more his skin grows pale and stretches over his bones.

Without a doubt he has fallen victim to a dark curse.

He has been seen slipping out into the night, leaping and yapping as he runs towards the woods. He comes back in the morning, dazed and covered in scratches and mud; his eyes are blank, as if he had

left his gaze back there, somewhere in the dark shadows.

Those who try to follow him lose his trail after only a few paces.

Finally, his father goes to Ikakata to consult an inyoshi sage, to whom he reports the boy's follies.

"I hope it is not too late, my good fellow, but you should have come to find me at the first signs of bewitchment, for he is under the spell of a Kitsune—a fox-woman—and unfortunately, the description you have given me of his condition only accentuates my fears. Hell is already in his soul! When you get home, nail up the doors and windows, and prevent him from going out, at least for three nights. Tie this *mamori*, this amulet, around his neck and make sure that he does not escape, or you must give up all hope!"

On his return to the village, the father does everything that the inyoshi sage has told him to do. He nails up the doors and windows, ties the *mamori* around his son's neck, and keeps watch to make sure that he cannot get out.

The nightmare lasts two days and three nights. The unfortunate lad exhausts himself throwing his body at the walls and scratching the ground until his nails bleed. He yaps and howls in answer to the heart-rending calls that come from far away. But the *mamori*, which he tries in vain to tear off, acts like indestructible shackles, always pushing him back towards the center of the room, onto his mat. So he struggles like this, ceaselessly, until his strength betrays him, and he falls back with a broken heart. At that moment, the red moon passes across the smoke-hole in the roof, laying a ray of its light upon him as he dies.

According to the custom of the land, the body of the Kitsune's betrothed is placed in a large terra-cotta jar—called a *kamé*—and the jar buried in a deep hole, dug into the side of a hill. As for his soul, people say that it journeys a great deal before it takes form again . . .

The form of a fox . . .

HABITAT:
The Japanese countryside and, in the last few years, the cellars, sewers, and embankments of towns. She sleeps very little. Her lair is just a simple hole where, as a vixen, she goes to digest her meal and regain her strength.

FOOD:
She is a vampire, an ever-greedy carnivore; she is not content just to suck the vital essence from her victim, but also his blood. She devours a lover once or twice a year.

BEHAVIOR:
The Kitsune come from China, where they are called Huli Jing. They are infernal creatures, cruel and cunning, who are eager to do evil. They seduce and bewitch young men (Kitsune Tsuki: possession by a fox) in order to feed, but equally for the pleasure of watching them suffer. They also like to reduce men to the state of zombie-foxes, attached to their pack.

ACTIVITIES:
In recent times, the Kitsune have seemingly taken up residence in town, where their acts of violence attract less attention. Numerous urban legends are a mere echo of their bloody reality.

NOTES:
They are held responsible for so much misery that each year, in mid-January, in the Totoni province, the Kitsune Okuri ceremony is held: after a procession, the priest and villagers burn effigies of foxes and straw dolls to drive them away and counteract their curses. The expression Kitsune-no-yomeiri— "the fox's marriage"—whose equivalent in our culture is "The devil beats his wife and marries his daughter," is used when there is rain and sunshine at the same time. It is at this moment— so people say—that the Fox-Women go back to their mother's houses, deep in the forest.

HEIGHT:

Big. Very very very very big.

APPEARANCE:

Impressive. The quaintness of his face does not reduce his ability to unsettle the observer. Nevertheless, this untrammeled, excessive, and grotesquely huge Elf with its pink and blue body is not wholly devoid of beauty. His hairy, bearded, crimson face is split by a greedy mouth which stretches from one ear to the other. Three markedly protruding eyes seem to roll about below his bushy eyebrows. He has three fingers on each hand and three toes on each foot, all ending in sharp claws. Majestic horns are set high on his forehead.

Despite his colossal height and weight, he attempts to fly as effortlessly as the birds, whose grace he much admires. His efforts at imitation inevitably fail, and soon his carnal appetite brings him to his vulgar senses. Done with grace, he falls back to earth with a loud bump.

He often changes shape, according to his needs—to become a cloud, a wave, a tree, or a dog—but, even in these disguises, his distinctive characteristics are always easily recognizable.

CLOTHING:

He is very proud of his expensive clothes, which he wears very loose.

The Oni

Human flesh is still subject to distress!
Such feasting tonight!
Let us slip away without being seen.
—Tapanmohan Chatterjee

Once upon a time there was a young bride who was captured by an Oni on the very morning of her marriage. She had risen very early to prepare for the wedding. Her mother had bathed and perfumed her, and clothed her in a ceremonial kimono. She went to pick a bouquet of tamarisks, which grew at the end of the garden, to decorate her belt. Such beauty as hers can seduce and attract the lustful desire of demons. An Oni, a slowpoke dawdling there, happened to see her and changed himself into a black cloud that enveloped her. When the sky cleared again, there was no one to be seen in the alley, for the Oni had whisked away the bride-to-be.

"I assure you that we shall celebrate a wedding: yours and mine!" the Oni proclaimed, and he made the young tamarisk girl his wife.

When the mother realized that her daughter had not returned, she searched the whole garden and the neighboring areas, then went to consult Renosha—a virtuous sage—to whom she brought rice and fresh fish each morning.

"Your daughter is now the Oni's wife," the sage told the mother. "If you want to free her, go and follow the path of rain that he left when he departed as a cloud. Stop near the lake that he deposited when he dried himself. The large black house reflected in the lake belongs to the Oni. If you want my help again, talk to the oyster shell that you find under your feet. You will hear my voice within it."

The girl's mother summoned all her courage and followed the path left by the Oni. It was so sodden with rain that it ran into the fields lying along the course of the river. It continued to grow, and grew bigger and bigger. When the mother came to a halt on the second day, she discovered that she was on the edge of a great lake in which she could distinguish the form of the Oni's residence. Her beloved daughter was somewhere behind its walls, but unfortunately she could not simply walk in and reclaim her child. The Oni would laugh in her face or, even worse, serve her to his fellows as the dish of the day.

She thought it would be better to hide and wait.

"What should I do?" she had whispered into the empty shell.

"Wait," replied the voice of Renosha, from somewhere deep within.

In the morning, she saw the door open and the Oni leave; he was dressed for hunting, with his horns erect on his head and his hairy red face lit up by his eyes and teeth. She waited until nothing stirred on the horizon before calling to her daughter.

They cried with happiness and embraced each other as they were reunited.

"We must hurry, as he never stays away for long."

They had to hurry, but the poor mother was very tired after her journey. She had walked so far, and the hunger and effort had exhausted her legs. She had to eat, rest, and sleep a little. Just for a moment.

But that moment was an hour, and the Oni's hunt lasted no more than a moment.

The Oni had gotten the scent of the beast he was tracking. He had taken it. He had killed it. The beast was laid across the Oni's shoulders when he returned to the castle and cried: "Wife, open the gate!" The mother barely had time to slip into a stone chest which he sniffed at nosily, his nostrils close to the ground like a pack of hounds scenting the quarry they are tasked with tracking. As he turned back to the stone chest again, he grunted: "I can smell flesh somewhere here... a mortal's flesh."

"It's mine," the girl claimed.

"It's not yours... It's like yours, but it's not yours."

"Perhaps then it's the smell of the child I am carrying in my womb."

When the Oni is happy he acts like a jolly child, with the ways and gestures of a simple creature. He laughs, dances, and claps his hands. And that is exactly what the Oni did on this occasion. He embraced his new wife and cried that he was thirsty and hungry. He called for a celebratory dinner, for an opportunity to eat and drink in a style worthy of his joy. After much festivity, quite drunk on saké, he rolled under the table, and set to snoring in a deep sleep.

The mother and daughter stole a small boat and rowed across the lake to the river's mouth. They were already far away when

the Oni woke up. He wondered where his wife was. He turned red with anger when he saw that one boat was missing and that the others had been cast adrift. He saw the women disappearing in the distance. But how naïve and ignorant they were to believe that they could escape from an Oni's claws! He put his mouth to the water and drank. He sucked the water up in a series of great gulps. He quickly wolfed down the lake and then swigged away until the river was gone as well. This brought the boat to a stop. However hard they worked at the oars, the current pulled them ever backwards toward that enormous gullet. The Oni was about to swallow them alive.

"What should we do?" the mother hastily asked the shell, which she had kept in her pocket.

"Didn't I teach you the secrets of the Oni the last time we spoke?" said Renosha. "You know how some minor ruse can disconcert the little intelligence he has. If you distract him, he will be at your mercy."

The two women took off their kimonos until they were stark naked and began to dance and sway their hips.

When the Oni is surprised, he behaves like a child. Confronted by the unexpected vision of the two women, his eyes became two moons and his mouth opened wide, until he had such a hiccup that it brought up the lake and the river in one vast cascade. The surge of water was so strong that it swept the Oni away and he was drowned.

In the distance, carried on the current created by the Oni, the little boat bore mother and daughter onward to the young woman's wedding.

HABITAT:
The Oni's house is in the center of Japan.

FOOD:
Excessive. Overindulgence in sukyaki with shoyou sauce, sashimi, and sushi, of course, but also too much game dowsed in saké. At one time he would round off such a meal with a few infants.

BEHAVIOR:
The Oni is a terrible species, and certainly one of the most well known in Japan. He has a bad reputation. He's a predator, a drunkard, and a thief. He spends his time searching for adventure and seducing young women, with whom he behaves in a scandalously gross way. He possesses all the powers of a black Elf, but, luckily, like most Scoffer-Elves, he is rather stupid and falls headfirst for the most rudimentary tricks.

ACTIVITIES:
The Oni are always present when disasters strike, and are associated with floods, earthquakes, sickness, and epidemics. They bear the souls of the wicked to the depths of the infernal regions. On the last day of the year, the so-called Oni-Yakari *ceremony keeps all Oni at bay and wards off all the evil that they represent for the coming year. A fistful of peas thrown in four directions is sufficient to chase them away.*

HEIGHT:
Between four and twenty-eight inches (10 to 70 cm), but when puffed up in his aggressive state, he may tower over the whole forest.

APPEARANCE:
Greenish skin and a vast disheveled tuft of emerald green hair adorned with twigs, leaves, and lichens. Muscular forearms and legs ending in deer's hooves. Piercing green eyes. He sports a majestic crown of branches, roots, and horns on the top of his head.

CLOTHING:
A coat of goat's hair and sheepskin.

HABITAT:
In winter, he sleeps curled up in thick bearskins at the back of a cave. In spring, he lodges in huts which he occupies only once. But when he has abandoned a cabin, any hapless lumberjack or woodcutter venturing inside will be pursued by furious winds and end up torn to pieces.

FOOD:
The Lechiy doesn't eat wild animals, which he sees as friends or subjects, but has no scruples about attacking the herds or flocks of neighboring farmers.

BEHAVIOR/ACTIVITIES:
He is the guardian of the forest, claiming to protect its fauna, its flora, and its allies: woodland Fairies, Dwarfs, Dryads, and sylvan Nymphs. In his happy summer state, he forgets his royal duties in favor of fleshly enjoyment in the fields; he climbs rocks, does somersaults with the field Liechiy, and pursues an affair with the pretty and faithful Liechatchika close to the river Roussalkas. He has only one son and one daughter, the two of whom he teaches all the secret lore and his love of the forest.

He has two vices: anger and a great propensity for drunkenness.

Liechatchika is very gentle and very gifted with her nimble fingers, carving neat little dollies in parasitical tree mushrooms.

The Lechiy and the Forest Spirits

There are marten cats and badgers and foxes in the Enchanted Woods, but there are of a certainty, mightier creatures.

—W. B. Yeats

The Lechiy is the djinn of the forest. He was the first denizen to emerge from the overgrown soil of the vast Russian and Czech woodlands, where he is known as Lesni Muzove. He rules there as king along with his companion known as Dine Zeny, or Lesfli Pany. Nothing happens under those vast vaults of vegetation without his awareness. Green blood runs through his gnarled body. He is the creature that assigned a magical name to each tree, grass, plant, and animal. All manifestations of life, even wolves, obey his rule of law. The bear is his bodyguard and confidant. The birds keep him informed of the movements of humans, whom he despises and from whom he claims payment for the right of passage when they drive their flocks and herds through his realms. He hates the lumberjacks even if they do no more than make a clearing at the edge of the woods. During his fits of anger he whips up tornadoes. The inhabitants cower, as tree trunks shattered into volleys of splinters are as formidable as spears and arrows.

In the month of May, when the lily of the valley, hyacinths, and other flowers spread on the mosses, the Lechiy, recently awakened from his hibernation, is deeply touched by the little folk of the forest. He sees the hinds leaping and mating, the hawthorns in blossom, and the birds nesting. The Mustelidae and fleecy-furred squirrels surround him, and Lisunki, Lirchatchika, Liessuika, Liechika, all his alluring subjects, naked yet adorned with a multitude of gold buttons, dance in a circle in a glade inviting him to come to them. It is time to make love!

Shedding his rough skin, he croons the nuptial melody most harmoniously, and chooses the prettiest of the throng.

During these periods of raw happiness and wild exaltation, he offers humans one of his kind deeds. Thus he might provide silver-birch spirit for the still brutish and unadventurous members of certain tribes.

With his claw, he rips a slit in the silvery bark of the tree, causing the sap to run. Collected in a terra-cotta pot, the liquid is allowed to ferment. The frost distills it. It is a simple process at which the Lechiy is quite expert.

It offers the old warmth and a surge of well-being brought on by intoxication, for those who drink this concoction believe that they have heard the voices of the gods. The Lechiy have always been intermediaries between humans, the elements, and the gods.

The Libotchnik

The Libotchnik (from the Russian word for "cradle") is a Lechiy cyclops so named because he likes to swing in a hammock of branches tied to the very tops of trees. He is often heard at night whistling to encourage the winds to blow and rock the hammock.

Galleret le Brun

This former feudal lord of the forest is suffering from amnesia because he has lost his powers. He persists in trying to rule over bunches of nettles. Armed with a long-handled scythe he unsuccessfully harangues armies of indifferent mushrooms.

The Guerliguet

Very comely and lively, he is inoffensive and lives in the foliage and hollows of trees. He has nut-colored eyes and a reddish-brown pelt, with pointed ears and muzzle. He stands guard over the foliage, is an excellent hand with a catapult, and repels predators trying to raid birds' nests.

The Touttus

A bad variety of Lechiy. They act as agents for Trolls by using their music to attract young people into the woods, where the Trolls take over and carry them off.

The Maricoxis

Bizarre little creatures from the Southwest of the Matto Grosso, they were encountered by the explorer Colonel Fawcett, who described them as greenish, and hairy like monkeys. They are excellent archers.

The Béréguines

The Slavic peoples placated them with offerings so that they would not terrorize them. These Lechiy vampires lived in groups amongst the trees bordering the River Dnieper.

The Bocquillons

These white creatures are found most often in silver birch plantations.

The Wudewasa

They were numerous in the Middle Ages. One of them kidnapped the daughter of a feudal lord and gave her such a hideous and deformed child that she died of fright during childbirth.

The Lumantrophes

Products of the dreams of Lechiy. Pale and without mouths, they can only be found in the deepest hours of damp nights, flying around mossy old oak trees.

Rhi'Mellen

It was not satisfied with troubling us for a single season, but will do so until the end of time . . .
—Walter de la Mare

The Elf came from an enchanted island, off Douarnenez. Accompanied by his dog with golden fur on its heels, he crossed the waves to reach the continent, but how he did so remains a mystery. Overnight, he was seen coursing from one byway to another, sowing wild pansies along the ditches, red and blue berries in the branches of hedges, water lilies on the ponds, and butterflies in profusion over the meadows.

Sitting on the edge of stone fountains in village centers, alongside his dog with golden fur reclining on its haunches, he gathered people around him by telling stories illustrated with phantasmagoria drawn from his hat.

He recounted legends permeated with the perfumes of those moving islands that slide unceasingly on the waters. He described the fabulous fauna and flora, the grass that cuts iron and will only grow on the last stroke of midnight, and the white flower of wisdom upon which only unicorns graze. He invited the listeners to reunite in a dream and join the whirling dance of Goblins and Nymphs when, crowned with garlands of woodruff, they celebrate the return of May.

At certain times, encouraged by thunderous applause, he would spread the wings hitherto folded on his back and fly up to the weathercock on the church tower. He would then make his way to another village, his golden-furred dog always at his heels.

It was a strange dog—large, but thin and angular—whose almond-shaped eyes seemed to reflect its master's feelings. When the Elf evoked some obscure scene, the dog's pupils clouded over, little by little. When the story was rich with joyous dawns, the darkened pupils glowed anew. They filled with tears; they sparkled with laughter. Those who dared stroke its back felt a sensation of happiness course through their veins, and their fingers glowed for a long time afterwards, having received the golden dust of their caress.

In the evening, the Elf wove a kind of hammock from spiders' webs between two willow trees and, covered by his wings, went to sleep with his golden-furred dog lying at his side.

One morning, a group of children came across the fields and woke him. They shared a meal of walnuts, hazelnuts, and mushrooms. Then the Elf showed them how to make a magic wand from a simple elder branch, and a Gnome's whistle from the dried roots of a parsley plant.

The Elf with the golden dog told them then and there that they should not harvest a field without leaving at least one sheaf of corn for the Sylphs to nibble.

He added that it was unreasonable to tear out the hedges, for they are the larders of Elfins, birds, and Ouphs. If they were deprived of a living and a home in that way, they would take their revenge.

The Elf also said that they ought not to cut down *all* the forests: they are the homes of the Dryads, the Nymphs, the Green Man, and the wild fauna of the woods. If these were banished from their realm, they too would take their revenge.

Filled with the wisdom of the Elf, many of these children displeased their parents, the wealthy farmers, who had appropriated the earth, who had subdued the waters and the woods and the fields, who had domesticated the flora and the fauna, and who had ignored the spirit that blows on all of this bounty. They displeased the feudal lords and rulers in every realm. One day, those in power decided to converge on the Elf with the golden dog and to silence him. With the aid of churchmen, they seized him and accused him of witchcraft, heresy, and black magic. Then they threw him and his demonic dog onto a bonfire.

As soon as the Elf's foot touched the embers, there was a great flash, followed by claps of thunder. Then darkness descended. The wind rose and, howling, it swept up logs and blazing bundles of firewood; it threw them down again onto thatched roofs and wooden timbers. The whole village was set on fire under the watchful eye of the golden dog, sitting in the middle of the ashes. The Elf had disappeared, but his hateful glare shone from the pupils of his dog.

The years have passed and the burnt-out town has now disappeared under the concrete of other buildings. The country-

HEIGHT:
The height of a greyhound.

APPEARANCE:
That of a menacingly lean dog with a shifty, low-slung lope. Its splendid golden coat is transformed into yellowish hair. Mangy. Its mood is sometimes sad and sometimes dangerous.

HABITAT:
In Brittany, on piles of old rigging, in the rotting carcasses of decommissioned boats. Doctor Yves Blaise reported the presence of the Ar Hi Mer'nn in the Poullaouen region.

FOOD:
Desperately gnaws bone after bone.

BEHAVIOR/ACTIVITIES:
Formerly known as the Elf of the Light. He came from one of those enchanted isles whose current sometimes sweeps close to our coasts, bringing a dream of happiness and wisdom with it. But, put to death by men, he is now the shadow of a gloomy Elf and, in the guise of a dog, he brings a trail of distress, misfortune, and bad luck in his wake.

side, devoid of seasons, is just an industrial zone, with its car parks and its maze of inner and outer roads. The horizon is lost forever under transient cultures. Now and then, the ocean throws up streams of black blood, known as oil, onto its coasts. It snows in summer and it rains at Christmas; it drizzles throughout the year. News flashes have replaced the stars, and advertising has replaced birdsong.

An emaciated dog wanders through the streets of towns and cities, down the alleys, and along the docks and seawalls. It comes and goes, ceaselessly and aimlessly. It hovers in front of cafés and shops, and growls if it is approached. Those who encounter it in the morning are struck with misfortune or death by the evening. Once the color of gold, its coat is now yellowish and tinged with plague. Its ribs are visible, and it has an unpleasant smell. The Bretons call it Rhi'Mellen—the yellow dog. It brings bad luck and tragic misfortune.

The Isitwalangcengce

If I catch it I eat it.
—Jean Rollin, *The Bloody Nun*

HEIGHT:
Six and one-half feet (2 m) and over.

APPEARANCE:
He looks like a big monkey crossed with a hyena. He has an enormous head on his shoulders, which resembles a laundry basket woven from bones, bristles, skin, and hair. This wicker-esque bric-a-brac mask is pierced by a mouth from which bloody fangs protrude.

CLOTHING:
Naked.

HABITAT:
South Africa; they live in frightful caverns encrusted with congealed blood, which are so malodorous that even vultures and carrion crows, sickened to their stomachs by the sheer mustiness of these lairs, are bound to vomit.

FOOD:
All human flesh, from the most delicate baby girls to the toughest and most wrinkled crones. They consider the brain to be the greatest delicacy. They eat it as humans eat crab, smashing the head on a rock to open the forehead and scooping out the inside.

BEHAVIOR:
The Isitwalangcengce are loners and antisocial. They detest each other and eat their own kind; the male eats his mate once the act of reproduction is completed—with difficulty.

ACTIVITIES:
They are delinquent bogeymen Elves, who forget to frighten children into obedience, and dream only of refilling their stomachs. In the same way that a sheepdog that has tasted a sheep's blood remembers the taste indefinitely, the Isitwalangcengce have developed this bad habit from eating a little too close to the unruly babies for whose discipline they are responsible.

The Isitwalangcengce is a delinquent Zulu Elf who slyly oversteps the mark by exceeding the boundaries of its duties. Instead of just frightening cheeky, wayward, disobedient children, he eats them, and also attacks their relations: babies, fathers, mothers, grandfathers, even great-grandfathers. The whole family could find itself crushed in the teeth of the Isitwalangcengce.

He is wicked, gluttonous, and ugly; he has a head like a basket.

The Isitwalangcengce doesn't play tricks. He is incapable of doing so. He lurks around the villages and in the bushes lining pathways; as soon as a victim passes his hiding spot, he flings himself upon the poor soul and carries it off. He will carry his victim back to his nauseating den, trapped in his basket-head.

This is how he lives. The Isitwalangcengce always operates in this same way, the way in which he traps and eats his prey. At least the way in which he *used to* trap and eat his prey because, luckily for the prey, this ogre Elf is very stupid. A little child managed to outwit him, many years ago, so now he is rarely feared.

It was in the days of yesteryear, and the child Do was called the water-child, because he lived near a river that he used as a bed, house, garden, and orchard. From dawn on, he could be seen swimming, splashing about, fishing, cooking berries, and drinking the nectar of flowers that grew on the river banks; in the evening, when the last glimmers of dusk turned to stars, he would choose a large aquatic leaf as a bed and would entrust his dreams to the rocking of the waves.

Once, when he went to the village to sell some fish, an Isitwalangcengce caught him in his basket-head and started to make its way through the forest towards its cave.

Clutching the sides of the hideous, long-haired lobster pot, the child Do, though shaken about by the great jolting strides, saw beneath him the long arms and large feet of the restless monster and above him the canopy of trees as he passed through them.

The child Do was so clever that he had no trouble in finding a way to escape. While his head skimmed the leafy branches, he picked all the fruit that he could throw into the basket-head. He picked and picked without stopping until he had harvested the equivalent of his own body weight. Then he seized a low vine, slipped out of the basket, and ran off among the undergrowth. Meanwhile the Isitwalangcengce sped on its way, not suspecting for a moment that he was only carrying fruit.

When he arrived back home and discovered the deception, his cries of rage could be heard from more than a hundred miles away.

He howled, crackled, and boiled with anger. He trumpeted, bellowed, and cursed the child Do. And he still curses him today because, when the child returned to the village, he told the story of the ruse that saved his skin. The story was spread so efficiently that whenever anyone was taken by the Isitwalangcengce, they played the same trick. Then the ogre, too stupid to understand the joke, was left feeling a fool.

And if the Isitwalangcengces have practically all disappeared nowadays, it's because they died of hunger.

The Abatwa

And here is an Abatwa!
—Jean Aillery de Saint Gilles

The Abatwa is small—very small, smaller than an ant. For the Abatwa, a blade of grass is a baobab tree; an ant is a zebra. It is its small size that has made it bad-tempered. Long ago, at the very beginning of the world, when none of the creatures of the desert reached even to its shoulder, the Abatwa dominated all the wild fauna and spirits of the air of what would become South Africa. It surpassed all the creatures in size, but not to the point of being a "dominating force." On the contrary, the Abatwa people had a generous nature, shared their goods with the tiniest and the weakest, and came to the aid of anyone who was in need.

When the ants came out of the earth, they made an alliance with the Abatwa, and nothing ever happened to break or spoil this coalition. From the beginning, the ants always served the Abatwa, and the Abatwa always served the ants.

Then valleys and mountains and bodies of water began to form, and trees began to push up out of the ground; at the same time, Elves and beasts of all types—all the way to humankind—were poisoned with the desire to subjugate others. Soon this evil infected everything that ran, crawled, or walked. Every creature was driven by the desire to subjugate and control its brother, or else to consume it.

Despite their tiny size and their puny appearance, the Abatwa, who were overlooked by the entire world, feared nothing and no one because they had sprung from the most powerful magic origins. However, finding themselves relegated to the doorstep of the infinitely small—just a little above microbes and mites—their character turned nasty.

Nowadays, the ferocious Abatwa are the sworn enemies of the "White Canker" which—with good reason—they hold responsible for terrible crimes committed against the old and venerable races of black Elves. Their invisible poisoned arrows of revenge never miss their targets.

There is only one known way to escape their anger: that is to flatter them.

Anyone who has the misfortune to encounter one of them on his or her way through the bush will immediately be asked, "Have you seen me before?" One should reply without hesitation, "I am certain I have seen you before." A negative answer is a fatal mistake . . .

"Where did you see me?"

"You see that mountain, far away over there? Well, I came over the plain and saw you sitting on the very summit."

Then the Abatwa can afford to be magnanimous, satisfied that, in spite of his infinitely small size, it is clearly visible to the point of being recognized from so high up and from so far in the distance—as long as the tone of your asseveration is sufficiently convincing.

HEIGHT:
Small, small, small, small, small.

APPEARANCE:
It is difficult to give an idea of how small they are.

CLOTHING:
They are like their Zulu friends, and have imitated their hair, tattoos, and clothing.

HABITAT:
A nomadic people who follow the "ants' paths" across the South African stretches of desert, they find refuge under rocks and abandon their improvised camp the next day. They cut across the granite plateau, the chain of the Drakensberg Mountains, the gold mines of the Transvaal, and the Witwatersrand, the Kimberley diamond mines.

FOOD:
Hunters of game, which they eat whole on the spot. They move around on the same "steed," sitting one behind the other. When the Abatwa cannot find any prey, they eat their mount.

BEHAVIOR:
Naturally gentle and generous, they become enraged and extremely dangerous when they are riled. If they are stepped on inadvertently because they have not been seen, they immediately punish the uncouth offender with their invisible arrows, which are dipped in a withering poison made from unknown plants and ant venoms.

ACTIVITIES:
They are always on the move and sleep very little. They hunt, breed ants, and constantly hone their skills in the art of witchcraft. They guard the reserves of sacred ores from the greed of corrupting human influence.

The Trolls

Ho! The Trolls are all over the country!
—Karl Holter, *The Parchment*

Tore Kyrkjebo and Tallak Brenna tell such lies about the Trolls! Like all the other old people from the mountains, they see them everywhere! That may have been the case in years gone by, in the wildernesses of the world, in the animal and forest milieu that must have disturbed their minds. So thought the young Endre, who hails from a large town down in the valley where these legends have lost their meaning and are no longer believed in.

Tallak said that humans from below had long ago come to build a chapel on the heights, in order to chase away the Trolls and demarcate the limits of the new religion. But the shepherds of the alpine pastures hadn't noticed a decline in the lowlanders' numbers since that time. They still yapped and swarmed in all the neighborhoods, of course, and they did more than simply pile up a few stones to be dominated by a wooden cross. They sought to dislodge those that had lived there before humans: the old founders—who were on no account to be annoyed—like the Jutul of the blue mountain and Trunt Trunt, the father of the Trolls. Endre had been warned never to follow the Trolls, or to reply to the arm gestures made by their women—otherwise he would turn out just like them.

Endre laughed at all this in the loneliness of the chalet that he had to look after because the two old shepherds had gone down to the valley for a week to sell cheese. He didn't have much to do high up there: the flock looked after itself on the alpine pasture, and Endre killed time by repairing the things that he had always fixed in the old cabin. He only had to follow the old men's instructions and everything would carry on as normal. However, he was annoyed because he had been told to go each evening and stand squarely in front of the mountain that, according to Tore and Tallak, the Trolls now cared for. To the question that the Trolls would ask, he should reply, "Oh! You can keep it," and then he could go back to bed again and sleep without worrying. Endre had never heard the Trolls' question, and it greatly annoyed him to talk to thin air as the old men, brats, and village idiots did. But as he had promised to do this, he had to go. He stood in front of the dark summit, and the question from the depths of time caught him off his guard: "Can we let it go?" and instead of replying "You can keep it," he was incapable of making any more suitable reply than an ill-considered: "Oh! Do what you want!" With that, the Trolls let the mountain go.

Trolls are everywhere: where the torrent rumbles, where the mountain is at its

HEIGHT:

A Troll can be a giant or a dwarf: the size of a mountain, or no bigger than a hare. Sometimes they are invisible.

APPEARANCE:

The Troll is rock, mountain, glacier, moss, lichen, roots, and gnarled tree all at the same time. A Troll may be confused with mushroom stumps, with swarms of insects, or with the bestiaries of childhood. They are long-haired, unkempt, and rough, with eyes like stars, like brilliant stones, or like stagnant water, depending on their moods. Some have been seen with a tail, others without. They are hideous and hunchbacked, but the Fairies and naïve people think they are beautiful. Insects, birds, and even little beasts live amongst their folds. They use the universal language of the spirit.

CLOTHING:

Naked under its ridiculous mineral and vegetable outfit. They have even refused to wear any headgear. However, though they do so with ill will, the Troll can take on the appearance of a human being: then they dress themselves in what appear to be short trousers held up by leather straps.

FOOD:

Ants' eggs, larvae, dung beetles, slugs, and carrion. They are excessively fond of horse liver and rancid fat. In winter, they are satisfied to eat what is under their nails and in their ears.

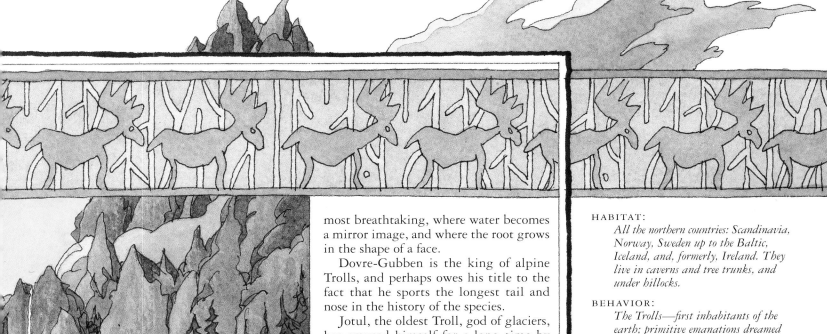

most breathtaking, where water becomes a mirror image, and where the root grows in the shape of a face.

Dovre-Gubben is the king of alpine Trolls, and perhaps owes his title to the fact that he sports the longest tail and nose in the history of the species.

Jotul, the oldest Troll, god of glaciers, has amused himself for a long time by playing skittles. He has used as his target the churches that peasants built on his domains.

Sjotroll, or Drang-Drangen, is the giant Troll of the seas. His mouth is always open over an abyss covered with spiky teeth. His body, covered with algae and sea grasses, comes out of the water on stormy days and creates a tidal wave by hitting the water with its vast palm-leafed hands.

The Brotrollet is normally found under Norwegian bridges, which he shamelessly commandeers, demanding price of passage from everyone, even other Trolls, who dread his anger.

Fossgrimen, or Fidler: *Foss* means "cascade" or "rapids;" *grim* means "ugly" or "hideous." However, there is nothing ugly about this Troll of the torrents. His hair is blond, his body is harmoniously silky, and he plays its violin marvelously. Perhaps he plays too divinely, because his magical melodies summon passersby to their death in the tumultuous currents.

The Tuftefolk are among those Trolls that, by alliance and marriage with the Nisse and Tomte, draw close to human houses and farms, but never become domesticated.

The Velse Tomten is a Troll who has lost his physical characteristics—to his own profit—but who has preserved his trollish instincts. He persuades the animals to regain their freedom, by encouraging bulls to gore, goats to kick, dogs to bite, cats to steal, and horseflies to sting.

The Tusslader—the rascals of Tunnel—are very, very small: they are so small that they go unnoticed, but their misdeeds are so terrible that it is preferable to abandon a home that they have infested. No trick, talisman, or exorcism can dislodge them.

HABITAT:
All the northern countries: Scandinavia, Norway, Sweden up to the Baltic, Iceland, and, formerly, Ireland. They live in caverns and tree trunks, and under hillocks.

BEHAVIOR:
The Trolls—first inhabitants of the earth; primitive emanations dreamed up and then abandoned by stammering inchoate deities, or an early trial species in the creation attempt made by the Supreme Being—multiplied like weeds before becoming the spirits of the forest. They are gentle and serene, or extremely violent and choleric, depending on the influences of the atmospheric movements governing their souls, which are both divine and brutish, made up of shadow and light.

ACTIVITIES:
They are the protectors of nature. They trigger hail, avalanches, and storms that they ride while letting out great cries. They can kill the wicked with their gaze or illuminate what they are searching for. With a mere cry they can dislodge a mountainside onto an irreverent alpinist.

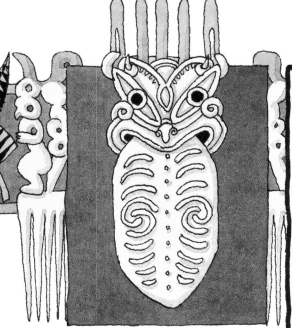

The Patupaiarehe

I detest this monster and its awful children.
—Joann Sfar, *Professor Bell*

HEIGHT:
About six feet (1.9 m).

APPEARANCE:
Tall, slender, very pale, with very white teeth and an icy look. A voluminous mop of red hair. Regular but fierce features. They are not ugly, but they inspire fear. The Patupaiarehe women also inspire fear.

CLOTHING:
Something similar to loincloths, and cloaks of white feathers. They give the impression of being enveloped in mist.

HABITAT:
They live in the mountains and on hilltops in New Zealand, in areas wreathed in mist. The few mortals who have been successful in escaping them have never wanted to describe the appearance of their dens.

FOOD:
They eat fruit, roots, fish, and (always raw) game; the smell of cooked food makes them run away.

One day a young Maori fisherman complained that he hadn't caught anything all morning. It certainly isn't easy to catch fish by hand when they have decided not to comply, for they somersault tauntingly in the water and, on this occasion, they let him approach very close; and just when he thought he could catch them, they tossed their silver tails and leaped off into the distance. The young Maori fisherman fumed and kicked the pebbles. Before long, he saw a heap of beautiful fish lying on the beach, all freshly hauled from the sea and gutted. Whoever caught them must have been very astute, or must have started at dawn to have caught so many. The young fisherman had risen early too, but he had come back empty-handed. There were so many fish just lying there that he soon lost patience counting them. Without a doubt this wasn't the work of one fisherman: there must have been several of them to make such a catch. How-

ever, the beach was empty. No one was in the vicinity, no one to eat them. It was as if they had been abandoned there, quickly. They must have been in a terrible hurry— as if they were fleeing. And so the young fisherman thought of the Patupaiarehe, the pale, redheaded Elves who were frightened of the dawn, because the sun's rays turned them into stone.

It was exactly as he had thought: a little farther on, he discovered some very, very light footsteps in the sand, where they had arrived from every side on tiptoe.

The young Maori fisherman was very courageous and loving; when he returned to the village with the secret of the Patupaiarehe, he would become as important as the chief. He was going to be able to marry the beautiful woman whom he had long desired without ever daring to tell her so. Now that he was more than just a fisherman, this could be arranged. He would come back here, that night. Definitely.

The skin of the young fisherman was already paler than that of the rest of the Maori, but that night he bleached it even more by tinting it with chalk. He also put red pigment in his hair and, thus disguised, came back to the beach at midnight.

The Patupaiarehe were so busy fishing—throwing their magic nets into the

waves, then bringing them back to the shore filled with thousands of fish—that none of them took any notice of him, or worried about him at all; on the contrary, as he mixed with the others, and got involved in the work, he was given a net that he pulled in, completely full. He carried on in this way all night. He fished and fished, going farther and farther into the waves, throwing the net far off and hauling it in so heavy that he had to drag it. He became so engrossed in fishing that he forgot to be careful. He forgot that chalk paint disappears when it comes into contact with water, and soon his brown skin reappeared. Even if it was lighter than that of the Maori, in the eyes of a Patupaiarehe it was as black as coal. Hundreds of pale eyes turned towards him and raised their eyebrows. The dye from his hair ran onto his shoulders. The chief of the Patupaiarehe let out a cry, and his claws came out, menacing.

No pity could be expected from these livid spirits; the tribe's medicine-man had told him everything he knew about them. He knew that they only came alive at night and that they detested humans, whose women they stole by attracting them with lively flute playing. Once in the lairs of the Patupaiarehe, all humans—even the most faithful wife—forgot the past and relinquished themselves willingly to their new masters; it was almost impossible to escape. He knew that the Patupaiarehe reign over nature and animals, and that they don't tolerate humans touching them. The young fisherman also knew what to expect when the gauntlet of warriors closed around him. On his knees with his eyes shut, he waited for the fatal blow, ready to bear the image of his beloved with him to his death.

But the blow never came.

He dared to open one eye, then the other . . . Everyone had disappeared. He saw rocks bathed in the dawn light, but nothing else. The beneficent sun had turned them all into stone . . .

The young fisherman took the magic nets of the Patupaiarehe back to the village, and that was how the Maori learned to fish.

BEHAVIOR:
Black Elves, but white in color, these nocturnal spirits remain very mysterious and inaccessible. They have never practiced their wiles on men, whose women they abduct. Albino Maoris are born of these unions. Protectors of nature and of all that lives there, they declare war on everyone who enters their territories. They are very seldom seen, and then only on moonlit and foggy nights. They fear the sun that petrifies them, as well as iron, ash, and the color red.

To keep the Patupaiarehe away from one's household and from one's wife, the house should be painted red and something should always be left cooking in the pot: a missionary would be very suitable!

ACTIVITIES:
Marvelous musicians. They are such powerful magicians that they can influence the moods of the weather and the seasons.

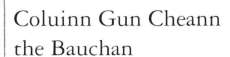

Coluinn Gun Cheann
the Bauchan

*Go . . . go yourself to see it! It's at the end of
the corridor.*
   —Sheridan le Fanu,
      The Destiny of Sir Robert Ardagh

There was no deeper forest, no sky more tormented, no night more somber. There was no wilder scenery, no rocks more precipitous, and no castle more remote or more gothic than those of Macdonald of Morar. There was no midnight more sinister, no corridors more windy . . . and no lovers more excited than Fionna Macdonald and her Bauchan of Morar.

There is no sadder story than the story that follows:

As a child, the gentle Fionna had been sold in marriage by a greedy father to the brutal Robert Macdonald of Morar. She lamented her state, crying and wandering as a prisoner from tower to tower and along the full length of the wet battlements. Her husband went hunting, and when he returned in the evening, drunk with the blood of the beast he had hunted, he would stare at her and then treat her like his quarry.

Long ago, when her nurse had lulled her to sleep by singing fairy ballads and heroic tales to her, there was always a prince who came to save the young lady imprisoned in her dungeon. Day after day, she looked into the murky distance in vain; the much-desired horseman did not appear . . . Fionna wandered among the shadows.

In Scotland, it is rare that the shadows are uninhabited. At the castle of Macdonald of Morar, a Bauchan haunts those shadows—a solitary and rather morose Elf that sadness makes good or wicked in turn.

Mutually attracted by their loneliness, they met each other under the red stained-glass window of the chapel. At the center of the rose window, a golden column spread its wings as if to bring them together. The Bauchan was only a shadow, but it was possible for the girl to create a lover from these gentle shadows. In the evening, when her husband returned, his coat permeated with the stench of wild beasts, all she had to do was to turn her head a little to know that the creature was there, floating in the semidarkness.

Sometimes, intrigued by her vacant stare at nothingness, the hunter also gazed into the same invisibility, looking for the reason for the smile on her sealed lips.

Sometimes, he came upon her unexpectedly as she was speaking to herself, murmuring as if repeating the prayers of the rosary, or the nonsensical words that children sing to angels and Fairies.

Sometimes, he saw the ends of her fingers dispatch a kiss or a caress into the air.

Hunters possess the same mysterious

sensitivity to the presence of the hidden world as wild beasts. He knew that because the drawbridge was always raised, because the walls were too high, and because his wife never went out, the lover could scarcely be an individual from the world below. He spread ashes in front of Fionna's room and in the morning discovered some footprints.

There was no deeper forest, no sky more tormented, no darker night.

He got up stealthily at the twelfth stroke. Bauchans take visible shape by moonlight. The hunter tore open the bed curtain and found the couple entwined. He raised his sword and, with one blow, he cut off the lover's head.

There is no worse story than this.

Shortly thereafter, Fionna died, giving birth to a son. It was a strange creature, without a head. It was given a name: Coluinn Gun Cheann . . . *the Headless Trunk*.

It is said that Coluinn Gun Cheann attached itself, like a Banshee, to the widower, Macdonald of Morar, whom he protected while remaining hostile to anyone else. He threw himself on all who crossed his father's path; women and children were spared, but men were beheaded.

This situation continued for a very long time, until a certain Big John Macleod of Raasay decided to put a stop to the massacres. He took up arms and one night left to meet Coluinn Gun Cheann on the Morar House Road. His intention was to keep the fight going until dawn, because he knew that his adversary would be annihilated by the light of day. They fought each other all night long but, seeing the dawn break over the hills, Coluinn Gun Cheann asked Big John Macleod to let him leave, and as he refused to do so, the Bauchan told him his story. He told the tale so convincingly that Big John Macleod took pity on him and said, "If you swear on the Bible, the candle, and the dagger that you will never come back to haunt the *smooth mile*, you can go."

The Bauchan knelt down on one knee and swore on the Bible, the candle, and the dagger that he would never be seen again.

Should anyone see him again, it is certain that the shadow of the young girl who died of love has summoned him.

Not long afterwards, woodcutters, alerted by swirling crows, found the body of Robert Macdonald in a ravine, half eaten by wolves.

HEIGHT:
A *full head shorter than a living man.*

APPEARANCE:
The Bauchans are not beautiful, having indistinct features and vague contours. They are slovenly, gray, and unsociable. Some of them resemble vague, innocuous phantoms.

CLOTHING:
Their clothes are nothing special, and are like those of human beings, except that they appear always stained, dirty, and crumpled.

HABITAT:
The Bauchan above all prefers the houses in the West of the Scottish Highlands. The Bocan haunts Ireland and America.

FOOD:
The Bauchans only pretend to eat.

BEHAVIOR/ACTIVITIES:
These somber Elves of the shadows are easily offended and dangerous. In general, like the Banshees, they are attached to a house, and to a clan, whose members they protect, or torment. They sometimes alternate between good and wicked but, from the example of Fionna's Bauchan, we know that they are even capable of committing murder.

The Trows

HEIGHT:
That of children between the ages of ten and twelve.

APPEARANCE:
Very ugly. Flattened muzzle, crunched-up forehead, and sugarloaf skull. Completely hairy, with long arched arms. Thick skin. Hands like carpet beaters and limp legs ending in broom-like protrusions. Their piggy stare lights up and their eyes open wide, like almonds, when they play or listen to music. The lugubrious Kunal-Trows are like gray shadows. They often take on the appearance of the places in which they live, becoming sandy on beaches, rocky on peaks, and bushy in woodlands.

CLOTHING:
In their original state they wore branches, moss and lichens, furs, and the hides of cows that they had slaughtered; nowadays, however, they are more inclined to wear secondhand clothes discarded by the Fairies and Elves of the hills. Because of their club feet, their right shoe is bigger than the left, and they use the iron heel to beat time. They carry numerous bags filled with their loot and very beautiful fiddles.

HABITAT:
The Highlands, the Shetland Islands, the Faeroes, and the Orkneys. They live under hillocks, hills, and tumuli, near lochs, and in cliffside grottos.

The people called Drows, being a corruption of duergar or dwarfs, and who may, in most other respects, be identified with the Caledonian fairies.

— Sir Walter Scott,
Letters on Demonology and Witchcraft

On one occasion, in the foggy month of January, old Gibbie Laurenson of the village of Grutting in the Shetland Islands made his way to the water-driven mill of Fir Vaa to grind his grain. It was still very early in the dawn hours, and only the white hoar frost showed him the way in the dark. It was like the dreadful winter of 1803, a cruel winter indeed, and the old man was freezing as he waited for the millstones to do their work. He approached the chimney nook to stack up some little blocks of peat, and lay down near the fire to sleep on a mattress of old sacks. He was just settling himself, when he heard a noise that at first he supposed was the tock-tock of the mill, which could easily get out of kilter. Perhaps the millrace was wobbly. But soon raucous hiccups and bizarre little whistles were exchanged in something like conversation. He recognized the language of the Trows, who must be nearby. You could never be sure what was going to happen with them: something a little bad, or the worst possible outcome. He quickly looked for somewhere to hide, but it was too late, and all he could do was pretend to be asleep.

He cursed his eagerness in hurrying to arrive there before the others to grind his flour. But, of course, he should know that the night belonged to the creatures of the night.

Through his half-closed eyelids, old Gibbie saw at least a dozen Trows enter, with their wives and their children. They thudded the ground with their lame feet: they were bushy-haired, with mucus dripping from their noses, and they were inconceivably ugly. He thought he would die of fear as they gathered around his fire, put on their cooking pots, and threw in the chunks of bloody meat that they drew from their large pockets. One of the pieces of meat fell to the ground, and he saw that the skin was covered with the reddish-brown spots of a cow that he recognized as belonging to the neighboring farm. He trembled, thinking of the sad end that awaited him if they ever decided to get

rid of the witness to their larceny. What if they knew that his village had invited the *Trowie Doctor* to chase them away altogether? Maybe the Trows already realized that the day was near when they could no longer sneak through the streets at night, without coming upon a straw cross, or a Bible, or one of those cursed talisman-knives that made them powerless.

He nearly jumped up when one of the women put the dirty nappy of the baby she was changing on his right leg. Praying to God and all the saints in Heaven, old Gibbie forced himself to stay as still as a tree stump.

Suddenly, one of the Trows asked, "What shall we do with the sleeper?" and it started to sharpen its meat-knife.

"Leave him be," said the mother, fondling the child. "He's not so bad. Tell Shanko to play a tune for him. That'll give him sweet dreams."

With that Shanko took up his fiddle and played a tune so joyful, so original, and so sweet: no mortal ear had ever heard anything of the kind before. Gibbie would later say that the mill vanished, ceiling, roof, and all, and that nothing remained except pure melody. It was so beautiful and moving that, without moving his lips, Gibbie silently sang along with the fiddler in his head, imprinting the tune on his innermost mind before falling asleep.

When he woke up later, there was no one there, and nothing to remind him of what had happened. All that remained was a magical melody—so original, so soft and enchanting—and Gibbie began to dance, keeping time with his right leg.

When he got back to the farm, he whistled the tune to his fiddle-playing son, who named it "Father's Tune."

The Trows, or Drows, are lesser Trolls. When the Vikings set out to conquer the nations beyond their seas, they took the Troll sprites with them in their dragon-ships.

The first coastline that they came to was that of the Shetland Islands. The earth in those parts is very verdant and rich, so they settled there, and the Trolls did so along with them. Their former mountains were replaced by hills, and in this new countryside the Troll people acquired a more appropriate size, though without any reduction of the maleficent powers they had previously enjoyed.

On the contrary, as they grew accustomed to the undulating Shetland landscape, the Trows gained in strength what they lost in height.

FOOD:

> The Trows, or Drows, eat a lot. They greedily consume everything that they consider to be their game: seals and fish, as well as chickens, sheep, and cattle from neighboring farms. They like beer and strong spirits but hate vegetables. They find bread particularly dry and tasteless.

BEHAVIOR:

> The name of the Trolls has given rise to a number of related names: Trollawater is a loch in Unst, Trollhoulland is a group of hills to the West of the mainland, and Trollegio is a creek of the Shenies. The Trows, Jean Renaud assures us, appeared there in a dramatic and memorable way. The Trows are at their most powerful and dangerous around the winter solstice.

ACTIVITIES:

> Trows adore music. They play the fiddle ceaselessly and divinely. Moreover, it is said that a large number of folk tunes from the Shetlands, including "Hyltadance," "Winjadepla," "Vallfield," "Aith's Rant," "West Side Trows' Reel," and "Trowie Spring," are actually based on melodies composed by the Trows.

HEIGHT:
*Fourteen to sixteen inches
(35 to 40 cm).*

APPEARANCE:
*Yesterday, an arrogant Elf, a formidable
warrior, and the Grand Duke of the
black mountains. Today, owl and
Grand Duke of ruined towers. Retains
fifty percent of yesterday's stance.*

CLOTHING:
*Some fragments of plate-mail over his
plumage, and a gold chain sporting
his coat of arms around his neck.*

HABITAT:
*The Upper Alps. In 1848, Ladoucette
drew attention to the presence of one of
these creatures in the rocks at the heart
of the little town of Serres, where you
can still see the remains of the ramparts and a sort of rocky door called
"The Dûphon's Hole."*

FOOD:
*Hunts squirrels, rabbits, snakes, and
weasels, but also eats Sprites, Fades,
and the little Fays of the region.*

BEHAVIOR:
*This sinister spirit of the midair—
half Elf, half owl—is a survivor of
the warrior races and predators of the
High Ages, of battles and conquests
between Svartálfar and Liosálfar.
Fierce, haughty, and cruel, it waits
for death and even provokes it. The
extinction of the Dûphon is inevitable;
it knows this and hastens its destiny
by confronting adversaries that are
stronger than it. The few remaining
females are all barren.*

ACTIVITIES:
*Hunting, nightly warmongering, and
spending its days dreaming of former
glories. The last Dûphons don't hunt
with hounds. They never get together,
preferring to live out in solitude the
ultimate indulgence of an obscure quest,
both murderous and rotten.*

The Dûphon

*It is a more lugubrious cry than a rook's being
strangled by a fox . . .*
—Thomas Radford, *Country*

Gradually the rustling of leaves breaks the spell of silence. On the edge of the waning day, the birds fill the deep and peaceful air with their song. Choir and soloists recall the little joys of the day and already demand the birth of the next day. Thickets, mournful valleys, and gardens echo with these trills and songs, accompanying the melody with the murmur of a clear stream. The goldfinch sings of the thistle's color, the swallow of the joy of its comings and goings, the sparrow of the modest crumbs of its routine, the tasty morsels from the hedgerow, and, in the fields, the lark celebrates its mystical ascension. Deeper in the woods, in secret, the cuckoo struggles to perfect its silvery outburst of two notes.

Then a shadowy presence falls from the trees, ascends the sides of ditches, and spreads out; it passes across the bushes, snuffing out each song like an icy breath blowing out candles one by one.

It is the hour of the Dûphon.

The cracked sound of its cry sears the limits of beneficent day and brings closer the abyss; it shatters the last warble of the magpie and scatters its pearls. Everything is hushed; they have all have fled or gone to ground. It is the hour of the hunt. From the height of its perch on a jagged fragment of the ruined tower, it prepares its spurs for the chase. This baroque silhouette of swordsman, Elf, and Grand Duke is ready for action. It takes up a firm and arrogant stance before the moon, like the black spot on a target, like a challenge. Its eyes glowing, it positions itself and struts, puffing up its chainmail and feathers, whose luminescence dusts the night with phosphorescent emanations. It is a robber baron; below, right down there, are the black expanses of the nocturnal kingdom that it will soon fly over in search of enemies and victims. Simultaneously, it sharpens its sword, beak, and talons like steel on a stone; now the Dûphon is reciting war litanies composed of metallic hisses, raucous yelps, and cavernous hooting. As many curses as echoes reverberate from mountains to precipices, from valleys to burrows, to nests, to villages, and right to the back of alcoves.

Tu whit tu woo! A last cry warns both the normal forest and the bizarre fauna of the High Alps.

The Dûphon is a mercenary of high places, a scourer of the skies. A recalcitrant object of Oberon's pacification methods, it remains a rebel, preferring to see its race

degenerate and become extinct rather than ally itself with the conquerors. From century to century, from decline to decline, in the guise of a bird of prey, the foolhardy jouster of the tournaments and battles of yesteryear has become a pathetic brigand taking refuge in the ruins of Serre. The citizenry fears its cry, which has always presaged doom.

Although it no longer attacks humans, there are numerous village stories of its past misdeeds: of shepherds attacked; solitary riders set upon, unseated, and clawed to death; ploughmen lacerated; and young shepherds with their eyeballs torn out. It descended on their flocks, causing mayhem among the animals, pushing them into ravines by lacerating their backs and pecking out their eyes,

then flying off again towards the peaks, and sowing the funereal hiccup of its laugh throughout the valleys.

Constantly longing for scuffles and duels, it searches all night for enemies of similar size. Confronting the last Matagots, Arassas, Rafagnaoudas, Patchitchatchas, Villaouts, winged snakes, and other "terrors" of Alpine fabulists in monstrous assaults, it does not always emerge as the winner.

Often, at dawn, rodents have fought each other over the torn and bloody remnants of one of these crepuscular ruffian warriors.

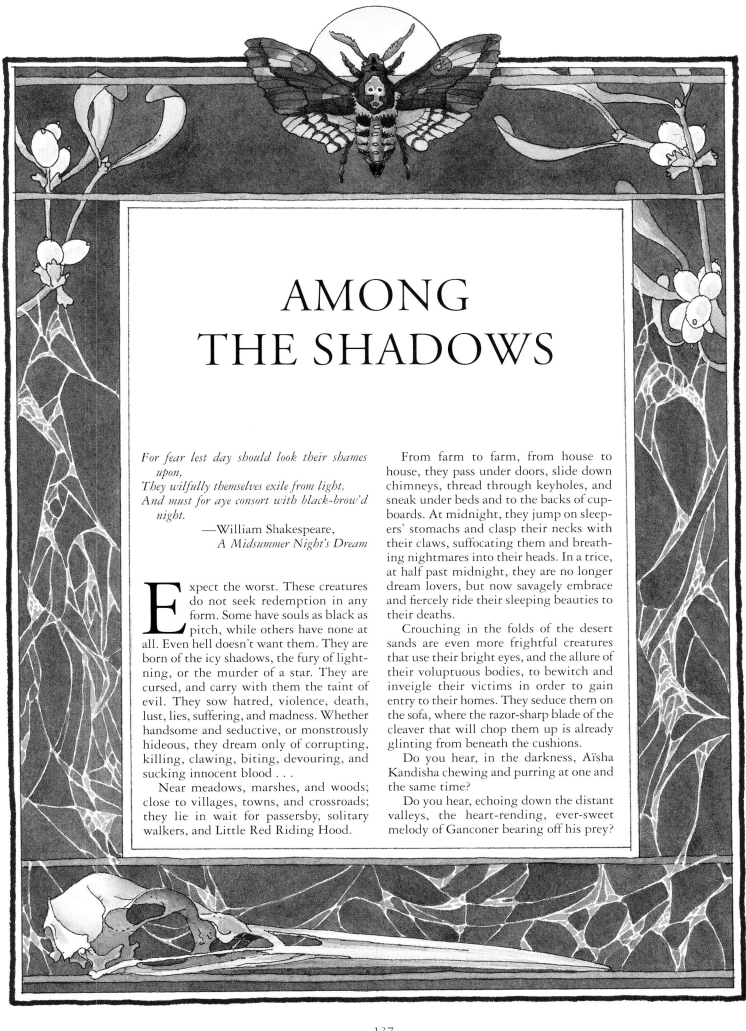

AMONG THE SHADOWS

For fear lest day should look their shames upon,
They wilfully themselves exile from light,
And must for aye consort with black-brow'd night.

—William Shakespeare,
A Midsummer Night's Dream

Expect the worst. These creatures do not seek redemption in any form. Some have souls as black as pitch, while others have none at all. Even hell doesn't want them. They are born of the icy shadows, the fury of lightning, or the murder of a star. They are cursed, and carry with them the taint of evil. They sow hatred, violence, death, lust, lies, suffering, and madness. Whether handsome and seductive, or monstrously hideous, they dream only of corrupting, killing, clawing, biting, devouring, and sucking innocent blood . . .

Near meadows, marshes, and woods; close to villages, towns, and crossroads; they lie in wait for passersby, solitary walkers, and Little Red Riding Hood.

From farm to farm, from house to house, they pass under doors, slide down chimneys, thread through keyholes, and sneak under beds and to the backs of cupboards. At midnight, they jump on sleepers' stomachs and clasp their necks with their claws, suffocating them and breathing nightmares into their heads. In a trice, at half past midnight, they are no longer dream lovers, but now savagely embrace and fiercely ride their sleeping beauties to their deaths.

Crouching in the folds of the desert sands are even more frightful creatures that use their bright eyes, and the allure of their voluptuous bodies, to bewitch and inveigle their victims in order to gain entry to their homes. They seduce them on the sofa, where the razor-sharp blade of the cleaver that will chop them up is already glinting from beneath the cushions.

Do you hear, in the darkness, Aïsha Kandisha chewing and purring at one and the same time?

Do you hear, echoing down the distant valleys, the heart-rending, ever-sweet melody of Ganconer bearing off his prey?

That of a large mouse or a small rat

APPEARANCE:

Tiny, slender, and grayish-white like all nocturnal Elves. Very wrinkled skin, with green phosphorescent eyes to pierce the darkness of cellars and food cupboards. Dirty hair and long beards covered with dust and spiderwebs. Large, greedy mouths. They are very light.

CLOTHING:

Badly dressed, with their shirt hanging down to the middle of their thighs. Green hoods and stockings. They carry a grappling hook in a sling to enable them to scale the highest shelves. A goblet and a pewter bowl hang on a chain around their neck. They bear a long iron needle sheathed in their belt as protection against predators in cellars, lofts, and salting rooms. They are also very agile deflectors of Elf-shot.

HABITAT:

Cellars, lofts, food cupboards, prosperous abbeys, and the houses of the wealthy in England and Ireland.

FOOD:

As a general rule, it is known that Elves, like Fairies, appreciate the food of mortals, unless it is marked with a cross. The Buttery Spirits, or Abbey Lubbers, only eat food that has been stolen from people, or has been otherwise obtained dishonestly. They particularly like all dairy products: cream that they skim from the milk before it has been churned, and fresh butter. Despite their puny appearance their appetite is prodigious. They are capable of consuming all the reserves of a large abbey in less than a week.

BEHAVIOR/ACTIVITIES:

During the Golden Age these Elves of the dusk were cooks and master stewards of the kingdom of Elfiria. The decline of the legendary ages has transformed them little by little into shadows of their former selves, so that they have become parasites on the homes of the nouveaux riches *and on opulent abbeys.*

Abbey Lubbers and Buttery Spirits

I shudder at the recollection {Horresco referens}.
—Virgil

At the first note of the lark, Friar Rush half-opened his eyelids, which were still puffy with sleep. Normally, only the din of the morning bells, which, on his orders, had been pushed back to eleven o'clock, would force him to rise from his silky pillows and feathery eiderdowns; but today a question of the utmost importance awaited his reply in the cellar.

By St. George, the slayer of dragons, soon he would get to the bottom of it! Damned bugs, he was going to give them a roasting! And a wicked grin surfaced over the ruddy, chubby cheeks of the Father Abbot of Spout Grace Priory. Slipping on his nightshirt—a comfortable, lined pelisse of fur—Friar Rush threw off the bedcovers. He yawned, put on his slippers, and, ferreting around in the fireplace, took out a formidable-looking poker. This would stave off a whole army!

From each side of the corridor that he passed along, the monks in their comfortably furnished cells emitted noises not normally associated with places of prayer. Here and there, the joyful clink of cutlery resounded under the arches, and this music mingled with a medley of succulent aromas—odors of roast meats and stewing pots, golden juices, spiced sauces, and oven-baked pastries.

As he passed the kitchens, Friar Rush noted the aroma of flambé pancakes and an elixir of quinces.

He really had to force himself to repress his longing to enter the heart of the holy of holies, to pick at this, taste that, and, under the pretext of checking the quality of the products and the smooth working of the office, snatch and consume the thigh of some greasy capon.

But this was not the moment to appease his culinary taste buds; he was faced with the serious task of hunting, tracking, and eliminating a scourge on this house of God!

Abuse is no argument against the use of anything *(Abusus non tollit usum).* That should have been the creed of the brother priors of Spout Grace Priory, whose debauchery and extortion were notorious, and dreaded for miles around. It was said that they enriched themselves at the expense of the serfs; that they abducted and raped young girls, cut the throats of those who opposed them, and sullied the holy altar with blasphemous masses. But nobody dared to confront them with their wrongdoing, because these demonic monks *were* the law of the land, and their executioners were never out of work.

The poor peasants could only cry with hunger, while the cursed monks of Spout Grace Priory made merry behind their walls. No one would come to disturb their pleasures, or to sooth the peasants' suffering.

Nevertheless, for some time now, Friar Rush had sensed mysterious presences

entering and insidiously roving hither and thither in the abbey basements. They seemed to emerge at nightfall and to haunt the deep maze of wine cellars and grain storerooms. They proceeded to rise to the level of the salting rooms, the pantries and larders, and the fruit and vegetable reserves, before visiting the dairy and the cheese-making room. They stole everything they could, leaving tooth marks on whole cheddar and Cheshire cheeses, and miniscule finger marks in the butter, as forms of signature.

At first they were thought to be mice, then large rats, and finally, when tons of pickled herring began to disappear, a variety of voracious cat. And then, one evening, Friar Rush—routinely peeling the vegetables—dropped his load of turnips on seeing a grayish and contorted shadow, as if some furtive imp were there!

To accuse a demon of theft would be like libeling a fellow accomplice! That wasn't reasonable in the circumstances of the monks' behavior. What was to be done?

Down below, the grayish and contorted shadows seemed to have taken possession of the place, impressing their fingers on the butter, and emptying the storerooms. It was time to put a stop to this as quickly as possible.

Friar Rush had decided to take the bull by the horns. No matter who the enemy was, there would be no limit to the amount of money spent on poison. No expense would be spared in eliminating these rats! Friar Rush spread the poison everywhere: in the grain, in the milk, the vegetables, and the meat. They would die at the first mouthful . . . and the poker that he held in his hand would finish off the toughest holdout!

Friar Rush pushed open the basement door with a heavy kick, directing the beam of light from his lantern into the shadows, but there was not a single corpse to be seen . . .

There was nothing but a multitude of little green eyes shining in the dark.

The Abbey Lubbers rang the bells of Spout Grace Priory for three days and three nights, announcing to the locality the end of the corrupt monks. Henceforth, all that remained of the once-imposing abbey were some ruins haunted by the ghost of Friar Rush. He was seen endlessly coming and going under its arches, now open to the sky, and walking around the cellars, now with a candle of repentance in his hand.

Ganconer, the Love-Talker, and the Black Elves of Love . . .

I met The Love-Talker one eve in the glen,
He was handsomer than any of our handsome
young men . . .
— Ethna Carbery, *The Love-Talker*

Ganconer, the Love-Talker, always lurks near paths, sometimes on a gray horse, sometimes walking with the ease of a dancer, with a *dudden* in his mouth to blow puffs of smoke into the air. He loiters near farms where there are girls, and always outside dance halls, where his indefatigable high spirits seduce poor lasses with far too tender of hearts. Of course, there is always a naïve and unsuspecting person ready to invite him in out of the shadows, for he tells the old stories well and sings the ancient laments beautifully. You have to ask him to come in, or else Ganconer cannot cross your threshold. This is the only barrier he knows. Once he is inside, the fox is in the chicken coop, and he will choose the prettiest girl, bewitch her, and offer to accompany her out for the night. On their return, he will marry her in the darkness and carry her off, body and soul, to the gray country of Elves.

Once, near Kinvara, he heard the sound of a fiddle through the open window of a house. The master of the household was on the doorstep and, seeing his good looks and beautiful clothes, invited him in. Immediately, he went over to Oona, the youngest daughter, and purred his way into her heart, proving that his sigh was like the murmur of a hidden stream. Oona wanted to listen to it forever.

Her mother started to worry because she saw him cough some small glowing cinders into his handkerchief, in the interval between two songs, just to clear his voice. She sent some attractive young men over to her daughter to break the spell. But Oona didn't even see them, because she had eyes only for the fireflies in the Love-Talker's gaze. The mother recognized him, and knew that once he was inside, nothing could make him leave, not even a priest . . . unless a trick was played on him that made him decide of his own volition to cross back over the threshold. So she thought up the notion of a challenge, a game in which all the boys would join: "The one who weaves the longest rope the quickest will win Oona's kiss!"

The mother went to fetch some hanks of flax from the barn, and she placed them in the middle of the room. All the suitors hurried to weave them, placing three or four strands one over another, knotting and pulling, until their ropes grew longer and longer . . . .

As Oona watched Ganconer weave, the thought of having her made his fingers run so quickly that their action could scarcely be followed. He seemed to lose himself in his work, weaving once above, once below, and pulling out to make the rope longer, over and over again, until he left the other suitors well behind. Oona did not guess her mother's strategy and the trap she was laying, so she encouraged him and hurried him more and more. He reached the wall with his rope, but this was not enough, for there was still some flax left, so he went on until the rope began to pass over the threshold and he was outside. Then Oona's mother rushed forward, threw the rope out with him, slammed the door, and closed the shutters.

Two terrible cries were heard at that moment: one a cry of rage from Ganconer outside, and the other a sad lament from Oona, who never smiled again.

"Play, fiddlers, play as loud as you can!" cried the mother. "Play your most joyful tunes around Oona, and muffle the coax-

HEIGHT:
Perfect.

APPEARANCE:
He is more handsome than the handsomest of our young men. His eyes are blacker than the ripest berries on blackberry bushes, and his mouth is a red fruit, full of milk teeth. His hair is long, black, wavy, and shoulder-length. His complexion is that of the day after the flood. To girls he seems as handsome as the devil.

CLOTHING:
Elegant, yet not too sophisticated. Not a dandy. His sober and well-cut clothes resemble those of a young gentleman doing the Grand Tour. He wears boots and always smokes a short clay pipe.

HABITAT:
The gray country of Elves, when not tracking his innocent game through the remote valleys of Ireland.

FOOD:
The breath and vital energy of young virgins.

BEHAVIOR/ACTIVITIES:
Ganconer, or Gean-Cannach, or Love-Talker, is a predator, a vampire Elf of the shadows. Everywhere he goes, in a wake of fog, he leaves behind the lifeless bodies of the souls he has taken. Very little is known about him because he disappears as mysteriously as he appears. Making the sign of the cross sends him packing, and he can't enter houses unless invited in. While sucking up his victim's life energy in the middle of a fatal kiss, he continues to charm her with tender words of love, and with a sort of very gentle, yet very disturbing, whistle.

ing voice of the dark Elf of love whose voice is heard in the night."

Sir Halewyn

When Sir Halewyn sang a song, everyone who heard it wanted to be near him. This Ganconer of Flanders emerged from the fog in his white clothes and silver armor, and rode along singing. His tunes seemed like the wind's rending lament, and were irresistible to young girls. He carried them off on his pale horse to the banks of the river, undressed them, and cut off their heads. Then he returned to the fog with great fanfare.

Herne the Hunter

Similar to the Févert—the green Elf of Spring—if only because the ladies, young girls, and young boys that he seduces and drags off to the woods are never seen again.

Zburãtorul, Zhurãtoarea

In his remarkable *Dictionary of Popular Rumanian Mythology (Dictionnaire de mythologie populaire roumaine),* Ion Talos describes a twin of the Hungarian Liderc. This black love Elf usually appears in the guise of a male or sometimes a female demon; less often as a flame, a bird, or a whirlwind. He slips down the chimney into houses during the night, and couples with those who are pining for love. It is said that the marks of his nocturnal frolics—bruises, traces of scratches and kisses, and so on—are visible the next day. These visits have ill-fated consequences for his partners: the victim soon falls ill, sinks into depression and madness, and then dies. To protect against these erotic nocturnal visitations, all exits from the house must be blocked and four knives placed in the form of a cross at the entrance to the chimney.

Luidag
(pronounced "lootchak")

The rags on this dangerous seductress, nicknamed "the Rag," barely cover her nakedness. She tempts walkers around the Lochan of the Black Trout, on the Isle of Skye, then attacks them sexually and savagely—"like a tornado"—until they are left lifeless on the heather.

The Gyre Carlin

It is the lament for an eternal being . . .
—Rainer Maria Rilke

The work of the Gyre Carlin is to make November more somber, the Pass of Glencoe windier, and the howling of the strong gusts that blow thereabouts even more lugubrious. She makes the horizon lower, the waters of the loch colder, the stretches of peat bogs more treacherous, the snow more icy, and the frost more biting. She makes furrows deeper and draws out the bad winter days to the point of deep distress. She makes cats fight each other by moonlight, and she starves the crows. She spoils grain once harvested, dampens wheat, sours milk, entices children toward ravines, and loses flocks and their shepherds in fogs. She inserts fevers deep inside beds and calls death to the doors of houses. She plays the funeral march on an organ of old bones. This is indeed the work of the Gyre Carlin. She drools over her misdeeds as if they were the sweetest of sweetmeats and notches them on her stick.

Yesterday, she blew the roofs off three cottages, froze a mountain dweller and his child to crystals in front of their hearth, set a thunderbolt on a coachman, and split the wall of a garage in two; today, she is penetrating foundations in order to undermine the keep of her neighbor, Blasour.

He didn't realize that he was playing with fire when he declared his love, poor Blasour! He never guessed that the old Queen of the Shadows was so hysterically cantankerous about everything to do with romance. Holding tight to the battlements, peering into the depths below, he regretted the little gesture he had performed so nimbly on the sulky buttocks of the glacial Amazon. The Gyre Carlin was born old, already dried up, on the highest of the Scottish highlands. She emerged like a spindle of wickedness from a black rock broken by ice. In her talon she grasped an iron rod so heavy that the wind preferred to obey it rather than get a thrashing. Then there were the clouds, showers, snow, and wolves that it had tamed. Now there is the army of moles urged on by her cudgel blows; ceaselessly, they must dig and dig, until they succeed in bringing down the ramparts of that old swine Blasour. A fitting punishment indeed! You can hear his cry of distress as he falls to his death in the depths of the abyss.

HEIGHT:
> *Large, gangling, and emaciated. Her nose sometimes touches the stars.*

APPEARANCE:
> *A hideous shrew, with contorted bones, hair, and toenails. Her skin is wrinkled with sties, and pocked with the types of crusty, scrofulous psoriasis and eczema reserved for the wicked. Big teeth and varicose veins round out the portrait of this beauty. When she isn't found sufficiently terrifying by those whom she plagues, she promptly becomes a dragon-like cloud monster, spitting out storms and icy flames.*

HABITAT:
> *Betokis Bower, a citadel of black clouds, at the summit of the mountain hidden from the view of mortals by bewitched smoke screens. She often lurks in the Lowlands and the Shetland Islands.*

CLOTHING:
> *A coat of iron armor. Black, tawdry, worn-out rags.*

FOOD:
> *Eats human flesh, pink babies, newborn lambs, and young sows.*

BEHAVIOR:
> *Like the black Fairy Cailleac Bheur, with whom she is often confused, and other stormy women and ogresses, she personifies winter.*

ACTIVITIES:
> *Presides over the cruelties of winter. She is also very much present at Candlemas and on Shrove Tuesday (Mardi Gras). At these times, you are advised to put the spinning wheel in the cupboard, for otherwise the Gyre Carlin will come down the chimney to terrorize the family.*

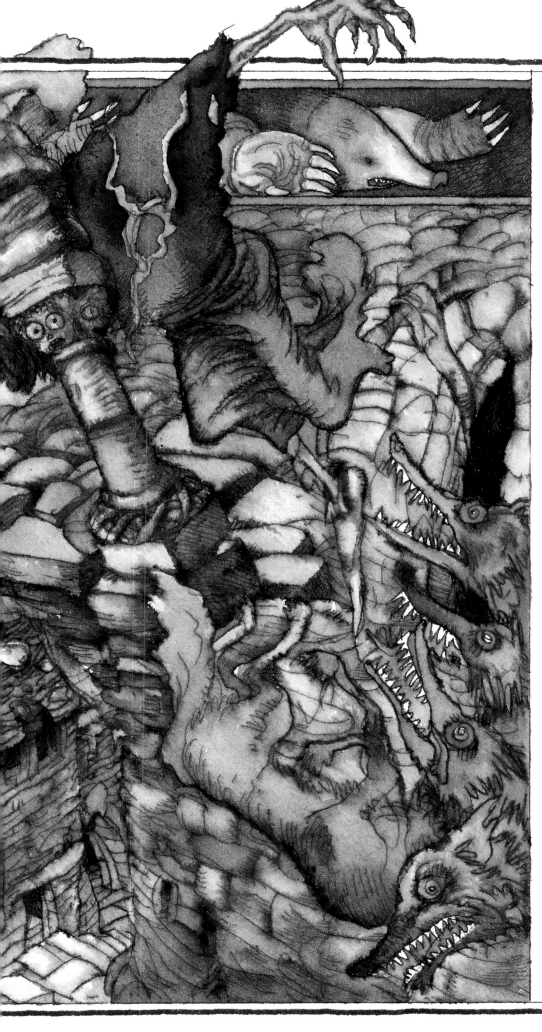

Another notch on her cane marks this new deed of daring undoing, and there she goes to survey the peaks and prepare for other misdeeds. There will be plenty, for she has the black heart needed for such work.

"Something must be done to get rid of this witch!" cried the people of the valley. They asked the minister to exorcise her at the top of the mountain, near Betokis Bower, where she goes to ground.

The good man of God wasn't even granted time to leave his house, for he was found hanging from his degree hood at its door.

In despair of anything being done to preserve them, and with their fear rising, they went in a very humble delegation to the King of the Elves' castle, and asked his protection against the terrible ogress. In exchange, they offered sacks of tobacco, rolls of beautiful tartans dyed with heather flowers, and barrels of beer.

A deal was quickly struck. The King gladly led the punitive expedition. He knew that it was necessary to fight evil with evil. A whole army of dogs of the abyss—black mastiff Elves with manes and tails of fire, and mouths full of saber-like steel teeth—were dispatched to assail the walls of the old ogress. In no time, they had devoured a heavy door of studded oak, invaded the courtyard, and hurtled down the winding maze of corridors. A great heaving mass of dogs of hell rushed the castle stairs.

Sitting on her throne of stone, the Gyre Carlin watched in her magic mirror and espied the shadows of the enemy advancing; she watched the fiery breath of the fierce hellhounds melt all the ice barriers pounded into shape by her iron rod. Before long they reached her lair, and found nothing there but a mean mouthful of a meager carcass.

"They haven't managed it, after all that effort!" the ogress sniggered, cursing them, expertly.

In fact, she emitted so terrible a curse that the whole countryside, and all its flora and fauna, was transformed in a trice into a frozen landscape. Simultaneously, the monster changed herself into a winged horror with a girth so vast that the castle cracked. She took off into the sky, pouring down strong gusts of wind and hailstones with each beat and thrust of her wings. Soon, she was nothing but a black cloud wedded to the black emanations of the night. Although she was compelled to flee from the Elf of light, she hadn't lost the war. She would be back—sooner rather than later.

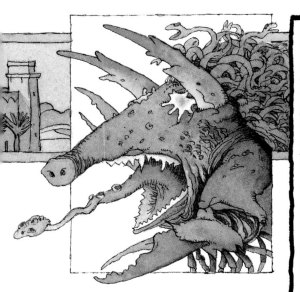

HEIGHT:

Expandable. He can pass through the keyhole and simultaneously fill the house so that the roof comes off.

APPEARANCE:

Horrible, because he is made of the things that most frighten children. He combines various characteristics of the hairy ogre, the spider, the crab, and the scorpion. A horned lizard's head with a pig's snout and lion's mane plaited with snakes. Black and red with green scales, he sports a hump, stinking pustules, eyes like splats of fiery spittle, a leechlike tongue, an overwhelmingly shit-smeared tail, and a crustacean's pincers.

CLOTHING:

They make long, long, long caped coats from all the tiny clothes of the children they have killed.

HABITAT:

Originally a bloody cave in subterranean Algeria. The Budjemah Djedid (or Arab Mythologies*) situates him more precisely on the border between the Sahara Desert and modern-day Morocco: between Béchar, Aïn Sefra, and Tiout.*

FOOD:

The flesh of small children and disobedient adolescents.

BEHAVIOR:

Very little is known about him except that he's the most horrible, frightful, angry, crafty, cruel, voracious, and frightening of all bogey Elves. He likes his work and carries it out knowledgeably.

ACTIVITIES:

Punishes, whips, lacerates, burns hands, nibbles toes, tears out fingernails and hair, flays, kills and devours, sleeps, digests, and gets up only to go back to work again.

The H'awouahoua

No threat is worse than that of the H'awouahoua!
—Rachid Buchtaka

When he was very young, Budjemah's mother threatened him with the H'awouahoua as her father had been threatened, and before him his father's father, and so on, from generation to generation. Budjemah had never seen the H'awouahoua, although if you are a wild and disobedient child, there is every chance of seeing him, because he doesn't spare a single rascal child. Once a fault has been committed and the mother catches it, the beast descends, blacker than the darkest night, redder than blood, with his eyes flaming, his teeth grating, and his claws ready to rend and tear. He throws himself onto the wicked little human imp, carries it off to his underground lair, and eats it raw.

It seems that as yet Budjemah has not sinned seriously enough to have met this ghastly demon. More than once his mother threatened to summon him: the terrified Budjemah heard the earth breaking open and claws being sharpened, and he saw the horned shadow creeping over the wall, but his mother was moved by his sobs to send the monster back.

But of course he hates being disturbed for no reward, and his patience is as limited as a spider's web is fragile. It should be known that every time an angry mother calls on him and wakes him, the name of the errant child remains engraved on the creature's memory. Every report goes down in the accounts, and a due number of bites and lashes of the whip is recorded. On the day when an exasperated mother explodes with anger and lets the H'awouahoua loose, the resulting bloody mess is an unpleasant sight.

Budjemah grew up and moved to the Mediterranean with his family to escape the violent conflict that marred the history of his country. They lived in some gray suburb surrounded by hills of slag from the former coal mines. There the sky was oppressed by rain and clouds, but at least children laughed when the butterflies emerged. When he went out with a group of children to play on the slopes of the slag dump, his mother reminded him of the H'awouahoua and his meticulous accounting system.

Budjemah had never seen him, but he knew that the H'awouahoua existed, for on one occasion he had definitely heard him getting closer. There he was, waiting for his hand to move out and steal something.

Budjemah knew that he would soon be old enough to put fear of the H'awouahoua behind him, but it was at this point that he was most in danger . . .

Because, you see, the H'awouahoua was waiting for him at the corner supermarket . . .

Aïsha Kandisha

The offspring of a union between a jackal and a sow.

—Abdul Raziz, *The Black Sisters*

Aïsha Kandisha is certainly a witch and a vampire. She lives in the desert. During the day, she sleeps in a grotto, and she comes out as evening approaches. She parades her wares near water outlets, and makes her way round the encampments. She belly dances in public, to provoke men into keeping her with them for the night. She shares a bed with whomsoever she likes but, when her partner falls asleep, she spreads herself over him and with her tongue sucks all the life from him. Even worse, at the moment when she deprives him of his soul, she also takes the souls of his nearest and dearest. She vacuums up his father, mother, wife, and children, even though they may be asleep miles away. No matter—they will all die at the same time, and become shriveled sacks in their own beds.

Observers swear that Aïsha Kandisha possesses many guises, that she can multiply at will, and that her sisters are as powerful as they are dangerous. Some of them left Algeria with the French and their associates, and made their way to metropolitan France, where they still frequent the suburbs, embankments, and towns and cities.

There are Aïsha Kandishas in Marseilles, Lyons, and Lille.

One of them is said to haunt the deserted parking lot of a large superstore at night. The first thing you hear is the metallic screech of a shopping cart's wheels approaching from among the shadows. You feel the presence of an icy breath, and then she appears, wrapped in a pale shroud of fog. She drifts past the vehicles occupied by lovers, parked discreetly where they hope not to be seen, and she presses her hideous face to the window. Then she scratches the windshield with her sharp nails, shakes the doors, and tries to enter . . .

When she fails in such attacks, her howling terrifies the masses for miles around.

In that particular suburb, they claim that she is the ghost of a young girl who, on the day before her wedding, was run over by a driver distracted by his purchases. Because she was deprived of *her* wedding night, she now takes her revenge by attacking young couples making love here, where she was killed.

That's what they say here in this neighborhood, but we all know that in reality Aïsha Kandisha has assumed yet another guise to terrorize people.

On Saturday nights, when young people go clubbing for fun, she slips a white raincoat over her naked body and walks the roads into town trying to hitch a lift. Once she has entered a vehicle, she seduces the driver and makes him drunk with her perfumes. She kisses him and grasps him in her firm embrace. By the time he loses control of the wheel and crashes into a tree, the demon is already some miles away.

NOTE: The story of the Aïsha Kandisha of the parking lot was collected and narrated by enthusiastic students of the Jules-Ferry primary school at Maubeuge, France.

HEIGHT:
Gracefully tall.

APPEARANCE:
All the attractions of evil. All the devil's seductive charms. But her voluptuousness and passionate beauty actually hide a grotesque ugliness. A human mouth, teeth strong enough to crush bones, a tongue to suck blood and draw out the soul, and claws to tear skin. She can multiply in infinite numbers under different forms: snake-woman, winged hyena or, on other occasions, palm tree under whose shade one goes to rest without being aware of the danger one is running into.

CLOTHING:
Suggestive clothing as worn by a belly dancer, under the bright, diaphanous veils of the White Lady.

HABITAT:
In the past, she existed only in the deserts of the Middle East. Today, she also haunts our suburbs, for she is there among us, panting in the shadows.

FOOD:
She is a vampire, a man-eater, and a vulture.

BEHAVIOR:
Frightful. Abdul Raziz opines that she was born from the union of a jackal and a sow, but ancient legends claim that she existed a long time before jackals and sows, which, anyway, she is said to have created to nurse and breastfeed her young. Some commentators say that in the olden days she was a little benefactress Elf of quiet waters, which she filled with fish and all manner of benefits. She provided humankind with water from an inexhaustible spring, but these ungrateful beings, instead of thanking her, destroyed her kingdom with their waste. So the story goes . . .

ACTIVITIES:
Ghastly.

The Yara Ma Yha Who

HEIGHT:

There are two varieties: the Yara Ma Yha Who that eats children, and is the size of a precocious marmot; and the Yara Ma Yha Who that eats adults, and is much bigger.

APPEARANCE:

Disgusting. Entirely red, from head suckers to toe suckers. He is a sickly red color, with crimson patches and alopecic cavities. He is given to scratching his body on rough tree bark, and his incessant itching makes it all the more evil-minded. He is also covered in varicose veins and oozing pustules. When he lies in wait of prey in trees, he looks like an old, squashed-up leather bottle. He swells as soon as he begins to move and gets ready to attack. Long hanks of hair hang down on either side of his disproportionately large head. He has two vast, rheumy, red eyes from which tears run out between bloodshot lids. His two short legs terminate in damp feet that leave viscous marks on the ground.

CLOTHING:

Unashamedly naked. He is like some sort of rugged rock during the rutting season. The female creature, like any cow, is also unclothed.

HABITAT:

The trees of Australia. He also goes under other names and is a shape-changer.

FOOD:

Surely this is obvious!

BEHAVIOR:

Unspeakable.

ACTIVITIES:

Unmentionable.

NOTE:

The Yara Ma Yha Whos have no redeeming features.

It was the Thing, the Creature, the Horror concealed in outer darkness, the emissary of a god of vengeance and anger.

—Edward Frederic Benson

Since, as you must by now be aware, this manual has to cover the whole field of elficological knowledge, this particular horror has to be mentioned and some information about it (succinctly phrased and cautiously inserted at a relatively safe point in the middle of the book) must be conveyed, even though one is tempted to erase or ignore it. Read this page quickly and be especially careful not to moisten it, not even with a dot of saliva on your finger, for any kind of water attracts this vile Elf and brings it to life. This black Elf is blacker than black, although only in spirit, since it is red. It is the worst kind of monster, an eater of men, a loathsome and totally depraved demon. When they see it, even those entities conveyed to us through the genius of Lovecraft are sickened to their stomachs; and, it must be admitted, even Roland Sabatier, who has vast experience dealing with the nasty denizens of Elfland, was extremely reluctant to draw this particular brute.

The Yara Ma Yha Who is a disgusting combination of a flaccid, leathery maggot through which there runs a single, enormous gut, and a mouth packed with teeth and suckers. He spends the day snoring in a tree, waiting for someone to pass below.

When you first see him, you take him for a moldy old leather bag with some kind of trap on top that a hunter has abandoned there. Of course you are wrong, for if you sit nearby, he falls on you, wraps himself around you, and with vile sucking sounds draws every drop of water from your body. Then he opens his mouth to the last crack and swallows his dessicated victim in a single gulp.

That's it. All that remains is to digest the meal. Such a large piece of meat is difficult to get through the system, even for a Yara Ma Yha Who.

In his fine work, *The Song of the Didgeridoo* (*Chant du didgeridoo*), Marie-Pierre Chenderowsky describes the slow and painful process of his digestion. First of all, supporting his gross paunch in both hands, he moves off on his short legs and, in another single mouthful, swallows an entire slimy slough of stagnant water. The mud helps the food to slip down and stimulates the gastric juices.

Now on his back and anchored to the spot by the weight of his potbelly, the Yara Ma Yha Who is overcome by torpor and drops off to sleep. If our Jonah-like victim imprisoned within has any life left in him, now is the time to make a very cautious climb up and out of the horrific mouth that the beast leaves open in order to breathe. But it is important to feign death until this point, and not to wriggle or jerk around when the filthy creature is actually swallowing you.

Once you are outside, you have to replace yourself by the equivalent of your weight in rocks and stones, which the beast's intestines will try in vain to digest during its sleep—a sleep that, one has reason to hope, will last forever.

Now it is time to tiptoe away to safety. You should be advised that only one in a hundred attempts to carry out this delicate procedure ends in success.

The Mamu

It was black, tall, and carried clubs and a didgeridoo on its shoulder.
—Marie-Pierre Chenderowsky

The hunter had been foraging in the bush for a long time without finding any game. The sky over Baïame was beginning to grow dark; he was a long way from his village, and he was exceedingly hungry. When he looked up, he saw a fire burning at the top of a sand hill, and an old man sitting in front of the flames, cooking a kangaroo. After welcoming him, the old man told the hunter to take a rest and said that he could share his meal. The night would prove more enjoyable if they were to spend it telling one another tales of former times, the old man said. The hunter agreed and warily decided to sit on the other side of the fire, since he was well aware of the all the tricks used by the Mamu to enable them to devour their prey. They are able to change shape many times, and to look quite different on each occasion. The son of Wayamba, one of the young warriors of the village, had been deceived in this way. He went fishing and found a superb flat stone, which he carried to a spot on the riverbank where he had already prepared a fire. While waiting for his meal to cook, he began sharpening the point of his spear on the fine, flat stone. Suddenly, it changed into a Mamu. There was no time for Wayamba's unfortunate son to flee before the Mamu had strangled him and added him to the other ingredients of

the meal he was cooking. Another time, a Mamu had adopted the appearance of a young man squatting near a campsite in order to surprise a solitary traveler on just such a night as this. That victim, too, had been overcome, and his sun-bleached bones were now lying in the sand of the outback.

Perhaps his fears were totally unfounded, and the old man before him was a wholly inoffensive bush nomad. But as he waited for the meal, all the while poking at the glowing embers with a stick, he watched his companion's every move. Perhaps the old loincloth thrown carelessly to one side concealed the Mamu's finely sharpened stone knife and his frightful club? The meat was nearly ready now and was emitting the most tantalizing odors. "Would you like a piece?" asked the old man, and he ripped a generous morsel from the roast kangaroo.

The hunter grasped the hot hunk of meat, but as he bore it to his lips he noticed a big red hole, full of pointed teeth, all but hidden in the smoking flesh. He pretended to eat it and chewed noisily. When the old man, pleased at his guest's excellent appetite, rose to look for something in his knapsack, the hunter threw the meat into the fire, where it began to change shape and to twist this way and that with pain.

The Mamu's wife was burning in the midst of the flames. Whenever someone ate the meat, she would attack his or her heart from within, cackling: "Ah ah ah! I'm not a kangaroo steak—I'm the Mamu's wife!" Then the male ogre would jump on his victim, rend his flesh, and tear open the belly to free his wife.

That is how Mr. and Mrs. Mamu had treated many travelers before encountering this cunning hunter.

HEIGHT:
Varies. Very tall when he reveals his true self.

APPEARANCE:
Capable of appearing in any desired shape: that of a twig, stone, or everyday object. He draws the hunter on by taking the shape of an animal, of a bird, or of another hunter. It is not unknown for him to deceive his own kind by using the appearance of a friend or a brother. He has murderously sharp teeth. His great pointed head is covered with a thick crepe turban. His face is cruel, red, and bestial—somewhat like a monstrous monkey.

CLOTHING:
That of the person he simulates. Essentially naked, he may wear a kind of skirt made from the skulls and bones of his victims. He carries a club and a didgeridoo on his shoulder, and uses the latter to seduce the equally hideous and bloodthirsty females of his species.

HABITAT:
Deep holes hollowed out in the Australian outback.

FOOD:
Human flesh.

BEHAVIOR/ACTIVITIES:
The Mamu is a nighttime Elf, the black Elf of the Aboriginal nations of Australia. He was born alongside the moon and the sun in the arid desert; he was born with the thirst of sand and the hunger of stones. A drop of blood enticed him from the bush; since then he has used any means to provide for himself appropriately.
He has several points in common with his cousins, the Nadubi, which are other man-eating Elves as ancient as the Mamu. They frequent the same spots, but do not hunt together.
The Nadubi lure their prey with honey. When they attack their victims, hooklike claws emerge from their spines, knees, wrists, elbows, and foreheads. Once they have seized their prey, they devour it on the spot.

APPEARANCE:
They are as attractive or as repellent as sin, for they can look like voluptuous succubi one moment, and the very next moment, they take on the appearance of the most hideous sorceresses. Everyone sees them as his or her own inclinations dictate. They wear their tresses long, but shave below their waists.

CLOTHING:
Naked, but they also wear see-through veils, stockings, and nun's black coifs, or an old sorceress's apron and moth-eaten skirts. They prefer long fingernails and boots—thigh-boots, or big galoshes. They are quite prepared to wear studded leather gear. Their broomstick serves both as a mount and as a magic wand. On their second fingers they wear rings made of lizard skins, twisted into plaits with green goat's hair.

HABITAT:
The evil powers of the Makrâlles extend to the Ardennes region of France, whereas the Chorchîles cover the Ath area and its hills. To ordinary mortal eyes their caves are no more than extremely gritty dens, but the clairvoyant can make out the splendors of a royal palace behind this facade of decay and neglect.

FOOD:
They are excessively greedy and fastidious, and also appreciate the forbidden pleasures of vampirism and cannibalism.

BEHAVIOR:
The Makrâlles and the Chorchîles are related to the Larvae, Black Ladies, and Fallen Fairies. They are sorceresses of the first rank. King Oberon exiled them to the countryside eons ago because they threatened to disturb the peace of the fairy realm with their diabolical scheming. They still equal each other in power and wicked designs. They rule over the little folk of the shadows.

Makrâlles and Chorchîles

They drink wildly and attire themselves in various guises, and their nails are red with blood as they rend and consume the flesh of infants.

—Marie de Sains

"Now we are in Belgium, among the Walloons, and the Makrâlles—half Elves, half sorceresses—dance the *cramignon* in the forest, on the banks of the Amblève," writes Karl Gruen, in his *Elemental Spirits (Elementare Geister)*.

The Makrâlles of Oisy spend the entire night in sabbat revelry. After feasting on freshly slaughtered meat, they dance their mad rounds, flinging their limbs every which way. Mounted astride their broomsticks, dead drunk, they enjoy themselves by sailing close to the rooftops, twisting the weathercocks, shaving any remaining foliage from pollarded willows, and throwing stones down chimneys. One morning, a hunter, who espied one of them gliding over the woods, took aim and shot twice at the Makrâlle above him, crying:

Clickety-clickety-clack,
The Makrâlle is in the sack!

Not so, you dolt! As fast as anything she turned the bullets back, slew the hunter, and carried off his head in her bag. All she could think of from then on was how to get her revenge for this attempt on her life, and she immediately started raining curses and spells down on local houses, stables, fields, and cradles.

But all this labor proved exhausting and tedious. The Makrâlle decided that what she needed was a good pint of ale, wine, or milk to cool the sweat and save the day.

Wherever they are working, Makrâlles like to draw their beer from the cask. How is this done? Nothing could be easier: they merely point the end of a broomstick in the direction of a village or a house; then stick it in the ground, broom end uppermost; insert a wooden tap they carry for the purpose into a hole in the shaft and turn it; and then empty by remote control the priest's cask, the reserve stock of a brewery, a farmer's barrels, or the entire cellar of a bar or restaurant.

If the Makrâlle prefers milk, the method is no more complicated. She hangs a milking pail from a convenient branch, and sets to work manipulating the udders of a distant cow, and the milk flows most copiously.

In Flobecq, where curdled milk tart is the local specialty, Chorchîles acquire it in a similar fashion. If the dairyman is to counter their spell and prevent his herd from drying up, he must boil milk and, just when it comes to a boil, use a fork to prick the white skin forming on the surface as often as he can. Then the old hide of the greedy Chorchîle suffers as many pricks as the man can manage, and she has to cease her thieving.

On the other hand, we must not malign all the Chorchîles. The oldest specimens certainly have leathery skins, and are justly said to resemble monkeys in aprons. But some of these sorceresses are remarkably sexy creatures.

Like the Makrâlles, the Chorchîles are very powerful and fear neither prayers nor a cross held up by a priest. On one occasion when a priest tried to confront one of these sorceresses in order to exorcise her, she blew a cloud of poisonous dust into his nose. It took him nine days to die, consumed from within by black vermin.

In the morning, when they see wraith-like mist or fog above the meadows, peasants say that that it is the dirty washing which the Makrâlles and Chorchîles have hung out to dry after their evil celebrations.

The Sprêtin, a nighttime Elf, is the male equivalent and lover of the Makrâlle.

ACTIVITIES:
They glide through the night astride
their broomsticks, or in black-dressed
carriages with all the adornments of
hearses of centuries past, unless they
decide to ride on the backs of young
people whom they saddle and harness
like horses.

They slip under doors and through
locks to disturb the sleep of innocent
folk, caress the bodies of their sleeping
victims, and carry them off over hedges
and streams, farther and farther
away, until they reach the ultimate
sacred haven of the shadowlands.

The Skogsrå

Women of the wood dancing naked in the depths of the wood deprive us of wood.
—Clarabelle, *Where the Woodruff Grows*
(Le trou des aspérules)

Einar, Skord, Erker, and Torn entered the verdant forest under a blue sky. There were four of them, all singing the same song. As they passed under the first fir tree, Skord scattered the few coins he had in his pocket on the ground. There were four of them, all singing the same song. On an old mossy tree trunk lying across their path, Erker set the chunk of smoked beef and the remains of the bread he carried in his knapsack. It was a good, round loaf of white bread, which he had carefully baked the night before without adding the least suggestion of a caraway seed to the dough. There were four of them, all singing the same song. When worried thoughts came fluttering about his head like so many butterflies, Torn brushed them away. Then, when the wind blew up from the depths of the forest glade and battered down the ferns in the clearing, all but one of them said the Our Father backwards. Though they were four in a company singing the same song, the Skogsrå had come to banish it from Einar's lips.

All those who had their footwear and waistcoats inside-out saw her exactly as she was, with her deep hollow in the back, cow's tail, and long rapacious claws; but it was too late for Einar to perceive her as anything other than a beauty beyond comparison. They tried to tie him down, hold him back, and snatch him from the lure of the woman of the woods. But Einar heard nothing now save the song of the wind and the leaves, the torrent and the wolves, to which he joined his own voice, with all the strength of his captive heart. He might still have saved himself if he had drawn his knife and plunged it in her while shaking a red handkerchief before her green eyes, but Einar did none of these things. On the contrary, he held out his arm and followed her.

Now there were only three men singing the same sad song. Though they followed the pair for a long time, calling their companion repeatedly, their cries and prayers soon returned to them as derisive echoes from the depths of the night. There was still a tiny possibility that Einar would not lose his mind forever, if only he could make love to the Skogsrå and escape afterwards without actually sleeping with her. But Einar was already lying clasped in her arms. Now he was sleeping a deep, deep sleep. Cradled in moonbeams, he dreamed that he was king of the forest, and the trees and wild beasts understood all that he said; that the lightning would strike when he ordered it, and bears would come to stretch themselves out at his feet . . .

There were three of them now, singing the same song, waiting for dawn as they hid in the thickets around Nemeto, where Einar and the Skogsrå were sleeping in one another's arms. Skord, Erker, Torn, and Einar were inseparable, for they had all been born on the same day at the foot of the same bell tower. No wild woman of the woods would separate them. They had entered the forest all singing the same

Variable. Female Skogsrå prefer the average height of a woodcutter's wife, whereas the males, who are more ferocious, like to frighten people by exceeding the height of the tallest fir in the forest.

APPEARANCE:

Variable. It depends on the person observing them and how they want to be seen. They have many traits in common with the Huldre, including a hollow in their back and a long cow's tail. Unlike their cousins, theirs is not a simple, pastoral prettiness, for they enjoy the sensual characteristics of savage beauty: big, deep green eyes; full, sensual lips; a forest-maiden's pointed face; a taut and supple body with extended muscles; prominent curved buttocks; large firm breasts; very tanned skin; and jet-black hair. They are richly endowed with attractive pubic hair.

CLOTHING:

The male Skogsrå wears a rough outfit, a combination of old skins and moth-eaten furs, whereas the female's dress is superbly decorated with floral motifs, and adorned with tiny carved-bone jewels, feathers, and fine furs. They wear bracelets of plaited leather and necklaces of multicolored pearls. Instead of rings, they have several thin ribbons knotted round their slender fingers. Their impressive breasts project freely above their broad belts or sashes.

song, and they would leave it in the same way.

Finally dawn arrived, chased the darkness from every corner, and reached into the forest depths until it came to the circle of ancient pagan standing stones where the Skogsrå slept. She woke up as the first ray of light touched her eyelids. She shook her long hair and, without looking at her lover, who she now knew was bound to her henceforth by invisible bonds, left his side. He would not escape. She could run the whole day long, engage in her wild activities, and in the evening return to find him lying in the same spot, lustfully awaiting her return. But the others were watching and, once the Skogsrå had departed, all three jumped on Einar and carried their sleeping companion through the woods.

They took him to his house, barricaded the door with a heavy log, and crammed red verbena into the lock and into any cracks in the window frame to prevent the Skogsrå from gaining entry.

They placed Einar on his bed, and surrounded him with flowering garlic plants and a circle of iron breastplates.

When the moon reached the highest point in the sky and took hold of all the nighttime creatures subject to its rule, the wild woman left the woods and came scratching at Einar's door. She summoned him with a song of the same mysterious power as those sung by sirens when they try to entice sailors into the ocean's depths.

Einar let loose so deep and melancholy a groan that everyone's hair stiffened. The three of them could not restrain their frantic companion as he lay there: he beat about him with his arms and legs, tried to jump so high in the air that he threatened to break his own back, and foamed at the mouth as he rained curses upon his companions. Then one of the three picked up a gun and took aim at the Skogsrå through the window.

They say that everyone in the village who lived through what ensued, even the very youngest children, found their hair had turned white in a single instant. A vast cry rose from the surrounding woods, forests, and thickets. All the Skogsrå descended from the trees and came down into the streets to look upon their dead sister, lying there so beautiful and so pale in the white moonlight.

Torn, who had killed the woman of the woods, lost an eye, the very one with which he had taken aim. It simply disappeared from its socket. But Torn knew that this was the price he had to pay for his friend Einar to escape the Skogsrå's clutches.

Once again there were four of them, all singing the same song.

HABITAT:
Usually in the trees of the Swedish forest, or in inaccessible sacred glades and clearings. The oldest of them rarely leave their old tree-trunk lairs. They have also been observed along the Baltic coast.

FOOD:
Laurel and bay leaves, roots, and offerings made by woodcutters and hunters: they bring meat and bread guaranteed to be caraway-free, since a single caraway seed can bring down on the unwitting culprit's family a curse that will last several generations.

BEHAVIOR:
The Skogsrå come between the Trolls and Huldres. They are very ancient Elves who emerged from the dark, hostile, primeval forests. The Skogsråt, extremely solitary and extraordinarily savage, avoid human company, whereas the Skogsrå spend much time pursuing and seducing them.

ACTIVITIES:
They enliven the forest with their presence; it is said that the more Skogsrå there are in the forest, the further it extends, the more it thrives, growing greener and more fragrant. They have a certain power over wood, tempests, wind, and anything combustible. In the winter some Skogsrå, less wild than others, descend from the forest and frequent farms and isolated houses, where they repair wooden implements in exchange for jewels or lace.

The Spunkie

He played a melody which evoked, one by one, the gracious dances of the Fairies and the Spunkie's cunning sarabandes.
—Sikes MacLeod,
The Almanac of the Borders

HEIGHT:
The Spunkie is not much taller than a bottle of whiskey.

APPEARANCE:
His skin has been reddened by the fires of hell. He is as thin as a rake, and looks dry and gnarled. He has a pointed head, a mouth that stretches from one side of his face to the other, deep eyes emitting beams like lightning flashes, and no nose. He acquires and wears the hands of condemned men.

CLOTHING:
He sometimes wears a big, blood-red hood or cape that makes a bright show against his otherwise black-clad silhouette. His unpleasant head is surmounted by a coachman's hat.

HABITAT:
He is an infamous visitor to, or inhabitant of, all parts of Scotland. He is said to have dwelled for some time beneath one of the arches of the bridge that leads to hell.

FOOD:
The Spunkie is voracious. It is reported that by using the hand of a burglar he makes his way at night into the best inns and restaurants.

BEHAVIOR:
Although Spunkies are said to be merely another name for Will-o'-the-Wisps, their excessive brightness and heat are marks of the black flames associated with the tribe of greasy Horned Elves, which fell from between the buttocks of the most fallen of fallen angels.

ACTIVITIES:
It is far from inconceivable that all the pacts that they are so intent on having signed might help them to obtain the favor of the devil himself, thus opening the gates of hell at last, so that Spunkies can do the work of stewards and chefs in the infernal grill-room, offices which they have aspired to hold for centuries.

Anyone who comes up against a Spunkie will find that the Spunkie always gets the better hand.

John Malcolm of Lochmarsum was the most hardened bandit in the entire region. His disgusting old mother would cry out from the depths of her scullery: "John! John! You can see the bottom of the pot!" At this signal, John would get up, comb his red hair, tie the cords of his eagle-feathered hat beneath his chin, throw his green tartan plaid over his shoulder, put his sharp dirk in its leather sheath, and charge his two pistols with two bullets apiece. He would then lead his neighing mount through the threshold, and quietly leave the mountain so that no one could see which flock he would approach to steal sheep and rams, and which manor he would raid for cash and clothes.

But a thief's life is a hazardous one, and sooner or later he is liable to be caught. Indeed, one evening John was arrested by a powerful laird and thrown into a dungeon with a massive rock as the door and a tiny aperture as the window. He had committed so many burglaries and slain so many good people that his execution seemed inevitable. In the evening, you could hear the executioner's men in the courtyard setting up the gibbet's gloomy supports. There was no doubt that the rope attached to the main beam above the platform would cause John's death as he swung there early the next morning. Seeing no way out of his predicament, he cried, "I would give the Spunkie my hand if only he would save me from this fate!" Immediately, an ugly face with piercingly bright eyes interrupted the light from the narrow window.

"As you are aware," said the demon, "I will protect any criminal on condition that while he is alive he gives me his hand, for half an hour a day, and assigns it to me forever when he is dead! Decide now, John Malcolm, for you have very little time left: the rope is there ready for you," the Black Elf said with a mocking laugh, before disappearing from the cell.

An hour later the laird's archers came to fetch the condemned man from the dungeon and lead him to the gibbet. When he reached the foot of the gallows, just when the executioner was about to place a filthy sack over his head, he heard the Spunkie's voice once again, repeating the offer in his ear:

"Do you want to be freed?"

"Yes!"

"Shall I have your hand?"

"You will!"

At the very moment when John Malcolm was about to be catapulted into eternity, the crowd and the old laird who presided over the scene trembled at the sound of a sudden burst of supernatural laughter; the onlookers were surprised to see not the bandit hanged, but a straw man dangling like a jumping jack at the rope's end.

Shuck

I counsel you by way of caution to forbear from crossing the moor in those dark hours when the powers of evil are exalted.
—Sir Arthur Conan Doyle,
The Hound of the Baskervilles

Lord Windleby of Lydford Manor would never give up when he lost the scent of a fox, even if it turned out to be the devil incarnate. Now, however, his infernal quarry seemed certain to evade him within its labyrinth of winding paths and refuges. All morning, wily Reynard had succeeded in exhausting the hounds with his dodges up hill and down dale, leaving no more trace than a flash of lightning.

The day was fading. In spite of all their efforts, the hunting party had lost sight of the fox and darkness was gradually closing in on the countryside once again.

Before long, it would be impossible to see anything; the secret retreats of the area would be obscured by brambles and briars. The only thing that made sense was to abandon the chase and ride back to the Manor. It would be crazy to ride at full tilt through the depths of the night, risking the calamities of mud pits and ravines. Some huntsmen had already begun to pull up their horses and turn back.

Soon the only rider still in the saddle was Lord Windleby, whose principles forbade him to quit; he was leading a group of four inveterate, dedicated companions. It seemed that their determination was about to be rewarded, for a triumphant tallyho told them that the fox had been scented again. It was cornered near the

remains of the old gibbet at Watching Place. Even in broad daylight, locals shunned this highly sinister spot like the plague. And now—Lord save us!—something very different from a mere moldy corpse was about to strike terror into the hearts of these hardened huntsmen.

The wild baying, the snapping of whips, and the fierce shouts of men about to flesh the hounds suddenly gave way to cries of fear, and then silence. The dogs' tails were pressed to their flanks, the huntsmen's hair was standing on end, and everyone's gaze was on the outlandish figure of a rider on a fiery-eyed mount.

He seemed to have appeared from out of nowhere, threatening in the voluminous black garments of another age. He wore a full-length, bat-winged cape, and his featureless white face shone like an ivory mask beneath a tricorn hat.

It was the misfortune of Lord Windleby of Lydford Manor to have led the remnants of his companions and pack toward the satanic fiefdom of Shuck, the "Midnight Rider."

Although they longed to escape by flogging and spurring their horses into flight, it was too late. Before the year's end, they would all be dead.

They had come up against a merciless fiend from the very depths of hell.

On other occasions, he would change shape and become a gigantic black hound patrolling the countryside, though he was as likely to take on the appearance of a black horseman accompanied by his boarhound. Shuck belongs to a murderous company of "black huntsmen" and their dogs, including the Gabriel Hounds, Squire Cabell's hellish pack, and Hugh de Baskerville's infernal hounds.

HEIGHT:
Tall and menacing.

APPEARANCE:
A black rider with a flaming red or chalk-white face. Sometimes a demonic hound with fierce teeth and fiery eyes. Sometimes in both guises at once.

CLOTHING:
Dressed as a highwayman in Dick Turpin style, in voluminous black attire. He carries two pistols on the pommel of his saddle. He wears a sword, and constantly brandishes and cracks a powerful plaited whip.

HABITAT:
Those parts of Britain where a doleful spirit conjured up by grim events in the past still lingers, such as a dark cave, a deserted crypt, or a mysterious ruin at the end of a shadowy lane.

FOOD:
Sumptuous meals, fine wines, beer, and strong spirits, but, sad to say, when he takes the form of a mastiff, he eats the tender flesh of young shepherdesses.

BEHAVIOR:
Gross and appalling. Elfin lore tells us that the Shuck's damnable soul was not always so black. During the reign of King Ullin, he was thought to be essentially a person of integrity— a courageous and just huntsman. Unfortunately, he fell passionately in love with a lady who deceived him. This angered him so greatly that he punished her by drawing out her guts and eating them while she was still alive. A court of his Elfin peers sentenced him to become an eternal wanderer, and he was thrown directly into the outer darkness.

ACTIVITIES:
The same as other demonic hounds that roam the countryside and the same as the most infamous Black Huntsmen, but also Devil's Dandy Dogs, Gabriel Ratchets, and the Wish Hounds.

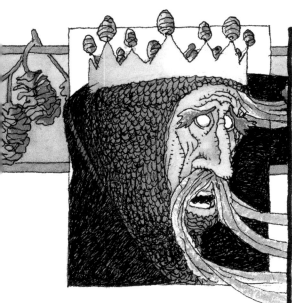

HEIGHT:
Tall.

APPEARANCE:
Dark and gaunt, but of noble mien. He is wan, disheveled, ageless, and appears as a kind of wandering knight; formerly angelic, he is now decadent and definitely fallen. His deep-set eyes are like two frozen tears. He is sometimes apparent as a drifting fog, or as ragged shadows from which two trembling hands and an entreating face emerge. He slides through space with the same facility as ghosts.

CLOTHING:
A vast black cloak or huntsman's coat, with black lapels and a black tabard on a hauberk of black steel mail. He completes the gloomy ensemble with black highwayman's boots.

HABITAT:
The German countryside, as described in Goethe's poem "The Elfin-king" ("Der Erl-König"). An abandoned and near-ruined castle in the midst of overgrown gardens, pools without reflections, and forests where the birds are silent. Set in a region of fogs and mist, unaffected by time or season, it lies in the outermost reaches of dismal Elfland.

FOOD:
He sups on children's souls once they have given way to his entreaties.

BEHAVIOR:
That of a dismal Elf of the shadowlands. His past is a mystery: the exact nature of the hurt that made him so pathetic a monster, and his daughters such sad harpies, is unknown.

ACTIVITIES:
He can enchant his victims yet his spell brings misfortune. He captures children and bears them off to his dark kingdom, vainly hoping that their innocent, happy souls will bring about the rebirth of his former joy. He also rules over the souls of all those who die in the forest.

The Elfin-king

Ach!

—Dittmar Arschloch,
Der Kampfgruppe Frisör

"Who rides so late through the midnight blast? 'Tis a father spurs on with his child full fast. He gathers the boy well into his arm. He clasps him close, and he keeps him warm." Roundabout them the wintry moon reveals unending forests inscribed in the clouds above. Though he is enfolded in his father's cloak, the child's heart almost stops when he espies the ghostly visitant approaching and surveying them both.

"My son, why thus to my arm dost thou cling?"

"Father, dost thou not see the Elfin-king? The Elfin-king with his crown and train?"

"My son, 'tis a streak of the misty rain!"

Shivering between the heavy folds of his father's wrap, the child alone hears the soft, deep voice of the spirit now accompanying them.

"Oh father, dear father! And dost thou not hear what the Elfin-king whispers so low in my ear?"

He listens to that beguilingly sweet voice right up against his ear, as the infernal sprite offers him a snow-white horse, a golden sword, figurines and puppets to play with, and a future of infinite joy:

"Come hither, thou darling! Come, go with me! Fine games know I that I'll play with thee. Flowers many and bright do my kingdoms hold. My mother has many a robe of gold."

"Calm, calm thee, my boy, it is only the breeze!"

But to the boy's frightened gaze the trees grow pale and wraith-like, disclosing the unmistakable image of the Elfin-king: "Wilt thou go, bonny boy! Wilt thou go with me? My daughters shall wait on thee daintily. My daughters around thee in dance shall sweep, and rock thee, and kiss thee, and sing thee to sleep!" And he asks the boy to choose the most beautiful of them as his companion.

"O father, dear father! Dost thou not mark the Elfin-king's daughters move by in the dark?"

"I see it, my child, but it is not they, 'tis the old willow nodding its head so gray!"

The spirit's cold hands reach out to search for the child in the folds of the father's cloak. Its starlit eyes promise an eternity of pleasure in a realm of gray slopes.

Perhaps the Elfin-king uses these captive children to replant gardens where nothing blooms, to ensure that the echoes of their innocent laughter enliven the fading spirits, and to repopulate the imageless dreams of the inhabitants of his ghostly palace. His voice seems irresistible as his hands close on the child:

"O father, dear father! He's grasping me—my heart is as cold as cold can be!"

Suddenly, the sky grows darker and the air colder; the boy's body is frozen and lifeless in his father's hands. Two black wings beat their way upward, and a whirlwind passes overhead.

Now, in a distant enclosure, a beautiful child with faded golden locks is mechanically pacing out the steps of a

mournful dance. He has entered the service of a monarch in a realm where no bird will ever sing.

The Elfin-king's daughters are bored with the tedium of their father's court. Sometimes, after nightfall, they put on their finest dresses, adorn themselves, and dance through the forest in search of a handsome suitor. They seek one who will strike a loving spark in their gloomy hearts and ignite a fire they have never known.

They form a fairy ring and dance until Sir Oluf rides by. One of them beckons to him:

"Now welcome, Sir Oluf, tarry with me! Step into the ring. Yes, dance with me."

"I must not dance, and I dare not stay. Tomorrow is my wedding-day."

"Light down, Sir Oluf, and dance with me, and two gold spurs I will give to thee. A shirt, too, of silk so white and fine. My mother bleached it in pale moonshine."

"Well I like the golden glance, but not for that with thee I'll dance."

"And if thou wilt not dance with me, a bane and blight shall follow thee."

With that, she struck him a blow right over the heart. It chilled him through, his color faded, and he began to falter. Scornfully, she cried, "Now get thee home to thy winsome bride!"

When his bride-to-be lifted the red mantle she found on the forest floor, there lay Sir Oluf dead. Traveler, beware, for the Elfin-king's daughters never cease dancing!

HEIGHT:
It is the same size as a water lizard, but can extend itself until it is strung out like fog.

APPEARANCE:
Entirely black and repulsive. A Pali also has wings like a bat's. The tip of its vast glutinous tongue is equipped with suckers and two stingers packed with numbing venom.

CLOTHING:
It has none.

HABITAT:
In the deserts of Araby once night has fallen.

FOOD:
Blood.

BEHAVIOR:
It is a primitive larva thrown up by the primeval chaos of the Elfin universe. The black Elves of the shadowlands thought it best to abandon it in the wilderness, far from all other living things.

ACTIVITIES:
It is a dedicated predator. Once daylight has faded it fears nothing and no one. It will even attack Djinn and Shaitan. Fortunately, it is devoid of intellect and will not suck upon a victim that has been foresighted enough to rub its body against a stone containing alum.

The Pali

There are more things in the desert, Prospero, than are dreamt of in your philosophy.
—Burette de Sévigné,
Niaiseries et mignardises
(Entertainments)

The caravan came to a halt somewhere in the desert wastes. Fires were lit between two expanses of sand and sky. Both sand and sky glittered. A tiny phosphorescent glimmer on the horizon announced the vastness of the starry universe. As tea leaves were infused and gradually released their scent into the night air, nomads and camels alike relaxed tired limbs and tense countenances. In these cool moments at the day's end, a melody plucked from a simple instrument might break a silence interrupted otherwise only by secret dreams.

Gossiping and joking, all the travelers stretched out by their fires, except for one. The face of the oldest man among them seemed grooved with as many pathways as were hidden by the desert's monotony. He knew every dune, stone, and trace of vegetation. He knew the secret watering-places, the spots which a sudden wind might reach, and the areas where mirages were rife. He was aware that when the prospect seemed most bare it most surely concealed unpleasant surprises.

Somewhere in this particular desert waste, only a few paces away in fact, something dangerous and full of deep cunning awaited them.

The old man wrinkled his nostrils and scrutinized the darkness surrounding them, searching for some odor or other manifestation of evil slithering from the depths of time.

"I am sure," he told his companions, "that a Pali is close by, watching us. As soon as we are asleep, it will slip among us and start licking our feet, pierce them, and suck our blood to the last drop. We shall never wake up, for the Pali's sting and bite are painless. Just now it is lying low, waiting for the right moment. We shall have to sleep together, foot against foot."

And they followed his advice, for they all knew the old man and respected his knowledge of the desert.

They dropped off to sleep in a circle, end to end, thus ensuring that the sole of no foot was exposed, but was firmly planted on another. When the Pali reached them, though it turned this way and that, it could not find a single sole to suck.

"I have traveled through millennia and thousands of deserts, and drunk the blood of thousands of travelers, but never before have I seen a man with two heads."

And when the morning light began to appear to the east of the dunes, the Pali returned to some place beyond the shadows and the night, where it had dwelled before it found the caravan.

The Muzayyara

The Woman of the Desert is swifter and her starlit kiss colder than the frozen wind at night.
—Zenobi, *The Astrolabe*

One night Idris was on his way back from Barshoom, the city of poets, liars, and camel-drivers. He was crossing the desert more quickly than the wind, and not even a Djinni could have overtaken him. "Get along, get along, my beauty," Idris sang to his mare.

Idris adored these crossings. He felt like a monarch whose realm grew all the greater as his mare covered the miles, and that nothing could bring him to a halt.

"Idris, O Idris! Idris, do you hear me?"

Someone was calling him. It was an appealingly soft, woman's voice. Yet, wherever he looked in the surrounding darkness, he could see no one.

Once again the voice summoned him: "Idris, O Idris, help me!"

He had to make an effort to control the mare, whose nostrils were flaring and flanks trembling. "There, there, my beauty!" But she snorted, pranced, and pawed the ground, however reassuring the words he whispered in her ear.

The woman who now emerged slowly from the darkness was tall and beautifully formed under her white veils. Her shining eyes pierced those of Idris. She pointed to a jar at her feet, which was so heavy that she could not lift it to her head.

"What are you doing here so late?" asked Idris.

"I was looking for water. It was hot so I bathed and went to sleep. Time passed and when I woke up night had fallen. I live in the village next to yours, to the east, and more than once I have seen you mounting your white mare in the market-place. Will you see me home?"

To Idris, her mouth looked as sweet as a juicy orange. He took her by the waist to swing her onto his saddle.

But the mare was nervous, and kept twitching her head and giving frightened looks.

"Idris, Idris, you are strong and handsome, and your blood is rich and brightest red," said the woman.

The wind seemed to make the beautiful stranger behind him shake and tremble; he turned to see that she was no longer totally unfamiliar, but the all-too-recognizable Muzayyara. She flexed her steel nails and tore open the ribbons on her chest that restrained her breasts of iron and their fiery emissions. Within seconds, he might have succumbed to the Muzayyara's seemingly irresistible embrace, as she sought to tear his lips, suck in his breath, pierce his chest with her armored nipples, and devour him in the greedy flames that burst from her.

But Idris gripped reins and mount with all his might, and sank his spurs into its flanks so that it reared and cast the she-demon to the ground. She laid there on her back long enough for Idris to pull back his mare, turn, and race away.

Even at some distance he could hear the angry creature screaming: "Son of a dog, you have escaped me for the moment, but I shall not let you get away a second time." Idris rode like the wind. When he reached home, he awakened his wife and told her how he had defeated the Muzayyara.

"What was she like?"

"A ghoul with iron teeth, iron hair, and flaming iron breasts."

"Like these, Idris?" the Muzayyara cackled, throwing back the sheets . . .

HEIGHT:
Tall.

APPEARANCE:
Muzayyara is very beautiful, but once she grasps her victim firmly in her arms, the beauteous mask disappears to reveal a hideously ghoulish countenance. She has sharp iron teeth, vile bloodshot eyes, and a great shock of iron hair. Her generous iron breasts bear nipples with dagger-sharp points and emit jets of fire.

CLOTHING:
A cloak and white veils. She never wears jewels but sometimes carries a few chains, which she enjoys using to tie up her captives.

HABITAT:
The Egyptian desert. She haunts oases, watering-places, and pyramids.

FOOD:
The flesh and blood of the men whom she hunts after nightfall.

BEHAVIOR:
She is said to be a water spirit (cf. Hasan El-Shavay, Folktales of Egypt, University of Chicago Press, 1938), but the waters she frequents are dark, brackish abysses. This blackest of Elves is said to have been fashioned from iron ore, sow's blood, and camel dung.

ACTIVITIES:
She haunts, seduces, enchants, and kills eagerly. She moves faster than thought.

HEIGHT:
   Not less than six feet (1.9 m) tall.

APPEARANCE:
   Seductive and frightening. Very beau-
   tiful, with regular features and a
   tendency to smile. Its tall figure and
   dignified bearing, perfectly shaped
   body and limbs, and charming mien
   never betray the monstrous reality of
   this sprite. The Kishi's generous shock
   of hair conceals the truly demonic
   countenance of a hyena with a jaw
   full of long and incredibly sharp teeth,
   strong enough to rip any metal. As
   soon as it throws back its hair, and
   hides its deceptively pleasing face, its
   head twists round on its shoulders, it
   flexes its legs, and its stance changes.
   Groaning and screeching, it behaves
   like a starving wild beast.

CLOTHING:
   Finely woven and richly colored fab-
   rics. Kishi wear broad, plaited leather
   belts and sandals decorated with
   shells. They adorn themselves with
   bracelets of copper and gold, necklaces,
   and headdresses studded with enor-
   mous diamonds.

The Kishi

O, what a panic's in thy breastie!
—Robert Burns

A very long time ago, a mother and her daughters lived in Angola, home of the scaly anteater. One day she sent them to the river to fetch water.

The eldest daughter walked in front, swinging her hips carefully, with a water-jar poised on her head, which she kept quite erect. She was very beautiful. The way boys looked at her assured her of this, and her mother complained that she knew more than was good for her.

The second daughter followed the eldest, dragging her feet and looking for openings in the brush. She was lazy and greedy; her mother was always telling her that all she did was sleep and grow fat.

The youngest daughter trotted along cheerfully. She was certainly the prettiest of the three and still at an age when her mother's assurance of this fact was enough to make her supremely happy.

Eventually, they arrived at the river-side. The eldest admired her reflection in the water. The second lazily bathed in the water. The third rescued a little bird from the mud in which it was stuck.

On the other bank, mysterious and alluring hills stretched into the distance. There were many tales of the wonders to be found there: of great trees bearing every kind of delicious fruit, and of encounters with brave and handsome warriors.

"What about crossing over?" said the eldest daughter. "It isn't far."

The second eldest hesitated, but then thought how marvelous it would be if truly all you had to do was open your mouth to let juicy fruit drop into it. No, it wasn't far.

"Not a good idea!" said the youngest daughter. "Mother said we mustn't go there. You know that it's off the beaten track, and the Kishi are watching us from behind the black brush."

"But we would see the Kishi coming a long way off. We'll have plenty of time to run away."

"But you won't recognize them."

Her two older sisters disregarded her fears and began to make their way across. They passed between two immense rocks, and before long ascended into the great valley from which the Kishi had observed the whole procedure.

"Yes, yes," they murmured to one another as they saw their next meal approaching. "That's right, my dears. One of them will make superb chewing meat, another looks as if she will taste very sweet indeed, and the little one will be a nice tidbit for nibbling at."

The Kishi are two-faced, demonic ogres. They use one attractive face to appeal to women, and the other, a hyena-like hor-ror hidden under long thick hair, features the jaws with which they devour their prey. As the sisters came closer, the Kishi put on their very best attire and wel-comed the girls as if they were royalty.

The sisters were most impressed and followed the Kishi into their great assem-bly-hut, which was roofed with fresh straw. Sumptuous carpets covered the walls and ground around a fire, before which a superb meal was about to be served. Tooth-some, spicy, and delicately crisp dishes were passed from hand to hand. The greedy sister's mouth was scarcely big enough to swallow all she shoved into it, before she was grabbing the next mouthful. Her older sister was beaming with joy at the fine compliments and ingenious flattery of her admirers. They were both far too busy with their own interests to listen to their little sister say over and over again that they ought to get away before it was too late. "Oh, do be quiet!" they said.

The fun went on so long that they did not notice time passing and night falling.

"If we started back now, we would lose our way."

"Of course you can sleep here," said the kind Kishi.

The youngest sister was about to drag the others away by their dresses, since she saw the demons' true faces scowling beneath their black locks. But the eldest girl was reluctant to quit the most atten-tive of her suitors, and the second sister was almost asleep on her feet.

"Here is a hut and some carpets for you to sleep on," the Kishi told them. Then they shut the entrance and barricaded them in, as they made ready to fire the hut and roast their captives.

Almost too late the girls realized that they were trapped; acting quickly, they managed to slip through the window and made their way into the night. They had come to their senses just in time, for when they turned around, they saw flames ris-ing and the Kishi rubbing their bellies in anticipation of a tasty repast. But the sis-ters were not safe yet: they were in very real danger until they crossed the river. The Kishi raked the ashes of the hut without finding any trace of their roast supper. Without wasting a moment, they picked

up their sharpest spears and set off in pursuit.

The girls foolishly imagined that they would be safe when they arrived at the river. But disobedience brings its own consequences, and during the day the water had risen. It was now far too deep and wild to attempt a crossing. What were they to do? Where could they go? The only refuge they could see was a giant baobab tree. They climbed it by mounting each other's shoulders and lay there trembling between the branches, entreating the tree-spirit to make them invisible and inaccessible.

But the tree-spirits only respond to mothers and adults of a motherly aspect. The girls had been told so often not to leave the confines of the village, and to shun the realm of the Kishi. For the tree-spirits, the sisters' fate was their own fault and would serve to warn others not to do the same.

At dawn, the light of a vast red sun lent these bumps in the tree the appearance of delicious ripe fruit—which the Kishi below could not wait to try. As soon as they shook the tree, down fell the eldest daughter, right into the arms of the warrior she had found so attractive the day before. He found her appealing too, and so he ate her. After a few similar assaults, the two remaining sisters, scared out of their wits, fell to the ground.

Suddenly the youngest girl saw a big black eagle swooping and turning above them. "Get on my back, little one; it was you who saved my eaglet, and now I shall repay you fittingly." With a single beat of its great wings, the bird bore the child to the other bank of the river.

When she asked the eagle to save her sister, it flew back to find her. "Get up on my back and hold on to my neck." The girl mounted its back and grasped its neck, but she was so fat that the eagle could not carry her all the way. She fell not far from the bank, and the Kishi devoured her.

Only the youngest survived to tell her tale and warn others of the Kishi and their tricks.

HABITAT:
Old Angola and what remains of its great plains and luxuriant forests. They live in pleasantly furnished huts designed to achieve their nefarious ends.

FOOD:
Recently-slain raw meat.

BEHAVIOR:
These flesh-eating Elves are superb musicians, dancers, and versifiers. They do not balk at composing elegant couplets for the sole purpose of seducing young girls, but are true storytellers and poets. The contrast between villainy and accomplishments is all the more appalling when they are observed on all fours, howling.

ACTIVITIES:
Ogre-like. They are the black brothers of the Ganconers.

HEIGHT:
Variable.

APPEARANCE:
When Shaitan appear as Djinn, they look like hideous beasts, with features borrowed from winged serpents, cats, camels, and long-snouted rats. They are said to have "blood pouring from all the black hairs of their bodies. The faces of some of those who paraded before Solomon were twisted back to their tails, and fire emerged from their mouths. Some walked on all fours, whereas others had two heads—or a lion's head on an elephant's body."

CLOTHING:
Naked, though sometimes wrapped in shrouds, or rich and gorgeous robes cleverly adjusted to arouse lustful desires.

FOOD:
Souls and blood.

HABITAT:
Mounts Aja and Salma, the plains of Tihama, the mountain of Aby Qubays, which dominates the Meccan valley. The regions of Ubar between Yamana and Shirhr. Djinn inhabit both the wilderness and populated areas, and also groves and thickets along the trade routes.

BEHAVIOR:
Unions between Djinn and humans have produced Balqis, the Queen of Sheba, and Dhu-l-Quarnayan, whose mother was a woman called Fira and whose father was an angel named 'Ibra.

ACTIVITIES:
They travel through the heavens and across deserts, and pass from village to village and town to town, looking for victims, and instigating death, crime, sickness, and epilepsy. Some of them specialize in misfortune, theft, crippling, lies, and domestic strife.

The Djinn

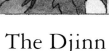

And we created the Djinn with fire so bright . . .
— The Qur'an

"No one knows your Lord's Hosts but the Lord himself." Beyond the seven heavens, in the infinite voids, hidden behind veil upon veil, God created angels with two, three, and four wings: "The heavens burst apart, says the Prophet, and rightly so, for not even the smallest space is without its angelic inhabitant." Together their voices resound like thunder. There is no atom in the universe that is not placed in the care of one or more angels; not a single drop of water comes down from the sky unless an angel descends with it in order to place it on the spot where God intends it to fall. "If that is true of atoms and of drops of water," Toufy Fabd asks, in his magisterial work on the spiritual implications of Islam, "what are we to say of the celestial bodies, the air, clouds, winds, rain, mountains, deserts, lakes, springs, rivers, minerals, plants, and animals?" In fact, the angels are guarantors of the persistence of order in the universe and of the due maintenance of all existing things.

According to Ibn Abbas, Iblis was the leader of a group of angels, known as Aj-Djinn, who were created from a very intense fire. The other angels were made from lights, the bulk of the Djinn from a lesser tongue of fire, and humankind from clay. Iblis was known as Al-Harith and was one of the guardians of Paradise. The Earth's earliest inhabitants were the more common variety of Djinn. They introduced corruption, drew blood, and killed one other. Allah sent Iblis to them at the head of an army of Aj-Djinn angels who fought them, defeated them, and dispatched them to islets at the center of lakes and to the summits of mountains. After his victory, Iblis said, "I have succeeded in doing something that no one else could achieve."

Iblis was blinded by pride.

The transformation of Iblis into a Shaitan (a demon) was the result of his sin. Similarly, all Djinn guilty of disobedience became Shaitan. Cohorts of Djinn and Shaitan flew off into the heavens, filled the deserts of the earth, and multiplied among human beings. "Never drink from the neck of a chipped jug, for it is a Shaitan's hindquarters," says the Prophet, who advised believers to pray in tightly closed ranks lest the Shaitan seek to occupy the intervals between them.

Shaitan generally attack in a group. Djinn are more individualistic and cunning, for they resort to seduction in order to "possess" their victims. Their semen produces monstrous and bloodthirsty creatures, such as An-Nasnas, a legendary entity with only one foot that proceeds in leaps and bounds like a bird, or Ash-Shiqq, which is half human, half animal. They also send their animals to inseminate beasts belonging to humans, in order to populate the earth with wild animals subject to their will, like the type of camel known as Hawshiyya.

One day a woman came to see the Prophet, saying, "My son has been pos-

sessed by a Djinni that overwhelms him by day and by night." The Prophet passed his hand over the boy's chest, and then the child vomited up a little animal, which promptly ran off. This time the Djinni was defeated, but it returned, and continued to return, until the unfortunate boy was completely entranced. The Djinn, you see, are extremely dangerous, and it is only in pretty tales from the *Arabian Nights* that they can be confined to a lamp or stoppered in a bottle.

The Wendigo

"The Wendigo is simply the Call of the Wild personified, which some natures hear to their own destruction."

—Algernon Blackwood,
The Wendigo

When night falls and the mountain folk—trappers and members of parties hunting moose in the far north—gather round the fire, which seems like a single star lost in the immensity of the surrounding darkness, when they pass the rough moonshine from hand to hand, when they tire of singing along to a concertina or harmonica, they set to telling ghost stories that suit their drunken melancholy and loneliness.

They take turns telling stories of wolves and bears, scalp-hunting natives, and the murderous trapper who made necklaces of gold teeth. These campfire storytellers also draw from the fearsome depths of the forest's history the phantoms of massacred Hurons, and the ghostly presences of giant badgers and female grizzly bears. There is some laughter—probably the only way to ward off fear—but it is followed by silence.

The silence creeps because someone has let too much time pass between tales, and deathly quiet has taken advantage of the hush, changing the mood of the company.

Then they realize that that *he* is somewhere close by, and that one of those present will be unable to prevent himself raising the subject. Who among the six of them will be the first to speak? Smoky Bellew, old Defago, Punck the little Frenchman, the Major, possibly that buccaneer Charbonneau, or Balfour from Aberdeen? Anyway, it is too late now to hold back, and the longer they delay, the more the silence becomes adept at feeding on their fears. Charbonneau sniffs nervously this way and that, sneezes, and then wipes his nose in his fingers as if to banish the suspicion of an odor that might betray the creature's presence. The cold threatens to put the fire out, and each of them senses the darkness trying to envelop him.

"I remember…" says old Defago.

Even he knows who it is they are about to talk of. They would rather forget the nature of the vast ear that it must be stretching out to listen to them above their campsite, the huge misshapen organ that accompanies a visitation by the Wendigo.

The old beaver trapper gazes beyond the glowing embers and into the depths of the past, into those times before fire was invented, which wild, inchoate divinities filled with a company of deviant, vile creations, some survivors of which still haunt the sloughs of the ages and the silt of distant riverbanks. His jaw trembles and his speech is interrupted by moments of terror as he speaks, but no one listens, for everyone is fearfully intent upon his own memories of meeting that "old muck-eater," the Wendigo.

"They say," says one of them, "that it haunts campsites at night, and that your heart freezes at its approach. Then you must keep the fire going and stay awake, because sleep is a trap. Before long you will hear a soft voice that calls each of you by name, whispering in the tones of a distant friend, male or female, or of some dead acquaintance you would dearly love to see again. But if you leave the protective circle of the encampment, immedi-

ately a gigantic hand will grasp you and sweep you through the air to the jaws of the Wendigo, ready to rend your vitals before spitting out your remains."

"Sometimes it seizes you and bears you off at such a dreadful speed that you bleed from the eyes, the friction on your feet as you are dragged along burns them until they drop off, and new ones form on the burning stumps so that the torture can recommence."

"During the winter months," says another, "when food is scarce, they eat one another."

"One Wendigo has been known to choose a solitary hunter, a backwoodsman, pursue him intently, enter his head and drive him insane. Another among them knows a story about smelling a Wendigo, turning round only to see nothing but the leaves moving, and finding his head full of horror. Or maybe the Wendigo will prey on his emotions, recall nightmare events and everything he has tried to forget, prevent him from sleeping, and surround him constantly with that stench with which it impregnates the air you breathe, the clothes you wear, and the food you find you can no longer eat."

"You try to shake it off, but it's impossible."

"The lonelier we are, the more the strength of the Wendigo grows. Then you begin to lose your head, firing your rifle into the heart of the woods and shouting out, or you cast yourself into the foaming waters or a ravine, only for the Wendigo to pick you up and let you down gently on the bank, and begin again. He never lets go. Sometimes, in the backwoods, you come across men who he's driven to the point of madness; staring straight ahead, they carry on walking with the dead eyes of zombies."

"It infects some people as if they were bitten by a rabid dog. As soon as the poison enters their system, they start to change, become hairy, stop washing, roll in the muck, smear themselves with dried blood, and start haunting camps, the villages of the local tribes, and trading posts, in search of human flesh. They can't stop. I've heard it said that some victims even return home to eat their own families."

Smoky Bellew, old Defago, Punck the little Frenchman, the Major, Charbonneau, and Balfour from Aberdeen sit by the fire, talking and exchanging stories, until early light. This is one way of exorcising the fear of the Wendigo and of keeping it at bay. Perhaps you will manage to elude him for a night, but he will always be back the next day.

HEIGHT:
Taller than the highest tree in the forest.

APPEARANCE:
A hideous giant with a vile head, enormous sea-green eyes, a mouth as big as an oven, and a body like the decaying corpse of a long-dead bear. It has hooves and its heart is cold as ice. Its voice is like the wind and its stench is that of the hellish pits of the ultimate wilderness.

It bounds like a flying demon from tip to top of forest firs and tears down trees to use as snowshoes.

CLOTHING:
Its corpselike bearskin.

HABITAT:
The wildest stretches of the Canadian North.

FOOD:
Cannibals that do not hesitate to devour their own kin.

BEHAVIOR:
The Wendigo, Windingo or Witiko, known to mountain men as "that old muck-eater," is an Elf from the abyss of Elfin horror that considerably predates the great Troll of the northern celestial hemisphere.

Its name comes from the Algonquin term for "demonic spirit" and "cannibal." "Windingo" stands both for the demon itself and for its demonic action.

ACTIVITIES:
Its sole ultimate designs are madness and death. It draws from the depths where primeval atavisms lurk, and can infect an entire group of travelers, indeed a whole village. Forts have been found burnt to the ground by their occupants, driven to murderous anarchy by one of their number imbued with the nature of the Wendigo that has haunted him.

The Duergar, The Spontaïls, and Other Malicious Black Elves

Most of those who incur the enmity of natural demons are solitaries.
—Marie-Louise von Franz,
Darkness and Evil in Fairy Tales

HEIGHT:
"Knee-high."

APPEARANCE:
Vile. Black and hairy-coated, hump-backed and pustular, with a horse's snout, crocodile teeth, and vampire ears. They have twisted limbs and run on all fours, but are extraordinarily strong. They stink to high heaven.

CLOTHING:
They steal clothes drying on washing-lines. These are too big for them, but they cut them down with their teeth, then dip them in a mixture of leaves, moss, and clay to make them water-proof.

HABITAT:
Ordinary holes in the Simonside hills of Northumberland, between Rothbury and Elsdon.

FOOD:
Extremely fond of water-buffalo meat, having cured their prey in great stone vats where they have previously dumped a quantity of Will-o'-the-Wisps or Jack-o'-Lanterns caught in surrounding swamps and peat bogs.

BEHAVIOR:
The behavior typical of wild black Elves. Duergars fear only the Black Huntsman, whose pack sets off in pursuit of them whenever there is a full moon.

ACTIVITIES:
They pursue, frighten, and fight one another. They terrorize travelers, both humans and Fairies, who stray into their territories. They chase, beat, and scare them almost to death, yet never slay them.

After nightfall, solitary walkers in lonely places attract demonic Black Elves, which crowd in on them like so many echoes of their moments of fear. The victims almost always try to reassure themselves by snapping their fingers, whistling, or singing, which inevitably arouses and disturbs the creatures of darkness. They immediately prick up their ears, open their eyes, and flare their nostrils to catch the scent of fear, thus sharpening their appetite. A great number of them haunt the countryside, plains, and woods. The Duergar and their associates live under the rocks of the Simonside Hills, an isolated area between Rothbury and Elsdon in Northumberland. As soon as they hear footsteps drawing close, they wake up the other members of their band and rush to meet the stranger, who is soon lost to them, however fearfully he might beat a makeshift iron gong and shout, "Hey there!"

On one occasion, a drunken bet had enticed a tipsy traveler to make his way from the village inn to a marshy area to play with the Will-o'-the-Wisps. He started to flail about him with his cudgel and cried out to impress anyone who might be listening: "As for Duergars, all I need is this to make them run for it!"

This foolish challenge could not go unanswered. He stood there in a defiant stance, his hackles up, brandishing his oaken stick and threatening the deepest darkness with chastisement. The response soon came: a light started up in front of him, between the rushes, and flickered and shone out like a candle in the window of a shepherd's hut. Unperturbed, the yokel approached the light and soon arrived at a mud pit from which a load of peat had been dug, leaving a deep hole full of water, on the surface of which the flame trembled.

"I'll damp you down, you devilish flame!" he shouted, and gathered a hand-ful of moss and mud from the ground. He threw it at the flame, which was immediately extinguished, leaving nothing but the deepest darkness around him.

"That'll teach you!" cried the drunk. But another flame was now visible, and beyond it another, then yet another; then a fourth, a fifth, a sixth, until the foolish man could count no further because fear had replaced his unreliable drunkard's bravado. All around him, wherever he looked, there was a shimmering bouquet of lights. They began to fly toward him, and then they grasped him, revealing their shapes and threatening faces.

He was surrounded by a countless number of hideously malicious creatures of the same type, each bearing a flaming torch in one hand and a bludgeon in the other.

He decided that the best solution to the problem was to show a clean pair of heels, but they were stuck fast in the marshy ground. He soon realized that the bog was slowly devouring him. One of the Duergar let out a cry of attack and the whole crowd surged forward.

He replied, like some knight of old, as best he could by striking back at the Elfin host, but however and wherever he sought to strike them, his cudgel fell on thin air, striking neither flesh nor bone. Instead, each attempted blow met with an increase in the number, height, and ferocity of the demons.

Eventually, he lost the last traces of composure beneath this onslaught. He stood a stupefied and bruised victim until the gray light of morning dispersed his unholy opponents and enabled him to find his way back to the inn.

The Spontaïl

This is the Breton version of the Duergar. It also haunts bogs, marshes, sandy river-banks, and circles of standing stones. In winter it besets villages, entering cottages to slip stealthily between the sheets and bring about the death by terror of unsuspecting sleepers.

Biard Bheulach

This monster of Odail Pass on the Isle of Skye is the Duergar of the Highlands of Scotland. As described by J. G. Campbell in *Witchcraft and Second Sight in the Scottish Highlands*, it was the most frightening of creatures to meet. Sometimes it pursued its victim as a small man with only one leg, whereas on other occasions it appeared as a fiery-eyed greyhound or hellhound. At night, when uttering frightful shrieks and howls, it can be heard even at a great distance.

The Biard Bheulach is not only ghastly to see or hear, but also constantly needs to assuage its longing for blood.

Buggane

This monster, like the Picktree Brag, is a vicious Hobgoblin. It is a shape-shifter, and on occasion gains entry to the fairy realm by taking on the appearance of an ordinary Goblin or Pixie. It cozies up to softhearted and naïve inhabitants of that world and, once in their beds, frightens them to death by resuming its hobgoblin appearance.

Cipennapers

"Cipennaper" is merely an attempt to reproduce "Kidnapper" in Welsh. Kidnappers are any mischievous or evil Elves that carry off children.

Athach

This is the Duergar of the lonely lochs and waterfalls of the Scottish Highlands. It hides under the torrent or in the depths of a gorge, and is liable to tug on a fishing line to persuade the angler that a salmon has been caught. As soon as the fool leans over the water to see what has happened, the Athach lunges from the flood—half Elf, half reptile—and, howling most discordantly, chases the unfortunate fisherman until his heart fails.

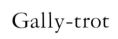

Gally-trot

An English horror known in parts of the North Country and in East Anglia. *Gally* means "to scare," and the Gally-trot, a ghostly doglike apparition, chases after anyone who takes to his or her heels in fright.

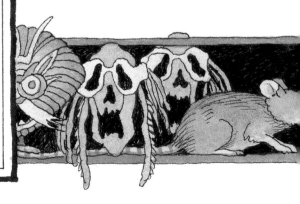

HEIGHT:
That of a goat, a young girl, or a bent old woman.

APPEARANCE:
That of a goat, a young girl, or a bent old woman.

CLOTHING:
A snowy woolen coat over skin as clear as an April day, or the ash-colored rags of an old sorceress. They wear black aprons and high-pointed hats on top of their stiff gray hair. They carry a large cooking pot gripped tightly in their emaciated arms.

HABITAT:
An ancient scullery or cave in the Welsh hills and mountains, and also along the borders with England, near the ruins of Tintern Abbey and the Sarnesfield area of Shropshire. They are especially fond of the Llanhilleth Hills, not far from Abertillery and Abersychan, where they occasionally assemble at the command of their ruler, the Old Woman of the Mountain.

FOOD:
Grass, sorrel, mountain basil, soups, laurel and bay infusions, and weird mixtures which they simmer for a week in their traditional cauldrons. They do not despise human food and particularly appreciate a drop of Double Dragon Ale.

The Gwyllion

She sat down and heard "a funny kind of crying" behind her, the crying of a lost child.
—Arthur Machen,
The Strange Tale of Mount Nephin

You have set out to climb a mountain, such as Mount Nephin, by Lough Conn, in County Mayo, Ireland. Before long you hear something like a child crying. The sound comes from a stream. You go over to investigate, but there is nothing there. It must have come from a more distant spot. The crying now grows all the more urgent. You begin to worry about the fate of this child—certainly lost—that has perhaps fallen into some crevice; or has broken a leg and is resting on a ledge a few inches from a fatal descent into the ravine below; or is possibly suspended above the abyss merely by a fragile piece of clothing, which is about to tear, if the branch does not break first. Good Lord! The cries now seem to come from every direction simultaneously! You hasten hither and thither, scratching your legs on brambles, slipping on the wet moss, and spraining your ankle as the path rises abruptly. The voices are still audible as you stagger among the stones, stumble, and then almost take a bad fall. You barely manage to catch at a protruding root in order to keep yourself upright.

A lucky escape! But you are not safe yet, since the providential root begins to loosen as you hear the leaves rustling, and then a child's derisive laughter . . .

But it is not a child.

Not only in Ireland, but also in Wales—the country whose national emblem is a Red Dragon, whose language changes shape so often and so subtly, and that elevates the fairy harp to high musical status—it is dangerous when mountain climbing to respond to mysterious cries and entreaties, even if they resemble the appeals of a lost child.

Especially if they resemble the appeals of a lost child!

You are drawn by the cries to the edge of a cliff, above a deep ravine, where you see not a wounded infant, but a mountain goat. It seems to dance on its dainty hooves. You thought its bleating was a child groaning!

Luckily, you managed to save yourself from falling headlong, just in time, and here you are, still on your own two feet, even though you feel rather queasy. You have been more frightened than hurt, and set about gathering plants and grass in an attempt to attract and feed the elegant little creature over there, rearing up on its back legs with its beard fiercely erect.

You address it softly and approach quietly. But the goat keeps its distance and somehow treats you not only with disdain but also with amusement. It seems about to let you stroke it, and lowers its head for the purpose, then bounds away, right to the cliff edge.

You have no time to escape when it turns, lowers its horns, and charges.

If you are foolish enough to behave like this, you will join the ranks of the climbers who disappear completely, and your bones will grow ever whiter beneath the water where they will lie for years to come.

You see, the goats that haunt the wooded slopes of Gwent or Mount Nephin are not goats at all, but Gwyllion, or their Irish equivalents.

Gwyllion are sly and crafty. Even those humans born in the lands they inhabit are hoodwinked by them, even though there is an abundance of cautionary tales.

When the weather grows stormy, Gwyllion sometimes decide to shelter in human habitations. It is customary to greet them hospitably as they arrive, and to offer them fresh-drawn water. But all cutlery and metal objects must be hidden for fear of offending them.

To protect yourself from their attacks, you must draw a knife and point it at their eyes, for they are sensitive to the power of cold iron or steel.

BEHAVIOR:

The word Gwyllion *is possibly derived from the Welsh* gwill, *meaning lurker, vagrant, or bandit. Gwyllion are extremely evil renegade Elves, subjects of the Old Woman of the Mountain and sworn enemies of the diaphanous and kindly Ellyllon. They are daughters of the great sorceresses of the Gramarye, or Black Book, epoch and were the associates of dragons, demons, and basilisks. For centuries, their powerful spells, charms, and perfect knowledge of the black arts enabled them to rule over the lands of Death beyond Death, Shadowland Fairies, and Redshanks, yet they retain only the faintest traces of those eons of glory. Initially, they succumbed to fatefully innovative ideas, then the demythologizing tendencies of a skeptical age, only to be dethroned by the Tylwyth Teg, or Fair Family, who replaced their silver horns with goat's horns. Even though they are but shadows of their former selves, they represent an ever-present danger for humans.*

ACTIVITIES:

Very wicked. They disguise themselves as old women, or take goat form and emit the plaintive cry "Wub, wub," in imitation of infants in distress, in order to tempt decent folk into pits and over cliff edges. They shape-change adroitly in order to make silly boys commit acts of bestiality with them.

The Gwyllion own vast herds of goats, whose beards they have been said to comb on Fridays.

The Shedim

You could still hear a few footsteps as gentle as distant waves; then, all of a sudden, everything was silent and empty.

—Nikolai Gogol

HEIGHT:
Varies.

APPEARANCE:
Wild. They look as if they are up to no good and harbor evil intentions. Their mouths are slack and blubber-lipped, and their tongues hang out. One eye is vicious and the other inquiring. They are horned, bearded, hairy, and scaly-skinned. Physically, they look somewhat ungainly, having three legs with three toes apiece, but they are evidently very agile.

CLOTHING:
Parti-colored rags and tatters, usually fragments of clothes stolen from peasants, sewn together any which way and dyed using forest plants and berries. They are fond of wearing cloth or fur headgear in the Russian style, decorated with feathers and little bells. They favor broad plaited and colored belts.

HABITAT:
Crude huts, poorly tended grottoes, dens hollowed out under banks, and the roots of big trees in the great dense forests and distant regions of Russia.

In times long past, when Czar Saltan reigned over Old Russia, there were two twin brothers. One was rich and envious, and the other poor and happy. One kept a village shop and the other was a woodcutter. Each had a hump: one on the belly and the other on the back.

On one occasion, when the woodcutter was dead tired and sleeping with a smile on his lips in his hut made of rough branches in the middle of the forest, he was awakened abruptly by music, singing, and joyous footsteps. He set off in search of all this merriment, and soon found himself at the center of a Shedim dance.

It is dangerous to encounter the Shedim, who are bizarre forest demons. While in their company, you never quite know what will happen and what you risk being changed into: a dog, cow, or rock. On this occasion, there were at least a hundred of them laughing and knocking about. They were horned, mop-haired, filthy, drunk, and quite grotesque as they danced the *hopak* on their three, three-toed feet.

The poor woodcutter wanted to run for his life, but before he knew it he had been grasped by iron-strong hands and tugged into joining the dance. In such cases, one just has to hop along with the crowd and copy the principals, and since the poor woodcutter was inclined to laugh and joke anyway, he followed their example. The Shedim have big, broad, twisted mouths and lolling tongues, so the woodcutter made haste to let his own hang out and began to grin revoltingly. He imitated their little jumps, splits, and rough shouts so meticulously that the Shedim were quite won over. They issued an invitation for the next day at the same time.

To cross a Shedim is as foolhardy as tugging on the devil's beard, so the woodcutter agreed to join them. Nevertheless, the Shedim guessed that his heart was not in the acceptance, and they demanded a token: something which he had with him and would be forced to come back for.

He suggested his sheepskin *tooloop* jacket, but they rejected his proposal. Instead, they said they would take his hump, which must surely be very dear to him, for he kept it stuck close to his back. At dawn, they melted away like dew.

Never in the whole history of human-kind had anyone seen another man as

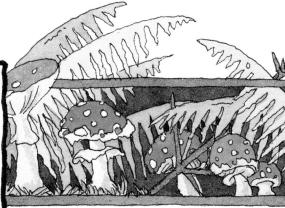

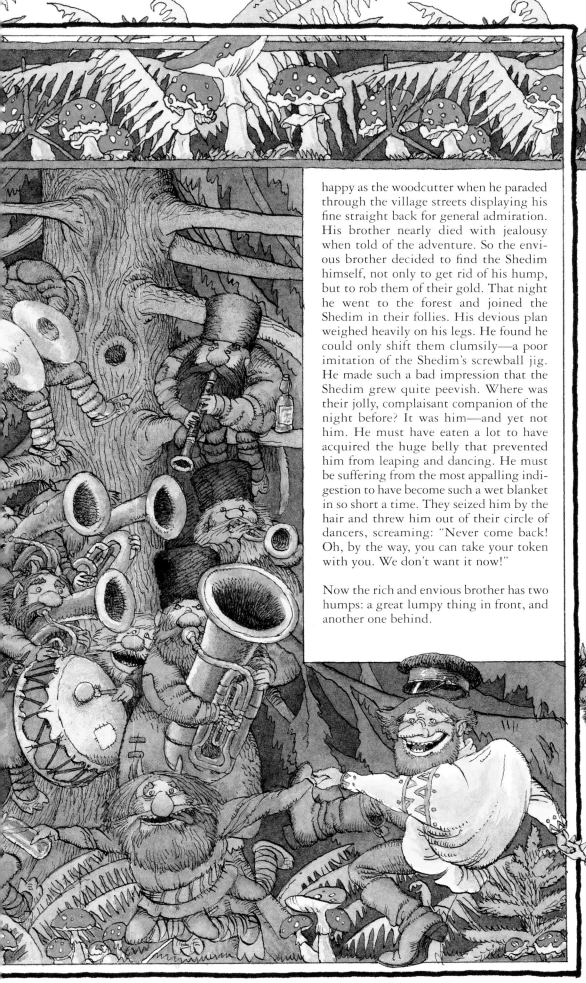

happy as the woodcutter when he paraded through the village streets displaying his fine straight back for general admiration. His brother nearly died with jealousy when told of the adventure. So the envious brother decided to find the Shedim himself, not only to get rid of his hump, but to rob them of their gold. That night he went to the forest and joined the Shedim in their follies. His devious plan weighed heavily on his legs. He found he could only shift them clumsily—a poor imitation of the Shedim's screwball jig. He made such a bad impression that the Shedim grew quite peevish. Where was their jolly, complaisant companion of the night before? It was him—and yet not him. He must have eaten a lot to have acquired the huge belly that prevented him from leaping and dancing. He must be suffering from the most appalling indigestion to have become such a wet blanket in so short a time. They seized him by the hair and threw him out of their circle of dancers, screaming: "Never come back! Oh, by the way, you can take your token with you. We don't want it now!"

Now the rich and envious brother has two humps: a great lumpy thing in front, and another one behind.

FOOD:

They stuff themselves with the same food as humans, with a preference for kulebiaki, *or tarts made mainly from egg and fish, and* kissel, *a fruit jelly with a topping of potato flour. They are fond of liquor and can knock back a phenomenal quantity of kvass or vodka in a single night.*

BEHAVIOR:

The Shedim were originally black sheep among the gray Elves. They were drawn to pleasures of the flesh and, under cover of night, resorted to the brothels of the Netherworld. There they coupled with Demons, Gnomes, and Salamanders before venturing into this world to continue their antics. This tale of a hump removed from the back of a pleasant, innocent boy and placed on that of a recalcitrant, bad-tempered twin is also found in Japan and in Brittany. It shows that the Shedim are related to the Oni and the Korrigans.

ACTIVITIES:

All those activities engaged in by malign Sprites of the forest and plains. They like to mislead or play abominable tricks on delayed travelers; they tempt them into joining the Shedim in their dancing and drinking, and sometimes even into accompanying them back to their lairs.

The Jouroupari

Once again the devil has been outdone.
—Abbé Denis Grivot

One night a young girl asleep in her hammock was suddenly awakened by the feeling of someone or something on top of her. She thought she was in the process of being smothered, and was about to die. But when she awoke she could see no one around her, and merely recorded the fleeting impression as a nightmare.

Some time later, she found that she was pregnant, even though she had never had any kind of relations with a man. Following Tupi custom, the old men of the village blew their breath onto her repeatedly to help her deliver the child without difficulty. Nevertheless, she did not give birth, even though some months passed after the usual time of delivery.

This caused some consternation among the tribal wise men, who made sure that a group of the tribe's most responsible women watched over her every day.

One day, when she was bathing in the middle of the river, a turtle bit her stomach savagely, and she gave birth through the wound. The women seized the infant immediately and carried him to Tuxaua, who was struck by his frightening appearance. He had a big ugly head, rough skin, and horny twisted feet. Tuxaua ordered him to be exiled to the depths of the forest.

No one knows how the little monster managed to survive in the hostile jungle, or what kind of creature took pity on him and fed him, but he succeeded in growing up away from all human habitation. When he reached manhood, he masked his face and began shooting flames from every part of his body, all the time cursing those who had sent him into exile.

So the elders of the tribe told the women never to look at the monster.

They were afraid that this demon might impregnate a woman with a single glance and that she would give birth to nightmarish infants as a result.

They called the monster Jouroupari, which means "hand on mouth" or "creature that comes to our hammock."

Then the Jouroupari began to commit a whole series of misdeeds.

HEIGHT:
A little taller than a man.

APPEARANCE:
The Jouroupari looks hideous and repulsive, like the vilest creature you might imagine rising from the blackest pool. He has a thick, knotted mass of fibrous hair. He has a face reminiscent of a toad, with globular eyes, running nostrils, a mouth distorted by excessively ferocious laughter, protruding fangs, and steaming, warty gills. All this is even more grotesque and shocking than the unbelievably ugly features of the ghastly mask with which he seeks to cover his actual countenance.

CLOTHING:
His speckled, warty skin is weirdly tattooed, and covered in horny, leathery scales that serve as a kind of armor.

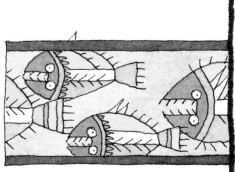

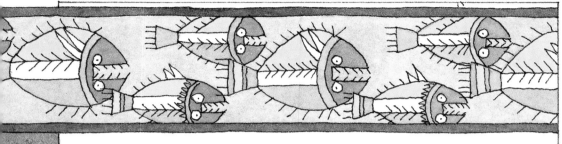
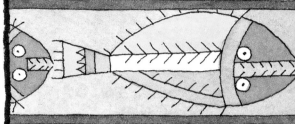

At night, he left his lair and approached the village at the pace and in the manner of a wolf. He slipped into the huts and hovered over the hammocks where men, women, and children were sleeping, and throttled them to death. Alternatively, he sucked their blood, inserted demonic snakes into their heads, or took advantage of virgins in their unconscious state.

He cackled hideously in the night at the consequences of his wicked exploits.

How could the village folk rid themselves of the monster? Whatever they did seemed ineffective. They tried fire to drive him away, gifts to seduce him, and traps to imprison him. He tripped every trap and saw through every ruse. Arrows bounced ineffectually off his enchanted skin.

But it was this same hard, scaly skin, with its weird tattoos and impenetrable leather plates, which the Jouroupari removed and laid on the stump of a *mamburizeiro* tree while he bathed in the river.

While he was swimming and scratching his flesh under the water, a hunter happened to pass by. He caught sight of the Jouroupari's magic skin, grabbed it, and covered himself with it, hoping to acquire the creature's strength and resistance to wounds and blows. He had scarcely finished adjusting it to fit when the Jouroupari, whose body sensed the theft of his skin, jumped out of the water, red muscles and tendons tautened. "Vile creature! What have you done? You certainly do not realize the danger in which you are now firmly wrapped. Now you too are a Jouroupari and must constantly feed your skin, which will always remain hungry, and may even consume you one day!"

And one day the stolen skin did eat the man. Then it returned to cover the body of the Jouroupari once again.

HABITAT:
A stinking hole packed with bones and decaying carcasses, in the most overgrown, least accessible, most impenetrable, most dangerous, and most deserted part of the Brazilian rain forests.

FOOD:
The Jouroupari is a vampire and a man-eater.

BEHAVIOR/ACTIVITIES:
An Elf of the darkest regions, and a nightmarish imp. As a nightmare-creature he considers all means of provoking bad dreams to be permissible. He haunts the native Tupi tribe, but also the Jawi and Mundurucus. He is also known as Izi.

NOTE:
Not so long ago, wooden images of Jouroupari were carved and then hidden in streams and rivers. On certain days, they were fetched from the water and displayed on the riverbank for special ceremonies. These were occasions of celebration and rejoicing. Only men were allowed to see and touch these idols—a favor forbidden to women. If curiosity prompted a woman to try to see or touch the image of Jouroupari, she was sentenced to death.

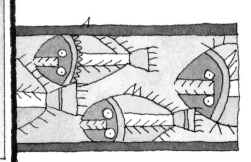

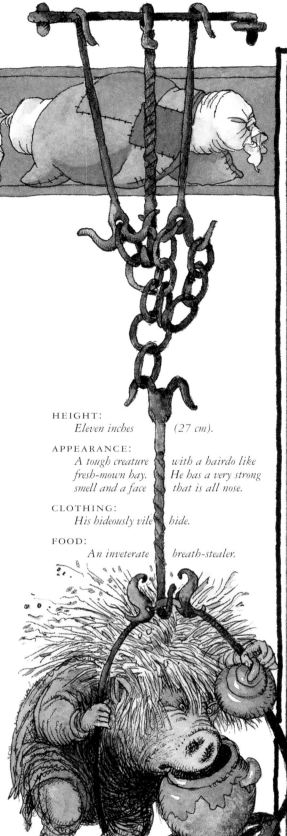

HEIGHT:
Eleven inches (27 cm).

APPEARANCE:
A tough creature with a hairdo like fresh-mown hay. He has a very strong smell and a face that is all nose.

CLOTHING:
His hideously vile hide.

FOOD:
An inveterate breath-stealer.

HABITAT:
Occupies hollows beneath hearthstones of houses in the Auvergne, in France.

BEHAVIOR/ACTIVITIES:
Gluttonous.

The Betsoutsou

A Cinder-elf is hard at work under the eider-down, burning the poor fellow's belly.
—M. C. Aze

At midnight, this nightmarish Elf of the Auvergne region of France wakes up from his slumber under the traditional hearthstone. He shakes himself, cackles fiendishly, and finishes the dregs in any glasses left on the table before setting off on his nightly rounds. Thus invigorated, he looks for a stray thorn, mounts it, and sails over hills and villages, sniffing the breeze. He flies around the bell tower of Ruyne in the Margeride district and circles the turrets of the town of Saint-Flour. He sniffs curiously at the perfumed remains of the smoke rising from each chimney, for he is searching for a particular mixture of odors.

Suddenly, his nostrils flex as they are assailed by and greedily inhale the desired scent.

Then he descends on the favored farm below.

He slips noiselessly under mossy shutters and window frames. Following the scent, he arrives at the chosen bedroom of that night's unfortunate sleeper.

He bounds up onto his victim's stomach, sits astride it, and allows his quivering snout to rejoice in the rich garlicky breath rising to delight it.

He grips, presses, and massages the belly he is riding and sups on the savory

exhalations enriched by stuffing, sauces, rare mushrooms, and chives. He greedily devours the scent of sugarplums.

Then, totally sated, he abandons the body he has pounded to extinction, and departs on foot, hiccupping and tottering along the stony pathways that lead to its retreat.

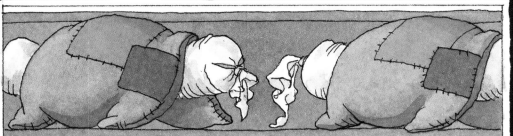

The Alp-Luachra

They draw the bed-curtains at midnight, when the moon is out.
—Robert Kirk

Four posts to my bed,
*Four Angels round my head.
Matthew, Mark, Luke, and John,
Bless the bed I lie upon.*

This is the prayer repeated by a character in a work by Elisabeth Goudge who is asking for protection against the black Night-Elves. Of course it is a very old bedtime petition taught to English children for generations. Though this prayer might well have sent a lesser nocturnal demon flying, it is not certain that it would have repelled an Alp-Luachra. It has been said that no crucifix, no blessed palm, no open pair of scissors on the pillow, no rural charm, however sacred, could ever foil their wicked plots.

Throughout the day, the Alp-Luachra slumbers rolled up in a ball in a kind of viscous cocoon; he emerges only at dusk when the eyes of infants begin to close, for he specializes in assaults on children.

When the household is asleep and snoring, the now fully awakened horde of mini-demons attacks the inhabitants' beds. Astride house spiders—climbing the folds in sheets or dropping from the ceiling—they reach their victims and settle down to enjoy the gasps of snore-breath that they find so delicious.

Other Vampire Elves of Nurseryland

The Retsousu

Grandsons of the Betsoutsou, sons of the Tsoutsu, they are born of unions with beauteous female nightmare Elves. They only attack infants, whom they scarcely nibble. Their appetite must surely fade as generations pass. They are cowards, and flee at the slightest sign of their victims waking up.

The Sucker

The tiniest of all Elves. It is smaller than the least of gnats, lives in the nursery, and greedily feasts on the sweet dreams of the newborn.

HEIGHT:
No bigger than a midge.

APPEARANCE:
Hideous, scrofulous, hydrocephalic, and suffering from ringworm. He has a sucker mouth, and his chin ends in shards of spongy flesh. Also has a rat's tail, threadlike claw feet, and three nauseatingly damp antennae.

CLOTHING:
Wears a spiderweb coat in frosty weather.

HABITAT:
Cellars, attics, thatched roofs, floors, wainscoting, and beds. At the bottom of deserted mouse nets, wall crannies, and cupboards. They reproduce in vast numbers on hot June nights, above marshes, mud holes, and peat bogs.

FOOD:
Alp-Luachra, also known as Joint-eaters or Just-halvers, use their sucker-antennae to suck up and breathe in the energy of their sleeping victims. Kirk says that they sit beside their victims and feed on "the pith or quintessence of what the man eats" (Robert Kirk, The Secret Commonwealth).

BEHAVIOR/ACTIVITIES:
The Alp-Luachra is a vampire Elf that frequents bedrooms and appears at the first sign of sleepiness. Van Helsing maintains that it is born from the union of a Psylle and a Scarbo.

Other Nightmare Elves

The Tsoutsu

"The Presser" is the son of Betsoutsou. He is much idler, more sedentary, and less selective than the other nightmare elves. He is satisfied to snatch once a week some of the breath of the members of the household where he has taken up residence.

The Papoires

Hideous gargoyles that depart from the Last Judgment reliefs on Amiens Cathedral like demonic flies, and plague honest folk as they take their well-earned rest.

The Scarbo

These are another manifestation of horror that assault their victims, those already bitten by vampire hordes, by crudely cauterizing the neck bites with iron fingers, made red-hot in a blacksmith's furnace.

The Morphores

Miniature Harpies and sleep parasites born of the nightmare imaginings of Morpheus, the son of Sleep. During the midday nap, they attach their deceptively warm, comforting, and lovely selves to the necks of reapers sleeping in ditches and drain their blood.

The Agathion

A male Morphore whose nightmarish specialty is to appear at the twelfth toll of the midday Angelus bell on the hottest days during harvest time in the Beauce region of France, driving the harvesters insane.

The Chauceur

On the last stroke of midnight, this nightmare demon of the Jura region of France emerges from the long-case clock where he has slumbered through the day. He then makes his way to the bed of the master of the house in order to torment him mercilessly. He sits astride his chest, rams his spurred feet into his flanks, seizes his throat, and roars with demonic laughter at the contorted facial expressions of the man he is strangling. Still seated on him, he takes his final pleasure by releasing his hold on his victim at the last possible moment. Sad to say, those whom he plagues scarcely ever live longer than a year under this torture. Upon the death of his host, the lustful Chauceur leaves the household in search of another mount.

The Mark

A nocturnal demon of the Walloon areas of Belgium. During the day he slumbers like Lumçon, the dragon of Mons, in the depths of belfry cellars. At dusk, with a great cloud of his companions, he emerges from the tower above and flies out in search of victims in the Fagnes area on the borders of Flanders.

The Cauquemare

He takes on the appearance of a lizard two feet long, slips between the sheets, and sucks out sleepers' souls. He causes insomnia, fits, cold sweats, and a considerable number of heart attacks.

The Marautule

He haunts headboards and sometimes appears as a hideous cluster of fluffy cobwebs. He falls from the ceiling into any available open mouth, where he repeatedly inserts his stinger into the larynx until a savage sore throat ensues. The victim often dies.

The Waarbuter

An etiolated and somewhat snobbish creature of ages past that haunted only canopied four-poster beds in old manor houses. He preferred the comfortable glow of candles and disappeared with the first glimmers of electric lighting.

The Rudge-Pula

Something of a practical joker rather than a truly dangerous creature, he died as a result of his sense of humor—he swallowed a set of false teeth left in a glass of water, which he consumed before replacing it with vinegar.

The Marni

A murderous demon. One can detect his recent presence by finding the marks of his claws on the belly of his victim.

Toggeli

A tentacled hydra and haunter of the sleeping, whom it asphyxiates with its embrace. It leaves a revolting whiff of carbon monoxide behind it.

The Quaeldrytteriude

On four occasions the image of this usually invisible creature has been captured in a mirror. Maupassant describes a version of this horror in his story *The Horla*.

The Nachtmanule

A fastidious creature that preferred to feast on the enchanted dreams of Fairy folk rather than mundane human imaginings. Oberon managed to capture the Nachtmanule's legions by setting a trap of sticky threads and imprisoning them in lead urns.

The Schrecksele

Rinus van Worms tells us that for many years you could see the dried-up remains of a Schrecksele at Wafelaarts Castle, impaled on the point of a rapier. The Schrecksele is a form of distressingly ugly butterfly with venomous characteristics.

The Wegaleyo

This creature hid his unpleasant features beneath a vast curved forehead and tortoise-like hunchback. He was known to slip into Native American tepees and sap the braves' courage before battle.

The Chort

Like bats, wrapped in their membranous skin, Chorts sleep upside down all day between the curtain folds of bed canopies. As soon as the sun goes down behind the Carpathian Mountains, Chorts unfold their parchment-like wings, stretch their vile mouths, and let out multiple yawns between their tiny fanglike teeth. Oupires and ancient Vourdalacks may no longer stain embroidered pillowcases and coverlets with their bloody kisses, but Chorts continue to mark the jugulars of young virgins with two ruddy pearls.

The Endormillon

One night he arrived to haunt the Sleeping Beauty, but he was entrapped by the unfathomable dreams behind those ever-closed eyelids. He remained imprisoned by her glistening blonde tresses, with his paws, wings, and dragon tail caught up in the linen folds and threads. In time, he withered there, leaving the imprint of his horny rump on her forehead and shoulders.

175

It

HEIGHT:
Difficult to judge.

APPEARANCE:
Invisible, but also a veritable apparition. It assumes the appearance of our deepest, most visceral, and uncontrollable fears. *It* has great, livid staring moons instead of eyes.

CLOTHING:
Hazy.

HABITAT:
The darkest, most obscure recesses of our lives and dwelling places. It favors sinister spots: infamous and filthy holes, deserted parking lots, and all corridors of vice.

FOOD:
It feeds on our fears.

BEHAVIOR:
It is the blackest of Black Elves, but also the most ancient and atavistic, and has many faces. It *borrows the features of Trunt-Trunt, Kurupira, the Wendigo, the Bogey, the Mask of the Red Death, bugbears, Chthwllu, werewolves, Old Leather-jacket, the Gaslight Vampire, Babheu, Captain Hook, and the very Demon of Demons; none of which can rival the vileness of* It.

ACTIVITIES:
It awakens our fears, from the most fleeting suspicion of apprehension to the most terrifyingly dominant obsession. It *gently coaxes, nourishes, feeds, goads, and brings them on to the point of total panic. It* hastens through winding streets to the crossroads, where It *waits for the victims* It *will slay with the sudden shock of recognition.*

Our alpine cowherds believe that "It" lives in a hut left uninhabited, as is usual during the winter months.

—Marie-Louise von Franz

One day someone who had never known the meaning of fear decided to set off along the trail of who-knows-what-will-happen in order to face and slay fear itself, and bring its head home as a kind of trophy. He gained victory after victory and piled up slaughtered dragons and ogres, beasts both fantastic and colossal, hydra-headed monstrosities and bogeys galore. He proved to be another "Green Breeches," the redoubtable hero whose achievements are celebrated by Charles Deulin in his *Tales of a Beer-drinker* (*Contes d'un buveur de bière*). Green Breeches managed to defy and vanquish the most monstrous and vile inventions of any world here, beyond, or below. He defeated everything, but not fear itself, which still gave him the slip, sniggering and grimacing as vilely as ever. But of course fear, better known simply as "It" (or, when multiple, as "Them"), has many faces. *It* assumes many shapes. *It* lives here, but also there, for *It* has no fixed dwelling-place.

However, one drunken night during his travels, an amiable demon whom he met in a tavern told our intrepid adventurer that *It* had taken up temporary residence in a shepherd's hut very high up, right over there, in the solitary mountain wastes. He set off promptly in that direction. His heavy saber, which not long before had sliced the bellies and spilled the entrails of a mass of bestial demons, was newly honed and sharpened. *It* would not elude him for long now. *It* would soon know the strength of a resolute demon-slayer.

He made his way to the distant heights and eventually reached the empty hut in the wasteland up there. He made himself at home, lit a fire in the hearth, and then sat by the window and waited. As he waited, he looked out into the depths of the darkness surrounding the hut, and with daybreak tried to pierce the wraith-like mists. Although he waited patiently, *It* did not appear. But he guessed that *It* was indeed there, for it crawled over the hut, rubbed itself on its walls, and scratched them. When *It* screamed horribly and shook the roof, he rushed outside grasping a turfing iron, and shouted, "Show yourself!" But nothing appeared. *It* was certainly there in the darkness close by, laughing derisively, watching him, and, like our hero, waiting. But *It* was waiting to see who would give way first.

Of course, *It* was a champion performer in this respect. This was its natural pursuit. It had all the time in the world, for *It* is the darkest and oldest of all the ageless Black Elves. The night delivered *It*, and the darkness suckled *It* and sang *It* to sleep with the ghastliest of all lullabies.

It can wait and wait without betraying its presence. The powdery snow covering the mountain slopes is made of the long-faded bones of all those who have ascended there, confident of their ability to smoke *It* out. But *It* continues to haunt the visitors' huts, weaving its silent plot against them, and exhaling the breath of pure solitude. *It* knows that the spirit now

caught between its fingers can only peck pathetically at the gaps, for *It* has imprisoned this human soul.

This continued for many languid days and many interminable nights, while the man who had never known fear tried to address, defy, and attack—though in vain—this faceless, disembodied thing enclosed in the circumambient darkness.

The time had come for *It* to slay its victim, and to allow the empty gaze of two moonlike eyes to appear on the window glass.

They say that the man who went in search of fear found *It* right up there, in a deserted hut among the silences, and that since then his steps have been dogged by terror, for the least creak or sigh startles him, drives him to the very edge of dissolution.

It was in a far-distant refuge-hut at the summit of a snow-clad peak that Marie-Louise von Franz, Jung's brilliant disciple, met *It*. The phantom completely took her over, when, not realizing that this was the very creature she had come in search of, she gradually succumbed to total panic.

It always answers if you call *It*. Dr. Jekyll found *It* at the bottom of a test tube. Polly Nicholls met up with *It* one August 31 at two-thirty in the morning at the corner of Osborn Street and White-chapel Road. Children sometimes come upon *It* crouching in the bottomless reaches of a bedroom wardrobe.

On the Other Side of the Pages

Firiel rises with the dawn
As magpies start their morning chatter
And puts her golden ball gown on
Embroidered everywhere with pearls
Barefoot in the morning dew
Dancing down the river long
Enchanted by the song anew
This light, beguiling Elfin song

Come, come, and walk on water
If you choose to, walk on water
Until you reach the vessel grand
Sailing to the Elfin land

—Patrick Ewen

There is no end to the making of books on the Elves, for there is so much more to come. There are the countless ranks of Afreets and Peris, and along with them the multitudes of other Caetchen, Laighrin, Gailoin, Fir Morca, Goborchin, Niao-Shih, Ta Hao, Rocots, Nayes, and others, amassed in all their myriad companies. Now that you have passed along all the Elfin corridors of this book, and met with so many Goblins, Fairies, and Elves, none of these sprites, whether already introduced or yet to be described in some future encounter, will seem quite so alien as beforehand. Having traveled a journey woven in imagination, having entered realms so distant from this cheap world and its tired millennia, and having cast off the arrogant pretenses of your own dominant species, you will have learned how to slip out of place and time and steal away to the hills and islets not only of Elfin oblivion but of infinite dreams and lovemaking.

The last page of this part of the book should be like a white sail on the far-reaching seas of Elfiria, pointing to an Ever-land whither the least breath of magic will bear you at any moment and a new tale must surely begin . . .

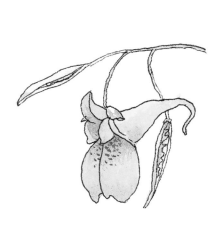

PART II
GOBLINS
AND
OTHER LITTLE
CREATURES

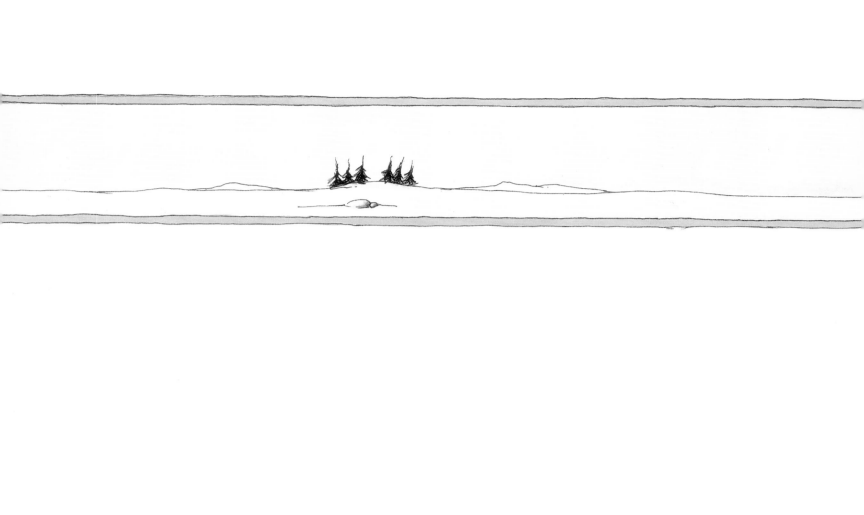

Invitation to the
Unknown Kingdom

Little thoughtful creatures sit
On the grassy coasts of it;
Little things with lovely eyes
See me sailing with surprise.
—Robert Louis Stevenson,
A Child's Garden of Verses

I began this book long, long ago, as they say in stories. I no longer remember exactly when. At first, there were just impressions, travel diaries and readings gleaned here and there, including those from the archives of Petrus Barbygère. I've run the gamut of elfology books! Without my realizing it, this book must have taken shape from those haphazard encounters. However, it is not an encyclopedia in the conventional sense of the word. We cannot classify unclassifiable species. That would actually be the height of rudeness. We can merely sketch alleys, trace vague paths in the inextricable labyrinth of their garden, and talk about them and describe them while respecting their nebulous and whimsical rules. But we must also be careful never to hurt their feelings, pride, or sensitivity. We would be wise to cover our tracks, to overuse trite expressions and wordplay—which they merrily trample underfoot—and become simple souls. Science degrees

and ethnological research are of little use in gaining entrance to the universe of Elves. A better approach is to lay aside the magnifying glass and the butterfly net. How far off track are the current works undertaken by scientists and specialists, who feel no compunction in being limited by etymology and restricting to Greek and Latin roots the origins of those "Others" who predate human language! Reading their works still flabbergasts me. Delving deep into musty libraries and stacks of books amuses me. Serious Dodgsonian mythologists pore over the infinitely small, extrapolating to the infinitely large, learnedly dissecting turns of phrase in nursery rhymes to reach sweeping generalizations. Their painstaking approach amazes me. Sometimes one stumbles upon wisdom through a perfunctory glance inside a wolf's den.

Save the works of Katherine M. Briggs, *The Personnel of Fairyland* (1953), *An Dictionary of Fairies* (1976), and *The Vanishing People* (1978), which remain the most complete and "beautiful" approach to the universe of Fairies, and other rare exceptions, how much more "real" and evocative are the strolls of William Butler Yeats at the foot of Irish raths, the reveries of Kathleen Raine, the premises of Diane de Margerie, the meditations of Gaston Bachelard—who so often unknowingly followed in their footsteps—or the simple act of listening to a story. An Arthur Rackham drawing, a Pre-Raphaelite detail, an Edith Holden pastel, a dangling Emily Dickinson verse, a sentence in a Mary Webb text, a mantra repeated a hundred

times, the contemplation of a plant, the rediscovery of a ritual gesture, a melody carried on the wind, these are all equally invitations to the Luminous Passage . . . To each his own, so long as he does not abuse the privilege and aims anew to deserve entry each time.

Furthermore, let us not forget to look up from the page and follow the Leprechaun road zigzagging through the lakes of Kerry . . . Let us leap the Pixie Bridge at Postbridge in Dartmoor; let us not hesitate to spend a day in hot pursuit of a Farfarelli flight over the fragrant slopes of Berbeno, to enjoy the shade of an oak at Comper in Brocéliande, to relentlessly pursue the Tourmentine, right to the back of her own garden . . . Let us learn how to breach the frontiers of the Kingdom cracked open by an April sunbeam.

As I am about to see these pages printed, these leaves bound and enclosed between the covers of a book, it feels like many creatures are about to slip away. Some will hollow invisible tunnels through the tome; others will escape through gaps in the binding or vanish into thin air by the magic of a single gesture. I almost want to incite them to escape, or even help them, by blowing beneath the silken wings of still-drowsy Fayettes, by shoving the rear of that enormous and slow Piot-Chan scarab.

I know what these creatures are like. They will choose this moment to stay just to be contrary, and they will line up neatly, assuming the spurious air of rare specimens. But I pay no attention; I am not so easily fooled. I have dealt with them for too long. For twenty or thirty years—no, without a doubt more—I have allowed them to stray onto my desk. I have used everything to attract them: pictures, old books, fairy-grass, tree bark, lichens, mosses, fossils, arrows, magic lanterns, flowers, marbles, pebbles, grains of tobacco, big-bottomed creatures, thousands of objects likely to captivate them, even figurines sculpted in their image. What a playground! The only thing left to do was pretend to see nothing while observing everything.

Surely, they are not gullible, but fair is fair: a paper clip for a small secret, sledding on the curve of a pipe for a formula from the depths of the ages. I have also groomed myself, adopted an Elfin beard and some traits that should please them. In the woods, I fortuitously meet a majestic stag that lets me approach almost close enough to touch (I feel like the man who talks to the animals), but once the invisible frontier is breached, he disappears. Nothing is ever certain with the "Little Neighbors." They make the decisions. Contact comes slowly, and only when you no longer expect it, when you no longer reason, and the spirit is inadvertently led astray to inside their way of thinking. Of course, nothing is permanent.

"I have made you rich
Ear by ear,
Sheaf by sheaf
I will ruin you," they say.

The Fairy World dissipates with the slightest lapse, the most innocent blink of an eye: the golden comb reverts to a seashell, the leaf received as a gift dries up, the mountain shuts, and the path

disappears. The secret voice may be silenced forever, and it feels like the Golden Age is lost once again.

Sometimes they come at dawn, loaded with stories, generous with their affection. They laugh to find among themselves a person who thought he was lying in bed. They are capable of offering lasting hospitality. Waking, still lit by the luminosities of green kingdoms, impregnated with perfumes of saffron, we can believe it possible to transmit the fullness of the experience, describe the marvelous clear flow of the moment, but they have changed the magic words into locutions so dull and commonplace that they crack under their own weight.

When I reach the threshold of my last twilight, will you welcome me for all eternity under those blessed hills? I will be sure to slip my best tobacco into my pocket and to slide a primrose into my left shoe and a yew berry under my tongue.

To illustrate the notes gathered during a kind of "Elf nature stroll," we need a purveyor of images with an eye precise enough to draft a herbarium or a bestiary, but equally bedazzled by a perception of the "Invisibles." It was not at all easy, especially since it is quite the fashion to replace feeling with thought, to intellectualize "conceptual and formal research" to the point of absurdity. After much searching and many detours, I finally found one couched in the humus and the gills of the mushrooms, playing the bombardon in order to make them dance, while busily adding a nose and ears with strokes of a lively pencil. Tinkerbell came along as the colorist who would summon dawn pigments like butterfly wings.

The Dwarfs, the Gnomes, the Goblins were our closest neighbors; we have followed in their minute footsteps.

To the fairy land afar,
Where the Little People are
—Robert Louis Stevenson

Pierre Dubois, Elfologist

On the Origins of the Little People: the Alfs, the Dwarfs, the Elves, and Their Existence

They rank in the number of the gods those alone whom they behold.
—Caesar,
The Gallic Wars, vol. VI, 21, 2

Before the "Golden Age" of the memory of heroes, before the "Other Time" of the memory of Men, the Alfs greeted the same dawn as the gods.
—Claudius Expansyvhe, Manx le Shentocieux Ruadh—
Trilly Twyll Wiel—Barbygère Dhû,
The Haegtesse Chronicles

Genesis

There, in the North, before the beginning of the world, gaped the Abyss: Ginnungagap. To the north of the North was Niflheim, the world of ice and fog. To the South was Muspelheim, the world of fire and infernos. They met above the void in an explosion of snow and flames, of lava and cloudbursts. The fusion of contrary elements caused the impact which welded shut Ultima Thule.

In the midst of outbursts, fiery icebergs, petrified fumaroles, and steam tornados, gushed a great shudder of life. First a bubbling, a roaring, then a form . . . a rough shape began to grow under clouds punctured by lightning flashes. From these cosmic antonyms, accidentally united by a ridiculous mating, were born Ymir the Giant, Aurgelmir the narrow-minded, and Hrimthurse, the repulsive hoarfrost Thurse who vomited his son Thrudgelmir from his clay entrails.

That is not all. From the overly fecund alluvium sprang forth a big fat lumpy cow with the dulcet name of Audhumla, who presented the starving Ymir with a breast flowing with four rivers of milk.

It is a strange story, this cud-chewing wet nurse who, lacking blades of grass to chew, started to lick the snowdrift desert, munching on the stones, sucking the hailstones, placidly polishing the ice floe, and at the end of three days of lapping, turned up the loose stones—and uncovered a god! The first god of creation revealed by the rough tongue of an innocent bovine!

This god, Buri, went on to sire Bor, who then married Bestla, the daughter of Bolthorn. She gave birth to Odin, Vili, and Ve.

In the meantime, the creative forces did not stop at only one Thrudgelmir. Bergelmir was brought to life. That alone was too many people for that small and sacred plot, and the largest was destined to die. Odin, Ve, and Vili assassinated Ymir, whose sobbing cries flooded and drowned the old Thurses of the ice, too hoary to swim. Only Bergelmir escaped. He founded a race of Giants distinguished by hate and vengeance.

What could be done with the unwieldy cadaver but fling it into the bottom of the safest of hiding places, the abyss of Oblivion, where no one would ferret it out: the original void, Ginnungagap. Or better yet: to bury forever the crime in earth that does not yet exist. The infernal trio used the corpse to concoct a planet. Unseen and unknown, the dismemberment went well.

The pale snippets of Ymir's brain spread as clouds to the four corners of the chasm. Here and there the quilted circumvolutions, the tattered fringes of the brain's lobes now hang subject to the cumulus, stratus, nimbus, and rabbit-fart winds of the atmosphere! The gravedigger gods were ever more ingenious. The flesh was soon reduced to compost, a ball of earth where the skin disappeared under a very well-disguised camouflage. The tresses, the superfluous hair, and the beard became forests, prairies, heaths, and thickets. The knucklebones and the teeth were scattered in the form of lava flows and rockslides along the spine and the skeleton. The tumultuous blood was channeled into rivers and streams; hemorrhages ran between the ribs, creating promontories and turning the thighs into downy beaches.

Nevertheless, you can never be too careful! Dull, supercilious uni-browed Ymir would serve as a fortress against the eventual invasion of the vengeful Giants. A wart would be the keep of that improbable bastion: Midgard, the middle moat. To finish the job with a delicate and artistic touch, they collected sparks of Muspelheim's glow and affixed celestial orbs and stars to the summit.

Of Ymir there was no longer any trace.

They patted themselves on the back, they celebrated, they sprinkled ambrosia beneath the fairy lights of their celestial citadel of Asgard . . . But, alas, the cadaver still rose to the surface; one can still see the skeleton in the closet. A swarm of larva and maggots soon blossomed from the entrails of the rotting Thurse. Nibbling the putrid clay, a pallid blind swarm groped its way to daylight.

Odin saw the twisted black shadow on the land that signaled their approach. What could be done with this fermentation of Ymir rising toward the light to testify to their crime?

"Placate them! Treat them as allies" (*The Other Side of Alfaheimr*, Petrus Gardsvor). Give a face to the searching snout of worms, a voice to that inarticulate croaking, a shape to those crawling guts, intelligence to that devouring instinct . . . why not powers? Extraordinary strength?

Odin distributed a vast number of divine gifts and magic.

This is more or less how the Dwarfs were born, according to the Eddas, the mythological Norse recitals (*The Edda of Soemond*, 38 songs attributed to the bard Soemond Sigfusen; *The Edda of Snorri*, Snorri Sturluson, 1178–1241).

The Golden Age of the Dwarfs and Their Fragmentation into Species

There is a place called Alfaheimr, where the Elves of light reside, but the Elves of darkness reside below, under the earth.
—*The Deluding of Gylfi*

Some of "Them," bound close to Muspelheim—the luminous side of the world—during a long period of gestation, were delicate and well balanced. The contact with fire made them stunning, each shoulder sporting bunched spindles of wings ready to unfurl.

Long live their wondrous ability to escape like so many butterflies taking to flight in the spring. These were the White Alfs (Liosalfar, Elves, Elbs, and Alves), the aerial Genies of the light who peopled Alfaheimr and whose descendants founded "the Elfin people," the Holdes, Huldres, Sidhe, Tylwyth Teg, and Sylphs.

Svartalfaheimr, realm of caves, chasms, and the bowels of the earth, was home to the Black Alfs, the Svartalfar, and the Dwarfs. They reigned over mines, metals, treasures, esoteric sciences and forces. They tamed fire and became master blacksmiths. They tempered Durandal for Roland, Gungir for Odin, the broadsword of Doolen de Mayence, the cursed blade of King Heidrek . . . and the lightning hammer of Thor. The four strongest held up the four corners of the celestial vault formed by the cranium of Ymir: Austri to the east, Nordri to the north, Vestri to the west, and Sudri to the south.

They crisscrossed the heart of the planet, excavating and exploring immense caverns planted with stalagmites where rivers and torrents sung and foamed; they dug, hollowed, scrabbled, and extracted from creases in the rocks diamonds, blocks of emeralds, and iridescent stones

they hewed and carved. At the bottom of their volcanoes they melted veins of gold, hammering and embossing dishes, jewelry, arms, coats of mail, crowns, Njörd's boat, the shimmering, flying boar of Freyr, the timepieces of Weedysheim of the Antipodes, and the Thrymgjölf "Grates of Hell." And they drilled even deeper. They industriously dug coal. They were solitary and kept to themselves in lairs, to meditate and devote themselves to experiments and alchemy

A tribe, a clan seduced by the gleam of a tunnel of minerals, stopped and settled: Nibelungen, Kobolds, Stille Volk . . . From east to west, from north to south: Berggeister, Kloks'Tomtes, and Velus established themselves in the mountains. In banks, caves, and hollows: Nutons, Sôtés. Under rocks and upturned stones: Korrigans and Kourrils. In the darkness of the forests: Ohdows and Trolls. Less cave-bound and venturing to "the outer limits": the Gnomes. On the surface, buttes, and hills: Bergfolk, Sangres. The most reckless found a place in the hedges, the branches, and the simple shelter of the grasses; there, in the light of day, they regained the graceful flight of their Elfin brothers, and the most inspired mated.

Some centuries afterward, later generations appeared in the mines, the courtyards of chateaux, the abodes of men—the sorcerers' laboratories and farms, cellars and attics. This was the Golden Age; the decline was still only a blurred image in the premonitory dreams of Gwynd'hylwnn the Visionary.

Other Versions of the Origin of the Dwarfs

And their love was so great, so great that they had giant children!
—J. Lenoir and J. Larue, *The Dwarfs*

Queen Maeve: "*In which Edda do you appear?*"
—W. Otnit Brainellyou, *The Happy Age*, Act II, Scene VI, Ed. Oxenedes, 1703, Leiden

"One must also know why God created the Dwarfs first, then the Giants and the Heroes.

"He began by creating the minuscule Dwarfs because the earth and the mountains were savage, wild lands, and hidden under the mountains were large amounts of gold, silver, precious stones, and pearls. That is why God gave the Dwarfs science and great wisdom—so they could distinguish good from bad and understand what these things were good for . . . and so that they could be kings and lords just like the other valiants.

"Why did God create the Giants? To fight the great dragons so the Dwarfs could live in safety and cultivate the earth. After a few years, the Giants began to harm the Dwarfs, becoming villains and traitors. Then God created the vigorous Heroes as intermediaries between the other two. We should remember that the vigorous Heroes were long loyal and good-natured, and God made it their duty to help the Dwarfs fight the traitorous Giants, wild animals and reptiles."

Even though this fifteenth-century Teutonic text (*Das Deutsche Heldenbuch*) gives a different origin for the Dwarfs from that given in the Eddas, the Black Alfs were nevertheless always associated with science, wisdom, and the knowledge of underground riches. Still, there exist even more contradictory ideas, since from Pliny, Homer, Hesiod, Saxo Grammaticus, Doctor Johannes Faust, Paracelsus,

Petrus Barbygère, Heinrich Heine, Jacob and Wilhelm Grimm, Paul G. Stanwood et al. to F. Pfister, Eugène Dubois, J.R.R. Tolkien, de Saussure, Karl Grün, Brian Froud, Gould, de Boor, Ronan, Sir Walter Scott et al. through to strange Claude Lecouteux's[1] Sherlock Holmes-Garnacki, there is no agreement on the birth of the Alfs (black or white)!

In the *Völuspà* Edda, the Dwarfs Modsognir and Durinn are the Adam and Eve of the Elfin world who created the race in their image.

"The first inhabitants of the earth were the Giants; the second, physically weaker, but dominating by virtue of their lively spirit, possessed the art of divination and, thanks to their magic, were able to pass themselves off as gods. Man was born from the mixing of these two races and was falsely acclaimed a god." (*Gesta Danorum* I, V, 5, ed. J. Olrik and H. Raeder, Copenhagen, 1931).

"Since the time when the peaks of those mountains rose high enough to snag the infinity of the skies, the sea was vast enough to swamp the sun and spit it out on the other side of the world, the crevices and the chasms bit so far into the earth that the dragons, the salamanders, and the monstrous fauna of the original fire rose to feed freely at the surface, Giants have reigned over the Age of Innocence. There were good and peaceful spirits, cruel and savage spirits, and evil conquering spirits who fought the neighboring gods: Détyas, Asouras, Osymandias, Titans, Nephilim, Thurses and Chrymthusars, Joten, Hüsses, Trolls, Trolde Cyclopes, Ogres, Kokas . . . When the new ages ground, polished, withered, and gentled the natural raw state to prepare for the Age of Man, the Giants, vanquished after a rebellion, adapted to nature by shrinking. Since then, they would live for a long time, becoming—through magical powers stolen from the divinities—Dwarfs, Elves, Fairies, Sylphs, Goblins, Undines, Dews, demigods, elemental spirits, or heroes. Their physical appearance changed according to the tendency of their species and types: they changed into

trees, fire, rocks, beasts, wind or often into a knight or a sorcerer among humans. Some regained their height owing to various reasons of heart and soul."

The text by an anonymous eleventh-century Englishman (in *Aelfsidem*, translated and annotated by W. T. Dodgsons Luchtat, 1334, Meinster p. 526) can easily explain unnerving wonders incomprehensible to our limited rationalism, such as a Goblin metamorphosing into a horse, Trolls decompressing into Forest Dwarfs, a Dwarf-Giant, a Giant-Dwarf, a female Dwarf mating with a Giant, and Giants seducing slender princesses! In Saxo Grammaticus's *Gesta Danorum*, Harthgrepa the Colossus salaciously whispers to a being smaller than she: "Twice blessed: my great size will frighten the brave, and your small size will attract the caresses of men." The *Aelfsidem* later notes that "the Original Ones, whom the ancient English grouped under the general name of Fairies, Fairy Beings, or Little People, and the French more vulgarly and inexactly called Lutins, be they gentle Sidhe, pale Alfs, Pixies of the moors, Boggart of the

dust, Kouril of Britannia Minor, or far-off Akkas. All are issue of a similar flesh, of a unique seed, of a kindred soul. From the first Alf to the last descendant of the Pillywiggin line, despite the chaos, the disruptions, the genocides, the persecutions, and the most unbelievable mixtures, nothing has yet degenerated {the text dates from the sixteenth century}, because all are brothers or offspring of those who rubbed elbows with the gods."

Therefore, the Dwarf is an ancient Giant, rival of the gods. Despite his smallness, he has retained his powers, his supernatural strengths. He is practically invulnerable, immensely rich, a skilled blacksmith and metalworker. A powerful weathermaker, he controls the elements. He protects or decimates and destroys livestock and plants. Familiar with the buttes, the cairns, the subterranean worlds, he has links to the dead, perhaps demons. A passionate lover, irascible and formidable, he has deliberately chosen to shrivel up, to distort himself, and to diminish to the point of vanishing—all in order to "fool" the newcomer: man. Is this why man—who will never cease to overtake, to destroy, then to deny the very existence of Dwarfs—has described them etymologically as a false midget, deformed, dark, and evil?

And what of the Elves? . . .

"The Elfs are Snarks who will not be blamed."[2]

1. The indispensable *Fantômes et Revenants au Moyen Age, Les Nains et les Elfs au Moyen Age,* (Paris: Ed. Imago, 1988) and *Les Monstres dans la littérature allemande au Moyen Age,* 3 vol. (Goppingen, Kummerle Verlag, 1982).
2. Message written in chalk, in the large handwriting of a novice, found on the door of the desk of Reverend Charles Dodgson in Christchurch, and erased almost immediately by Mr. Heaphy on Tuesday, 9 October 1888. Extract from the *Diary of Little A.L.* inserted into the files of "Jack the Ripper," File R. 7, eta. 4., closed by order of Watson, Sirius, Pemberton.

CREATURES OF THE EARTH AND THE CAVERNS

I have often been the discreet host of the border regions.

—Cassilde Tournebize

Let us descend with our geologist guides along the forked branches of underground passages; let us breach the stone gates etched with fossil spirals from Time Immemorial. Let us mine through the ages, petrified layers of earth, where a spirit materializes from an ancient memory. Let us enter the heart of a cosmos hewn into the matrix of the Earth itself in order to understand the metaphysics of its depths.

Like the spreading branches of a giant tree, the path splits and arcs into a labyrinth of rows and colors—a rosette of tunnels carved with ancient signs. Let us lose ourselves there in the grid of myriad honeycombed caves, crypts, and cells leading towards distant regions peopled with underground beings.

HEIGHT:

Twenty-six inches (66 cm).

APPEARANCE:

Beings of clay, of the subterranean waters, and of iron and ores, as revealed by their Appearance: eyes of coal or diamonds, a pasty complexion with mineral scabs, wrinkles resembling hollows emphasizing the bubbly, gay or intense personality of a face bounded by hair and thick iron-gray side-whiskers. Large ears that stick out. Robust body with gnarled limbs, calloused and skillful hands, and webbed feet.

CLOTHING:

Shirts, coats, overblouses, tunics, frock coats, breeches of flax, silk wool, and velour; thick velvet, and frill and lace skirts for the ladies; caps, hats, and leather overalls for the men. They like browns and grays.

Quiet Folk
and Stille Volk

A being that is joined with the subterranean powers. By dreaming of them, one harmonizes with the irrationality of the depths.

—Gaston Bachelard,
The Poetics of Space

Crack, bam, bam, crack! The world below resounds with noisy activity, echoing through molehills, crevasses, mountain shafts, hills, buttes—even houses suddenly leap at the shock of an underground explosion rocking their foundations! After all, the work will not cease just because the men above had the damnable idea of building hamlets and villages right on top of the quarries and forges of the Middle Kingdom. There were so many other places available, and yet men were so bold as to shatter heads and ears, to shake all the buildings of the hidden city, and to pollute the atmosphere with the most revolting wastes.

Stille Volk and Quiet Folk, peaceful and industrious Dwarfs of the Bergfolk race, do not hesitate to be extremely rowdy, even late at night. What does it matter what time it is, if it is day or night, for these dwellers of darkness not governed by the sun?

Wham, bam, crack, smack! The obstinate crowd trots, crawls, and bends to the task. There are hundreds of them in the mine, at the forge, limping on their short web-footed legs, their shadows lit by the dancing flames of the braziers. Merry, their faces split by ear-to-ear grins, they buzz, singing, around the red-hatted crew leaders. They excavate, dig, drill, saw, hew, push carts, feed the fires, work the bellows, cast and beat iron, hammer, forge, temper, harden, hone . . . During the breaks announced by trumpets, they stop and gaily gather in a circle, taking their lunches from their satchels.

The Stille Volk detest idleness. They work for themselves, but also for the neighboring Sidhe, Sith, and Huldres: the

Mound Folk, the subterranean Elves for whom they forge arms, breastplates, sumptuous jewelry, crowns, and golden armor. They also accept orders from humans with whom they have cordial relations.

It is considered a great pleasure to be invited into human homes and to be allowed to borrow beautiful dining sets for celebrating weddings and banquets. In return, the Stille Volk will readily distribute sacks full of gold, diamonds, rubies, and other precious stones taken from deposits only known to them.

Every one of the small attentions paid to them will be amply rewarded. A well-informed man who is smart enough to choose one as the godfather of his child may be assured that his infant will always be rich, in good health, and endowed with every talent. The Guarchelles of Wales, the Yarthkins of northern England, and the small Djambos of Borinage are the most reluctant to venture into the reality of daylight "where the sun lays bare the prosaic quality of things. They prefer to 'sink' even further into the primordial unfathomable shadows, and, seated on the edge of a chasm, dream while listening to the harmonic dark tones of the Musica Reservata."

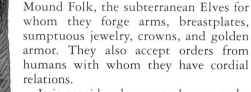

HABITAT:

Middle Earth is divided into two important kingdoms: Erdluitle on one side, encompassing the Bergfolk, Ederweibchen, Bergmanlin, the peaceful Stille Volk and Quiet Folk, and the Little Miners, Nicolins, or Earth Dwarfs; on the other side the chthonic Elf people of the Mound Folk encompass the Bienveillants, Bons Voisins, People of Peace, People of Daoine Sidhe, Sith, Huldres (certain offspring, crossbred from the Thurses, become Trolls on contact with sunlight). The Trpaslik are the Little Miners of the Eastern Mountains.

FOOD:

The Stille Volk women are fine cooks and do particularly well with tasty spice bread sold at the "goblin market" on Saint Eloi's Day.

BEHAVIOR:

The Stille Volk are industrious, inventive, and benevolent. They know all the material and spiritual resources of the earth. They are immensely rich, but miserly, and they gladly accept the help of humans on the condition that the latter never pronounce the word "church" in their presence, never beat a drum, and never ring bells near the entrance of their abodes. They are less and less tolerant of the noise of cities and the proliferation of trash.

The Pidimuzik, engendered when a comet strikes the earth, are crazy!

ACTIVITIES:

Miners and blacksmiths, they are also herbalists, concocters of an innumerable variety of philters and magic powders, and they treat themselves with the help of selected stones they place on injured spots.

HEIGHT:
Fourteen inches (36 cm).

APPEARANCE:
Pockmarked. Very long, dirty body hair which they purposely drag in the milk. Skinny legs. Deep voice. The women do not lack charm.

CLOTHING:
Although they prefer to go naked inside their dens, the Wichtlein show themselves to humans dressed in red jackets and stockings, coal hats perched on the edge of their pointy heads. Their wives wear very tall headdresses made of lace. Out for a stroll, they always carry a metal-tipped club that can, from a distance, put snakes, foxes, badgers, and feral cats to sleep.

The Wichtlein

3 knocks, it is a Knocker!
24 knocks, it is a Wichtlein!
— Mass. W. Hertzbrudre,
The Anvil of the Gods,
Magdebourg, 1802

In contrast to the Knocker, the unceasing digging of this south German Rapper is not meant to guide miners to rich deposits, but to break down the foundations, stays, and buttresses and bring passages crumbling down on their heads. It is true that the Wichtlein warn miners of these catastrophes, which they themselves cause, by imitating the bang of an explosion, but they only do so when there is no one left alive!

Strangely, they are often classed with household and domestic Dwarfs. Perhaps this is because after leaving the humid quarries they settled in the cellars of houses, living at man's expense and tormenting him in every possible way: sticking a cow's tail on his rear end or a pig's ear on his forehead during the night, overturning beds and crockery, undermining the house's foundation to bring it down! They are very like the Putzen, who are veritable plagues on peaceful houses.

The Fanfrelons

The Fanfrelons were dressed in red like English soldiers and they wore red and yellow scarves knotted around their heads. The strangest thing was that they were almost the same height as humans, but they looked more like dwarfs and could only be dwarfs.
—Wirt Sikes, *The Goblins of England*

The Fanfrelons are insane Knockers; they struggle to excavate, dig, and turn over entire mountains without ever removing the smallest particle from the most evi-

dent and richest lodes. When a gold nugget accidentally falls into their hands, they immediately go to the nearest pub to drink, dance, and fornicate as much as they can. Even the most gouty and toothless Welsh hags fear the "raids" of the Fanfrelons.

The Telchines

The Greek Telchines, or black Telchynes, are sorcerer Knockers and blacksmiths for the gods of Olympus, for whom they forged the first bronze statues and legendary tools like Poseidon's trident and Chronos's scythe. Their knowledge of magic allows them to transform themselves into monsters, humans, fish, birds, and insects—and to command the demons of fire.

They live inside volcanoes, and they work with their bare hands, handling the lava and beating the metal with their fists. It was a Telchine captured by the Canaanites who cast the hideous sacrificial statue of Moloch. They are responsible for many volcanic eruptions, but they are not fire spirits.

The Cabires

These creatures are the link between the spirits of earth and of fire. They are ruddy, heavyset Dwarfs armed with hammers and honored in Asia Minor, Phoenicia, and Egypt. Their origins are lost in Elfin memory, but according to Sophus Oehlenschläger (*Elverskud*), they are "a sort of divine hybrid of the blood and sperm of Knockers, Incubi, Koboldes, Gnomes, and the son of Cyclops cleverly combined to guard, exploit, and sort out the soft and fertile stones of Chaos."

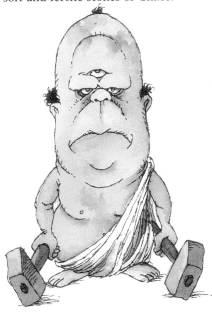

The Bergleutes

These beings first appeared in the diamond mines of Germany around the sixteenth century. They do not mix with other Miner-Dwarfs, but live communally in tiny hidden thatched cottages in the forest at the foot of the mountain where they work. Cheerful and generous to the weak and the unfortunate, they take in wounded animals, starving vagabonds, and lost children. It is now recognized that the Bergleutes were the "Dwarfs" who sheltered Snow White.

The Knockers

Knock, Knocker, knock
The singing crystal of pale rock,
The black rosettes of the ferns of coal . . .
Under the tomb of Chaw Gully.
　　　　　　　　—*The Ring of Selma*

Ancient tales have it that good spirits of the mine called Solilubki protect the treasure of salt against the savage waters and warn miners of imminent danger. They also decorate the gray rocks with a white patina of salt to make the miners' stay inside the dark tunnels more agreeable. This tribe of Dwarfs has a queen, a charming lady named Bieliczka. She lives in an underground palace made of the most beautiful salt crystals and never grows old (Julian Majka, *Wieliczka*, Krakow).

The Polish Solilubki are Knockers—just like the Welsh Coblynau, the Nickel, the Austrian Schacht Zwergen, the German Berg-Monche and Meister Hammerling (Master Hammer), the Scottish Back Dwarfs, the French Gommes and Petit Minou—a species of Rapper, who should not be confused with the racket-making Rapping Spirits: Poltersprites, Poltergeist, Tapageurs.

The Knocker is a Dwarf of the mines and quarries. Lucky and attentive miners may perceive the musical sound of their picks and axes at the bottom of the tunnels and shafts as they hammer the rock faces in search of valuable lodes. The Knocker, who was born along with the ores, knows the richest lodes like the back of his hand, and in return for a small offering (a bit of food, a slice of bread, a small mirror, some cheap jewelry for his coquettish wife), he will make tinkling noises to guide his human "miner brothers" to the best spots.

When they "sense" a catastrophe, such as a firedamp explosion, through their amazing instincts, the Knockers begin to shout, blow horns, and rap with all their might. Many "black faces" and prospectors of gold, silver, and copper have escaped being suffocated or crushed by cave-ins by taking the Knockers' warnings seriously.

The Knocker is obliging but sensitive; if you forget just once to compensate him, however humbly, or if you swear, whistle, fight, or disturb the peace of his silent kingdom, the response will be quick: the guilty party will be drawn into a narrow tunnel and risks being buried alive. But a Knocker is also loyal: if a miner who has become a friend is about to die, he will warn family, friends, and neighbors by "rapping out a death knell" under their houses and will not stop his funereal accompaniment until the dying person passes on.

HEIGHT:
　　Twenty-four inches (60 cm).

APPEARANCE:
　　The Knockers have all the traits of Dwarfs. Thin, dark body, stringy and dried-up but muscular limbs, strong and hard as steel. Large, gnarled, calloused hands and feet. Piercing, nearly white eyes. Abundant body hair. The females are very beautiful, like all the subterranean Dwarf females.

　　Certain trapper and miner Knockers sometimes appear different. Those from Thessaly have copper heads; others have diamond, quartz, or iron heads. In Rubli, the Gommes take the form of meteors when they visit their brother Rappers on another mountain.

CLOTHING:
　　Rags that Gnomes and Wichtlein no longer use. Also a long leather apron and a kind of studded helmet reinforced at the nose and the nape.

HABITAT:
　　All working or abandoned quarries and mines: coal, salt, diamond . . . all the ores.

FOOD:
　　They eat what they are given. The Knockers are restrained. Their only vices are crepes and sweet waffles.

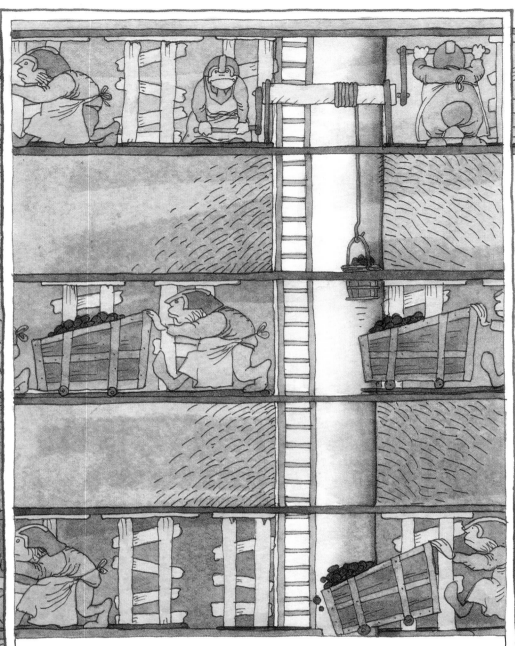

BEHAVIOR/ACTIVITIES:
The Knockers live in tribes. Each Knocker has two wives: one elderly, another younger. They have only two children, whom they abandon in the deepest mines for thirty years to toughen them. The Knockers live so long as to be almost immortal, but eventually they crumble into the dust of the ore of the mine that sheltered them.

They are friends of the Wichtlein and the Brownies who sometimes visit underground. They detest the Kobolds and the Anneberg, a demon from the mines of Germany with an immense neck who hunts them down through the labyrinths of the tunnels, and Loki, the Scandinavian demon of earthquakes. They also fight the Sitich (wicked Welsh Kobolds) who encourage the brave coal miners of southern Wales to spend all their pay in the pubs of Cardiff.

There are some renegade Knockers:

The Buccas and Bockles: These belong more to the category of Poltersprites . . .

The Rock Cracker: Ousted from his tribe of quarry Rappers for an unknown sin, he is solitary and spends his nights slamming a sledgehammer against stones bleached by moonlight around Penanru, near Morlaix.

Little Father Bidou: A Knocker crossbred from a Flemish Kobold, he is the crafty hero in the woefully underappreciated masterpiece by Charles Denlin, *The Tales of a Beer-Drinker*. It would be good sometimes for academics to come down from their ivory towers and take a tour of the carillons and belfries of the low countries, even if the once-bold Flemings have sold out their Giants and Gayant for a weak and flabby Quinquin.

The Kinnaras: These noble Knockers from the forest of Laka in India protect the subterranean resources but leave the trouble of extracting them to the inferior Dwarfs.

The Cluricaune

Yesterday I stopped in a broad place on the road to Kilkartan to listen to Irish songs.
—W.B. Yeats, *The Celtic Twilight*

HEIGHT:
Approximately twelve inches (30 cm).

APPEARANCE:
Tubby and paunchy. Florid face, spotted nose. Eyes vacant or gleaming with a rather twisted mischievousness. Hairy, with a long beard. Long, broad, and flat feet. The American Cluricaunes are more robust, bronzed, with strong limbs.

CLOTHING:
A hat adorned with a buckle. A gray cape over a vest, loose breeches, and stone-gray wool stockings. The American Cluricaunes are distinguished by black pilgrim hats and very stiff brownish topcoats, buttoned under their chins and embellished with white bands; they may also dress "mountain-man style" with skin tunics, leather stockings, and colorful scarves on their heads. They are always armed with cutlasses.

HABITAT:
The cellars, or more precisely, the casks of the houses, pubs, and inns of Ireland, from Kerry to Donegal, from Mizen Head to Malin Head (John Ford, John Wayne, and Victor McLaglen saw masses of them leaving the bars of Cong during the filming of The Quiet Man*), and, of course, the caverns of Kentucky.*

FOOD:
They have small appetites, so whiskey, along with a grilled mouse, a bit of cheese, and a crust of bread suffice to satisfy the "Sedentary One." In contrast, the "Adventurer" likes to eat and cures fish and game, treating himself to buttered grog with gunpowder. We must not forget that they built the first bourbon distillery.

The Cluricaune is a subterranean Dwarf and a distant cousin of the Gnomes.

At the end of the Golden Age, when the Elfin people began to fade into invisibility or to mingle with humans, the Cluricaunes left their enchanted caves to take up housekeeping in the cellars of inns and to become "household and domestic dwarfs." In exchange for this human hospitality, they revealed the secret of whiskey, already confided to the Brownies of Scotland.

In 1620, a colony of Cluricaunes, homesick for the green valleys of their lost paradise, secretly embarked in the bilges of ships leaving for the virgin prairies of America. Some joined the long lines of covered wagons; others forged an alliance with the Puckwudgies and mated with a race of "demon-pygmies" that Lewis and Clark, in their *Travels to the Source of the Missouri River*, located on a hill near the Whitestone River that the Sioux called "The Mountain of Little People." It must be noted that most of these immigrants turned wicked.

Allying themselves with previously arrived Red Caps, Dutch Nickapacks, and Kabouters, they threw themselves into alcohol trafficking and piracy along the Ohio River, on the Red Banks wagon trail, and along the Natchez Trace to Shawneetown. The underground Cluricaunes are good and merry sprites who do not disdain the boozing company of humans. Their favorite pranks are tripping up café waiters, blowing fuses, and drawing Guinness behind their backs. They are essentially lazy and spend hours sleeping off their excesses and dreaming of olden times. The Kentuckian variety is a true plague, sly and cruel. The reign of the Cluricaunes of Kentucky did not end until 1775, when the celebrated and no less bloodthirsty Samuel Mason expelled them from Cave-in-the-Rock in order to settle there himself, as is well known.

However, we must not damn the whole line, since it is true that many immigrants did not follow in the footsteps of the "outlaws," but married decent native women, founding respectable families that live today in the foundations of the best American bars. Like the Leprechauns, they know innumerable songs and, if invited, will perform a thousand services around the house: cleaning the cellar, brewing beer, telling stories, looking after and cradling children, and putting them to bed. (Rip Van Winkle met Cluricaunes and Kabouters on the mountain.)

The Leprechaun

Brother of the Cluricaunes, with whom they are often confused, Leprechauns are the most popular and best-loved of the Little People in all of Ireland. People open the cat flap for them and leave milk on the windowsill. Leprechaun figurines are found in every souvenir shop, and one opens Saint Patrick's Day parades among Irish-Americans . . . although the American strain does not always have a lighthearted personality.

Guardian of the buried riches of Thuatha De Danaan and of Elfin treasures and cobbler to the Sidhe and the Little People, the Leprechaun is incapable of finishing work at human request and will only repair one shoe of a pair. If you spot one first, he is obliging and will regale you with pretty stories, lovely songs (his repertoire is inexhaustible), and excellent beer—and may even slip you a purse full of gold. But watch out if he sees you first, since these fellows can be dangerous and transform you into whatever they wish or transport you to wherever they please.

To avoid trouble, Leprechauns should be approached politely and offered a pinch of snuff or a handful of MacQuaid for the long clay pipe stuck in the band of their hats.

Brilliant violinists, they taught the great Irish musicians how to handle a bow. Nowadays, we do not know if the Sidhe or the Leprechauns invented hockey, but the Leprechauns are hurling virtuosos who can play blindfolded. They may, indeed, cheat, but it is best not to point this out.

The Lurikeen

The Lurikeens are wandering Cluricaunes, eternally regretting Paradise Lost. Descendants of the great bards of the Golden Age, they are the pathetic offshoot of the legendary era and the new ages, the jarring note of the violin bow, the decayed teeth of a singer from Pogues, the household spirit of tinkers and Gypsies. Elves of misery, famine, and defeat, they are melancholy and mad and proffer endless speeches in the strange Shelta tongue. When they sing and pluck strings stretched across a crate, all grows quiet, and the tar on the streets swells and splits as if to allow the reemergence of the glass cupolas of engulfed cities.

APPEARANCE:
Rather thin and dry, Leprechauns are very strong and can knock out a steer with a blow or with a swipe of their trusty hammers. Long and red or very bulbous nose. Tanned face, long hair, and sly eyes.

CLOTHING:
Tricorn hat. Green jacket adorned with thick copper buttons. Green breeches, stockings, and vest. Leather apron. Shoes with a silver buckle. Plaid handkerchief sticking out of their pockets.

HABITAT:
They are now found in all the counties and small islands of Ireland, but they first emerged on a mountainside in Ben Bulben. They build their comfortable and neatly laid out dwellings in the shelter of hedges or of upturned stones on banks planted with trees, whose roots serve as the frame. There they stitch, nail, and work, warmed by the rays of the sun that filter through the skylights hollowed out of the trunks.

FOOD:
Gourmands, they often gripe about Irish cuisine, since they detest potatoes. They make herbed soda bread, meat, mushroom and fruit pies, and delicious stews.

BEHAVIOR/ACTIVITIES:
Aside from their trade as more or less competent cobblers, the wily Leprechauns take pleasure in mocking the greedy and attracting thieves to traps from which they will never escape. They mark the hiding places of their pots and cauldrons of gold with rainbows that they constantly shift and move.

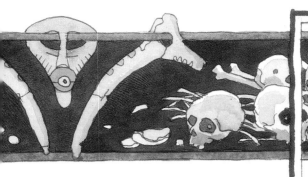

The Bone-Crunchers

Crack, crunch, munch . . . What are those strident, sinister sounds emanating from behind the walls of the cemetery, frightening the passersby? It is a Bone-Cruncher feeding! The Bone-Crunchers are truly repugnant Dwarfs of the night, horrors haunting the darkness and sowing fear: midget bogeymen, scarecrows. Even during the great era preceding the present age, the era when animals talked and when Elves and Fairies, dragons and sorcerers still lived, they were already deformed, ugly, cruel, appalling. They were the gravediggers of the battlefield. Taking pride of place over Harpies, Ghouls, vultures, and hyenas, a Bone-Cruncher was the first to fly over the charnel house, mounted on a screech owl.

At that time, they were very powerful, and Goblins and Fairies dreaded the armies of these carrion eaters who haunted the burning heavens during the nights of war, falling on the cadavers with a rustling of wings and the cawing of the mobs of crows that followed them, finishing off the wounded with their clubs, tearing off armor, opening helmets to pluck the still-fresh eyes and to feast on the tongue, ripping coats of mail, sinking their teeth into pulsating flesh, pulling out steaming entrails, picking clean the skeletons, crushing the bones, sucking the marrow. The hungry who demanded part of the bloody loot were driven away with blows of the sword. They thrived during famines and plagues, haunted the gallows and pillories of execution grounds, and often attacked and carried off to their lairs lone Nymphs, Elves, and Follets. Building their nauseating cities on the slopes of cliffs and the most inaccessible ridges, they drove away assailants by throwing streams of sulfurous pitch on them.

With the advent of man, the Bone-Crunchers, like many other Goblin and Fairy races, disappeared beneath the ground of cemeteries.

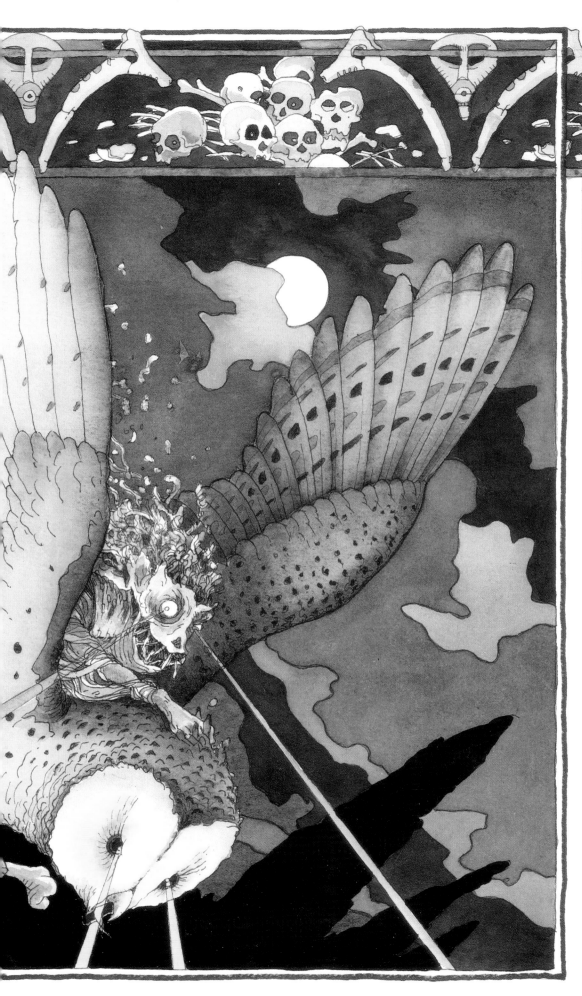

HEIGHT:
Twenty-six inches (66 cm).

APPEARANCE:
Repulsive, pallid, hairy. One hand is in the shape of a spatula for digging; the other strong hand is for breaking things. Impressive jaws. Emits a pestilential stench.

CLOTHING:
Scraps of patched armor stolen from corpses.

HABITAT:
Subterranean hollows under cemeteries, especially in the French Ardennes, Ireland, and Bavaria.

FOOD:
Leaves nothing from either fresh or fleshless cadavers.

BEHAVIOR:
A degenerate race that is disappearing. There are not enough females to perpetuate the species.

ACTIVITIES:
Excavate endless tunnels linking many cemeteries, sometimes up to a distance of sixty miles. Hunt moles to tan the skin into delicate parchment on which are written the history and the legends of their people, beautifully illustrated with the help of crushed roots lopped off at the surface. The Bone-Crunchers also trap vipers and make a heady alcohol from the venom.

Gnomes

HEIGHT:
One foot (30 cm). They can shrink in order to edge through the narrowest crevices. Enormous Gnomes of around forty inches (1 m) in height are seen in the Carpathians, in the Ukraine, and near Tschirnau in Bohemia.

APPEARANCE:
Muscular and gnarled, with broad shoulders. A large head, very lumpy forehead. Hair and beard as thick as iron filings. A very dark skin, almost as "black as tar." Eyes that are both piercing and dreamy. Because of crossbreeding with evil spirits, the Gnomes have changed in appearance to reveal their character: nosy Gnomes have six extra pairs of eyes; the greedy, four mouths; and the quick, eight feet.

"The female, the Gnomide, is even smaller, admirably beautiful, superbly dressed, walks in silence; you hear nothing other than the whisper of her slippers, one in emerald and the other in ruby."

CLOTHING:
A hood and a tough leather tailcoat adorned with precious stones.

Little mother, the Gnomes hardly love you.
Little father, the Gnomes do not love you.
Little Pidozka, the Gnomes do not love you anymore.

—Old Ukrainian song

Much has been said about Gnomes in stories that are still told, but there is yet more to tell. Like the French "Lutin," "Gnome" is the name that comes to mind for the classic Dwarf—bearded and wearing a pointy hat. This is the garden Dwarf or the Swiss chalet Dwarf, pushing a wheelbarrow, astride a deer, imprisoned in a snow globe. The little "Carabostron" hunchback trotting through picture books is identified as a Gnome. He is the irascible midget with his beard wedged in the trunk of a tree from which he will be freed by Snow White and Rose Red. It is with Gnomes, lantern in hand and in single file, that pretty decorations are made along the alpine peaks. He is placed on the Yule log; he sits on red mushrooms with white polka dots. He is the only Dwarf in primers, the only object that a writer ignorant of *Fairy Species* can pull from his poor bag of tricks. He is boon companion to the substitutes of Perlimpinpin or the miserly mountain Gnome with pieces of gold! Sometimes good, often nasty, innocent or sly, always "deceitful"!

In short, the illustrations of legends generally show the French Lutin as a mischievous, nimble, young, and smiling Green Dwarf of the forests, while the Gnome is the old, deformed, ugly, and bearded Dwarf of the mines and mountains.

Everything small is gnomish. The puny kid at recess is called a gnome, as is the deformed, sickly, scrofulous, overbearing, mangy grown-up! Sometimes they are considered mean or nasty gnomes: "But what on earth is that gnome there?"

Is this any way to speak of the famous and powerful Genies of the Earth?

Philippus Aureolus Theophrastus Bombatus von Hohenheim (1493–1541), called Paracelsus, in the first tentative human effort to classify the beings of the Fairy World (*Liber de Nymphis, Sylphis, Pygmoeis et Salamandris et coeteris spiritibus*, Basel, 1590), makes the mistake of designating Gnomes as "the" earth spirits that, along with Pygmies, Dactyles, Goetes, Monacielli, Sôtés, Kabouters, Wichtlein, Kobolds, and Knockers, are no more than a branch of the main tree of black Alfs and Dwarfs. The Gnomes are a special, very complex species from the manifold empire of the subterranean Genies. "The natural philosopher Paracelsus used the terms Sylphs, Undines, Salamanders and Gnomes because these terms were known to the public," says Heinrich Heine (*Elementary Spirits*). He adopted them, even though they do not quite represent his ideas. Let us likewise be careful to not be misled down one more of those obvious false trails.

As invoked by Jewish cabalists, the belief in Gnomes seems to have been introduced to Europe from the Orient, along with Pythagorean philosophy, at the beginning of the sixteenth century by Jean Pic de la Mirandole, Marsile Ficin, Girolamo Cardan, Johannes Reuchlin, and, of course, Paracelsus. The name "Gnome" is completely absent from Greek and Germanic mythology, and supposedly comes from a mistranslation that confuses the Low Latin *gnomus* and the Greek *gignosko* (to experience, to know), indicating their gift of foresight. It has also been suggested (Brian Froud and Allan Lee) that "Gnome" comes from *yevouos,* meaning "from the earth." In Germany, the word *gnomen* was borrowed in the thirteenth century from France, oddly enough a country where no Gnomes existed. Since the eleventh century, the mountain dwellers of the Balkans have avoided the quarries exploited by *gnomas* (*Neptunu*s, Vrieslander).

The last word seems to belong to Petrus Barbygère: "*Gnome* is a contraction of three words in their own language: *guwiyau*, meaning 'guardian,' 'watchman,' and also 'visionary'; *gwiaul*, 'brilliant' or 'luminous'; and *nhôm*, 'good.'"

In the cabala, the Gnome, although mischievous, is benevolent. He knows the

secrets of the earth; he brings to life the plants and animals, who would wither and die without him. In contrast, demonologists very quickly treated him as a henchman of Satan, a lower demon whose main characteristic is cruelty: "They are akin to the Foul Fiend, just like the Sylphs are akin to the Angels." Karl Grün mistakenly thought that Caliban was a Gnome: "Shakespeare popularized an atrocious Gnome by the name of Caliban. In *The Tempest*, he puts a part-human, part-sea-cow monster on stage." Caliban is an Incubus, spawn of the devil and the sorceress Sycorax, and a worshipper of the horned Setebos, gods of the Patagons.

What is known for certain is that it was not until the second century of the great Alfic partition that many Allyens (clans) ventured out of the depths into the light of day. Dazzled and disoriented, they settled in the cool, shady caves of mountains, mines, hollows, and the vast forests of Russia.

It took less than one hundred years for these new industrious and obliging Gnomes, who had earlier been benevolent towards humans, to form an alliance with demons and turn against man.

The Russian Gnomes are the most formidable and powerful. Their king, whom the Ukrainians call Vij, strikes down his enemies with a glance. Nikolai Gogol described him as a "stocky being, strong, clumsy. He was completely smeared with black earth. His hands and feet, covered with earth, were like strong roots grooved with thick veins. His gait was ponderous and he stumbled constantly. His long eyelids reached the ground. His face was iron."

In India, the Arbhas are very skilled Gnomes to whom the upper gods have assigned the most delicate tasks and work. Their Yakschas guard the treasures hidden in the mountains.

The Kaukas of Lithuania love fresh flesh.

The Dhoërs live in cellars in the old quarters of Prague and are skilled alchemists.

The Dactyles (from the Greek for "finger") are divided into two types: the Good, who are jewelers and adepts of magicians and physicians of Cybele, and the Evil, who are allies of the Phrygian demons.

The Goètes are evil Gnomes who forged bewitched iron shoes and led their victims in an exhausting fatal saraband. "Long, long after the Goètes had disappeared, their shoes still walked the streets" (Anonymous).

HABITAT:

They live in clans in spacious and well-kept caves in the mines and on the peaks of Germany, Bavaria, Poland, Flanders, Russia, and the uninhabited regions of the northern hemisphere. A race of Gnomes, the Schroettelis, still survives in the Swiss mountains. Even though Elizabeth Goudge often mentions them (The Singing Valley, The Smoky House)*, Gnomes do not exist in England any more than they do in France. In 1911 W. Y. Evans Wentz* (The Fairy-Faith in Celtic Countries) *discovered a family living in Ireland.*

FOOD:

Gnomes raise goats for milk and meat. They make cakes flavored with lichen and cave plants. They cultivate mushrooms and use grafting to produce particularly tasty giant species.

BEHAVIOR/ACTIVITIES:

In olden times, many artisan Allyens worked metal and precious stones, polishing and sketching out the work that the master metalworker Dwarfs would then finish.

Gnomes have the gift of penetrating the soul of both living and inanimate creatures: flora, fauna, and Fairy creatures, as well as the cosmos. They have often been asked about their "art of mind-reading."

They have long helped men, giving them formulae, secret magic, and ways to exploit subterranean resources.

HEIGHT:
*From five to twenty-four inches
(12 to 60 cm).*

APPEARANCE:
*Red-faced, chubby, chunky, plump,
potbellied, and short-legged. With a
triple chin, a big snub nose, a smooth
face, a cheerful slit of a mouth, lively
eyes with dark circles under them, and
a bald head.*

CLOTHING:
*A tailcoat and a monk's hood—both
red—like the sandals and the round,
flat bishop's hat they wear on rainy
days.*

HABITAT:
*Monacielli are squatters in beautiful
ancient dwellings, where they are so
rowdy that no one dares enter, but they
must spend three hundred days a year
near the treasure in the caverns and
caves. For the remaining sixty-five
days they invade all of Italy, Greece,
Sardinia, and sometimes Switzerland.*

FOOD:
*They greedily stuff themselves with
anything from polenta to meat. Love
wine and liqueurs. Despise pale and
anemic vegetables.*

The Monaciello
and the Guardians
of Treasure

*Nature has enfolded gold and precious stones in
the deepest hiding places of the Earth.*
—Erasmus

The depths of the Earth overflow with treasures: golden calves, golden goats, chickens and hatchlings of gold, barrels of gold, coffers of coins, jars of silver, stones, jewels, carbuncles, pearls, coral, and crowns. They are found at the bottom of caves, cliffs, mountains, chasms, and rivers; hidden in the deep; under cairns, standing stones, fairy chimneys, rocks, ruins of spitefully haunted castles, and monasteries—even more frighteningly haunted! There are even places where one has only to bend down to pick up riches—at least that is what quite a few reckless people have said before disappearing. It is not enough to find the spot, strike with spade or pick, and help yourself: you must also know all the secrets and tricks of the guardians.

Those who wish to venture forth must first relearn saintliness—understood as a soul of innocence, the eyes of a child—and let themselves be guided by instinct and the direction of the wind. Nonetheless, it is helpful to know that a likely place to look is where the grass grows greener and thicker, where the mosses and St.-John's-wort abound, or where gossamer threads form a rainbow, and the White Ladies and the Fairies stop to chat about clothes. The sounds of bells, the insistent chirping of crickets, the babbling of a brook, or strange voices could all lead one to favorable paths. But that is not enough. The invisible doors must still be opened. It is said that the inscriptions and the designs carved on the stone indicate the path to follow—but to decipher the message, it is necessary to understand the language and writing of The Others.

You should be aware that a seeker of the treasures of Dwarfs, Elves, and Fairies is exposed to inconveniences, risks, and dangers—unless he is chosen or born lucky, or an amulet protects him. Otherwise, it will be difficult . . . And above all, he must confront the guardians. Nevertheless, it is well worth the risk. In the end you can lay hands on the riches of the wrecker Sorgues, Tan Noz, and Tud-Gommon; here are stacked the marvelous timepieces of the Kloks'Tomtes, the gold of giants. But you must first take the keys of fire from between the transparent but

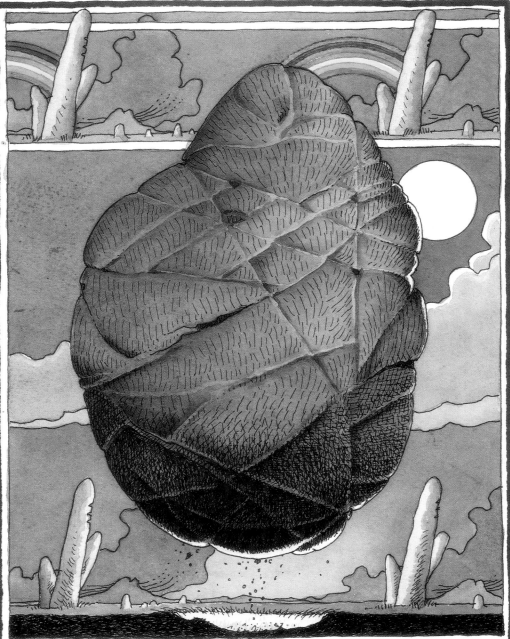

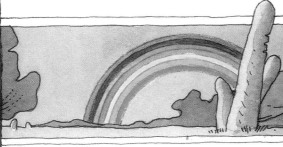

The Neapolitan Monaciello or Manchetto, the Silician Mamucca, and the Calabrian Monachicchio are only monks insofar as dress is concerned. They are noted scoundrels, thieves, imps, bottom-pinchers, and terrors of convents, where they harass the nuns early in the morning, during prayers—and especially at night!

ACTIVITIES:

They guard (badly) the treasures of the Dwarfs and Fairies: The Poulacres, or "little gray monks," watch over the loot left behind by the dead. The Pundacciù are in charge of the gold of the Tomtes. Hâwitz, the "little green monk," protects the property of the mountain Dwarfs. Crispinus is the custodian of the treasures buried by misers. Frosta and Fjalar watch over the hoard of the Nordic hero-gods. Grobelhlon uses a herd of wild boars to guard the Elfin gold of Romande Switzerland.

sharp teeth of the Fairy Milandre or from the claws of the demon Gaziel and overcome the vigilance of the Zwerglacher, the master of Harz, or wait patiently for the right moment . . .

Timing is everything: The white quartz rocks of Pyrome (Deux-Sevres) lift at midnight on Christmas Eve. Jadron's Rock opens on Palm Sunday. When the procession enters the church on Saint John's Day, and the priest says: "Et Homo factus est," the cellar in Robin Castle opens slightly. The wood cairn of Morlhiou remains ajar during the twelve strokes of midnight mass. You must be quick, leap in without hesitating, and pocket as much as possible without thinking, careful not to be overcome by the fever of taking it all. Once the twelve strokes have sounded, the doors close again, the guardians return—and many people have thus left their bones.

Many setbacks, risks, and worries await treasure hunters, unless they capture a Monaciello and steal the red hood that contains his joie de vivre, thus obliging him to open the strongboxes.

The Monaciello, the little monk, is supposed to protect the treasure of the Dwarfs, but he is not a good guardian . . . There are so many other interesting things to do in Italy, besides remaining eternally beneath the dismal spigots of stalactites, benumbing his rear on the uncomfortable edge of a strongbox, however golden.

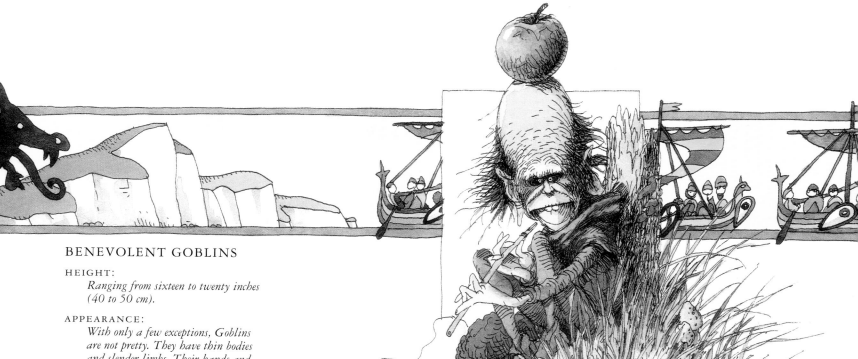

BENEVOLENT GOBLINS

HEIGHT:
Ranging from sixteen to twenty inches (40 to 50 cm).

APPEARANCE:
With only a few exceptions, Goblins are not pretty. They have thin bodies and slender limbs. Their hands and feet are long and bony. They have huge, egg-shaped heads, curved foreheads, and very dirty, prominent cheekbones. Their great mug of a mouth sometimes reveals large rabbit teeth. Their tiny, flat noses protrude out of an apple face. Shiny eyes like ankle-boot buttons align with their long, pointy ears.

CLOTHING:
Goblins' everyday attire consists of green overalls, a brown and rust sort of leotard, and a large gray-blue cap. For the holidays they dress in traditional Goblin garb, the color yellow being the only detail we know.

FOOD:
The same as we people eat, except for meat.

BEHAVIOR:
Benevolent Goblins first appeared in Normandy, France, where everything from water and forest to clouds united to facilitate their development. Goblins, charmed by the white cliffs of lush green Albion, set sail on small Norman craft and Viking vessels to cross the English Channel. Fascinated by life at sea, the Goblins, as the Phoenician Patakoï before them, cleaved to the ships and became the "dwarf divinity of the ship's hold and its decks." Warmly welcomed by the Druids, the Goblins, by whispering a tiny rhyme ("Robert-Robin-Rob-Hob"), became Robin Goblins . . . and then Hobgoblins!

Goblins

*From haunted spring and grassy ring
Troop Goblin, elf and fairy,
And the Kelpie must flit from the black bog-pit,
And the brownie must not tarry.*
— Henry Jenner,
*Glenber of the Gorsedd of
the Bards of Brittany,* 1910

In Scotland, the Goblin carries the image of a shrunken, weakened, long-dead man. But Goblins and men existed side by side all along: they are our shadows! Once a man died, his shadow took possession of his remains, made them come to life, and then lived in them.

For W. Y. Evans-Wentz, the French Goblin was the equivalent of the Pixie of Cornwall, the English Robin Goodfellow, and the Brownies of Scotland. For Albert Doppagne, it is a sort of Boublin, a Bogeyman and mischievous cave-dwelling spirit of the same order as the Drows or Brownies of Scotland, German Kobolds and Trolls, Swiss Servans . . . and, strangely, according to Karl Grün, Scandinavian Elves (spirits of the air), whom he classifies among earth Genies. Dom Lucae nails them down to none other than the doors of hell, like Incubi. Christina Giorgina Rossetti sees them "climbing fire and bog, mines and lakes." The kindy Scheffel takes them up high into the clouds, flanking Fairies and Seraphim.

Even if they are a breed unto themselves, Goblins (Gembelin, Goubelin, Gobin, Goblinus, Gobliniot, Gobino, Hobgoblin), similar to Lutins, Farfadets, Follets, and Nissen, owe their mongrel stock to the ancestral union of Dark and Light Alfs. Deeply influenced by their parents' luminous or gloomy chromosomes, these half-breed offspring—crosses between Dwarf and Elf—were begat during the second quarter of the immigration wave with a singularly complex genealogy that has not ceased to develop through battles, voyages, and degeneracies.

Goblins are certainly a vigorous bunch from the fourth generation after the Golden Age, bringing together a lesser part Elf impregnated with several genes of benevolent spirits of land and forest, but dominated by the negative, nocturnal Bogon, one of the Others, who reproduced abundantly over time until the two opposites separated, never to meet again. The result was two fairly distinct orders of Goblins.

There were two vassalages of Goblins, divided in the fashion that already existed on land and in the heavens: those of the Seelie Court, relaxed and limpid, and those of the shameful Unseelie Court, fat like larvae . . . But the layperson will not be able to distinguish the good ones from the bad, because the latter confound man in the shrewdest of ways. After one hundred years on the Alfic calendar, the two branches were easier to distinguish, as the evil traits of the Dark Goblins became increasingly pronounced. However, three or four hybrid species remain—up to the present day—very difficult to distinguish.

Some malevolent Goblins:

Grascos: The dark Castilian Goblin who hid out in dank dungeons, graveyards, cloisters of cursed monks and bleeding nuns at the time when Walpole, Ann Radcliffe, and Monk Lewis plunged into the sulfuric Gothic and Spanish crypts. Clad in a large red hood, he left deep tracks with his claws on the colored pages of tiny prayer books.

Agnen: The irascible Brazilian Goblin who continually stole sweets and then boiled the blood of those who tricked him into taking pepper instead.

Three-Toothed One: "Badger-Goblin living in the country, with a squat but elongated body whose unsightly skin is covered with warts. He destroys gardens and yards and makes sheep bleed through enormous incisions" (*Strigis, Sirix, Draco,* Dom Eon de Bréchiliant).

Cockeyed One: A Goblin of the moor and wasteland.

The Angry One: A cyclops Goblin of the marsh.

Femming: A cross between a Goblin and a Troll. He frightened the evil mother Raklidz in *Morbacka* by Selma Lagerlöf.

El Trasgu: Spanish vampire-Goblin.

Tause: A cross between a Goblin and the nightmarish Alp (also known as Alb) in Germany.

Zwerglacher: Goblin-demon of the Harz. He travels whichever way the wind blows and harasses hapless passersby who should, with the rap of a cane, send his hat flying to get rid of him.

Jimmy Square-Feet: Not much is known about this brutish, repugnant Goblin, more stupid than dangerous.

On the other hand, the Berstucs, Markropet, and Slavic Coltk are excessively alert and cruel.

The Dark Caraquins live between walls, under floors, in blocked chimneys, and sometimes in cellars.

The Crapoussins and the Nobiots are often confused with the Latusés.

While contemporary, Snunks still have all the ancient and monstrous traits of their ancestors. They haunt subways, parks, and tiny, dark backstreets. They have chosen to set up house in vents, public mailboxes, and garbage cans. The false Goblin of Evreux (a Goblin-demon, according to Collin de Plancy), chased out of town in the sixth century by Saint Turin, took refuge in Caen.

MALEVOLENT GOBLINS

HEIGHT:
Ranging from twenty to twenty-four inches (50 to 60 cm).

APPEARANCE:
These Goblins are swarthy, hairy, and deformed. They are hardened and nervous, composed of re-cooked and smoked devil flesh. They have bumps, points, and claws everywhere. Their small bodies are wrinkled, spindly, and folded over.

CLOTHING:
They love enveloping themselves in dirty, smelly rags.

HABITAT:
Malevolent Goblins live in sewers, dumps, cesspools, and other sickening places. They are also found in cellars, run-down buildings, haunted houses, and leper colonies where crime and vice run rampant.

FOOD:
Spoiled meat and confectioneries.

BEHAVIOR/ACTIVITIES:
In olden days, Goblins enjoyed frightening humans in a thousand different ways and used to disturb them by impish tricks scarcely better than fairy-tale naughtiness compared to the devastating powers of the modern-day Goblins. In contrast to the majority of Alfs, who have fallen by the wayside in modern times and have been consigned to superstition, Goblins have never worried about using electricity or any number of the many modern man-made inventions. Their fusion with Kobolds, through whom they acquired the art of the magical sciences and knowledge of subterranean resources, allowed Goblins—as well as Gremlins (spirits who have invaded machines and Genies of technology)—to compete with men in the race for power . . . and aspire to conquer the world!

Kobolds

One day, on grassy sidewalks, children will again play at Kobolds and Indians...
—*La Genèse future,* Charles Störm

In twelfth-century Germany there was a cult dedicated to the Kobold, in which this small domestic Genie was worshipped in the form of a small statue made of wood and leather. The cult faded, however, and with time, like so many other pagan gods, Kobolds came to be considered as simply a fabled Goblin.

At the dawn of time, Kobolds, Cobale, or Kolfi were "doubles" for the Alfs, sent out from the depths by them as keen observers of the outside world: the universe above. Thanks to Paracelsus, we know that these Dwarfs traveled from one place to another through the ground with as much ease and speed as a bird in the air. Kobolds moved up toward the light while spinning like a top, making holes in different strata of the earth, and were similar to small, upright statuettes fixed in the soil, which came to life when approached.

The Kobolds were a peaceful force and performed and distributed numerous, wondrous gifts and kindnesses in return for information or simply out of a desire for fraternity (Alfs were Love, after all, without hate or malice). It is therefore probable that men considered the Kobolds to be gods and devoted certain rituals to them, such as arranging circles of stones dedicated to their memory and adorning altars where they appeared and where they could be most often found.

Men tried in vain to keep them close by flattery, gifts, and even force! Nevertheless, one day the Kobolds just didn't come back. Sufficiently educated about the world above, the Alfs prepared for the Big Expansion and no longer sent out doubles. The Kobolds disappeared, and mankind felt as abandoned as orphans.

With the Kobolds vanished precious stones, gold, abundant harvests, vast skies, and fertile flocks. Prayers and sacrifices were no help, and so men turned to wizards and witches. It was under these circumstances that the first Kobold dolls appeared, crafted in virgin wax, molded symbolically in the soft part of bread, sculpted in mandrake roots or in the wood of sacred trees. And each man was to take one of these models of "little gods" home to attract a blessed and happy presence to his house. Decorated in the finest clothing and placed carefully inside beautifully crafted boxes, Kobolds were implored every day to come back to life by means of special rites, and these practices lasted for one hundred years.

Finally, during the Alfic metamorphosis, Dvergr, Dwarfs, Gnomes, and Elves separated from one another in search of their own destinies. The lost Kobold Spirits bored away in the earth and felt drawn to these nostalgic calls that reached them from so far away. But what was left up there of their luminous time except for dusty old dolls, as useless as any forgotten toy?

Well, no matter. The Kobolds chose the course to take and never looked back. They found themselves on the threshold of cobwebbed memories, shut like sealed windows. They reentered the lives of men through chimneys, attic windows, and

cat-doors. The dull gaze of the elderly and other humble souls perceived their presence. Even if certain stubborn human masters with too many material worries ignored the Kobolds, the daydreaming grandfather, the shepherd, the wise man, the fool, the servant, and the little boys and girls welcomed the spirits as understanding friends from far away. In exchange for a piece of their heart, a drop of milk, or the last crumbs of a meal, the humans bartered for the Kobolds' services, which would take away difficult tasks and household drudgery. But the Kobolds had lost their appearance and their substance. They were now only bluish vibrations whose physical form had once again been taken by the Alfs. They were "invisible phenomena" who haunted houses by night, creeping into the kitchen to clean it, turn on the water, or put away the dishes. The owners of these "haunted" houses, that is, the upper classes, were crazed, confused them with Poltergeists and other malicious and noisy spirits, and threatened to drive them out of the house!

If they wanted to stay, the Kobolds had no other choice but to find other living bodies as soon as possible. And where could they find one nearby? They could perhaps borrow the wandering souls of accident victims or ghosts of those killed by assassination or by suicide, who prowled inside the walls . . .

Despite their good intentions, this led them to be taken for demons and malevolent Goblins. The situation became so critical that these unfortunate ones, searching earnestly for a solution, only ended up invoking greater human wrath. Forsaking human ghosts, Kobolds tried to inhabit anything that came into their hands: remains of animals, Gnomes, Farfadets, Nutons—and sometimes all at one time! Horror was at its peak; there were shakes of the holy water brush, and the incantations didn't stop! Anything was fair game at "fair" people's houses for the removal of devils! Hemmed in, smoked out, and embittered by this great ingratitude, the Kobolds were determined not to concede one inch of the dwellings they considered theirs and, putting all hope in their magical powers, they turned on humans in droves. The Kobolds were able to use the many, very efficient powers and tricks borrowed from the various species whose identity and exterior they had adopted to further their cause.

Today, Kobolds, completely assimilated with Goblins, Gremlins, and Dark Tomtes, continue their ruthless underground fight, which can—they say—only end in their own triumph.

HEIGHT:
Ranging from sixteen to twenty inches (40 to 50 cm).

APPEARANCE:
In the beginning Kobolds were Alf doubles, luminescent and slightly tinged with blue. Then they had to take on the appearance of the different ghosts they inhabited.

FOOD:
It has been ages since Kobolds were content eating crumbs and meager table scraps. Instead, they gorge themselves on our vital sources of food and water.

HABITAT/BEHAVIOR/ACTIVITIES:
Once upon a time Kobolds reigned in and protected the houses of Germans and other Northern Europeans. Nowadays, they are everywhere . . . and everywhere they are the enemy, with householders trying every means to evict them. The Heinzelmännchen in Cologne, for example, were at once annoyed and enraged as they slid and tumbled over the dried peas that the owners of the house had scattered cunningly all over the stairs.

On the other hand and in an earlier age, the friendly, russet Hutkins, dressed in clean green clothes and with red bonnets, were careful and active servants so much appreciated by families that they were even given a comfortable corner of the attic in which to live and surnames and nicknames by which to be called.

A Haedeken, or Hutkin, (from the German Hütchen, meaning "small hat"), was present in the court of Bishop Bernard d'Hildesheim.

Erdluitle and Infernal Dwarfs

HEIGHT:

About twenty-four inches (60 cm).

APPEARANCE:

These spirits are a mixture of Elves and Dwarfs. Little by little, they have lost their aerial grace the better to burrow and shrink. The Erdluitle have large, heavy heads and features that, contrary to popular belief, are straight and regular. Their high foreheads are set off by a long nose. Their faces contain clear and well-shaped eyes, large ears, white hair swept back off their foreheads, and silver beards. They have long, muscular arms with skillful hands of steel. Their skin is extremely resistant and glows in the dark. Their feet are webbed.

CLOTHING:

The Bergfolk of Denmark wear red coats and blue caps. The Gurivz from Northern Italy, of Bergame and the Aoste Valley, prefer long embroidered black shirts; the Patasson prefer green blouses. The mischievous little women of the country, Erdbibberli, Erdweibchen, or Heidenweibchen, don aprons with multiple flounces. When they go out (which is rare), all of them try to conceal themselves under huge capes to hide their duck feet, because they are quite ashamed of them. They also cover their heads with hoods or huge leather hats.

"In the sky above our heads, there was another land. But the land below objected to the fact that the celestial beings polluted the lower world with their excrement. Therefore, it swapped places with the world of up-above. What had been above was now below, and what had been below was now above." Or that is what is says in the legends of Tobas. The Kajadeh cite the same phenomenon: "Since this upset, Magonia, the underground crystal city, is located somewhere under the canopy of heaven between Yee-Dun and Venus."

For spirits as whimsical, free, and illogical as the Fairies—whose very nature it is to turn everything on its head and upside down—the fact that the world below could become the world above and vice versa is without a doubt seen as a very simple and banal occurrence. So instead they distorted the equilibrium of above/below by reversing the below of the above, the above of the below, and the below of the above of the below.

Numerous tales give the same origin to the reversal of the Alfic universe and its repercussions: the Ancients of the below kingdoms, angered by the superior and haughty attitudes that the inhabitants of the above kingdoms displayed in their presence and even more infuriated by their untimely dumping of garbage, reversed the world order. It is for this reason that we find airborne spirits, Elves, and "creatures of light and sky" at the very center of the cave-dwelling areas, and, conversely, infernal spirits and the Dark Dwarfs in the purple of the skies. This is why it is possible to find forests, oceans, clouds, skies, and stars under the earth's crust and diamond mines, caverns, stalactites, stalagmites, and black holes higher up than the galaxies.

The marriage of the Fairy People with the ancient dark dwellers brought forth the Erdluitle, or Bergfolk or Shadow Elves (underground Elves), that Barbygère called Seïth Du, or even Erdaun . . .

Since then, the underground has given rise to luminous, flowering, musical, and celestial places. You can hear the clanging

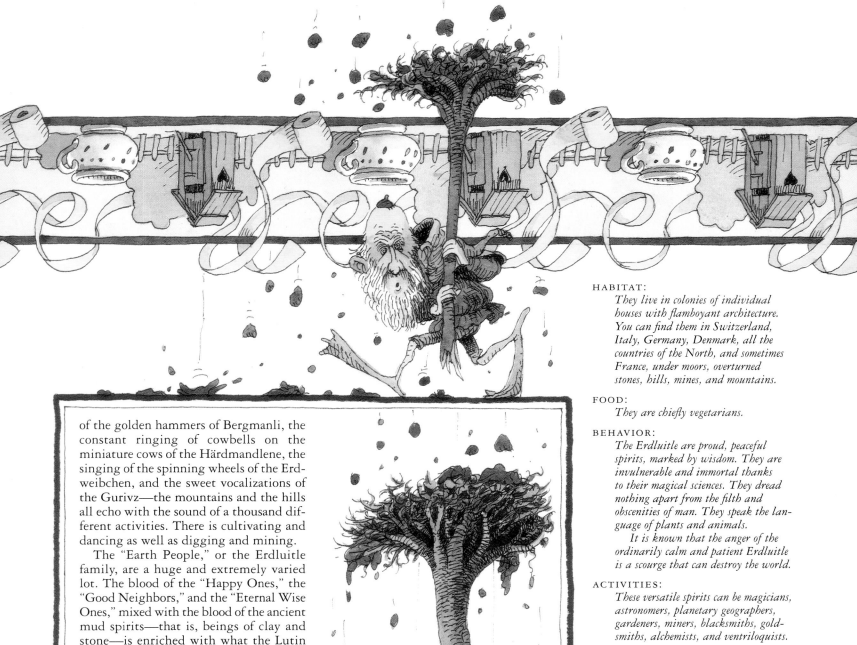

of the golden hammers of Bergmanli, the constant ringing of cowbells on the miniature cows of the Härdmandlene, the singing of the spinning wheels of the Erdweibchen, and the sweet vocalizations of the Gurivz—the mountains and the hills all echo with the sound of a thousand different activities. There is cultivating and dancing as well as digging and mining.

The "Earth People," or the Erdluitle family, are a huge and extremely varied lot. The blood of the "Happy Ones," the "Good Neighbors," and the "Eternal Wise Ones," mixed with the blood of the ancient mud spirits—that is, beings of clay and stone—is enriched with what the Lutin and Gnome species bring to it, along with wild and exotic transplants. Hence the Quiet Folk, Stille Volk, and the Patasson came into being by climbing back up onto the mass of Sphinx fossils. Pipintu and Tacanachus climbed back into the trees; Espiales and Solèves fell from the heavens. And today, they all complain about the arrogance of the men-from-above, and the fact that trash and waste of all kinds is always falling on top of their heads.

HABITAT:
They live in colonies of individual houses with flamboyant architecture. You can find them in Switzerland, Italy, Germany, Denmark, all the countries of the North, and sometimes France, under moors, overturned stones, hills, mines, and mountains.

FOOD:
They are chiefly vegetarians.

BEHAVIOR:
The Erdluitle are proud, peaceful spirits, marked by wisdom. They are invulnerable and immortal thanks to their magical sciences. They dread nothing apart from the filth and obscenities of man. They speak the language of plants and animals.
It is known that the anger of the ordinarily calm and patient Erdluitle is a scourge that can destroy the world.

ACTIVITIES:
These versatile spirits can be magicians, astronomers, planetary geographers, gardeners, miners, blacksmiths, goldsmiths, alchemists, and ventriloquists.

Rübezahl

HEIGHT:

Thirty-three inches (80 cm), but may grow to the size of a Colossus, over six feet seven inches (2 m) tall.

APPEARANCE:

Rübezahl wears so many disguises it is impossible to describe him clearly. Still, he is seen most often as a stocky, ruddy little man, with a long, unkempt beard. He can be recognized by his "greener than green" eyes.

CLOTHING:

A large hat, a brown-colored overcoat, leather stockings, a hooded red cloak, and a whip.

HABITAT:

He lives in a huge room decorated with bronze columns in the midst of his riches gathered over the centuries, in the center of the Riesenberg.

FOOD:

He gorges himself on pâté, sausage, stuffed pies, game, red meat, cooked beets, sauerkraut, beer, and brandy. According to the Elfin Chronicles, there is such a thing as a Rübezahl elixir: very "stiff," black and bitter, excellent for the voice and to combat sore throats.

BEHAVIOR:

He is the uncontested king of the Hey-Hey-Men, the Callers, the Appeleurs, the Houpeux, the Hejkadlo, the Hoihoi Mann, the Rôpenkerl, the Hüamann, the Hurleurs, the He-Männer, Pleureurs, Hurlous, etc. Fierce and ferocious, he lives surrounded by monstrous fauna of demons and spirits, both earthly and of the mountains, and Velus, Gnomes, and Knockers who

Many people think that the Schrat is a small child as fast as the wind, and yet he is a poor soul.

—Hans Vintler, fifteenth century (Jacobs Grimm, *German Mythology, op. cit, t.* III, p. 422)

The Genie of the mountain took a young country woman prisoner. "If you love me," she said to him, "tell me how many turnips there are in this field." The Genie started to count them. Meanwhile, the woman escaped and ran away.

The Genie was the most famous "Big Dwarf" in Germany. Rübezahl ("turnip counter" in German) was also the king of the Hey-Hey-Men, and his exploits are recounted anywhere his people can be found.

He prefers to be called "Master Johannes, Lord of the Mountains" and becomes enraged when people call him the ridiculous nickname "Rübezahl"!

He lives in Riesenberg in the German province of Silesia. Although he only occupies a small portion of land, he owns vast swathes of underground territory, extending several hundred miles. He leaves his underground lair by various secret doors, known only to a few old Hey-Hey-Men, Shouting Spirits from Prussia and Austria, and certain Gnomes and Knockers. When he shakes his enormous bunch of keys, he calls up violent storms. Once a week, he surveys his kingdom and designates duties to all the underground Genies under his rule. The main task of these hard workers is to look after his ores and treasure and to keep humans away from them.

When Rübezahl is seen on Riesenberg, woe betide all who cross his path.

Once upon a time, when this mountain was still a desert, he used to have fun letting the deer run wild, exciting and pitting the bears against the buffalo, and fighting the high-dwelling Giants and Dwarfs, reducing them to slavery. Then, when the first farmers and woodcutters came, he considered them mediocre, or intermediary beings between the spirits and the animals, and out of curiosity he studied them up close. Disguised as a fat peasant, he tried to offer his services to the closest farm. He was hired under the name of Rips and worked so efficiently that everything he touched prospered. But his master was an exploiter who liked to live off the hard work of others and pay his servants with ingratitude. So, Rübezahl left that master for another, whose herd he ended up tending. Under his supervision, the livestock flourished and not one animal strayed. However, this master, who loved food, stole the fattest lamb out from under his servant's nose for his own greedy pleasure. He charged his servant for the cost of the lamb, accusing him of having lost the animal. Ire-filled, Rübezahl then went to work for the judge of the township and became the terror of the thieves, ruffians, rogues, and paid assassins who ravaged the countryside. This new master was an avaricious glutton who sold justice to the highest bidder. Worn out, Rübezahl threw in the towel. The judge was so annoyed that he locked Rübezahl in a dark dungeon, from which he escaped by

turning himself into a tiny Goblin and sneaking to freedom though the keyhole.

After these distressing experiences, Master Johannes, contemptuous of all humankind, retired once more to his subterranean world . . .

Since then, when Rübezahl haunts the mountain, it is for revenge—destroying harvests, bringing on storms, making it rain or snow, raising the wind, and causing infernal droughts and floods. He can make people's ears grow, make beards and mustaches sprout on young girls and goat horns on men, or transform fruit into dung. He is capable of making noses longer, changing wigs into donkeys' tails and hair into straw, and transforming tree roots into venomous snakes. He also sends Changelings to steal children and force them to work in the gold mines.

He orders his Callers to get rid of solitary voyagers by luring them with their cries and hurling them over precipices.

During the Thirty Years' War, he amused himself by sinking the musketeer troops in the marshes in their Sunday best and then removing all the ornaments and feathers that had weighed them down.

Collin de Plancy also tells of a time when Rübezahl would pretend to be an assassin condemned to death by hanging. In a town square filled to capacity with curious souls, he allowed himself to be hanged on a tree branch. But, suddenly, instead of being strangled by the rope, he would start to dance and kick so hard and well that everybody ran away in all directions, trampling one another in an all-out stampede. When this happened, Rübezahl would laugh and sing merrily and continue to dance on the gallows the whole night through. The next morning, when the townspeople cautiously approached to take down the rebellious Rübezahl who had finally quieted down and was hanging there motionless with his disgusting black tongue sticking out . . . all they would find was a lifeless puppet!

work either in the mines or protecting their treasures. Immortal, he changes his wife every fifteen years, choosing from among the prettiest females of the Appeleurs. His divorced wives are fed to the guardian dragons of the bowels of the world in accordance with a pact signed at the beginning of time.

ACTIVITIES:
He rules over the subterranean world when he is not playing abominable tricks on humans.

Schrats, Callers, and Appeleurs

Three days before, three horrible, sharp cries were heard.
　　　　　—Brantôme, *Vie des dames illustres,* "Mélusine"

Callers, Appeleurs, and Houpeurs are characterized by their terrible cries to passersby, intended either to steer them away from danger or to lure them to their deaths . . .

The original meaning of the name *Schrat* was the notion of the dead and those who have come back from the dead, but in the ninth and tenth centuries, two more connotations were added, that of the mask—*masca*—signifying sorcery, and that of *thalamasca*, which means a mask that one wears at a masquerade ball. One hundred years later in England, the Scraettes (ghosts come back from the dead) became "nightmares" (*Ephialtes*), before developing into Goblins. They are often mistaken for Lutins or Follets, and they are sometimes good, but occasionally also sly. Give the Schrat-Follet what he wants, in case you should offend him. Many people believe that every house has its own little Schrat who brings luck and fortune.

What is certain is that such Callers and Appeleurs are not easy to describe with any certainty, due to their multiple forms. They descend from no particular family of Goblin and can be found haunting mountains as often as they are found in forests, moors, marshes, houses, and shores. They mix with the spirits of the air, water, and earth and can adopt the guise of a demon, a fish, a Goblin, a pale lady . . . or even an owl! Their inconsistencies run to such an extent that the eighteenth-century Elfologist Bridoux came up with the following thesis: "If there are so many differences among the Appeleurs, and if sometimes they appear in the form of a Féetaud of the Sea and other times in the form of a Dryad of the Forest, or a Pygmy of the Earth and

Sylph of the Air, it is only because they are their 'spirits'—they are the wandering Souls of the Korricks, Houziers, Nutons, Sidhe, and Kelpie, who disappeared centuries ago."

This is not true. That is not to say that Fairy or Elf ghosts do not exist—and why not even a ghost of a ghost?—but the origin of the Appeleurs dates back to the aftermath of the last Battle of the Hundred, when the armies of the hundred strongest Elfin people battled fiercely among themselves for one hundred days in a bloody fratricide provoked by the gods. One of the kings of the Tuatha De Danaan felt remorse when he saw "as far as the eye can see, bodies lying on the mist-covered plain, as pale and cold as dead fish floating on the gray waves of the Final Tide, their armor like tarnished scales." He gathered the surviving tribes around him and asked each of them to chose, from among his men, one Sad Hero, who would live forever, wandering the earth and the heavens, the seas and the moors, calling out to everyone as a sorrowful example of their folly. It would be their task to warn living beings away from such blind and murderous acts—and to punish them if they remained deaf

to their calls and stubbornly persisted with their evil deeds.

As the millennia of the Golden Age tumbled by and the fortunate races declined, the mission of the Appeleurs was wiped from even their own memories by the sands of time. Soon, only cries and wordless moans remained in the empty heads of these pathetic, despairing messengers.

And this is why I sojourn here
Alone and palely loitering,
　　　　　—John Keats,
　　　　　La Belle Dame Sans Merci

Hutzeran: The name derives from French common parlance (*hutsi, hucher,* meaning "to call out in great shouts"). Dressed all in green, they hide in the forests of the Vaudois Alps. In a sometimes sonorous, sometimes masked voice, they release echoes and wake the sleeping Fairies of the blanketed forests. They sleep on the soft moss or perch in one of the highest pine trees. When a dead branch falls, it is the Hutzeran who has touched it and made it drop. When the snow cascades from branch to branch and spills like flour, again it is the Hutzeran who provokes the avalanche. If you are walking through a silent wood, be careful: sing, whistle, or shout, but do this no more than twice. If you do, on your third cry one will descend upon you! In Parcey, the habits of a particularly raging and remorseful Genie are told of in the stories. He will come towards you and tear off a leg or an arm. But fear not: the limb will be returned to you the following day, left outside the door to your dwelling.

The cries of these Callers can be heard ripping through the silence in regions of Maine in the United States and Anjou in France. The Lady of Garenne also releases awful cries, searching for her lost slipper in the Ardennes countryside.

The Huyeux: They live in the Bredoulain woods and resemble small altar boys The Bauieux of the Prix forest dance dressed in red at night in the forests of Ardennes, shouting, "Ah! Oh!" and the Caramaras shout beneath the

Chawatte stone. In the seventeenth century in the Ardennes forests, an Ouyeu once joined a hunt and diabolically lured the hunters with his cries. Around 1835, people spoke of an "Overseer of Evil" who could be found crossing the woods walking a black dog on a metal leash. His eyes became red as flames as he uttered these horrible words:

Beasts, stay out of the passageways.
Foul and game, leave stride by stride.
Make room for the cursed souls of the
countryside!

Lucibaut: The Lucibaut and their kin announce death and despair by barking and howling at the moon. They drag chains along behind them, and on All Saints' Day, they devour little rascals traveling on the roads of Noyon, near Compiègne. The Indian Chaïtanes look like hairy demons, raging on the night of the full moon. They carry away those who respond to their calls and rip them into pieces. The next morning, the victims' parents find a shower of blood outside their door. Drawcansir are swaggering Goblins who spread panic throughout British armies. They gather together and shout at the moon during Mass and when the bells are ringing for Saint Hubert. The "Chatterers" and "Whistlers" cry out, chirp, and growl in despair and anger in tropical forests. The "Cart-drivers" imitate the sounds of overloaded carts. The "Whisperers" moan in the pipes and walls of houses; the "Watchers" screech on the coasts of England. The Beûbeus pounce upon people, scaring them with cries of "Beuh! Beuh!" which is how they earned their names. They often wear brown hoods.

The Monk of Saire: He is often seen in the harbor of Cherbourg looking like a little man who is drowning. He shouts, "Save me! Save me!" If a sailor goes to help him, the Monk seizes the hand that the sailor extends to him and drags the poor wretch beneath the waves. Sometimes the Monk hides among the rocks and shouts out at those who walk along the shore, "Go that way! Come this way!" in order to push them into the sea. He also appears on the shore, recognizable by his white tailcoat, to chat with passersby and challenge them to a race. If any accept, he draws them little by little toward the sea . . . (A. Bosquet, *La Normandie romanesque*).

Dama Dagenda: These are the Appeleurs of the jungle of New Guinea. They understand the languages of the Papuan tribes who have invaded their territory, and they take their revenge by leading them astray into the wilderness with their imitations of animal sounds. The only way to escape them is to learn a sorcerer's dialect that they don't know and to speak and sing loudly in it while crossing their territory: by the time they work out the dialect, the person in danger will have had enough time to escape. Whoever hears the "Weeper of the Woods" enters into a state of perpetual languor. The "Crier of the Woods" appears as a white figure that is half human, half animal.

Lubin: Tearful and timid, the Lubin runs along the roads of Lower Normandy on Christmas night, crying out "Robert [the devil] is dead." He vanishes as soon as a finger is pointed at him, but if you respond to his cries, he will drag you along behind him.

The Saurimonde: The mountain dwellers of Tarn consider them to be among the Fassilières (spirits who can exercise either a positive or evil influence). They appear as beautiful children (usually female, but sometimes male) with curly blond hair, abandoned at the crossroads of a forest or on the edge of a fountain. They call out with their sweet voices. Often, kind boys or sympathetic shepherdesses rescue them. If a shepherd marries a Saurimonde, he soon finds himself to be the husband of a demon, and if the child is adopted by a kind woman, the evil creature forces her to pledge her future to hell (A. de Chesnel, *Usages de la Montagne Noire*).

The Houpoux: The Houpoux of Upper Brittany imitate the "hoohoo!" sound that is customarily repeated by villagers as they call out to each other in the evenings. Often they change their tone of voice to sound like a little girl who might be lingering on the bank of a pond or a canal in order to seduce boys (P. Sébillot, *Traditions de la Haute-Bretagne*). Those who have seen the Houpoux from far away describe them as a gray shadow without a definite form but with big white eyes.

The Houpeurs: The Houpeurs live in remarkably large, strangely shaped rocks in the proximity of standing stones. Mischievous and sometimes even malicious, they are cunning spirits. At a late hour of the night their shrill cries can be heard. Those who imprudently respond are seized and torn into pieces (Durang-Vaugaron, in *Mémoire de la Société d'émulation des Côtes-du-Nord*).

The Houpeurs of Picardy, or the "Squawkers" of Pas-de-Calais, call out to anyone who comes along and drag those who respond around by their hair.

The Scrigérez Noz of Lower Brittany pursues people, moaning mournfully.

The Lutin of Condes enjoys feigning the cries of a drowning child.

The spirit of Fiestre (Champagne) perfectly imitates animal sounds, so that when the shepherds run after their herd, they fall into his clutches.

Ian an Ôd: John of the Shore, or Ian an Ôd, is the best known of the Houpeurs of Lower Brittany. He dwells on the banks of rivers, continuously making the guttural sounds familiarly used by the rural inhabitants of Breton when they return to their homes in the evening. If someone responds to him, Ian an Ôd travels half of the distance that separates him from his naive victim in the blink of an eye and repeats the same sound. If the person responds to him again, the Goblin again covers half the remaining distance that separates them. If the hapless fool responds a third time, Ian suddenly moves to strangle or drown his prey (Le Men, in *Revue Celtique,* t. I, p. 419).

The Krieren Noz: The Krieren Noz, night criers, moan among the large rocks on the coast of Tregor. In the late eighteenth century, the doors of the homes on Sein Island were only closed during storms. When the inhabitants of the island heard the faraway murmur of thunder that preceded a storm, the elders would exclaim, "Let's close the doors and listen for the 'Krieren' and the whirlwind that follows them."

In the region of Cape Sizun, the Chouerien are said to make such a racket that the area is basically uninhabitable.

The Chouerien-Porzen are found in a little creek off the southwestern coast of Lescoff, near the lighthouse at Raz Point. There are seven of them, and they always walk in a single-file line. They never do any harm, but deafen people with their loud chant of "Ho! la! la! tenna ar bagou da séc'ha!" (Ho! la! la! Take the boats out to dry!)

The Conjuré haunts the mouth of the Douron River in Plestin.

Pautre Penn-er-Lo: The sandy peninsula of

Penn-er-Lo in Quiberon was once the domain of a type of spirit with a melodious voice named Pautre Penn-er-Lo. He called out to travelers who had been trapped by the tides or the falling of night at the ford of the river before the Plouharnel road in Quiberon had been constructed. He offered to carry them across on his back. If they accepted, he would take them right to the middle of the ford and throw them into the sea (Abbé Collet).

Colle Pohr-En-Dro: Colle Pohr-En-Dro is a protean Goblin from the region of Carnac who cries out for help as if he is just about to drown. When he finds that someone has jumped into the water to help him, he rushes out to the middle of the waves and bursts out laughing (J. Buléon, in *Revue des traditions populaire*, t. IV, p. 273).

Begul an Aod: In the dark of the night, the people of Arz Island (Morbihan) sometimes hear the sound of their boats being caulked. But nobody knows where these boats go, for there is no sign of them when the first moonbeams begin to shine. The Begul an Aod cuts the ropes, lifts the anchors of the boats in the harbor, and pushes them out toward the breakers. Sometimes, he challenges the sailors by shouting, "All aboard! All aboard!" with open arms. Whoever takes him up on his invitation inevitably perishes by drowning (L. F. Sauvé, in *Mélusine*, t. II).

Dr. Viaud Grand-Marais mentions that at Devin Point near Noirmoutier, the small boat of an Appeleur approached the coastline at dawn. A voice shouted, "All aboard! All aboard! Let's go to Galloway!" and the boat appeared to be so overloaded that it seemed near to sinking. It is believed that the land of Galloway, or Galloways, meant Galilee, where the dead are judged.

The Bawlers: The Bawlers wail at night, when the wind violently tears through the island of Noirmoutier. Sailors, who believe that they are hearing victims of a shipwreck crying out for help, jump into the water and swim in search of them; but the farther out the sailors go, the farther

away the Bawlers seem to be. (P. Sébillot, *La Mer et les eaux douces*).

The Howlers: In Carteret there is a spirit that is called the Howler. The night before a storm, a man whose face is never seen and who wears a brown cloak and rides bareback on a black horse travels through corn cockles and large rocks, filling the air with ominous screams. Neither quicksand, nor slippery kelp, nor the depths of the sea, nor the peaks of gigantic rocks can stop the swift progress of this man and his black horse. Their passing leaves any water sizzling, smoking, and blackened for a long time after they have gone by, for the black horse's shoes are red, as if they have come out of an infernal forge (Barbey d'Aurevilly, *Une vieille maîtresse*).

The Lupeux: The Lupeux of Berry manifests its presence by repeating in a small, clear voice, "Hah! Hah!" Whoever is curious enough to ask him three times "What?" or "What happened?" will hear him babble like a chatterbox, telling of strange or scandalous adventures. He finishes by leading the questioner to a body of seemingly shallow water and saying "Look!" Then, the Lupeux pushes his foolhardy victim in and, perched on a branch, calls out to his drowning victim, "Hah! Hah! . . . Well, that's what happened!" (Georges Sand, *Légendes rustiques*). Another kind of Lupeux is a supernatural being with the head of a wolf and a human voice; he lures travelers into holes (Jaubert, *Glossaire du Centre*). It has also been said that certain Lupeux resemble a big, soft, wrinkly owl with clipped, membranous wings.

The Borlô or Bawler of the Abbey: According to Armand Pellegrin (*Le Folklore brabançon*, 1921), in the days of old there was an aquatic monster that lived in the lakes of the Prémontré Abbey of Opheylissem (Belgium): the Borlô or Bawler of the Abbey. On dark and stormy nights, his calls and menacing screams were heard for miles around. No one ever managed to make him disappear by force; he left of his own accord after the water in the lake

receded. It has also been said that the Borlô was a Dwarf who had "a mad and mediocre mind, who engaged in lots of

vain discourse, and often made a fuss, trying to raise himself up to the lineage of the kings." A dangerous megalomaniac, he found a place among the political "Dribblers," "Babblers," and "Orators."

The Hugon (or Huguet): He was a Caller who appeared in the city of Tours and threatened children: "Some have claimed that in Tours the Huguenots took their name from the Hugon tower where they gathered, or from a goblin of the same name, who threatened the children in this city" (Agrippa d'Aubigné, *Histoire universelle depuis 1550 jusqu'en 1601*, I, 96).

The Cougher: In the swamps of Poitou, a small, mysterious boat appears, called the "anguish-carrier." The boat passes through the canals that divide the swamp, covered in a white sheet laid out like a shroud. At the stern of the boat is a ghost called the "Yellow Cougher" (a kind of plaintive personification of swamp fever). As the

conductor of the chariot of the dead, the spirit, between coughing fits and a few moans, says to those he meets, "Turn around, or I will turn you over." Those who encounter him are sure to die within the year. With the Cougher we enter into the dismal circle of familiar, ominous messengers, including night singers, Merluisaines, Damettes, White Owls, and Banshees.

Damettes: Damettes, as described by Bérenger-Féraud (*Superstitions et Survivances*, Paris, 1896, t.I, p. 7), appeared at the windows of the château of Maubelle near Hyères. Small, young, pretty, and lavishly dressed, they sang, talked, and danced when there were happy occasions in the family. One could hear their sobs and moans when the family was stricken with misfortune. Similar ominous messengers, Merluisaines, would come out of the chimney of the chateau of Piney in Champagne; they would scream so shrilly that they could be heard in the neighboring village, and one could be sure that one of the lords would die within the year. The children were told, "The Merluisaines will take you away," when moans were heard while the Hainaut winds were blowing. All of these messengers of happiness, or more likely of death, were attached to houses, families, castles, ruins, and places where battles, crimes, and executions had taken place. More recently, they are found attached to places where accidents have taken place, like the "White Hitchhiker" who has been encountered by many travelers (see *Invitation au château de l'Étrange*, Claude Seignolle).

These specters, who appear in whitish, evanescent forms; weeping, screaming, howling at the moon; or cloaked in bloody shrouds, haunt the Vendée, Brittany, Flanders, England, Scotland, Ireland, and Germany in various forms. Banshees are the most well known.

THOSE OF THE WOODS AND THE FORESTS

All theory is gray; the only thing that remains eternally green is the tree of life.

—Goethe

The forest is the birthplace of fabulous beings: a place of deep immensity where both light and shadow reign, where the four elements meet. The intercessory trees thrust their branches into the air and their roots into the secret depths of the underground where fires perpetually blaze. Here, paths branch out in steady succession, and the green peacefulness allows the discernment of quiet voices and the eternal education of young shoots.

Behind this barrier of trees, which were planted in the very heart of the world by the Age-Old Legendaries, where the original tree grows, the ancient guardians of the forest faithfully watch over the Golden Herb and the Branch of Life.

White Alfs, Black Alfs, Dwarfs, Fairies, Elves, unicorns, animals and labyrinthodores, Lechiy, Trolls, Fayettes, Puckwudgies, and slight, tiny fauna of the forest all live together beneath the divine cluster of trees—evidence of their rich, romantic harmony.

HEIGHT:
About eight inches (20 cm).

APPEARANCE:
A rough, greenish ball of grass with four big eyes just above the ground. The root, which is buried in lichens, has eight long legs covered with trailing rootlets. Tourmentines do not have a mouth, but a kind of stomach-pocket that bounces around amid the nodules.

HABITAT:
Tourmentines have always existed in every forest, except for the fir tree forests and other places where conifers are planted.

FOOD:
Earthworms, insects, Elf-Dwarfs.

BEHAVIOR:
Banished by Flora, they live in clusters which are isolated from the other forest spirits. They are jealous of the Parisettes' beauty, and for this reason, they detest them and fight tirelessly against them.

ACTIVITIES:
Misleading people and imprisoning them by touching their shoes. In May, when the lilies of the valley and the hyacinths are in bloom, they can be heard making a flutelike sound. There are many varieties of Tourmentine.

The Tourmentines

I can evoke it through the effects of chiaroscuro.
—Umberto Eco,
La Production des signes

Bladé tells the story of a man who fell asleep at the foot of a fir tree in a forest in the Grande Lande nature reserve in France on the eve of St. John's Day: He woke up at midnight, hearing noises that came from the treetops and from underground. He saw spirits in various forms fly and fall through the air, including flies and glowworms, and from the earth, along with lizards, frogs, and salamanders, little figures of men and women emerged, as tall as a thumb and clothed in red, carrying three-pronged golden forks. And these spirits danced and sang:

> *The little plants thrive*
> *In the fields whereupon*
> *They flower and seed*
> *On the day of Saint John.*

Long ago, the forests were teeming with "different kinds of life" both by day and by night. The air beneath the canopy hummed with spirits, Elves, and winged Genies, and the soil stirred with a secret, multicolored abundance. Whoever strayed from the main paths and wandered into the meandering trails of the forest risked falling under the spell of the Little People. If he lost his senses, then his fate was already sealed—he would disappear! But if he was marked by certain graces, the dancing Nymphs and Elves would drag him along in a circular dance which would wear out his feet, and he would be left to die.

A wanderer might walk along a path without noticing the presence of the Dwarfs, since, with the slightest sound of a step, the watchmen of their kind whistle out a call for general withdrawal. Then from among the foliage, thousands of sharp eyes watch the intruder until he leaves.

But that does not mean that he is safe, because he could still come across the Tourmentines, which grow during the eve of summer solstice in magical parts of the forest. Born of the melodious bird whose song erases time and the Nettle Nymph, Tourmentines are also called the "Plant of Forgetfulness," and the "Grass of Distraction." If he steps on one of them, he will be lost forever.

Whoever tramples the Tourmentine becomes something like a ghost and is no longer conscious of himself. He will walk around in circles for the rest of his life unless fortune smiles upon him and the Sylvain and the Sidhe have the goodwill to lead him to a Parisette, who will break the evil spell.

Around the beginning of the last century, young people were getting lost in a particular part of the Forest of Chûtrin, helplessly attracted by magical herbs, and the Timeless Beings would choose their husbands and wives from the most suitable of these youths. The Grass of Distraction has often served as a pretext for rambling, licentious young women when they must explain to their impatient fathers why they returned home at such a late hour!

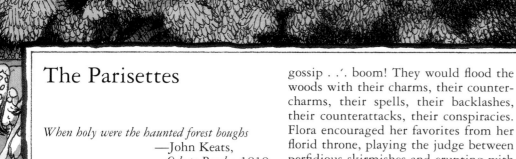

The Parisettes

When holy were the haunted forest boughs
—John Keats,
Ode to Psyche, 1819

Back when Flora reigned over the world of vegetation, the Fayettes, Demoiselles, Nymphs, Little Bacchan Sisters, Huldres, Gianes, Vilys, Vouivres, and their followers lived out their Golden Age in the vast realm of the woods and forests; each one had their own castle of greenery: their own lake, clearing, rock, oak grove, row of willows, bank of flowers, yew. Of course, although these creatures were excessively feminine, they were not completely ethereal to the point of being mere pure winged evanescence. To the contrary, these rascals, under their transparent veils, angelic faces, and sunshiny locks, never missed a chance to pull each other's hair out. And these beauties, each one an expert in magic, were not afraid of using their powers and dueling with sorcery. They cast spells, concocted love potions, and waved magic wands, and, beneath the forest foliage, one spark of magic could turn a peaceful copse into a battlefield . . .

For the offense of a borrowed comb, some stolen eye shadow, a copied style of dress, a rival love interest, a triviality, an annoyance, a cross-eyed look, a piece of gossip . . ´. boom! They would flood the woods with their charms, their counter-charms, their spells, their backlashes, their counterattacks, their conspiracies. Flora encouraged her favorites from her florid throne, playing the judge between perfidious skirmishes and erupting with laughter at the outcome of certain bouts: a supple Water Nymph becoming a huge-nosed tadpole with tiny feet grown into flippers, a Sylph taken down in mid-flight turning into a flabby toad, a svelte and slender Gwyllion shriveling up into a scrofulous runt.

This is how Carbuncle-the-Blonde became Dame Agaisse, who took her revenge on the oak trees by turning them into Hennefêtes. This is also how grotesque and monstrous hybrids were born: Nymph-fish, mushroom-Fairies, Elf-snails, an entire preposterous, embittered, and vengeful collection of flora-fauna.

The eyelash-batting Parisettes annoyed the Nettle Nymph with their youthful grace and success with charming princes and handsome shepherds and were shrunk by her from five feet five inches down to ten inches. Fortunately, Queen Flora loved them and preserved their beauty.

From this time on, Parisettes have not stopped thwarting the traps laid by the Tourmentines, the Plant of Forgetfulness and daughters of the Nettle Nymph. Their epic battles always attract a crowd of amused onlookers, who love to see the pretty Nymph triumph time and time again over the hateful and hideous plant.

HEIGHT:
Ten inches (26 cm) tall.

APPEARANCE:
They are adorable. They have long hair like grass, dotted with flowers, and very flexible bodies with pink skin. Their eyes are blue.

CLOTHING:
Often nude, they like to adorn them-selves with flower-petal garlands, pet-ticoats with tiny bells sewn in, and a cape in the shape of butterfly wing.

HABITAT:
Parisettes are found in forests in all countries with a temperate climate. They particularly prefer warm and humid places.

FOOD:
Wild strawberries, berries, bilberries, pollen, and dried fruit.

BEHAVIOR:
Joyous, playful companions, they fre-quently cavort among Elves and Dwarfs. Nostalgic about their past loves, they are attracted to woodcutters, whom they caress in their sleep while lamenting their own diminished size. They only live for one season. At the first sign of spring, a new Parisette is born from the frozen remains of its pre-decessor, killed by the cold of winter.

ACTIVITIES:
Among other things, they release wan-derers from the magic spells cast upon them by the Tourmentines.

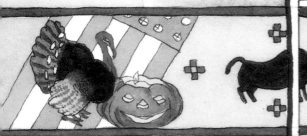

HEIGHT:
Twelve inches (30 cm) tall.

APPEARANCE:
They possess all the grace and beauty of nature, which is their soul. Their bodies are supple and well proportioned, their skin golden. Their faces, while keeping their pure oval shape, somehow resemble each and every animal. When they plunge into an empty space, two wings sprout from their backs. They have pointy ears. Their females are still tinier and prettier.

CLOTHING:
They wear tunics woven from the fibers of various plants, decorated with seashells, small polished stones, turquoise, and the spines of porcupines. Their long black hair is plaited and, like the Indians', decorated with feathers and ribbons studded with pearls. They wear fringed and embroidered chaps and moccasins made of moss. They are never without bows, and their arrows unleash lightning and storms.

HABITAT:
They live in America, which the Ageless have named "the Beautiful Land." They are found all over the place, even in Canada. In the wintertime, they cover themselves with a very thick and silky fur on which they draw plants and animals.

FOOD:
Berries, fruit, corn, sweet potatoes, pumpkins (of which they are particularly fond), and a delicacy made of maple syrup and flavored with the juices of plants and flowers.

The Puckwudgies

Was somebody asking to see my soul?
See, your own shape and countenance, persons, substances, beasts,
the trees, the running rivers, the rocks and sands.

All hold spiritual joys and afterwards loosen them;
How can the real body ever die and be buried?
　　　　—Walt Whitman,
　　　　"Starting from Paumanok"

When Old Sam was very old, he sat down in front of his veranda and began contemplating his existence and what his life had thrown at him, things that he wished to rediscover and things that he wanted to see just as he had done in the first days after he arrived there. He didn't know anymore when that was! Had he come there alone? In leather chaps with a Kentucky rifle under his arm, or maybe before, dressed in a black overcoat? Or was it later, when he broke from the caravan of covered wagons? He really could not say. Old Sam had become so light that he no longer needed to tip the rocking chair with his feet; the breeze took care of it by itself. Perhaps even the soft rhythm of the universe turning was enough to set the chair a-rocking. His old hat seemed permanently screwed onto his wrinkles, or maybe the hat had sat on his old head for so long, it was now a living extension of it: rain, snow, sweat, and sun had glued one to the other. After all, was it not under this felt skullcap that all of Old Sam's ideas and flashes of intelligence took seed?

It had been a while since the dog had come around and stuck his big nose into the creases of Old Sam's worn overalls. The dog was now buried somewhere at the top of that hilly outcrop where he liked to sniff the fresh air. Martha was also asleep there, under the giant, outstretched arms of an oak tree. For a long time Old Sam had taken flowers up there, both morning and night, but the seeds had spread over the land now. It was no longer necessary to bring more flowers to add to the massive bank of white petals, an expression of his love. Now a trail of blooms led down the hill and back to the house. They had traveled so close that they gave the impression that the joyous, virginal petals were about to climb the porch steps.

In bygone days, his younger brother would come to him

to ask if he wanted to go for a walk, but he had long since fallen to gunfire, along with his two sons. Old Sam could no longer remember when or where: Yorktown? Vicksburg? Big Black River? Or over there, in Bastogne or in the hell of Vietnam? So many battles, so many brief letters received! The bodies never came back . . .

Three butterflies come flying around him now and land on his shoulders. He does not chase them away. A snake slithers up and wraps around his ankles, and a skunk frolics on his knees. Old Sam welcomes them with a brotherly spirit. A huge burst of merriment suddenly takes away the sad memories, and Old Sam opens his eyes to the forest at his land's boundary. The leaves seem greener, the grass more luscious, the mountains in the background closer and more welcoming; their peaks, yesterday insurmountable, now bend toward him . . .

When one of Martha's flowers alights on his nose, Old Sam smiles a nearly toothless grin. He blinks. Has he been sleeping?

He must have been sleeping like a log because the sky looks more vast than usual, beginning to be marked by stars, while simultaneously the sun displays its most beautiful sunrise in the east and stokes its fires for an amazing sunset in the west; meanwhile, the

moon, in the middle, is becoming its fullest for Christmas.

The aroma of ploughed land, of cut hay and morning snow, wafting toward his nostrils carrying the smell of cherry blossoms doesn't disturb him any more than the strange silhouette of a little being crossing the pasture with a big smile on his face. Old Sam has seen him once before when, as a child, he freed a rabbit from a poacher's trap. Oh, but he didn't see him for long! Only the flicker of an eye. But he never forgot this tiny man, so handsome, so majestic, so happy, and so kind! All of his life, Old Sam had hoped to meet up with him again . . . but then he had forgotten him.

But this very day or night—Old Sam does not know the time anymore, nor the date, nor even the season—the little figure appears to him once more with a big smile and signs of friendship and . . . No, Old Sam isn't dreaming, it sure is Martha following the Puckwudgie, as pretty as she had been on their wedding day, draped in her fringed shawl, and there is the dog at their heels. Roune is there as well, the first cow that Old Sam ever bought and whose milk he always shared with the old Indian who used to live next door, and who was said to have a little witch in him . . .

And it is so good to find everyone here, once again reunited!

BEHAVIOR/ACTIVITIES:

Puckwudgies live in couples over the entire range of "the Beautiful Land," which they try and protect from pollution and acts of vandalism. They control the elements. They protect the harvests, the fauna, and the flora. They are intermediaries between the spirits, the gods, the elements, the animals, the plants, and humans.

They appear to those who live in harmony with nature and who maintain and protect it. They also appear to those who, on their deathbeds, have made peace with themselves and with the world. They offer them all their unconscious desires in the space of an eternal second.

Puckwudgies gather together once a year, when their grand council meets. They discuss the future of the universe. If they ever become disappointed with humanity and no longer meet, this will be the end of time.

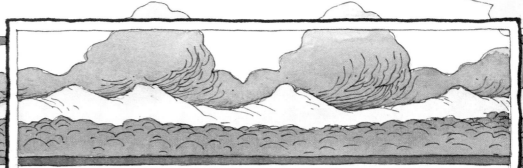

HEIGHT:
Seven inches (18 cm) tall.

APPEARANCE:
*They have jutting jaws, receding
foreheads, and prominent, arched eyebrows. They have an apelike gait and
are very hairy.*

CLOTHING:
*They are nude, without jewels or
weapons.*

HABITAT:
*They live in a particular corner of the
Ardennes in France and are not found
anywhere else.*

FOOD:
*Most likely herbivores, eating roots,
leaves, and berries.*

BEHAVIOR:
*Their primate morphology would
suggest that they belong to the Hairy
Mountaineers and Little Savage Men
like the Sasquatch. The reason for
their theft of laundry (even though
they themselves are nude) is not entirely
clear, though it may be part of a ritual of a particular cult. Or maybe,
as certain popular beliefs lead one to
suppose, they were attempting to dress
the corpse of a female Druid woman
who fled religious persecution and was
found deep within a cave mummified
and tattooed from head to foot by
them. In his* Grand Répertoire des
Déchus *(Repertoire of the Fallen),
Brigid Soror describes them simply as
"venomous dwarfs of the forest."*

The Couzzietti

*At least twelve Couzzietti lived in this
underwood . . .*
—Abbé Goffaux, *Les Hauts brûlés*

Up until the beginning of the
twentieth century, when the
women of the Ardennes region
of France went to wash their
clothes in the waters of the Goulets, it was
never without apprehension. They always
arranged to go down to the river in large
groups, because when they found themselves in the depths of the woods in groups
of only three or four, they would hear
strange noises emanating from all around.
The leaves would shake, creaking sounds
would reverberate beneath the canopy, and
they would hear a voice screeching the
same phrase over and over: "Oh, Couzzietti! Cowardly Coutteni! Oh, Couzzietti!
Cowardly Coutteni!" The cries would get
ever louder until they became deafening.

Then there would be a stampede!

Crazed out of their minds, the washerwomen would bolt, followed by an
excited horde of scoundrels still shouting
the words, "Oh Couzzietti! Cowardly
Coutteni!" They would quickly catch up
with the fleeing women, jump on their
shoulders, grab the ribbons of their bonnets, pull their hair, hold on tight to their
petticoats, and try to grapple the women
to the ground. Sometimes they would
throw sticks under their clogs to make
them trip or push them towards prepared
traps beneath the trees: trip wires just
above the level of the soil, "ankle-break-
ers" covered with leaves, balls of pine needles, stakes driven into the ground, and
dangerous points in the air. These tiny
but dangerous traps would leave the
unfortunate ones limping or wounded on
the ground. When the decimated group
reached the village, rescuers would run
out to help, but all they would find in the
woods would be trampled grass and
empty baskets: the laundry and the small
creatures would be gone. They would beat
the thickets, smoke out the holes, and
search the cracks in the rocks, but the
Couzzietti were nowhere to be found!

Sibaras

*Cozy and warm beneath the eiderdown, I heard
the rumble of the storm and the cry of the Sibara.*
—Mes Ardennes

One stormy night, worn out by
the evil deeds of a wizard, the
inhabitants of a hamlet in the
Ardennes region of France
chased the sorcerer, intending to burn him
at the stake. They finally cornered him at
the edge of a precipice. The wizard raised
his iron fork to cast one final spell, but a
bolt of lightening struck the black
enchanter instead, reducing him to carbon.

There he remained, welded to the rocky
ridge, shrunken and shriveled, molded to
his spear, shreds of clothing whipping in
the wind like on a scarecrow. The townspeople left him up there and soon forgot
about him, until the day when a woodcutter thoughtlessly brought him down from
the embankment to his yard to chase the
pesky birds away from his cherry trees.

And then, once again, a storm raged
above the orchard. Again, a bolt of lightning struck the mummified carcass of the
wizard. But this time, by some sort of
magic the mass of bones came to life.
Smoking, skipping, squeaking his hatred
to the four corners of the earth, the scarecrow ran and took refuge in the woods.

For a long time he stayed here; he spied
on the comings and goings of the villagers, waiting for the right moment to
take his revenge. They called him Sibara
("scarecrow" in the local dialect). He was
hideous, dwarfish and deformed, his skin
ravaged by burns, and he crawled endlessly along paths. He struck everywhere,
throwing showers of arrows, provoking
avalanches, and setting fire to haystacks.

One day he kidnapped a young girl and
brought her to his lair; in this den Sibara
offspring proliferated. They, in turn, kidnapped other shepherdesses . . .

On stormy nights the caves of the
Ardennes now resonate with the sound of
more than one terrible cry. Three hundred
years later the descendants of that first
Sibara still possess an inherent fear of
storms. They never miss an opportunity to
throw a lonely hiker down a hole, but the
great hatred of their wizard ancestor is
reduced, and, for the moment, the Sibaras
remain hidden from humans, allowing
themselves to   be seen only rarely.

HEIGHT:
*Twenty-two to twenty-four inches
(55 to 60 cm) tall.*

APPEARANCE:
*Formerly of normal height, Sibaras
have become a sort of living mummy
with red hair. Their faces are burnt,
without nose or lips. They have bare
teeth and eyes sunken into their sockets.
They are a repulsive sight, with the
grimacing faces of corpses on stunted
burnt bodies. Where their skin is torn
you can see their skeletons.*

CLOTHING:
*They wear fur hats peppered with
daggers and carry a quiver about the
shoulders and a bow. They dress in
rags with high leggings attached to
their calves by laces. They have bare
toughened feet. They use a forked branch
tipped with the blade of a sickle.*

HABITAT:
*They live in all the old ridges in the
Ardennes mountains.*

FOOD:
*They hunt, dry, and smoke game and
cook bread made of ferns. They also
eat cheese.*

BEHAVIOR/ACTIVITIES:
*Since the beginning of the twentieth
century, not much has been heard from
the Sibaras. They keep to themselves in
wild tribes, and they do not let others
approach them. They still kill from
time to time, but they no longer kidnap
young girls. They fear storms and,
paradoxically, scarecrows.*

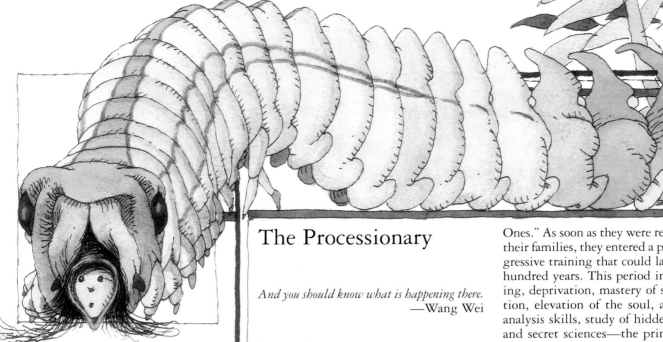

The Processionary

And you should know what is happening there.
—Wang Wei

The Processionary is a most strange and rare creature, whose mysterious origin dates back to the dawn of Elfin times. In that age, insects, caterpillars, birds, and numerous other animals were of a considerably more imposing size than they are today. When the contemporary artists and painters of this fantastic age depicted Elves gamboling about on top of scarabs, flying through the air on the backs of cockchafers, and battling with enormous wasps, it was not that these creatures were small, but rather that the insects were huge. It was only over the course of many centuries that these creatures grew smaller. In his *De la croissance du coléoptère et du parallélisme chez l'Alven* (The Growth of Coleoptera and Parallelism among the Elfin People), Romélius Barbygère states that by 1415 insects and other flying and crawling creatures—with a few exceptions—had already achieved their final size, "as had the forest goblins of the fairy world." Thus, when such important artists as Arthur Rackham, Richard Doyle, and Cecily Mary Barker depicted Fairies and Sprites as smaller than or approximately the same size as dragonflies, butterflies, and flowers, they were simply representing the reality of that time.

In the olden days in the Fairy Forest, curious monasteries lay hidden among circles of hollow tree stumps that were connected to one another by a complicated network of underground passages. These passages were the home of wise but strict Lutins, who had not one ounce of impishness and who authored austere and turgid tomes concerning the genesis of the Elfin species. These diminutive Sprites were recruited at birth by stern masters who searched the whole of the Fairy races in order to select those who were most suitable for receiving the teaching of the "Wise Ones." As soon as they were removed from their families, they entered a period of progressive training that could last up to one hundred years. This period involved fasting, deprivation, mastery of self, meditation, elevation of the soul, astral travel, analysis skills, study of hidden universes, and secret sciences—the principal grand themes of knowledge. They left their abode once a month, just for enough time to complete a circuit of the glen and to inhale the air necessary to sustain them. They moved forward one after the other in a long line, heads lowered within their large hoods, lips sealed, hardly breathing for fear of falling down completely drunk, giddy to the hilt from a vigorous and overly hasty gulp of fragrant air. Thus, they moved along, in deep contemplation, cautiously, all orifices closed.

But alas, a Nymphet, fresh from her bathtub and scantily clad, who was dancing around to dry herself collided heavily with the last in the line of Fairy folk, causing him to fall down. She helped him up, dusted him off, and laughed as his feelings came to life. She laughed even harder to see him struggling within the tangle of his cowl and attempted to help him, tentatively, but somehow also managing to get inextricably tangled there. Meanwhile, the remaining hooded beings returned home, not having noticed a thing!

Of course, the disrobed one never returned to his abode, preferring instead to gallivant with his delightful new friend, making up for lost time and causing such a racket that his former masters dispatched a troop to punish the rogue.

Hunted by this ragtag army, the unfortunate fugitives, cradling a tiny newborn, attempted to reach the refuge of a swamp. Hounded and desperate, they hid the baby in the cocoon of a silkworm in an attempt to save it. They then embraced and together slipped into the quagmire.

The following spring, the young child emerged from its now-worn cocoon, half fairy and half caterpillar, not caterpillar enough to become a butterfly, and insufficiently Fairy to flutter around the forest. The creature was destined, as his father once had been, to a life of solemn procession.

LENGTH DURING THE ELFIN AGE:
Nine inches (22 cm).

CURRENT LENGTH:
Eight inches (20 cm).

APPEARANCE:
A long and attractive caterpillar, brightly hued and downy. It is mainly azure blue, purple, and mauve in color. It has the tiny face of a Lutin within a cowl, formed by a membrane of orange skin, from which emerge the long, silky hairs that cover its head. Two Nymph arms and legs sprout from the middle of its body.

HABITAT:
In dense forests around swamps.

FOOD:
Foliage, buds, pine needles.

BEHAVIOR:
The Processionary has very few morals, living alone, away from the Fairies and other little creatures. It is fertilized once every hundred years by a moonbeam, but the egg which it carries only rarely hatches.

ACTIVITIES:
It is in constant procession from dawn until noon the following day. On certain August nights, it emits a wondrous, light-filled musical note and radiates intense light alternately from two orbs. In November, it weaves a cocoon of silk between curled leaves.

HEIGHT:
Thirteen inches (34 cm), according to the Greeks.

APPEARANCE:
Burned, pitted skin. Spindly, skinny bodies, narrower at the shoulders than at the pelvis. Flat chests. Huge bumpy heads balanced precariously upon necks as thin as a chicken's. Feet turned inward. Hindered by their puny build, Akkas have developed a tough outer skin that has allowed them to endure for millennia and to face the numerous dangers of the wild savannahs.

CLOTHING:
Nude, with the exception of a loincloth that is frequently decorated with shells, or wearing a penile tube. Feather and bone decorations are worn in the hair. Some Amazonian Akkas paint themselves green from head to toe and then decorate themselves with flowers and creepers. The Kossobala dress themselves in a cloak made from their own beards.

HABITAT:
Small cabins, troglodyte caves, or grass huts constructed in trees. Homer, Aristotle, and Herodotus described them as living at the source of the Nile. Later, the British explorers Henry Stanley and Dr. David Livingstone encountered the Vaouta population in the Congo. As for the Akkas, the "founding fathers," the German traveler George Schweinfurth (1836–1925) stumbled across them during his excursions in southern Arabia, the Nile region, and Eritrea.

FOOD:
Fruit, game, everything that grows "outside" the soil. They reject anything that grows or comes from "Ymir's entrails"—sweet potatoes, roots, larvae, snakes, and so on. This rule appears to have been left by the wayside for the last three hundred years among those Akkas who live in close proximity to humans.

Akkas

"The gods themselves tell the stories of creation . . ."
—Kathleen Raine

Picks and axes chopped at earth, rock, and forest, formerly the flesh of the giant Ymir. The Alfs, in their earliest physical form, moved forward in the darkness. Clumsy, yet powerful, they struck at blocks of granite. Their movements were lumpish and stilted. Only yesterday, they lacked arms and crawled about like blind larvae. It was Odin who sculpted them, and some still bore the imprint of those divine fingers on their skin.

Their gaze was out of focus, the intelligence behind their eyes still nothing but a dull glow, but that did not matter. They had the whole of eternity in which to learn! Already driven by an uncontrollable instinct, they advanced, dug, and broke out of their initial mold, drawn by an irresistible glow that only they could sense. Throughout the eons—that is how they measure time—of their development underground, slight differences emerged.

Those who came into being in Niflheim (a cold, dark world) craved the shadows, while those from Muspelheim (a place of fire and heat) craved the light.

Akkas were created so close to the furnace in Muspelheim that they were all but turned to carbon. Unlike the White Alfs, who were exposed to the radiant light, Akkas never had the chance to become living arcs of luminescence. It was only when a frozen chunk of rock from Niflheim unexpectedly struck the place where the Akkas lived that they were saved from cremation at the very last moment and were released.

This close brush with death steeled the courage of these charred spirits, and they immediately began to carve out escape tunnels. After baking for so long, Odin had suddenly buried them beneath arctic ice, and, more accustomed to waves of heat, the Akkas were quick to up and leave what had hitherto been their home, unwilling to freeze one second longer on the ice pack. They shoveled and dug as hard as they could, their efforts alone sufficiently warming them. As a result, once they established their domain, they despised hard work thereafter.

Eons passed and the Akkas were the only ones still digging. They dug and dug for an eternity. They dug through mines of lead, coal, and salt. They ignored the diamonds that they passed, so great was their desire to discover a new Muspelheim, somewhere in the bowels of the earth.

Finally, as they slowly dug deeper, the ground began to feel warm beneath their feet, becoming ever hotter, until, almost

BEHAVIOR:

The original Akkas are now nothing but a memory. Unions with cannibalistic demons have given rise to numerous breeds. The Ashanti from Ghana fear small Genies with enormous heads. Along the Ubangi, Mandjia hunters say that they sometimes encounter a deformed Dwarf accompanied by dogs. In the Gulf of Guinea, the local inhabitants fear tiny red Dwarfs with white beards. The inhabitants of the forests of northern Brazil run away from the red-capped, black Saci, who are capable of killing from a distance.

ACTIVITIES:

Akkas hardly bat an eyelid when confronted with big game, crocodiles, or even elephants, which they hunt with bows and arrows and javelins. Very mindful of perpetuating the species, the Akkas of the Congo like to pursue young Water Nymphs frolicking at the river. These Nymphs, not wanting to bring into the world the offspring of a demon, wear a false penis on their stomachs in order to deflect the interest of their stalkers.

at the surface once more, the ground was nearly boiling! They clambered out of their underground tunnels beneath a scalding sun. Slow, sluggish waters lapped against cracked banks before evaporating towards deserts of torpor. This scorched landscape filled the Akkas with joy, and they drifted off into the savannah, beneath the baobab trees, and were lost in the mirages of the dunes . . .

The Akkas were ready to found the great Pygmy races, races that still exist today. They had arrived at the gates of Eden. They were its soul. The gods of the north disliked the Akkas and regarded them as mongrels, but the southern gods cherished them as favorites. The indigenous creatures were respectful and fearful and venerated the gods, making ritual offerings of livestock and young virgins to them. This custom continues to the pre-

sent day. Throughout Africa, tom-toms resound to announce the arrival of these little masters of the elements, who are constantly wandering along the great rivers, the Niger and the Congo, in pursuit of the scorching jungles of the equator and the plains of Cameroon and Gabon. They have crossed the warm seas and gotten as far as Bengal and the Philippines, and they have also spread to the incarnadine villages of the Americas, along the Rio Grande and the Colorado River.

On the way, they married dark-skinned girls with eyes the color of tinder and spawned the Okna, Buhuha, Watta, Datoua, Alta, Micopi, and other tough subspecies that have escaped the attentions of explorers.

Their survival, like that of the last equatorial paradises, is currently under threat.

HEIGHT:
  Under twelve inches (30 cm).

APPEARANCE:
  Graceful. Coppery skin, curly golden hair, Greek profiles. They grew uglier throughout their long decline, becoming hideous, deformed Dwarfs.

CLOTHING:
  First attired in light, white materials, silky tunics and peplums, they later strapped on small bronze coats of armor that, alas, glinted like prawn shells in the grip of enemy beaks and talons.

HABITAT:
  Before the war of Dënoe, they made do with flimsy flowered cottages on the perfumed hills of Thrace. They were later forced to disappear under the rocks of Bulgaria.

FOOD:
  They were not averse to crane meat before they themselves became the cranes' preferred food.

BEHAVIOR/ACTIVITIES:
  Struck down by the goddesses, this once rich, cheerful, and creative civilization never again experienced happy times and degenerated. Besieged by the murderous diving of the birds, the Pitikos relentlessly tried to destroy crane broods perched on the crags by inventing ineffective weapons.

The Pitikos and Other Pygmies

About bodies that seem like the transient spirit of ever-changing nature.

—Kathleen Raine

"The resounding voice of the winged people of the cranes rises to the sky as they flee from torrents and celestial tempests and clamorously traverse the raging sea to rain death and destruction on the Pygmy race, waging a tremendous battle from above," recounts Homer. "The cranes, resonant clouds of Thracian birds, suddenly swoop down on the Pygmies, who run into battle poorly armed with light weapons. Unable to resist, they are clasped in the hooked talons of the merciless cranes and carried into the air," adds a caustic Juvenal in a description of the cruel confrontation between the cranes and the Pitikos. An interminable and absurd battle, born, like so many others of the era, of a whim of the gods . . .

The beautiful Dënoe enjoyed a wonderful romance with the small but sweet Pitikos Nicodamas. They wed under the blooming olive trees, and the union produced a baby, whom they named Mopsus. The christening was a very elaborate affair, typical of mythological times. There was no skimping on the resources, the entertainment, or the guests: hordes of heroes, goddesses, demimondaines, and demigods crowded ceremoniously around the cradle. They ate mutton with sweet peppers, whole roasted sheep, stuffed grape leaves, taramasalata, and baklava. But just like the interruption of the Wicked Witch in the story of the Sleeping Beauty, uninvited callers appeared, veiled in wrath and anger: shrewish and oversensitive Artemis, goddess of the hunt, and Mistress Hera, wife of Zeus and queen of the skies in all her festering splendor. Poor little Dënoe barely had the time to mutter an excuse, blaming a slow messenger or a mistaken address, when her lovely voice began to caw and cackle, her regular features began to elongate into a beak, her rounded thighs narrowed into the feet of a wading bird, and her magnificent buttocks feathered into plumage.

Nicodamas desperately rushed to his transformed wife, but a wind called up by the goddesses carried her into the air on her new wings. Dënoe's brain was reduced to the size of a pea, and only one thought crossed her mind: to recover the fruit of her womb. She knocked her Dwarf husband to the ground with one blow of her claw and lunged toward the cradle. An army of Pitikos immediately sprang to defend it, confronting her with anything near at hand: forks, ladles, knives. They crippled and wounded the bird, forcing her to abandon her prey!

To end the story here would be to underestimate the heart of a mother and the stubbornness of a crane. She sailed through the heights seeking reinforcements among her fellow wading birds, and returned to launch a pitiless war. This was the start of an era of hatred, attacks, and massacres. Even after time had erased the memory of the quarrelsome couple and the reason for the vendetta, the cranes and the Pitikos would never cease to do battle.

NOTES:

Besides the Pitikos, Greco-Latin Lutinologists also mention Mirmidons or
Myrmidons.

THE SPITHAMIENS

Evasive Dwarfs situated by Pliny
along the Ganges after they fled Chios;
hunted by the great owls, allies of the
cranes.

THE LONG-EARS

Another species of big-eared Dwarf,
whose exact name has been lost; they
likewise fled the persecution of the
avian avengers by taking refuge in
untamed lands. In the sixteenth century, Magellan's associate Pigafetta
described an encounter with these
tiny troglodytes, whose ears
were so large that when
they bedded down, one
ear served as a mattress
and the other as
a blanket.

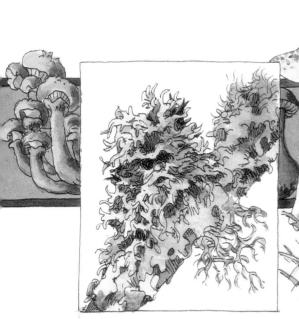

HEIGHT:

> *Some are microscopic; others are as tall as twelve inches (30 cm).*

APPEARANCE:

> *They appear in many guises: gray aerial microbes, minute acrocephalics, winged Souriquets, plumed corpuscules, mossy stunted homunculi. Both vegetable and animal, Fairy and Dwarf, they can be covered with down, plants, or ladybug shells; have butterfly wings, weasel's snouts, or squirrel's tails; or resemble little old greenish men with long lichen beards and hair. The Kientibakori, dreaded by the Jivaro Machiguenga, appears as a head constructed of vegetation topping a large heap of intestines and gelatinous roots. The Cipbelu is almost invisible, disguised as a part of the tree that harbors it. The Moss Gatherers are graceful little beings no larger than a Capricorn beetle.*

CLOTHING:

> *Most have no need of clothes; some of the Finzweiberl or Verdier dress in gowns, jackets, coats, and bonnets of moss, lichen, sewn-together leaves, feathers, or furs. The Mushroom Sabateus dress in red leather in order to blend in with the glistening autumnal tints of the mushrooms.*

FOOD:

> *Herbivore, insectivore, carnivore. The most minuscule gather rose nectar and pollen. The Mouthless Ones feed on the perfumes of the undergrowth and the vapors of the dawn.*

The Little Moss People

It is fair that the moss of shady spots and the hollows of rocks belong to the subterranean dwarf people. Entrusted to their care, it quickly becomes glossy, fresh, saturated with spring water and nascent rain showers.
—Marie Gevers,
The Legendary Herbarium

With the aid of keen hearing, silent observation, and knowledge of behavior in the sylvan kingdom, anyone who is familiar with the forests will soon hear, see, and be able to approach the secret world of invisible fauna.

Once the "Mysterious Barricades" have been breached and the peephole laid bare, the forest panorama comes alive. The guest can part the ivy to reveal a multitude of winged Nymphs; those hyacinth mosaics one sees are actually azure Fairies, and the dragonflies are not dragonflies but swarms of slender Fusaylles. If you remove the large caps of the silver dollar mushrooms, you will find a whole army of stemmed Fijn. The same is true for the helmeted and skirted troops of "Coprinus disseminatus and glistening ink caps," and all the ferns, butterflies, toads, and bouquets of honey mushrooms turn out to be Mycenaean platoons. The grand, cohesive mimesis dissolves to reveal faces crowned with tiny antennas, shoulders indented with elytra, silks, wings, thighs, backbones, furbelows: maidenhair ferns, sybaritic Fujoles, female Fairy-Dwarfs, Heather Dwarfs, tiny cavalry, woodruff, ashen Carquinets, moss sprites, and all the Dwarf fauna of the minuscule hills of the mossy "undergrowth."

The sylvan Little People searched for many years for the perfect habitat and settled in different places according to their character: wooded areas, where the dense trees limited the light and rationed the air, provided the perfect home for the groups of so-called "air creatures" or "Alf-air creatures." Those who remained on the ground were called the "earth creatures," either adapted to life on the surface (epigeous) or underground (hypogenous). The "Furry Foot" is a hypogeal species, and the Verdier is epigeous. Then there were those who spanned the two classifications, spending time on the surface and taking refuge in burrows during part of the day.

Those who live a hypogeal life have adapted their bodies accordingly and have developed slender frames perfect for digging tunnels. The subterranean existence has also affected their organs of sight, as

Dreamy and mysterious. They often gather around the Buschgrossmutter Huedren, the Vieille Mère, and the Fay-trees teeming with Dryads. Once a month, during the full moon, the Little Moss Women, the Moss Maidens, the Moswyfje, and the Lohjunfern visit the hillocks of the Huldres. In other respects, Elfologists agree that they do not know what these Dwarfs do.

Their greatest enemy is the "Savage Hunter."

has a nocturnal epigeous life, leading to atrophy or hypertrophy.

The forest provided shelter for many earth creatures, but this dark habitat sometimes forced them to seek the air and light outside, whether in flights across the plains, ascents into the foliage, or leaps from branch to branch. Undergrowth fauna became climbers and gliders.

To reach the branches, the gnawing Dwarf, who fed on hazelnuts, eggs, and pinecones, developed monkey arms with nimble clawed fingers; a plume of hair on his tail now serves both as a balancer and a parachute. This creature is called the Guerliguet, a type of Silomeel forest creature that can both climb and fly.

The insectivorous Veluvoltins used their skin parachutes to climb, leap, and glide to freedom, no longer needing any terrestrial support, and they have become free batlike creatures of the air. On summer days, they take refuge in the crevices and clefts of trees, from which they emerge at dusk; in winter, as the aerial plankton that sustains them becomes scarce, they don their silky membranes and hibernate in the deepest of caves.

The Gatherers, Hattia, Little Men, Gardenets, Berthes Dwarfs, Moss Manikins, Moss Sylvains, Green-Hoods, Vergris, Pchwist, Minimes, Mirlurons, Tottus, Roncins, Rododeras, Waldzwerge, and Skritek, who do not travel through the dense forest, take refuge in burrows or sleep in "forts" or "bastions" of impenetrable shrubbery.

The Hupitoo and the Mushii rarely leave the bushy wild lands of the "Wind Lichen."

The life of the Little Moss People is discreet, regulated by the clock of flowers and animal nontime. They generally wake at "flight time," when the ducks pass over the marshes, and they emerge when they sense the twilight fragrance that precedes the livid hour of the sandpiper, when men return home at the first chill of night.

Robin Goodfellow

Not Robin Goodfellow, nor Robin Hood,
But Robin the encloser of Hatfield Wood.
　　　—Algernon Cecil,
　　　　Life of Robert Cecil, London, 1915

Robin Goodfellow, also known as Robin Goodfriend or Robin Goodchild, is a last-generation Goblin. However, this robust fellow, described by W. Fisher as being "born on an oak seedling" just like his cousin Puck, is no ordinary fellow, and Elfin chroniclers have written page after page about him, just because he is so elusive.

He appeared in Nottinghamshire in England in around 1200. His origins are very bizarre and maddening to sensible Lutinologists and scholarly Elfologists who have tried to follow his zigzagging spoor! Not one can give precise details, and each one endeavors to buttress his very own version of the green "Goblin."

Is Robin Goodfellow the "spirit," the impish ghost, of Robin Hood, born in 1247 in Kirkless? Was the "good-hearted bandit" actually a Robin Goodfellow? His friend? A colleague? A relative? A twin? And the famous cheerful companions, the "merry men," were they Hobgoblins? So many unanswered questions. But the legends of the Goblin and the famous archer often cross; they blend, they intersect, and they intermingle.

Just like the Robin Goodfellows, Robin Hoods exist everywhere! There is a Robin Goodfellow hillock and a Robin Hood hillock in Dorset. Two crosses marking the border in Lincolnshire carry their names, as does a hill near Gloucester. They are particularly evident in the English counties of Nottinghamshire, Derbyshire, Cumberland, Cheshire, and Staffordshire, and they have built dolmens near Chard, as well as at Tilston Fearnall.

In his *Mythology of the Fairies*, Thomas Keightley tells us that Robin Hood is a name for Robin Goodfellow. A drawing from 1638 shows him with a horned head and goat legs dancing like a Puck in the center of a circle of sorcerers. When Dame Alice Noon went on trial in 1316, she admitted that she worshipped a spirit named Robin Artison, under whose auspices she cast spells while practicing black magic! Nyls Wicanton notes that Robin Hood is sometimes known under the nickname Robin Round-Cap and is so called because he wears a headdress similar to that of the Gnomes, and his companions wear green, the traditional color of the Little People! The English saying "around Robin Hood's barn" means to take the long way around or to use an indirect approach.

The same clothes, the same appearance, the same companions, the same places visited, the same ability in archery, the same inclination for thievery, laughter, and practical jokes: the two really have a lot in common!

Joseph Hunter insists that Robin Hood was born between 1285 and 1295 and was declared an outlaw for having participated in an uprising by the Duke of Lancaster. Wakefield town records establish that Robin Hood married a

certain Matilda in 1316. J. M. Outch has him being born in 1225. In the *Paleographia Britannica*, Dr. Stukeley traces his family tree back to Waltheof, Earl of Cumberland and Huntingdon, who married the niece of William the Conqueror. There is a place called Loxley in Staffordshire where Robin is said to have once owned land, before it was lost to him. Robin, who was none other than Robert de Fitzooth, took the name Robin Hood to travel through the forests in disguise.

Growing weak, he took refuge in a convent in 1247 and died there. In a last effort before death, he shot two arrows through the window and asked to be buried where they fell. One was swept away on the Calder River; the other fell in a park, and to this day marks his tomb.

Once Robin was buried, the Robin Goodfellows also disappeared. The world had to wait another hundred years before they reappeared with very pale faces lined with sorrow.

HEIGHT:
Twenty-four inches (60 cm).

APPEARANCE:
Red-haired, sharp eyes, pointy ears. Some tales and beliefs occasionally depict them with two small horns and even a goat's tail.

CLOTHING:
Caps adorned with a feather; green tunics and overcoats. They carry a bow and arrows slipped into a deerskin quiver.

HABITAT:
The countryside and the magic forests of England. In trees, rocks, and fern cottages.

FOOD:
Game, cheese, beer, and cider.

BEHAVIOR/ACTIVITIES:
They are rogues. They are very active in May, playing the bagpipes and pinching the young girls. They live in groups. They mix with the Fairies of the mosses and the undergrowth. Practical jokers, agreeable and lighthearted, they can take up arms if provoked. They rob criminals and villains, piercing them with arrows. It is said that they plant the roots of spring that the woodpecker brings back each March.

HEIGHT:
*From two to eight inches
(5 to 20 cm).*

APPEARANCE:
*The Dwarfs with no anus are very
small. The Pipintu have long beards,
but they are bald because of all the
garbage that the humans living above
drop on their heads. The Idsetti-deha
have red hair. Some of them look like
sloths. In contrast to the South American Dwarfs without anuses, the subterranean Dwarfs of North America
are better formed and slightly larger—
the size of a squirrel. The Coeurs
d'Alene, who owe their name to the
Salish-speaking Indians living in the
present state of Idaho, look like tiny
humans and rapidly shin up trees
headfirst. They carry their babies on
their backs swaddled head-down. The
Ohdow are as pretty and elegant as
the Elves.*

CLOTHING:
*Coarse, red clothing. Those from North
America are generally dressed in
Indian-style tunics made of squirrel
skins.*

HABITAT:
*Claude Lévi-Strauss considers the
domain of these subterranean Dwarfs
to cover the northern Amazon region,
stretching from the Xingu basin to
Central America.
The Algonquin, the Sioux, the
Iroquois, the Creeks, the Cherokees,
the Delaware, the Nez Perce, and
Amerindians from the Rio Grande
to Canada recognize many species of
Dwarf quite similar to the Abatwa
of South Africa, who reign over the
entire underworld.*

The Pipintu,
Idsetti-deha,
and Oneitib

*He entered a world where everything was
small, even the door that closed behind him . . .*
—Anselme Krook, *Lower Space*

Seven leagues from the Gnomes,
Kobolds, Wichtlein, Erdleute, and
Sidhe, the Lower Worlds are home
to other tiny Dwarfs, children of
the "Backwards World," the most famous
of which are the Pipintu, studied in detail
by Claude Lévi-Strauss in his remarkable
work, *The Jealous Potter.*

They are so minuscule and go out so
little that they remained unknown for
years and years. When their sharp cries
burst forth from the impenetrable forest
vegetation, they were taken for the squeals
of animals; when one skittered through
the shingle of a cliff, it was thought to be
the scrabbling of rodents—until the day
an Indian, pursued by an enemy, hid at
the back of a deep cave. He slipped farther
into the cavern and emerged into the
heart of the land of the Pipintu, Dwarfs
without anuses who feed on steam. They
welcomed the intruder so amiably that he
stayed with them for quite a while; he was
stunned to see them bustle about, taking
care of business and hunting, but doing it
all backwards . . . They also reversed the
meanings of words: "heavy" meant "light,"
"hot" meant "cold," and "day" meant
"night." They entered to exit and exited
to enter. When they felt hungry, they
placed food on the nape of their necks and
let it slide down their backs. They would
sit in circles to sniff the aroma of food
simmering in a large pot. They begged
the Indian to give them an anus just like
his. He tried to operate on them, but the
patients died one after another. They
lacked not only an anus, but also intestines;
the food they had thought they could

swallow shredded their insides. The man
returned home and told his people of his
adventures. The story circulated from
bivouac to village and from hut to teepee,
and other nomadic Indians added tales of
similar experiences.

A Tukuma spoke of a Dwarf people
who inhabited a subterranean world and
fed on the aroma of food. A human married one of their women. She wanted to
eat like her husband, but the food caused
her horrible pains. The man used a knife
to cut an anus for her so that she could
have a bowel movement, but she died
shortly afterwards.

The Lipan Apache discovered an iden-
tical race, whose anuses were no larger
than the head of a pin; they were so small
that the poor things could not relieve
themselves, so they subsisted on only the
steam rising from food. In the Indians'
eyes, these Dwarfs were half-baked beings
who had escaped from the nether regions
before the Creator had time to finish them.

The Tacana told the story of a hunter
who went down an armadillo burrow and
found himself in the other world. It was
occupied by Idsetti-deha, also without
anuses, who lived on drops of water and
the aroma of food. To them, the wasps
were hostile Indians and the jackrabbits
were jaguars. The hunter saved them from
these fearsome enemies, but even in their
gratitude, they felt such deep disgust at
seeing him defecate that they led him up
to the surface again and sent him away.

The Arapaho described tiny cannibals
with childish voices who left their hearts
hanging in their houses before going out;
the Algonquin described the "little men,"
or Makia'wis, who were able to transform
themselves into nightjars; and the Sanema
described Dwarfs called Oneitib, who
lacked an anus and intestines and were
hollow inside, which made them perpetually hungry.

Likewise, a well-traveled trapper confided that he had seen a Yaanaite who ate
through his tail, defecated through his
mouth, and copulated with his nose.
But since he was a paleface, no one
believed him.

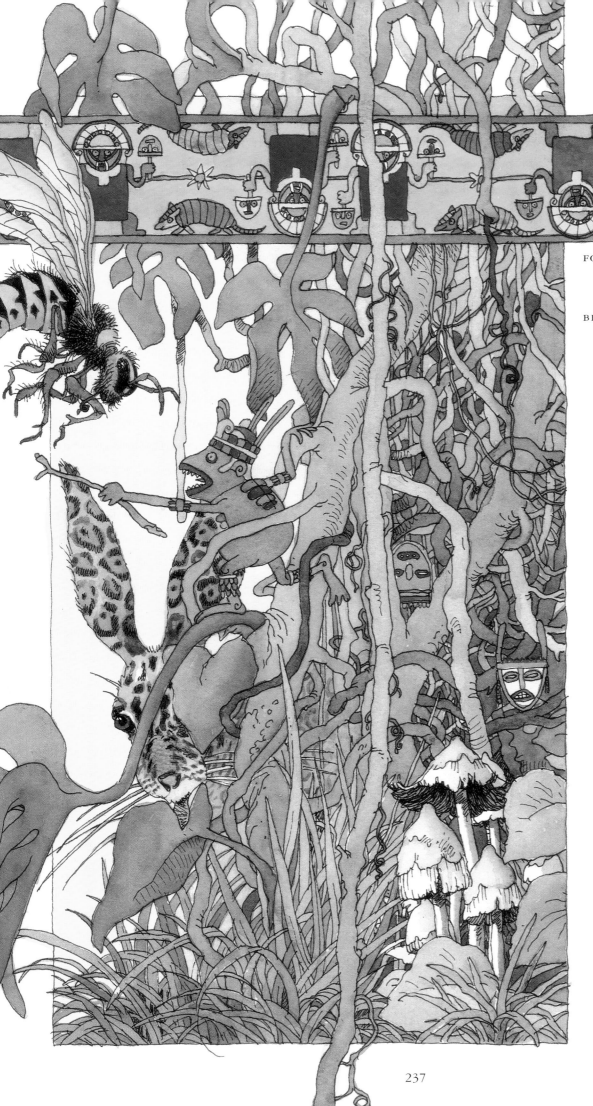

FOOD:

While the "anus-less Southerners" are satisfied with the steam rising off food, their Northern cousins hunt and fish.

BEHAVIOR/ACTIVITIES:

They love to play. Nonetheless, some may be malevolent: they lead hunters astray in the forest or kill them with arrows that leave no trace of a wound. They willingly marry humans or Elves. The women cannot give birth naturally; their abdomens must be cut open to remove the child. The Nunkui protect gardens. Thanks to judiciously employed magical powers, the Ohdow control the earth spirits. According to the Iroquois, these chthonic Dwarfs are good hunters. They bathe in water containing mashed human fingernails in order to take on a human odor and more easily approach their prey.

THOSE OF
THE HEATHS AND
THE HILLS

Seasonal life rises from the depths of geological time to an unimaginable future.

—H. Dalmon

In the middle of a field, at a crossroads, in the fold of a hill, in a copse, or in the divisions between fields, sit the gods of the "Octre Forest," motionless and meditative. Coiled inside an age-old oak, a rotting tree stump, a shrub, or a tuft of grass, they observe what humans do to their untamed realm.

On once-forested land watered by rivers, settlers have gradually cleared and subdued the terrain, but the old arborescence persists, and at the first sign of neglect, the forest reappears in rhythmic stages: a prairie thick with brambles, scrubland with blackthorns, a small wood where oaks move to dominate the earth. Just one growing season is enough to turn a wood into a forest. The frost, the rain, and the sun lay down the law in the fields, but Nature tamed is never irrevocably so. The wrath of water spirits can sweep over a field in less time than it took to plant it; through the ages, farmers have learned to respect natural cycles and practices.

Today's agricultural engineer, perched on the rising curves of excess production, would do well to come down from his ephemeral pedestal and contemplate the true face of wheat.

In fact, although it is extremely difficult to describe a Lutin, everything becomes crystal clear once you understand its rules.

HEIGHT:
A Lutin is both short and tall at the same time, ranging in height from half an inch to one foot (1 to 30 cm).

APPEARANCE:
They are both unique and multiple, visible and invisible, clean but with dirty noses and ears. Lutins are scrawny yet slinky. Their eyes are sparkling and as round as little cobnuts. Their fingers are long and dexterous, and their thick hair grows in tufts. Lutins begin to get old at the age of around three hundred. Their beards grow and lengthen, and at the same time their hair falls out, and their narrow, almost chinless faces with their rounded cheeks begin to crumple like an overripe apple. Lutins also gain weight and acquire a potbelly with age.

CLOTHING:
Brightly colored green and brown rags. Very tall pointed red or green caps. Long pointed patched shoes. Lutins like to run around naked in the forest. If you offer them new clothes in exchange for their services, they get offended and will never return. In the summer, they wear jerkins dyed green with sap from the leaves.

Lutins

Like black flying serpents, the hideous Noitins (Lutins) reveal themselves to be perilous.
—Benoît de Sainte-Maure,
Roman de Troie (c. 1160)

What is a Lutin, said Estonne. *Sire,* said Nascis, *it is a spirit that one can see and that enjoys deceiving people.*
—*Perceforest,* Vol.II, f° 13-XVI
(second half of the fourteenth century)

Only a Lutin would do battle with the dead.
—Michel de Montaigne,
Essays, III-112 (1588)

L utins are the French equivalent of Elves, Sprites, Goblins, Hobgoblins, Imps, Pixies, or Cornish Piskies. Lutins gambol, tease, jest, make mischief, sneak around, plot, change their shape, and ride on the backs of related species. They have scattered under myriad identities; they migrate, proliferate, and disappear down holes—reappearing in a hundred different guises. Lutins are unclassifiable, inexplicable: you may think

you have gotten hold of one, but just then you accidentally open your fingers slightly and all that remains is the impression of liveliness and a few green threads.

"They are singularly diverse spirits. On the one hand, they are similar to Elves and Lemures, as well as to the Kobolds and to the Lares. In this last guise, they should preferably be called Follets or Farfadets," claims Grün, who, like most Elfologists, even the most ancient, has never quite known how to pin them down! "The character of the Lutin is hard to fathom," the chorus of Lutinologists chants desperately: they are spirits of both the air and fire, sprites of the woods, the streams, the dunes, the meadows. One may be a peaceful Penate who turns into a demon on werewolf nights, or he may be a highwayman, the plunderer of men and seducer of women, a master of mischief-making and trickery, a practical joker, or a kindly imp, the protector of children and animals.

Lutins are not Kobolds, Nutons, Brownies, Goblins, Annequires, Laùru, or Gnomes, but a race in their own right. They are so numerous and lively that in France the name *lutin* is commonly used to designate all kinds of Little People. They have haunted legends, country traditions, and folktales since the dawn of time! Philologists claim that the name

lutin derives from that of Neptune. Jean Markale, author of *L'Epopée celtique en Bretagne* (The Celtic Saga in Brittany) invokes the god Nudd and its variations Nodons, Nuadu, Nut. "Some derive the word *lutin* from the medieval French words *luits, luiton, luicter, lutter,* meaning 'to fight,'" writes Grün. Others claim that *lutin, luton, nuton,* and *netun* all have the same root, the French word *nuit,* meaning "night." Grandgagnage believes that the derivation is from the English word *little. Hutin* is a word which means someone who is quarrelsome. The word *utinet* means a cooper's hammer, and Utin the Lutin is a sprite who beats people up! Barbygère, on the other hand, claims that Lutins are descendants of King Lutt (known in English as King Lud), ruler of the "Hooded Genies" (*Geniicucullati*), and of Eyllyn, Fairy of the morning miracles.

Even before the year 1000, the monk Eon prophesied that "daymons and Noituns [Lutins] beasties will soon all the town invade." In c. 1212, Gervais of Tilbury explained that Lutins are demons or beings of a secret or unknown nature who get along well with the simple country people, attend their celebrations, and help them with their domestic chores. As soon as the doors are closed, they warm themselves beside the fire and take small frogs out of their breast pockets, which they eat after roasting them in the embers. They have a vicious air and wrinkled faces and are no more than half an inch high, yet they effortlessly perform the hardest manual work. It is in their nature to make themselves useful, although this does not stop them from playing a few nasty tricks on mortals.

Der Schretelund der Wazzerbär, a thirteenth-century German fable, tells of the Herculean strength of a Schretel, the German form of a Lutin: "A Norwegian accompanied by a bear stopped at a peasant's house to spend the night there, but the home was haunted by a Schretel, who was described as measuring three spans and having extraordinary strength. He wore a red cap and was in the habit of turning furniture and household implements upside down. In the middle of the night, he would emerge from his hiding place and warm himself at the fireside. This time, seeing the bear asleep by the hearth, he hit it, and a terrible fight ensued. In the morning, the Schretel informed the peasant that he was leaving and would not return as long as the big cat (the bear) remained in the house."

In 1402, the French Dominicans were forced to abandon their retreat because it was possessed by a Lutin named Bronzet.

HABITAT:
> They live in warrens that are as active and busy as huge termite nests, but where playing and capering about replace work. Their homes are solidly built, being made from adobe with added moss and fragrant herbs. The warrens stand on hilltops, embankments, and standing stones, and in the woods between the roots of giant oaks or yew trees. They rarely leave home, although they can sometimes be found here and there in cellars and lofts, under beds, at the back of cupboards, or in workboxes.
>
> Lutins live mainly in France, but a few, attracted by the "green Fairies," have settled in southwest England, where they have merged with the Pixies. A cousin named Brag who wears a cap with bells on it lives in Yorkshire; there are two or three Kwelgeerts Plageerts in Flanders, and a few related species in Germany and Italy.

FOOD:

They are greedy and take several helpings of everything.

BEHAVIOR:

Imps, wags, pilferers, teases, loafers, and pranksters, they are also brave workers and redoubtable warriors. Although they gad about after young girls and Fairies, they remain faithful to their Lutines and follow them in death. Lutins are not entirely immortal: they can succumb to a violent accidental death or to grief.

Thanks to the Tarnhelm (a sort of hat), they can disappear or transform themselves into humans or animals—or even inanimate objects.

Lutins are not timorous, but it is said that they will never tangle the hairs of a donkey, because they refuse to touch the animal, owing to his role during the birth of Christ. The smell of a mane burned by a blessed altar candle will keep them away from the stables.

Prayers were completely ineffectual other than to increase his savagery.

The Parlement of Bordeaux, held in 1595, issued an order canceling the lease on a house haunted by Lutins. Some time later, a woman who lived nearby found herself pregnant by one of them.

The Lutin living at Château de Callac always harassed an old woman who looked after the château in the absence of the owner. He rolled huge balls in an upstairs room to disturb her sleep, he tangled her thread, he set her dirty-blond hair on fire with a candle, and he put salt in her milk soup. On other occasions he mussed her headdress, knotted her hair, or traced lovely black mustaches on her face with charcoal. One night, he stood right in front of her and laughed as he held a red-hot iron cauldron to her neck.

In his correspondence with W. Y. Evans Wentz (*The Fairy-Faith in Celtic Countries*), Anatole Le Braz, author of *La Légende de la mort* (The Legend of Death), describes the household Lutin of his childhood: "Each house had its own. It was like a little Penate god. Sometimes visible, sometimes invisible, he presided over all aspects of family life. Better yet, he participated in the most helpful way. Inside the dwelling, he helped the servants, fanned the fire in the hearth, watched over the cooking of

food for humans and animals, comforted crying infants bedded down inside the armoire, and kept worms from the pieces of bacon hanging from the beams. It was also his duty to guard the cowsheds and the stables: thanks to him, the cows gave creamy milk, and the horses had robust hindquarters and glossy coats. In a word, he was a good family spirit, but only on the condition that people showed him the respect he deserved. In the face of any slight, his benevolence changed into mischief, and there was nothing he would not do to those who had offended him, including overturning the kettles on the hearth, knotting wool around the bedposts, spoiling pipe tobacco, inextricably tangling horses' manes, drying up cows' udders, and peeling the wool off sheep's backs. His customs and his whims were carefully respected by everyone. At my parents' house, our old maid Filie never stored the iron cauldron without taking the precaution of sprinkling a little cold water on it to cool it off before setting it in a corner of the hearth. If you had asked why she performed this ritual, she would have told you, 'So the Lutin doesn't get burnt if he sits on it.'"

It was the custom in Brittany to respectfully call them Nantrou (Sir) or Moestre Yan (Master John). It was best

not to "muss" the manes or tails that the Lutins had tangled during the night, for fear of having your own hair tangled. The curly-maned horses, whose necks had served as mounts for the Lutins, were very much in demand in the markets.

The story goes that the Lutins, in whose veins coursed the valiant blood of King Lutt, joined some brave wandering knights and shared their adventures while perched on the croups of their white palfreys. If seduced by a gentle damsel, they would uninhibitedly defend her colors, the magic resourcefulness of their steely arms compensating well for their unimpressive size. The beautiful Locathelye, who took the Ardennes Lutin Nourcine — ironically decked out in black—as her spouse, had no reason to be ashamed of him.

On the other hand, Hodekin the Scounnunck (the household Lutin of a noble German house) had less luck with his poor cuckolded master. The latter, about to leave for a trip, called the Lutin who served as his page and told him, "My friend, I leave my wife in your hands, keep an eye on her." As soon as the husband had crossed the drawbridge, the adulterous wife shamelessly sent for her lovers in turn. But Hodekin did not allow any of them to approach her; he spent the day beating them back with blows of his sword. When the husband finally returned, the Lutin ran quite a distance to meet him and said breathlessly: "My prince, I rejoice at your return, because I will be released from the heavy task you set me. It was only with extreme difficulty that I succeeded in preventing your wife from falling into infidelity. Therefore, I beg you not to ask me to watch over her again. I would rather spend my days guarding all the swine in Saxony than such a hussy!"

As long as grass does thrive,
The Lutins will survive.

ACTIVITIES:

Female Lutins (Lutines, or more precisely Lupronnes), love to take on the appearance of simple weasels. They cross the path in front of strollers and mock them from a distance with many frisks and capers. If their beauty is complimented, they delightedly strut and blow kisses.

Lutins are never still. If they are not working, they are playing; they rarely rest. They are often seen gliding down the rivers on water-lily rafts, but they never get wet, as we can see by their rather dirty faces.

The Bona, Lutins from the Auvergne, like to take on the appearance of bagpipe players. Despite using magic to try to increase their height, they have never managed to grow beyond seventeen inches.

The Chorriquets, Bonâmes, Penettes, Gullets, Boudig, and Bon Noz are mostly employed in looking after livestock and horses.

Lutins are very clever dyers, and they know the coloring properties of tree barks. The small inhabitants of the forest kingdom frequently bring them clothing to be dyed in season.

Their main activity is pulling pranks.

The Jeannette Lutin and the Fighting Lutins

Now then, who will take me on?

Taken at random, the first Fighting Lutin to mention is Big-Shoulders. As tiny as he is, if he does not like your face, he will jump on your back, and—bang!—he will crack your spine as easily as if it were a bit of wood.

The second is a protector of flora and fauna and a righter of wrongs when people barbarously mistreat animals. For example, if you inflate a frog by sticking a blowtorch up its rear, if you break the eggs of a clutch, or pull the legs off a fly, your life isn't worth a wooden nickel!

As for the Sorgues, they are the highwaymen; even smugglers fear them. It was, in fact, French smugglers who named them Sorgues, which means "night" in the lingo of delinquents. They are very small, hooded in black, and it's impossible to pinpoint their location. They advance noiselessly in the darkness, and then the game is on! It is impossible to stand up to these Fighting Lutins whose strength increases tenfold when their feet touch the ground or their hands brush against a tree.

The Spunkies attack only those who wear uniforms and cassocks.

The last one is the Jeannette Lutin. Small, yes, but he is a tremendous swashbuckler. He is invincible: a boxer, a redoubtable hand with the cutlass, a notable thief, and an excellent horseman.

These qualities also make him a relentless seducer. This daring eighteenth-century Lutin used his audacity and natural authority to become the leader of the most bloodthirsty gang of renegades. One fine day he went to the cave that served as their lair.

"What do you want, you little rat?" sneered their leader, drawing up to his full, hairy, giant height and peering down in surprise at the reckless runt. "I'm going to—" Wham! Already off the ground, flung into the air, cut down with a brutal jab, and spitting teeth, he had not even finished his threat when he found that the triumphant Lutin had already taken his place as leader.

"Come on! On your feet! To work!" commanded the Jeannette Lutin, and they all leapt to follow him, galloping across the countryside. Clinging to the mane of a robust black horse, he led the band of masked wretches, attacking stagecoaches, robbing travelers, and assaulting fortified farmsteads . . .

Is there anything more fickle than a mercurial Fighting Lutin?

Of course not! However, this particular Lutin suddenly, after seven fruitful years of thievery, grew bored of playing the highwayman! Tired of riding the moors, he betrayed his comrades and had them arrested. Captivated by a young and beautiful marquise in the neighborhood, he settled down with her in the elegant manor of Hautes-Bruyères in the Loire.

From that moment on, Jeannette became a household spirit and companion, and he took good care of the manor with the help of the wealth he had amassed during his wild years.

HEIGHT:
Some twenty-four inches (60 cm).

APPEARANCE:
Massive heads, thick red hair. Squinty, phosphorescent eyes, snub noses, long, mocking mouths, pointed ears. Their bodies are thin and twitchy.

HABITAT:
The southwest of England: Cornwall, Dartmoor, Exmoor. They swarm around the bogs of Granmere, from Bodmin to Launceston, in the Doone Valley. They are found from Moreton-hampstead and Tavistock to Wide-combe, Princetown, and Bovey Tracey, where they ride Tom Pearce's old mare and the ponies that abound there. Pixies live in the open air and are happy with the shelter of a briar or a hole under the tors, even in the depths of winter. Sometimes they cuddle up in the warm fur of a wild beast of the moor, or they may occasionally occupy the corner of a barn.

FOOD:
Cider, local sheep's milk. They stuff themselves with what they have stolen during their raids on gardens, orchards, and pantries. They eat platefuls of whortleberries with Devonshire cream in the summer.

Pixies

Pixie fine and Pixie gay
Pixie now will fly away.

Robert Hunt, in his *Popular Romances of the West of England,* divides the small Fairy People of Cornwall into five main species: the Small People; the Spriggans; the Buc-cas, Bockles, or Knockers; the Brownies; and the Piskies . . .

Piskies, Pisgy, Pixy, Pix, Piks, Pics, Picky, Picts, or Pixies: are they the descendants, the spirits, or the ghosts of the divinities of the mythical Picts? So many scholarly theories have crumbled amid the changeable winds of the moors!

The very name sounds like a nickname, evoking a cunning vivacity. There is both mischievousness and cruelty in this malevolent Goblin of the Devonshire heaths and moors, the bogs of Somerset, the slopes of Brown Willy. Their mops of red hair covered by red caps dance among the shrubbery and on the rocks with the molten fluidity of a Will-o'-the-Wisp. They untiringly ravage the countryside, leaving behind soured milk, sick cows, empty henhouses, and plucked orchards. They steal, pinch sleepers, push harvest workers, and throw young girls into ponds. Pixies make fun of decent folk, scolding them, insulting them, and driving them mad with the discordant din of their flutes and the racket of frenzied jigs.

They are even more fearsome to the prisoners of Dartmoor. They burrow in the limitless gravelly heaths that surround the gray walls of this infamous jail, waiting for an inmate to make the fatal mistake of trying to escape. The fangs of the guard dogs and the whips of the guards—even the rope—are preferable to the games of the Pixies. No witness has ever been able to report the details of their manhunts, but inarticulate, strangled cries from the bogs of Grimpen hint at their "devilry"!

Pixies are all the more dangerous for being intangible. You think you have one trapped in the corner of a barn, but even if you move quickly as you grab at him, you will come up with empty hands. He is already far away.

Many legends say that they are descendants of the Red Heads. If their supposed ancestors were indeed the offspring of the master builders of Cornwall, they have certainly changed over the course of centuries. Like the Elves and other Lutin races, their "normal" height has continued to decrease. While this process eventually halted in the majority of their cousins, the Pixies continued to shrink until they disappeared completely.

Well and truly gone? Er . . . that would be to underestimate their infinite capacity for resistance. Once they were reduced to nothing, blending with the cosmos, the elements, and the invisible forces, they began to inhale all of the extractable forms of energy from the heaths: wandering souls, Will-o'-the-Wisps, bog specters, auras of pagan kings laid beneath the burial mounds or circles of stone. They were regalvanized by the peat and the rocky peaks and drew power from flashes of lightning. They then reemerged, wizened and minuscule, but a hundred times more powerful, diabolical, and feisty.

Today, the laughter of the Pixies once again echoes terrifyingly through the hills.

BEHAVIOR:

Irascible and peevish, they shun their Fairy neighbors and detest most humans. Nevertheless, they can be moved by sad love stories; they protect the unlucky, the hopeless, and the rejected and every morning unfailingly put flowers on the grave of Kitty Jay, who hung herself because of a disappointment in love. Some children may also touch them; they leave small gifts in the road for them: coins and brightly colored eggs. Doddiscombleigh farmers Charlotte, Bean, and Charles Lacey have seen them many times. Children in the southwest of England often wear a bronze figurine of them around their necks in an unavailing attempt to encourage their favors.

If it should occur to one to stay in a house, the owners will not be especially happy, since they will then be compelled to overflow with gratitude and expensive gifts in exchange for sloppy work.

The Pixies swept the Gullins, a red-haired tribe of cannibalistic Little People, from the cliffs of Lydford Gorge, and they chased away the evil spirit of Benjamin Grayer by ordering him to empty a pond using a tea strainer; he "returned," however, in the form of "Binjie, the black Goblin." Squire Richard Cabell's infernal pack of dogs, which still haunts the region and inspired Sir Arthur Conan Doyle's The Hound of the Baskervilles, *devastated the Pixie broods.*

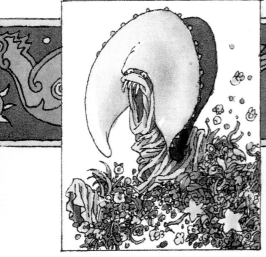

HEIGHT:
Variable. Small when he tackles the moon, he fattens and swells according to the size and extent of his meal.

APPEARANCE:
A kind of loose, pale material; he swells like an empty balloon and turns crimson with each mouthful. Slightly luminous toward the end of the month.

CLOTHING:
An indescribable coat made of Magonian plants and flowers. Wears a cocked hat with braiding, trimmed with gold tassels.

HABITAT:
A hidden island on the neighboring planet of Magonia.

FOOD:
The moon. He drinks ether, the sparkling fermented water of the astral lakes.

BEHAVIOR:
Colin Rosset remains an enigma even to the great Elfologists, as they have never been able to get near him. He is lost in the depths of extraterrestrial bestiaries, along with the little green men from outside and the ethereal silhouettes of "close encounters of the third kind."

ACTIVITIES:
Devours the moon each month.

Colin Rosset

He is a dwarf lost in the clouds.
—Robin Yerby

"The beings who evolved in space and sail through the heavens and the beyond are not all Fairies, Sylphs, Seraphim, and air spirits. It is a crass error to limit the Great Repertoire of Lutyns, Elves and Dwarfs to our planet and solar system," Petrus Barbygère tells us in the introduction to his *Repertoire of the Invisibles.*

In a region of the sky the "color of time" lies the imaginary land of Magonia, mentioned by Grimm in his *Teutonische Mythologie.* Here the firmament consists of mountains and valleys covered with grass and forests. The stars are not fixed, but march through the heavens like beasts grazing on a prairie: the vaporous air rising from the earth and the mountains holds them up and keeps them from falling. A beautiful blue ocean near these peaks is dotted with the ships of the Stormers, who sail from port to port and trade in storm-ground grains. Gervais of Tilbury confirmed the existence of these extraterrestrial spirits when he described an anchor that had fallen to the ground in England while still attached to a cable lost in the clouds.

Many animals, Goblins, Fairies, Dwarfs, and stupendous unknown creatures abound in this secret kingdom, but we know very little about them, since nowa-days only Colin Rosset dares to visit our solar system. Old narratives of the "People of Oblivion" found in Rovergue explain that "the moon used to be a sun: when it was no longer good for the day, it was put out at night." In other words, when it could no longer perform its daily task, it was sent to light the night. More recent Elfin legends affirm that our moon, which passes close to Magonia, is in fact a large cake of light made by the Fairy Queen and her daughters using the luminous milk of the Milky Way and the flour of the nebulas. A Magonian Lutin named Colin Rosset, riding a rocky asteroid and covetously peering at the monthly preparation of the golden pastry, dives down and greedily devours it as soon as it is finished and glowing in the sky. Despite the inevitable gorging by the piggish Dwarf, the good Fairy pastry cook is never discouraged and each month remixes and rebakes the shining cake that Colin Rosset nibbles quarter by quarter, sometimes on one side, sometimes on the other. Once sated, he returns to his rock to digest it and sits entranced and satisfied, contemplating the beauty of the galaxy and the stellar phenomena playing on the musical waters of the infinite.

HEIGHT:
From one to two cubits (18 in/48 cm to 36 in/91 cm).

APPEARANCE:
Small, very wrinkled, puny, black, and hairy, with prodigious strength. Long hair, sometimes braided. Some have a forehead ornamented with small horns, to which they attach their suspenders. Goat feet, iron hooves, hands with cat claws. Small tails that wag unceasingly. The "Little Coalman" from Bryère resembles a reddish-brown monkey.

CLOTHING:
In the tenth century, when Samson saw "those pagans dance around a menhir" for the first time, he described them as savages dressed in animal skins. It was not until the eighteenth century that they adopted the local peasant dress and a curiously large and round hat. An old manuscript brought to light by Claymorius says that they deliberately showed themselves to humans in "uncouth rags and kept their true and noble finery for the intimacy of the Kouril domain that extended under the earth, below the sea and the rivers."

HABITAT:
Dolmens mark the location of their homes. Korandous inhabit the cliffs from Belfort to Paimpol. At Coat Bihan, the tumuli are called Poulpican castles. A burial mound in Saint-Nolfen is the retreat of the Bouléguéans; it was once their capital, where they lived by the thousand. The moors of Plandren have been completely excavated and house a Couril metropolis. The monumental and strange constructions of Carnac delineate the borders of the mother city: the shore people, "the Blacks," live in holes in cliffs; the last Teus disappeared into

Korrigans

Forsan et haec olim meminisse juvabit. [Someday it will please us to remember even this.]

—Virgil

When Bugul Noz, the shepherd of the night, led his herd of ghosts to pasture at dusk, it was time for the Breton farmer to return home and lock his door. The Bugul Noz was not evil; he was simply a watchman making his rounds, fastening the doors and inviting good people to go to sleep. He patrolled the moors, announcing to those still out that it was time to let the spirits reclaim the shadows: "Come, the day is yours; the night belongs to us." And humans hurried, because following on the heels of the Nocturnal Shepherd came the friends of the Ankou—the Treo Fell and the Korrigan gangs.

Once, a young man from Morbihan who had lost track of time with his beloved took a shortcut while hurrying down a cobblestone alleyway and fell in with a band of Korrigans. Even though they pressed around him in their thousands—all black with cat claws—he was not too frightened, since he was carrying

a carsprenn (a small wooden fork used to clean a plowshare), which protects a person from their wickedness.

The "little-horned ones" carried on in a great uproar, while indefatigably bellowing the same singsong tune:

*Monday, Tuesday, Wednesday,
Thursday, Friday, Saturday . . .*

Warmly invited to join in the dance, the newcomer added in his best voice:

*And come the eve of Sunday
The week is complete, Hooray!*

The clever rhyme sparked widespread enthusiasm. He was thanked, he was congratulated, and he was offered a reward of a sack of dried leaves, which the following morning turned out to be pieces of gold.

In some variations of this tale, the hero is a hunchback, and the Korrigans remove his hump in gratitude for this added couplet that delivered them from the curse of having to dance to the end of time. In a longer version, they deck an avaricious hunchback with this second hump that they have taken off their benefactor. This story of the Korrigans and the seven days

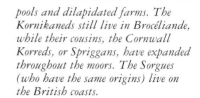

of the week has been told for a long time, and even though modern children have "expanded" the story with many events and adventures, they claim it is true for the benefit of tourists.

The people of the Kôrigans, Korrigans, Kouricans, or Corrigans are divided into four tribes who inhabit the woods, the moors, the dales, and the landholdings. Those who inhabit the woods are called Kornikaneds, since they sing into the small horns they wear hanging from their belts. Those who inhabit the moors are called Korils, Courils, Corrics, Kriores, Kéréores, Kourils, Korrils, or Kannerez Noz, since they spend the nights dancing round by the light of the moon; at dawn they leave behind immense circles of burnt grass.

Those who inhabit the dales are called Poulpikans, Poulpicans, or Poupiquets, which means that they make their burrows in low, humid places. The Teus or Teuz hide in the meadows or in ripe wheat. But whether they come from the forests, the moors, the marshes, or the fields, they all gather under the cromlechs, the cairns, the menhirs, the dolmens, and the vaults of stone to perform their rites.

Travel, alliances, and marriages between clans and with other "children of the night" have given birth to the Tumuli Goblins; Hoseguéannets; Guerrionets of the circles of stone; Arragousets and Bolbiguandets of the sea and the shores; and Boudic, Boudiguets, and Bouffon Noz of the farmlands.

pools and dilapidated farms. The Kornikaneds still live in Brocéliande, while their cousins, the Cornwall Korreds, or Spriggans, have expanded throughout the moors. The Sorgues (who have the same origins) live on the British coasts.

FOOD:
They demand no more than a little grease for their broth and their porridge. However, many people have seen the smoke from under the stones and have smelled the delicate aromas of banquets wafting through the vents of their dwellings.

BEHAVIOR:
We actually know very little about this ancient race; contact with humans has been limited to a few encounters: services, dances, and maritime calamities. The women sometimes call on human midwives for difficult births and pay them in gold.

ACTIVITIES:
Some say they dance the night away around the menhirs; humans pulled into the circle rarely survive. Others say they guard the treasures piled under large rocks that open when they are tapped with a certain rusty key. When a person has lost something, it is enough to go to their residence at nightfall and say, "Poulpican, I have lost such and such an object." The next day, the object will appear on the doorstep.

HEIGHT:

Some sixteen inches (40 cm). Descendants have shrunk to the size of a May bug.

APPEARANCE:

In the nineteenth century, they resembled small dried and wrinkled demons with white body hair. The Follets from Berry were the size of a small rooster with a red crest; their eyes were fire, and they had claws instead of fingernails. Their tail looked a little like a rooster's, a little like a rat's, and they used it as a whip to spur their mounts.

The Scottish ones, of which the most famous was Maggy Moulach, have retained the charm of the Farfadets of old: slender and hardy, brown-skinned, with shiny eyes and red, rebellious hair, pointy ears, aggressive chins, mouths both mocking and willful.

CLOTHING:

Their beautiful clothes of yore have become rags; they have never wanted to give up those splendid vestiges of the revolutionary era. Some prefer to go naked, clad in just a strip of shirt. It irritates them when a prudish dowager remarks on this.

The P'tit Davy of Beaupréau, the best known of the Farfadets of Maine-et-Loire, appear to women in gray felt hats, while the Frérots have a very hard time keeping their brown hoods pulled over their heads.

HABITAT:

Scotland, Belgium, Switzerland, France.

Farfadets, Follets, Fols, and Fradets

Brother Frérot,
Does my cowl fit well?

The Farfadet race is of royal lineage. It is a great and ancient branch of the Fairy Kingdom. They could have rivaled those innumerable and dominating Lutins if they had not been so individualistic, rebellious, and inflammatory.

While humans have often tolerated the pranks of the Lutins, they have never accepted those of the Farfadets. However, children are an exception. Both children and Farfadets have played many tricks, while putting the blame squarely on the other!

They descend from a slightly bastardized Elfin line. W. Abernathy traces their migrations back to Scotland, on the rough slopes of Mel Choire Bui or Ben-y-Gloe between the Glas Mol and Glen Beg. H. Dauzat claims that they originated in the Vendée in France, and the *Elfin Chronicles* say that they came into being in both places at once. Barbygère claims that two Farfadet families came together at the time of the great Franco-Scottish alliance, and the two blended into one romantic and whimsical race. Together, they rallied to the "party of honest men" (the Jacobites) to follow the heroic troops of the 1715 Uprising and the great rebellion of Bonnie Prince Charlie in 1745. Most returned to the Loire region after the unfortunate disaster at Culloden. It seems they tried to foment a new uprising, but it did not succeed for lack of support from the humans, who were demoralized by their bloody failure.

Was it this rebuff, seen as a sign of stubbornness, which caused the Farfadets to distance themselves from humans and spend their time amassing riches stolen from seigneurial and princely strongboxes, including those belonging to the Dwarfs and Genies who associated with humans? Did they perhaps intend to arm Elfin reinforcements and take up combat again? Still-vivid beliefs testify to the existence of these buried treasures accumulated over the centuries and indefatigably guarded by the Watchers, Farfadets or

their ghosts, especially near the Pyrome fountain in Deux-Sèvres, under numerous castles in Poitou, at Noirmoutier on the tip of Lugeronde Cove, under the dolmens of Saint-Gravé, and at Cancoët (Morbihan). "The treasure of the Allier Fols is entombed under the cave inhabited by the tribe. The slab covering it rises of its own accord at the moment of the Elevation during midnight Mass, and on Palm Sunday, when the priest knocks three times on the church door, but you must have sold your soul to the devil before you can seize the treasure." Nonetheless, you would do well not to approach the caches, since the invisible lances brandished by the Watchers never miss their target.

All the same, time has blunted the Farfadets' warlike longings. The ancients have grown too old to whip up the crowds or died, and the vindictive young Frérots have turned their marvelous combative

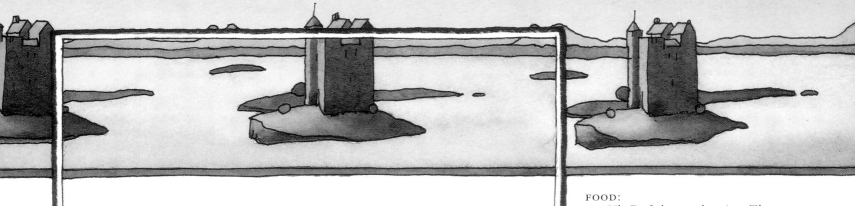

spirit to mischief-making and use their energy to play cunning pranks on mortals. They have married Fades and Fadettes, small Fairies of the region, and the Follets, Fradets, Frérots, Folatons, Foulets, Ferrés, Fols, and Fursey have blended and reblended and, very much pacified, have

prayers, they will not escape the Follets, who emerge from the stones, run and dance on the moors, and take pleasure in seizing or leading astray those caught unaware by the darkness.

The children of the Farfadets still exist: In Poitou, even at the end of the nineteenth century, the women of the Sèvre

FOOD:

The Farfadets are abstemious. They eat and drink little: smoked fish, oats, milk. They wait for the gargantuan Mardi Gras banquet held every year around a large basin hewn into the bedrock at Chambretaud in the Vendée.

BEHAVIOR:

Courageous to the point of recklessness, they were once teasing and noisy. They have, however, grown silent. Bigmouthed orators, they were generous and romantic. They have now grown petty—except with children, with whom they regain their spirit of adventure and dreams.

ACTIVITIES:

At night they enter houses, draw beer, sour the milk, and smear butter or soft soap on the stairs. They listen and repeat the secrets they hear while hidden under the beds. The archives of the Swiss town of Vevey mention a Follet spirit, the Tschanteret, who lived behind the Villeneuve in 1551 and got into the Boillet tower, where he engaged in all kinds of mischief. After due deliberation, the village council advised the master builder to seal all exits to the tower so that the Tschanteret could neither enter nor leave. The Allier Fols rattle chains, make dogs howl, and block the chimneys so that smoke pours back into houses.

They flee from a cross carved in volcanic rock.

disappeared into the thread of time only to be remembered in evening tales.

A handful of diehards settled in Brittany, teamed up with Korrigans who had "gone bad," and took to crime on the moors of Morbihan. Local peasants who cross the moors know that if they do not reach the stone cross erected by the side of the road before night falls, and if midnight strikes before they have said their

valley met at night to spin or knit in the caves created by the quarrying of stone; the caves were sought after during that thrifty era for their pleasant temperature that did away with the need for a fire. They settled in as best they could, but the Farfadets, disturbed by this noisy intrusion into their domain, took revenge with a multitude of tricks. These were very childish acts of retaliation and laughable deeds of provocation for a brave race who in days of yore had taken claymore in hand to follow the white cockade of the Young Pretender.

Red Caps

Bonnie Charlie will never come back to me.
The Red Caps have dyed his cockade white.
　　　　　　—"The Lament of Catriona"

Angus led Molly through flowered glens to the ruined tower
overlooking a lake sparkling
with dancing sunlight. Spring
tinged the hills green, kindling quivering
purple heather. Leaping from rock to
rock, the May lovers laughed in the lovely
weather, in the happiness of their wild

engagement celebrated under the Scottish
sky according to the rites of Brigadoon.
Their bonnets beribboned, their plaids
displayed, they embraced, they kissed, and
they rolled in the grass near the turret,
where in the hollows of shadowy stones,
the "Bloody Caps" waited to murder them.

The Red Caps, or Dunters, Combs, or
Powries, are hideous Goblin Dwarfs from
the Scottish border region, but they are
also found in the High- and Lowlands.
They hide in castles, keeps, abandoned
manor houses, and blood-soaked crime
scenes that are haunted by specters, whose
company they love. Like the Bone-
Crunchers, the Red Caps were an important warrior race, fearless even to the point

HEIGHT:
Twenty-five inches (62 cm).

APPEARANCE:
Robust. Prominent muscles. Eagle talons for hands. Long gray hair and braided beards. Fire-colored eyes. The females proudly display abundant manes of red hair.

CLOTHING:
Red caps decorated with goose feathers. Sheepskin tunics. Tartans torn from cadavers. Gaiters. Copper and tin jewelry. They carry targes *(shields) and* claymores *(swords).*

HABITAT:
Ruins, haunted castles, towers where the walls still ooze fresh blood from crimes committed over the course of centuries.

FOOD:
Bannock and game. Rannoch deer pâté.

BEHAVIOR:
Cruel and fiery, they detest humans. When misfortunes are about to befall their enemies, the visionary Red Caps feast and dance to the sound of bagpipes until dawn. A person who hears them may warn the nearby town that a great disaster is imminent. Nothing frightens Red Caps except for crucifixes, crosses on sword hilts, and certain biblical phrases. When they flee, they always leave a talon behind.

ACTIVITIES:
Hunting and waging war. They also forge metal collars, wristlets, and above all daggers: dirks and skin-dhu. The Swiss Red Caps are amiable servants attached to cottages, whom the Capuchins turned back to whence they came.

of defying the Giants of the Heights.

During the reign of Uther Pendragon, father of Arthur, they fought the Picts and the serpent people of the dark lochs. It was only after the defeat at Culloden that they disappeared among the old walls, unable to accept occupation by Englishmen, whose gleaming attire gave them ideas . . .

Since then, they continually shove travelers, tourists, and lovers of beautiful romantic ruins off cliffs and squash them under enormous boulders.

They use human blood to dye their caps. Once the color has faded and dulled, they go on the lookout for victims to revive the shimmer.

The Mourioche

Houou houou houououou.
— Umberto Eco, *Foucault's Pendulum*

HEIGHT:
Eighteen inches (46 cm).

APPEARANCE:
Little devil with small horns, cloven feet, pointed ears, baleful eyes, and hooked fingers. Hunchback. Very energetic. Can assume the appearance of whatever he wishes or become invisible.

CLOTHING:
Cap with bells. Ragged court jester's costume in faded colors, twisted stockings, worn pointed-toed shoes.

HABITAT:
Burrows, tree hollows, and the rookeries of crows during the summer and haylofts, cowsheds, and stables during the winter.

FOOD:
He pilfers what he can find. He hates fish and seafood, which remind him of his youth under the sea.

A tease, a rogue, a mischief-maker, a mastiff: the Mourioche is a true little devil, a joker who will drive you up the wall. Here and there, he flits, appears, disappears, changes into whatever comes into his head, and plays a thousand pranks, amusing or nasty, depending on his mood.

Here we see him in the evening, watching from under the hedge as the workers leave the fields. Having finished his work, a farmer whistles as he heads home for supper with his scythe on his shoulder. "Whistle, whistle at your ease, walk, walk, your mind empty, hearing nothing, seeing nothing," says the Mourioche to himself, snickering and waiting inside the shrubbery for someone on whom to play his evil tricks. "Whistle, whistle, but your lovely scythe is mine." Nimble, light-footed, he leaps onto the farmer's back and takes the scythe so adroitly that the peasant goes home without having noticed a thing! Roguish Mourioche laughs and bounds through the meadows and forests, the tool gleaming like the last blaze of the crescent moon.

There, the demon Mourioche follows a farmer who ambles by peacefully. "Boo!" he says behind the man's back to scare him. "What's that?" cries the startled peasant, seeing nothing but the road snaking under the brilliant stars. "Boo, who goes there?" The peasant is even more frightened; his teeth chatter. And the Mouri-

oche laughs and becomes a leaping stone that clatters against the shoes of the stroller, who tries to use his stick to defend himself against the diabolical pebbles!

Wham! The stick cracks the Mourioche on the head, and he immediately changes into a toad. Wham! The toad becomes a caterwauling cat. Wham! Now he is a biting dog! Wham! Another blow—he metamorphoses into something bigger this time: a stamping goat. Wham! Now he is a bucking horse. Wham! Bigger and bigger: a bull charging down the unfortunate farmer, who dies of fright.

And the Mourioche regains his impish form and laughs and capers and somersaults with wicked joy.

It is like this every night, winter and summer. This Goblin from Haute-Bretagne in France works himself up to play his nasty pranks whenever he can!

The Mourioche used to be a jester to Triton, king of the sea, and was a favorite of the great court magician who had initiated him into black magic. But the Mourioche was banned from the kingdom for using a magic potion to seduce the youngest princess. Condemned to be beheaded by her enraged father, but having succeeded in fleeing owing to the magic intervention of his protector, the wretched villain had to leave the watery kingdom behind forever. Since then, the banished Goblin has wandered the moors, taking his anger and his temperamental moods out on the humans he meets.

He leaves his hideout at nightfall to begin his evil raids: he burns furniture, ravages gardens, plucks orchards clean, enters farmhouses through the dormers and pillages the pantry, pinches young girls as they sleep, blows nightmares into

the ears of children, smashes precious objects in the house . . . At last, he disappears through the chimney, covering the furniture with sticky clouds of soot; he steals the weathervane from the steeple, changes the water in the washhouse to blood, dries up wells, and sows panic in the village.

Not too long ago, a man from Ville-Orien in Saint-Cast was returning from Matignon when he saw a sheep not too far from his home. He shut it in the cowshed. The next day, when he went to give it water, he found a cow. The day after, a horse. "Heavens," he mused, "what's going on here?" The next day, it was a black dog with red eyes that bared its fangs, laughed, and said: "Why do you come to see me every morning? You are very strange!" The frightened man went to find his shotgun. By the time he returned, the Mourioche had left with all the cattle and half the cowshed. The farmer tried to rebuild, but what the masons did during the day, the Goblin undid during the night. Despite exorcisms and prayers, holy water and boxwood crosses, he always came back in just as much of a rage. Finally, he tired of this and punctured the tires of a nearby tractor.

Today, he lives on the moors, ready to leap over the shrubby broom as soon as the light fades and the night grows dark.

HEIGHT:
Eleven inches (28 cm).

APPEARANCE:
Wild, ugly, very hairy. The female Fadettes are more elegant, but still quite rough.

CLOTHING:
Thick beige wool breeches. Short robes for the Fadettes.

HABITAT:
They love stony ground and gentle hills. They live in the Fadet Cavern near Lussac-les-Châteaux (Vienne). They also live in the impressive cave of the Fadets at Verryues (Deux-Sèvres), and the most famous metropolis of the Fadets is at Biare, in the Moussac district of Poitou.

FOOD:
Millet soup and seagull stew, broad beans from the Poitou marshland, snails in red-wine sauce.

BEHAVIOR/ACTIVITIES:
Not much. The Fadets were plentiful during certain epochs. They were part of the coppices just like sparrows, mushrooms, snails, and eels. They have more or less disappeared. The Fadets, threatened by inbreeding, replaced their progeny with Little Men.

Fadets

The Fadet brothers, close cousins of the Farfadets and cousins once removed of the Fradets, date from long ago. Even during the adventurous early Middle Ages, they hardly had any powers. They are not Genies or spirits, but a race of small beings that lived under the rocks of Poitou before humans arrived. They smell of sulfur, but they are not Satanic. If they have often been seen in the company of the Devil, it is because he has used them as a workforce, but the Horned Master has never entrusted any important missions to them. On the Fadet Dolmen on the island of Yeu, it is still possible to see the traces of the three-legged stool used by Satan on Saturday nights as he gave weekly instructions to these grisons, who were limited to minor acts of villainy; he saved the most diabolical plots for the superior Goblins. It was not in the nature of the Fadets to be cruel, and once the Gothic era of devilry had passed, they naturally turned to good actions.

They have accomplished nothing miraculous or memorable: they build neither bridges nor castles, nor any other construction, but once night has fallen, they lead the farmers' herds to pasture in lush, secret meadows. Sheep as beautiful as the ones they guard are not to be found anywhere.

Pucks

Even though William Shakespeare and later Rudyard Kipling named and knighted the Pucks, these attractive laughing and dancing Elves, these delightful products of the impish amorous encounters of the Poucs, these bacchanalian Goblins and Little Bacchan Sisters existed even before the Five Hundred Years' War. Blowing on their conch shells, foxglove fingers, or giant bluebells, they heralded the return of the Elfin Spring Festival (then held on May 30), showering the Fairies with flowers and throwing them garlands of hyacinths and cowslips. They were then followed by the Elves who announced the start of the Flora Games, their butterfly chariots fluttering over the meadows and woods.

Curiously, poets, writers, and painters have always described male Pucks, malicious horned satyrs, without ever dwelling on female Pucks, pert brunettes with pointed ears, sharp teeth, and cloven hooves, who are a hundred times prettier and have manifestly more sparkling personalities than those randy old goats whom they never marry anyway.

Female Pucks are Sun-Elves of the wild and rugged regions; they blossom in summer, while winter finds them curled up in the warmth of their snug caves carved out of hillsides. There they knit, darn, dream, play house, cook, dream, embroider, paint, dream, and make plans for when the weather improves . . . After the first rain shower in March, they show their faces, and their childish laughter is heard as they come and go from hillside to garden, followed by a few Elves, as well as by their goat friends, whose language they understand. In April, May, and June, they sow plants and flowers on their plots of land, rock on their porch swings, and along with Flora—who cherishes them and is amused and charmed by their wild grace—preside over the summer fairs of the Little People.

Unlike male Pucks, female Pucks have always avoided the company of humans, except for a few young witches as wild as they are, who purchase the secrets of plants from them in exchange for the marzipan of which they are so very fond. After interminable Elfin tragedies, the pacification of Oberon, and the arrival of Merlin, these beautiful little creatures decided to leave their territory in the enchanted hills for the confines of remote verdant regions, the entrance of which was covered by Flora with thick forests in order to keep them secret.

HEIGHT:
Twelve inches (30 cm).

APPEARANCE:
Adorable little brunettes with hazel eyes and abundant jet-black hair. Except for their cloven hooves, they strongly resemble Zunia, the heroine of René Hausman's fantasy comic strips.

CLOTHING:
Short woven woolen tunics with adornments of flowers, fruits, stones, and shells.

HABITAT:
Of old, the regions of hilly moors. Their caverns were artistically carved and hewn into circular cities by the ancient Hobgoblins of the Stones.

FOOD:
Goat cheese, lots of vegetables, fresh and dried fruits. They are crazy for marzipan.

BEHAVIOR:
Pretty, but with fiery characters. It's easy to make them mad: they can sulk like a bear or laugh all day. Their anger is devastating, but it amuses Flora, who forgives them anything. Female Pucks do not marry male Pucks. In the seventieth year of the reign of Titania, the most famous queen of the Pucks married King Urlus, thus founding the families of Lallia, Nasturtium, and Bygail, who are still around, as well as the Poulpiquets.

ACTIVITIES:
Weaving, gardening, sometimes fishing, dreaming, and playing a lot.

THE LITTLE PEOPLE OF THE MOUNTAINS

*Gods and dwarfs with beards of snow
still survive on the highest peaks.*
　　　　　　　—Ludwik H. Becker

Beyond the forests, beyond the high mountain pastures and the valleys tamed by man, where leaves shrivel into needles, where the grass grows sparsely and reverts to its wild texture, where the flora is reduced to Elfin petals, where the green slopes crack and fold into crevices, shingles, and scree, where the mountain ranges meander and split, where the mountain streams trip down all the way to the ancient banks of snow and crystallize in the vast, furrowed snowfields, that is where time freezes and the Ancient Times arise again.

There the fossils breathe at the foot of celestial walls that top even the turrets and dungeons of the eternal snows.

Each being has remained in its rightful place for millennia. Nothing has changed and nothing will change—unless one day the People of the Summits descend to the plains . . .

HEIGHT:

Ten to fourteen inches (25 to 35 cm).

APPEARANCE:

Attractive, well-proportioned, lively, and smiling. Pointed ears, curly blond hair, dark skin, and white spiky teeth. Their expression reflects the brilliance of mountain peaks in the sunlight. They smell pleasantly of hay and fresh milk.

CLOTHING:

Green shirts, vests embroidered with flowery designs. Caps knitted by the Fairies, Tyrolean hats, and the red or black breeches of Swiss peasants. Fur-lined goatskin coats in winter.

HABITAT:

They make their nests in haylofts, in old hollow tree stumps, or under rocks that shelter them from the wind. During bad weather, they hibernate in abandoned cottages. For three weeks every May, they share the high alpine meadows with the graceful Fairies.

FOOD:

They like whatever they are given; they are not picky. They are happy with soup, bread, cheese, butter, and milk; they find their dessert in the mountains.

The Servans

I have often seen your earthly eye
Fall thrice on the herdswoman
From a pasture on high,
So bewitch her
That I saw death on her
And worms on her skin.
— L. Richer, *L'Guide bouffon*, 1651

After an initial period of distrust, the Servans, little mountain Wood Nymphs, quickly grew accustomed to the arrival of humans. They descended from the mountain crests and settled near the pastures and the cottages. When the mountain people are away from home, these kindly Dwarfs, friends of the hearth, enter the houses and perform a multitude of small tasks. They sweep, wash and tidy the dishes, churn the milk to make butter, watch over the ripening Gruyère, look after the animals, put flowers on the tables and the windowsills, and prevent thieves and evil spirits from entering.

In the Vaudois Alps in Switzerland, the Servans, or Serfous, are the friends of the pastures. They lead the cows to the fields and never allow them to come to any harm. The leader of the herd says: "Pommette, Balette! Go where I go—that way no rocks will fall on you." And miraculously, the animals climb to where even a chamois dare not go and graze on the most

inaccessible summits where the grass is sweetest.

When the Fouletots of the Jura Alps notice that the shepherdess is asleep, they draw the prettiest cow into the deep woods, and after letting the shepherdess search for a long time, they bring her back with swollen udders, sated with the best forage.

In Alsace, once the last herdsman takes his winter leave of Mount Kerbholz, which overlooks the Munster Valley, the Servans, accompanied by their magnificent, well-fed livestock and well supplied with all the equipment needed for making cheese, settle in the deserted cottages and labor day and night. Then, in the darkest part of the cold season, they descend into the valley and stealthily enter the huts of the poor to leave them pats of tasty butter and large rounds of the most savory cheese.

It is extremely dangerous not to follow certain rules in exchange for these services. At the approach of the first snows, when people hurry to spend the winter down below, they should always leave the cottage clean and a dormer window ajar in order to prepare a place for the Servans who will come and hibernate in the warmth. This ensures a good harvest and protection from the mountain spirits when the good weather returns. You must

never make a Servan angry—never insult him, make fun of him, play mean pranks on him, or try to capture him. It is very unwise to forget to place his small portion of food on the cottage doorstep in the evening; just one bewitching glance from him could make the cows keel over, and one gesture of his hand and lightning might strike and pulverize everything. It is not difficult to keep the Servans happy, but they hold dear these small and traditional rewards.

In the mountains of Vaud, it is usual to give them the first layer of the best morning cream. Once, on the edge of little Lake Loison, the master cowherd had left the cottage early after having reminded his herdsman to see to the Servan's portion. During his absence, the young herdsman ignored the advice. This is what happened: The night after the master returned, a storm blew up and a voice was heard to cry, "Jean, get up, get up for a surprise." In the morning, the master and his foolish cowherd went in search of the herd and found it crushed to death at the bottom of an abyss. It is also said that the Servans so detest slovenliness that they left a farm that had prospered owing to their help, after disrespectful people befouled the milk placed in a bucket on the roof for them.

BEHAVIOR:

Lively, sociable, gently mischievous. The Servans, Serfous, Folatons, Persevay, Serveins, Little Shepherds, Jeannots, Foultas, Napfan, Fameili, Chanterais, or Jean de la Bolieta are hostile to the nasty mountain spirits, from whom they can escape owing to their outstanding climbing skills and their imperviousness to vertigo; they are also helped by animals such as bears and eagles.

ACTIVITIES:

They help the mountain dwellers in their work. They make butter and cheese, and they devote themselves to the pleasures of magic. They are fond of animals, and it is not unusual to see them traveling through the precipitous peaks on the back of a chamois or seated between the horns of an ibex. They whistle with the marmots and the birds.

The Kloks' Tomtes

HEIGHT:
Fifteen inches (39 cm).

APPEARANCE:
Pale and puny with bony faces. Their left eye is squinty and inquisitive; the right is enormous, deformed by the perpetual use of a goldsmith's or watchmaker's loupe. Very long hands, delicate and nimble fingers. Pointed beard thrown back over the shoulder like a scarf.

CLOTHING:
Quite elegant with thick cloaks, cashmere shawls, silken velvet doublets, and collars and cuffs of lace. They also wear embroidered caps or shakos, to which they attach their most delicate and indispensable tools, and fur-lined boots.

HABITAT:
Steep mountain peaks in Germany, Austria, and the Tyrol. They have been seen as far away as India.

FOOD:
They are happy with very little, but they are not averse to sparkling wines and fruit liqueurs.

BEHAVIOR:
They live together in a village in which each house is separate from the others. They do not visit with each other. They are happy in solitude and rarely leave their workshops. There are no female Kloks'Tomtes; instead they build graceful and adorable automata dolls that are regularly replaced instead.

ACTIVITIES:
All the most skilled tasks of clockmaking, watchmaking, goldsmithing, and creating fantastical things.

The iron hand, a fivefold spring adapted to Goetz von Berlichingen's stump, was the work of the mysterious and skilled dwarfs that Colonel Scheerbart called Kloks'Tomtes.
—Paschasius,
Tagebuch eines Beobachters seines selbst

The Kloks'Tomtes live on the most inaccessible peaks in tiny cottages of chiseled and carved stone that look like cuckoo clocks, the playthings of Fairies, or the music boxes of the Follets. They are the most skilled metalworkers of the Ageless World.

Since the dawn of Sylphic times, they have made grandfather clocks, musical jewels, mechanical birds, automata, striking-Jack timepieces, barrel organs, bell-clocks, glass bells, and "self-propelled armor" for all the courts of the kings and magicians of the Elfin nations. Merlin, Titania, Mab, and Oberon were known to have patronized them.

The Kloks'Tomtes often travel invisibly and can move from one point on the earth's surface to another in a fraction of a second, thanks to a marvelous machine with complex cogwheels that was invented by their Venerable Master. They price their work very dearly, but they can produce the gold castings necessary for a new commission in the blink of an eye.

The Kloks'Tomtes sometimes accept orders from humans, so long as the work suits them and presents a challenge. It is said that they built Goetz von Berlichingen's famous mechanical hand to allow him to wield a sword again and resume his battle against the Bishop of Bamberg and the burghers of Cologne. At other times, any reckless person who disturbs them at their work will be punished by being thrown into a crevasse.

Although they are naturally puny, a hypnotic power renders them invulnerable and fearless in the face of anyone bold enough to dare confront them. Thanks to their unique and complex mechanical windmills, they can also produce winds, tempests, gales, and tornados of ice or fire.

A museum exhibiting the most beautiful and priceless of their works once existed in a vast mountain cave, but this dusty, cobwebbed museum will never again receive visitors. The Kloks'Tomtes' few requests for services are dwindling to none, which will eventually lead them to lose their amazing knowledge.

There remain just a few feeble Kloks'-Tomtes, capable only of crudely carving edelweiss of horn for the souvenir stores that attract tourist buses.

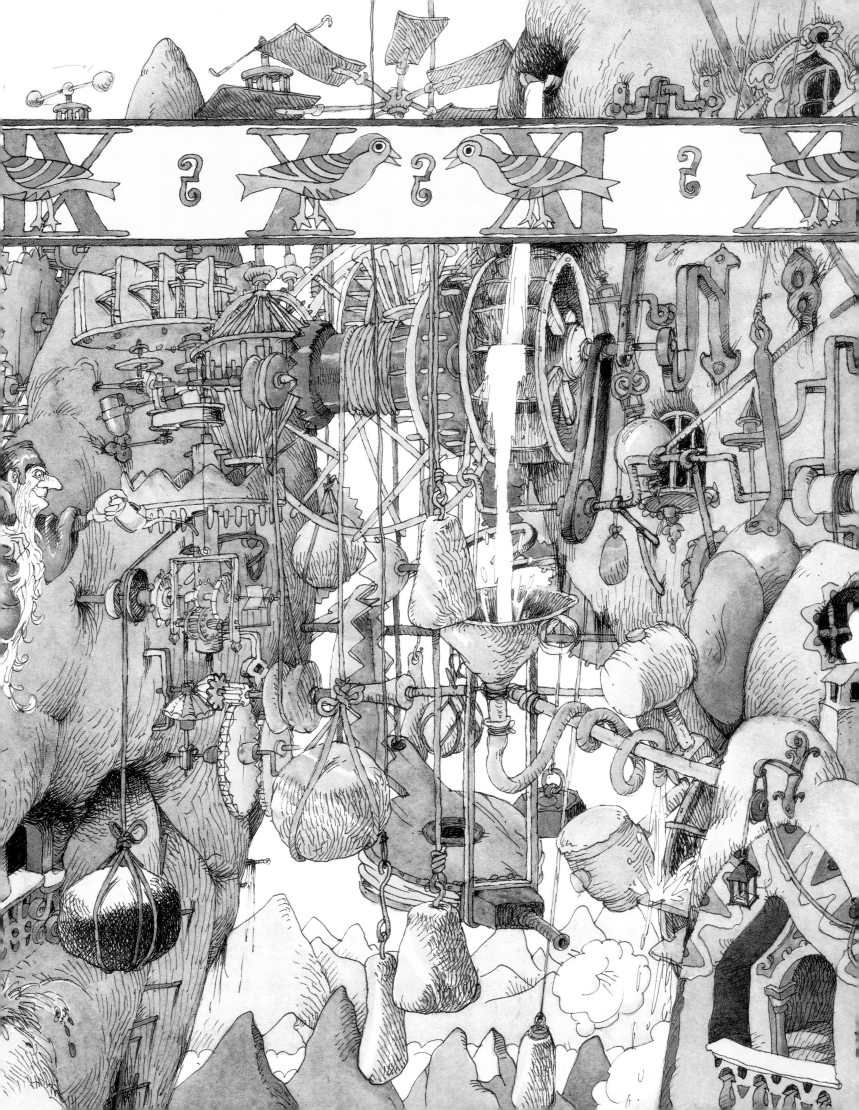

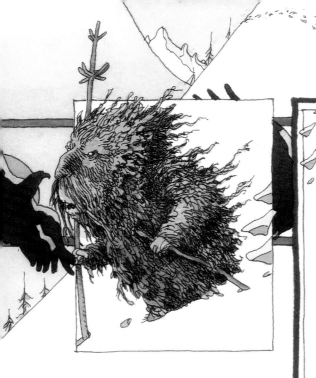

Diablats, Diablerets, Dahuts, Barbegazi, and Other Furry Devils

Kingdom of the soul, beyond the peaks and the ages.
(Reflection of our own dream enclosed in a star of ice.)

—Capucine Locatelli,
L'Almanach des enclos

What do mountain Dwarfs look like? Smickity-smackity, smickity-smackity, thwack! Infantile imagery, the folklore of Mother Goose, and snow-covered Christmas cards have etched them on our mind's eye. They are short-ish, bearded, wear pointed hats, and carry picks on their backs and lanterns in their hands as they descend in single file from the summits to their dollhouse cottages. That is how Dame Tartine described the Eismandel, the Bergleutes, the Rougeverts, and the many little Tyrolean miners of Switzerland and the Carpathians. But the multitudes teeming over the rocks, moraines, and peaks are blacker, untamed, hairy . . . and often web-footed or cloven-hoofed.

Entire mountains teem with Fairies and Dwarfs, Elves and Gnomes. The Hairy Ones are scattered along the crests. They are true living fossils, as ancient as the rocks, as hardy as the lichen, as tough as the Chocards of the crevices. Companions of the first marmots, they were there before the Fadets, the Saracens, and the Servans.

Humans always climbed the mountains respectfully, depositing gifts and offerings to the Genies and gods in exchange for passage through to the mines and green valleys and paths to new, infinitely pure realms. More timid climbers only hoped to be protected from suffering from altitude sickness. But we must never kill an animal or pick a plant on any one of the sacred peaks, otherwise the sun will heat up, avalanches will rain down, and the glaciers will move together again.

For Man was never alone in the mountains; he was watched by a thousand presences, a thousand Hairy Ones hidden under the stones, the mosses, the snow . . .

A young herdsman often left his father's cows to hunt chamois on the cloud-covered alpine peaks. His parents tried to forbid it, but in vain. He continued to passionately pursue this dangerous pleasure. One evening, amid the steepest precipices, he unexpectedly encountered a violent storm. The snow and ice caused him to lose his way, and he lay down on a rock, afraid, tired, cold, and hungry. A mountain spirit suddenly appeared in the form of a "Hairy Tornado" and cried in a menacing voice: "Reckless fool! Who let you come to kill the flocks that belong to me? I don't hunt your father's cows; why do you hunt my chamois? I will forgive you this time, but don't come back." He suspended the storm and sent the herdsman on his way back to his cottage. From that day forth, the herdsman never left his cows. The Hairy One reigns supreme up there. He knows all, sees all, hears all; he is an extension of the mountain—the protector and destroyer.

The mountain dwellers of yore so feared him that they imagined him as a kind of miniature devil, a Diableret, a Diablat, a black Man of the Mountains.

Modern humans—who no longer respect the peaks—have caricatured him and reduced him to an object of ridicule. To mock them, he sends them on nocturnal hunts for Dahuts, who take revenge for his vexation at being so badly treated by throwing them off precipices, making them lose their way, or freezing them in timeless snowdrifts.

There are several species of these little devils:

The Basa-Jauns, or wild lords, live in the deep chasms of the Pyrenees. The bodies of these creatures are covered with long silky hair. The little Storm-makers of the Nelhou peak destroy crops when humans have angered them.

The Diablats of the Valais are experts in dancing the Coraule or Devil's Dance.

The Dusies have silver hooves and furry caps.

The Mimis of northern Australia are sometimes cannibals.

Although the red Btsons are not mean, these Mo-sin-a, or Hairy Spirits, appear to solitary mountain dwellers on Chinese summits.

The Barbegazi, or "Frosty Beards," do not leave their beds of ice until winter comes.

HEIGHT:
Twelve inches (30 cm).

APPEARANCE:
While those of the snows have white body hair, those of the high mountain meadows are green; those of the crests are reddish; those of the crevasses black or gray. All the Hairy Ones have bodies covered with a dry fleece similar to lichen or the coat of a marmot or mountain goat. Mountain dwellers who have seen them always describe them as small, ugly, very active, robust, and sometimes horned, with webbed or hoofed feet.

CLOTHING:
Their all-season fleece is a coat styled after the "Wildlings," who sometimes walk around inside a great ball of lichen in which they nest to sleep.

HABITAT:
They are found on mountains all over the globe, never in only a single cave, but dispersed throughout cracks in the rocks.

FOOD:
Roots, plants, game.

ACTIVITIES:
From the moment a stranger sets foot in the hills, the hairy lookouts warn the others by whistling like a marmot. Anything goes to protect the mountain if they feel it is in danger. To rejuvenate themselves and renew their vigor, they like to tumble down with avalanches. When they climb up again, they are one hundred years younger. (It is said that Samivel, the prince of the summits, had Diableret blood.)

Bidon

At the foot of the stony distaffs of the "fairy chimneys" of Saint-Gervais, hidden at the foot of a white mountain stream, there is a hole in the ground. It is the Bidon's lair. It was once inhabited by this mountain Dwarf, a lively weasel with a pointy snout, furtive and cunning, who could rob a cottage of a crispy fritter or a piece of sausage in one bound and rival the chamois by cavorting along the crests on the next bound. His race, crosses between a marmot, a weasel, and an ibex—possibly even remotely descended from a noble alpine line—emerged from the rocks, boulders, and sparse heather.

Bidon committed villainies here, there, and everywhere. All just for fun! (Certainly he didn't do it to get rich!) What else could he steal from a herdsman or woodsman besides a feather from a hat, a crust of dry bread, a pinch of tobacco, a scrap of cheese rind? It was the thought that counted! Yet he always left them their knives.

Later, he played many nasty tricks on tourists, amateur climbers, and the earliest skiers. He never liked people encroaching on the musky paths he had crossed, denuding the hills of bluebells, and he hated to see fashionistas crisscrossing the virgin expanses of snow. He funneled stony scree into rockslides, diverted streams towards shelters, and threw the careless into the void. The echoes of his squealing laughter and the victorious cascade of notes on his xylophone always announced fresh misdeeds to those below.

At first, he spared the women who came to sit in the snow in their long skirts and large hats; he was satisfied with stinging them from afar with a peashooter loaded with bunches of pine needles. The women thought the pinpricks were horseflies or hornets—so he stung them even harder and stole their ribbons, which he then presented to the Fadettes.

As more and more stylishly clothed ladies appeared, Bidon grew evil and began throwing them down from the heights. This furious madman dotted the Haute-Savoie with traps that placed all mountain folk in danger. The accidental death of an innocent Fadet, strangled by a perfidious snare, made the Little People decide to put a stop to this guerrilla warfare. One night, the hunter Servans, Diablerets, Dahuts, Fadets, and Aguanes from other mountainsides chased Bidon to the summit of Mont Blanc, from whence he jumped rather than submit to their justice.

HEIGHT:
  Sixteen inches (40 cm).

APPEARANCE:
  *All legs and shoulders. Reddish, with
  a weasel head and piercing eyes.*

CLOTHING:
  *Covered with moss and brush, shod
  with delicate shoes of carved goat horn.*

HABITAT:
  *A lair nestled in the rushing course
  of a stream that incessantly babbles
  his story.*

FOOD:
  *He took from here and there; he was
  not fussy. A hazelnut, beechnuts, a
  handful of huckleberries, a mishmash
  taken from "visited" pantries.*

BEHAVIOR:
  *Spent the spring chasing ladies,
  the Fadettes, or the Fadets.*

ACTIVITIES:
  *He once charmed the heights with his
  crystalline xylophone concerts improvised on stalactite organs.*

Sotrés

HEIGHT:
Twenty-four inches (60 cm).

APPEARANCE:
Skinny and clumsy. Long, pointed noses. Shaggy hair and beards. Daylight-blind. Bright-eyed. Barefoot, with long, flat, horned feet, and dewclaws on their ankles. Huge mouths without lips, stretching from ear to ear.

CLOTHING:
They sometimes appear wearing only a red greatcoat and a tall black hat. At other times, they wear a black greatcoat and a tall red hat. They always wear a necklace of dried mushrooms.

HABITAT:
Former badger sets, quickly converted into feather beds using materials stolen from henhouses. They only live in the highest parts of the Vosges mountains, near chalets and farms.

FOOD:
They devour the contents of cupboards and pantries, love mushrooms, and are fond of milk and "potée," a pork-and-cabbage stew.

BEHAVIOR:
Their method of reproduction remains a mystery since there are no female Sotrés. The inhabitants of the Vosges claim that they grow naturally, like the mushrooms, or by the light of the moonbeams on the soil—or even that they are born of laughter, and "as long as there are tricks to be played, there will be Sotrés."

ACTIVITIES:
Sotrés eat, sleep, have lots of fun, and sing lots of incomprehensible melodies into human ears, which humans know without ever having learned them.

Who steals all of the eggs one by one from the nests in the henhouse? Who hides boots and tools, tangles and braids shoelaces, and opens the doors of the hutches at night? It is the Sotrés (or Sotrets, Souttrés, or Soltraits).

While everyone is sleeping, they make a tremendous racket and turn everything topsy-turvy. Then at dawn, weary, their bellies aching from laughing too hard at their own tricks, they run off screaming, causing the startled farmers to fall out of their beds! These rowdy little imps from the Vosges region of France are not very fierce, but they are gluttonous, thieving, lazy, inquisitive, insolent, short-tempered, and devilishly bawdy! If by chance someone surprises one, either in the stable while he is pestering the horses or in the kitchen while his long nose is buried in a block of butter, it is wise to pretend not to notice him and, above all, to avoid speaking to him; if not, the Sotré will carry him off in a whirlwind that he produces from his disproportionately large mouth. When Sotrés, who are very fond of milk, want to milk a cow, they begin by removing its horns, which they will not put back if they are disturbed.

Sotrés love children, however—a fact that has often been affirmed by the chronicles: "The little girls whom the Sotré-imp has abducted and has 'known' are always simpleminded and distraught when they return from their stay. They remain single for the rest of their lives, mournfully singing to themselves, and having conversations with rats and mice." Otherwise, they enjoy going into children's bedrooms and doting on them while they're sleeping, rocking their cradles and singing sweet, never-ending lullabies. Fortunate are those whom the Sotrés surround with their thoughtfulness, because they open their hearts and minds and give them skill, agility, and strength—and a knack for finding wild mushrooms.

Women, at the very least those who are annoyed by their visits beneath the eiderdown and desire to maintain peace in their households, must safeguard themselves against the Sotrés' familiarities by crossing their arms over their breasts right before they go to sleep and chanting, "Sotré, Sotré, come not where I lay: outside you shall stay. Sotré, Sotré, leave us in peace!" Some women place a knife on their chests, the point facing downward. If an imp hurts himself, he may escape, but will never return.

Jumpers

Jump, Jumper, Jump
Over the hedges and the bushes
Jump to the Diâl and farther beyond!
—Witches' Spell, J. Van de Wattyne

Jumpers, also known as Sotês or Sotais, are troglodytes, or Belgian Dwarfs. Grün considers that the root of Sotê is in the Basque word *Soto* (cave). Barbygère made an ironic comment: "Let's make a standing jump into the etymology of the leaping Jumper or Sotê, the origin of whose name is obvious, like that of his accomplice, the lustful Massotê, Massotai (whom the women always notice when it's too late), who is the Walloon alter ego to Massariol."

Jumpers would like to work, but choose not to wear out their noble old age and risk slimming down their round little potbellies constructing towers, churches, and bridges like the Kabouters, Lamignacs, and other Dwarfs engaged in construction. They hate hard manual work, and when they lived among humans, it was always something of an ordeal to convince them to pick up a scythe or rake during haymaking and harvesting. They preferred helping out in the kitchen. With a big apron wrapped around their bellies, they bustle about, their noses twitching, their cheeks bright red, their mouths watering over pots and dripping pans. Happily, they had the plump, rosy kitchen maids sing for them, and they would cuddle them, tickling them with their long beards by brushing them against their necks and slapping their bottoms as they bent over the preparation of pâtés, stews, and pies. Jumpers weren't even averse to helping with the dishes, the laundry, or the ironing. In conversation, "telling the tale," with little cups of coffee, a cookie and a pipe in their hands, they would entertain their female audience with romantic tales of chivalry and love while their husbands went out to toil in the fields.

Agile dancers despite their height, these stout, potbellied midgets could be admired for their skill in pirouetting; the expression "playing the Sotê" still means playing a game of spinning tops in many parts of Hesbaye! They still attend all of the festivals, processions, and fairs and, in comic effigy, rock their big, hoary heads to the sound of the fanfares during the Malmedy carnival.

Joseph Wrindts (*Wallonia* vol. 4, p. 82) points out that the Jumpers were so much a part of village life that it was they who warned the villagers that Charlemagne and his mighty army were coming. The Emperor was astonished and yet impressed by the somersaults and acrobatics of these creatures and their gymnastic dexterity. He even tried in vain to recruit some of them as acrobatic warriors for his army; but the Jumpers, who are not very warlike, declined all of the offers on the pretext of suffering from "chronic sluggishness."

The two World Wars and the devastating madness of mankind have convinced the Jumpers to return forever to the tranquility and peace of their own secret subterranean world. Besides, the kitchen maids and housekeepers of today prefer to listen to the radio or watch television instead of attending the ramblings of the Jumpers that used to fire their imagination.

HEIGHT:
Sixteen inches (40 cm).

APPEARANCE:
"Little old men." Stout, red-faced, with large noses and twinkling eyes. Their handsome, legendary beards have left their name to the clematis of the Haies, called "Sotê or Jumper beard," and we call it "Old Man's Beard."

CLOTHING:
Mended and stylishly embellished worn garments discarded by the men of the household. They also sport top hats.

HABITAT:
They live in comfortable little bedrooms built into the depths of the caverns near the hamlets of Wallonia, Belgium, particularly in Hesbaye in the region of Liège in the Ardennes.

FOOD:
Gourmands and gourmets, Jumpers love to cook, either at home or in other peoples' homes when they are invited as guests. They are fond of beer, especially Gueuse, the Belgian beer they age in the coolness of "Jumper holes."

BEHAVIOR:
Old paintings found on the walls where the Jumpers lived are likely to be portraits of deceased wives, which proves the existence of females and suggests that perhaps they have been dead for a long time. Jumpers have become very rare.

ACTIVITIES:
They work as little as possible apart from helping around the house. Smokers, they cultivate some tobacco patches scattered throughout the woods, which the Nutons regularly destroy in order to take revenge for the fact that the Jumpers are on good terms with humans.

HEIGHT:

They were once large, strong, and handsome before they shrank to the size of squirrels.

APPEARANCE:

The Tartaros, or Tartare, of the Basques have hairy bodies. They are endowed with one eye in the middle of their foreheads, which is all that distinguishes them from the rest. Otherwise, they all resemble one another—the Mauriacs or Maures, Hairodes, and Saracens. They all have rictus-like, bitter grins and sad eyes beneath bushy eyebrows. Their tanned skin is flecked with soot. They have lanky bodies, hunched shoulders, hairy torsos and limbs, and webbed feet.

CLOTHING:

Miserable tatters of dormice and vole skins. The Hairodes wear the skulls of ermine on their heads and shoulders. The Saracens wear some kind of wooden skullcap which gives them the appearance of being helmeted, but in reality these "helmets" are nothing more than crude acorn cups.

HABITAT:

Communal halls in the caves of mountains large and small. They edge their way into their homes through narrow holes and crevices hidden by vegetation. The Caramaras live mainly in dolmens; the Fachans, cousins from the Highlands, live in the rocks of Ben Nevis and the Grampians.

Saracens, Mauriacs, and Hairodes

Marginalized groups, such as the Cagots, have existed and still do in the Extremadura region of Spain, deep in mountainous terrain, cut off from this century. They form a community of dwarves called the Hurdès.

—Samivel

Were the Tartaros, Hurdès, Cagots, Caramaras, Hairodes, Saracens, and Mauriacs, mysterious renegades of dubious origin who lie buried beneath the shadows and rifts of the mountains, the henchmen of evil? They have been deliberately confused with each other, mistaken for Bohemian tinkers, Gypsies who steal children, and nomads. They are marked or can be distinguished by their infamous crow's feet, a distinctive sign of outcasts, outlaws, lepers, and demons.

"The Saracens at the Dawn of the Ages haunted epic sagas and stories. The accounts of the Crusades tainted their gallantry, and they fell into disgrace in the eyes of the Christians . . . and the word 'Saracen' was eventually used to designate pagans of all kinds.

"As Guilhem was bringing back a relic of the True Cross to Gellone, he rode his horse down a slope in the Hérault district of France called Lou Pahon. Suddenly, at a bend in the path, he heard screams and gulping sounds coming from a rocky outcrop, and saw a band of Saracens rushing towards him. He galloped his horse across the river, but the movement was so violent that the head and right shoe of the horse left an imprint in the left bank, while his tail left a second imprint on the bank on the opposite side . . ." (Petrus Barbygère)

These races have gradually disappeared, leaving only a few representatives among the Nutons and Gnomes. Naturally, they are assumed to have been of a size compatible with their underground habitats, which would cause them to be hunched over, shrunken, dark, and animal-like. Oral tradition often recalls the confrontations they had with humans who tried in vain to wrest their sparse territorial possessions from them. The people of Colombugne tell the story of the Saracens driven from the Land of Montmaure, who took refuge in a cave where they died of hunger rather than surrender themselves, and threw into a well the skin of a dog which contained the tribe's treasure. Out of spite they impaled themselves on their own spears after they lost the battle of Roche-Migé. The underground refuge of Moubon in Saint-Martin-le-Mault is littered with bones of those whom the Saracens massacred.

The few survivors mixed with other banished races and live with them as mountain-dwelling Dwarfs.

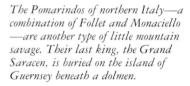

The Pomarindos of northern Italy—a combination of Follet and Monaciello —are another type of little mountain savage. Their last king, the Grand Saracen, is buried on the island of Guernsey beneath a dolmen.

FOOD:
They are said to be cannibals, and in Brittany Saracens are considered to be Ogres. They simmer stews and ragouts of ivy, ferns, clematis, asperules, moss, and wild mushrooms, flavored with moles, hedgehogs, or small rodents. The women bake bread in Saracen and Hairode ovens (which seem to be still in use).

BEHAVIOR:
Once valiant warriors, knights of the gods destined to perform cosmic tasks, they are now nothing but mere trappers of mice and shrews.

ACTIVITIES:
Hunting, working with metals, and mournfully contemplating the armor, helmets, shields, and swords that have become over one hundred times too large for them and that they cannot even lift any more.

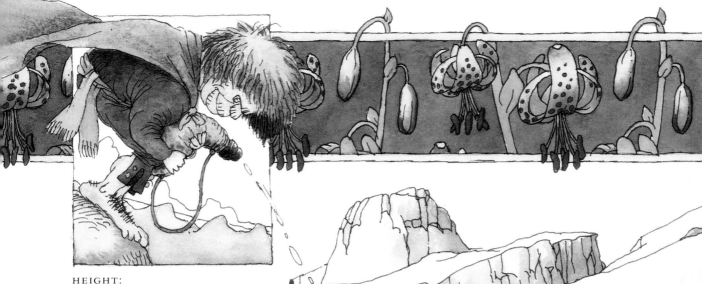

HEIGHT:
About twenty inches (50 cm).

APPEARANCE:
*The Lamignacs, or Laminaks, are
"similar to men, but smaller and not
quite as well built." Why? Because
"The good Lord created them before
men," they say. The Lamignacs are
not deformed, but they have crude,
coarse features and stocky, muscular
bodies on short stubby legs with abnor-
mally large calves that have been
strengthened from climbing. Their
bushy hair is powdered in gold dust.
The oldest of them have attractive spirals tattooed on their cheeks.*

CLOTHING:
*Tunics, capes, and robes of well-tanned
animal skins. Fur jackets in winter.
They do not need shoes or boots, because
their feet are naturally lined with a
substance that is as hard as horn.*

HABITAT:
*The mountains of Basque country.
They live in magnificent castles carved
into the caverns, their cellars overflowing with sumptuous treasures.*

FOOD:
*Those who have tasted their cuisine
say that such meals could not even be
found at a king's table—it was so
good that they can still taste the
incomparable flavors in their mouths.*

Lamignacs

*The martagon lily indicates the paths of the
Lamignacs.*

—Mgr Segrée-Fontaine,
Derrière les gentianes

One day, as a young shepherdess was watching her flock of goats in the mountains, a Lamignac came to her and carried her away on his back like a sack of potatoes despite his small stature. While she cried out with all her might, he took her down into his cave in Aussurucq. She remained there for five years. The Lamignacs gave her bread as white as snow which they had made themselves and other delicacies that tasted so good, there couldn't have been anything better. After two years she had a child by one of the Lamignacs, whom she taught to classify plants, following the custom of the Lamignacs. One day when the child was three, everyone went out hunting in the company of the Mau-riacs and Little Savage Men and left the young woman alone in the cave. She told

her son to play quietly while she stepped out for a moment and fled, running away to the valley. When she arrived back home, her parents had a hard time recog-nizing their daughter in the creature before them—she had become a Lamignac!

One night a beautiful young woman came to the door of a midwife's house, begging her to come and help a friend who was in labor. They traveled through the mountains, and upon arriving at a cliff, the young woman gave the midwife a wand and asked her to tap against the rocks. A door immediately opened. They went into a remarkably magnificent château, lit with elaborate candelabra of gold and dia-monds. At the far end of the most beauti-ful of a succession of rooms lay a Lamignac about to give birth, surrounded by a crowd of somber, still little creatures. As soon as the midwife had done her duty, she was given bread to eat that was as white as snow. Then the young woman led her to the door, but as it remained closed, she asked the midwife if she had brought something with her. She responded that she had kept a small piece of bread to show to her family. Once she gave it back, the door opened, and the young woman

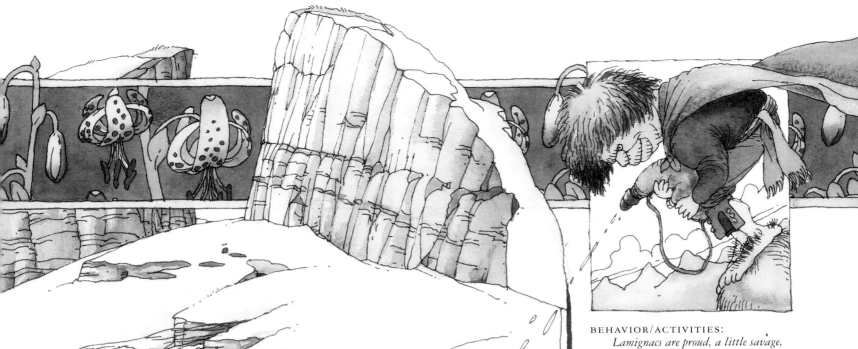

Lamignacs are proud, a little savage, and somewhat thieving, but also happy, contemplative, and helpful. They are not aggressive but can be provoked to anger, especially if someone destroys their territory (at which point they cause avalanches). They are great magicians, who can make people and objects disappear by tying their belts around them. They enjoy building replicas of human cities and villages. At night, they descend into human villages to steal the materials they need for these. The Lamignac women give a black chicken to their midwives or others whom they find to be deserving of a token. The chicken lays only one egg a day—but it is a massive, golden egg. So when fortune suddenly smiles upon someone, people say that "he has gotten a black chicken."

gave her a purse of gold coins and told her to put it in her chest at home. If she didn't speak of it to anyone, she would find it full every morning.

Many, many other stories are told about the Lamignacs. Not a day went by in the Basque country when someone didn't have something new to tell. It was enough to venture beyond the edge of the first gentians, and one was sure to encounter them—although hopefully not the kind that would steal you away on their backs! Their somewhat contradictory relationship with humans never went too badly, in spite of everything. And, frankly, if one wanted to avoid them, it was easy enough not go to where they hid out. In any case, they always made some kind of a trade: some treasure for some cows and sheep or a barrel of wine for a magic wand that lets one cross rivers without getting wet.

Sometimes, however, they went a bit too far. Once, when men blew up an entire section of mountain to make a quarry, the Lamignacs retaliated by causing an avalanche of boulders that resulted in the rerouting of a mountain stream right through the crops and fields. This almost resulted in Lamignacs and humans com-

ing to blows, but there was always a way of talking things out with them and making concessions. Little humans and little Lamignacs still did favors and ran errands for each other, driving the dormice away and chasing away the mountain goats, didn't they? After all, weren't they basically from the same great, ancient Family, that of the mountains, the rocks, and the peaks?

And then Roland, that old soldier with his heroic, swaggering airs, had to come along and ruin everything. Of course, the Lamignacs were wrong to devour all of his livestock in one and the same night. But matters could still have been settled. Knowing them, you can be certain that he would have been compensated. But no! That blasted Roland, who carried his sacred Durendal, would not tolerate this affront. "I'll show you up there what's what, I'll trap them and smash them to bits with my iron cudgel and stones . . ." Truly it was a war of madness. Even the children were dragged into it. There was no coming to an understanding. The surviving Lamignacs went back down into the depths of their dens and were never seen again.

Matagots

And suppose the cat wasn't a cat?
—J. B. Baronian, *Ode to Anne*

The great race of French cat-magicians known as Matagots long ruled over the mountain chain that surrounds the valley of Beyal-Trouble in Fairyland (nowadays known as the High Alps).

These excessively ferocious imps in animal form reigned from their mountaintop fortress, enslaving the peaceful little nations below—Dahus, Folletins, Troglodytes, and Whitecaps—and forcing them to forge weapons, extract precious metals from the rocks, cultivate the Matagon Herb, which was used to make magic potions, and herd the flocks of Joumeris (a cross between an ox and a she-donkey). Every mountain pass and gorge leading to their inaccessible mountain lair was guarded by the Arassas, grayish monsters with the bodies of lizards and the heads of cats, whose fiery glances would turn anyone who crossed their path into a mound of ashes. Yet the invincible Castle Rock eventually fell to the Saracens, who conquered the peaks thanks to an ingenious alliance they had with the hordes of the air.

Refusing to surrender, King Torte-Matagot was able to escape due to his thorough knowledge of the underground galleries of the mines that honeycombed the mountain. For thirty years he hid there, surrounded by his favorite concu-bines and a few loyal courtiers, before engaging in relentless and desperate combat.

There was a price on his head, and he was being hunted by those he had formerly enslaved. The pitiful tyrant was defeated once and for all at the Battle of Chaillot when the vengeful Folletins and Dahus captured him and dragged him, begging and weeping, to the Coulobre Precipice, from whence they flung him into the abyss.

Prudently abandoning armor, knighthoods, coats of mail, and the other attributes of war, the survivors changed themselves into ordinary, inoffensive black cats and settled in the French province of Dauphiné, taking refuge in the districts of Berry, Sologne, Touraine, Gascony, and Poitou, and at the mouth of the Rhone river, from whence they spread throughout southern France and still emerge for all sorts of devilry on nights when there is a crescent moon.

At midnight between Mardi Gras and Ash Wednesday, all the Matagots who have been scattered throughout the country come together to dance on their Black Sabbath, once again finding the gift of speech. They remain together until dawn, singing and telling the younger generations of their history, great deeds, and Matagon secrets.

Any person who seeks to abduct one of them must lie in wait every evening while fasting. The best way to succeed is to tie a chicken to a point at a crossroads. The greedy monster cat smells the creature and rushes towards it; that is when the hunter hidden in the hedge can pounce on his prey. He must grab the Matagot by

the tail and put it into a new leather bag without handling it roughly. He must carry the bag over his left shoulder and go home without speaking and without looking back, whatever sounds he may hear and no matter what happens. Whoever captures the demon cat can then lock it in a chest and feed it with a thousand kind attentions. If the hunter offers the cat the first mouthful of his evening meal, his fortune is assured because thereafter he will find a gold coin under his pillow.

But this could all end badly. When he is on the point of death, the Matagot's owner must get rid of it by bequeathing it to someone. As long as he fails to give this gift, one which his heirs may not want to accept, he is unable to die and experiences endless death throes, suffering horribly.

HEIGHT:
That of a large cat. They become longer on nights when there is a full moon.

APPEARANCE:
That of a large black cat. Their eyes turn red during the Witches' Sabbath, when they are capable of standing on their hind legs. The females have fiery patches between the ears.

CLOTHING:
In olden days, armor and magnificent robes. Today, beautifully shiny pelts.

HABITAT:
Southern and central France and the High Alps. Some nomadic families have spread almost everywhere, creating related races such as the Maragots, Mandagots, Coste-Matagots, and Montagos. They live in families in fortified foxes' dens from which they have chased the original occupants.

FOOD:
Small feathered and furred game and reptiles. They also raid rabbit hutches and henhouses, and they drink from the udders of cows and goats at night.

BEHAVIOR:
Matagots are cruel, pugnacious, and savage. When captured, they find themselves forced into servitude and forced to use their magic powers in the service of man, but their vengeance is terrible when they get the chance to gain their freedom. They choose a new wife every year during the nocturnal Mardi Gras festivities.

ACTIVITIES:
Hunting. They rarely engage in battle. Matagots cultivate the Matagon Herb and practice magic. They are constantly engraving the Matagon symbol on claws, teeth, and ornaments that have been inherited from the Ancients.

THE LITTLE FOLK OF THE MEADOWS, FIELDS, AND GARDENS

I contemplated the garden of the wonders of space, with a feeling of looking into the depths, into the most secret parts of my being.
—Czeslaw Milosz,
L'Amoureuse Initiation

Scattered beneath the immense canopy of the soul's foliage, places with forgotten meanings mark the boundary of the infrequently taken paths, the trails, the dirt roads that are now hidden, the roads traveled by the beings of the soil, whose long pilgrimage will traverse the pages of an herbarium that has returned to the wild like an ivy bookmark. Even the ancient trees can only confusedly remember the accounts of the Elders of the Moss with their hunched backs and long, lichen beards.

Before the land-clearance men and city planners, the enemies of expanses of grass and ruined splendors had remodeled and consolidated the primordial Great Forest with all of its superimposed layers of vegetation, which "Old Tree-Bark" reigned over—the forest canopy, the realm of magic; the lower, Elfin layer of the underwood; the Sylphidine layer of shrubs and bushes; and the layer of grasses and herbs, lichen of the thicket, and Fairy wands. A continuous curtain wall protected the forest within from the winds of the Massive Age and majestically extended along its "forts" of holly, from which unicorns, stags, the royal cavalry, and all the vassals of the sovereign Fairies and Dwarfs were driven by the first deep gashes of the plowshare.

Pan

Is that not old Pan sitting by the fireside?
— William Furse Kingwill

Nick, Puck, or Pan, he was in your bed, Madame!

— P. G. Salgati, *L'Incube*

Although it can be dangerously soporific to count sheep, we must run through the entire herd to cut loose a few of the tangled skeins of that mythological sheepfold.

To begin with, Pan is by no means that simplistic caricature of the lewd and lazy seducer to which he is too often reduced! He is a powerful and auspicious god, not to mention a hero and half-brother of the great Zeus!

When Pan was born, his mother was frightened by his little horns and his hairy legs, so she entrusted him to the pretty Nymphs of the tiny leafy trees. Ah, he was so cute with his wee cloven hooves and that premature downy goatee on his chin! Charmed, the Fairy Godmothers gathered about his mossy cradle to rock, cuddle, simper at, and delight over him. One of them pushed her tanned breast into his greedy mouth, one of them changed his diaper, another burped him . . . and Pan laughed.

With such lavish attentions, he grew fast and soon revealed those acrobatic and virile characteristics so superior to those of an ordinary goat.

He screamed and shouted himself hoarse when thwarted; his trumpeting was such that he has given his name to "panic" (and the disgusted Titans rue the day).

Shocked by the exploits of the clamorous little one, his father Hermes immediately took him to the gods of Olympus, who were dazzled by his vigor, his capers, his faun dances! But Pan was bored in those vast marble halls, so cold and tidy, among those affected megalomaniacs. He definitely prefers the company of the plump Dryads, the Centaurs, and the herdsmen. He needs to inhale the scent of clover at dawn, to roll down the cool valleys, to hear the bleating of goats—and to scratch wherever he feels like scratching. He dreamt of leaping into rivers, swimming under the duckweed to emerge farther down crowned with water lilies, and biting into the tender rump of a Naiad.

Pan did not think twice; he plunged into the divine cumulus and returned to earth!

His laughter echoed in cascades through the hills, woods, and valleys to announce his return.

"The Great God Pan is back! The Great God Pan is back!" All the farmers, herdsmen, household pets, and Fairy creatures and all spirits of the enchanted vegetation, the grass, and the violets salute the horned figure. He has come home! The earth covers itself with crops and abundant cattle. The ground once again resounds to his hooves launched in pursuit of a herd of fleeing female Centaurs . . . and there is pushing and shoving, billing and cooing, and mating. And flute concerts . . .

Yet Pan is also known to spend his days in silence and meditation. He remains perfectly still, breathing and allowing nature to permeate his limbs, his hairy body, and the vastness of his understanding. From dawn to dusk he meditates.

He can often be seen gardening, retouching the landscape here and there, giving a shadowy ditch a touch of bluebells, relieving the paleness of wheat with a sprig of poppies, placing festoons of ivy on old walls and barren places, and putting lilies-of-the-valley under a clump of bushes just for the pleasure of seeking them out later—with a female companion.

This solitary old being is known to have had "one true love." Of course, he had many other conquests, and they were none too shabby—even Selene, the haughty, frigid moon goddess, submitted to his charms—yet he had only one "great romance." That is the sad story he plays endlessly on his famous Pan pipes, the *syrinx*. That was the name of the young and pretty nymph—Syrinx. He loved that graceful Meadow Fairy dancing beneath the primroses, but she panicked in the face of the tumultuous passion of this bearded goat-bard and chose to flee! Trapped by a tumbling river, she changed into a reed bed. At the edge of the waters all that remained were the rustling tufts of reeds that Pan cut into different lengths and assembled to make the syrinx on which he sighs outs his inconsolable disappointment. Was it his fault she didn't know how to play the game?

The cry goes up: "The Great God Pan is dead!" The earth mourns. The animals, the plants, the spirits, the Nymphs, the Dryads, the Wood Nymphs, the little companions of the meadows, and the groves grow somber. The grass bows down, the birds fall silent at the fateful news: "The Great God Pan is dead!" Yet it is nonetheless a sort of coronation, since he was and will remain the only god who has access to eternal rest . . . and to the eternal return.

The Children of Pan

If Pan has disappeared, sucked into the mire, it is because times have changed. His bestial allure has become disturbing; it betrays his animal origins. The body hair, horns, and tail make a poor image for a progressive civilization. Ugh! The church made him into a devil, an Incubus fit for burning at the stake. Let us throw him in the fire and scatter his ashes; let there remain no trace. Glory to the One Celestial God with no trace of muck!

Pan departed on a high note. He went before seeing the ax fall on the old oaks.

During his solitary meditations, did Pan the visionary actually foresee the danger and prepare for his "survival" through a perpetual line of descent? Did not that other venerable vestige of the first ages, the Dragon-God, escape from the assaults of fundamentalist archangels by scattering himself like an earthworm, only to reemerge later in a plethora of "Batrachian Imps": tadpoles, frogs, toads, and lizards?

Hidden in the midst of his herds of goats and Nymph accomplices, behind the screens of myrtles and pistachio trees, Pan prepared his attack. His son Silene was the exact likeness of him in every feature, hair, and horn. The good Silene, companion of the Maenads, debauchedly repopulated the meadows with his namesake Silenes who begat the Satyrs with horns and hooves in their turn. The syrinx carried the triumphant song of the rebirth of Pan throughout the valleys and the groves!

Nevertheless, the assault on the Horned Ones grew fiercer and fiercer, and their territories continued to dwindle. The Goat People decided to disperse and disappear to await better times.

They burrowed beneath the ground; they hid in caves and on the most inaccessible heights; they even emigrated. In Ireland, England, Scotland, France, Belgium, Germany, Scandinavia, in the des-

olate heaths, in the woods and remote valleys, the Fairy People, some of whom were also refugees, welcomed them.

The mountain goats paired with the ibex, the chamois, the white goat, and the alpine deities of the Lamignacs and Fions; the forest goats mated with the charming Dryads and the sweet Wood Nymphs! They married Fairies, Elves, and spirits of wind and water—resulting in the most extraordinary crowd of exceptional mutants! Winged goats, goat-hoofed Silenes, chamois-goats, billy-nanny goats, nannybilly goats, goat-serpents, and more.

But it did not end there, since in the secrecy of their remote retreat, some daredevils ventured to spawn with Succubi, demons, the infernal consorts; they boned up on magic spells in books of black arts and invoked the most terrible entities, whom they then "came to know"! This shamefully acquired knowledge allowed them to change their appearance, shape, and color by chanting any incantation. None went back to the way they were.

Yet better times still failed to materialize, so those among them who were the most homesick, the most protective, and the most helpful cautiously started to descend gradually once more into the valleys and attach themselves to homes, barns, and orchards, aiding the farmer in the field and the herdsman with the herd, protecting—like Pan before them—the harvests and the animals, and, of course, seducing the mistress of the house.

You see with these long-lost heirs of Pan that "like father, like son!" The Schrats, those forest criers whose screams panic those walking late at night . . . And pointy-eared Pucks with their cascading laughter . . . The horned Fougres . . . the sly Faudoux of the haylofts . . . even Peter Pan with his reed flute . . . and finally, the tired old Verbouc Satyr, who even in the twilight of his years managed to impregnate a woman working in a fairground!

HEIGHT:

Pan measured sixty-four inches (162 cm), the first generation forty-seven inches (120 cm); the second regressed to the size of a goat.

APPEARANCE:

Abundant frizzy fleece. Pointed, waggling ears. Horns whose size depends on age. The oldest carry a fine pair of horns like those of a ram. Laughing mouths with no lips. Pointed beards. Very muscular, compact, hairy bodies. Wagging tails. Extremely strong goat legs. Highly developed genitals.

CLOTHING:

Nude, sometimes covered in skins or straw. They wear a kind of leather codpiece during jumping competitions, races, and encounters with goats. They often flirtatiously adorn themselves with crowns and garlands of flowers.

HABITAT:

Greek and Italian meadows. They sleep in the open air in both summer and winter.

FOOD:

Honey, fruit, flowers, milk, cheese, wine offered by shepherds.

BEHAVIOR:

Very uninhibited.

ACTIVITIES:

Bucolic, lovers of the countryside, faun-like. They are the protectors of natural flora and fauna. The Satyrs are able to command the winds. Good musicians, excellent dancers.

Fauns

Under the cold slabs of oblivion
Lies the insignificant faun . . .
—Strauss-Heinz-Strumme,
Das Volksleben der neugriechen und
das hellenische Alterthum,
vol. XI, Innsbruck, 1801

In the beginning, there was Faunus, the "rustic god" of the Romans—wrongly compared to the Greek god Pan—son of Picus, himself the son of Saturn and a rustic divinity who amused herself by adopting the lively form of a woodpecker. Faunus protects herds from wolves; hence his nickname Luperus.

From his loins were born the little hairy, horned, and cloven-hoofed beings who spread over fields and throughout the countryside and diverged into the other races of Kornböcke and various lines of succession, eventually becoming Fauns.

Twenty inches (50 cm). A forty-five inch (115 cm) wingspan.

APPEARANCE:
"Horned" heads of a bird of prey. Enormous beaks that can crack the skull of a sheep with one blow. Scaly, plucked necks. Plumage on the shoulders. Strong legs with steel-hard talons. According to those who have seen them, the rest of their bodies resemble a pallid, hairy chamois. Membranous wings. They hide two token arms as supple as slowworms.

CLOTHING:
Thick woolen mantles that they fling backward like a cape when they fly.

HABITAT:
Nests of bones on the barren crests of Slieve League, from which they survey the Irish countryside.

FOOD:
All sorts of game, crows, sheep, and small calves. They fish and attack other birds of prey in full flight, as well as devouring abandoned Cluricaunes.

BEHAVIOR/ACTIVITIES:
There are few Fougres left, since many Leprechauns, Fir Darig, and Cluricaunes, enraged by their raids, have decimated the species, crushing broods and burning nests. In our day, a last surviving one lurks in the form of a large red-and-black goat with the eyes of a sparrow hawk, armed with two enormous ibex horns.

Fougres

Fougres are the tragic result of a gang rape committed by a multitude of Hargnes spirits (Vassalerie of the Unseelie Court) on a Sidhe living in the heather. Before dying, the poor unfortunate Sidhe brought into the world a kind of small, hateful monstrosity, half predator, half demon, that allowed itself to be carried off by a Satyr that had taken refuge in the solitude of Donegal.

One or two broods later, Fougres infested the country.

In 1821, Thomas Macaulay, a farmer on his way to a hurling match, was attacked by one of them. Even though it gouged his face, he managed to overcome his attacker with the hurling stick; he exchanged his trophy for several bottles of raw whiskey from the owner of a shebeen who then nailed the beast up behind the bar.

Night after night, its "family" came to reclaim the body, creating a great rumpus, knocking on windowpanes, and overwhelming the innkeeper's children with so many aches and pains that the innkeeper decided to leave the withered corpse on the threshold. By the next day, the Fougre had disappeared, leaving behind only four deep scratches in the wooden door.

Kornböcke,
White Goats, and
White-Clad Ones

HEIGHT:

From the size of a ladybug to that of a goat.

APPEARANCE:

All the field Genies look alike. They are descended from the Goat People, Sylvains, Satyrs, and Silenes, and while here and there some traits have changed, they are characterized by flattened snouts, longish ears, red eyes, and brownish coats; in general, they carry the imprint of their progenitor Pan: half human, half goat, horned foreheads, goat legs, and hooves.

CLOTHING:

They are clothed in white linen. The Pavari wear pointed hats, the Catez shepherd's caps, the Pilwizes green felt hats, the Lysgulbar round hats with tassels. In the winter, they bundle up in coats of long white fur. The Pavari have sickles attached to their ankles. The Caraquins of the Highlands proudly wear their plaids and never let go of their dirks.

HABITAT:

Wherever crops are found.

In the countryside, it is the magic that remains when all is lost.

—Henri Pourrat,
L'Homme á la bêche
(The Man with the Spade)

Humans waste bread, since they would rather throw it away than give it to charity. They plant more and more to get rich while impoverishing the earth. After they had committed all sorts of crimes to usurp neighboring fields, a Genie grabbed a stalk of wheat (on which the grains used to stretch along the whole length) at ground level and drew it between his fingers, almost to the top. A Fairy stopped him, asking him to leave a little tuft of grain for the bread of the just. Since then, the wheat stalks have been long and the ears short.

The gods and the "friends" of the fields ensure that nature is neither spoiled nor destroyed, that its cycles are respected, and that its bounty is not exhausted for profit. A person who throws away bread is punished within the week. Lovers who crush the sheaves when they lie down, those who pick flowers or cut down wheat by slashing through it blindly across the fields, and children who run through the crops while playing are all punished. A snake bites them, they cut themselves badly with a scythe, they hurt their backs falling off a haystack, the midday demon fries their brains, or Roggenmöhme, the "Rye Fairy," sends them fever.

If people want a good haymaking season or harvest, it must be earned by honoring this partnership. The whole field should not be cultivated—a corner must be left fallow for the spirits of the earth. They must no longer mow down their circles, the tumuli inhabited by the Sidhe, or Elfin hills. They must leave a grassy area around the standing stones, cairns, dolmens, and menhirs where the Korrigans reside; they must not uproot a sacred tree to gain a few feet of earth in which to plant crops! They must make even more of an effort not to uproot the hedges, never redistributing them willy-nilly and disrupting the harmony of hedged fields to extend cultivated lands even further! The guilty will be charged with all these excesses of greater or shorter degree, and no Fairy hand will lighten the sentence— a black blight will scorch the golden stalks to cinders.

"One day at a time," as the saying goes. Man must tread lightly and patiently and respect the wisdom of the fields. The

earthworm, the insect, the bird, the hedge-hog, the flower—each has its task and its place. For the bucolic Böcke, the crickets are as magnificent and useful as they are themselves. Their chirping symbolizes peace and abundance. Even though these rural Genies spread their attention over thousands of acres, they do not think any less of the effort of the ant to carry a crumb. It goes badly for humans who fail to learn this lesson.

Once, when a storm threatened, an improvident farmer was completing his harvesting in haste. He tossed the sheaves into the hayloft in great swathes and fork-fuls, cursing the weather all the while. Suddenly, he noticed that a minuscule and puny Genie stood at his side to help him. Bent under the weight, the little creature made an effort to drag along a stalk and strip it grain by grain. "Get out of my way, you bother me, do you think you're helping me like that?" the farmer sneered in his face. This was not a good idea and was something the farmer would soon have reason to lament. "I have made you rich, ear by ear, sheaf by sheaf, and I will ruin you in the same way," declared the spirit—and thousands of weevils came every year to devour the farmer's crops.

The Pavari of northern Italy, who have dog's heads and iron teeth, make beans proliferate and grow, but if they see that the farmers under their protection refuse someone a plateful of them or waste them, the Pavari allow vermin to enter the seed-pods, they invite the great beast Ogress to help herself, or they themselves cut off the roots with snips of their scissors. They have sickles attached to their ankles; some Pavari carry a rather long cane with a pommel sculpted in the shape of a goat's head.

The Preinscheuhen do the same for oats and millet, as do the Yugoslavian Catez. Regardless of their country of origin, the Scottish Urisks, the German Kornböcke, the Swedish Lysgulbar, the Bavarian Pil-wizes, the Scandinavian Julbocks, and the Belgian White-Clad Ones all have the same duty to protect the harvest, as well as to conserve the Fairy-Earth.

The Scottish Urisks dwell on the moors and near streams. Others are found in the woods, but during warm weather they descend in groups to the fields and do not leave until the fall.

The Scandinavian Julbocks, who come around to the farms at the beginning of winter, are invited to eat as much as they wish on December 23. If they are not offered anything, they sour the beer, rot the grain, and turn the flour moldy.

FOOD:
Bread, milk, and cereals. The Scandinavian Julbocks, who visit farms in early winter, are invited to eat as much as they wish on December 23.

BEHAVIOR:
They still have their ancestors' keen amorous instincts, and they reproduce wildly. The old males are always attracted to pretty Nymphs, Fadettes, and young peasant girls in the area, whom they abduct at night on the roads.

ACTIVITIES:
When they are not watching over the fields, they can be seen riding and running in the wind on the crests of waves of rye, oats, and wheat, moving so fast that they leave long, luminous trails in their wake.

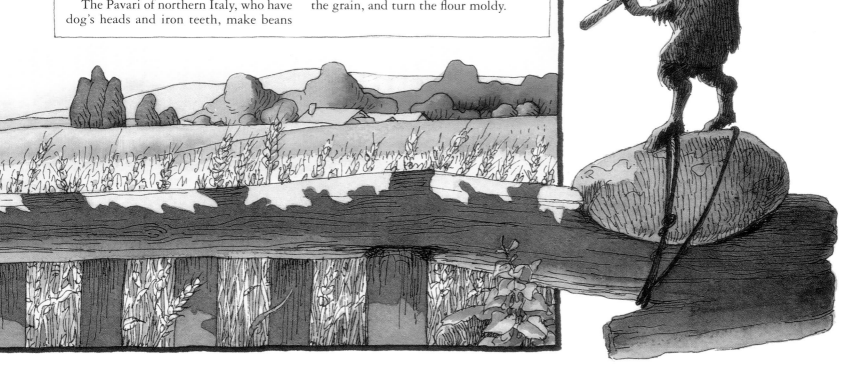

HEIGHT:
   Ranging from two feet (60 cm) to over thirteen feet (4 m).

APPEARANCE:
   Multiple appearances. His original appearance was that of a furry Gnome with a horse's head, whose mane was braided by the Moss Sprites. His right hand is large and wide to enable him to seize and strangle his prey; his left hand is sharper and steely to enable him to rip open flesh.

CLOTHING:
   He wears tunics of skin and fur, with heavy chains around his neck, which he rattles to frighten humans or to smash heads.

HABITAT:
   Throughout the whole of Ireland. Prefers uninhabited areas. When he stops and rests somewhere, he digs a hole in which he sheds his previous skin.

FOOD:
   He devours cattle and children but spares Dwarfs and Elves.

BEHAVIOR/ACTIVITIES:
   He is crazy, cruel, and gleeful. His enthusiasm causes him to play unpleasant tricks such as pulling off someone's head to play football with it, kidnapping a little child and taking pleasure in the grotesque sobs and lamentations of its parents, or throwing himself into a funeral procession and viciously kicking the mourners. But one hears his neighing cries less and less since he retreated to Kerry, where he now spends all his time smoking pipes beside his peat fire, having taken on the shape of a gentle old man with a strong and lively grasp.

The Phooka

The Phooka is a descendant of Pan. The Phooka's direct ancestor has been described as "a roaring serpent who seizes in his gaping jaws screeching flocks of stormy petrels, gulls, and puffins off the Skellig Isles." It is there, among the Skellig Isles, where the Phooka swims beside the dragon of Gougane Barra who was struck down by St. Finbarr. He launches himself into the air like a bird, soaring over the misty heights of the Sheehy Mountains and disappearing only to emerge lower down, covered in a snow-white pelt and bleating like a kid. He mixes with the goats and flatters the goatherd who caresses his soft pelt—which suddenly tears open to reveal a saurian monster. The Phooka can be found in the shape of a falcon in the Mountains of Mourne and as a belligerent Dwarf in the caves of Marble Arch, a seahorse on the stormy coast of Sligo, a chained ghost in Connemara, and a hungry Triton beneath the waters of Lough Key.

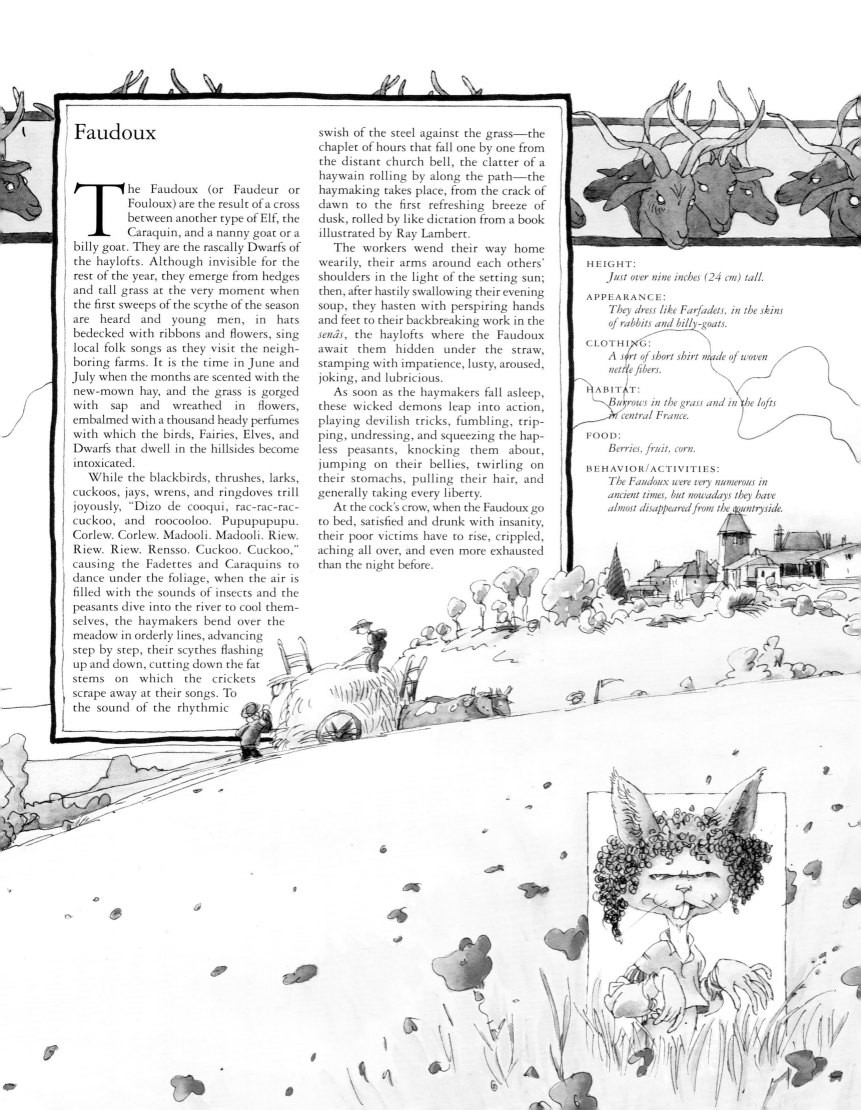

Faudoux

The Faudoux (or Faudeur or Fouloux) are the result of a cross between another type of Elf, the Caraquin, and a nanny goat or a billy goat. They are the rascally Dwarfs of the haylofts. Although invisible for the rest of the year, they emerge from hedges and tall grass at the very moment when the first sweeps of the scythe of the season are heard and young men, in hats bedecked with ribbons and flowers, sing local folk songs as they visit the neighboring farms. It is the time in June and July when the months are scented with the new-mown hay, and the grass is gorged with sap and wreathed in flowers, embalmed with a thousand heady perfumes with which the birds, Fairies, Elves, and Dwarfs that dwell in the hillsides become intoxicated.

While the blackbirds, thrushes, larks, cuckoos, jays, wrens, and ringdoves trill joyously, "Dizo de cooqui, rac-rac-rac-cuckoo, and roocooloo. Pupupupupu. Corlew. Corlew. Madooli. Madooli. Riew. Riew. Riew. Rensso. Cuckoo. Cuckoo," causing the Fadettes and Caraquins to dance under the foliage, when the air is filled with the sounds of insects and the peasants dive into the river to cool themselves, the haymakers bend over the meadow in orderly lines, advancing step by step, their scythes flashing up and down, cutting down the fat stems on which the crickets scrape away at their songs. To the sound of the rhythmic swish of the steel against the grass—the chaplet of hours that fall one by one from the distant church bell, the clatter of a haywain rolling by along the path—the haymaking takes place, from the crack of dawn to the first refreshing breeze of dusk, rolled by like dictation from a book illustrated by Ray Lambert.

The workers wend their way home wearily, their arms around each others' shoulders in the light of the setting sun; then, after hastily swallowing their evening soup, they hasten with perspiring hands and feet to their backbreaking work in the *senâs*, the haylofts where the Faudoux await them hidden under the straw, stamping with impatience, lusty, aroused, joking, and lubricious.

As soon as the haymakers fall asleep, these wicked demons leap into action, playing devilish tricks, fumbling, tripping, undressing, and squeezing the hapless peasants, knocking them about, jumping on their bellies, twirling on their stomachs, pulling their hair, and generally taking every liberty.

At the cock's crow, when the Faudoux go to bed, satisfied and drunk with insanity, their poor victims have to rise, crippled, aching all over, and even more exhausted than the night before.

HEIGHT:
Just over nine inches (24 cm) tall.

APPEARANCE:
They dress like Farfadets, in the skins of rabbits and billy-goats.

CLOTHING:
A sort of short shirt made of woven nettle fibers.

HABITAT:
Burrows in the grass and in the lofts in central France.

FOOD:
Berries, fruit, corn.

BEHAVIOR/ACTIVITIES:
The Faudoux were very numerous in ancient times, but nowadays they have almost disappeared from the countryside.

HEIGHT:
Two feet (61 cm) (Justave Sarcaud, "Legends of Bassigny in Champagne," 1880).

APPEARANCE:
Small plump, merry fellows with malicious, laughing eyes, pointed beards, and pointed, hairy ears.

CLOTHING:
Round hats, breeches, shoes with buckles, gaiters, coats, and purses all in red. The Felteus dress badly and are poor tailors. The women are a little smaller and pleasingly attractive, but they dress just as badly as their husbands do; they wear many bright red skirts, one on top of the other. They are also fond of cheap costume jewelry, for which they pay gold to hawkers, who are thrilled with this windfall.

HABITAT:
Champagne. They live in the deep woods in rather dirty little cottages badly built of limestone and cob and covered with moss and bracken.

FOOD:
They binge generously on whatever looks appetizing.

BEHAVIOR:
The Felteus are lazy Dwarfs without much of a temper and not very talented, but they are accommodating. Although given to theft and pranks, they are kind and never get angry.

ACTIVITIES:
The Felteus laugh and dance a lot. Completely under the thumb of humans, they are content to get along in the space allotted to them in fairy tales and bedtime stories.

The Felteus

One, two, three Felteus all in a row.
—Round from Verzy

Around two hundred years ago, a cook in the French province of Champagne was heading home through the Noyers forest after working at a wedding. In the midst of a clearing, she came upon more than sixty Felteus arranged in three concentric circles around a large fire. The largest circle consisted of Felteu-ostlers, brushing, currying, and braiding the manes and tails of the most beautiful horses in the land. The horses let them work while they plunged their muzzles deep into nose bags full of oats. In the second circle, fiddlers played frenzied melodies. The circle closest to the fire was formed of kitchen boys who were busy plucking chickens and peeling vegetables that the cook recognized as having been stolen from her during the wedding. As she indignantly noted this act of larceny, the Father Felteu, an old man with a long white beard, appeared. He signaled to the others, who bounded forth frisking, leaping, and laughing like madmen. They surrounded her like a dizzying whirlwind singing to the tune of "Marlborough" at the top of their lungs:

Here is the cook,
By the grace of God.
She will be a good friend
To the little Felteus.

The good cook trembled; after all, these Little People had a reputation for being practical jokers. Reassured, however, by hearing them sing "by the grace of God," she said to herself that they would not harm her. They told her that they had been waiting for hours for the Felteu cook to put in an appearance. "If that's all it is," she said, "I myself will cook for you!" Rolling up her sleeves and donning her apron, she immediately set to work to the jubilant applause of the crowd. After the party ended, the cook followed tradition and made the rounds of the company with her large ladle. Each Felteu put at least two pieces of gold in it, and the old man deposited his full purse. At that very moment, the first glint of dawn appeared, and with it the Dwarfs and all trace of their meal disappeared, leaving the good woman dumbfounded—and sufficiently rich to open "The Inn of the Good Felteu."

288

The Little Bell Ringer

A genie clarifies the golden wine.
 —Maitre K. Mattheus,
 La Vigne légendaire
 (The Legendary Vineyard)

Friend Fritz, the illustrious doctor Matheus, the pretty Myrtle, Zacharias Piper, and many others, all of them good Erckmann-Chatrian heroes, have had at least one meeting with this indispensable Alsatian imp, master of the golden vines, who leans on a vine-stock cane and lovingly watches the glowing morsels mature.

Kobus Wendling, his belly heavy with sauerkraut and meat, roast goose, and potatoes cooked in lard and his head reeling with a merry inebriation conferred by the magic mixture of many tankards of excellent beer and sparkling goblets of fruity wine, left the "Au Jambon de Mayence" inn to take a walk. The purpose was to tone down the crimson blush of his cheeks and dissipate the merriment that invariably exacted terrible repercussions from Mrs. Wendling. So he staggered around the countryside.

Leaving the village by a narrow alley, he climbed towards the Ettendorf hills, glancing at the tiny windows lit by bright fires or gleaming with lovely Bohemian glass ornaments.

A soft October breeze carried the scent of fir trees and shrubs from the nearby forest . . . as well as a slight tinkling sound from the vineyards.

Oh! Oh! Oh! Our suddenly sober friend burped three times, pricking up his ears with difficulty in order to better hear the faint chimes of the bell.

My God, yes! It must be! It is indeed the well-met Little Bell Ringer who is still around. The grape harvest is barely over, but he is already preparing for the next one. From his joyous ringing, it must be a good one. About time!

And Wendling gaily and exultantly ran back to announce and spread the happy news at the inn . . . and there you will find him still!

HEIGHT:
Twenty-four inches (60 cm).

APPEARANCE:
Corpulent Dwarf of the hills, well-built though slightly overweight. Pink skin. Bright eyes. Big nose. He has a short beard but no mustache.

CLOTHING:
During the week, he wears the typical clothes of the Alsatian vintner. On Sunday, he proudly sports the magnificent local costume: tricorn hat, red jacket with metal buttons, embroidered vest, white stockings, buckled shoes, and a chain of small silver bells.

HABITAT:
Eastern France.

FOOD:
He stuffs himself with cooked meats and almond cakes. He also treats himself to plates of sauerkraut flambé. He drinks excellent wines from the vineyards he protects.

BEHAVIOR:
Once he was the grandmaster of the wines and spirits storehouse, the keeper of the royal cellars, and the chief of the master tasters of the Kobold kings of the Rhine. After a quarrel over a vintage, he left his old benefactors to tend the vines of the Giants of Nideck. He will never leave his beloved slopes, which have fallen into the hands of humans. His wife is an Erdwiweleschlucht Fairy.

ACTIVITIES:
He watches over and protects the vines and announces successful harvests. When the wine is good, he dances and plays a happy tune. If it is not, he can be seen sitting sadly at the edge of the vineyard, clanging a bell with a doleful note.

HEIGHT:
Twenty-four inches (60 cm).

APPEARANCE:
Robust legs ending in deer hooves, piercing green eyes. However, their heads carry fewer antlers than those of their older brothers. A humble pair of spiral horns adorns foreheads covered with curly fleece. Their bodies are entirely covered with lovely silvery fur that they burnish every night in the still waters.

CLOTHING:
White linen tunics, thick woolen coats, and, in winter, a sort of balaclava made from all sorts of grains. When they feel amorous, the Little Mujik wear red caps topped with a bunch of wildflowers.

HABITAT:
They sleep in the open air in fields all over Russia. They do not feel the cold, and a bale of straw is enough to make them happy in winter. Snoring coming from under a hedge indicates that one has made his bed there.

FOOD:
Berries, fruit, cheese, game.

BEHAVIOR:
Merry, amusing, teasing, hardworking (sometimes). They are always seen around farmers, who fear them less than the Leshiye.

ACTIVITIES:
They protect the crops and ensure a good harvest. They join in the harvesting with the workers, and even though their sickles are little more than toys, they finish a field ten times faster than a human being. However, a sudden whim to frolic can make them leave work on the spot.

Dikonkyi Mujik

Thanks to the teaching of the fruit trees, the rain, and the sun, the rivers and the forests, the bees and the beetles, not to mention the lessons of the god Pan . . .

—Hermann Hesse

From a horizon studded with ancient forests, the slopes descend to meet large lonesome oaks, beeches, and poplars. These plant menhirs, these Easter statues crowned with living green tiaras, stand among the crops like vestiges. All has become a wooded landscape, interspersed with cultivated lands, orchards, water meadows, and dry lawns with rock gardens. The windswept expanses of gorse and heather recall the steppes. Two red curlews with large eyes take to the air from a distant stony, bald mountain. The two-note cry of these hermits of the rocks heralds their twilight hunt for the creatures that live in the crevices.

The oats, the thick wheat, and the silver-green swell of ears of rye cover the lower slopes. The hedges are overrun by woody nightshade, white bryony, and wild hops, and the dog roses mingle with the eglantine. The chestnut is the last of the great trees to flower.

Farther down, the Solomon's seal, buttercups, and daisies appear in ever more subdued light to cap off the herbal collection of flowering species of the undergrowth, where only the fragrant sage, hawkweed, and saprophytic orchids will soon emerge.

Yellow bursts of pollen escape from stamens throughout the undergrowth, looking like a sulfurous rain from afar . . .

This is the time when the stars and cosmic clouds of galactic matter sprinkle the celestial provinces with light from the depths of the ages and when the rambling Elfologist replaces the amateur naturalist. Before our very eyes, the seas glisten and stir.

Deep in the lunar waters dotted with marsh marigolds, rushes, sedge, and plankton, the skinny frogs—exhausted by egg-laying—are quiet, but the toads dressed in their emerald corsets begin to sing, croaking their interminable prayers to the gods and Genies whose first representatives will soon come to bathe.

The Dikonkyi Mujik, the rather wild "little Mujik," are the Leshiye of the fields. They are less touchy and temperamental

than the forest Leshiye, and the grin that splits their faces from goat ear to goat ear is indicative of their jolly natures. The peasants love them and often invite them to share their midday meal; a plate of stew waits for them at the farmhouse door each evening. But the Dikonkyi Mujik refuse to cross the threshold. Although they are deliriously happy in the open, the sight of four walls and a roof suffocates them! Young girls amuse themselves by teasing and tickling them; on harvest or haymaking evenings, they join the girls on the wagons loaded with sheaves.

When the winter snow keeps the peasant at home, the first snowflakes kick off the mating season for the "Ashy Little Mujik." Gliding along icy streams, they climb to the foothills, where the Babas, small wild women who have come down from the Carpathian mountains, greet them warmly. The products of these "snow marriages" are sent down to the plains as soon as the renowned ashy coat makes its appearance.

It is common for landowners to offer the Dikonkyi Mujik jobs as shepherds, since their relationship with the Leshiye—masters of the bears and wolves—keeps the carnivores from attacking the herds.

They usually refuse, since spending too much time with sheep bores them.

If they are seen running through the stubble fields in the morning, it is a sign of good weather, but if they sulk against a tree, it will surely rain.

The Dikonkyi Mujik are good and peaceful, but they do not stand for having their predictions doubted or their orders questioned. One time, when one had ordered that the harvest be gathered on a sunny, cloudless day, people mocked him, whereupon he allowed the crops to spoil when the storms and lightning fires came that night. It is also best not to comment on their bouts of idleness. Once vexed, they will never return, and disaster will continue to strike.

To be friends with the Dikonkyi Mujik, you must take him as you find him, whenever you find him.

HEIGHT:

Variable. They grow and shrink along with the rye and wheat that form their habitat, from a tiny shoot just visible above the earth to the size of a proud tufted ear of wheat.

APPEARANCE:

Powerful, with bronzed skin and brilliant blue eyes. Green beards and hair. They carry themselves in a stooping posture. The Poludnitsa are deep brown, pretty and lively, with "dreamy" expressions.

CLOTHING:

The males, like the females, are clothed in short tunics of undyed linen, tied about the waist with belts made of plants, green in the spring, full of flowers in summer, and threaded with reeds in the fall and winter. They wear leggings of grass.

HABITAT:

They are spread, like a comfortable overcoat, across all the cultures of Russia.

FOOD:

They eat lots of cereal broths and birds' eggs that are laid in the fields. Rye cakes filled with wild fruit jelly are one of their favorites.

The Polevoi

The history of wheat extends so far that it becomes entwined and entangled in the luscious hair of the Fairies who reigned over the wild prairies.

—H. de Fauconnier

In the beginning, the Leshiye reigned over the forest, and the Vodianoi over the waters. Domovoï kept watch over the fire spirits, and the Polevoi over the vast grassy plains of Old Russia. The millennia came and went, and creatures crawled out of the swamps, spread along the shores, and shed their scaly skins in favor of ragged clothes. They walked on two legs and went on to conquer the plains with stone and fire. The Peaceful Ones and the Contemplators, who preferred to graze peacefully on leaves, were pushed ever further back into obscurity. As man continued to evolve, the dreamy Bucolics remained unchanged and disappeared into the far reaches of the deserts, to the snowy borders of the Land of Legends . . . Their names vary depending on the region in which they are found: Yeti, Mi-Ghen, Goul-Biadasse, Djinni, Bigfoot, Kaptar, and so on.

The Polevoi saw their untamed domain, hitherto disturbed only by bison and long-haired ponies, slowly become covered by a new, cultivated plant. They were intrigued by the vast areas of segmented, plowed, planted, and domesticated land. At night, they carefully approached the fields to taste the green and yellow ears growing in rows and in plots—and it was good! The small grains cracked beneath their teeth and released a subtle floral flavor. The Polevoi were not spiteful creatures—they held sway over immense areas, and their soul was of the same dimensions. Men wanted to cultivate the earth. They let them do so. Domovoi already lived on farms and made the Polevoi try some of the bread that the strangers made from the plumed plants that swayed in the wind like the abundant hair of their wives the Poludnitsa . . .

The bread was good, the grains tender, and the songs that the workers sang in unison while they labored soothed the Polevoi in their reveries. They decided that they would help the humans to reap abundant harvests.

They were kings of the meadows, and it would not be the carefree Dikonkyi Mujik, their direct vassals, who would question their authority. In exchange for some grain and some cake, but mainly due to their generosity, the Polevoi went on to bless all the crops with their good deeds: they commanded the wildflowers to stay away from the useful plants, they made the three-colored violet lose its perfume so as not to distract the harvester, and they told the insects to stop their damage. The hail and wind lost their harmful force due to their efforts, the sky Genies filtered the sun's most powerful rays, Mistress Snow spread a protective

coat over the germinating seeds, and Mistress Rain restrained her vicious downpours.

Once the harvest was in and the last golden ear brought from the fields, the Polevoi were praised and crowned with poppies. They were offered a place at the head of the table and opened the ball. Life continued blissfully in this way, until one day a scythe sliced off the legs of a young Polevik. Then, despite warnings, agricultural machinery began to take over, and another small Polevik was ground to pieces by a combine harvester, and a Poludnitsa was swallowed up by a thresher.

Since then, the Polevoi have never been the same. They leave nature to take over the harvest; they let insects infest the crops and the elements freeze or scorch the ears. When human children stray deep into fields of wheat, they are strangled, and if the farmers venture far into uncultivated wastelands, they are sliced to pieces by vengeful families.

BEHAVIOR:
Since the accidents, the Polevoi are scarcely seen, except around midday, during siesta time, and in the twilight, when the farmers have left the fields. The Poludnitsa have become full of hatred and reveal themselves to women on remote paths, asking questions about the crops. They strangle those who cannot answer.

ACTIVITIES:
They dream and are nostalgic for the old days. In late September, they ride across the plains and barren steppes on the backs of small ponies, ritually marking out the limits of their domain. The Polevoi are more dangerous than the cheerful Dikonkyi Mujik and possess magical powers that their cousins do not have.

The Kabouters

Crash, bang!
The little fellow
Isn't dead!

In ancient Flanders there were as many "Kabouter houses" as there are molehills in the fields, rabbit warrens in the hillsides, and inns by the wayside. Kabouters are the best-known Dwarfs in that beautiful flat golden land of Flanders, where you can see so far that a Kabouter in a willow tree can communicate by signs with his brother, the Klabouter, perched on the prow of a ship far out at sea.

Till Eulenspiegel, Culotte Verte, and Cambrinus all shared a drink with a Kabouter at least once in their lifetimes, or else shared some tobacco or a couple of good jokes with one. It is said that "a Kabouter will never let anyone go thirsty"; it is enough to call for help, and he will come running, a pint of ale in his hands. At one time, a nook was set aside for a Kabouter in every pleasant inn. Here he could set his beer glass and his Gouda pipe on a small table near a coal-burning stove. It was certainly worthwhile taking good care of the little guy, because there was nobody else quite as skilled at flavoring the hops or distilling the perfect Dutch gin. He was forever the fun of the fair and the carnivals, the life and soul of any party, merrymaking, or shindig. He could be seen on the backs of wooden horses on carousels or clanging cymbals alongside Limonaire's mechanical figures. He would shoot down parrots with a bow and arrow or a crossbow, and catch pigs by the hind legs. He would lavish attention on the pretty Neleke and treat her at his expense.

Many countries lost their magic and their party spirit, but Flanders and Belgium still knew how to have a good time, and the lively Kabouters lost none of their joyful energy. The sails of the windmills spun round and round, young girls continued to dream, brass bands banged their drums, and men offered toasts when the bells rung, and although the Kabouters were seen less and less, the little chaps were never far away:

Crash bang!
The little fellow
Isn't dead!
Sausages and raisin loaf
Long live the Kabouter.

Where did they come from? Where were they born? Some scholarly studies claim that Kabouters were abnormal Kobolds, Goblins, Herodes, or Hairodes, and trace their mythological, genealogical, and etymological roots through convoluted paths to reach this conclusion. Some people say they were poplar spirits, spirits of the willow tree, found alongside canals and in the peaceful countryside. Grandmothers continue to weave a legend that has been told on many an evening over the years and claim that they originated in trees where the souls of dead children reside. They were spirits of the earth, Dwarfs of the marsh, of the Scheldt estuary, and of the fertile silt. They were spirits of the Artois hills, of the Hainaut plains, of the Brabant, right up to the bor-

HEIGHT:
A few inches (6 or 8 cm),
the height of a clog or a piece of
gingerbread.

APPEARANCE:
Stocky and powerful. Gnarled limbs.
Jolly paunchs. Pointed noses. The
eyes of a dreamer. Ruddy, veined com-
plexions. Very long beards, which are
the source of all their strength and
magical powers; if you can cut off his
beard, you have mastered him.

CLOTHING:
Gray morning coats, velvet breeches,
cotton stockings, red caps, and clogs. On
special feast days, they sometimes don
dark red jackets with long tails, deco-
rated with very large golden buttons.
They are often seen with tankards in
their hands. They carry a bag over
their shoulder.

HABITAT:
Small, very attractive homes under-
ground beneath hills, slopes, and
hedges. Rabbit warrens and mole bur-
rows act as the entrances and exits.
They are found in all parts of what
was once Flanders. Celibate Kabouters
prefer to set up homes in ruins, inn
cellars, and belfries. White Kabouters
(named for their white shirts and
morning coats) live near millers and
help with grinding the flour. There are
some families in Holland.

ders of the Netherlands. They were the spirits of the Antwerp countryside, which they plowed and cultivated with the aid of the Reuze (Giants).

With their golden tools, the Kabouters planted potatoes, Belgian endive, tobacco, and hops that reached up toward the amber, downy clouds.

All that remained was for them to carve stone cities with chiseled designs as elaborate as flowers and doilies of Fairy lace, whose secrets were revealed thread by thread by the Husses, the wives of the Kabouters. The cities had belfries as high as the tops of the poplar trees and resounded with celestial music. The networks of green canals carried processions of Swan Fairies, Nekkers, and Water Nymphs. Flanders was a harmonious place inhabited by peaceful men with strong family ties and good spirits. But they

were invaded by the Inquisition, led by a mad Spaniard, who replaced the windmills, maypoles, greasy poles, and archery with stocks, treadmills, and gallows, red with the blood of Mad Joan! Demons, leviathans, monsters, and the damned haunted Bruegel's joyful banquets and village fêtes. Since then, the stench of burning has hung over the Kabouters' meadows. But:

Crash bang!
The little fellow
Isn't dead!
Sausages and raisin loaf
Long live the Kabouter.
The ears of wheat will always grow back!

FOOD:
Hearty eaters. The Husses are wonderful cooks. They have too many recipes to list here, but, to mention a few, they prepare tripe and ale soup, vegetable soup, leek tart, fish stew with eels, and starry-gazey pie.

BEHAVIOR:
The Kabouters, also known as Kaboutermannekens, Aardmannetjes, Heuvelmannekens, Roodmutsjes, Jans met de roo de nauts, or Alvermannekens, depending on the region, live for two hundred years. The Husses or Laplanders are their wives and are very lively and active. At the age of ninety, their husbands bury them alive with a little bit of brioche, saying: "Don't grow old, mother; come back to me when you are younger."

ACTIVITIES:
They are very skilled and hardworking and are knowledgeable about art and magic. At night, they leave their homes to visit farms and houses. They are kind-natured and often help those in need, doing the heavy manual work. If you have an urgent task to complete, you need only take it to their hill, and in the morning the work will be meticulously done.

They borrow kitchen utensils: pots, pans, dishes, pie pans, and skillets; but they return them the next day, scrubbed clean.

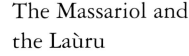

THE MASSARIOL

HEIGHT:
Sixteen inches (40 cm).

APPEARANCE:
The Massariol, or "Little Farmers," are stocky, potbellied, ruddy, and cheerful. They are so keen on contact with women that in order to get closer to them, they will transform themselves into a comb, a washcloth, stockings, or even undergarments.

CLOTHING:
They hide their rolls of fat under baggy, loose clothing, peasant shirts, and embroidered waistcoats. They wear large pants, clogs, and straw hats. They really like the color red.

HABITAT:
Apart from Italy, they are also found in the Southern Alps, in the Dolomites, and as far afield as Yugoslavia, where they are called Mamalic or Macic. The Massariol are mainly found in Italy, due to the great attractiveness of the Italian people. The Scazzamurieddu, similar to the Taiters, sneak in at night to suck on the breasts of pretty women. The sex beast of Barabao lives in Venice and hides in chamber pots.

FOOD:
They like cold meats and plates of pasta.

BEHAVIOR:
Insatiable.

ACTIVITIES:
They plow, seed, plant, scythe, harvest, and thresh the wheat. They love to help housewives with the laundry and the dishes. In May, they take engaged couples up into the mountains and make them dance to the sound of the piffero and the zufoli.

The Massariol and the Laùru

May your teaching enlighten the young souls . . .
—W. Cowper

Why group these two together, if the Massariol live on the plains of northeast Italy and the Laùru are only happy in the south? If the former are nothing but jolly round men, ugly and fat, and the latter are handsome devils with slim figures? One can do the work of ten men and ten women in one day, and the other shies away from work for fear of sullying his immaculate clothes. They are so different, it is hard to imagine a day when they will ever meet. But both are domestic Dwarfs that come and go with the seasons, and above all, they both leave behind a hint of magic—a slight air of rising panic.

These two jolly characters appear at harvest time and offer their help with the haymaking and the harvest. They check, discreetly and without even discussing a salary, as to whether the lady of the manor is pretty, if there are girls in the house, and if the serving wench has a twinkle in her eye. In other words, to use their expressions: "If the henhouse is well stocked," or "If there are pillows on the beds!" because it is not the promise of money that brings them here. They know the location of underground treasure troves and have all the gold they need. What they crave is the

friendliness of the farm. If the family is not hostile, the visitors will be generous; the farm will be prosperous, and the Massariol and the Laùru may well settle down there for good. But if the farmer's wife is too devout and faithful to her husband and prevents the Dwarfs from entering by hanging a bull's head above the door, they will move ever onward, offering their dual services elsewhere.

The Laùru are not very efficient at working in the fields, but on the other hand, their skill at herding livestock is unrivaled. They love the animals and take good care of the herds, which under their watchful eyes breed like bunnies in a bush. They are also able to predict winning lottery numbers and don't mind spreading the word between kisses and caresses. They teach children about the mysteries of love and hand out potions and recipes to the women and girls who come to them wanting to attract or repel a lover, win back an unfaithful husband, or make one more active in bed. They are extremely romantic and will only woo one conquest at a time. When one protests his undying love and devotion, he is speaking truthfully, but just for that moment.

The Massariol, on the other hand, have a sexual appetite as large as their big, fat bellies, and they prefer quantity to quality. Louis Marie Fraximus Touffette states that "in love there are gentlemen and there are dogs." The Massariol are dogs. For this reason, they prefer well-populated farms to small but charming thatched cottages and choose wild, unrestrained sex over romantic and tender passion. Enough sweet words—"He doesn't talk about love, he makes it!"

THE LAÙRU

HEIGHT:
About twenty inches (50 cm).

APPEARANCE:
Thin, slim, well-proportioned, bronzed skin, passionate eyes, long, jet-black, wavy hair. Their campy mannerisms hide their true character, which is slightly animalistic and disturbing. According to works on magic teratology by the demonologist Corvi, they are "cunning, with potent seed."

CLOTHING:
They dress very elaborately and adorn themselves with accessories and well-fitting clothes in bright colors. Pointed hats, frock coats. Shirts open at the chest. Hoop earrings in their ears. Castilian-style belts, decorated with ribbons. For show, they carry mandolins with mother-of-pearl inlay, but they are unable to play a single note!

HABITAT:
Southern Italy.

FOOD:
They eat whatever food is provided to them at the farm where they are staying. They prefer sweet dishes.

BEHAVIOR:
Insatiable.

ACTIVITIES:
They take care of horses and farm animals, but avoid household tasks. Old wives' tales would have it that they "take care of" unwanted babies and can return the "bloom" to anyone who has lost it, whatever their age.

HEIGHT:

Ten to twelve inches (25 to 30 cm). There are even some only four inches (10 cm) tall.

APPEARANCE:

Folleti are crazed and lively and look like little brats running riot in the countryside and on the roads. They have a twinkle in their eyes and turned-up noses. Their mouths are large and mischievous. Their teeth are very white and sharp, and their chins and ears are pointed. They are very proud of their wild beauty and golden, curly hair. Two small marks can be seen on their foreheads, the remnants of vestigial horns.

The Mantellioni skip around wearing just one clog. The Locatelli have goat's hooves for feet, decorated with red ribbons and bells. The Salvanelli, sons of the Sylvains and the Aguane, have heads that are half goat and half Fairy, and they are very hairy. The Salbanelli, sons of the Salvanelli and the mountain wizards, have very dark skin, almost black, and green eyes. The Farfarelli, fruit of the union between the Folleti and the spirits of the air, the Folleti del Vento, are very small and forever somersaulting around the windows of beautiful girls and around chimneys, fluttering their multicolored butterfly wings. The Fujettu are found in the Calabrian countryside and are great teases. The Barreti are slyer and cause nightmares. The melancholy Fuglietti of Sardinia will turn anyone who bores them insane.

CLOTHING:

Their favorite color is red, which they wear from the tips of their pointed hats (which make them invisible) to their dancing shoes. They usually wear shirts without collars, very short jackets, tight-fitting, knee-length breeches, and stockings. Knives hang from their studded belts.

Folleti

La not era consiglia da sara su l'usse parqué il Folleti agniva dentr . . .
—Lodovico Giovanni Corvi,
I Demoni nella tradizione populare,
Castel l'Arquato,
Provincia di Piacenza, 1120

Long ago, the Fauns and the Sylvains inhabited the forests of Italy. In the morning, flowers would open their petals when the Fauns played their flutes, and the grass would become greener beneath the capers of the Sylvains. When the sun burned above the countryside for too long, it would suffice for a farmer to place an offering at the edge of the woods, and rain would fall in reply to the high-pitched trilling of the syrinx. But when storms swept earth and rocks down onto the roads of the mountain villages, another small offering would transform the melody, and solemn chords would dry the sodden clouds as they waved on strings and clothespins suspended from swallows and draw a rainbow across the sky above the hills, quivering beneath the celestial laundry.

Sometimes farmers would add the sound of their tin whistles to the impressive symphony of forest music, and the herds would prosper on the lush grass. It was a time when farmers would sing while harvesting the golden wheat from the fields. Their moving chants would be repeated by voice after voice in valley after valley, and the hills would resound with the sound of infinite praises to Pan.

As the sun became less generous and walls began to divide the fields, signaling the end of the agricultural golden age, the Fauns made efforts to ensure that their descendants would be better adapted to the calendar of men.

Fauns bred with the Faunac and the Fatuac and gave rise to the Incubi. The Sylvains bred with the Sylvane, and the result of this divine coupling was the Folleti: beings with the spirit of the old world, rebellious and tough. The Folleti multiplied on the prairies and in the woods, orchards, mountains, villages, and cities, and they became, and remain to this day, the main Lutin race in Italy.

The Folleto is scared of very little, and even if he runs away, he will be back before long. He can survive anything: wars, poverty, grief, catastrophes, and even the egocentricity and evil acts of men. The Folleti were originally well-meaning creatures, but they have become touchy and evil-tempered.

Traits shared with the Incubi have made the Folleti sex-obsessed creatures, who reproduce endlessly in order to ensure the survival of the species. They ignore the cries of protest from the partners they assail, whoever they are: humans, Fairies, Water Nymphs, Stregges. Folleti chromosomes are very strong, and no matter whom one breeds with, the offspring will be pure, unadulterated Folleti.

Man has tried to restrain their passions and stop them from reproducing, but he has tried in vain. Every region, every village, and every family has its own method for exorcising the Folleti, but just as insects become immune to toxic products, the Folleti resist these attacks, recover, and spring back to life in a new form.

At the start of the nineteenth century, an Elfologist set about trying to complete a full inventory of the different forms of the Folleti, but he soon lost his nerve—and his head—because the genealogy and mutations of these pesky critters were so anarchic, they caused him to despair. "It was like trying to weed out the bad seeds and grasses from the enchanted fields of a mad gardener!" he exclaimed, before throwing his manuscript into the nettles. Despite their numerous forms and differences, there is only one way to class these beings: as Folleti.

HABITAT:
All over Italy. They do not have their own houses, but sleep wherever they happen to be when they feel tired.

FOOD:
They are crazy for polenta with sausage or grilled with cheese. They love mozzarella with anchovies and cold meats from the mountains.

BEHAVIOR:
The Folleti do not possess any great powers, but they do know some magic secrets. However, the Sicilian Fudditu can be incapacitated simply by removing his jacket.

ACTIVITIES:
They wander about, amuse themselves, perform some services for the rare humans who ask, and spend an immense amount of time on debauchery.

In Lombardy, when a human is turned mad by a Folleto, he can be cured by eating eggs. One hundred and one eggs should be collected by one hundred and one families, and the patient must eat thirty a day . . . on his last mouthful, the "Mad Spirit" leaves him.

HEIGHT:
Five inches (12 cm).

APPEARANCE:
Very thin, with dark and hardened skin, toughened against nettle stings, thistle spikes, and bramble thorns. They are beardless and have many wrinkles. Their noses resemble the snouts of moles. They have sharp, prominent teeth and mole claws. Their mates never come out during the day and have dirty white skin.

CLOTHING:
They wear breastplates constructed from overlapping insect skins. Their helmets are the hollowed-out heads of stag beetles, and their shields are the wings of june bugs. They use the claws of mole crickets as swords.

HABITAT:
Vast, deep holes below gardens and toolsheds. They are found all over Europe.

FOOD:
Vegetables, fruits, roasted snails. They distill a strong liquor from the slime of the slugs that they breed.

BEHAVIOR:
There is only one Piot-Chan family per garden. The females spend the entire year shut away, except on March 1, when they leave their homes to greet the moon. They give birth to huge numbers of offspring who accompany the Piot-Chans on their expeditions almost from birth, galloping behind the troops of slugs and learning their skills.

ACTIVITIES:
Destroying orchards, fields, and gardens. They fight toads, lizards, and slowworms. They are prone to murderous rages during the red moon.

Piot-Chans

Innumerable goblins were fighting the fairies for the Garden Kingdom . . . Piot-Chan, the keeper of the slugs, led his troops toward our lettuces.
—Paul Bruzon,
Simple histoire de mon verger
(The Simple History of My Orchard)

Gnomes, Dwarfs, Kabouters, Wichtlein, and Kobolds divided the land between them, digging tunnels and mines. The Dwarf people enjoyed a happy life, living beneath hollow hills and in caves, extracting ores, and cultivating the rich soil on the forest edge. They slowly acquired a great deal of knowledge through their observation of nature, and they respected the cycle of the seasons, living in harmony with the beating heart of the planet. But everything changed when mankind arrived and cut down, ripped up, cleared, and plowed the delightful forest, uprooting the sacred Elfin trees in order to construct their homes and plant their potatoes.

Some Lutin races formed a pact with man; others withdrew, disappeared, or launched an unequal battle. The Piot-Chans chose to do battle.

Piot-Chans (ancient French for "little sorcerers") were a hideous mongrel of Dwarf-Elf species and field Genies and were hounded by the incessant spread of human farmers. They went underground in the gardens, and for centuries each small family has been waging a pathetic war in their own particular garden by sabotaging peaceful rows of cabbages, radishes, and carrots; spinach plantings; strawberry fields; prim lines of beetroots; and bushy bundles of parsley. With one blast of their icy breath they can turn frail, early shoots brown; they freeze the first growths and buds and are constantly reseeding weeds, even in freshly hoed soil. The sound of their flutes attracts moles, voles, and mice to fields and gardens and dormice to orchards. Piot-Chans herd their slugs towards the lushest lettuces and harangue the Hargnes spirits, encouraging them to burst their clouds of hail over cherry trees, apple trees, and roses. They call starlings down into the vineyards, let the blackbirds attack the wild cherry bushes, and allow Jack Frost to nibble at the delicate greenery. Their piercing whistles attract famished armies of caterpillars, aphids, and insects to the flower-filled borders and rose gardens, and, once there, the swarming armored hordes are encouraged to chomp at the plants and attack the roots and fruits. Once they have finished, the vines, petals, and leaves carry a black mark: the symbol of the Piot-Chan's eternal anger.

Hojemænnels and the Inhabitants of the Herb Garden

A narrow fellow in the grass
Occasionally rides;
You may have met him

—Emily Dickinson

Hojemænnels left the forests of Germany long, long ago and firmly established themselves in the herb gardens and vegetable plots of the countryside. These wrinkled Dwarfs, dressed in green and with hair and beards of gray moss, once frolicked about among the dew-covered ferns, intoxicated by a liquor made from bluebells and moon lichen, which filled them with vitality.

The Hojemænnels came into being as a result of the "attraction" between the secret seeds of the mosses and tree sap, mingling in the fertile, humid atmosphere where both the dew and the soil were rich with the remains of centuries of Elfin magic. The Hojemænnels were more plant than animal, and this allowed them to discover all of nature's resources and secrets. They also benefited from "the vision of the undergrowth," which enabled them to locate and to cultivate the invisible and extremely rare "moon lichen," a lichen that disappears under the light of the moon and when humans approach.

It is said that this lichen originally sprang from the dust raised by Selene's footsteps as she went to join her beloved Endymion. The adoring couple had five children, but nothing is ever said in the legends of their names and of their descendants. Occasionally a hint is given as to the identity of one of their grandsons or granddaughters in the stories of the various sleeping beauties.

It is known that moon lichen grows on the trunks of trees caressed by moonbeams. This phosphorescent lichen feeds from the lunar energy, and unicorns and other sick or wounded creatures rub against it to cure themselves. The Happy Spirits draw their immortality from the lichen, and the Fairies "energize" their feet upon it. And it was from this very lichen that the first Hojemænnel obtained the juice necessary to brew their special grog.

The Hojemænnels, like many others of their kind, have now been forced out of their natural habitat, but they ask little of the gardeners who welcome them. All they require is a small corner of fallow land and a small dish of milk left beside the toolshed. For this small remuneration, their services and ancient knowledge can be yours, and they will protect and enchant your gardens.

HEIGHT:
Twelve inches (30 cm).

APPEARANCE:
Gray faces covered in wrinkles. Hair and beards of gray moss. Long, thin noses. Phosphorescent eyes. Large, protruding ears with pointed lobes and skin that is almost transparent, allowing the veins to be seen clearly. Their bodies are worm-eaten trunks. Attached to these are four thin and knobby limbs, which look like branches.

CLOTHING:
Tunics made of moss, leaves, and lichen. Large, buckled boots. They wear hats with scales that look like pinecones.

FOOD:
Milk and vegetables. They used to drink the tea of life.

HABITAT/BEHAVIOR/ACTIVITIES:
They originated in the vast forests, but now live in gardens and in the countryside in Germany and Austria. They help protect and cultivate their chosen abodes. Two or three families can peacefully inhabit one herb garden, but they avoid orchards inhabited by other spirits.

If a Hojemænnel is particularly happy and comfortable in his abode, this can be seen by flowers bursting with pollen, the large number of bees, and the abundant honey harvests. It is recommended to leave some honey behind in the beehives, to keep them clean, to decorate them with flowers on March 21, and to mark each death within the hive by attaching a black mourning ribbon to it.

THOSE
WHO LIVE IN
HOUSES

"Shh . . . let's not disturb the dreams of the spirit in the attic."

—Joyce Ashton

Whether one lives in a cave, a hut, or a cabin; whether far away in an isba lost on the threshold of a taiga forest where the tundra begins, or farther away, beneath the cold dome of an igloo, in a cottage on the moors, in a wooden house, in a stone structure, or in a cube built of concrete, the first to live in one's house were not of humankind. Other inhabi-

tants were already there, mixed with the spirits of the forests, the mosses, and the heaths, searching for the heart of the four elements and surviving in the most prominent but ephemeral fortresses.

The spirit of the home, the little god Penate, is not a cricket, a lucky charm, or a farmhand; he is as invisible as a worm, tucked away within the wood. And just like that worm, he can get the best of even the most solid structures. He watches, attentive and immortal, and his eyes, as red as a brand in the fireplace, heed the movement of the clock, while outside, those of the "plains" call out for him.

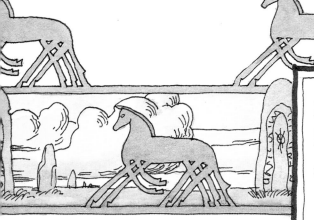

Brownies, Boggarts, Buccas, Bwiocd, and Bogies

HEIGHT:
   Eight inches (20 cm).

APPEARANCE:
   Brownies, whether they are from the Lowlands or the Highlands of Scotland, or from Wales, Northumberland, Ireland, Shetland, or the Orkney Islands, are all part of the same divine race and all look alike. In their gruff and primitive appearance one can distinguish a conglomeration of all of the elements of which they were born. They have a mineral and earthy complexion. Their bodies are covered with a brownish fleece, which looks somewhat like the vegetation in glens and moors; their gaze is both bright and dark, like two mountain lakes into which the heavens have plunged their legendary luminosity and deep mysteries. As light as air and as quick as a ray of light, they can come to a halt and sit silently on stones for hours.

CLOTHING:
   Their thin natural fur covers them like a warm cape, but sometimes they also put on cast-off clothing that is worn and brown.

HABITAT:
   They live among rocky peaks or on hilltops, covered paths, standing stones, and knolls. They may also be found in ruins, barns, attics or lofts, henhouses, hollows in walls, and broken-down fireplaces.
   The Brownies love old objects and the scent of old papers, and they like to inhabit bookstands in the back of antique stores, old libraries, and the desks of writers who are inclined toward the supernatural or fantastic, to whom they confide their fantastic inspirations.
   They were taken to the United States by emigrants from England and Scotland and live there in mines. Robert Louis Stevenson scattered them around during his journeys throughout the South Pacific, the Cevennes, and all along the Sambre, mainly in Hachette, where they multiplied beneath a tumulus in the forest of Mormal in Avesnois.

And yet conceive us robbed of it, conceive that little thread of memory that we trail behind us broken at the pocket's edge; and in what naked nullity should we be left!
—Robert Louis Stevenson

Who are these Little People? "They are near connections of the dreamer, beyond doubt; they share in his financial worries and have an eye to the bank-book; they share plainly in his training; they have plainly learned like him to build the scheme of a considerate story and to arrange emotion in progressive order; only I think they have more talent; and one thing is beyond doubt, that they can tell him a story piece by piece, like a serial, and keep him all the while in ignorance of where they aim. Who are they, then? And who is the dreamer? Well, as regards the dreamer, I can answer that, for he is no less a person than myself . . . and for the Little People, what shall I say they are but just my Brownies, God bless them!"

In an essay written in October 1887 and published in *Scribner's Magazine* in January 1888, Robert Louis Stevenson, author of *Treasure Island*, acknowledges all that is owed to the intervention of these familiar little creatures: Brownies, "who do one-half my work for me while I am fast asleep, and in all human likelihood, do the rest for me as well, when I am wide awake and fondly suppose I do it for myself . . . the whole of my published fiction should be the single-handed product of some Brownie, some Familiar, some unseen collaborator, whom I keep locked in a back garret, while I get all the praise and he but a share (which I cannot prevent him getting) of the pudding." This is not the first, nor the last time that Stevenson alludes to his tormenting insomnia. He would later open up to Dr. Frederick W. H. Myers . . .

The Brownies have a "liberated" and savage double called the Boggart, and this Goblin may be the inspiration behind the strange case of Dr. Jekyll and his evil "chemically induced" doppelgänger, Mr. Hyde.

Brownies are the soul, the "super-unconscious" of Scottish dreamers. There is no doubt that Brownies flew down the chimneys of Abbotsford, where Walter Scott lived, and entered via the fireplace of Boris's cottage in Alloway. And what about James Barrie's Peter Pan: is he not the immortal spirit of the Brownie?

The Brownies were the first Elfin inhabitants of Scotland. They were the gardeners of the glens, the planters of the heather and dark purple thistles, the alchemists of the clear waters, and the spirits of the whiskey, who, with a handful of barley malt and a scent of peat or kelp, distilled the heart of legend into a golden liquor.

They emerged out of the stones and crystallized from the open air. They approached the fires of the Picts and the Scots, and inspired lonely men with encouraging stories and songs in order to help them combat the cold, the wind, and the desolation. They discovered the hidden valleys and desolated peaks; they sat beneath thatched roofs near rudimentary huts, providing the most timid and destitute people with heroic and marvelous inspiration so they could cling to the rocks. They convinced them to cultivate this proud Elfin land and to emblazon their sad cloaks with the purple hue of the hills and the blood of the gods and to wear on their forehead, like a royal seal, the only flower that bloomed there. With a bit of brush, the stomach of a sheep, and the moaning of the wind, they sang the ballad of the glory of a Fairy Land emerging from the gravelly haze, and from the snowy sea, a powerful storm struck, and the sun shone through the clouds and ran along the land, shining down on the clans and the low walls, illuminating the countryside with a blazing plaid pattern.

As man has evolved in a material sense, he has come to see these spirits as nothing but domestic spirits, ancient Sprites, servants who have become increasingly useless, Bogies who have become more and more quick-tempered as they try to prevent men from polluting everything. The Highlanders are not what they used to be, and now it is only the poets, dreamers, ghosts, and nostalgic gallants who still lend an ear to their song.

FOOD:

Brownies ask for little from humans in return for their precious help: a bit of black bread or a bowl of cream. Among themselves, they like to be treated to black buns, baps, tawts slaw, quarg, raw onions, jannock, singing hinny, bacon flavored with scotch and whiskey. They chew on a longevity herb, called "Green," which they pick at the summit of a peak known only to them.

BEHAVIOR:

They are unsubtle and allow themselves to be guided by instinct. They ignore vice and evil, and if by some chance they happen to indulge in bad behavior, it is always innocently.

ACTIVITIES:

Before they were angered by man's ingratitude, they had numerous activities: brewing beer and planting, cultivating, and enriching arid regions. They have now become turbulent, noisy, and as mischievous as Poltergeists, but they continue to distribute their services and to sustain and nourish well-intentioned people with stories.

Church Grims

*A ring of diabolical fiends dances a rampant,
lugubrious farandole around the room.*
  —Léo Perutz,
    Le Maître du Jugement dernier

Help! He moved! It is impossible! But, but . . . yes! He is moving!

The hideous demon sits straddling the sculpted gargoyle at the top of a shadowy arch and winks a heavy eyelid, partly veiling a bulging, shifty eye. He stretches out his twisted limbs and yawns, revealing the entirety of his thick-lipped, toothless mouth. The Church Grim waits until the parish priest leaves the church before jumping down from the back of his reptilian mount, his calloused heels clicking on the black sandstone paving stones.

He blends perfectly with the grimacing masks and basilisks grouped around the tops of the pillars. The Church Grim stays hidden there during all church services, peering at the devout ones, amusing himself with his somber gift of predicting who will die within the year.

Unlike other Goblins, who are afraid of crosses, crucifixes, chapels, and church bells, the Church Grim enjoys himself in the heart of the sacred precincts. This is where he comes out and lets his ferocious joy burst forth as he soils the altars, committing all kinds of profanities!

As soon as the holy building is empty, Church Grims spring out from every corner, and they all enjoy themselves as they skate along the aisles, playing leapfrog in the central nave upon the prie-dieux. They climb around in the pulpit, swing from the thuribles, and splash themselves with holy water from the baptismal fonts. They engage in fencing, cutting and thrusting with candles. They enjoy looting the sacristy, where they tear open the closets containing holy robes and caps, dressing up in surplice and lace, getting drunk on the wine reserved for Mass. They jostle each other as they romp up to the top of the bell tower so that, at midnight, they can awaken the parish by setting off a concert of bells and chimes! They prepare, plot, organize, and play nasty tricks on the priests: running strings across the aisle to make the priests stumble, putting soap on the stairways of the crypts, tying the sleeves of the robes together, and scribbling profanities into the notes that they use to deliver their Sunday sermons!

The origin of Church Grims is uncertain. Spirits who live in holy places generally originate from Greece, and it is believed that they are perhaps manifestations of the souls of animals sacrificed at the sites of ancient temples upon which churches were later constructed.

Church Grims can be found in Scandinavia and in England. In Denmark they are called Kirkegrims; in Finland, Kirkonwaki; and in both Switzerland and Finland, Kyrkogrims. The Arc'-Houskeziks of Brittany have the power to put flocks of people to sleep during Mass. Once, the Church Grims of the church of Sweetfield were terribly drunk on wine and whiskey (a charitable parishioner's gift to the parish priest to warm him during the chilly winter nights). The excessive inhalation of the incense fumes had driven them mad, and they leapt out into the middle of the annual procession and started pulling women's hair, hoisting up the innocent maidens and jostling them around, scratching people's faces, breaking the reliquary containing the holy relics, tearing crucifixes and candles from the hands of the choir children and using them like swords and maces, jumping down from the arches onto the chaotic, jumbled crowd that was trying to escape outside. But the Church Grims' rear guardsmen were amassed together, forming a hideous barrier in front of the doors, and they pushed the crowd back, turning everything upside down by swinging the Easter candles in a propeller-like motion. Reverend Montague G. Drut mentions in *Les Chroniques paroissiales* that after this scene of horrific carnage, the inhabitants left the tranquil village for good, and it has been erased from today's maps.

HEIGHT:
Two feet (61 cm) tall.

APPEARANCE:
Animal-like. Tough, blackish skin. Giant egg-shaped skulls. Protruding foreheads. Crumpled ears. Big hanging mouths. Receding chins. Flat noses. Stooped posture. Crooked limbs. Cloven feet. Tails.

CLOTHING:
Nude. Sometimes they wear sparkling stoles and golden chasubles, miters, and barrettes with pompons.

HABITAT:
They never leave the church where they nest. They live in the church tower, beneath the altars, in the deepest corners of the transept, or in crypts and other underground places.

FOOD:
They gorge themselves on candles and incense, lap the oil from the lamps, drink the wine reserved for Mass, swallow eggs whole, and devour the crows and owls that sleep in the attic.

BEHAVIOR:
They live in anarchy and never stop arguing. They are monstrously self-centered and have no sense of family or friendship. The females, who are impregnated randomly, give birth once a year to their young, who, once weaned, are abandoned in the central nave.

ACTIVITIES:
Overactive. Always moving around, Church Grims sleep little, except for during the week of Christmas, when, inexplicably, they bury themselves in a corner and fall into a sort of lethargy for seven consecutive days.

HEIGHT:
Fourteen inches (35 cm).

APPEARANCE:
Pretty, plump, nimble, supple. Look very much like Flower Nymphs, apart from their slightly heavy hips and rather strong hands.

CLOTHING:
Clinging bodysuits, in the style of a circus unitard, which they have embellished with flounces and lace.

FOOD:
They dine exclusively on sweets. They claim that anything will make them gain weight.

BEHAVIOR:
These furtive Sprites, who live in solitude with only their reflections for company, remain shrouded in mystery. They have been sighted most often in the "sophisticated" eras. They flourished in the seventeenth and eighteenth centuries, at the time of beautiful demoiselles and marquises. The Marquise de Pompadour boasted of having one in her linen closet. Danthienne were forgotten during the late eighteenth century, reappeared around 1870, became scarce, and then reappeared again to invade armoires in 1900. Sulked. Returned in 1930. Disappeared again. Have not noticed the arrival of jeans . . . but are bashfully succumbing to the allure of retro, little by little.

ACTIVITIES:
Preening themselves.

Danthienne

And they thought they could hear
from the bottom of the keyhole's chasm,
a distant sound, a vague and joyous murmur . . .
　　　—Arthur Rimbaud,
　　　　The Orphans' New Year's Gifts

Inside the pink room, underneath the duvet, the master of the house snores loudly, and the lady of the manor snores faintly. Atop the downy quilt, the cat purrs. The door to the wardrobe makes a little squeak and opens slightly. A crimson ribbon rolls out from a pile of sheets, and a charming Danthienne descends its length silently. She moves with little dancing steps, jumping from an ottoman to the vanity table, where she will spend the night looking at her reflection and batting her eyelashes.

Danthienne are female Sprites who live in houses, apartments, and castles. Whether the city or the country variety, Danthi-enne have only one occupation: to make themselves beautiful!

Very little is known about them. These pretty Sprites appeared in the middle of the prehistoric era at the time when young women first started to dress up. Their arrival coincided with the invention of the bone comb, the first wooden necklace, and the first garland of woven flowers. Despite their long blond hair, their physical attributes, and their grace, they are not Fairies—and this is something they greatly regret. They do not have any special gifts and, sadly, do not possess wings, which would perhaps be useful to them in their various acrobatics. Alas! With too many trips to the candy store and too many boxes of pralines, these gourmands think that their hips are too large and their posteriors somewhat burdensome. As soon as they know that they are alone, they emerge from their hiding places and ransack the bedrooms and attics, opening the drawers and taking out ribbons and lace, unfolding petticoats, and fastening all kinds of silky flounces to their waists. They do their hair, make themselves up, pluck the teeth of tortoiseshell combs like a harp as they dance, swim in the bottles of perfume, and dry off amid clouds of powder . . .

But at the slightest sound, at the merest alarm, the Danthienne furtively go back to their little hiding places, leaving behind an unbelievable mess.

The Little Red Man of the Tuileries

When Philibert Delorme began construction on the Tuileries Palace in 1564, it was noted that there was a Goblin dressed in red, who had been seen in the morning and in the evening strolling through the rooms, salons, and corridors. He would investigate, surveying the work as if he were the proprietor and coldly scrutinizing all who crossed his path from his diminutive point of view. As soon as anyone approached him or called out to him, he would disappear with a laugh.

Over the course of the years, the Tuileries residence was modified again and again by wig-wearing architects, and the red Dwarf would follow them, stealing their plans so as to add his own arrangements.

For centuries, he remained alongside the crowned heads, haunting the history of France. He would lean over the cradles of kings and announce the good news and the bad. When the grandiose Louis XIV left the palace walls for those of Versailles, he was furious. Refusing to move, he remained there to sulk until the time of the Revolution, when he could be seen dancing a vengeful *carmagnole*: they should have listened to him!

And then he redirected all of his affections to the little Bonaparte, whose tiny silhouette stirred him. "I will make an emperor of this midget," he decided. The sedentary sprite left his comfortable quarters for the "little corporal," following him to all four corners of the globe and giving him council and guidance. On the night before the Battle of the Pyramids, he led him into one of them and forced him to sign a treaty that would bind him to the Little Red Man for ten years in exchange for victories. The Little Red Man took him away to Mount Sinai and assured him, "Everything is fine." On the 18th of Brumaire, the red Goblin, this time dressed in green, suggested the coup d'etat. On coronation night, he was there, triumphant! However, although the strange guardian offered Bonaparte another pact at the battle of Wagram, he reproached, lectured, and scolded (often violently) the "shrimp tyrant." The Little Red Man disapproved of the butchery of the Spanish War, opposed his divorce, and condemned the campaign in Russia. On the eve of the Battle of the Moskva, he told Napoleon: "My son, you are going too quickly, you are lacking men, and your friends are betraying you." Before the defeat at Waterloo, Napoleon sighted the little Goblin astride a large black cat, making the rounds of the battlefield three times.

The Little Red Man died in the fire that destroyed part of the palace in 1871, but he "returns" sporadically in the form of a little hobbling phantom.

There are numerous examples of other Dwarfs who likewise offered their services to kings, knights, and heroes all throughout history and in the great legends: Hutgin, Oberon, Alberich, Laurin, Iubdan, Bifurr, Ruddllwn Gorr, Gwyddolwn Gorr, Gnu Dheireoil, Guivret, Lacey, Gribalo, Walberan, Lorandin, Alfrikr, Picolet, Malabron, Soutache, and Agrapart the Bearded. The most famous of these are red Dwarfs, black Dwarfs, and green and yellow Dwarfs, some handsome like gods, others ugly like monkeys, but all powerful ones that have emerged from the Enchanted Realms to distribute power, glory, and magical grandeur.

HEIGHT:
Just under thirty-four inches (87 cm).

APPEARANCE:
Bowlegged and misshapen. Long, hooked nose. Pointy chin. Squinty eyes. Sallow complexion. Left leg shorter than the right. Clownish physique.

CLOTHING:
His clothes, which change with fashion, have always been bright red, except on one occasion. The only authentic engraving depicting him, which dates from the Empire, shows him strapped in a frock coat that is decorated with epaulettes and buckles. He is wearing breeches and riding boots. He wears an enormous triangular hat and has ridiculously curled hair.

HABITAT:
Posh hideaway among the rafters of the Tuileries.

FOOD:
Eats very little. A cookie or a macaroon per day, followed by a glass of white wine (his preference is for a Touraine Sauvignon).

BEHAVIOR/ACTIVITIES:
Participated up close and from a distance in the lives of the French "Greats" who lived in the Tuileries, up to the death of Louis XVIII, which he witnessed.

HEIGHT:
Twelve inches (30 cm).

APPEARANCE:
*Attractive, lean bodies, large heads
(like most Dwarfs) that are nonetheless handsome, large foreheads, regular,
distinguished features, dreamy and
melancholy expressions, pale complex-
ions, long, curly hair, Musketeer's
moustaches and goatees, fine and adept
hands. When they reach the old age
of five hundred, they wear their beards
in their full splendor.*

CLOTHING:
*Very well groomed. Brown waistcoats,
dark green vests, linen shirts, black
corduroy breeches, elegant shoes made
of pearly gray leather. Wide-brimmed
hats.*

HABITAT:
*The holes, cracks, and pits in the
Ardennes lead to vast, tidily arranged
caverns. They all live together around
an enormous hearth and a communal
table flanked by single-unit dwellings
fashioned out of the giant oaks. Each
one has his own room, a little parlor,
and a workshop. They are reserved and
quiet; disturbances among them are
rare.*

FOOD:
*Hotchpotch, venison soup, game stew,
pâté, ham, smoked sausages: all the
savory Ardennes dishes, which they
know how to prepare with care.*

Nutons

All of my hopes, offered like a harvest of gold . . .
—Charlotte Brontë,
The Spell

The Nutons have never had much
luck with mortal men, and even
less with women. They are gifted,
intelligent, hardworking, wise,
and sensitive, and they make excellent
blacksmiths and cobblers. They make
positive contributions to society and will
bend over backwards to help and please
mortals. In addition, Nutons are attractive, smartly dressed, considerate, and
usually very quiet. And yet the ungrateful
clods who live in the French Ardennes are
always poking fun at these little jewels.

At night, people will set out iron to be
forged, pots to be resilvered, shoes to be
resoled, and the next morning, instead of
thanking the Nutons for their good work,
they will mix dirt and ashes into the
bread that they give them in exchange!

And if a Nuton should be unlucky
enough to fall in love with a local girl,
everyone will do what they can to make
sure that the chosen one, instead of succumbing to her suitor's charms, will end
up disgusted by him. Yet his attentions
will be nothing but courteous. He will
bring flowers, give the mother a costly
gift, assure the father that there will be an
abundant harvest—and ask only that he
be able to sit by the hearth and lovingly
contemplate the "little sparrow" as she
sews and knits. At midnight, when everybody goes up to bed, he will bow to them
all and graciously take his leave.

Once, there was a young farm girl who
was touched by his admirable ways,
which were so different from those of her
neighbor, who was always ready to flip her
onto her back. She was not against the
Nuton's visits, and her family, scandal-
ized, went to tell the parson, who rushed
over to threaten the madwoman. The
elders in the region still remember the

speech that he gave to her, which Jérôme
Pimpurniaux also wrote down: "A Nuton!
In love with a Nuton! But what are you
thinking, poor child? Are you insane?
Aren't you aware that Nutons aren't
Christians, aren't even human? Associating with him is the same as associating
with the devil. Break as quickly as you
can, yes, break these ties that are against
nature, these ties that our mother the holy
church condemns; if you don't, like a dis-
graced member of the flock, you will be
cast out from the community of believers."

Then, the priest had her boil some
beans, crush them with bran, salt, and
sulfur, then steep the paste in onion juice
to make a cake for the "pagan" to eat the
next time he came around!

The treacherous effects of the "engagement cake" made the poor Nuton's stomach expand like a balloon. Despite his
Herculean efforts to contain himself, the
moment came when he could no longer
master his clogged system, and he let out
an interminable series of increasingly resonant explosions while the delicate lady's
company hooted and laughed. This made
him so ashamed that he never dared to
show his face to her again.

A girl who wants to get rid of a Nuton
suitor only has to show herself to him,
squatting on a pile of dung in an eloquent
position while eating a slice of toast. The
prudish little toad, shocked, will never
return. An even more effective method is
to heat up the iron trivet under the pot
that he's just sat down on; his ass aflame,
he will never come back.

Another time, a girl from a good family promised to marry a smitten Nuton
once her granary was full of wheat, her

BEHAVIOR:
A very ancient race. The Nutons are peaceful, but they can also be warriors. Inventive and ingenious artisans, they have crafted very powerful crossbows that use four stretchers and rocks.

ACTIVITIES:
Working leather and metal. They also write and make engravings. They are now extinct, but the Nutons have nonetheless left their traces all over the Ardennes countryside and in the local expressions. You can see their towers, their holes, their trunks, their bowls. Of Warmifontaine inhabitants, they'll say, "It's a Nuton from Warmick, who eats lashes and sticks!" In the area between the Sambre and Meuse rivers, nuggets of pyrite are called "Nuton turds," and in Comblain the fruit of the Cotoneaster vulgaris *is called the "Nuton apple." Those who are on the fringes of society are said to "live like Nutons."*

armoire full of dresses, and her chests filled with gold! Once the "little squirt" had fulfilled all of her requirements, she laughed in his face and threw him out. Now that she finally had a rich dowry, she married her fiancé, a young notary clerk.

Today, the Nutons no longer exist in the Ardennes region; everything was done to get them to move—persecutions, exorcism prayers at the entrances to their grottoes, and crosses placed on the roads they would take on their way to the village.

NOTES: The scatological methods for combating the Nutons' amorous attentions, as well as courtship from any other type of sprite, are not exclusive to the Ardennes. The disgust that creatures of the Fairy Realm have for "below the belt" humor, as well as allusions to natural functions (numerous species of Pipintu don't even have anuses), is well known. Italian beauties have warded off the nocturnal advances of the Linchetti, Buffardelli, Caccavecchia, and the Mazapegoli by showing themselves seated on their toilets, eating cheese and reciting the following dependable formula: "Crap on Linchetto: I'm eating my bread and my cheese, and I shit in front of him."

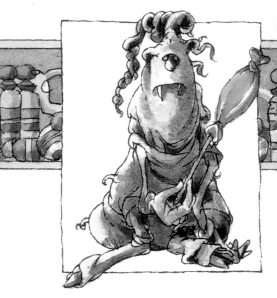

HEIGHT:
Five or six inches (13 or 15 cm).

APPEARANCE:
The Latusés look very much like the evil spirits depicted by Arthur Rackham in the wonderful illustrations he drew for Washington Irving's Rip Van Winkle: *wide mouths, grimaces garnished with fangs, and big bald heads with a kind of fleshy curl at the top of their skulls. Their bodies are thin and grayish. Their hands and feet, which have claws, are enormous in proportion to their size.*

CLOTHING:
Nude, but this is not shocking, as, like the Closantêtes, they are asexual.

HABITAT:
They hide away in the woodwork. Most often, they can be found underneath the slats of antique hardwood floors and in the compartments under stairwells. There, they set up comfortable, warm nests lined with balls of yarn, down, dog hair, bits of wool, and cobwebs. That way, they can comfortably watch the comings and goings of the household through the cracks in the floor.

FOOD:
They feed exclusively on children's psychic emanations, yet they have all of the external attributes of solid carnivores. They sharpen their long, useless incisors on old oak planks; it is this monotonous grating of wood fibers that can sometimes be heard at night.

Latusés

Wasshout myboy if your'nt careful the Latoosay'll come 'n getchyoo!
(Watch out, my boy, if you're not careful, the Latusé will come and get you!)

How many times have mothers in the North called out this prophetic formula? As soon as the sound of this threat penetrates the woodwork, beneath the planks of the old wooden floors, the Latusés awaken: a group of tiny Goblins that are all teeth and claws.

The scamp so addressed has no other choice but to apologize right away and promise to be as good as gold. Only the mother—who holds the magic powers of the home—can say the magic word to send the assailants, whom the errant brat has already heard moving under his feet, back under the worn floorboards (or *lattes usées* in French—hence the Goblins' name).

The Latusés and their neighbors, the Closantêtes, are not descendants of the "great races" of the People of the Light. They come from out of the shadows, from creaks, from the fears of children, from plays on words. They originate in a combination of little ingredients that, when added one to the other in the crucible of the subconscious, give rise to a gray phantom, a sort of squishy larva, which the imagination then deems to be the definitive appearance of these Ogres that occupy homes.

The Latusés only live in houses where there are children. When the children grow up, leaving the house to go and study or to get married, if the nursery is not replenished immediately, the unfortunate

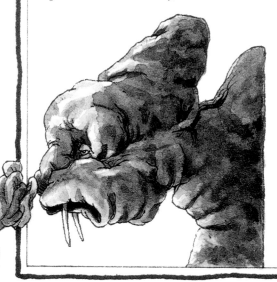

Latusés will waste away, endlessly wandering the length of the rooms where games were once cheerfully played. They will sleep in the places where the little beds were located, seeking out contact with a handkerchief, a forgotten toy, a last trace of life. And, forlorn and drained of energy, without anyone to crank their psychic wheels, they grow skinny, weaken, and die.

All that remains of them is a piece of tough, grayish skin somewhere in the attic. The Latusés cannot leave the houses in which they were born. They are the product of the "atmosphere" of the house, comprised of odors, sensations, and murmurs, and are extremely fragile. Any contact with the outside and the Latusés will immediately disintegrate. Therefore, it is impossible for one to follow those children who made it out into the world or to find the spark necessary to its existence in another home. But, if the home is never lacking in the presence of young people, the Latusés can live for extraordinarily long periods without showing the least amount of age. The first cry of a newborn turns their internal clocks back by one hundred years.

However, there is no need to be alarmed for their future. Their race is not nearing extinction—and more's the pity for us!

They continuously spy on the children and tell the parents of the stupid things they do. They cause nightmares. It is they who, cloaked in the darkness, will amuse themselves by scaring children who are going up into the granary or down into the cellar, breathing on their necks or making the stairs creak and then causing them to drop the milk, knocking over their inkwell, or leaving footprints or paint on the carpet. They tyrannize little scamps by doing bad things before they get the chance to.

There is only one positive thing about them: the Latusés are the ones who tell the famous Tooth Fairy when a child has lost one of its milk teeth, and they help her place candies underneath pillows.

On the other hand, it is impossible to say what they would be capable of doing to a disobedient child if an exhausted mother were to turn him over to them completely. Up until now, overcoming their wrath at the last moment, no mother has ever done more than make the simple threat . . . The rapacious speed at which they respond to the summons, the clatter of their claws, their carnivorous smiles that nonetheless have a trace of a pleading puppy—these all suggest the worst!

BEHAVIOR:
No sexual activity. They are friends of mice and warn them of traps that have been set for them underneath the furniture. They love the end of the semester, when they can harass the dunces who are cramming for their final exams. They dread vacations because the children desert the house. They kill time with their pals the Closantêtes, with whom they play house, although they don't actually understand the meaning of the actions they have only observed from their hiding places.

ACTIVITIES:
With a certain perversity, they compensate for mothers who wield little authority.

HEIGHT:

Domovoï measure around twenty inches (50 cm) high. The house Sprites are smaller, reaching the size of a mouse.

APPEARANCE:

All of the domestic Sprites look like the Domovoï, of which they are the miniaturized descendants. The great artist and illustrator Bilibine depicted them as hairy, with bulbous foreheads and prominent, bushy eyebrows. Round and tender eyes. Very long arms, and their fingers have claws. They are covered entirely with a silky, brown or black coat, even on the palms of their hands. Their female counterparts, the Domovikhas, or Volossatkas or Maroukhas, are smaller, graceful, and less hairy.

CLOTHING:

They do not like to wear anything. However, they consent to cover themselves with white tunics fastened with blue belts if necessary so as not to compromise the modesty of the girls in the home.

FOOD:

Milk, honey, cheese, blinis, borscht; they especially like very fat geese, cakes, and sour cream.

HABITAT:

Domovoï are happy behind the stove or in any other location where they have enough room to stretch out and where there is a warm carpet of dust.

Domovoï and the Inhabitants of the Isba

This divinity, and even others still, haunted my childhood.

—Herman Hesse, *Traumfährte*

It takes very little to keep the Domovoï at home and be assured of eternal happiness. All of the powers of the forest and the lakes, of earth, air, water, and fire, are united in the heart of these good domestic Sprites: observe their gentle and benevolent gaze, in which you can read the intelligence and wisdom of those who lived through the Golden Age.

According to literature, and, in particular, Nadine Teffi's *Village Chronicles of Vourdalak*, everybody in Russia knows the Domovoï.

Ritually, in order to attract them, it is sufficient to set out a bowl of freshly cooked borscht on a clean, white napkin accompanied by some sour cream and a few blinis. In front of the bowl, add a hard-boiled egg dyed with red beetroot juice and say, "Master, old Master, come before me like the bud before the flower, neither black nor green, but just like me.

I offer you this red egg!" And the Domovoï will then distribute the household tasks to the other kitchen, barn, and stable Sprites, who may otherwise be lazy or troublesome.

The Domovoï require a plate of stewed grains on January 28 and a white sheet on March 30, which is when they molt and shed their old skin.

Nobody is afraid of the little house Sprites; they are the Domovoï's subjects. Actually, it is the Sprites themselves who are fearful. They have great difficulty establishing their nests. While one of them may find a nice pile of dust to claim in a forgotten corner, all is lost when somebody comes to give the room a sweeping. Then it is necessary for him to find another hideaway without displacing his brothers occupying all of the other nooks and crannies. One who has lived all of his life behind the commode will find it difficult to be happy in the oven fan. Patiently, they wait for the dust and the cobwebs to settle and form new places which they can call home. They also hope that the house will not change owners, since it is very difficult—even impossible—for them to move with the proprietor. Sometimes the younger ones will follow the family, but the oldest ones will keep their places of privilege.

As for the Domovoï, they never ever leave the home that they belong to. They are sold along with it and pass from one proprietor to the next. Sometimes they will violently display their discontent when the new tenants are not to their liking, and they can also exhibit great regret when a family that they like leaves the house forever. But no matter how afflicted they may be, they cannot follow people.

Other times, when families live for centuries under the same roof, all of the various domestic gods establish them-selves there, according to their hierarchy, and they have a thorough knowledge of how the household operates. Likewise, from one generation to the next, each member of the family will know that in one room you may hear whining, in another you may hear stomping, and in a third you may hear something that sounds like hazelnuts rolling—and this is where the Ovinnik, the Vasily, and the Domovoï live.

The Spark

A Polish Domovo who looks very old. He is less furry, and his coat is white. He wears a blue jacket, boots, and a flat cap with a rooster feather in it. He lives in the fireplace, and at night his red eyes may be mistaken for the coals in the hearth.

Iskrzycki

A Domovo who lives in eastern Germany. He is lazy and susceptible to cold, and he never leaves the hearth. He spends his days at the bottom of it, snoring. He does the dishes, but he breaks a lot of plates.

BEHAVIOR:
Cheerful, obliging, and courageous, they are efficient reapers and excellent doctors. Sometimes they may also prove to be irascible, skittish, and hot-headed. Their fiercely conservative spirits sometimes seem like pure mean-ness: they accept no innovation and will attack new furniture so as to destroy it. Anxious about maintaining their supremacy over the entire house-hold, they refuse the presence of another Domovo in their home and require that a bear's head be nailed above the door to keep away any that may covet their position.

Domovoï are sedentary, unlike the females, who prefer the open air. The Domovikhas will join them when they are in heat and remain with them in the granary for just enough time to procreate. Once the babies are about to be born, the Domovikhas will go to give birth in the peaceful forest and will not return until three years later.

ACTIVITIES:
Domovoï take care of the household business. They chase away lightning, sickness, and bad people. They preside over all of the other Sprites in the house. They also watch over the educa-tion of young children.

Ovinnik and Vasily

These stable Sprites groom, rub down, and braid horses' manes and tails. When a horse eats oats touched by their hands, it is calm and obedient and never gets tired out. These Sprites are lanky and have legs that taper into hooves. It is said that one Vasily, after drinking all of the dregs of vodka and ratafia left on the table, could not find his bed. Wherever he went, the spot was occupied by another inhabitant of the Isba, because each one had an assigned place. After making the rounds, whining, and kicking up the dust, he found the dish that had been used to serve the sour cream. He crept inside and pulled the lid over him. The next day, he faced all kinds of sneering from his own kind. There were little white prints every-where—under the bench, on the stove and the hearthstone, daubs of cream left here and there by the poor little guy who had wallowed in the dish. Outraged by this behavior, the Domovoï banished him from the house, and ever since then the Vasily have stayed in the stable.

Niejits

Smaller than the Domovoï, they very sel-dom go into houses and remain in barns, stables, and grain silos. They idle, tend to the fodder, change the animals' bedding, and milk the cows.

They bring prosperity to the livestock in the morning and at night, and they are given bread and vegetables in return. They don't like meat or cheese. When

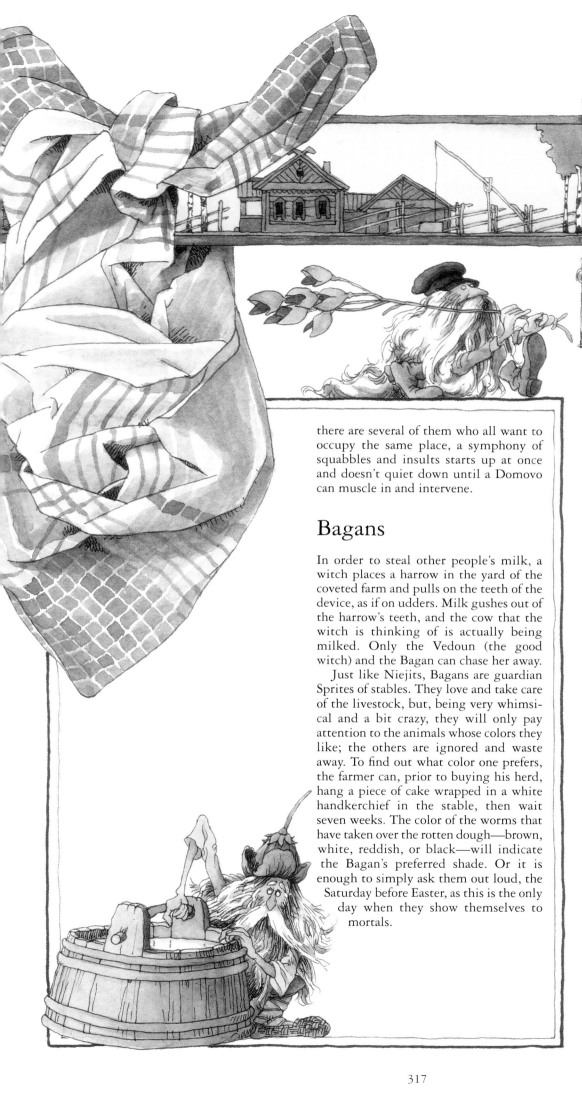

there are several of them who all want to occupy the same place, a symphony of squabbles and insults starts up at once and doesn't quiet down until a Domovo can muscle in and intervene.

Bagans

In order to steal other people's milk, a witch places a harrow in the yard of the coveted farm and pulls on the teeth of the device, as if on udders. Milk gushes out of the harrow's teeth, and the cow that the witch is thinking of is actually being milked. Only the Vedoun (the good witch) and the Bagan can chase her away.

Just like Niejits, Bagans are guardian Sprites of stables. They love and take care of the livestock, but, being very whimsical and a bit crazy, they will only pay attention to the animals whose colors they like; the others are ignored and waste away. To find out what color one prefers, the farmer can, prior to buying his herd, hang a piece of cake wrapped in a white handkerchief in the stable, then wait seven weeks. The color of the worms that have taken over the rotten dough—brown, white, reddish, or black—will indicate the Bagan's preferred shade. Or it is enough to simply ask them out loud, the Saturday before Easter, as this is the only day when they show themselves to mortals.

BEHAVIOR/ACTIVITIES:
These little Sprites know no evil: they are entirely benevolent. They sometimes engage in a little mischief: they knock over the salt or the milk, or they hide an old grandma's glasses or sewing needles or a young girl's ribbons and combs. In these situations, all you have to do is tie a knot in their belt or their handkerchief, or even just twist it around the leg of a table, repeating, "Little devil, go and have a good time/But return to me what is rightly mine." Immediately the object is returned, because the knot or the twist paralyzes the Sprites. Just remember to undo it once the object has been returned; otherwise, you might not be able to count on them anymore.

They pay a lot of attention to honest folk and try to warn them when they are in danger. This isn't easy for them, since they can't speak to humans, so they stomp, sigh, and groan in the corners, cry in the chimneys, pull on skirt hems, and try their best to be understood.

When people move to a different home, it is advised to set out bowls of milk and honey for them in front of the fireplace. You also have to give them treats on Christmas Eve, because on that night they are sad and sigh, since it is the anniversary of the birth of He who provoked their decline. They are also offered tidbits on Mardi Gras and just before Lent.

HEIGHT:
That of a small monkey or a cat.

APPEARANCE:
Banniks resemble the Domovoï, but are a bit smaller and shiftier looking. Their apelike faces are cruel and lustful, with low foreheads and small darting grey eyes burrowed beneath heavy V-shaped eyebrows. Their large mouths move ceaselessly, and their spindly bodies, humpbacked and stringy, are covered in coarse hair, always damp. The index fingers and thumbs of their elongated hands are more developed, with an inward curl from pinching the fleshy backsides of bathing women.

CLOTHING:
Naked, because they always feel warm. They may steal boots that they find to their liking—especially red ones. Plunging both their legs into one boot and clinging to its top, they can amuse themselves the whole night long by jumping about.

HABITAT:
Found throughout Russia and the Baltics. The proliferation of saunas in Western countries has spurred an unfortunate increase in Banniks. They live in the damp dark regions populated by demons but prefer to lurk within bathhouses.

Banniks

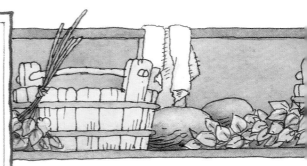

"He finally believes now," she said.
"In what?"
"In the demon of the bath."
—Nadine Teffi, *Vourdalak*

The bathhouse played an important role in Russian daily life, particularly in the outlying provinces. While public baths in the cities were fairly tranquil places—with private changing rooms, sofas, chandeliers, bathtubs, and dressing tables—in the villages every "smoke sauna" was haunted by one or more Banniks.

The smoke sauna was a tiny, windowless log structure with a straw-covered dirt floor. At its center, water was heated by casting red-hot rocks into a large cauldron, producing a cloud of vapor. Families gathered here, steaming in the thick mist.

The *petit bourgeoisie* or those who were well-off used to build more elaborate saunas in the middle of their gardens, sheltered on three sides by raspberry or black-currant bushes. In summer they made their way to the sauna on narrow walks edged with fragrant fennel and large-leaf cucumbers; in winter, they arrived wearing felt boots, following a path left in the crunching, well-packed snow.

No icons were hung within the smoke sauna, because it was considered a haunted place. Since the Middle Ages staunch believers had been wary of personal hygiene—after all, preoccupation with the flesh was a sin. Many religious orders used to take vows to live without washing. Because the place was unsanctified, all kinds of demons could reside there. No one ever dared to enter alone. It was said that some nights the dead, led by "one who walks," would come to wash their emaciated bodies.

During the Christmas holidays, young women would slip inside to listen to mysterious sounds. The boldest used to file in at night to "consult the mirror." They placed it on a shelf behind two lighted candles, and then balanced a second mirror at chest level so it reflected the candles, creating an infinite line of fire. The supplicant's fate for the New Year would appear out of the flames. This magical consultation was made while naked, of course, without protection from one's cross, and at times it became a frightening experience when, instead of images of fiancés or happily-ever-after lives, vile creatures swarmed from the burning depths. The bold one, fear-struck, would quickly hurl the mirror to the ground and try to flee the bathhouse, but the nasty Banniks would block her escape.

FOOD:
Little is known of the diet of Banniks, who are believed to feast on refuse found beneath the smoke sauna.

BEHAVIOR:
Cruel and vicious, they latch onto the backs of women (and sometimes men) and are quick to possess them against their will. Because they are eternal, born of an "evil spirit," they are not concerned about setting up households and raising children.

ACTIVITIES:
Banniks are credited with only bad behavior. As soon as bathers are peacefully enveloped in the sauna's opaque cloud, the Banniks, fond of air currents, throw open the door—so one finds oneself wondering why it is suddenly freezing in the midst of this torrid vapor! But the Banniks' greatest pleasure is to block up the smoke shaft, asphyxiating those inside. Boukas, other wicked spirits that used to dwell in the darkened corners of the home, were able to shrivel up small children with just one glance.

Nissen, Tomtes, and Assorted Housewights

HEIGHT:
About that of a four-year-old child.

APPEARANCE:
Chubby, gleaming, but wrinkled faces. White beards and hair. Well-proportioned, robust bodies. Fairly large heads, illuminated by large, mischievous smiles and bright little eyes.

CLOTHING:
Jackets and short pants in shades of dull gray with pockets and cuffs in bright green, the color of holly; caps and socks in lively red; birch-wood clogs.

HABITAT:
Housewights (also known as Niskes, Niss, Tomtes, Tomtru, Para, Tomtewütte, Nisses, Nissegodren, Tomtegoble, Tomtra, and Niägruisar) can be found throughout the magical northern lands, from northern Germany to Denmark, Norway, Sweden, and Finland, even as far as Ireland and the Faroe Islands.

I, who had come from the other side of things to see so little that's pleasing in this pale absence of light.

—Jacques Réda, *L'Herbe des Talus*

. . . Put a spirit of youth in everything.
—Shakespeare, *Sonnet XCVIII*

The ancient Chaldeans used to sing accompanied by harps that long ago, after thirty-five days of stormy weather, the sky remained dark and heavy, and the earth was as lumpy and black as night. Evil creatures emerged from the shadows and, with their frost-breath, killed all plants and animals; wolves blew out the lights of campfires with one exhalation.

After huddling in their huts for thirty-five dawnless days, gripped by terror, the inhabitants of the North sent a messenger to the highest mountaintop to look for light, a sign of the Sun's return.

At the news that the Sun was approaching, there was a collective shiver of impatience—men, women, young, and old rushed from all over to greet it. Even the dead shook off their dust and pulled themselves to the openings of their burial mounds to join the universal rejoicing.

To bring the day back to life, the Messenger of the Winter Solstice began by planting in each heart the first shoots of Yuletide, small sprigs of evergreen studded with red berries.

The Swedes, Icelanders, and Danes called the Winter Solstice Fil, Feul, or Fol; Anglo-Saxons called it Gehol, Geol, or Gehrul; to Finns and Estonians it was known as Joulov or Joulo; to the Celts, Guyl or Gwell; and to Laplanders, Joula. It is said that in the North, it wasn't until the tenth century that the celebration of Christmas supplanted that of the Winter Solstice. Whatever its various names or religious attributes, the messenger of the solstice emerges from dark peaks and plunges down slopes and valleys into each home, where it re-illuminates the household, throws open the curtains to reveal luminous fields, and gives gifts to children who—deep down—always believed it would return.

This little herald, a Tomte or a Nissen, is much more than a household spirit: he

is hope for a new day, a "messenger of life"; the grass begins to grow again after him, and, before him, those who sleep begin to stir. There is no better craftsman, no more skillful worker! He can plant a field from a piece of straw and a forest from a pinecone, and by knotting or unknotting a piece of string, he can start or stop the wind.

Once the miraculous times of December pass, once the wreaths, golden balls, and candles are put away next to the buried memories in Paradise Lost, the Nissen limit themselves to the tasks of a humble servant. They work at the everyday tasks of any day laborer, digging up and mowing down, taking cattle to pasture, sifting flour, churning butter, grooming and currying horses, shining silver. But should they go away, everything would go downhill.

Unbeknownst to anyone, they initiate the children of the house into their secrets—but not all the children. They single out those who are receptive to their discourse, and in doing so don't hesitate to invoke all sorts of apparitions. Did a Tomte really lead Nils Holgersson to make his long exploration of Sweden, or was he merely an armchair traveler? Only the clever Nissen can tell us.

It is said that Tomtes and Nissen are descended from Huldres and Trolls, divinities shaped from darkness and light. This establishes their connection with the thirteen little Icelandic visitors of December, the Yuletide Jolasveinar, children of the Trolls Gryla and Leppaludi, whose names (like the jingling of a celestial harness) are music to young ears:

Stekkjastadur (who carries a sheepfold fence),

Giljajadur (who shouts into fjords),

Stúfur (who is itty-bitty),

Thvörusleikir (who licks ladles),

Pottasleikir (who scrapes the bottoms of pots),

Askasleikir (who sips bowls of curdled milk),

Hurdaskellir (who slams doors),

Skyrgámur (who bleats for a bowl of yogurt),

Bjúgnakrækir (who snatches sausages),

Gluggagægir (who peeps in windows),

Gáttathefur (who sniffs about doorways)

Ketkrókur (who steals meat),

Kertasníkir (who filches candles).

FOOD:
A thick soup of milk and cereal with butter, consumed four times each day at very precise times. On Christmas Day, an enormous tureen of Julegroden *(Christmas gruel)—boiled milk and flour—must be prepared for the housewights.*

BEHAVIOR/ACTIVITIES:
Over the last two or three hundred years, the Nissen have experienced some unfortunate character changes. Many reports have accused them of brawling or fighting among themselves, allegedly to "gain the good graces of their mortal masters by having only their interests at heart."

While the Nissen or Tomtes remain as hardworking as ever, still bringing domestic prosperity to the home, they have become demanding: they won't tolerate much noise and on Sundays refuse all activity except dancing and music making. (The Maciew of Russia are very similar, and the Tomtes of Torely insist that their farmhouses be well kept.) It is customary to politely ignore them. Selma Lagerlof wrote that they are "small and gray, in short pants and a gray jacket with silver buttons, wearing a red cap."

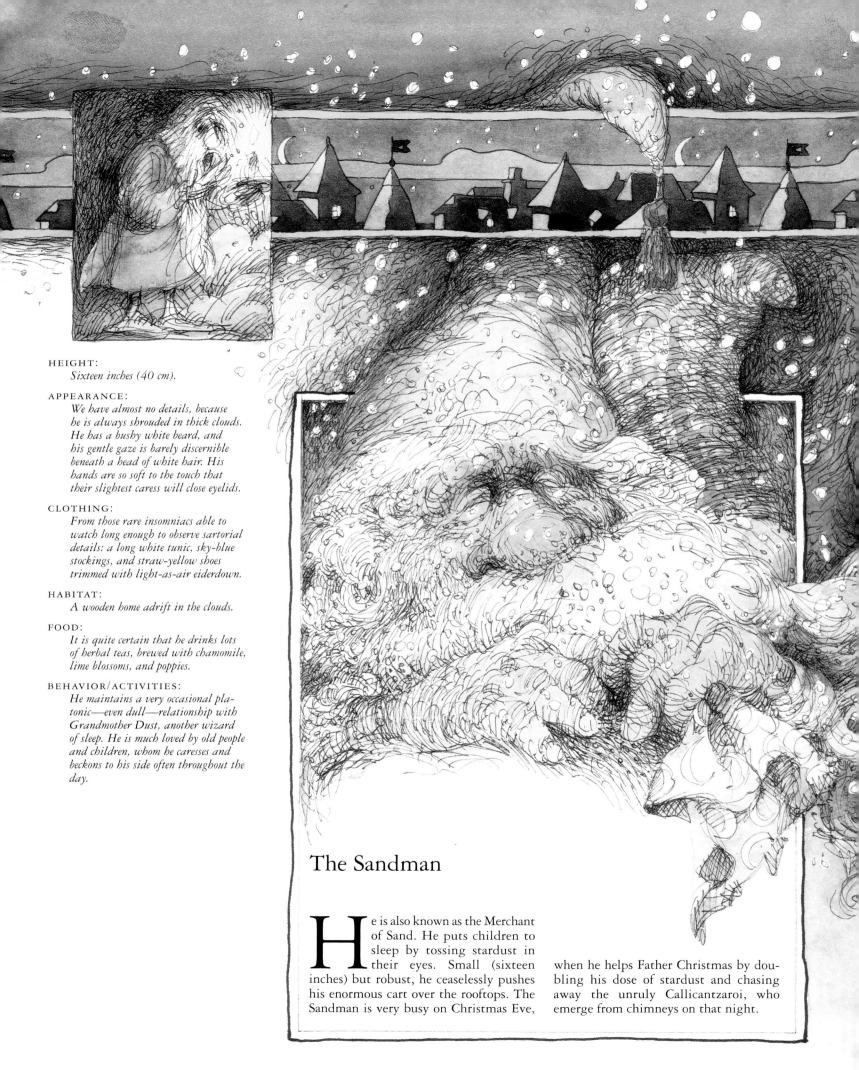

HEIGHT:

Sixteen inches (40 cm).

APPEARANCE:

We have almost no details, because he is always shrouded in thick clouds. He has a bushy white beard, and his gentle gaze is barely discernible beneath a head of white hair. His hands are so soft to the touch that their slightest caress will close eyelids.

CLOTHING:

From those rare insomniacs able to watch long enough to observe sartorial details: a long white tunic, sky-blue stockings, and straw-yellow shoes trimmed with light-as-air eiderdown.

HABITAT:

A wooden home adrift in the clouds.

FOOD:

It is quite certain that he drinks lots of herbal teas, brewed with chamomile, lime blossoms, and poppies.

BEHAVIOR/ACTIVITIES:

He maintains a very occasional platonic—even dull—relationship with Grandmother Dust, another wizard of sleep. He is much loved by old people and children, whom he caresses and beckons to his side often throughout the day.

The Sandman

He is also known as the Merchant of Sand. He puts children to sleep by tossing stardust in their eyes. Small (sixteen inches) but robust, he ceaselessly pushes his enormous cart over the rooftops. The Sandman is very busy on Christmas Eve, when he helps Father Christmas by doubling his dose of stardust and chasing away the unruly Callicantzaroi, who emerge from chimneys on that night.

Nukku Matti

Scattered in the middle of the Gulf of Botnia are several small islands: the *Fjäderholmarna,* or Feather Islands. Those who draw near find themselves on a cottony lawn, the domain of Nukku Matti, the great-great-great-great-grandfather of Sleep, younger brother of Death.

He is so old that when Adam stretched out to sleep at the close of the first day, the Sleepmaster had already flung sand from the *Fjäderholmarna* into his eyes. He sings lullabies, protects those who slumber, and keeps watch over dreams. But he is so very, very old that sometimes while working, he is overcome by the lethargy of the thousands of sleepers he safeguards. He dozes off, letting some drift into nightmares and forgetting others, who become sleepwalkers.

Giants

This one killed him,
This one fricasseed him,
This one ate him.

Long before animals came to graze on the green hills and make themselves heard, the Dwarfs dug the earth's cellars, and the Giants, supervised by the gods, smoothed its rough edges.

The gods had created the clever Dwarfs and the simpleminded Giants, who were good only for digging rivers, raising mountains, planting forests, sowing rocks (while playing ringtoss), opening canyons (by sneezing), and hollowing out valleys (by lying down to nap). At least that is what the old tales say, recalling Gogmagog, Goliath, Ymir, Kronos, Polyphemus, the Cormoran and Bolster Giants, the Cyclopes, Sinnagog, Antaeus, Atlas, Gargantua, Ferragut, the Thunes and the Titans, and so many others of iron and fire!

Mythology describes them as the equals of the gods, irascible and forever in rebellion. In the *Gargantuan Chronicles,* they appear both monstrous and easygoing, "quick-tempered builders of high mountain chains, natural fortresses." Legendary heroes ranked them with the powerful dragons, great Centaurs, and kidnappers of princesses. In the *Elfin History,* Giants are sweet and innocent, the "working hands" of the Elves. They had a divine and Fairy-like nature, but lacked "sense." As soon as they obtained it, though, whether in payment for their labor or through their regular association with spirits, the Giants began to revolt, for good:

"They pull out with their hands the very
walls they've built!
They arm themselves with tall trees, planted
by their own hands!
And walk upon the fortress of the gods."
(Wilken, *Baldr*)

Tales, legends, chronicles, major and minor myths, and stories, despite their divergent views of Giant psychology, all agree on the Hundred Year Rebellion: when they became acquainted with that which the gods, by prudence, had concealed from them—that they had minds as well as strength—they turned against their creators and wanted to take over the place of the gods, to make laws and construct the world in their own way." "But," adds Evans Bowes, "while they had acquired sense, they had not acquired wisdom."

In short, the Giants became crazed with pride, destructive, and cannibalistic: those who were assigned to celestial work unleashed chaos in the heavens; those in the oceans spread bitterness and anger on the small islands that they populated with monsters in their own image; those on the land used frost and fire to make the grass die and, through the terror that they inspired, rendered men spineless and deceitful. To exterminate them, the Ancients then created the Heroes: demigods, warrior Elves, paladin Giants in shining armor. Joseph Arndt explains that the disappearance of Giants was due to "a comet sent by the gods to wipe out evil races."

Whether it was by the sword or by an actual divine meteorite, the reign of the Giants was well and truly over. Hemmed in on all sides, they scattered (despite some vain individual resistance) and gradually disappeared from the surface of the earth . . . not completely, however!

HEIGHT:
Some reach the sky, scraping their heads on the stars. They can straddle the oceans with one stride.

APPEARANCE:
They are generally quite ugly, with low, severely dented foreheads and prominent horsehair eyebrows. Some have one nostril, very large and deep, which they use to unleash storms and blow away enemies like wisps of straw. They have typical carnivore teeth and are bearded, hairy, and heavy lidded, with cruel, piercing gazes. Aside from the celebrated Bolster (the very thin Giant of Saint Agnes), they are big, fat, and powerful. For a long time the Cormoran Giant was considered the best example of the species; it continually kidnapped young girls in hopes of using its obvious advantages to seduce them.

CLOTHING:
Unkempt and untidy. Other than the regal line of Gargantua and Pantagruel, wealthy enough to spend a fortune on yards of expensive fabric, we know very few stylish Giants. They limit themselves to only one real luxury, seven-league boots.

HABITAT:
Immense iron castles ringed by magic beanstalks, on mountain peaks, or deep within forests.

FOOD:
Fresh flesh—with fingertips as a special delicacy.

BEHAVIOR/ACTIVITIES:
The Ancients knew them first as courageous and hardworking, then as brutal and bloodthirsty. Tales and legends often describe them as mean, greedy beasts. But apparently the Giants' character is more varied: there are good ones, naïve ones, and sentimental ones. After taking centuries to build valleys, erect mountains, and plant forests, they finally disappeared. But some inspired observers claim that the pale, melancholy gaze of surviving Giants can be seen in the sky as they glide behind the clouds.

They had enough intelligence and magical power to employ trickery, becoming smaller so they could metamorphose and thus mingle with the good Elfin races in such a way that the Fairy Folk could not always succeed in exposing them. You could be dealing with an Elf or a most charming prince, only to find that you are in the company of a Giant in disguise, a Falconer, a Pacolet, an Alder King, an Allewyn, and are being led from the marital bed into the salt marsh . . .

Whether beside the fire in a gingerbread house, in a cottage thatched with carnivorous plants, in an aerie, in a toy store, or in a slumbering tower atop a magic beanstalk, the Giants smoke peacefully, leafing through poorly-printed books and honing their knives as they wait for fate to guide a plump child across their threshold.

"Who's knocking there, the wind?
It's a tiny child, an infant.
Come in and say good night!"

In nursery rhymes, this "good night" can then be made to rhyme with "fright," "plight," "bite," "take flight," and so on and so forth . . .

The Giants have features and faces familiar to all children who have seen their images in storybooks and on the big screen, such as the Giant in "Jack and the Beanstalk" and other huge gluttons with overflowing potbellies. They include, to name only a few, Orco, Orchi, Saalah, Balardeu, Galaffre, Fine Oreille, Dents Rouges, Grand Colin, Ourgon, Raminagrobis, the Red Man, Tartaro, and Craquehle.

HEIGHT:

Bogeymen are short with stunted legs: about five feet three inches to five feet five inches (1.6 to 1.65 m).

APPEARANCE:

Lots of hair, heavy browed, long and thick beards, hairy skin that is rough and ruddy, well-formed white teeth. They all have prominent bellies and are heavy boned. It is said that their fur bonnets hide their horns and pointed ears, just as their boots hide their hoofed feet.

CLOTHING:

Bearskins, boots of straw and bark, shipboy's coats, horned masks of the Körbopche, before they adopted the greatcoat and waders; reddish-colored tunics. They carry large baskets on their back and a stick or a green branch in their hand.

HABITAT:

In the past, mountains, caves, forests; today, cellars. They live in bourgeois houses. Some have permanently established themselves in the east of France, Switzerland, Bavaria, the Tyrol, northern Italy, and Lapland.

FOOD:

They have recently stopped consuming the flesh of little children, it seems.

Christmas Bogeymen

Children? Children?
—Davis Grubb,
The Night of the Hunter

"What is that loud noise we can hear coming from the plain? It sounds like a chain being dragged along stones . . . It's the great Lustucru passing. It's the great Lustucru who will eat all little boys who are not sleeping soundly, all the little boys who don't sleep at all!" Thus goes the song about troublesome children. The Ogres are no longer simply lying in wait—not now that the laurels have been cut and the children no longer visit the wood (unless the parents go there to lose them), not now that the confectioner makes home deliveries so that the children no longer have to run around looking for pastry stores. No! The Ogres have removed the lanterns from their doorways since they fail to attract people to them. They are busy going around from house to house.

Disguised as hawkers with baskets on their backs, they first turned to selling nice pictures, puppets, spinning tops, and rag dolls. Disguised as the Sandman, as Fütter Männchen, as the Sand Merchant, as a candle blower, it was they who closed the eyes of children, who ruled and made the laws in the nursery. These Ogres of the city were very clever and, with their ribbons, horoscopes, and "sweet talk," fooled many mothers. Thanks to their dark clothes, their stern looks, and their "love of children," they were taken for old retired schoolteachers, the kind of prefect for kids who misbehaved. At any sign of naughtiness they were summoned immediately, simply by saying, "If you are not good I will tell Zwarte Pieter to come!" And of course, they did come . . .

Now they live permanently in houses: in the cellar, in the attic, in the broom closet, at the bottom of the wardrobe. They see all, hear all, know all. At night you can hear their voices coming from the basement and their nails scratching at the woodwork. Only the little ones know their true nature, but they only wear themselves out trying to expose their bad intentions. The adults never believe it. The children are the only ones to have seen the contents of their bloody baskets and wait pale and trembling for their turn in the dark . . .

Oh! If the moms could only guess the double meaning behind the songs of the Bogeymen:

"Little lamb, where are you going?
–To the slaughterhouse.
–To do what?
–Spill my blood.
–Will you be back?
–Oh! No never.
If I come back,
I'll come back
With my head chopped off,
My tail minced,
In the butcher's wagon."

The Luggage of the Bogey Man (a painting by Timoléon Lebrichon, Salon of 1874) tells the story so well with an enormous basket of coarse wickerwork out of which jut the tearful faces of five or six little girls.

The Bogeymen, Croque Metjiens, or Croque Mädchens hide behind several other identities whose names all the children of the world have shared: Bâbou, Jean the Grey, Lowethme, Galaffre, Father Whipper, Big Eyebrows, Grumpy Monk, Mister Louis, Olentzaro, Croquemitaine, The Redhead, Father Frost, Bouman, Hans Trapp, Boublin, John the Green, Pépé, Isola, Papa Goulu, Rat Catcher, Father Chalande, Nose Man, Zwarte Pieter, Krampus, Pelznickel, Hairy Nicolas, Beelzebub, Aschenman, Lent Fresser, Lustucru, Butzenberckt.

Oh! But how is it that these names are also used in some countries for Saint Nicolas and good old Father Christmas?

BEHAVIOR:

It is claimed that they have all become very good and obliging and excellent educators (for all that, rather strict).

ACTIVITIES:

They are skillful and ingenious toy makers, and they distribute these every year to children who write to them. They come only at night, moving across the sky with the help of shoes that are as fast as the sandals of Mercury, slippers of air, and seven-league boots, unless of course they are traveling through the firmament on reindeer or donkeys or behind a Sylph-like team. They enter as they wish the homes where they are invited and place their presents in front of the fireplace (where a kind of altar is laid for them) in exchange for a humble present.

Changelings

HEIGHT:

> *That of a six-month-old baby. Even when they have reached their adult size, "the exchanged children" (Changelains, Changelings, Wechsel Kinds) resume their childlike measurements in the presence of children or those who love them. (Certain Elfologists postulate that Peter Pan was a Changeling.)*

APPEARANCE:

> *There is hardly any difference between the Dwarf Changelings (the children of the Dwarfs among humans) and the human Changelings (the human children among the Dwarfs). Grotesque and spiteful imagery always strives to depict the Dwarf Changelings as horrible little runts, black and wrinkled, no doubt to terrify mothers. The Dwarf Changelings are a mixture of an old man and a baby; they are ageless. Even as adults or as old men, they give an impression of youth. Their deep, large eyes reflect the images of sunny valleys in bloom. Their mouths pass readily from a smile to bitterness.*

CLOTHING:

> *Although Changelings wear the local costume when they are among humans, in their own environment they wear tunics and long moss- and earth-colored coats.*

Like the Fairies of the swells off the coast of Brittany, the Fairies of the caves of Guernsey also practice the habit of switching children. A fisherman from Erée placed some limpets that he had just collected from the shore over a big fire. He went off for a few minutes while they were cooking. His wife, who was busy in the house, heard a strange, raucous voice coming from the cradle where her newborn baby lay. She turned and saw a horrible wrinkled Goblin standing there, looking with deep attention at the house and saying:

> *I am not of this year or of another,*
> *Nor of the time of Rouey Jehan,*
> *But in all my days and in all my years,*
> *I never saw so many little pots boiling.*

She had heard old women saying that Fairies sometimes took advantage of the absence of mothers in order to steal their sleeping children and substitute their own babies, and the only way for the mother to recover her baby was to throw the child on the ground and hit it. The woman did this, and the Changeling started to cry. Straightaway, a Fairy jumped over the half-door, gave the woman back her baby, and carried off his own offspring.

It was not so long ago that Dwarfs used to amuse themselves by kidnapping children and replacing them with nasty little creatures. Despite being breast-fed all the time, they remained sad and puny, with the faces of old men, and drank the milk nurses dry of their milk. Once the Jetins took a little boy whose mother had carried him to the fields and placed him to the side. They swapped him with one of their own. The baby did not grow, despite being fed baby bottles and baby bottles, and the woman took him to a wise man, who advised her to put a dozen shells (these could be the shells of shellfish, the shells of nuts or hazelnuts, or acorn cups) filled with water to boil in front of the fire. Upon waking, the runt squealed with round eyes, "I am more than a hundred plus a hundred years old, I saw the acorn before the oak, the egg before the chicken, but I never saw so many little pots boiling." The good woman asked him where her little boy was, and he replied that the Jetins had taken him away to their place "to have a share of human blood." She went once again to ask the advice of the wise man, who had her carry the Dwarf to the entrance of the Goblins' abode, crying out that she was going to kill him if they didn't give her back her little one. She started to beat the poor creature, and it began to cry loudly. After a few minutes, a Dwarf appeared holding the hand of a handsome, bright-faced little child. He took the Jetin child in his arms and carried him off quickly to his home of moss and stones.

These stories are the same everywhere. Only the expressions of the Changelings are different: "I have many days and many years. Never did I see so many little white

pots," exclaimed the one from the forest of Jailloux. "I saw the forest of Ardennes, all in rye and in wheat. The forest of Brekelien was not planted yet, but I have never seen so many little pots!" said the Fersé Goblin. The words do not matter; what counts is to make them admit their great age and, in the same breath, their Elfin origins.

Some say that when they break their silence, it is because they are annoyed that people are laughing at their little size by preparing miserably small utensils for them. Whatever the case may be, this is the only way to get rid of one and retrieve the stolen baby. They disappear up the chimney, and if you mistreat them, their parents will run and fetch them.

"Sometimes, however, the adoptive family gets used to him or even gets attached to him, and the Changeling grows up among humans. He becomes then a musician, a hermit, a poet, a visionary, or a cow doctor, but he never marries. He is an 'Intermediary.' Formerly they were saints and were respected, and people came from afar to consult them," writes Barbygère. As for the human children who stay with "Them," another life begins for them.

The people of Livradois in France say that, contrary to what the legends state, it was the Christians who started it all by stealing the offspring of the Fairies. In retaliation, the Fairies then carried off newborn human babies, and when the mothers came to beg for their return, the Fairies replied:

Give us back our little sprite
We'll give you back your oily mite
[an allusion to the oily baptismal
 water].

An old Elfin story recalls other examples of Féetauds and Fayons taken away by villagers, but the Dwarfs and the Elves readily admit that it was the Black Alfs who were the first to empty cradles. One cannot ignore passages about the terrible Bogeymen and the meat-eating dwarfs: the Hebrew Schabta, the Burmese Ponnaka, the bloody Dzonoqwa and other Chichefaces, Rounff, Calin-Minou, Tirelovis, Babarouchi, Caragnaou, Piquious, Babarabaüs, Tschanteret, Stalker, and the bad Niques, who crept out of the shadows of the Erlking and the Ellekongen, his Danish twin.

But the idea that our Goblin neighbors stole children "to have a share of human blood" is definitely a theory devised by humans, whose arrogance goes as far as considering all of nature to be their own environment, whereas they are really only specks of dust in a vast universe. In the eyes of Dwarfs and Elves, children are precious. Age has no meaning; they belong only to themselves. Their spirits can still "choose." Just like the Indians (so close to the gods, the simple spirits, brothers of the fauna and flora), they take away little white children not to torture them, but to raise them; these well-wishers take away a chosen few in order to open doors for them to other worlds, in the hope that when they return later to their own people, they will direct them toward a more harmonious and better future. They leave in exchange their own children, to whom they are so attached that they run to fetch them at the slightest danger, in the same spirit of generosity and for the same utopian ideal!

HABITAT:
Dwarf Changelings, just like human Changelings, prefer isolated cabins among the trees, in the woods, or near ponds and springs. They are scattered throughout the world.

FOOD:
They are vegetarians. The beliefs about their Ogre-like appetites and their insatiable thirst (they would dry up the milk of two nannies and a cow in less than a week without ever gaining an ounce) come from the same wish to show them up as unsightly and dangerous monsters.

BEHAVIOR:
Changelings love their adoptive parents as much as their natural parents. They are silent and meditative but can also be good-humored. They are reputed to be excellent musicians. They are in general unhappy in love and seek the companionship of little girls with whom they maintain tender relationships until the girls grow up and start to prefer boys who are more "normal." The same is true with very young Fairies!

ACTIVITIES:
Whether in one world or the other, the Changelings seek harmony and communion with nature and the elements. The Kaybora of the American forests steal babies and hide them at the bottom of tree trunks so that they can learn the language and the wisdom of the trees and the Dryads.

But watch out! Not all Changelings are angels. Some, disguised as humans, corrupt, violate, and assassinate. They are recognizable by their yellow eyes and red nails. A hypothesis of C. Marmadulee Perthuvee (The Changeling of Whitechapel) suggests that Jack the Ripper was one of them.

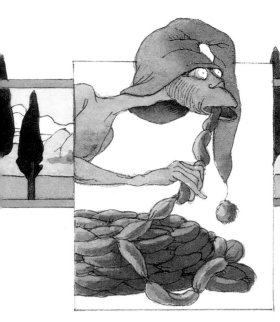

The Callicantzaroi

The month of Advent
Is subject to wind.

HEIGHT:
> *Twenty-four to twenty-eight inches
> (60 to 70 cm).*

APPEARANCE:
> *Pale, emaciated children. Bulging eyes
> that look almost blind. Many have
> white eyes. Toothless mouths devoid of
> lips stick out like beaks. Bald, no
> ears. A long tuft of hair sticks out of
> the bottom of their backs. One of their
> two legs has the characteristics of that
> of a pony. They shiver nonstop.*

CLOTHING:
> *Naked. Only hats which are too big
> for their bald heads and hide half of
> their snouts.*

HABITAT:
> *Strange earthenware amphorae molded
> in the form of a Callicantzaros. Kout-
> sodaimonas stack them in layers at the
> bottom of narrow passes in the Greek
> mountains.*

FOOD:
> *Once a year, they greedily devour
> whatever appetizing Christmas food
> they have time to peck at.*

BEHAVIOR/ACTIVITIES:
> *Some claim they are descended from
> the Centaurs. Others say they are the
> souls of bewitched children born at
> Christmas. The Reverend G. Carolus
> puts forward the thesis of little still-
> born offspring of the ancient gods of
> Parnassus. There is a great chance
> that the Callicantzaroi are the "spir-
> its" of the great Greek gods, determined
> not to sink into oblivion. Preserved in
> jars in a larva-like state, they come
> out of their enforced slumber to affirm
> their existence on the birthday of the
> One who displaced them.*

The month of Advent is also when the Callicantzaroi begin their tormenting. When the first window in the Advent calendar is opened and the miracles begin to swirl around the hedgerows, spreading Fioles and Foufus by the roadside, the Callicantzaroi rush down from the Greek mountains. Under the sleeping summit of Mount Parnassus, somewhere in the southwest of Doris and Phocis where the memories of the ancient gods lie forever dormant, the Callicantzaroi awaken from their slumber.

Throughout the whole of Advent they will disturb the population, piously occupied with preparations for Christmas. They spread anger, annoyance, and disorder among the fathers, peasants, and priests in order to spoil the arrival of the infant king. A village decorated with silver angels, straw, and branches of plaited silver paper flowers is turned upside down. Having devastated the Nativity scene and the string of glittering pictures, the pack of fiends bustles toward the houses, forcing doors and windows and blocking chimneys, smoking out rooms made ready for the festivities. They pee in the fire, the soup, the water tank. For three, almost four weeks, they wander from house to house and terrorize the children.

When the cock crows at dawn, they disappear, leaving the women to repair the devastation, but it will be repeated the following night. The men prepare reprisals: pigs are immediately slaughtered and cut up. They are a necessary sacrifice, since only their jaws hung in the hearth will repulse the assailants.

Everywhere, the air is full of the sound of piercing squeals; the hatchets, red in the light of the torches, set the ritual in motion. Bah! The meat won't go to waste—it will be salted to last all winter. The most disinherited who have nothing to kill come to reclaim the feet: the smell of burnt hooves also disperses the strange invaders.

A line of old women with black hats wander around the square, their heavy baskets oozing blood. Talismans and rosaries nailed to door lintels drape down among the pious streamers, scapulars, mistletoe, stars, and holly.

Now let them come . . .

And of course, they do return to find the forbidden barriers, which they cannot overcome. They run here and there. Everywhere, it is the same impediment they meet. They come and go and try to enter through the barns or the dormer windows. They climb the gutters and inspect the chimneys. Repulsed by the smell of smoking pork, they fall, disabled, among the crowd, and bit by bit a monotone groan arises. They knock gently at the doors, moaning, demanding, and scratching at the windows.

And although defeated and pitiable, the Callicantzaroi wander around until the triumph of dawn takes them back to their entrenchment at Parnassus for another year. The families salute the Chosen One and enjoy the well-earned feast.

Koutsodaimonas

Behind the pathetic troupe of Callicantzaroi trundle along the bandy silhouettes of the Koutsodaimonas, guardians of the Callicantzaroi's hive.

HEIGHT:
  Thirty-one inches (80 cm) without the horn.

APPEARANCE:
  Obscene mixture of Faun and Caliban: hairy, hunchbacked in front, big-bellied behind; bandy-legged, donkey-eared, with enormous bovine heads, the slit eyes of a goat, goatees, hanging tongues, huge genitalia, the weight and size of which make walking difficult, and serrated horns in the middle of their foreheads.

CLOTHING:
  Naked, except for crude nets of clinking medals stamped with the effigies of the lost gods.

HABITAT:
  Stationed in Parnassus, they sometimes travel to the coasts of the islands of Andros, Samos, and Kalimnos in search of bathers who are not put off by their anatomy.

BEHAVIOR/ACTIVITIES:
  Very dangerous on Christmas night, they sneer at the talismans of pork; only fire and torches keep them at a distance. They chase and disembowel those who attack the Callicantzaroi. They spend Advent contaminating the slaughterhouses, the wells, and the springs by taking baths in them. Sexually insatiable, their stranglehold can be fatal, especially for unwary young shepherds. They play the panpipes well.

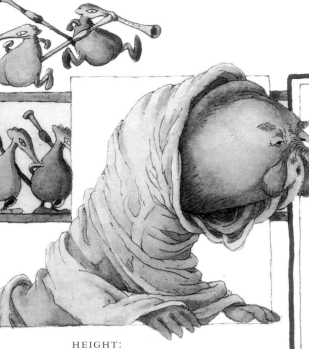

Hosenteufel

HEIGHT:

About six inches (15 cm) at rest, but they can reach fourteen inches (35 cm) and sometimes more when very active.

APPEARANCE:

Even though those men or women who are enthralled by their charms find them beautiful, seductive, and well-formed, Hosenteufel are, in fact, repulsive. They are soft and wrinkled "like a slug in the sludge" when they are resting and digesting their victories; they stretch like salamanders when the "Spiritus Incubus" (Barbygère) wakes them up. They are disgusting wrinkled, sweating cylinders. They are covered with warts; their ears are soft, their noses the shape of a trumpet, their eyes oozing. They have the tail of a macaque, whose features they share more or less. Their genitals are covered with suckers. Their backs are hairy, and their hands and feet are webbed. They can take on the appearance of a handsome young man, an incomparable lover. They appear symbolically on a canvas by Hieronymus Bosch as a pair of ears straddling a knife in the form of a nose.

Banners, flags, and gonfalons flap in the wind. The clamor covers the sound of the fifes. Plumes dance behind the captain of the warriors, who moves forward, mounted on his charge. Both captain and horse appear as if forged from one solid casing of steel. His nose, as beaked as a helmet, leads the victorious troop through the village overwhelmed with joy.

With wide-open eyes, young Gretel admires the handsome plumed soldiers. Following the heavy foot soldiers and the pikemen come her favorites, the Swiss lansquenets from southern Germany, walking to the rolling rhythm of the drums. It is a pleasure to see their tall silhouettes stand out, with their broad-bladed partisans or double-edged swords at the shoulder and their scalloped felt hats placed gallantly on their heroic heads. She has eyes only for them, especially for a huge coarse sergeant with white teeth and coal-black eyes, walking to the right of the group and leading these gentlemen of war, who are as beautiful as the warriors of Holbein or Dürer, erect like those of Peter Flötner and Hans Burglemain.

With their torsos sculptured in their skintight jerkins and their shoulders made even larger with the rolls of cloth, these glorious dandies turn the heads of girls with their male coquetry. Just think, these resourceful fellows, encumbered by the restraints of their extremely tight-fitting clothing, have found nothing better but to open the material at the seams in a "deliciously primitive" manner. In order to stand at attention, to parry, thrust, or lunge, they cut their clothing at the armpits, the elbows, and the knees, exposing underwear and naked skin through these gaps to these gasping females! In response, bourgeois gentlemen, the jealous husbands of these excitable ladies, ask their tailors to provide the same innovations. These artisans clip like no one else can into the doublets and the corsets. A little slash here and a cut there: everywhere the eye may rest a while. And everyone parades themselves, peacock-like in a costume full of splits like splendid tattered rags. From the highest ranks through the cart driver, everyone is covered with slits and splits over a lining of silk to simulate a shirt. But real connoisseurs despise these pathetic fakes. Quite rightly, the women prefer the genuine article to these childish pretenders.

And the young Gretel cannot prevent herself being delighted at the view of the bawdy parade. Red, golden, white, yellow, they move forward, suntanned, molded in clothing through which long bicep muscles and strong thighs bulge. From behind the blond bangs escaping from her bonnet, she notices large sandals out of which sprout the glorious legs of the traveler: the bound contour of the calf, the firm thigh working under the coarse skin of the stocking, the swinging hip struck regularly by the greasy sheaf of a dagger. Timidly, she hesitates, but only briefly, on the ornate shell of the codpiece, its size exaggerated by the pressure of the belts. Seized with shame, Gretel returns to the study of the aglets and laces and mortifies herself by counting out the rows of buttons. But it is already too late! Her eyes have been captivated and return to stare at the knot of sin.

Jan Hus, the reformer burned in 1415 in Constance, had already condemned these gothic trimmings. After him, Andreas Musculus, the superintendent of the Mark of Brandenburg, also thundered from his pulpit during the feast of the Assumption against the unchaste fashion of these disciples of decadence, condemning the diabolical pants, the seat of sin, and stating that, gestating in their bowels, they contained the embryo of evil itself: the Hosenteufel.

Although Gretel could still hear the vocal harangues of the sermon, she had fallen.

My God! Holy Mary! Gretel realizes she is damned, that the evil is done. She forgot the warning, being totally immersed in her naïve and childish joy at watching the soldiers pass. Now, hypnotized, she can no longer tear her fascinated stare from the weeping eye peering through a crack. It is useless to try to escape the attraction of the demon that is quickening and imperceptibly unwinding, separating from the distended material, escaping, and beating up sulfur clouds with its tail! Now, whatever she does, it will meet with her that night. *In cauda venenum . . .*

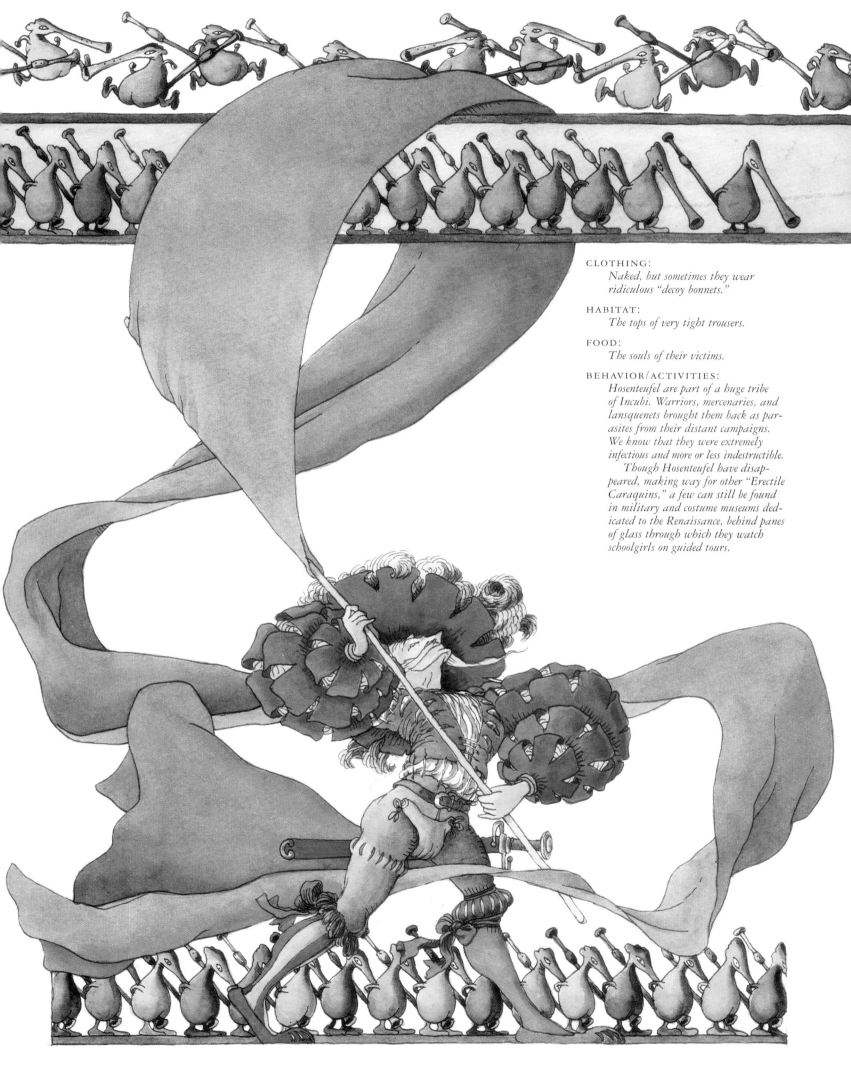

CLOTHING:
Naked, but sometimes they wear ridiculous "decoy bonnets."

HABITAT:
The tops of very tight trousers.

FOOD:
The souls of their victims.

BEHAVIOR/ACTIVITIES:
Hosenteufel are part of a huge tribe of Incubi. Warriors, mercenaries, and lansquenets brought them back as parasites from their distant campaigns. We know that they were extremely infectious and more or less indestructible.
Though Hosenteufel have disappeared, making way for other "Erectile Caraquins," a few can still be found in military and costume museums dedicated to the Renaissance, behind panes of glass through which they watch schoolgirls on guided tours.

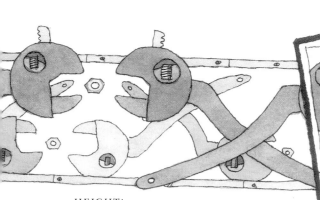

Gremlins

The motor won't work,
The Gremlins are berserk!

The alarm clock didn't ring; the bedside lamp shorted, as did the electric coffeemaker and the toaster; the transistor radio crackles with static, the microwave oven shorts out, the washer won't work, the TV has imploded, the iron has burned out, the refrigerator has stopped, the stove is smoking, the sink is stopped up, the shower is scalding, the water heater is frozen, the garage door is stuck, the car won't start, the bus is late, the subway is blocked, the train has derailed . . . There is no use fretting or giving the contraption a good shake. There is no point fooling around with the outlets; it is better not to insist, better to avoid accusing, insulting willy-nilly, because things will just get worse! Ears are listening, eyes are spying, hands are ready to deal ruthlessly with you. Better to take a deep breath, calm down, smile, humbly apologize, and admit gently that it's all your fault, that last night before falling asleep you simply forgot to have a grateful thought for the kind household Goblins, the watchmen, tinkers, protectors, repairmen of the house-hold appliances, of electric circuits, of gas and water lines, of all things mechanical: the Gremlins! They are the experts in all things that turn on, are plugged in, function, light up, operate, start up, rev up, suck up, wash, grind; they are the spirits of all machinery, from the smallest to the largest, from the most simple to the most sophisticated. Assuage your guilt. Offer them a bouquet of compliments for their ingenuity, for the incomparable kind deeds they generously bestow on you . . .

Central heat: instead of having to gather wood in rain and wind, fell trees, chop logs to feed a furnace that smokes or burns your face and freezes your rear end and vice versa!

The faucet: a simple invention that avoids the outdated fetching of water—the heavy bucket, the frozen fountain, the Drac-infested well!

The beatified vacuum cleaner: such a comprehensive friend to the housekeeper; elegant, easy to handle, efficient, abolishing the exhausting task of sweeping that creates clouds of dust!

The dishwasher with an almost inaudible hum, that erases the vain efforts of reddened, cracked hands, broken glassware, and disgusting splashes of greasy water!

How much hard labor, how many obscure chores have been avoided thanks to Gremlin magic? And we have so easily forgotten them!

HEIGHT:
From three and one-half to five inches (9 to 13 cm).

APPEARANCE:
Very small, slim, and exceedingly flexible, they can contort, flatten, and lengthen themselves, make themselves noodle-thin, and slip inside of the narrowest mechanical works. They can become invisible, shrink to the size of a speck of dust, of rust, of a virus (in order to pirate, erase, or transform computer data). They are sharp, smart, wise, visionary, and their eyes are as small as a pinhead. They are very successful with young girls who are impressed with their creativity, technical expertise, and staggering philosophical-epistemological discourses.

CLOTHING:
Overalls covered in a patchwork of pockets in metallic colors, and wide belts on which hang hundreds of carefully maintained fine tools. A kind of aviator's cap, very fitted. They are never far from their oilcan and rag.

HABITAT:
Gremlins nest in machinery, engines, and all kinds of appliances.

FOOD:
Gremlins eat very little; a kernel of popped corn can sustain one all day. They appreciate the pieces of chewing gum left for them by knowing children, amateur do-it-yourselfers, and builders of small-scale models and electronic games.

BEHAVIOR/ACTIVITIES:
Just like their brothers, the Goblins, they were originally kind and generous towards men; then they grew disgusted by their ingratitude after having inspired them to the best of scientific inventions. Frightened by man's destructive instinct, Gremlins have become suspicious and try desperately to caution him of the risks incurred by giving successive warnings, from a simple electrical short to a nuclear catastrophe.

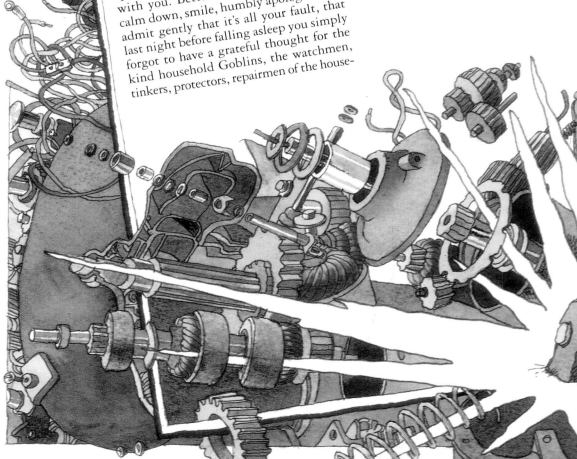

It was so long ago that man has forgotten the day when Gremlins spontaneously offered their services to the first human chieftain and gave him the idea for the first invention—what was it again? A rudimentary tool: a stone embedded in a piece of wood, or a sharpened bone inset in another. Such a simple idea! Man could have thought it up on his own. But there had to be a spark, the intervention of geniuses of "Thinking Matter," little divinities of "Psychomatter." They asked for almost nothing in exchange: that men would recognize their contribution at each new invention. The Elves, Dwarfs, and Genies of the Golden Age were so trusting, so generous, and demanded so little. For each gift given, they required that man always leave an ear of wheat in the field, a fruit on the tree, a drop in the fountain, a tiny part left to Nature, a kind thought toward the Invisible—a simple thank-you.

Then there was fire and another tool and another: the wheel, the hub, the mill, ball bearings, the screw, the first mechanical contraption, the steam engine, the internal combustion engine, the motor, the propeller, electricity, the telegraph line, the airplane, the atom, bombs, the computer—and the tragic consequences and fallout when the proud inventors ignored the Gremlin Pact.

Catastrophes, wars, accidents, viruses, and pollution never fail to remind scholars, scientific minds, brilliant mathematicians, atomic scientists, computer technicians, electrical engineers, and astrophysicists that the future of the planet (just as the humble home of the housewife is jeopardized by her ingratitude) depends only on a simple, friendly thought towards the little Gremlins.

THOSE OF
THE PONDS AND
RIVERS

Follow me to the source and discover its secret.
—Patrice de la Tour du Pin

In the murmuring of the stream running between the rocks and in the current of the raging waters where polished flints roll along the bottom, the practiced ear of the solitary rambler hears a soft and mysterious music. Who then is this person singing in the waves? And who is this person who menaces those who fall in the water? Who draws them with an irresistible force toward the deep? These were the questions asked by Leopold Rancke around 1840 as he investigated the rumors surrounding the aquatic and sonorous locations.

Whom do the monks of the river resemble with their spongy, hooded frocks? When the sun fleetingly revealed the world of water lilies, the washerwomen saw them in a procession, following each other, heads bent, revealing nothing of their appearance except for the pale, star-shaped footprints made in the mud by their invisible feet, which disappeared just as quickly as they had appeared. Hardly perceived and already vanished! It is always the same with the elusive water creatures; they are as liquid as shadows, just as capricious, dangerous, and evasive as their kingdom. They attract you with a melody or a diamond, and when you have barely bent over them, they grab you and pull you down, dragging you into the oblivion of the gray turbulence.

Louis the Courteous

HEIGHT:
Thirty-one inches (80 cm).

APPEARANCE:
A pretty boy with a pale complexion; nicely proportioned. Mouth the shape of a heart. Powdered. Beauty spot on his right cheek. Dark eyes with makeup.

CLOTHING:
Wears, both in winter and summer, a well-fitted silk suit in the style of an eighteenth-century Marquis. Sports a tricornered hat with a white feather. He wears a wig with sausage curls, tied with a ribbon of azure blue that he exchanges for a scarlet one when he has committed a murder.

HABITAT:
The marshes of Poitou and, more especially, the banks of the Mignon, and the region of Saint-Hilaire-la-Palud. He haunts pathways, groves, and conch shells. His manor, visible only at Christmas, moves around all the time.

FOOD:
Feasts once a year; otherwise he is satisfied with taking snuff. A string of delicate sneezes reveals his position and gives the signal for taking flight.

BEHAVIOR:
Louis the Courteous is a lakeside Goblin, like the Guiben, the great wrestlers and drowners of people; he is a bad "Spirit of still waters" (Barbygère). His first sighting was noted around the beginning of the eighteenth century.

ACTIVITIES:
He collects murders of all types. Excellent fencer and a witty poet. Although he doesn't mix with the Water Sprites and his cousins the Goblins, he has, on the other hand, great success with the Fairies, the Vouivres, the Fayettes, and even women.

*One, two, three, here comes Louis the
  Courteous!
Too bad for you,
Too bad for me,
Too bad for little father Francis!*

The sound of a soft sneeze causes a poacher fishing for eel by lantern light to freeze. He doesn't have time to react before two little manicured hands catch his flat-bottomed boat and capsize it. The man disappears under the silver duckweeds of the swamp, surrounded by bubbles. Louis the Courteous has just committed another crime.

The inhabitants of the Niort region of France and the marshes of Poitou christened this naughty Goblin Louis "The Courteous" because he seems to have a gentle allure and polite manner. If he meets you, he will gallantly salute you with a profusion of bows, and will politely offer you a pinch from his snuffbox, only to stab you later with his short rapier or drown you or break your neck or throw you into a dungeon or down a well. He could also hang you at the first branch you reach, and it is useless to resist. This Goblin has incredible strength!

He leaves little traces of his murders behind him and washes his bloody blade in the water of springs, which then remain red colored.

This seasoned killer is to be avoided at all costs all year round, except on Christmas Eve, when he opens the doors of his castle to whoever wishes to follow him. There, he offers copious meals, an exquisite bar, fireworks, and gifts and will chauffeur back to their homes in a golden carriage all those who have drunk a little too much alcohol and are unable to walk straight.

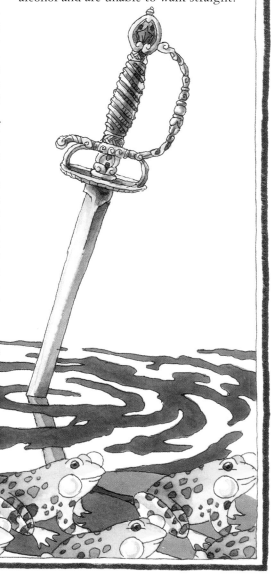

Houziers

The rivers were alive . . .
—Octave Grévin,
La Pêche au très petit
(Fishing for the Very Young)

A very long time ago, in Hardoye in the French Ardennes, there lived on the bank of streams and by bridges a type of aquatic spirit nicknamed the Houziers, meaning "Men of the waters."

Being so small, they could easily hide: in summer in bulrushes, in winter in a hole. By no means nasty, they were simply mischievous. Their great pleasure, when people passed by without seeing them, was to splash them and to cover them with mud, especially young people dressed up for Mass in their "Sunday best" or in beautiful white dresses.

On the sly, they would tease female bathers, pulling at their swimsuits, making them swallow water, tickling their stomachs from underneath while they were swimming, and hiding their clothes on the shore. They pushed the joke a little further sometimes: covering themselves in algae and leaves and imitating the cry of the water Ogres, they would bite their toes. If a bather wanted to spank one, the Houzier would already be out of reach, with a peal of laughter and a splash like that made by a big frog in diving, creating a ring of rippling waves. For a long time in the region of Hardoye, no one dared to walk along the edge of the rivers for fear of getting splashed. Even if the Houziers no longer exist in our time,

their memory lives on. In some remote places, when a child arrives home wet and muddy, his mother will always say to him, "Look at you, you're completely houzeled."

The Colinots of the rivers and Imps of the marshes are all alike, but none can ever rival the kindly Houziers. The Saris of the Semoy are "handsome hunchbacks." The Berges-Jeannot are green. The Pied-Pied-Vent-Vent of Igres is a likeable joker who repeats everything that people say. The Pretty-Heart is a splasher with silvery skin. The Father Bigournet (pronounced "Bigournette") wades through the rapid waters of the Loire. The Water Duz swims in lively waters. The Cracas prefer puddles. The Guldentrop from Anvers haunts roads flooded by rain. Ian an Ôd from Brittany hides under bridges; the one from Bayeux in wells. The Lantarnier, disguised as a Will-o'-the-Wisp, lights fireworks of sparks and water by plunging into the rivers. The Chantcrai (the one who leaps about) tumbles down and climbs up again all day long at the waterfalls in Valais and splashes the mountain dwellers. The Engouttés, like beavers, flood and change the course of rivers by constructing dams in the middle. The Bergeron spend hours in the sun lazing about on the moss. Aubin of the Loire-Atlantique region of France sprays all the shaved heads that pass near to him. Algol drinks water in oases. He is responsible for the mirages that draw thirsty people further into the desert: wherever the ground is cracked, Algol has been at work. To chase away a Gabinot or Gobineau of Morbihan, it is necessary to remark on his muddy odor by shouting at him, "Get out of here, Stinky."

HEIGHT:
Eighteen inches (46 cm).

APPEARANCE:
Pretty, laughing, and harmonious. Their backbones consisted of thin, fishlike scaly spines. They had big, round, and gentle eyes. Their ears were pointed but finely rimmed. Even though they spent a lot of time underwater, they lived on the banks of rivers, and although their feet and hands were webbed, their respiratory system was like ours, without gills. The Houziers expressed themselves in a very precise way and spoke the local dialect in rhyme.

CLOTHING:
Naked, with the exception of boots hiding their webbed feet.

HABITAT:
Cradles of bulrushes, dried and woven, buried under the roots of alders lining the river. They could be found in every lake, ditch, pothole, spring, and oasis in "both worlds."

FOOD:
Berries, flowers, roots, wild honey. Suckled cows and ewes.

BEHAVIOR:
They were the "turbulent creatures of fresh water." They were not at all nasty and thought only about having fun and playing tricks.

ACTIVITIES:
Houziers, like all creatures of their kind, enjoyed teasing female bathers and washerwomen, splashing passersby, jumbling up fishing lines, pulling on the corks to make it look like there was a big catch on the line, and freeing caught fish from their hook and attaching any object at hand.

HEIGHT:

From that of a flea to that of a giant tree.

APPEARANCE:

Before metamorphosis, the three cronies have no appearance: they are like the night; they have neither limbs nor face nor eyes. They wander in the silence of shadows. They wrap themselves in a cloak of pitch. Otherwise, they can be a man with claws, a nocturnal bird of prey, a black dog, a wolf with long stiff fur, or a deformed calf. In Schelle, they are described as having large heads and bulging eyes.

CLOTHING:

They sometimes cover themselves with chains, bells, or fishermen's hooks; their skin is as rough and smelly as a Spinner shark. Occasionally, they sport wide-brimmed fedoras, to make fun of a Dutchwoman's headdress, and they wear heavy wooden clogs.

HABITAT:

In "shamefully filthy" hovels in the Brabant, Waas country, in the Lijskenreer, near Haren. In Limburg, Hanover, by the Gravejand dike, in Kuokkre, at Kieldrecht, not far from Anvers, in Hamme, in the community of Doel. In all of Flanders and the western Netherlands, at Herchten, by Alost. Dender, in the region of Dendermonde, is the home base for the Kludde.

Kludde, Osschart, and Roeschaard

There are three little demons, the Kludde, the Osschart, and the Roeschaard, who are nasty Luchtgeesten (Spirits of the air) from Flanders—three rascals, all "blood relations," within a few hairs of being Werewolves. When night ties its black hood over villages, extinguishes the steeple candles, and encloses the fields in the pleats of its cape, the first of the diabolical trio comes out of his hole and screams four times: "Kludde, Kludde, Kludde, Kludde!" That is how he announces his presence; then he goes and waits under the eves to find himself a mount.

"O Maer, gij leelijk!" somebody cries. "Oh nightmare, nasty beast!" Osschart follows close behind *"met zijn bellen"* (with his bells). His two blazing blue eyes leave behind a crackling trail. He is wearing his darkest fleece—that of a crow's wing—and is looking for a humped willow from which to overlook the path. Each step he takes makes a sharp ring, like tin.

Then Roeschaard rises out of his well and trails behind. He is an air Spirit, but due to his contrary and morose nature, he has elected to dwell in damp places. This night, he sports a black calf's head with chains looped around its neck and the body of a large reddish dog with well-clawed paws, the better to grab his prey.

Each one of this Goblin trio, in a daily rite settled many moons ago, is prepared to perform his specialty, that for which he was created, and is stationed there in full view! Is it damnation, or a job ordered long ago by some crazed infernal prince, whom no one can remember anymore but whose orders are conscientiously and stubbornly carried out invariably each night on some unsuspecting client? They respect neither age, nor walk of life, nor status. The passerby may be a child or an old person, a lawyer or a vagabond, thin or obese, who cares! As soon as he is within reach, they all jump on the prey's shoulders, stick to his back, and are carried until the victim falls, exhausted, or succumbs. It is not very smart, and it is also mean, but "they don't know any better," as they say around these parts, and if by chance they do something new, it can only be "worse and more stupid!"

Kludde, Osschart, and Roeschaard can change into wolves, nipping at your heels, or a horse with a welcoming back that will just throw you into the water or a swimmer, so as to drown the fisherman, or even a flea, so as to ruin your sleep!

They are called "Aufkocher spirits," a lame translation of which would be "Lying-deceiving spirits." *The Chronicle of Night Frights* lists other examples: the Belleman, the Dromedaris of Groningen "who from behind the Hoornse Dike jumps on the back of passersby and wraps his trunk around their necks," and the Bozenherel and Boezekappert of Holland. Germans have to endure the terror of the Pojel of Burgwindleim and Beitl, known as Hoimann, after the cry he utters as he throws himself on the unwary traveler. The French countryside resounds with the thunderings of the Lil' Dog, the Mallet Horse, the Galipade, and the Pharamine Beast. Even the faraway Babylonians tried to use prayers to exorcise the Alu demon "who crushes a man like a crashing wall." The Amazonian Indians fear Jurupari, who, to add insult to injury, belches and farts loudly and sings at the top of his lungs in the ears of his carrier.

Kludde (also known as Klurre, Kleure, Klodde, or Klödde) can take the shape of plants or animals. He is often a very thin horse and is the terror of every farmhand. When one thinks he is jumping into the saddle, he is in reality jumping onto Kludde, who throws him off into the nearest bog. While the victim tries to climb out, Kludde can be seen rolling in the grass, laughing out loud.

The name Osschart, Osschaart, Ossaart, or Orsaart is thought to be derived from the suffix *hard* (strong, valiant), and *os,* which derives from *ors* (a word meaning "a mount" or "a horse," but which, according to A. Van Hageland, is now only found in proverbs). As he latches on to the victim's back, he burns

him with his fiery breath and suffocates him with his putrid odor.

It is commonly thought is that he is the only one of the trio who is dead: "In Sjije, an area of Malines," writes Jonas van Leckant, "the believers are still shown Osschaart's coffin and are still convinced that this demon is buried there."

As far as Roeschaard is concerned, *roes* is derived from the Scandinavian *ruske,* which means "to rush, to attack someone," similar to the English. But this word may be a corruption of the Anglo-Saxon word *brcosan* (to frighten) as well as the Dutch *roezen* (to make a racket).

Fear of being caught by Roeschaard was so strong at one time that the inhabitants of Blankenberge and its surroundings would get rebaptized and change their names in order to escape him. It was traditional that before a young man climbed into a boat to begin his career as a fisherman, he was sprinkled with seawater. During the baptism, the following formula was intoned:

I baptize you
and may Roeschaard
the three times ugly one,
turn away,
away, away, away.
Your name is
[the person's name was said].

FOOD:
Small birds caught in flight or flushed out of hedges; raw fish; lost dogs; prowling cats. They also eat out of trash cans.

BEHAVIORS:
They tend to be meaner than they are mischievous. They don't dare cross paths with the Lange-Wapper or any other water demons, who are the terror of the polders on the banks of the Escaut river: the Nikker, the Haleman, the Slokker, and the Krolleman.

ACTIVITIES:
Aside from wearing out their human mounts, they frighten the evening strollers in any way they can. One of their favorite pranks is to replace the contents of a fisherman's nets with large amounts of excrement.

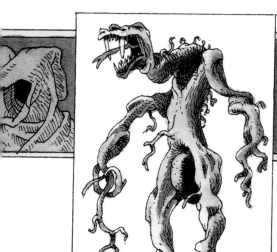

HEIGHT:
About four inches (10 cm).

APPEARANCE:
*Fluid and blackish serpentine shapes.
Two elastic arms. Head of a lizard
with a dog's maw.*

CLOTHING:
*In winter, the Animalitos coat them-
selves with mud and shreds of snake-
skin, which they shed during the
molting season.*

HABITAT:
*Marshes and rocky areas of Spain.
They roll themselves into gluelike
knots and insert themselves in the
cracks of monasteries and ruined castles and in the tombs of abandoned
graveyards.*

FOOD:
*They immerse themselves deep in the
middle of clumps of reeds. Motionless
in the muck, their eyes just on the surface, the Animalitos stalk swimmers
or cattle that come to drink. They slip
under their stomachs and, like fat
leeches, suction the blood of their prey.
In captivity, they clamor for human
flesh—all the better if it's damned.*

BEHAVIOR:
*They are said to be the lost souls of
the "ungodly" dead who were tortured
during the Inquisition. They were
originally Will-o'-the-Wisps without
any light, extinguished frozen sparks,
but they then materialized by snug-
gling up to nocturnal vermin.*

ACTIVITIES:
*Similar to the Genies in lamps and
bottles, homunculi, witching roots,
and tamed demons, they manage to
drive men to damnation by granting
them their most shameful wishes.
At bedtime, Mexican children slip
under their pillows little wooden toys
called Animalitos that prevent them
from having nightmares. People also
lay these toys on top of children's
gravestones.*

Animalitos

In Spain, cunning sorcerers secretly sell pieces of reed, knotted at one end and corked up at the other. Inside these reeds are little creatures who can grant you whatever you desire. But as Vicente the guide explained to Prosper Mérimée: "And you know as well as I do what to feed them, Sir: the flesh of an unbaptized child. And if the master of the reed can't obtain any, he must cut off a piece of his own flesh. He must feed the creature every twenty-four hours. I once knew a Zagal [a kind of footman who holds the reins and runs alongside the mounts as he guides his master. When the animals are at a full gallop, he cannot stop, or else the cart will run over him.]. This Zagal had a sickness that made him short-winded and prevented him from running. He then bought one of these 'vile genie' reeds from a wizard . . . and thus could run in front of the carriage team without even getting out of breath. He could run from Valencia to Murcia in one shot. But now, you can see what it cost him by just looking at him. His bones practically come through his skin, and if his eyes sink any farther into his head, he will soon be able to see through the back of it! The creatures are eating him alive!" And the Animalitos have a ferocious appetite!

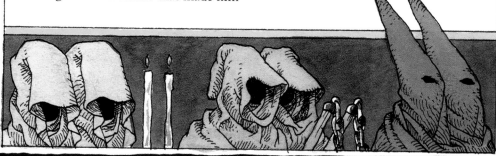

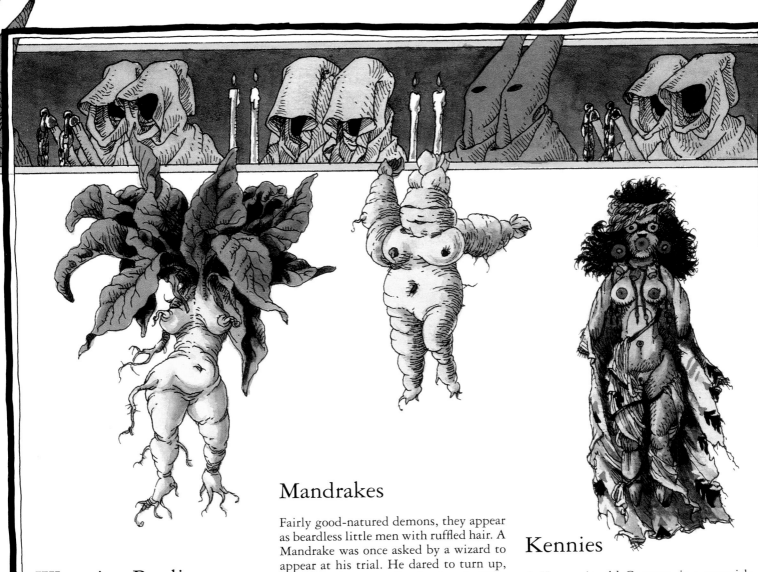

Wermine Pouline

Another kind of half-Goblin, half-plant entity that the dark wizards carried in their pockets and would grow as big and as fat as they fancied. The Indians called them Honowah and would replant them in the snow.

Débruma

Little demons from the Basque country. Smugglers would hire them in exchange for tobacco and earrings in order to guide them through inaccessible paths known only to them. They change into blood-thirsty monsters at certain times of the year.

Erles

An Alf-plant that the wizards cultivated in Germany to spread fear throughout the countryside.

Mandrakes

Fairly good-natured demons, they appear as beardless little men with ruffled hair. A Mandrake was once asked by a wizard to appear at his trial. He dared to turn up, and the judge immediately ripped off his arms and threw them in the fire (*Infernal Dictionary*, Collin de Plancy).

Ginseng

A Chinese Mandrake. She screams as soon as she is uprooted.

Alrunes

The ancient Germans owned Mandrakes called Alrunes. These wooden figurines held man's destiny and fortune in their power. They were nicely dressed and laid with dignity in nice little cases. Every week, they were washed with wine and water, and at each meal they were given both food and drink, lest they start screaming like children suffering from hunger and thirst. They would predict the future, either by a nod of the head or by expressing themselves very intelligibly (*The Secrets of Big and Small Albert*).

Kennies

A Kenne, in old German, is a greenish stone that forms in the eye of a dying stag. The lucky man who plucks it out can survive any venom or poison. If a Kenne is buried while following a certain ritual, after seven years a Kennie will appear: a tiny transparent spirit, who will open any lock for its master in exchange for communion wafers.

Terragon

A Clever spirit born of a sorcerer's manipulations. A test-tube Gnome-like creature, resulting from the crossbreeding of a fool and a Dryad. It was released around 1576 in the secret corridors of the Chateau de Blois. It tried hard to terrorize the French king, Henri III, by resembling a court pet, a sprightly swordsman of the Forty-Five, and then suddenly reverting to its former monstrous shape. It pushed the King to vice and vile deeds before guiding the hand of the conspiring monk, Jacques Clement, to be his assassin.

HEIGHT:
Six feet (1.8 m) tall.

APPEARANCE:
According to Professor Boris F. Porchnev, the Vodianoi, Vodni Moz, Povoduji, Hougga-Ma, the Water Ones, are old naked men, with either black or glaring red, unkempt hair. They are invariably endowed with the same vocal expressions as the Leshii and the Dikonkyi Mujik as well as the Liechatchikas: bursts of laughter, whistling, coaxing whispers. Their faces are blotchy and sticky. Their bodies are obese and spongy. They have prominent canines. They may appear as a pike fish, a carnivorous Gudiu, or a wealthy, red-faced peasant.

CLOTHING:
Naked underwater. When they saunter around as earthly and wealthy landowners, they are recognized by the soaked bottoms of their tunics and the puddles they leave behind or by the pungent sludge odor that permeates them. In Bohemia, they appear on the surface of lakes as a bouquet of red flowers.

HABITAT:
They are usually found in holes dug near windmills, in the reach or under the wheel. They sun themselves occasionally on the locks. They are found in northern and southern Russia, in Yugoslavia, and in Belarus.

Vodianoi

Among the niejit there is a water Tchort called Vodianoi.
—V. Baikov, *The Vurdalack*

"To make a really good shkembe tchorba, you must start with a well-spiced broth; add a red pepper, an onion, garlic, ripe tomatoes, flour, butter, marjoram—for fragrance—parsley, bay leaves, and tripe that was cooked the day before and minced fine—and I add some overripe sheep's cheese. But it is not enough to have the right ingredients. You have to have some skill with the pot!" And on that account, old Tatia fears no one! It is not the first time she has given out her recipe for tripe soup, but there is not a single one of those old country cooks, barely able to make blinis or prepare an ever-red beet borscht, who can come close to her skill! This is why all the men come to her inn to dine, in spite of its remote location. She inherited this gift, instead of a dowry, from her mother, who was from the Balkans, and she also inherited an impressive stack of recipes: sataras, three-meat goulash, sarma, the sis cevaps, the patka sis sele (duck stuffed with sauerkraut). It is because they ate so much of her good food that she has managed to send three husbands to their graves.

From time to time, old Tatia would leave the kitchen and wander through the dining room to see the result of her efforts on the delighted faces of her customers.

"A little drop with us, lil' mama?" offered Akaky Marribov Akakievich, great-grandson of Pavel Ivanovich Vakhramei Licachev, a regular, whose wife Anna Ivanovna Grigorievna did not even know how to boil a turnip.

In spite of her age, she will not be hanging up her apron at any time soon. The serving girls Olga and Foma do not balk at hard work or get offended when

they receive sly pinches on their behind in exchange for a kopeck slipped into the repository of their generous neckline. "Another good evening!" she sighs, satisfied. And yet, something perturbs her: that fat man over there in the shadows who downs one vodka after another. A strange countenance he has. Even though she is more than capable of chasing off the drunks with a soup ladle, this one looks like he is up to no good. This is the first time she has seen him here, and she hopes that it is the last.

Sullen, he doesn't eat and doesn't even answer kind offers to dine. She sends brown-haired Olga over to him three times to check him out. He has a cap pulled down to his eyes that hides his face, and he has downed enough bottles for ten tables without batting an eye.

She has to know for sure: she really can't stand the guy, so she strolls and lingers by the tables, discreetly approaching the stranger to see him up close. "Hmm, he really stinks, this sly dog!" By chance, she drops the ladle that she never lets out of her hand—and as she bends down to pick it up, she has just enough time to glance under the chair: "By Saint Nicholas and all the holy saints!" It is what she feared all along. The left corner of his shirt is soaking wet and a large puddle is forming between the monster's feet.

"Vodianoi!" she screams, pointing an accusing finger at the "aquatic Mujik" who is already overturning the table. He lifts it up at arm's length and throws it on the more intrepid who have come running to tackle him. They fall in a clump. With a roar, he throws off his heavy coat to reveal an obese body, spongy and blotchy; in two strides he reaches the door that he breaks down with one shove and

disappears into the night toward the nearest river. A roar of laughter, followed by a noisy splash, indicates that he is now at home.

The Rusalki: A good number of legends describe the Rusalki as ravishing Water Nymphs who are fair-haired and great consumers of wandering monks and saintly hermits.

The Rusalka "roussyi" is dirty blond. The Rusalka "ryjiy" has glaring red hair. The brown-haired Rusalki are Vodianikhas, the female companions of the Vodianoi—their playmates and bedmates as well. They are not just aquatic; they live in fields, in trees, and in rye and flax fields of the Toula and Orel regions. These Babas (wild women), with their luxuriant hair, are very flirtatious, and if offended, they can strangle the young men who don't respond to their advances with their very long breasts.

FOOD:
At the beginning of spring, when the whole countryside is still covered in snow, the village people buy a horse, fatten it up, braid its mane, and beribbon it after having covered its head with honey. On a certain Sunday, the "gift" is led to the river, and its legs are hobbled. Two millstones are tied around its neck, and it is pushed—at exactly midnight—through a hole in the ice beneath which the Vodianoi await. This offering is supposed to preserve the people from the Vodianoi's huge appetite for raw flesh. They are unfortunately always hungry and swallow anything that dives in and swims within its range, even the corpses of drowned people, whose souls they collect and deposit in a string of jars. It is customary to regularly offer them a black pig and the first beehive of the year in order to calm their spring madness and prevent the floods they cause just for fun.

BEHAVIOR:
The merest feminine presence splashing around in the water brings them running—sometimes from far away: their sense of smell is very keen. They propose to each bathing woman to become their Vodianikha or else be devoured on the spot.

Humans must not try to save someone who is drowning: that would offend the Vodianoi who will come sooner or later to seek vengeance.

ACTIVITIES:
The Vodianoi fish for girls and children with a long stick, adorned with pretty ribbons, that they shake under their noses: when they want to catch them, the Vodianoi clobber them and drag them down to the bottom. They give dropsy to any fisherman who would disturb their rest.

THOSE OF THE SEA AND COAST

Athi of the long beard,
Athi in the deep sea.

—Zacharius Topelius

How very little we know about the ocean depths! During the last century, times have certainly changed, and many an apparatus has penetrated the brine to get a closer look at the uncharted depths. Oceanographic technology has begun to shed some light along the ocean floor. Satellites plowing through the firmament of the stars, aided by hardworking surveyors, are busy mapping the Great Sea Terrebrorum, domain of the aquatic gods. But what sonar, refined though it may be, can penetrate the soul of the Vast Vertigo? Who, other than Neptune or Athi, can trace the borders of the undulating waves and calculate to the last drop where the Pacific Ocean begins and the China Sea ends?

Yes indeed, we know very little beyond what mythology has deigned to reveal to us in tales such as the *Chronicles of the Foam*, "Sinbad the Sailor," and "Sadko the Traveler" and those told by old dying Tritons who, with failing eyes, became stranded onshore.

347

HEIGHT:

A few inches (6 or 8 cm), no larger than the Kabouters.

APPEARANCE:

The Klabouters, Klaboutermanneken, or Klabbers are more robust than the Kabouters. Their skin is copper toned, and their blue eyes are quick and piercing. They wear no beards, but their long hair is wrapped in tarred leather on the nape of their necks, where their supernatural strength resides. Their hands are very large, and their feet are palm-shaped.

CLOTHING:

They wear oilskin hats, warrior's shirts, red pea coats, baggy pants, and, when they go ashore, short jackets with clay pipes inserted in the button-hole. They always have large knives hanging from their belts as well as boatswain's whistles. They wear ear-rings and have many tattoos.

HABITAT:

They left their native Flanders early in life to roam through Holland and northern Germany as far east as Leipzig. They were often seen roaming about in the large harbors of Ostend, Antwerp, Amsterdam, and Copen-hagen before putting out to sail the seven seas. They live in barrels, or more often in lighthouses, where they can enjoy the vast panorama.

FOOD:

Everything that is normally eaten on board ship, but they really adore waffles, Dutch pastries, and hard can-dies (the real ones, on a string!).

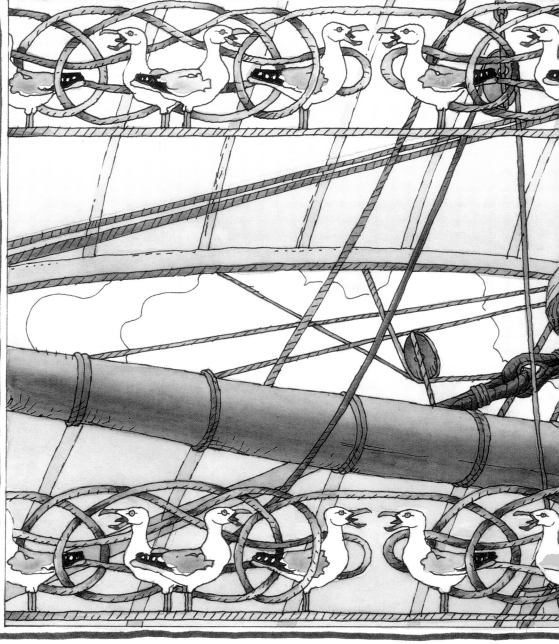

Klabouters

Do you see the land, little Klabouter? And what is it?

—Jan Timmermans,
The Beggar of the Sea

Klabouters are the sea brothers of the Kabouters. When they arose out of the primordial silt, one possessed genes more suited for life on the soil, while the other was immersed in water even then. Some mali-cious gossips assert that by dint of weak flesh, overindulgence in festivities, and a soft life, the Kabouters have become somewhat frivolous and lazy and it would take three Kabouters to do the work of a single Klabouter. That is both inaccurate and unjustified.

The Kabouters have left significant traces of their labors, for example, the Saint Gertrude Tower of Louvain and the many jagged gables found in Ghent, Bruges, and Antwerp, and they should not be insulted in that way. They are espe-cially reproached for having become stale and for no longer inspiring dreams, in contrast to the Klabouters, the real thun-derbolts of the seas.

The Klabouters felt themselves imme-diately attracted to the liquid element. While their land brothers weeded and spaded, as happy as larks, they were inhal-ing the free and open spaces, fishing and exploring the rivers, canals, and streams while journeying up the Escaut, the Elbe,

They have a girl in every harbor, but they also keep a kleine Husse Verloof *(a young fiancée) at home whom they promise to marry whenever they return. Although Klabouters and Kabouters are not enemies, one finds in them some of the same character traits found in the two heroes of Robert Louis Stevenson's* Master of Ballantrae. *One is as gregarious, wise, and economical as the other is adventurous, daring, and wasteful.*

ACTIVITIES:

We have seen on many occasions how the sailor, rising to meet the challenge of the elements and having good reason to do so, never fails to respect the laws of the sea: never eat rabbit nor even pronounce its name, nor take on board a woman or a black cat, avoid crossing a clergyman before embarking, never damage a Bible nor listen to the Sirens, have the ship exorcised regularly for fear that a curse may have become attached. And thus it was with great relief and appreciation that the sailors welcomed on board the "protective spirits" in flesh and blood! But Klabouters are not just good-luck charms. Their eagle eyes make them vigilant lookouts and incomparable gunners, while their liveliness and hardiness render them exceptional swordsmen.

and the Oder. While Kabouters sat on milk stools or dropped in to taverns to discuss the latest dairy prices, the Klabouters sailed into harbors and tied up at docks, all the while yearning for sea voyages with vibrantly colored flags hoisted and flapping in the breeze on board the *Zwarre Haai*, *The Wolf of the Seas*, *The Whale Who Smokes*, and the *Zeemeerminne* as they sailed away to adventure! While seated on a bollard, they would contemplate the outbound ships and the seagulls winging out to sea. They would wander through the alleys steeped in the odor of nets filled with drying fish and would linger at the display windows of the *schipwinkel* (maritime supply stores), spellbound by the bric-a-brac of copper-plated telescopes, sextants, and compasses, and the blue steel of the cutlasses, intoxicated by the incense

and the spices. When evening came they would settle themselves in a *tafelhorn* or a smoky *kabedoloesje* (gambling den) full of *zeekappers* (buccaneers), drinking dog-nose, *dobbel knollaert*, *kuyt*, or *bruinber*, while toasting the islands, the Marie-Clapettes, and the devil sacks.

"Verdekke and Potverdekke!" They would be buccaneers! Climbing that first step of the gangway, they made up their minds for good! Although they never quite became the gentlemen of fortune they had imagined, they nevertheless became the mascot and the good-luck charm for the ships' crews.

The ever-superstitious sailors never refused a virtuous spirit on board to protect them from the evil eye, from the Saint Elmo's fire, from shipwrecks, from tobacco ailments, or from Trafalgar!

HEIGHT:

From nine inches (22 cm) to 220 yards (200 m).

APPEARANCE:

A small, slimy ball, barbed with prickles and sharp pincers, sliding on fibers equipped with plungers. Two large red eyes and a sort of sucking mouth. Sometimes a huge monster with paws and a tail, armed with claws and an excessively large tongue. David Jones can also appear on land in the guise of an old sailor. He can be recognized in this form because of his soft and spongy green hands.

HABITAT:

He lives along the Côtes-du-Nord and the English Channel in drifts of plaited algae hidden under heaps of floating kelp.

FOOD:

Gobbles up small fish when they pass within his grasp. Four times a year, when the season changes, he devours an entire ship's crew.

BEHAVIOR:

He murders water creatures in cold blood and belongs to the Dismal Bestiary of the Damned. He reproduces quickly, with a life span of six years. He is legion and exists as a tribe of minute entities.

ACTIVITIES:

Those who have tried to learn more about David Jones have never returned. Even the writer William Hope Hodgson, the preeminent specialist in marine horrors, only lured him out with the utmost caution.

David (Davy) Jones

Those intrepid ones who would dare to take to the sea without being first reconciled with the gods and the goddesses will, without a shadow of a doubt, find death beneath the waves.

—Albert Van Hageland

A schooner skims the foamy seas, silvery in the moonlight. The helmsman dozes, gently rocked by the rolling waves, a small pipe between his teeth. Suddenly, a slight rustling scrapes the hull, causing him to jump up, staring into the eddies of the night. Some flaccid being encircles the hull. A feeble shuddering is felt beneath the prow, and the port light reveals a long, shimmering, rustling stream of algae.

Look out, dead ahead! Too late! The kelp trap has snared its prey, and the thousand sneering laughs of David Jones proclaim his triumphal boarding.

David Jones is the scourge of the ocean, well known to English sailors and those familiar with the waters of the North. He is by far the worst of the monsters that wander the seven seas. He approaches concealed in viscous folds of tentacles of plant mass, and without warning, "they" become a whole troop of teeming and yelping, slightly luminous Dwarfs. Thousands of small famished creatures similar to gelatinous sea urchins stack themselves to assemble a repugnant swarm. And thus it is that the mass rises up, transforming itself into a Giant besieging the bridge of the ship. Its clawed arms rise from the serpentine trunk, sweeping away the mast and ripping out the sails and shrouds. Four rows of teeth snap down on the chocks and pull out the bulkheads. Jaws grind and chew; the brawny tongue crawls through the steerage, moves through the catwalks, invades the storeroom, and carries away the unhappy seaman, deckhands, helmsmen, chicken handler, carpenters, pilot—in fact, the entire crew, from the cabin boys to the captain.

Satiated and satisfied, David Jones crushes the wreckage into the waves with a stroke of his tail and, once again, breaks up into a thousand small creatures. When all is consumed and the sea is rolling quietly, a placid bank of algae travels towards the horizon, emitting from time to time a discreet gluttonous belch.

Boschs

HEIGHT:
Fifteen inches (37 cm).

APPEARANCE:
Large, soft heads, coifed with white algae. Faded, deep, sad eyes. Hooked and flabby noses. Large drooping mouths. No body, but short tentacle-like paws and a long arm ending in a powerful hand.

CLOTHING:
Wrap themselves in remnants from old sails and flags.

HABITAT:
The forward part of the ship, most often in the rigging locker.

FOOD:
They eat rats and the tallow smeared on the lines.

BEHAVIOR:
Withdrawn, with a weak and melancholy nature, they acquire their strength from the fear that they incite. They are themselves the first victims of their own destructive powers, which undermine and poison their sad existence. They can endure this hellish life for seven years. However, if by chance a Bosch discovers the thief who caused him to be born and kills him, he then slips happily into the waters and becomes a luminous shellfish.

ACTIVITIES:
When they aren't busy provoking disasters, they cling to the end of the jib singing such slow and melancholy chants that even the Sirens cry. There may even be a domestic Bosch born from the treason of love and a broken heart. Insidious and tenacious, he would be that much more difficult to drive out, very likely pushing his abandoned lover to suicide.

For the sailor knows of nothing worse than having a Bosch on board . . .
—Ship's log of the *Corentin*,
Captain Louis Marie Fa—[illegible]

On the coasts of the French Finistère region, a theft committed on board a ship brings misfortune to the victim, not to the thief, who leaves behind his fatal influence as "the personification of the evil eye." These Boschs, troublesome parasites of ships and fermenters of misfortune, bring by their very presence the worst disasters, tempests, scurvy, accidents, bad fishing, pirates, fires, mutiny, windless seas, drownings, shipwrecks, and every other misery of the salty sea!

They are not really malicious, but if someone attempts to kill one, he becomes enraged at being threatened and strangles whoever dares to approach him.

As soon as one appears on the bridge, misfortune follows: a deckhand falls over the bulwark, a cannon comes loose from its moorings, the rudder breaks, the spanker rips, or the sea engulfs the ship!

Several methods are known to dislodge one, the simplest being to move some object to another vessel. The Bosch immediately rushes on board the "contaminated" ship. Fortunately, many honest captains reject this type of extreme practice. The second consists of filling the entire hull from stem to stern with smoke from wet straw. But beware! A Bosch can shrink himself small enough to hide in a thimble, so you have to be very careful and make sure that the smoke penetrates every crevice. The most efficient means to exorcise one is the technique called "thrashing." Once the crew is asleep, the captain lashes a large bundle of straw to the foot of the foresail mast, which he then sets on fire, crying out, "Devil on board!" The sailors, springing out of their hammocks and frightened by the infernal flames, grab bars, toggles, oars, and swabs and begin to beat everything at random on all sides. Overcome by smoke, spitting, coughing, badly beaten, burned, and threatened from all sides, the Bosch, terrified and bleeding, relinquishes his territory and throws himself into the sea.

Finally, to ensure that, once repulsed, he doesn't come back on board, briny and half-rotted nets should be spread out along both sides of the hull.

Fions, Jetins, Fois, and Folgoats

HEIGHT:
Fions, Fois, and Folgoats are tiny. Jetins are about six inches (15 cm) tall.

APPEARANCE:
It is said of the Fions and the Fois that "they were so small that their swords were hardly longer than the pins of a corsage." Lively, gracious, and dark-skinned, they are nicknamed "The Men Born {Black}." Hidden under their hair are two extra eyes. Slender, short, and hirsute, they have beards and long hair.

CLOTHING:
Under long brown coats, they sport elegant livery in sparkling colors, emblazoned with their master's coat of arms. They carry spears and swords. The Jetins dress somewhat more simply, donning fur caps and silver-colored wooden shoes. The Folgoats dress all in gray.

HABITAT:
The coast of Brittany, the Island of Baix. Noteworthy are the Fion abodes in Pleurtuit and on the banks of the Rance Maritime region. The Jetins first inhabited the Bec-Dupuy cave near Sulniac, but after the departure of the Fairies, the Fions, Fois, Folgoats, and Jetins all abandoned the cities for a more primitive life in setbacks and rock caves. Some Fions took up residence in Northern Ireland, where, having become somewhat mean-spirited, they entertain themselves by heckling passersby.

The Irish Fion is fearsome!

—Sotai's joke

"Back in the days when Fairies appeared often on the earth, a good woman was awakened in the middle of the night by a tiny dwarf wrapped in a large coat. When the woman turned on the light, the dwarf moved towards her, explaining that she was needed to care for a sick child. The woman followed the dwarf, but soon noticed that they were headed toward the Bay of Vozon, which surprised her, given that there was nothing along that coast but a long uninhabited cliff. She suggested more than once that they must have taken a wrong turn, but the dwarf insisted that they were going the right way. After crossing the sands, they arrived at the rocks near the Hournet tower. As night began to fall, the dwarf took the woman's hand and led her over the rocks. They entered a cave so black that she could not see even one step ahead. After they had walked together for quite some time through this darkness, the dwarf asked the woman if she saw something in front of them. She never revealed what she had seen, but the next day she was holding a tender little baby in her arms. It was a fairy baby, whom she kept and raised as her own until he was fifteen years old, at which point he was receiving lessons from the pastor. One night while returning home, the pastor heard a voice calling out his name, 'John of Marescq! Tell Colin the Younger that Colin the Elder is dead!' When the lad learned what the pastor had heard, he told him, 'Master, I must bid you now farewell.' He then went to see his adoptive mother and told her in tears, 'I must go far, far from here, and never again will I see you, my earthly mother. Dearest, bless me as I part.' Then he disappeared so quickly that she had not even the time to reply, and she never saw him again."

Anecdotes such as this one told by Louisa Lane Clarke were often heard back when the Fairies and Féetauds lived all along the beaches and shores. It was not at all uncommon for a fisherman in his boat to spot a sea chariot drawn by blindingly white horses carrying one of these Fairies through the salty seawater.

"Long ago," goes another story, "one observed in the Rance region of France gracious creatures dressed in the colors of the rainbow, dancing about the waves. The strong current transported them towards the creeks, where soon even more of them appeared, following a woman even more beautiful than themselves. This woman, aboard a boat made from the shell of a nautilus from the southern seas and pulled by two crawfish, was their queen, and her companions, the Fairies, ruled the waters. She ordered the winds to blow less strongly and to throw back to the Rance shore the human corpses that had been swallowed up in the storm by the sea."

Through thick and thin, Fairies and men lived side by side, exchanging services, loving and hating, killing and forgetting one another. In the midst of all this, the powerful Fairies of noble blood kept their distance, leaving their lackeys and servants to act as go-betweens. The Folgoats were the messengers; the Fois served as squires for first the elder and then the younger Prince Colin of the Dunes. The Fions comprised the domestic staff, while the Jetins, ever capricious and indomitable, invariably refused to pay allegiance to the rulers of the sea, agreeing to help them only when they pleased. When most of the noble Fairy families left the shores of Brittany for England, the Jetins blocked the way by demolishing the path leading to their former palace.

FOOD:
Simple but savory food. In former times, they sold cookies and macaroons at the summits of the dunes.

BEHAVIOR:
Accustomed to following orders, the Fions have been of service to human beings. They rarely become angry and often play with the children, which bothers the mothers since they cannot tell them apart from the Jetins, who are known to be child-snatchers. The Jetins are instinctively Changelings; the Fions are hermaphrodites.

ACTIVITIES:
When they had finished their work with the Fairies, the Fions would take their small black cows out to pasture.

The Jetins, as strong as Giants, rip huge rocks out of the coast and hurl them in the air, which is why one sometimes sees large rocks falling from the sky onto fields and farmlands. This strange habit is what earned them the name "Jetins" (from the French jeter, *meaning "to throw").*

King of the Auxcriniers

Arok tremen Kraou Alberz
Grel ho kiniad govde kovez.

"Only an ignoramus could not know that the greatest danger in the waters of the English Channel is the King of the Auxcriniers. There is no more formidable sea dweller—anyone who sights this creature ends up shipwrecked. As a dwarf, he is small; as a King, he is deaf. He knows the names of all those who have perished in the sea, and where they are now. He knows the ocean cemetery very well indeed. The base of this King's head is wide, while the top is quite narrow. His body is stocky with a sticky and deformed belly, and his cranium is covered with nodules. His legs are short, while his arms are long; for feet he has fins, and for hands he has claws. This king, with a large green face, has claws that are webbed, and fins with nails. Imagine the ghost of a fish with the face of a man. The only ways to put an end to him are through exorcism or by reeling him in on the end of a line. But he ominously stands by; nothing is less reassuring than to catch sight of him. The King of the Auxcriniers, the gloomy strolling player of the storm, appears only in turbulent seas. One sees his form emerge in the fog, in the flurry, in the rain. He stands up straight, as tall as the rolling waves that crash under the pressure of the wind, curling like wood shavings peeled off by the carpenter's plane. He keeps himself out of the foam, and when ships in distress arise on the horizon, his ashen face, hidden in the shadows, lights up with a madman's frightening smile, as he begins to dance."

Victor Hugo made this ugly acquaintance and thus explains why he was obliged to retreat from the enchanting Channel Islands. Even if Sir Edgar MacCulloch, the bailiff and impassioned researcher of Guernsey folklore, hardly mentions the existence of the Auxcriniers, even if Louisa Lane Clark (author of *Folklore of Guernsey and Sark*, 1890) seems to have forgotten them as well, no one can dispute the testimony of this great spirit and visionary poet, creator of Quasimodo, Han d'Islande, and the moving "man who laughs."

Detailed investigations conducted by

HEIGHT:
> *Eight to ten inches (20 to 25 cm).*

APPEARANCE:
> *Small but hearty and well-proportioned. Dark-skinned with harsh facial features. Long, pointy noses and eyes of steel. Thick, iron-gray hair. They are neither handsome nor ugly and give the impression of being warriors, with a coldness characteristic of Fairies. The children produced by the "Comprachicos," the Auxcriniers, disgusted them so intensely that they tossed them into the sea. Through paddling about from such an early age, the Auxcriniers thus learned to walk on water in the manner of Orion, Jesus, and the Finnish god Vainaimoinen. Today they are nebulous and spindly creatures, similar to the Alleurs, living in difficult conditions.*

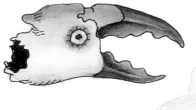

R. Claymorius have revealed that the Auxcriniers were the products of regrettable relations between the Arragousets, Sarregousets, and Sarregousetts and the "Comprachicos" or "small buyers," who according to Hugo were involved in the child-trafficking racket. What did they make of these children? Monsters. Why monsters? For amusement. The people need to laugh, as do kings. Children are sometimes fated to serve as the playthings of men, which is why this business exists. In order to produce such a toy, the child must be seized while quite young—a dwarf must obviously be made from something very small. A child standing tall is not funny; a hunchback is. From these principles emerges an art, along with its artisans. Imagine the reverse of orthopedics: one begins with a face and produces a muffle; one stunts the growth and molds the form. One crushes the cartilage while cratering the face. From two eyes a cyclops is created.

A load of these laughable creatures, departing from the impoverished island of Ireland and destined for Rome, where they were to amuse the Pope and his prelates, instead smashed into the coast of Jersey and Guernsey. The Arragousets gathered up these handmade Goblins. Thus were the Auxcriniers and their King born of happenstance. These children were so pathetic and hideous that the good island people were ashamed by their sight and preferred to ignore them. It took Victor Hugo, lover of "monstrous beauty," to bring them to light.

Arragousets

According to tradition, the Arragousets used to hold sway over a cave on the west coast of the island, called the Fairy Cavern, and it is from this cavern that they one day emerged. A man named Jean Letocq rose earlier than normal that morning to return to his farm. On the way he saw an immense number of Little People armed with all kinds of weapons coming out of the Fairy Cavern. Despite resistance from the island folk, they quickly spread throughout the area, killing the men and taking possession of their wives and homes. Only two of the inhabitants escaped this massacre: a man and a young boy from the Saint Andrew Monastery who had managed to hide themselves inside an oven. Over several years, the invaders from the Fairy race lived peacefully with the women. They made good fathers and had many sons and daughters. It is said that the small size but high intelligence of some families originates from this strange union.

However, the day came when, for some reason that has never been guessed but that is believed to have been an order from the king of the Fairies, the Arragousets had to leave the wives and the homes to which they had become attached. So one night, they all disappeared—or, more accurately, they became invisible. At night, they continue to visit their former homes to complete tasks that have been left unfinished. Then, they retreat into their hideaways on the coast, there where the Auxcriniers were born, only to return later in the form of small men who somersault in the clouds.

CLOTHING:
They have been sighted wearing coats of armor, short suits of mail, and iron helmets in the shape of shells, armed with lances and swords. Later, despite their "domestication" and their lives in homes, they never entirely abandoned their military dress, but leather slippers did replace their iron boots.

HABITAT:
Only found in the Channel Islands. Nothing is known about the inside of their current homes: they spit in the face of anybody who dares approach them, blinding them.

FOOD:
Originally, they ate raw fish and meats, but they later gave these up for local gourmet specialties.

BEHAVIOR:
Initially very overpowering and fearsome, even bloodthirsty, but contact with women has made them more domesticated and friendly.

The last Arragousets surviving on the island act as a sort of barometer. When they appear, a storm or some other kind of death of misfortune is brewing. "Ask them what path to take. They are good people. They are civil people. Friends of the earth." Maybe the old women who say this still carry within themselves a little bit of Arragouset.

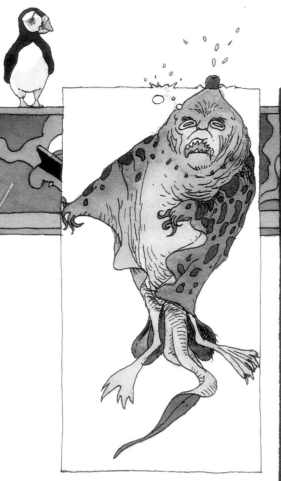

Tud-Gommon and the Wicked Spirits of the Seacoast

There are no worse starving persons
Than those in saltwater.

Danger lurks along the seacoast and shoreline in myriad forms well before the sailor reaches the open sea or floats into Leviathan's toothy mug. Waters are rough around the rocks of Fèlouére on France's north coast even in good weather. A ship loaded with iron oxide once ran aground nearby and boats that came too close, irresistibly drawn to its cargo, were also lost: this was the first shipwreck! And if a ship is lucky enough to escape the first snare, a second is always in wait close by. The whirlpool at the Fauconnière rocks, which terrified sailors avoid, was formed when a Fairy flung herself into the waves after a fisherman cast aside the love potion she had given him. Vindictive ever since, she lures ships into her bottomless abyss: the second snare!

Elsewhere, the tip of the diamond that is Brittany draws prows as if magnetized and fastens them onto rows of black reefs. On the coast near Tréguier, sandbars and shellfish may suddenly form a ring that rises up out of the water, trapping boats in its center; hordes of Cornandonets then scrabble aboard, devouring entire crews. At other times vessels bog down in algae banks that swarm with little cannibalistic beings, are overtaken by a bloody flotilla of Kolokinto pirates, or are guided onto the reefs at night by the deceptive lanterns of the Potret-ar-c'hill-krok, as other shipwrecking Gnomes play games: the umpteenth snare. The white sand of the beaches is said to come from the bones of men who perished at sea; in Brittany, they maintain, a storm isn't over till cadavers and foul bodies have washed up on shore.

With its slashes, tears, and splendors, the jagged coastline tells epic tales. Among the towers and slits of its cliffs, we can discover the vestiges of former Fairy palaces, crevasses created by dragon claws, and rock slides caused by combat between Dwarfs and Giants.

HEIGHT:
> *Ranging from the size of plankton to that of the sea monster Kraken.*

APPEARANCE:
> *Flat heads with slit eyes and suction-cup mouths, with flabby flanks, spindly limbs, and whiplike tails. Their flaccid and scaly skin is greenish-black—off-white on the belly.*
>
> *Tud-Gommon are protean, able to become smaller or larger, taking on the proportions of whales or the lizard-like mosasaurs; they can also simply fool everyone by appearing in the guise of mild-mannered fish. Some of these "little men of the sea," who travel on or under water, have nostrils and gills (the Treo Falls, Dud-vors, Bolbiguan-dets, Kolokinto, Red Dwarfs, Diavwlo dû, and Cornandonets).*

CLOTHING:
> *They wear sea grasses, with seaweed hoods and algae caps.*

The rocks, anthropomorphized, become monks, Fairies, Dwarfs, Giants, and sailors turned to stone. As for the golden dunes at Portsall, they say that Fairies who committed murder were condemned to count the grains of sand in the sea, until they reached a number beyond comprehension. The hillocks between Portsall and Lampaul are remnants of the piles that each Fairy counted.

And there are columns and arches emerging from the sand of the mudflats like the ruins of swallowed-up cities, watched over by hunchbacked sentinels. These tiny neighboring islands harbor so many demons, monsters, and tormented souls that birds don't even dare to land there!

When a ship's crew finally succeeds—through skill, prayer, and incantation—in escaping the seacoast's deathly lure and demonic pitfalls, they still have to confront their obsessive fears on the high seas, where the Beasts of Bizeux, Décollé, and Ebihens were among the first to accost them.

The fisherman who cast a last backward glance at the fast-blurring land would notice pale and tapering bodies swimming behind his ship.

"They're following us!" he would say, referring to Groac'h vors, Dud-vors, and the Bolbiguandets, creatures from Breton folklore who, refusing to let loose their prey, surrounded the stern like a pack of wild dogs: the vultures of the sea. Beyond them waited huge octopi, their long tentacles primed for passing ships that headed for the Triagoz archipelago.

In the past, any boat that would dare to go too close to them would be fatally lost unless it threw into the sea a wooden clog belonging to a crew member, a cockleshell, or a lock of hair from the youngest sailor, while reciting:

Botez, cogeu, cogeu vihan,
Et da gavout an erovan,
Et da vavout ar potru,
Kerset dezan ma blew dû.
[Clog, shell, little shell, / Go find the devil! / Go find the red man; / Take my dark hair to him.]

. . . because it was better to collaborate than to fall into the webbed claws of the wicked spirits of the seacoast.

HABITAT:
Only the Tud-Gommon dwell in the depths, where they bury themselves in the sand; other spirits haunt the coasts but don't venture too far for fear of sharks, orcas, octopi, and the fauna of the high seas.

FOOD:
They devour sailors and the flesh of the drowned.

BEHAVIOR:
Nasty and sneaky. They reside in groups, sometimes serving as guard dogs for the Fairies, Sirens, Tritons, Morgans, and gods of the waves.

ACTIVITIES:
They are able to provoke storms and fog. The Cornandonets dance merrily upon the waves in order to amuse ships' crews while they unknowingly drift treacherously close to danger. The demiurge Poisson Nicole keeps very busy, pulling up ships' anchors and cutting mooring lines. While most spirits attack at night, the Kolokinto pirates are not afraid to confront boats in broad daylight, traveling on their little skiffs made of hollow gourds and tar. The most often-used ruse of the Cornandonets is to change their appearance into that of schools of fish, let themselves be caught, and, once on board a ship, overcome the crew. They are the terror of smugglers.

Hooks

Wherever there's shadow, there's Hook.
—James Barrie, *Peter Pan*

March 17, 1580: The caravel *Santa Josefa* disappears.

July 20, 1668: A galley and all its crew are reported missing.

May 29, 1744: The principal vessel of Commodore Anson Philips sails into a patch of fog and never emerges.

November 6, 1758: The corsair *La Trinité* takes its turn, vanishing on the sea.

August 28, 1781: The frigate *Serapis* disappears in the open water of Chesapeake Bay.

December 14, 1840: Disappearance of a whaling ship from Nantucket.

May 27, 1855: The captain of the clipper ship *Sorcière des Mers* notes in his log "while drifting from island to island, we came upon a deserted clipper, mysteriously abandoned by its whole crew. A tea kettle was whistling on the stove, still hot."

Closer to home, on July 28, 1909: the *Waratah*, a two-propeller liner capable of carrying more than 9,000 nautical tons, disappears inexplicably while en route from Australia to Great Britain by way of Durban.

March 16, 1920: The *Asiatic Prince*, a cargo ship with a 7,000 nautical ton capacity, leaves Los Angeles bound for Yokohama and vanishes. A vessel at sea near Honolulu picks up a distress signal, undecipherable except for the word "pirate."

In maritime history, the list of ships that have disappeared mysteriously is too long to enumerate. All research to recover crews or vessels that were literally "erased" from the ocean's surface in calm weather has been in vain. No wreckage has been found: only ghost ships, drifting with no one on board. There is only one explanation: Hooks.

Hooks are not souls of those lost at sea, specters of pirates killed in combat, or the drowned who sometimes haunt ships' bridges. Instead, they personify the accursed souls of buccaneers who were executed on board ship. The Hook is the materialization of the buccaneer's last breath of agony, his cry of revolt as he was flogged, made to walk the plank, or was keelhauled in the "torture of the hold."

A tiny embryo will emerge from the cadaver thrown into the seawater and, over the next year, feed on plankton and swim in still waters. When it reaches full size, it draws itself up and boards the first vessel it encounters.

Once on board a ship, the Hook makes its way to the hold under the first bridge. Then as soon as night falls, it emerges from hiding to engage in invisible and irreversible acts of sabotage.

Alone, Hooks don't attack men, but if their numbers grow during the course of a ship's travels, expeditions, and errands, they can become very dangerous.

Led by their eldest, bands of Hooks can silently take over the bridge each night to continue the slow but inexorable destruction of the craft: cutting cables and the topsail line, damaging the hull, or tampering with the rudder. The hardtack container is soaked; foodstuffs are spoiled; dead rats are thrown into water barrels. The strongest Hooks, surging unexpectedly, can throw the watch overboard. They sow terror, sickness, and death throughout the ship—until there comes the inevitable mutiny. As the vessel is abandoned (for rowboats that are spitefully scuttled), any mutineers remaining on board are quickly seized and thrown to the sharks.

The conquered boat is either set adrift or reduced to ashes using its own stored munitions. The Hooks, floating away by raft, are already searching for new prey that they can overcome under the cover of darkness.

HEIGHT:
Sixteen to twenty inches (40 to 50 cm).

APPEARANCE:
Large cone-shaped head with a face contorted in a grimace like that of a tortured person at the moment of death. White eyes. Outer skins the color of algae. Broad-backed and strong. Enormous crablike claws are located where hands or feet would be, or they may extend from the shoulders or even from one side of the skull.

CLOTHING:
Sailor's uniforms, smeared with tar in order to blend into the night.

HABITAT:
They are found on oceans the world over, hiding in ships' holds and storerooms, except for those protected by seagoing Elves and spirits like the Goguelins or Klabouters.

FOOD:
They have no need to eat or drink and do so only out of revenge. If by chance you surprise one getting drunk on rum, it's a "memory reflex" in response to the spirit that drives him.

BEHAVIOR:
Hooks live communally. They can't be exterminated but can be chased away by a complicated and exhausting incantation that (in days gone by) was handed down by old bosuns who were born on a Friday.
In the sixteenth century, a handful of wandering Hooks reached Brittany and, by kidnapping the mates of the lower class living along the shore, established the carnivorous race of the Tan Noz.

ACTIVITIES:
The Hooks are not ready to give up their sinister takeovers, as proved by the steady disappearance of even the most modern and sophisticated ships.

HEIGHT:
About thirty-one inches (80 cm).

APPEARANCE:
Solid, dark-skinned, scarred, bestial. Threatening hands reminiscent of their ancestors' crab pincers. Their female companions, although just as ferocious, were also often pretty.

CLOTHING:
Tricorn hats. Colorful scarves. Sailor's pants. Pea coats and slickers, jackets tailored from the clothes of their victims. They loved silks and lace and draped themselves with loads of jewelry, earrings, necklaces, and shells.

HABITAT:
Used to haunt the Breton coast.

FOOD:
Man-eaters. They used to smoke the flesh of murdered sailors, then dry it by laying it over piles of gold and precious stones.

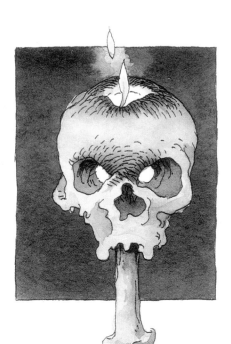

Tan Noz

As soon as night fell, the Tan Noz came out of their fortress carved in the cliff; they slipped and slid out of holes, crevices, and cracks, and they spread along the shimmering rocks. They scanned the horizon with a sharp eye, looking for sail. If there was no storm or wind, they then went out into the waves and released the swirls of old Norse winds that had been locked up in leather bags. Or else they provoked and angered the tempest spirits by insulting them, their tricorn hats pointed toward the skies. They also whipped up the surface of the water where the Sirens live. If the moon was too full and its beams lit up the landscape as if it were plain day, they masked it, gathering black clouds in front of it by blowing into the conch shells of sorcerers. Thick masses of smoke, which they conjured up from flameless fires of algae, spread along the shore, compensating amply for the absence of fog.

Once the coast and its surroundings had been booby-trapped and the lighthouse fires extinguished, the Tan Noz could turn on their fake lights. Lanterns and lamps shone peacefully, imitating a village with lighted windows. Torches hanging from the horns of cows acted as reassuring beacons. Ships, blinded by the fog, shaken by the waves, and lost in the darkness, were guided in all confidence by the redeeming glow on the coast, and then all hell broke loose!

The trumpeting Tan Noz responded to

BEHAVIOR:
*Chased away from a ship they were
haunting, the Hooks washed up first
at Kelaorou and quickly conquered the
coast, using all their ferocity against
the Little People of the shores, massacring whole families, and carrying
off the Morgans, Lusines, and Mermaids with whom they procreated to
create the Tan Noz, worthy sons of
their fathers!*

ACTIVITIES:
*Attracted ships, only to dash them on
the rocks in order to pillage them.*

the distress signal and brought the fragile prow about towards the rock spurs. A thousand little joyous laughs greeted the cracking of the hull onto the rocks. The Goblins were once again victorious, and they certainly loved a good shipwreck!

A whistle-blow from the Goblin leader gave the order for the ship to be pillaged and the survivors to be massacred. Finally, two flashes of a lantern reassembled the murderous spirits. Before the wailing widows who had guessed at the tragedy could arrive, preceded by a few policemen, everything was finished!

Having returned with great stealth to their invisible hideaway in the bottom of the cliffs, the Tan Noz divided up the spoils, snickered, wasted a few barrels of rum, and feasted on their catch to the tune of accordions, wailing through the cracks of the coast all the way to the deserted moor and filling the population with terror.

They were vultures of the shore, and these pirate Goblins bloodied the Breton coasts until the end of the eighteenth century, at which time, infuriated by their abuses, rapes, kidnappings, and incessant raids, the Mériens, Crierens, Féetauds, Arragousets, and a few other coastal sprites decided to annihilate them. Ripping out the throats of the guards and blocking all exits out of the cliffs, they entered in force by night, into the heart of the enormous stronghold previously reputed to be impregnable. Fighting for two days and nights, they left not a single Goblin alive, putting an end to the piracy of Tan Noz, which no human army, however powerful, had ever been able to vanquish.

Towards other borders . . .

Other echoes inhabit the garden;
Shall we follow?

—*T. S. Eliot*

"It so happened that the hill hid another valley, and in that valley another spring burst forth, seeming to stretch out forever among the low walls, enclosures, meadows, and secret forests, its bouncing reflections lighting up the world beneath the visitor's footsteps." Thus ends each volume of the *Elfin Chronicles*, signaling that the borders of the Elfin kingdom stretch ever further.

And so it is as well with this *Great Encyclopedia of Elves, Goblins, and Other Little Creatures.* This is not the end. For wherever the primrose blooms on Goblin territory, the honeybee will carry on its breath of a wing the seed of May toward other lush environs, and the wanderer who has not found here a shoe that fits will there step into glass slippers, winged sandals, or seven-league boots.

Whoever was looking for the sinister shadow of the Troll will find it sitting beside the old Alfs. The reader who has not found the Lumerels, the Vouivres, or the path he sought, nor the Elf or the Fairy whom he wished to discover; he who expected to hear the cry of the Banshee in the deep nocturnal thicket or who expected to share the love couch of a Fayette for a hundred years will discover them as he browses through books yet to come. They can be found among the Fairies and the Sith, among those from the Air kingdom and those from the Middle Kingdom.

He will cross the path of the Dryad, the lovely Herbycelles, the Luzerniers of the legendary Forester, the Fenettes and Gwagged Annw in the deep of the fabled Fairy ponds, the Willies, Bogunshies, and Lake Ladies with Flowers in the Mist, or the Charmuzelle hidden away beneath the cover of the Lunar Bestiary.

We have taken three little, quick steps, but the dance has yet to begin!

It is so difficult to approach them, so complicated to know what's what in this forest of genetic illogic, where origins are lost, purposely muddled in the contradictory interlacings of mythological hogwash, in a history too spectacularly ancient or time-warped to be dated and verified, that it appeared to us wise to cautiously check everything five times before proceeding further.

Why five times? Because it is the number that suits them. If twelve is the Giants' number, twenty that of the Unicorns, and seven the magic number of the enchanters and sorcerers, five is the golden number that any agreement with the Elfin people rests on, the territorial edge on which negotiations must be contemplated.

Five because of the four cardinal points and the fifth territory that must always be left free and fallow.

The fifth corner is sacred—it is the portion of the gods—it must always remain virginal and wild in the care and convenience of the Elementals.

All through the five volumes devoted to Sprites and other Dwarfs, Fairies and Elves, demons, Succubi, shadows and intermediary beings, legendary flora and fauna, we can thus get to know ourselves better and be mutually tamed, through time and association with the enchanted places, without drama or bumps: we can learn to breathe, sleep, dream, see the way Elves see, return to the source, to the tree, to the moss—to the harmony of the Lost Kingdom. And the mountains and the forests and the hills will open up. The language of the Others will be as clear to the reader's ear as the song of a reed flute, and if he then wishes to further lose himself, to untangle the mystery, to raise the grass behind his footsteps, it will be in the full complicity and knowledge of the Ageless Ones of whom he has become a familiar companion.

Bibliography

PART I
ELVES

*A Bibliography of Elf Books
for a Magic Library*

This is our entrance to certain refuge, a dream, or a novel idea: a comforting text that will fortify us and enable us to continue on the right path. To find the wise guidance and loving message that will open up a heart and reveal its innermost desire, we follow magical glyphs to the shores of the inspiration we crave . . .

At the end of the garden, beneath the old yew trees and the mysterious vaults of deep pathways, stands a pavilion with ivy-mantled, moss-clad steps. Its doors are bound by shadows, yet seem to open by themselves, impelled as they are by the early morning light we bear within our hearts.

A bouquet of images is scattered before us, and from these petals rise the sight and sound of joyously trembling wings, and here, and there, too, a firefly flits and pauses to reveal the kindly face of an old acquaintance. These ancient sources and perfumed pages take us upward, ever upward to the imagined walls of a castle keep, the bridge deck of a galleon, and the forests of Elfiria.

I am most grateful to Julien Darmian, Nicolas Brucker, and Cédric Morant for their invaluable help in preparing this manual.

Abrahams, Roger D. *African Folktales: Traditional Stories of the Black World.* New York: Pantheon Books, c. 1983.

Achour, Christiane, and Zineb Ali Benali. *Contes algériens.* Paris: L'Harmattan, 1981.

Algarin, Joanne P. *Japanese Folk Literature: A Core Collection and Reference Guide.* New York: R.R. Bowker, 1982.

Alleau, René, ed. *Guide de la France mystérieuse.* Paris: Tchou, 1964.

Allingham, William. *The Ballad Book.* Cambridge: Sever and Francis, 1865.

———. *The Fairies: A Poem.* New York: H. Holt and Co., c. 1989.

———. *In Fairy Land.* London: Longmans, Green, Reader & Dyer, 1870.

Almanach belge dit de Liège. Paris: Editions Casterman, 2005.

Amilien, Virginie. *Le Troll et autres créatures surnaturelles dans les contes populaires norvégiens.* Paris: Berg International, c. 1996.

Andersen, Hans Christian. *The Classic Treasury of Hans Christian Andersen.* Philadelphia: Courage Books, 2002.

Arbois de Jubainville, Henry d'. *L'Épopée celtique en Irlande.* Paris: Thorin, 1892.

Arrowsmith, Nancy, and George Moore. *A Field Guide to the Little People.* London: Macmillan, 1977.

Asbjørnsen, P. C., and J. Moe. *Norwegian Folktales.* Oslo: Dreyer, 1990.

B. B., *The Little Grey Men.* Oxford: Oxford University Press, 2001.

———. *The Little Grey Men Go down the Bright Stream.* London: Methuen, 1977.

Bachelard, Gaston. *La Poétique de la rêverie.* Paris: Presses Universitaires de France, c. 1960.

Barbygère, Petrus. *Les Chroniques elfiques.*

Barbygère, Saskia. *Laliocha.* Le Chemin herbu.

Barham, Richard. *The Ingoldsby Legends.* Philadelphia: Porter & Coates, 1848.

Baring-Gould, Sabine. *A Book of Dartmoor.* New York: Metheun & Co., 1900.

———. *Curious Myths of the Middle Ages.* London: Rivingtons, 1866.

Baroud, Ghalem. *Contes d'Algérie.* Paris: EDICEF, c. 1985.

Barret, René. *Contes populaires d'Afrique.* Paris: Guilmots.

Barrie, J. M. *Peter Pan.* New York, Scribner, c. 1980.

Barroso, Gustavo. *Mythes, contes et légendes des Indiens: folk-lore brésilien.* Paris: A. Ferroud, 1930.

Basford, Kathleen. *The Green Man.* Ipswich: D. S. Brewer, 1978.

Bellamy, Félix. *La Forêt de Brocéliande,* 2 vols. Rennes: Plihon, 1896.

Berbiguier. *Les Farfadets.* Paris: Al. Vinc. Ch. Berbiguier et P. Gueffier, 1821.

Bérenger-Féraud, L.-J.-B. *Superstitions et survivances,* 2 vols. Paris: E. Leroux, 1896.

Birrell, Anne. *Chinese Mythology: An Introduction.* Baltimore: Johns Hopkins University Press, c. 1993.

Birrell, Anne, trans. *The Classic of Mountains and Seas.* London: Penguin Books, 1999.

Blackwood, Algernon. *Pan's Garden.* London: Macmillan & Co., 1914.

———. *The Wendigo.* Holicong, PA: Wildside Press, 2002.

Bonneville, H. de. *Le Folklore des sources et des fontaines.* Rouen.

Bordelon, Laurent. *L'Histoire des imaginations extravagantes de Monsieur Oufle: causées par la lecture des livres qui traitent de la Magie, du Grimoire, des Démoniaques, Sorciers, Loups-garous, Incubes et du sabbat; des Fées, Ogres, Esprits, Folets, Génies, Phantômes, et autres revenans; des songes, de la Pierre Philosophale, de l'astrologie judiciaire, des Horoscopes, Talismans, jours heureux et malheureux, Éclypses, Comètes et Almanachs; enfin de toutes sortes d'Apparitions, de Divinations, de sortilèges, d'Enchantements et d'autres superstitieuses pratiques.* Amsterdam: Chez Estienne Roger, Pierre Humbert, Pierre de Coup & les Frères Chatelain, 1710.

Brasey, Edouard. *Les Amours enchantées: contes et légendes de France.* Paris: Pygmalion, c. 2001.

———. *Démons et merveilles: fées, lutins, sorcières et autres créatures magiques.* Paris: Chêne, c. 2002.

———. *Fées et Elfes: l'univers féerique.* Paris: Pygmalion/G. Watelet, c. 1999.

———. *Sirènes et Ondines.* Paris: Pygmalion, c. 1999.

Briggs, Katharine Mary. *Abbey Lubbers, Banshees and Boggarts: A Who's Who of Fairies.* Harmondsworth: Kestrel Books, c. 1979.

———. *The Anatomy of Puck.* London: Routledge & Paul, 1959.

———. *The Personnel of Fairyland.* Oxford: Alden Press, 1953.

———. *The Vanishing People: Fairy Lore and Legends.* New York: Pantheon Books, c. 1978.

Brontë, Emily Jane. *The Complete Poems of Emily Brontë.* London: Hodder and Stoughton, 1910.

Brooks, John Attwood. *Ghosts and Legends of the Lake District.* Norwich: Jarrold Colour Publications, c. 1988.

———. *Ghosts and Legends of Wales.* Norwich: Jarrold Colour Publications, c. 1987.

———. *Ghosts and Witches of the Cotswolds.* Norwich: Jarrold Colour Publications, c. 1986.

Bruzon, Paul. *Simple histoire de mon verger.* Paris: Stock, 1935.

Burnett, Frances Hodgson. *The Secret Garden.* London: Folio Society, 1986.

Cabal, Constantino. *Mitológica ibérica: Supersticiones, cuentos y legendas de la Vieja España.* Asturias, Spain: Grupo Editorial Asturiano (GEA), c. 1993.

Campbell, Joseph. *The Masks of God: Oriental Mythology.* New York: Viking Press, c. 1962.

Cantraine, Roger. *Légendes et contes du pays d'Ath.* Brussels: Paul Legrain, 1990.

Carroll, Lewis. *Alice in Wonderland.* Mount Vernon: Peter Pauper Press, 1940.

Carter, Angela, ed. *The Virago Book of Fairy Tales.* London, Virago, 1990.

Cerquand, John-François. *Légendes et récits populaires du pays Basque.* Bordeaux: Aubéron, 1992.

Chambers, Dennis. *Haunted Pluckley.* Denela Enterprises, 1984.

Chaters, Daphné. *Le Côté caché des choses, l'occultisme dans la nature.* La Diffusion spirituelle.

Chavoutier, Abbé Lucien. *Contes et légendes de Savoie,* coll. Trésors de la Savoie.

Chodzko, Alexandre Borejko. *Contes des paysans et des pâtres slaves.* Paris: L. Hachette et cie., 1864.

Clegg, Pierre. *Les Elfes aux lanternes de Romney Marsh.* Éd. du Capitaine.

Clute, John, and John Grant. *The Encyclopedia of Fantasy.* London: Orbit, 1997.

Collin de Plancy, J.-A.-S. *Légendes des esprits et des démons.* Nîmes: C. Lacour, 1991.

———. *Légendes infernales.* Paris: H. Plon, 1862.

Colombo, John Robert. *Windigo: An Anthology of Fact and Fantastic Fiction.* Saskatoon, Sask.: Western Producer Prairie Books, c. 1982.

Conway, Moncure Daniel. *Demonology and Devil-Lore.* New York: Henry Holt and Company, 1879.

Cooper, Joe. *The Case of the Cottingley Fairies.* London: Pocket Books, 1997.

Corvi, Lodovico Giovanni. *Folleti, farfarelli, I Demoni nella tradizione popolare.* Bergamo.

Coyaud, Maurice. *180 contes populaires du Japon.* Paris: G.-P. Maisonneuve et Larose, 1975.

Coyaud, Maurice, ed. *Contes chinois et kanak,* Paris: Pour l'analyse du folklore, 1982.

Creanga, Ion. *Croyances populaires de Roumanie.* Paris: Maisonneuve frères, c. 1931.

Créméné, Adrien. *Mythologie du Vampire en Roumanie.* Monaco: Rocher, c. 1981.

Croker, Thomas Crofton. *Fairy Legends and Traditions of the South of Ireland.* London: William Tegg, 1870.

Dampierre, Saskia. *Le Sentier de l'Elpe.* Valenciennes.

Davy, Marie-Madeleine. *La Montagne et sa symbolique.* Paris: Albin Michel, 1996.

De la Mare, Walter. *The Dutch Cheese.* New York: A. A. Knopf, 1931.

Dixon, James Henry. *Ancient Poems, Ballads, and Songs of the Peasantry of England.* London: Percy Society, 1846.

Dobson, R. B., and J. Taylor. *Rhymes of Robyn Hood.* Gloucester: Sutton, 1989.

Dontenville, Henri, ed. *La France mythologique.* Paris: Henri Veyrier–Tchou, 1980.

Doppagne, Albert. *Esprits et génies du terroir.* Gembloux: J. Duculot, c. 1977.

Dottin, Georges. *Contes et légendes d'Irlande.* Terre de Brume.

Doyle, Arthur Conan. *The Coming of the Fairies.* London: Hodder and Stoughton, 1922.

Doyle, Richard. *In Fairyland: A Series of Pictures from the Elf-World.* New York: D. Appleton, 1870.

Dumas, Georges. *Le Surnaturel et les Dieux d'après les maladies mentales.* Paris: Presses Universitaires de France, 1946.

Dumézil, Georges. *Mythe et Épopée,* 3 vols. Paris: Gallimard, 1968–73.

Dunsany, Edward John Moreton Drax Plunkett, Baron. *The King of Elfland's Daughter.* London: G. P. Putnam's Sons, 1924.

Durville, Henri. *Les Fées.* Paris: Bibliothèque Eudiaque, 1923.

Eisengott. *Discours sur les passages de la Vendoise.* Ghent.

Ekman, Kerstin. *Les Brigands de la forêt de Skule.* Paris: Actes Sud, 1993.

Enthoven, R. E. *The Folklore of Bombay.* Oxford: The Clarendon Press, 1924.

L'Épousée de Mai, Les Carnets de Lalie. Le Clos des Huldres.

Escoube, Lucienne. *Contes du pays d'Eire.* Paris: La Nouvelle Édition, 1945.

Estès, Clarissa Pinkola. *Women Who Run with the Wolves: Myths and Stories of the Wild Women Archetypes.* New York: Ballantine Books, 1992.

Evans, Hilary. *Fairies and Elves* from the *Enchanted World* series. Alexandria, VA: Time-Life Books, 1986.

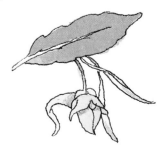

Evans-Wentz, W. Y. *The Fairy-Faith in Celtic Countries*. London: H. Frowde, 1911.

Ferdinand, Sylvie. *Au royaume du Dragon rouge*. Paris: Terre de Brume, 2001.

Franz, Marie-Luise von. *Archetypal Patterns in Fairy Tales*. Toronto: Inner City Books, 1997.

———. *The Interpretation of Fairy Tales*. Boston: Shambhala Publications, 1996.

Frazer, James George. *The Golden Bough*. New York: Criterion Books, 1959.

Frog, Walter. *Le Merveilleux de la mare*. Éditions du Fayt.

Froud, Brian. *Good Faeries/Bad Faeries*. Edited by Terri Windling. London: Pavilion, 2000.

Froud, Wendy, and Terri Windling. *A Midsummer Night's Faery Tale*. New York: Simon & Shuster, c. 1999.

———. *The Winterchild*. New York: Simon & Shuster, c. 1999.

Gardner, Edward L. *Fairies: The Cottingley Photographs and Their Sequel*. London: Theosophical Publishing House, 1966.

Garinet, Jules. *Histoire de la magie en France*. Paris: Foulon et cie., 1818.

Gaster, H. Théodore. *Les Plus Anciens Contes de l'humanité*. Payot, 1999.

Gaze, Harold. *The Merry Piper*. Boston: Little Brown, 1925.

Gennep, Arnold van. *Le Folklore de la Flandre et du Hainaut français*. Paris: G.-P. Maisonneuve, 1935–36.

———. *Le Folklore de l'Auvergne et du Velay*. Paris: G.-P. Maisonneuve, 1942.

Gervais de Tilbury. *Le Livre des Merveilles*. Paris: Les Belles Lettres, 1992.

Gevers, Marie. *L'Herbier légendaire*. Paris: Stock, c. 1991.

Gevin-Cassal, Olympe. *Les Légendes d'Alsace*. Paris: Boivin & cie., 1917.

Glot, Claudine. *Hauts lieux de Brocéliande*. Paris: Éditions Ouest-France, 1996.

Glot, Claudine, and Marie Tanneux. *Contes et légendes de Brocéliande*. Rennes: Ouest-France, c. 2002.

Glot, Claudine, and Michel Le Bris. *Fées, elfes, dragons et autres créatures de féerie*. Paris: Editions Hoëbeke, 2002.

Grahame, Kenneth. *The Wind in the Willows*. New York: C. Scribner's Sons, 1908.

Grégoire de Faulx, P. C. *Salamandriis*. Liège: l'Astrolabe.

Grillot de Givry. *Le Musée des sorciers, mages et alchimistes*. Paris: H. Veyrier–Tchou, 1980.

Grimm, Jacob and Wilhelm. *Grimm's Fairy Tales*. New York: Pantheon Books, 1944.

Grossier, Jean. *Les Elfes*. Éditions de Martimprey.

Grün, Karl. *Les Esprits élémentaires*. Verviers, Belgium: G. Nautet Hans, 1891.

Guillin, Sophie. *La Grosse Biesse*. Château Brillant.

Gutch, Mrs., ed. *County Folklore*. London: Folklore Society, 1899.

Hageland, Albert van. *La Mer magique*. Paris: Marabout, 1973.

Harf-Lancner, Laurence. *Le Monde des Fées dans l'Occident médiéval*. Paris: Hachette, c. 2003.

Harrison, Robert. *Forêts, essai sur l'imaginaire occidental*. Paris: Flammarion, 1992.

Hausman, René. *Croyances populaires en Wallonie*. Liège: Noir Dessin Production, 1998.

Heine, Heinrich. *Zur Geschichte der Religion und Philosophie in Deutschland*. Frankfurt am Main: Insel Verlag, 1966.

Henderson, William. *Notes on the Folk Lore of the Northern Counties of England and the Borders*. Wakefield: E. P. Publishing, 1973.

Hodson, Geoffrey. *Fairies at Work and at Play*. London: Theosophical Publishing House, 1976.

Hoffmann, E.T.A. *Tales*. London: Continuum International Publishing Group, 1983.

Hope, Elphinstone. *L'Étoile des fées*. Translated by Stéphane Mallarmé.

Howes, Edith. *The Cradle Ship*. London: Cassel & Company Ltd., 1916.

Hsou, Lien Tuan, and Simone Greslebin. *Contes merveilleux chinois*. Geneva: Slatkine, 1994.

Hulin, Michel. *La Mystique sauvage: aux antipodes de l'esprit*. Paris: Presses Universitaires France, 1993.

Hunt, Robert. *Popular Romances of the West of England*. London: John Camden Hotten, 1865.

Husain, Shahrukh, ed. *The Virago Book of Witches*. London: Virago, 1993.

Huxley, Francis. *Affable Savages: An Anthropologist among the Urubu Indians of Brazil*. London: Hart-Davis, 1956.

Jacobs, Joseph. *Celtic Fairy Tales*. London: D. Nutt, 1892.

Jézéquel, Patrick, et al. *Halloween*. Morlaix, France: Avis de tempête, 1997.

John, Brian. *More Pembrokeshire Folk Tales*, 4 vols. Newport: Greencroft Books, 1996.

Joisten, Charles. *Êtres fantastiques des Alpes*. Paris: Éditions Entente, c. 1995.

Judge, Roy. *The Jack in the Green*. Shropshire: Hearthstone Publications, 1996.

Kabakova, Galina. *Contes et légendes d'Ukraine*. Paris: Flies France, 1999.

Karadzi'c, Vuk Stefanovi'c. *Contes populaires serbes*. L'Âge d'Homme.

Karlsson, Paul. *The Trolls of Omberg*. Welcome Press.

Kauss, Alain. *Le Monde des Esprits*. BF Édition.

Keightley, Thomas. *The Fairy Mythology*. London: W. H. Ainsworth, 1828.

Kerner, Justinus. *Die Geschichte des Mädchen von Orlach*. Stuttgart, 1834.

Kierkegaard, Sören. *Christian Discourses*. London: Oxford University Press, 1939.

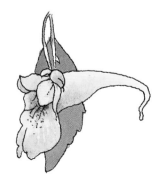

Kipling, Rudyard. *A Diversity of Creatures*. Garden City, NY: Doubleday, Page & Company, 1917.

———. *Puck of Pook's Hill*. London: Macmillan and Co. Limited, 1935.

———. *Rewards and Fairies*. London: Macmillan, 1910.

Kirk, Robert. *The Secret Commonwealth of Elves, Fauns and Fairies*. Stirling: E. Mackay, 1933.

Kitelsen, Theodor. *Troll I Norge som Th. Kittelsen så dem*. Oslo: Stenersen, 1968.

Laboulaye, Edouard. *Contes bleus*. Paris: Furie et cie., 1864.

Lacarrière, Jacques, trans. & ed. *Les Évangiles des quenouilles*. Paris: Imago, c. 1987.

Lagerlöf, Selma. *The Wonderful Adventures of Nils*. Translated by Velma Swanston Howard. Garden City, New York: Doubleday, Page & Company, 1913.

Lagerlöf, Selma. *The World of the Trolls*. London: Hodder & Stoughton.

Lally, T. M. *Tales Weird and Whimsical*. West Sussex: Merlin Books, 1991.

La-Motte-Fouqué, Friedrich Heinrich Karl, Freiherr de. *Undine*. London: W. Heinemann, 1912.

Lang, Andrew, ed. *The Lilac Fairy Book*. New York: Longmans, Green & Co., 1910.

Lapouge, Gilles. *Besoin de mirages*. Paris: Seuil, c. 1999.

Lascaux, Mikaël. *Contes et légendes de Bretagne*. Paris: Editions France-Empire, c. 1995.

Latham, Minor White. *Elizabethan Fairies*. New York: Octagon Books, c. 1930.

Leadbeater, C. W. *Some Glimpses of Occultism, Ancient and Modern*. Chicago: Theosophical Book Concern, 1903.

Le Bris, Michel. *Aux vents des royaumes*. London: Artus Books, 1991.

———. *Les Fragments du royaume: conversations avec Yvon Le Men*. Venissieux, France: Paroles d'Aube, 1995.

Lecercle, Jean-Jacques. *Alice*. Paris: Éditions Autrement, 1998.

Lecouteux, Claude. *Au-delà du merveilleux: des croyances du Moyen Âge*. Paris: Presses de l'Université de Paris-Sorbonne, c. 1995.

———. *Les Chasses fantastiques et cohortes de la nuit du Moyen Âge*. Paris: Imago, c. 1999.

———. *Démons et Génies du terroir au Moyen Âge*. Paris: Imago, c. 1995.

———. *Fées, Sorcières et Loups-garous au Moyen Âge: histoire du double*. Paris: Imago, c. 1992.

———. *La Maison et ses génies: croyance d'hier et d'aujourd'hui*. Paris: Imago, 2000.

———. *Les Nains et les Elfes au Moyen Âge*. Paris: Imago, c. 1988.

Lecouteux, Claude. *Dans l'eau, sous l'eau, le monde aquatique*. Paris: Presses de l'Université de Paris-Sorbonne.

Lecouteux, Claude. *Sauvons les Dieux*. Éditions Synapse.

Le Fanu, Joseph Sheridan. *In a Glass Darkly*, 3 vols. London: John Lehman, 1947.

Léger, Louis. *Recueil de contes populaires slaves*. Paris: E. Leroux, 1882.

Le Guillou, Philippe. *Livre des guerriers d'or*. Paris: Gallimard, c. 1995.

Le Rouzic, Zacharie. *Carnac: Légendes, traditions, coutumes, et contes du pays*. Vannes: Imprimerie Lafoye & J. de Lamarzelle, 1928.

Le Scouëzec, Gwenc'hlan. *Bretagne terre sacrée: un ésotérisme celtique*. Paris: Albatros, c. 1977.

Lescure, M. de. *Le Monde enchanté*. Librairie Firmin Didot et Cie.

Leser, Gérard. *Contes et légende de la vallée de Munster*. Strasbourg: Éditions Oberlin, 1979.

———. *Le Monde*

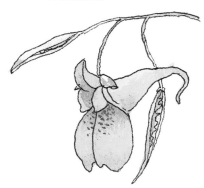

merveilleux et inquiétant des gnomes, nains et lutins en Alsace. Griesbach-le-Bastberg: Éd. du Bastberg, 2001.

Lórien, Ellen. *Elfes, Fées et Gnomes*. Paris: Arista, 1987.

MacDonald, George. *Phantastes: A Faerie Romance*. London: Chatto & Windus, 1894.

Mack, Carol K., and Dinah Mack. *A Field Guide of Demons, Fairies, Fallen Angels, and Other Subversive Spirits*. New York: Arcade Publications, c. 1998.

MacManus, Diarmuid A. *The Middle Kingdom*. Gerrards Cross: Smythe, 1973.

Malleus Maleficarum. Speyer: Peter Drach, 1487.

Marconville, Jean de. *Recueil mémorable d'aucuns cas merveilleux advenus de nos ans et d'aucunes choses étranges et monstrueuses advenus ès siècles passez*. Edited by Jean Dallier.

Markale, Jean. *Contes et légendes des pays celtes*. Rennes: Edition Ouest-France, c. 1995.

Marnier, Xavier. *Contes populaires de différents pays*. Paris: Hachette.

Martineau, Jane, ed. *Victorian Fairy Painting*. London: Royal Academy of Arts, c. 1997.

Mather, Cotton. *The Wonders of the Invisible World*. Boston: Benjamin Harris, 1693.

Matthews, John. *The Quest for the Green Man*. Wheaton, IL: Quest Books, 2001.

———. *The Winter Solstice*. London: Godsfield Press, 2003.

Maury, L.-F.-Alfred. *Les Fées du Moyen Âge*. Paris: Ladrange, 1843.

McGowan, Hugh. *Leprechauns, Legends and Irish Tales*. London: Gollancz, 1988.

Metraux, Alfred. *La Civilisation matérielle des tribus Tupi-Guarani*. Paris: P. Geuthner, 1928.

Meugens, Elisabeth. *La Vie des merles*. Paris: Stock, 1947.

Nahum, Peter. *Fairy Folk in Fairy Land*. London: Leicester Galleries, 1997.

Néroman, Dom. *Grande Encyclopédie*

illustrée des sciences occultes, I, II. Paris: Editorial Argentor, 1952.

Neyrac, Albert. *Traditions, légendes et contes des Ardennes*. Charleville.

Noctiflore, B. de. *Les Esprits de l'air: les Elfes, les anges, les Sylphes et les oiseaux*. Liège: l'Astrolabe.

————. *La Légende de Petit Fayt*. Le Chemin herbu.

Olcott, Francis Jenkins. *The Book of Elves and Fairies*. Boston: Houghton Mifflin Company, 1918.

Orain, Adolphe. *Contes de l'Île-et-Vilaine*. Paris: G.-P. Maisonneuve et Larose, 1968.

Osmont, Anne. *Voyage dans le monde astral*.

Outhwaite, Ida Rentoul. *Little Book of Elves and Fairies*. London: Michael O'Mara Books, 2001.

Owen, Elias. *Welsh Folk-Lore, a Collection of Folk-Tales and Legends of North Wales*. Norwood, PA: Norwood Editions, 1973.

Paasilinna, Arto. *Le Fils du Dieu de l'orage*. Paris: Denoël, 1993.

Paban, Gabrielle de. *Histoires des fantômes et des démons: qui se sont montrés parmi les hommes*. Paris: Locard et Davi, 1819.

Paracelsus. *A Book of Nymphs, Sylphs, Pygmies, and Salamanders, and on the Other Spirits*. Los Angeles: Philosophical Research Society, c. 1964.

Paulhan, Jean. *Progrès en amour assez lents, suivis de Lalie*. Paris: Tchou, 1968.

Perocheau, Joël. *La Sorcellerie en Vendée*. La Chaume, France: Le Cercle d'or Rivages, 1978.

Pilon, Edmond. *Contes anciens du Nord*. Paris: Henri Piazza, 1919.

Pineau, Léon. *Les Contes populaires du Poitou*. Paris: E. Leroux, 1891.

Porteous, Alexander. *Forest Folklore, Mythology and Romance*. London: Allen & Unwin, 1928.

Poulain, Albert. *Contes et légendes de Haute-Bretagne*. Rennes: Editions Ouest-France, c. 1995.

Pourrat, Henri. *Le Trésor des contes*. Paris: Gallimard, c. 1986.

Raine, Kathleen. *The Land Unknown*. London: Hamilton, 1975.

Randolph, P. B. *Magia sexualis*. Paris: R. Télin, 1931.

Reinsberg-Düsingsfeld, Otto von. *Traditions et légendes de la Belgique*. Brussels: F. Claassen, 1870.

Renaud, Jean. *Le Peuple surnaturel des Shetland*. Artus Nos. 21–22.

Rhéal, Sébastien. *Les Divines Fées de l'Orient et du Nord*. Paris: Fournier, 1843.

Rhys, John. *Celtic Folklore: Welsh and Manx*. Oxford, Clarendon Press, 1901.

Rolland, Christian. *Inisdoon*. Paris: Denoël, 1996.

Sagovärld, John Bauers. *Det var en gång...*. Stockholm: Bonnier Carlsen, 1995.

————. *För länge, länge sedan...*. Stockholm: Bonnier Carlsen, 2001.

Samivel. *Hommes, Cimes et Dieux*. Paris: Arthaud, 1973.

Sand, George. *Légendes et traditions du Berry*. Éd. de Montsouris.

Santa-Anna Néry, Frederico José de. *Folk-lore brésilien*. Paris: Perrin et cie, 1889.

Scott, Sir Walter. *Letters on Demonology and Witchcraft*. London: John Murray, 1830.

Scottey, C. *L'Infante retrouvée*. Éditions du Lieu-dit.

Scottish Fairy Tales. New York: Random House.

Sébillot, Paul. *Le Folklore de France*, 8 vols. Paris: Editions Imago, c. 1982–86.

Seignolle, Claude. *Contes, récits et légendes des pays de France*, 4 vols. Omnibus, 1999.

————. *Les Évangiles du Diable selon la croyance populaire*. Paris: G.-P. Maisonneuve et Larose, 1994.

Servais, Jean-Claude. *Déesse blanche, déesse noire*. Paris: Editions Dupuis, 2001.

Sfar, Joann. *Mythologie des Autres*. Dirck Editions.

Shakespeare, William. *A Midsummer Night's Dream*. Philadelphia: Lippincott, 1895.

Sikes, Wirt. *British Goblins: Welsh Folklore, Fairy Mythology, Legends and Traditions*. London: S. Low, Marston, Searle & Rivington, 1880.

Simiand, Stéphane. *Contes de la Montagne d'Or*. Le Rosier: Éditions Transhumances, 2001.

Sources Orientales, 8 vols. Paris: Éditions du Seuil, 1959–71.

Spence, Lewis. *The Fairy Tradition in Britain*. London: Rider & Co., 1948.

Stavig, Art. *Trolls, Trolls, Trolls*. Freeman, SD: Pine Hill Press, 1979.

Stone, Harry. *Dickens and the Invisible World: Fairy Tales, Fantasy, and Novel-making*. Bloomington: Indiana University Press, c. 1979.

Swedenborg, Emanuel. *The Earths in the Universe*. London: Swedenborg Society, 1875.

————. *Heaven and Hell*. New York: Pillar Books, 1976.

Taillepied, Noël. *Traité de l'apparition des Esprits*. Rouen: Chez Romain de Beauvais, 1600.

Tales of Forest Folk, 4 vols. London: Tiger Books International.

Talos, Ion. *Petit dictionnaire de mythologie populaire roumaine*. Translated by Annelise & Claude Lecouteux. Grenoble: Ellug, 2002.

Tarrant, Margaret W., and Marion and John Webb. *Wild Fruit Fairies, Forest Fairies, House Fairies, Twilight Fairies, etc.* Edited by Fiona Waters.

Teirlinck, Isidoor. *Le Folklore flamand*.

Terrasson, François. *La Peur de la nature*. Paris: Le Sang de la terre, c. 1988.

Thomas, W. Jenkyn. *The Welsh Fairy Book*. Cardiff: University of Wales Press, 1995.

Tieck, Ludwig. *Volksmärchen*, 3 vols. Berlin.

Tolkien, J.R.R. *The Hobbit*. London: Allen & Unwin, 1937.

————. *The Lord of the Rings*, 3 vols. London: Allen & Unwin, 1954–55.

Tonquédec, P. Joseph de. *Introduction à l'étude du merveilleux et du miracle*. Paris: Beauchesne, 1938.

Voisin, André. *Contes et légendes du Sahara*. Paris: L'Harmattan, c. 1995.

Wachtel, Nathan. *Dieux et vampires: retour à Chipaya*. Paris: Seuil, c. 1992.

Warner, Sylvia Townsend. *Kingdoms of Elfin*. New York: Viking Press, 1977.

———. *Lolly Willowes*. London: Chatto & Windus, 1926.

Werner, Alice. *Myths and Legends of the Bantu*. London: G. G. Harrap, 1933.

White, Carolyn. *A History of Irish Fairies*. Dublin: Mercier Press, 2001.

White, T. H., trans. *The Book of Beasts*. New York: Putnam, 1954.

Wilde, Lady. *Ancient Legends, Mystic Charms and Superstitions of Ireland*, I & II. Boston: Ticknor and Co., 1887.

Windling, Terri. *The Wood Wife*. New York: Tor, 1996.

Wirser, M. W. de. *The Tengu*. Transactions of the Asiatic Society of Japan.

Wullschläger, Jackie. *Enfances rêvées*. Paris: Éditions Autrement, 1997.

Yeats, William Butler. *The Celtic Twilight: Men and Women, Dhouls and Faeries*. London: Lawrence and Bullen, 1893.

———. *Irish Fairy and Folk Tales*. London: W. Scott, 1907.

———. *The Secret Rose*. London: Lawrence and Bullen, 1897.

Zipes, Jack. *Victorian Fairy Tales: The Revolt of the Fairies and Elves*. New York: Routledge, 1989.

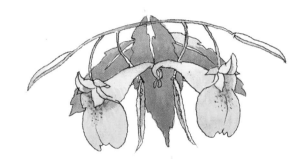

PART II

GOBLINS

AND OTHER

LITTLE CREATURES

Abrahams, Roger D. *African Folktales: Traditional Stories of the Black World.* New York: Pantheon Books, 1983.

Addiss, Steven, ed. *Japanese Ghosts and Demons: Art of the Supernatural.* New York: George Braziller, Inc., 1985.

Ady, Thomas. *A Perfect Discovery of Witches.* London, 1661.

Armstrong, Warren. *Sea Phantoms.* New York: John Day Co., 1961.

Arrowsmith, Nancy. *A Field Guide to the Little People.* London: Macmillan, 1977.

Bassett, Fletcher. *Legends and Superstitions of the Sea and of Sailors.* 1885.

Baum, L. Frank. *American Fairy Tales.* New York: Dover Publications, 1978.

Bord, Janet. *Fairies: Real Encounters with Little People.* New York: Carroll and Graf, 1997.

Bord, Janet and Colin. *Atlas of Magical Britain.* 1990.

———. *The Secret Country: An Interpretation of the Folklore of the Ancient Sites in the British Isles.* London: P. Elek, 1976.

Botkin, B. A., ed. *A Treasury of American Folklore.* New York: Crown Publishers, 1944.

———. *A Treasury of Mississippi River Folklore.* New York: American Legacy Press, 1955.

———. *A Treasury of Southern Folklore.* New York: Crown Publishers, 1949.

Briggs, Katharine Mary. *The Anatomy of Puck.* London: Routledge & Paul, 1959.

———. *A Dictionary of British Folk Tales in the English Language.* Bloomington: Indiana University Press, 1970.

———. *An Encyclopedia of Fairies: Hobgoblins, Brownies, Bogies and other Supernatural Creatures.* New York: Pantheon Books, 1976.

Bronner, Simon J. *American Children's Folklore.* Little Rock, AR: August House, 1988.

Browne, Thomas. *Pseudodoxia epidemica.* London: A. Miller, 1650.

Bruhac, Joseph. *Native American Stories.* Golden, CO: Fulcrum Publishing, 1991.

Brunvard, Jan Harold. *American Folklore: An Encyclopedia.* New York: Garland, 1996.

Byrne, Patrick. *Irish Ghost Stories.* Cork: Mercier Press, 1968.

Caesar, Julius. *De bello Gallico.* Translated by John Warrington. New York: Limited Editions Club, 1954.

Campbell, J. F. *Popular Tales of the West Highlands.* Edmonston and Douglas, 1860–62.

Campbell, John Gregorson. *Clan Traditions and Popular Tales of the Western Highlands.* London: David Nutt, 1895.

Cavendish, Richard. *Mythology.* New York: Time Warner Books, 2003.

Chambers, Robert. *The Popular Rhymes of Scotland.* Edinburgh: W. Hunter, 1826.

Chard, Judy. *Devon Mysteries.* 1979.

Clarke, Louisa Lane. *Recollections and Legends of Sark: An Account of Its First Settlement and Early History.* Guernsey: J. Redstone, 1840.

Clinch, Rosemary. *Supernatural in Somerset.* Bodmin, Cornwall: Bossiney Books, 1986.

Coffin, T. P., and H. Cohen. *Folklore in America.* New York: Doubleday & AMP, Company, Inc., 1966.

Conway, Moncure Daniel. *Demonology and Devil Lore.* New York: Henry Holt and Company, 1879.

Cooper, J. C. *Symbolic and Mythological Animals.* London: HarperCollins, 1992.

Crockett, Samuel Rutherford. *Red Cap Tales.* London: Adam and Charles Black, 1904.

Croker, Thomas Crofton. *Fairy Legends and Traditions of the South of Ireland.* London: William Tegg, 1870.

Curtin, Jeremiah. *Myths and Folklore of Ireland.* Boston: Little Brown, 1890.

Davis, James. *The Folklore of Mid and West Wales.* Felinfach: Llanerch, 1992.

De Lys, Claudia. *A Treasury of American Superstitions.* New York: Philosophical Library, 1948.

Dorson, Richard Mercer. *America in Legend.* New York: Pantheon Books, 1973.

———. *Folktales Told Around the World.* Chicago: University of Chicago, 1975.

Dunne, John J. *Irish Ghosts.* Belfast: Appletree Press, 1999.

Duxbury, Ken. *Sea Stories of Cornwall.* Bodmin, Cornwall: Bossiney Books, 1984.

Dyer, T. F. Thiselton. *Folklore of Plants.* London: Chatto & Windus, Piccadilly, 1889.

Eberhard, Wolfram, ed. *Folktales of China.* Chicago: University of Chicago Press, 1965.

Eden, Richard. *The History of Travayle in the West and East Indies.* London: Richard Lugge, 1577.

Erdoes, Richard, and Alfonso Ortiz. *American Indian Myths and Legends.* New York: Pantheon Books, 1984.

Evans, Hilary. *Fairies and Elves* from the *Enchanted World* series. Alexandria, VA: Time-Life Books, 1986.

Evans-Wentz, W. Y. *The Fairy-Faith in Celtic Countries.* London: H. Frowde, 1911.

Feversham, Anne Dorothy Slingsby, Countess of. *Strange Stories of the Chase: Stories of Fox Hunting and the Supernatural.* London: Bles, 1972.

Ford, Ford Madox. *The Brown Owl: A Fairy Story.* London: T. Fisher Unwin, 1892.

Frazer, James George. *The Golden Bough.* New York: Criterion Books, 1959.

Funk and Wagnalls. *Standard Dictionary of Folklore, Mythology and Legend.* New York: Harper & Row, 1972.

Gantz, Jeffrey, trans. *Early Irish Myths and Sagas.* New York: Penguin, 1981.

Gibbings, W. W. *Folklore and Legends, Scotland.* London, 1889.

Gibson, John. *Monsters of the Sea.* London: Nelson, 1894.

Glassie, Henry. *Irish Folk Tales.* New York: Pantheon, 1985.

Gould, Charles. *Mythical Monsters.* London: W. H. Allen & Co., 1886.

Green, Thomas A., ed. *Folklore: An Encyclopedia of Beliefs, Customs, Tales, Music, and Art.* Santa Barbara: ABC-CLIO, 1997.

Gregor, Rev. Walter. *Notes on the Folklore of the North-East of Scotland.* Published for the Folklore Society by Elliot Stock, London, 1881.

Gregory, Lady. *Visions and Beliefs in the West of Ireland.* New York: G. P. Putnam's Sons, 1920.

Grimm, Jacob and Wilhelm Grimm. *Grimm's Fairy Tales.* New York: Pantheon Books, 1944.

————. *Household Tales.* London: Methuen, 1973.

————. *Old Danish Songs, Ballads and Tales.* 1811.

Guazzo, Francesco Maria. *Compendium Maleficarum.* Mediolani: Apud Haeredes August. Tradati, 1608.

Guirand, Felix, ed. *New Larousse Encyclopaedia of Mythology.* London: The Hamlyn Publishing Group, Ltd., 1972.

Hall, James. *Dictionary of Subjects and Symbols in Art.* New York: Harper & Row, 1979.

Hamilton, Edith. *Mythology: Timeless Tales of Gods and Heroes.* New York: Meridian, 1989.

Hartland, Edwin Sidney. *The Science of Fairy Tales: An Inquiry into Fairy Mythology.* Detroit: Singing Tree, 1968.

Haywood, Charles. *A Bibliography of North American Folklore and Folksong.* New York: Dover, 1961.

Holt, J. C. *Robin Hood.* London: Thames and Hudson, 1982.

Huish, Marcus Bourne. *The Happy England as Painted by Helen Allingham.* London: A. and C. Black, 1903.

Hunt, Robert. *Drolls, Traditions, and Superstitions of Old Cornwall: Popular Romances of the West of England.* Felinfach: Llanerch, 1993.

————. *Popular Romances of the West of England.* London: John Camden Hutton, 1865.

Hyde, Douglas, ed. *Beside the Fire.* New York: Lemma Publishing Co., 1973.

Ingpen, Robert, and Michael Page. *Encyclopedia of Things that Never Were.* New York: Viking, 1987.

Ingram, John. *The Haunted Homes and Family Traditions of Great Britain.* London: Gibbings & Co., Ltd., 1897.

Jacobs, Joseph. *Celtic Fairy Tales.* London: D. Nutt, 1892.

————. *English Fairy Tales.* New York: G. P. Putnam, 1898.

James I, King of England. *Daemonologie.* Edinburgh, 1603.

Jobes, Gertrude. *Dictionary of Mythology, Folklore, and Symbols.* New York: The Scarecrow Press, 1962.

Jones, Allison, ed. *Larousse Dictionary of World Folklore.* New York: Larousse, 1995.

Jones, Sally Roberts. *Legends of Devon.* Bodmin, Cornwall: Bossiney, 1981.

Keightley, Thomas. *The Fairy Mythology.* London: W. H. Ainsworth, 1828.

————. *The World Guide to Gnomes, Fairies, Elves, and Other Little People.* New York, Avenel Books, c. 1978.

Kennedy, Patrick. *Irish Fireside Stories.* Cork: Mercier Press, 1969.

————. *Legendary Fictions of the Irish Celts.* London: Macmillan & Co., 1866.

Killip, Margaret. *The Folklore of the Isle of Man.* London: Batsford, 1975.

Lamont-Brown, Raymond. *Phantoms, Legends, Customs and Superstitions of the Sea.* London: Patrick Stephens, 1972.

Latham, Minor White. *The Elizabethan Fairies.* New York: Octagon Books, 1930.

Lauder, Rosemary Ann, and Michael Williams. *Strange Stories from Devon.* St. Teath: Bossiney Books, 1982.

Leach, M. *The Rainbow Book of American Folk Tales and Legends.* New York: The World Publishing Company, 1958.

Lee, Henry. *Sea Monsters Unmasked.* 1883.

Leeming, David Adams. *The World of Myth: An Anthology.* Oxford: Oxford University Press, 1990.

Linnaeus, Carl. "Anthropomorpha" in *Amoenitates academicae.* Stockholm, 1763, 6:76.

————. *Systema naturae.* Leipzig: Impensis Georg Emanuel Beer, 1788–93.

MacCullock, Sir Edgar. *Guernsey Folk Lore.* London: E. Stock, 1903.

MacDonald, George. *The Princess and the Goblin.* Philadelphia: J. B. Lippincott, 1907.

Mather, Cotton. *The Wonders of the Invisible World.* Boston: Benjamin Harris, 1693.

McManus, Seumas. *Donegal Fairy Stories.* New York: McClure, Phillips & Co., 1900.

————. *Favorite Irish Folk Tales.* Mineola, NY: Dover Press, 1999.

Morgan, Rev. T. M. *The History and Antiquities of the Parish of Newchurch.* Camarthen, 1910.

Murray, Margaret Alice. *The Witch-cult in Western Europe.* Oxford: Clarendon Press, 1921.

Narvaez, Peter. *The Good People: New Fairylore Essays.* New York and London: Garland Publishing, 1997.

O'Danachair, Caoimhín. *A Bibliography of Irish Ethnology and Folk Tradition.* Dublin: Mercier Press, 1978.

O'Sullivan, Sean. *Folktales of Ireland.* Chicago: University of Chicago Press, 1966.

————. *A Handbook of Irish Folklore.* Dublin: Folklore of Ireland Society, 1942.

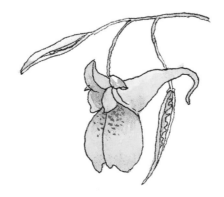

Ovid, *Metamorphoses.* Translated by Rolfe Humphries. Bloomington: Indiana University Press, 1955.

Paracelsus. *A Book of Nymphs, Sylphs, Pygmies, and Salamanders, and on the Other Spirits.* Los Angeles: Philosophical Research Society, c. 1964.

Pegg, John. *After Dark on Dartmoor.* Sevenoaks: John Peggs Books, 1984.

Pliny the Elder. *Concordantia in C. Plini Secundi Naturalem historiam.* New York: Olms-Weidemann, 1996.

Polley, J., ed. *American Folklore and Legend.* New York: Reader's Digest Association, Inc., 1978.

Rackham, Arthur. *The Arthur Rackham Fairy Book.* London: George G. Harrap, 1933.

———. *Fairy Tales from Many Lands.* New York: Viking Press, 1974.

Rose, Carol. *Spirits, Fairies, Gnomes, and Goblins: An Encyclopedia of the Little People.* Santa Barbara: ABC-CLIO, 1996.

Rydberg, Viktor. *Teutonic Mythology.* London: S. Sonnenschein & Co., 1889.

Scott, Michael. *Irish Myths and Legends.* New York: Warner Books, 1992.

Sikes, Wirt. *British Goblins: Welsh Folk-lore, Fairy Mythology, Legends, and Traditions.* London: S. Low, Marston, Searle & Rivington, 1880.

Snodgrass, Mary Ellen. *Encyclopedia of Fable.* Santa Barbara: ABC-CLIO, 1998.

South, Malcolm, ed. *Mythical and Fabulous Creatures: A Source Book and Research Guide.* New York: Greenwood Press, 1987.

Steele, Flora Annie Webster. *English Fairy Tales.* London: Macmillan & Co., 1918.

Stephens, James. *Irish Fairy Tales.* London: Macmillan Company, 1920.

Swainson, Charles. *The Folk Lore and Provincial Names of British Birds.* London: E. Stock, 1886.

Tezel, Naki. *Fairy Tales from Turkey.* Translated by Margery Kent. London: Routledge, 1946.

Tolkien, J.R.R. *Tree and Leaf.* Boston: Houghton Mifflin, 1965.

Turville-Petre, Gabriel. *Myth and Religion of the North.* London: Weidenfeld and Nicolson, 1964.

———. *Scaldic Poetry.* Oxford: Clarendon Press, 1976.

Underwood, Peter. *Gazetteer of Scottish and Irish Ghosts.* London: Souvenir Press, 1973.

Wilde, Lady Jane Francesca. *Ancient Legends, Mystic Charms and Superstitions of Ireland.* Boston: Ticknor and Co., 1887.

Williams, Michael. *Superstitions and Folklore.* Bodmin, Cornwall: Bossiney Books, 1982.

Williamson, Duncan. *The Broonie, Silkies and Fairies.* Edinburgh: Canongate, 1987.

Wreford, Hilary, and Michael Williams. *Mysteries in the Devon Landscape.* 1985.

Yeats, William Butler, ed. *Fairy and Folk Tales of Ireland.* Gerrards Cross, England: Smythe, 1888.

Epilogue

Elfland for the Elves...

"O mortal being with malign intentions and blighted soul,
you who have betrayed the confidence of the Little Folk,
and the loving covenant of the Fairies,
do not hope to subject us
as you have sought to enslave all that crawls, walks, swims, and flies on earth.
Take care lest the oaths and curses you direct against us
rebound upon you, with devastating effect!
Beware of the Elf's withering gaze
and of the Sith's unfailing power.
Stay far away from our realms which, knowing your ways,
We have kept free of your unsavory plans and corrupt spirit.
Mortal, I forbid you to draw near, to breathe the air of our domain!
Depart,
all mortals, mortal kin, and progenitors of mortal kind!
Do not tarry here,
but return to the other side of the hedge!
Go now!"